E. F. Benson

LUCIA IN LONDON

MAPP AND LUCIA

E. F. Benson was born in 1867 at Wellington College in Berkshire, England, where his father (who later became Archbishop of Canterbury) was the headmaster. Benson studied archaeology at Kings College, Cambridge, and at the British School of Archaeology in Athens, where he came to know Lord Alfred Douglas and Oscar Wilde. After visiting Henry James in the village of Rye, Benson eventually settled there until his death in 1940; Rye was the model for Tilling, the setting of his popular Mapp and Lucia novels. Benson published more than one hundred books on various subjects, but remains best known for Mapp and Lucia.

BOOKS BY E. F. BENSON

Lucia in London

Mapp and Lucia

Queen Lucia

Miss Mapp

The Worshipful Lucia

Trouble for Lucia

LUCIA IN LONDON

∞

MAPP AND LUCIA

E. F. Benson

LUCIA IN LONDON

MAPP AND LUCIA

VINTAGE CLASSICS

Vintage Books

A Division of Penguin Random House LLC

New York

FIRST VINTAGE CLASSICS EDITION, NOVEMBER 2015

Lucia in London copyright © 1927 by Doubleday, Doran & Company, Inc., renewed 1955 by Kenneth Stewart Patrick McDowall

Mapp and Lucia copyright © 1931 by Doubleday, Doran & Company, Inc., renewed 1958 by Kenneth Stewart Patrick McDowall

Published in the United States by Vintage Books, a division of Penguin Random House LLC, New York, and in Canada by Random House of Canada, a division of Penguin Random House Ltd., Toronto. *Lucia in London* was originally published in the United Kingdom by Hutchinson and in the United States by Doubleday, Doran & Company, Inc., in 1927. *Mapp and Lucia* was originally published in the United Kingdom by Hodder & Stoughton and in the United States by Doubleday, Doran & Company, Inc., in 1931.

Vintage is a registered trademark and Vintage Classics and colophon are trademarks of Penguin Random House LLC.

The Cataloging-in-Publication Data is available from the Library of Congress.

Vintage Books Trade Paperback ISBN: 978-1-101-91212-6

www.vintagebooks.com

Contents

LUCIA IN LONDON

Chapter One

CONSIDERING THAT PHILIP LUCAS'S AUNT who died early in April was no less than eighty-three years old, and had spent the last seven of them bedridden in a private lunatic asylum, it had been generally and perhaps reasonably hoped among his friends and those of his wife that the bereavement would not be regarded by either of them as an intolerable tragedy. Mrs. Quantock, in fact, who, like everybody else at Riseholme, had sent a neat little note of condolence to Mrs. Lucas, had, without using the actual words "happy release," certainly implied it or its close equivalent.

She was hoping that there would be a reply to it, for though she had said in her note that her dear Lucia mustn't dream of answering it, that was a mere figure of speech, and she had instructed her parlour maid who took it across to The Hurst immediately after lunch to say that she didn't know if there was an answer, and would wait to see, for Mrs. Lucas might perhaps give a little hint ever so vaguely about what the expectations were concerning which everybody was dying to get information . . .

While she waited for this, Daisy Quantock was busy, like everybody else in the village on this beautiful afternoon of spring, with her garden, hacking about with a small but destructive fork in her flower-beds. She was a gardener of the ruthless type, and went for any small green thing that incautiously showed a timid spike above the earth, suspecting it of being a weed. She had had a slight difference with the professional gardener who had hitherto worked for her on three afternoons during the week, and had told him that his services were no longer required. She meant to do her gardening herself this year, and was confident that a profusion of beautiful flowers and a plethora of delicious vegetables would be the result. At the end of her garden path was a barrow of rich manure, which she proposed, when she had finished the slaughter of the innocents, to dig into the depopulated beds. On the other side of her paling her neighbour Georgie Pillson was rolling his strip of lawn, on which during the summer he often played croquet on a small scale. Occasionally they shouted remarks to each other, but as they got more and more out of breath with their exertions the remarks got fewer. Mrs. Quantock's last question had been "What do you do with slugs, Georgie?" and Georgie had panted out, "Pretend you don't see them."

Mrs. Quantock had lately grown rather stout owing to a diet of sour milk, which without plenty of sugar was not palatable; but sour milk and pyramids of raw vegetables had quite stopped all the symptoms of consumption which the study of a small but lurid medical manual had induced. Today she had eaten a large but normal lunch in order to test the merits of her new cook, who certainly was a success, for her husband had gobbled up his food with great avidity instead of turning it over and over with his fork as if it was hay. In consequence, stoutness, surfeit, and so much stooping had made her feel rather giddy, and she was standing up to recover, wondering if this giddiness was a symptom of something dire, when de Vere, for such was the incredible name of her parlour-maid, came down the steps from the dining-room with a note in her hand. So Mrs. Quantock hastily took off her gardening gloves of stout leather, and opened it.

There was a sentence of formal thanks for her sympathy which Mrs. Lucas immensely prized, and then followed these ridiculous words:

> It has been a terrible blow to my poor Peppino and myself.
> We trusted that Auntie Amy might have been spared us for a few years yet.
>
> Ever, dear Daisy, your sad
> *lucia*

And not a word about expectations! . . . Lucia's dear Daisy crumpled up the absurd note, and said "Rubbish," so loud that Georgie Pillson in the next garden thought he was being addressed.

"What's that?" he said.

"Georgie, come to the fence a minute," said Mrs. Quantock. "I want to speak to you."

Georgie, longing for a little gossip, let go of the handle of his roller, which, suddenly released, gave a loud squeak and rapped him smartly on the elbow.

"Tarsome thing!" said Georgie.

He went to the fence and, being tall, could look over it. There was Mrs. Quantock angrily poking Lucia's note into the flower-bed she had been weeding.

"What is it?" said Georgie. "Shall I like it?"

His face red, and moist with exertion, appearing just over the top of the fence, looked like the sun about to set below the flat grey horizon of the sea.

"I don't know if you'll like it," said Daisy, "but it's your Lucia. I sent her a little note of condolence about the aunt, and she says it has been a terrible blow to Peppino and herself. They hoped that the old lady might have been spared them a few years yet."

"No!" said Georgie, wiping the moisture off his forehead with the back of one of his beautiful pearl-grey gloves.

"But she did," said the infuriated Daisy, "they were her very words. I could show you if I hadn't dug it in. Such a pack of nonsense! I hope that long before I've been bedridden for seven years, somebody will strangle me with a bootlace, or anything handy. Why does Lucia pretend to be sorry? What does it all mean?"

Georgie had long been devoted henchman to Lucia (Mrs. Lucas, wife of Philip Lucas, and so Lucia), and though he could criticise her in his mind, when he was alone in his bed or his bath, he always championed her in the face of the criticism of others. Whereas Daisy criticised everybody everywhere . . .

"Perhaps it means what it says," he observed with the delicate sarcasm that never had any effect on his neighbour.

"It can't possibly do that," said Mrs. Quantock. "Neither Lucia nor Peppino have set eyes on his aunt for years, nor spoken of her. Last time Peppino went to see her she bit him. Sling for a week afterwards, don't you remember, and he was terrified of blood-poisoning. How can her death be a blow, and as for her being spared—"

Mrs. Quantock suddenly broke off, remembering that de Vere was still standing there and drinking it all in.

"That's all, de Vere," she said.

"Thank you, ma'am," said de Vere, striding back towards the house. She had high-heeled shoes on, and each time she lifted her foot, the heel which had been embedded by her weight in the soft lawn came out with the sound of a cork being drawn. Then Daisy came closer to the fence, with the light of inductive reasoning, which was much cultivated at Riseholme, veiling the fury of her eye.

"Georgie, I've got it," she said. "I've guessed what it means."

Now though Georgie was devoted to his Lucia, he was just as devoted to inductive reasoning, and Daisy Quantock was, with the exception of himself, far the most powerful logician in the place.

"What is it, then?" he asked.

"Stupid of me not to have thought of it at once," said Daisy. "Why, don't you see? Peppino is Auntie's heir, for she was unmarried, and he's the only nephew, and probably he has been left piles and piles. So naturally they say it's a terrible blow. Wouldn't do to be exultant. They must say it's a terrible blow, to show they don't care about the money. The more they're left, the sadder it is. So natural. I blame myself for not having thought of it at once. Have you seen her since?"

"Not for a quiet talk," said Georgie. "Peppino was there, and a man who, I think, was Peppino's lawyer. He was frightfully deferential."

"That proves it," said Daisy. "And nothing said of any kind?"

Georgie's face screwed itself up in the effort to remember.

"Yes, there was something," he said, "but I was talking to Lucia, and the others were talking rather low. But I did hear the lawyer say something to Peppino about pearls. I do remember the word pearls. Perhaps it was the old lady's pearls."

Mrs. Quantock gave a short laugh.

"It couldn't have been Peppino's," she said. "He has one in a tie-pin. It's called pear-shaped, but there's little shape about it. When do wills come out?"

"Oh, ages," said Georgie. "Months. And there's a house in London, I know."

"Whereabouts?" asked Daisy greedily.

Georgie's face assumed a look of intense concentration.

"I couldn't tell you for certain," he said, "but I know Peppino went up to town not long ago to see about some repairs to his aunt's house, and I think it was the roof."

"It doesn't matter where the repairs were," said Daisy impatiently. "I want to know where the house was."

"You interrupt me," said Georgie. "I was telling you. I know he went to Harrods afterwards and walked there, because he and Lucia were dining with me and he said so. So the house must have been close to Harrods, quite close I mean, because it was raining, and if it had been any reasonable distance he would have had a taxi. So it might be Knightsbridge."

Mrs. Quantock put on her gardening gloves again.

"How frightfully secretive people are," she said. "Fancy his never having told you where his aunt's house was."

"But they never spoke of her," said Georgie. "She's been in that nursing-home so many years."

"You may call it a nursing-home," observed Mrs. Quantock, "or, if you choose, you may call it a post-office. But it was an asylum. And they're just as secretive about the property."

"But you never talk about the property till after the funeral," said Georgie. "I believe it's tomorrow."

Mrs. Quantock gave a prodigious sniff.

"They would have, if there hadn't been any," she said.

"How horrid you are," said Georgie. "How—"

His speech was cut off by several loud sneezes. However beautiful the sleeve-links, it wasn't wise to stand without a coat after being in such a heat.

"How what?" asked Mrs. Quantock, when the sneezing was over.

"I've forgotten now. I shall get back to my rolling. A little chilly. I've done half the lawn."

A telephone bell had been ringing for the last few seconds, and Mrs. Quantock localised it as being in his house, not hers. Georgie was rather deaf, however much he pretended not to be.

"Your telephone bell's ringing, Georgie," she said.

"I thought it was," said Georgie, who had not heard it at all.

"And come in presently for a cup of tea," shouted Mrs. Quantock.

"Should love to. But I must have a bath first."

Georgie hurried indoors, for a telephone call usually meant a little gossip with a friend. A very familiar voice, though a little husky and broken, asked if it was he.

"Yes, it's me, Lucia," he said in soft firm tones of sympathy. "How are you?"

Lucia sighed. It was a long, very audible, intentional sigh. Georgie could visualise her putting her mouth quite close to the telephone, so as to make sure it carried. "Quite well," she said. "And so is my Peppino, thank heaven. Bearing up wonderfully. He's just gone."

Georgie was on the point of asking where, but guessed in time.

"I see," he said. "And you didn't go. I'm very glad. So wise."

"I felt I couldn't," she said, "and he urged me not. It's tomorrow. He sleeps in London tonight—"

(Again Georgie longed to say "where," for it was impossible not to wonder if he would sleep in the house of unknown locality near Harrods.)

"And he'll be back tomorrow evening," said Lucia without pause. "I wonder if you would take pity on me and come and dine. Just something to eat, you know: the house is so upset. Don't dress."

"Delighted," said Georgie, though he had ordered oysters. But they could be scolloped for tomorrow . . . "Love to come."

"Eight o'clock then? Nobody else of course. If you care to bring our Mozart duet."

"Rather," said Georgie. "Good for you to be occupied, Lucia. We'll have a good go at it."

"Dear Georgie," said Lucia faintly. He heard her sigh again, not quite so successfully, and replace the earpiece with a click.

Georgie moved away from the telephone, feeling immensely busy: there was so much to think about and to do. The first thing was to speak about the oysters, and, his parlour-maid being out, he called down the kitchen-stairs. The absence of Foljambe made it necessary for him to get his bath ready himself, and he turned the hot-water tap half on, so that he could run downstairs again and out into the garden (for there was not time to finish the lawn if he was to have a bath and change before tea) in order to put the roller back in the shed. Then he had to get his clothes out, and select something which would do for tea and also for dinner, as Lucia had told him not to dress. There was a new suit which he had not worn yet, rather daring, for the trousers, dark fawn, were distinctly of Oxford cut, and he felt quite boyish as he looked at them. He had ordered them in a moment of reckless sartorial courage, and a quiet tea with Daisy Quantock, followed by a quiet dinner with Lucia, was just the way to make a beginning with them, far better than wearing them for the first time at church on Sunday, when the whole of Riseholme simultaneously would see them. The coat and waistcoat were very dark blue: they would look blue at tea and black at dinner; and there were some grey silk socks, rather silvery, and a tie to match them.

These took some time to find, and his search was interrupted by volumes of steam pouring into his bedroom from his bathroom; he ran in to find the bath full nearly to the brim of boiling water. It had been little more than lukewarm yesterday, and his cook had evidently taken to heart his too-sharp words after breakfast this morning. So he had to pull up the plug of his bath to let the boiling contents subside, and fill up with cold.

He went back to his bedroom and began undressing. All this news about Lucia and Peppino, with Daisy Quantock's penetrating comments, was intensely interesting. Old Miss Lucas had been in this nursing-home or private asylum for years, and Georgie didn't suppose that the inclusive charges could be less than fifteen pounds a week, and fifteen times fifty-two was a large sum. That was income too, and say it was at five per cent, the capital it represented was considerable. Then there was that house in London. If it was freehold, that meant a great deal more capital: if it was on lease it meant a great deal more income. Then there were rates and taxes, and the wages of a caretaker, and no doubt a margin. And there were the pearls.

Georgie took a half-sheet of paper from the drawer in a writing-table where he kept half-sheets and pieces of string untied from parcels, and began to calculate. There was necessarily a good deal of guesswork about it, and the pearls had to be omitted altogether, since nobody could say what "pearls" were worth without knowing their quantity or quality. But even omitting these, and putting quite a low figure on the possible rent of the house near Harrods, he was astounded at the capital which these annual outgoings appeared to represent.

"I don't put it at a penny less than fifty thousand pounds," he said to himself, "and the income at two thousand six hundred."

He had got a little chilly as he sat at his figures, and with a luxurious foretaste of a beautiful hot bath, he hurried into his bathroom. The whole of the boiling water had run out.

"How tarsome! Damn!" said Georgie, putting in the plug and turning on both taps simultaneously.

His calculations, of course, had only been the materials on which his imagination built, and as he dressed it was hard at work, between glances at his trousers as reflected in the full-length mirror which stood in his window. What would Lucia and Peppino do with this vast increase of fortune? Lucia already had the biggest house in Riseholme and the most Elizabethan decor, and a motor, and as many new clothes as she chose. She did not spend much on them because her lofty mind despised clothes, but Georgie permitted himself to indulge cynical reflections that the pearls might make her dressier. Then she already entertained as much as she felt disposed; and more money would not make her wish to give more dinners. And she went up to London whenever there was anything in the way of pictures or plays or music which she felt held the seed of culture. Society (so-called) she despised as thoroughly as she despised clothes, and always said she came back to Riseholme feeling intellectu-ally starved. Perhaps she would endow a permanent fund for holding May day revels on the village green, for Lucia had said she meant to have May day revels every year. They had been a great success last year, though fatiguing, for everybody dressed up in sixteenth-century costume, and danced Morris dances till they all hobbled home dead lame at the merciful sunset. It had all been wonderfully Elizabethan, and Georgie's jerkin had hurt him very much.

Lucia was a wonderful character, thought Georgie, and she would find a way to spend two or three thousand a year more in an edifying and cultured manner. (Were Oxford trousers meant to turn up at the bottom? He thought not: and how small these voluminous folds made your feet look.) Georgie knew what he himself would do with two or three thousand a year more: indeed he had often considered whether he would not try to do it without. He wanted, ever so much, to have a little flat in London (or a couple of rooms would serve), just for a dip every now and then in the life which Lucia found so vapid. But he knew he wasn't a strong, serious character like Lucia, whose only frivolities were artistic or Elizabethan.

His eye fell on a large photograph on the table by his bedside in a silver frame, representing Brünnhilde. It was signed "Olga to beloved Georgie," and his waistcoat felt quite tight as, drawing in a long breath, he recalled that wonderful six months when Olga Bracely, the prima-donna, had bought Old Place, and lived here, and had altered all the values of everything. Georgie believed himself to have been desperately in love with her, but it had been a very exciting time for more reasons than that. Old values had gone: she had thought Riseholme the most splendid joke that had ever been made; she loved them all and laughed at them all, and nobody minded a bit, but followed her whims as if she had been a Pied Piper. All but Lucia, that is to say, whose throne had, quite unintentionally on Olga's part, been pulled smartly from under her, and her sceptre flew in one direction, and her crown in another. Then Olga had gone off for an operatic tour in America, and, after six triumphant months there, had gone on to Australia. But she would be back in England by now, for she was singing in London this season, and her house at Riseholme, so long closed, would be open again . . . And the coat buttoned beautifully, just the last button, leaving the rest negligently wide and a little loose. Georgie put an amethyst tie-pin in his grey tie, which gave a pretty touch of colour, brushed his hair back from his forehead, so that the *toupée* was quite indistinguishable from his own hair, and hurried downstairs to go out to tea with Daisy Quantock.

Daisy was seated at her writing-table when he entered, very busy with a pencil and piece of paper and counting something up on her fingers. Her gardening-fork lay in the grate with the fire-irons, on the carpet there were one or two little sausages of garden-mould, which no doubt had peeled off from her boots, and her gardening gloves were on the floor by her side. Georgie instantly registered the conclusion that something important must have occurred, and that she had come indoors in a great hurry, because the carpet was nearly new, and she always made a great fuss if the smallest atom of cigarette ash dropped on it.

"Thirty-seven, forty-seven, fifty-two, and carry five," she muttered, as Georgie stood in front of the fire, so that the entire new suit should be seen at once. "Wait a moment, Georgie—and seventeen and five's twenty-three—no, twenty-two, and that's put me out: I must begin again. That can't be right. Help yourself, if de Vere has brought in tea, and if not ring—Oh, I left out the four, and altogether it's two thousand five hundred pounds."

Georgie had thought at first that Daisy was merely doing some belated household accounts, but the moment she said two thousand five hundred pounds he guessed, and did not even go through the formality of asking what was two thousand five hundred pounds.

"I made it two thousand six hundred," he said. "But we're pretty well agreed."

Naturally Daisy understood that he understood.

"Perhaps you reckoned the pearls as capital," she said, "and added the interest."

"No I didn't," he said. "How could I tell how much they were worth? I didn't reckon them in at all."

"Well, it's a lot of money," said Daisy. "Let's have tea. What will she do with it?"

She seemed quite blind to the Oxford trousers, and Georgie wondered whether that was from mere feebleness of vision. Daisy was short-sighted, though she steadily refused to recognise that, and would never wear spectacles. In fact, Lucia had made an unkind little epigram about it at a time when there was a slight coolness between the two, and had said "Dear Daisy is too short-sighted to see how short-sighted she is." Of course it was unkind, but very brilliant, and Georgie had read through *The Importance of Being Earnest* which Lucia had gone up to town to see, in the hopes of discovering it . . . Or was Daisy's unconsciousness of his trousers merely due to her preoccupation with Lucia's probable income? . . . Or were the trousers, after all, not so daring as he had thought them?

He sat down with one leg thrown carelessly over the arm of his chair, so that Daisy could hardly fail to see it. Then he took a piece of teacake.

"Yes, do tell me what you think she will do with it?" he asked. "I've been puzzling over it too."

"I can't imagine," said Daisy. "She's got everything she wants now. Perhaps they'll just hoard it, in order that when Peppino dies we may all see how much richer he was than we ever imagined. That's too posthumous for me. Give me what I want now, and a pauper's funeral afterwards."

"Me too," said Georgie, waving his leg. "But I don't think Lucia will do that. It did occur to me—"

"The house in London, you mean," said Daisy, swiftly interrupting. "Of course if they kept both houses open, with a staff in each, so that they could run up and down as they chose, that would make a big hole in it. Lucia has always said that she couldn't live in London, but she may manage it if she's got a house there."

"I'm dining with her tonight," said Georgie. "Perhaps she'll say something."

Mrs. Quantock was very thirsty with her gardening, and the tea was very hot. She poured it into her saucer and blew on it.

"Lucia would be wise not to waste any time," she said, "if she intends to have any fun out of it, for, you know, Georgie, we're beginning to get old. I'm fifty-two. How old are you?"

Georgie disliked that barbarous sort of question. He had been the young man of Riseholme so long that the habit was engrained, and he hardly believed that he was forty-eight.

"Forty-three," he said, "but what does it matter how old we are, as long as we're busy and amused? And I'm sure Lucia has got all the energy and life she ever had. I shouldn't be a bit surprised if she made a start in London, and went in for all that. Then, of course, there's Peppino, but he only cares for writing his poetry and looking through his telescope."

"I hate that telescope," said Daisy. "He took me up on to the roof the other night and showed me what he said was Mars, and I'll take my oath he said that the same one was Venus only a week before. But as I couldn't see anything either time, it didn't make much difference."

The door opened, and Mr. Quantock came in. Robert was like a little round brown sarcastic beetle. Georgie got up to greet him, and stood in the full blaze of the light. Robert certainly saw his trousers, for his eyes seemed unable to quit the spreading folds that lay round Georgie's ankles: he looked at them as if he was Cortez and they some new planet. Then without a word he folded his arms and danced a few steps of what was clearly meant to be a sailor's hornpipe.

"Heave-ho, Georgie," he said. "Belay there and avast."

"What is he talking about?" said Daisy.

Georgie, quite apart from his general good nature, always strove to propitiate Mr. Quantock. He was far the most sarcastic person in Riseholme and could say sharp things straight off, whereas Georgie had to think a long time before he got a nasty edge to any remark, and then his good nature generally forbade him to slash with it.

"He's talking about my new clothes," he said, "and he's being very naughty. Any news?"

"Any news?" was the general gambit of conversation in Riseholme. It could not have been bettered, for there always was news. And there was now.

"Yes, Peppino's gone to the station," said Mr. Quantock. "Just like a large black crow. Waved a black hand. Bah! Why not call a release a release and have done with it? And if you don't know—why, I'll tell you. It's because they're rolling in riches. Why, I've calculated—"

"Yes?" said Daisy and Georgie simultaneously.

"So you've been calculating too?" said Mr. Quantock. "Might have a sweepstake for the one who gets nearest. I say three thousand a year."

"Not so much," said Georgie and Daisy again simultaneously.

"All right. But that's no reason why I shouldn't have a lump of sugar in my tea."

"Dear me, no," said Daisy genially. "But how do you make it up to three thousand?"

"By addition," said this annoying man. "There'll be every

penny of that. I was at the lending library after lunch, and those who could add made it all that."

Daisy turned to Georgie.

"You'll be alone with Lucia then tonight," she said.

"Oh, I knew that," said Georgie. "She told me Peppino had gone. I expect he's sleeping in that house tonight."

Mr. Quantock produced his calculations, and the argument waxed hot. It was still raging when Georgie left in order to get a little rest before going on to dinner, and to practise the Mozart duet. He and Lucia hadn't tried it before, so it was as well to practise both parts, and let her choose which she liked. Foljambe had come back from her afternoon out, and told him that there had been a trunk call for him while he was at tea, but she could make nothing of it.

"Somebody in a great hurry, sir," she said, "and kept asking if I was—excuse me, sir, if I was Georgie—I kept saying I wasn't, but I'd fetch you. That wouldn't do, and she said she'd telegraph."

"But who was it?" asked Georgie.

"Couldn't say, sir. She never gave a name, but only kept asking."

"She?" asked Georgie.

"Sounded like one!" said Foljambe.

"Most mysterious," said Georgie. It couldn't be either of his sisters, for they sounded not like a she but a he. So he lay down on his sofa to rest a little before he took a turn at the Mozart.

∞

The evening had turned chilly, and he put on his blue cape with the velvet collar to trot across to Lucia's house. The parlour-maid received him with a faint haggard smile of recognition, and then grew funereal again, and preceding him, not at her usual brisk pace, but sadly and slowly, opened the door of the music-room and pronounced his name in a mournful whisper. It was a gay cheerful room, in the ordinary way; now only one light was burning, and from the deepest of the shadows, there came a rustling, and Lucia rose to meet him.

"Georgie, dear," she said. "Good of you."

Georgie held her hand a moment longer than was usual, and gave it a little extra pressure for the conveyance of sympathy. Lucia, to acknowledge that, pressed a little more, and Georgie tightened his grip again to show that he understood, until their respective fingernails grew white with the conveyance and reception of sympathy. It was rather agonising, because a bit of skin on his little finger had got caught between two of the rings on his third finger, and he was glad when they quite understood each other.

Of course it was not to be expected that in these first moments Lucia should notice his trousers. She herself was dressed in deep mourning, and Georgie thought he recognised the little cap she wore as being that which had faintly expressed her grief over the death of Queen Victoria. But black suited her, and she certainly looked very well. Dinner was announced immediately, and she took Georgie's arm, and with faltering steps they went into the dining-room.

Georgie had determined that his role was to be sympathetic, but bracing. Lucia must rally from this blow, and her suggestion that he should bring the Mozart duet was hopeful. And though her voice was low and unsteady, she did say, as they sat down, "Any news?"

"I've hardly been outside my house and garden all day," said Georgie. "Rolling the lawn. And Daisy Quantock—did you know?—has had a row with her gardener, and is going to do it all herself. So there she was next door with a fork and a wheelbarrow full of manure."

Lucia gave a wan smile.

"Dear Daisy!" she said. "What a garden it will be! Anything else?"

"Yes, I had tea with them, and while I was out, there was a trunk call for me. So tarsome. Whoever it was couldn't make any way, and she's going to telegraph. I can't imagine who it was."

"I wonder!" said Lucia in an interested voice. Then she recollected herself again. "I had a sort of presentiment, Georgie, when I saw that telegram for Peppino on the table, two days ago, that it was bad news."

"Curious," said Georgie. "And what delicious fish! How do you always manage to get better things than any of us? It tastes of the sea. And I am so hungry after all my work."

Lucia went firmly on.

"I took it to poor Peppino," she said, "and he got quite white. And then—so like him—he thought of me. 'It's bad news, darling,' he said, 'and we've got to help each other to bear it!'"

"So like Peppino," said Georgie. "Mr. Quantock saw him going to the station. Where is he going to sleep tonight?"

Lucia took a little more fish.

"In Auntie's house in Brompton Square," she said.

"So *that's* where it is!" thought Georgie. If there was a light anywhere in Daisy's house, except in the attics, he would have to go in for a minute, on his return home, and communicate the news.

"Oh, she had a house there, had she?" he said.

"Yes, a charming house," said Lucia, "and full, of course, of dear old memories to Peppino. It will be very trying for him, for he used to go there when he was a boy to see Auntie."

"And has she left it him?" asked Georgie, trying to make his voice sound unconcerned.

"Yes, and it's a freehold," said Lucia. "That makes it easier to dispose of if Peppino settles to sell it. And beautiful Queen Anne furniture."

"My dear, how delicious!" said Georgie. "Probably worth a fortune."

Lucia was certainly rallying from the terrible blow, but she did not allow herself to rally too far, and shook her head sadly.

"Peppino would hate to have to part with Auntie's things," she said. "So many memories. He can recollect her sitting at the walnut bureau (one of those tall ones, you know, which let down in front, and the handles of the drawers all original), doing her accounts in the morning. And a picture of her with her pearls over the fireplace by Sargent; quite an early one. Some fine Chinese Chippendale chairs in the dining-room. We must try to keep some of the things."

Georgie longed to ask a hundred questions, but it would not be wise, for Lucia was so evidently enjoying letting these sumptuous details leak out mingled with memories. He was beginning to feel sure that Daisy's cynical suggestion was correct, and that the stricken desolation of Peppino and Lucia cloaked a very substantial inheritance. Bits of exultation kept peeping out, and Lucia kept poking them back.

"But where will you put all those lovely things, if you sell the house?" he asked. "Your house here is so perfect already."

"Nothing is settled yet," said Lucia. "Neither he nor I can think of anything but dear Auntie. Such a keen intelligent mind she had when Peppino first remembered her. Very good-looking still in the Sargent picture. And it was all so sudden; when Peppino saw her last she was so full of vigour."

("That was the time she bit him," thought Georgie.) Aloud

he said: "Of course you must feel it dreadfully. What is the Sargent? A kit-cat or a full length?"

"Full length, I believe," said Lucia. "I don't know where we could put it here. And a William III whatnot. But of course it is not possible to think about that yet. A glass of port?"

"I'm going to give you one," said Georgie, "it's just what you want after all your worries and griefs."

Lucia pushed her glass towards him.

"Just half a glass," she said. "You are so dear and understanding, Georgie; I couldn't talk to anyone but you, and perhaps it does me good to talk. There is some wonderful port in Auntie's cellar, Peppino says."

She rose.

"Let us go into the music-room," she said. "We will talk a little more; and then play our Mozart if I feel up to it."

"That'll do you good too," said Georgie.

Lucia felt equal to having more illumination than there had been when she rose out of the shadows before dinner, and they established themselves quite cosily by the fire.

"There will be a terrible lot of business for Peppino," she said. "Luckily his lawyer is the same firm as Auntie's, and quite a family friend. Whatever Auntie had, so he told us, goes to Peppino, though we haven't really any idea what it is. But with death duties and succession duties, I know we shall have to be prepared to be very poor until they are paid off, and the duties increase so iniquitously in proportion to the inheritance. Then everything in Brompton Square has to be valued, and we have to pay on the entire contents, the very carpets and rugs are priced, and some are beautiful Persians. And then there's the valuer to pay, and all the lawyer's charges. And when all that has been paid and finished, there is the higher supertax."

"But there's a bigger income," said Georgie.

"Yes, that's one way of looking at it," said Lucia. "But Peppino says that the charges will be enormous. And there's a beautiful music-room."

Lucia gave him one of her rather gimlet-like looks.

"Georgino, I suppose everybody in Riseholme is all agog to know what Peppino has been left. That is so dreadfully vulgar, but I suppose it's natural. Is everybody talking about it?"

"Well, I have heard it mentioned," said Georgie. "But I don't see why it's vulgar. I'm interested in it myself. It concerns you and Peppino, and what concerns one's friends must be of interest to one."

"*Caro*, I know that," said Lucia. "But so much more than the actual money is the responsibility it brings. Peppino and I have all we want for our quiet little needs, and now this great increase of wealth is coming to us—great, that is, compared to our modest little income now—and, as I say, it brings its responsibilities. We shall have to use wisely and without extravagance whatever is left after all these immense expenses have been paid. That meadow at the bottom of the garden, of course, we shall buy at once, so that there will no longer be any fear of its being built over and spoiling the garden. And then perhaps a new telescope for Peppino. But what do I want in Riseholme beyond what I've got? Music and friends, and the power to entertain them, my books and my flowers. Perhaps a library, built on at the end of the wing, where Peppino can be undisturbed, and perhaps every now and then a string-quartet down from London. That will give a great deal of pleasure, and music is more than pleasure, isn't it?"

Again she turned the gimlet-look on to Georgie.

"And then there's the house in Brompton Square," she said, "where Auntie was born. Are we to sell that?"

Georgie guessed exactly what was in her mind. It had been in his too, ever since Lucia had alluded to the beautiful music-room. Her voice had lingered over the beautiful music-room: she had seemed to underline it, to caress it, to appropriate it.

"I believe you are thinking of keeping the house and partly living there," he said.

Lucia looked round, as if a hundred eavesdroppers had entered unaware.

"Hush, Georgie," she said, "not a word must be said about that. But it has occurred to both Peppino and me."

"But I thought you hated London," he said. "You're always so glad to get back, you find it so common and garish."

"It is, compared to the exquisite peace and seriousness of our Riseholme," she said, "where there never is a jarring note, at least hardly ever. But there is in London a certain stir and move-ment which we lack here. In the swim, Georgie, in the middle of things! Perhaps we get too sensitive here where everything is full of harmony and culture, perhaps we are too much sheltered. If I followed my inclination I would never leave our dear Riseholme for a single day. Oh, how easy everything would be if one only followed one's inclination! A morning with my books, an after-noon in my garden, my piano after tea, and a friend like you to come in to dine with my Peppino and me and scold me well, as you'll soon be doing for being so bungling over Mozartino."

Lucia twirled round the Elizabethan spit that hung in the wide chimney, and again fixed him rather in the style of the Ancient Mariner. Georgie could not choose but hear . . . Lucia's eloquent well-ordered sentences had nothing impromptu about them; what she said was evidently all thought out and probably talked out. If she and Peppino had been talking of nothing else since the terrible blow had shattered them, she could not have been more lucid and crystal-clear.

"Georgie, I feel like a leisurely old horse who has been turned out to grass being suddenly bridled and harnessed again. But there is work and energy in me yet, though I thought that I should be permitted to grow old in the delicious peace and leisure of our dear quiet humdrum Riseholme. But I feel that perhaps that is not to be. My conscience is cracking the whip at me, and saying 'You've got to trot again, you lazy old thing.' And I've got to think of Peppino. Dear, contented Peppino would never complain if I refused to budge. He would read his paper, and potter in the garden, and write his dear little poems—such a sweet one, 'Bereavement,' he began it yesterday, a sonnet—and look at the stars. But is it a life for a man?"

Georgie made an uneasy movement in his chair, and Lucia hastened to correct the implied criticism.

"You're different, my dear," she said. "You've got that wonderful power of being interested in everything. Everything. But think what London would give Peppino! His club: the Astronomer-Royal is a member, his other club, political, and politics have lately been quite an obsession with him. The reading-room at the British Museum. No, I should be very selfish if I did not see all that. I must and I do think of Peppino. I mustn't be selfish, Georgie."

This idea of Lucia's leaving Riseholme was a live bomb. At the moment of its explosion, Georgie seemed to see Riseholme fly into a thousand disintegrated fragments. And then, faintly, through the smoke he seemed to see Riseholme still intact. Somebody, of course, would have to fill the vacant throne and direct its affairs. And the thought of Beau Nash at Bath flitted across the distant horizon of his mind. It was a naughty thought, but its vagueness absolved it from treason. He shook it off.

"But how on earth are we to get on without you?" he asked.

"Sweet of you to say that, Georgie," said she, giving another twirl to the spit. (There had been a leg of mutton roasted on it last Mayday, while they all sat round in jerkins and stomachers and hose, and all the perfumes of Arabia had hardly sufficed to quell the odour of roast meat which had pervaded the room for weeks afterwards.) "Sweet of you to say that, but you mustn't think that I am deserting Riseholme. We should be in London perhaps (though, as I say, nothing is settled) for two or three months in the summer, and always come here for weekends, and perhaps from November till Christmas, and a little while in the spring. And then Riseholme would always be coming up to us. Five spare bedrooms, I believe, and one of them quite a little suite with a bathroom and sitting-room attached. No, dear Georgie, I would never desert my dear Riseholme. If it was a choice between London and Riseholme, I should not hesitate in my choice."

"Then would you keep both houses open?" asked Georgie, thrilled to the marrow.

"Peppino thought we could manage it," she said, utterly erasing the impression of the shattered nephew. "He was calculating it out last night, and with board wages at the other house, if you understand, and vegetables from the country, he thought that with care we could live well within our means. He got quite excited about it, and I heard him walking about long after I had gone to bed. Peppino has such a head for detail. He intends to keep a complete set of things, clothes and sponge and everything in London, so that he will have no luggage. Such a saving of tips and small expenses, in which as he so truly says, money leaks away. Then there will be no garage expenses in London: we shall leave the motor here, and rough it with tubes and taxis in town."

Georgie was fully as excited as Peppino, and could not be discreet any longer.

"Tell me," he said, "how much do you think it will all come to? The money he'll come into, I mean."

Lucia also threw discretion to the winds, and forgot all about the fact that they were to be so terribly poor for a long time.

"About three thousand a year, Peppino imagines, when everything is paid. Our income will be doubled, in fact."

Georgie gave a sigh of pure satisfaction. So much was revealed, not only of the future, but of the past, for no one hitherto had known what their income was. And how clever of Robert Quantock to have made so accurate a guess!

"It's too wonderful for you," he said. "And I know you'll spend it beautifully. I had been thinking over it this afternoon, but I never thought it would be as much as that. And then there are the pearls. I do congratulate you."

Lucia suddenly felt that she had shown too much of the silver (or was it gold?) lining to the cloud of affliction that had overshadowed her.

"Poor Auntie!" she said. "We don't forget her through it all. We hoped she might have been spared us a little longer."

That came out of her note to Daisy Quantock (and perhaps to others as well), but Lucia could not have known that Georgie had already been told about that.

"Now, I've come here to take your mind off these sad things," he said. "You mustn't dwell on them any longer."

She rose briskly.

"You've been ever so good to me," she said. "I should just have moped if I had been alone."

She lapsed into the baby-language which they sometimes spoke, varying it with easy Italian.

"Ickle music, Georgie?" she said. "And you must be kindy-kindy to me. No practice all these days. You brought Mozart? Which part is easiest? Lucia wants to take easiest part."

"Lucia shall take which ever part she likes," said Georgie, who had had a good practice at both.

"Treble then," said Lucia. "But oh, how diffy it looks! Hundreds of ickle notes. And me so stupid at reading! Come on then. You begin, *Uno, due, tre.*"

The light by the piano was not very good, but Georgie did not want to put on his spectacles unless he was obliged, for he did not think Lucia knew that he wore them, and somehow spectacles did not seem to "go" with Oxford trousers. But it was no good, and after having made a miserable hash of the first page, he surrendered.

"Me must put on speckies," he said. "Me a blind old man."

Then he had an immense surprise.

"And me a blind old woman," said Lucia. "I've just got speckies too. Oh, Georgie, aren't we getting *vecchio*? Now we'll start again. *Uno, due—*"

The Mozart went beautifully after that, and each of them inwardly wondered at the accuracy of the other's reading. Lucia suspected that Georgie had been having a try at it, but then, after all, she had had the choice of which part she would take, and if Georgie had practised already, he would have been almost certain to have practised the treble; it never entered her head that he had been so thorough as to practise both. Then they played it through again, changing parts, and again it went excellently. It was late now, and soon Georgie rose to go.

"And what shall I say if anybody who knows I've been dining with you, asks if you've told me anything?" he asked.

Lucia closed the piano and concentrated.

"Say nothing of our plans about the house in Brompton Square," she said, "but there's no reason why people shouldn't know that there is a house there. I hate secretiveness, and after all, when the will comes out, everyone will know. So say there is a house there, full of beautiful things. And similarly they will know about the money. So say what Peppino thinks it will come to."

"I see," said Georgie.

She came with him to the door, and strolled out into the little garden in front where the daffodils were in flower. The night was clear, but moonless, and the company of stars burned brightly.

"Aldebaran!" said Lucia, pointing inclusively to the spangled arch of the sky. "That bright one. Oh, Georgie, how restful it is to look at Aldebaran if one is worried and sad. It lifts one's mind above petty cares and personal sorrows. The patens of bright gold! Wonderful Shakespeare! Look in tomorrow afternoon, won't you, and tell me if there is any news. Naturally, I shan't go out."

"Oh, come and have lunch," said Georgie.

"No, dear Georgie: the funeral is at two. Putney Vale. *Buona notte.*"

"*Buona notte,* dear Lucia," he said.

∞

Georgie hurried back to his house, and was disappointed to see that there were no lights in Daisy's drawing-room nor in Robert Quantock's study. But when he got up to his bedroom, where Foljambe had forgotten to pull down the blinds, he saw a light in Daisy's bedroom. Even as he looked the curtains there were drawn back, and he saw her amply clad in a dressing-gown, opening windows at top and bottom, for just now the first principle of health consisted in sleeping in a gale. She too must have seen his room was lit, and his face at the window, for she made violent signs to him, and he threw open the casement.

"Well?" she said.

"In Brompton Square," said Georgie. "And three thousand a year!"

"No!" said Daisy.

Chapter Two

THIS SIMPLE WORD "NO" CONNOTED a great deal in the Riseholme vernacular. It was used, of course, as a mere negative, without emphasis, and if you wanted to give weight to your negative you added "Certainly not." But when you used the word "No" with emphasis, as Daisy had used it from her bedroom window to Georgie, it was not a negative at all, and its signification briefly put was "I never heard anything so marvellous, and it thrills me through and through. Please go on at once, and tell me a great deal more, and then let us talk it all over."

On that occasion Georgie did not go on at once, for having made his climax he, with supreme art, shut the window and drew down the blind, leaving Daisy to lie awake half the night and ponder over this remarkable news, and wonder what Peppino and Lucia would do with all that money. She arrived at several conclusions: she guessed that they would buy the meadow beyond the garden, and have a new telescope, but the building of a library did not occur to her. Before she went to sleep an even more important problem presented itself, and she scribbled a note to Georgie to be taken across in the morning early, in which she wrote, "And did she say anything about the house? What's going to happen to it? And you didn't tell me the number," exactly as she would have continued the conversation if he had not shut his window so quickly and drawn down the blind, ringing down the curtain on his magnificent climax.

Foljambe brought up this note with Georgie's early-morning tea and the glass of very hot water which sometimes he drank instead of it if he suspected an error of diet the night before, and the little glass gallipot of Kruschen salts, which occasionally he added to the hot water or the tea. Georgie was very sleepy, and, only half awake, turned round in bed, so that Foljambe should not see the place where he wore the *toupée*, and smothered a snore, for he would not like her to think that he snored. But when she said "Telegram for you, sir," Georgie sat up at once in his pink silk pyjamas.

"No!" he said with emphasis.

He tore the envelope open, and a whole sheaf of sheets fell out. The moment he set eyes on the first words, he knew so well from whom it came that he did not even trouble to look at the last sheet where it would be signed.

> Beloved Georgie [it ran]—I rang you up till I lost my temper and so send this. Most expensive, but terribly important. I arrived in London yesterday and shall come down for week-end to Riseholme. Shall dine with you Saturday all alone to hear about everything. Come to lunch and dinner Sunday, and ask everybody to one or other, particularly Lucia. Am bringing cook, but order sufficient food for Sunday. Wonderful American and Australian tour, and I'm taking house in London for season. Shall motor down. Bless you.
>
> *olga*

Georgie sprang out of bed, merely glancing through Daisy's pencilled note and throwing it away. There was nothing to be said to it in any case, since he had been told not to divulge the project with regard to the house in Brompton Square, and he didn't know the number. But in Olga's telegram there was

enough to make anybody busy for the day, for he had to ask all
her friends to lunch or dinner on Sunday, order the necessary
food, and arrange a little meal for Olga and himself tomorrow
night. He scarcely knew what he was drinking, tea or hot water
or Kruschen salts, so excited was he. He foresaw too, that there
would be call for the most skilled diplomacy with regard to
Lucia. She must certainly be asked first, and some urging might
be required to make her consent to come at all, either to lunch
or dinner, even if due regard was paid to her deep mourning,
and the festivity limited to one or two guests of her own selec-
tion. Yet somehow Georgie felt that she would stretch a point
and be persuaded, for everybody else would be going some time
on Sunday to Olga's, and it would be tiresome for her to explain
again and again in the days that followed that she had been asked
and had not felt up to it. And if she didn't explain carefully every
time, Riseholme would be sure to think she hadn't been asked.
"A little diplomacy," thought Georgie, as he trotted across to her
house after breakfast with no hat, but a fur tippet round his neck.

He was shown into the music-room, while her maid went to
fetch her. The piano was open, so she had evidently been practising, and there was a copy of the Mozart duet which she had
read so skilfully last night on the music rest. For the moment
Georgie thought he must have forgotten to take his copy away
with him, but then looking at it more carefully he saw that there
were pencilled marks for the fingering scribbled over the more
difficult passages in the treble, which certainly he had never put
there. At the moment he saw Lucia through the window coming up the garden, and he hastily took a chair far away from the
piano and buried himself in *The Times*.

They sat close together in front of the fire, and Georgie
opened his errand.

"I heard from Olga this morning," he said, "a great long tele-gram. She is coming down for the weekend."

Lucia gave a wintry smile. She did not care for Olga's coming down. Riseholme was quite silly about Olga.

"That will be nice for you, Georgie," she said.

"She sent you a special message," said he.

"I am grateful for her sympathy," said Lucia. "She might per-haps have written direct to me, but I'm sure she was full of kind intentions. As she sent the message by you verbally, will you ver-bally thank her? I appreciate it."

Even as she delivered these icy sentiments, Lucia got up rather hastily and passed behind him. Something white on the music rest of the piano had caught her eye.

"Don't move, Georgie," she said, "sit and warm yourself and light your cigarette. Anything else?"

She walked up the room to the far end where the piano stood, and Georgie, though he was a little deaf, quite distinctly heard the rustle of paper. The most elementary rudiments of politeness forbade him to look round. Besides he knew exactly what was happening. Then there came a second rustle of paper, which he could not interpret.

"Anything else, Georgie?" repeated Lucia, coming back to her chair.

"Yes. But Olga's message wasn't quite that," he said. "She evidently hadn't heard of your bereavement."

"Odd," said Lucia. "I should have thought perhaps that the death of Miss Amy Lucas—however, what was her message then?"

"She wanted you very much—she said 'particularly Lucia'—to go to lunch or dine with her on Sunday. Peppino, too, of course."

"So kind of her, but naturally quite impossible," said Lucia.

"Oh, but you mustn't say that," said Georgie. "She is down for just that day, and she wants to see all her old friends. Particularly Lucia, you know. In fact she asked me to get up two little parties for her at lunch and dinner. So, of course, I came to see you first, to know which you would prefer."

Lucia shook her head.

"A party!" she said. "How do you think I could?"

"But it wouldn't be *that* sort of party," said Georgie. "Just a few of your friends. You and Peppino will have seen nobody tonight and all tomorrow. He will have told you everything by Sunday. And so bad to sit brooding."

The moment Lucia had said it was quite impossible she had been longing for Georgie to urge her, and had indeed been prepared to encourage him to urge her if he didn't do so of his own accord. His last words had given her an admirable opening.

"I wonder!" she said. "Perhaps Peppino might feel inclined to go, if there really was no party. It doesn't do to brood: you are right, I mustn't let him brood. Selfish of me not to think of that. Who would there be, Georgie?"

"That's really for you to settle," he said.

"You?" she asked.

"Yes," said Georgie, thinking it unnecessary to add that Olga was dining with him on Saturday, and that he would be at lunch and dinner on Sunday. "Yes: she asked me to come."

"Well, then, what if you asked poor Daisy and her husband?" said Lucia. "It would be a treat for them. That would make six. I think six would be enough. I will do my best to persuade Peppino."

"Capital," said Georgie. "And would you prefer lunch or dinner?"

Lucia sighed.

"I think dinner," she said. "One feels more capable of making the necessary effort in the evening. But, of course, it is all conditional on Peppino's feeling."

She glanced at the clock.

"He will just be leaving Brompton Square," she said. "And then, afterwards, his lawyer is coming to lunch with him and have a talk. Such a lot of business to see to."

Georgie suddenly remembered that he did not yet know the number of the house.

"Indeed there must be," he said. "Such a delightful square, but rather noisy, I should think, at the lower end."

"Yes, but deliciously quiet at the top end," said Lucia. "A curve, you know, and a cul-de-sac. Number twenty-five is just before the beginning of the curve. And no houses at the back. Just the peaceful old churchyard—though sad for Peppino to look out on this morning—and a footpath only up to Ennismore Gardens. My music-room looks out at the back."

Lucia rose.

"Well, Georgie, you will be very busy this morning," she said, "getting all the guests for Sunday, and I mustn't keep you. But I should like to play you a morsel of Stravinski which I have been trying over. Terribly modern, of course, and it may sound hideous to you at first, and at best it's a mere little tinkle if you compare it with the immortals. But there is something about it, and one mustn't condemn all modern work unheard. There was a time no doubt when even Beethoven's greatest sonatas were thought to be modern and revolutionary."

She led the way to the piano, where on the music rest was the morsel of Stravinski, which explained the second and hitherto unintelligible rustle.

"Sit by me, Georgie," she said, "and turn over quick, when I nod. Something like this."

Lucia got through the first page beautifully, but then everything seemed to go wrong. Georgie had expected it all to be odd and aimless, but surely Stravinski hadn't meant quite what Lucia was playing. Then he suddenly saw that the key had been changed, but in a very inconspicuous manner, right in the middle of a bar, and Lucia had not observed this. She went on playing with amazing agility, nodded at the end of the second page, and then luckily the piece changed back again into its original clef. Would it be wise to tell her? He thought not: next time she tried it, or the time after, she would very likely notice the change of key.

A brilliant roulade consisting of chromatic scales in contrary directions brought this firework to an end, and Lucia gave a little shiver.

"I must work at it," she said, "before I can judge of it . . ."

Her fingers strayed about the piano, and she paused. Then with the wistful expression Georgie knew so well, she played the first movement of the "Moonlight Sonata." Georgie set his face also into the Beethoven-expression, and at the end gave the usual little sigh.

"Divine," he said. "You never played it better. Thank you, Lucia."

She rose.

"You must thank immortal Beethoven," she said.

∞

Georgie's head buzzed with inductive reasoning, as he hurried about on his vicariously hospitable errands. Lucia had certainly determined to make a second home in London, for she had distinctly said "my music-room" when she referred to the house in Brompton Square. Also it was easy to see the significance of her deigning to touch Stravinski with even the tip of one finger. She was visualising herself in the modern world, she was going to be up-to-date: the music-room in Brompton Square was not only to echo with the first movement of the "Moonlight" . . . "It's too thrilling," said Georgie, as, warmed with this mental activity, he quite forgot to put on his fur tippet.

His first visit, of course, was to Daisy Quantock, but he meant to stay no longer than just to secure her and her husband for dinner on Sunday with Olga, and tell her the number of the house in Brompton Square. He found that she had dug a large trench round her mulberry tree, and was busily pruning the roots with the wood-axe by the light of Nature: in fact she had cut off all their ends, and there was a great pile of chunks of mulberry root to be transferred in the wheelbarrow, now empty of manure, to the woodshed.

"Twenty-five, that's easy to remember," she said. "And are they going to sell it?"

"Nothing settled," said Georgie. "My dear, you're being rather drastic, aren't you? Won't it die?"

"Not a bit," said Daisy. "It'll bear twice as many mulberries as before. Last year there was one. You should always prune the roots of a fruit tree that doesn't bear. And the pearls?"

"No news," said Georgie, "except that they come in a portrait of the aunt by Sargent."

"No! By Sargent?" asked Daisy.

"Yes. And Queen Anne furniture and Chinese Chippendale chairs," said Georgie.

"And how many bedrooms?" asked Daisy, wiping her axe on the grass.

"Five spare, so I suppose that means seven," said Georgie, "and one with a sitting-room and bathroom attached. And a beautiful music-room."

"Georgie, she means to live there," said Daisy, "whether she told you or not. You don't count the bedrooms like that in a house you're going to sell. It isn't done."

"Nothing settled, I tell you," said Georgie. "So you'll dine with Olga on Sunday, and now I must fly and get people to lunch with her."

"No! A lunch-party too?" asked Daisy.

"Yes. She wants to see everybody."

"And five spare rooms, did you say?" asked Daisy, beginning to fill in her trench.

Georgie hurried out of the front gate, and Daisy shovelled the earth back and hurried indoors to impart all this news to her husband. He had a little rheumatism in his shoulder, and she gave him Coué treatment before she counter-ordered the chicken which she had bespoken for his dinner on Sunday.

Georgie thought it wise to go first to Olga's house, to make sure that she had told her caretaker that she was coming down for the weekend. That was the kind of thing that prima-donnas sometimes forgot. There was a man sitting on the roof of Old Place with a coil of wire, and another sitting on the chimney. Though listening-in had not yet arrived at Riseholme, Georgie at once conjectured that Olga was installing it, and what would Lucia say? It was utterly un-Elizabethan to begin with, and though she countenanced the telephone, she had expressed herself very strongly on the subject of listening-in. She had had an unfortunate experience of it herself, for on a visit to London not long ago, her hostess had switched it on, and the company was regaled with a vivid lecture on pyorrhea by a hospital nurse . . .

Georgie, however, would see Olga before Lucia came to dinner on Sunday and would explain her abhorrence of the instrument.

Then there was the delightful task of asking everybody to lunch. It was the hour now when Riseholme generally was popping in and out of shops, and finding out the news. It was already known that Georgie had dined with Lucia last night and that Peppino had gone to his aunt's funeral, and everyone was agog to ascertain if anything definite had yet been ascertained about the immense fortune which had certainly come to the Lucases . . . Mrs. Antrobus spied Georgie going into Olga's house (for the keenness of her eyesight made up for her deafness), and there she was with her ear-trumpet adjusted, looking at the view just outside Old Place when Georgie came out. Already the popular estimate had grown like a gourd.

"A quarter of a million, I'm told, Mr. Georgie," said she, "and a house in Grosvenor Square, eh?"

Before Georgie could reply, Mrs. Antrobus's two daughters, Piggy and Goosie, came bounding up hand in hand. Piggy and Goosie never walked like other people: they skipped and gambolled to show how girlish an age is thirty-four and thirty-five.

"Oh stop, Mr. Georgie," said Piggy. "Let us all hear. And are the pearls worth a queen's ransom?"

"Silly thing," said Goosie. "I don't believe in the pearls."

"Well, I don't believe in Grosvenor Square," said Goosie. "So silly yourself!"

When this ebullition of high spirits had subsided, and Piggy had slapped Goosie on the back of her hands, they both said "Hush!" simultaneously.

"Well, I can't say about the pearls," said Georgie.

"Eh, what can't you say?" said Mrs. Antrobus.

"About the pearls," said Georgie, addressing himself to the

end of Mrs. Antrobus's trumpet. It was like the trunk of a very short elephant, and she waved it about as if asking for a bun.

"About the pearls, mamma," screamed Goosie and Piggy together. "Don't interrupt Mr. Georgie."

"And the house isn't in Grosvenor Square, but in Brompton Square," said Georgie.

"But that's quite in the slums," said Mrs. Antrobus. "I am disappointed."

"Not at all, a charming neighbourhood," said Georgie. This was not at all what he had been looking forward to: he had expected cries of envious surprise at his news. "As for the fortune, about three thousand a year."

"Is that all?" said Piggy with an air of deep disgust.

"A mere pittance to millionaires like Piggy," said Goosie, and they slapped each other again.

"Any more news?" asked Mrs. Antrobus.

"Yes," said Georgie, "Olga Bracely is coming down tomorrow—"

"No!" said all the ladies together.

"And her husband?" asked Piggy.

"No," said Georgie without emphasis. "At least she didn't say so. But she wants all her friends to come to lunch on Sunday. So you'll all come, will you? She told me to ask everybody."

"Yes," said Piggy. "Oh, how lovely! I adore Olga. Will she let me sit next her?"

"Eh?" said Mrs. Antrobus.

"Lunch on Sunday, mamma, with Olga Bracely," screamed Goosie.

"But she's not here," said Mrs. Antrobus.

"No, but she's coming, mamma," shouted Piggy. "Come along, Goosie. There's Mrs. Boucher. We'll tell her about poor Mrs. Lucas."

Mrs. Boucher's bath-chair was stationed opposite the butcher's, where her husband was ordering the joint for Sunday. Piggy and Goosie had poured the tale of Lucia's comparative poverty into her ear, before Georgie got to her. Here, however, it had a different reception, and Georgie found himself the hero of the hour.

"An immense fortune. I call it an immense fortune," said Mrs. Boucher, emphatically, as Georgie approached. "Good-morning, Mr. Georgie, I've heard your news, and I hope Mrs. Lucas will use it well. Brompton Square, too! I had an aunt who lived there once, my mother's sister, you understand, not my father's, and she used to say that she would sooner live in Brompton Square than in Buckingham Palace. What will they do with it, do you suppose? It must be worth its weight in gold. What a strange coincidence that Mr. Lucas's aunt and mine should both have lived there! Any more news?"

"Yes," said Georgie. "Olga is coming down tomorrow—"

"Well, that's a bit of news!" said Mrs. Boucher, as her husband came out of the butcher's shop. "Jacob, Olga's coming down tomorrow, so Mr. Georgie says. That'll make you happy! You're madly in love with Olga, Jacob, so don't deny it. You're an old flirt, Jacob, that's what you are. I shan't get much of your attention till Olga goes away again. I should be ashamed at your age, I should. And young enough to be your daughter or mine either. And three thousand a year, Mr. Georgie says. I call it an immense fortune. That's Mrs. Lucas, you know. I thought perhaps two. I'm astounded. Why, when old Mrs. Toppington—not the wife of the young Mr. Toppington who married the niece of the man who invented laughing gas—but of his father, or perhaps his uncle, I can't be quite sure which, but when old Mr. Toppington died, he left his son or nephew, whichever it was, a sum that brought him in just about that, and he was considered a very rich man. He had the house just beyond the church at Scroby Windham where my father was rector, and he built the new wing with the billiard-room—"

Georgie knew he would never get through his morning's work if he listened to everything that Mrs. Boucher had to say about young Mr. Toppington, and broke in.

"And she wants you and the Colonel to lunch with her on Sunday," he said. "She told me to ask all her old friends."

"Well, I do call that kind," said Mrs. Boucher, "and of course we'll go . . . Jacob, the joint. We shan't want the joint. I was going to give you a veal cutlet in the evening, so what's the good of a joint? Just a bit of steak for the servants, a nice piece. Well, that will be a treat, to lunch with our dear Olga! Quite a party, I dare say."

Mrs. Quantock's chicken, already countermanded, came in nicely for Georgie's dinner for Olga on Saturday, and by the time all his errands were done the morning was gone, without any practice at his piano, or work in his garden, or a single stitch in his new piece of embroidery. Fresh amazements awaited him when he made his fatigued return to his house. For Foljambe told him that Lucia had sent her maid to borrow his manual on auction bridge. He was too tired to puzzle over that now, but it was strange that Lucia, who despised any form of cards as only fit for those who had not the intelligence to talk or to listen, should have done that. Cards came next to crossword puzzles in Lucia's index of inanities. What did it mean?

Neither Lucia nor Peppino were seen in public at all till Sunday morning, though Daisy Quantock had caught sight of Peppino on his arrival on Friday afternoon, walking bowed with grief and with a faltering gait through the little paved garden in front of The Hurst, to his door. Lucia opened it for him, and they both shook their heads sadly and passed inside. But it was believed that they never came out the whole of Saturday, and their first appearance was at church on Sunday, though indeed, Lucia could hardly be said to have appeared, so impenetrable was her black veil. But that, so to speak, was the end of all mourning (besides, everybody knew that she was dining with Olga that night), and at the end of the service, she put up her veil, and held a sort of little reception standing in the porch, and shaking hands with all her friends as they went out. It was generally felt that this signified her re-entry into Riseholme life.

Hardly less conspicuous a figure was Georgie. Though Robert had been so sarcastic about his Oxford trousers, he had made up his mind to get it over, and after church he walked twice round the green quite slowly and talked to everybody, standing a little away so that they should get a complete view. The odious Piggy, it is true, burst into a squeal of laughter and cried, "Oh, Mr. Georgie, I see you've gone into long frocks," and her mother put up her ear-trumpet as she approached as if to give a greater keenness to her general perceptions. But apart from the jarring incident of Piggy, Georgie was pleased with his trousers' reception. They were beautifully cut too, and fell in charming lines, and the sensation they created was quite a respectful one. But it had been an anxious morning, and he was pleased when it was over.

And such a talk he had had with Olga last night, when she dined alone with him, and sat so long with her elbows on the table that Foljambe looked in three times in order to clear away. Her own adventures, she said, didn't matter; she could tell Georgie about the American tour and the Australian tour, and the coming season in London any time at leisure. What she had to know about with the utmost detail was exactly everything that had happened at Riseholme since she had left it a year ago.

"Good heavens!" she said. "To think that I once thought that it was a quiet backwatery place where I could rest and do nothing but study. But it's a whirl! There's always something wildly exciting going on. Oh, what fools people are not to take an interest in what they call little things. Now go on about Lucia. It's his aunt, isn't it, and mad?"

"Yes, and Peppino's been left her house in Brompton Square," began Georgie.

"No! That's where I've taken a house for the season. What number?"

"Twenty-five," said Georgie.

"Twenty-five?" said Olga. "Why, that's just where the curve begins. And a big—"

"Music-room built out at the back," said Georgie.

"I'm almost exactly opposite. But mine's a small one. Just room for my husband and me, and one spare room. Go on quickly."

"And about three thousand a year and some pearls," said Georgie. "And the house is full of beautiful furniture."

"And will they sell it?"

"Nothing settled," said Georgie.

"That means you think they won't. Do you think that they'll settle altogether in London?"

"No, I don't think that," said Georgie very carefully.

"You are tactful. Lucia has told you all about it, but has also said firmly that nothing's settled. So I won't pump you. And I met Colonel Boucher on my way here. Why only one bulldog?"

"Because the other always growled so frightfully at Mrs. Boucher. He gave it away to his brother."

"And Daisy Quantock? Is it still spiritualism?"

"No; that's over, though I rather think it's coming back. After that it was sour milk, and now it's raw vegetables. You'll see tomorrow at dinner. She brings them in a paper bag. Carrots and turnips and celery. Raw. But perhaps she may not. Every now and then she eats like anybody else."

"And Piggy and Goosie?"

"Just the same. But Mrs. Antrobus has got a new ear-trumpet. But what I want to know is, why did Lucia send across for my manual on auction bridge? She thinks all card-games imbecile."

"Oh, Georgie, that's easy!" said Olga. "Why, of course, Brompton Square, though nothing's settled. Parties, you know, when she wants people who like to play bridge."

Georgie became deeply thoughtful.

"It might be that," he said. "But it would be tremendously thorough."

"How else can you account for it? By the way, I've had a listening-in put up at Old Place."

"I know. I saw them at it yesterday. But don't turn it on tomorrow night. Lucia hates it. She only heard it once, and that time it was a lecture on pyorrhea. Now tell me about yourself. And shall we go into the drawing-room? Foljambe's getting restless."

Olga allowed herself to be weaned from subjects so much more entrancing to her, and told him of the huge success of the American tour, and spoke of the eight weeks' season which was to begin at Covent Garden in the middle of May. But it all led back to Riseholme.

"I'm singing twice a week," she said. "Brünnhilde and Lucrezia and Salome. Oh, my dear, how I love it! But I shall come down here every single weekend. To go back to Lucia: do you suppose she'll settle in London for the season? I believe that's the idea. Fresh worlds to conquer."

Georgie was silent a moment.

"I think you may be right about the auction bridge," he said at length. "And that would account for Stravinski too."

"What's that?" said Olga greedily.

"Why, she played me a bit of Stravinski yesterday morning," said Georgie. "And before she never would listen to anything modern. It all fits in."

"Perfect," said Olga.

∞

Georgie and the Quantocks walked up together the next evening to dine with Olga, and Daisy was carrying a little paper parcel. But that proved to be a disappointment, for it did not contain carrots, but only evening shoes. Lucia and Peppino, as usual, were a little late, for it was Lucia's habit to arrive last at any party, as befitted the Queen of Riseholme, and to make her gracious round of the guests. Everyone of course was wondering if she would wear the pearls, but again there was a disappointment, for her only ornaments were two black bangles, and the brooch of entwined sausages of gold containing a lock of Beethoven's hair. (As a matter of fact Beethoven's hair had fallen out some years ago, and she had replaced it with a lock of Peppino's which was the same colour . . . Peppino had never told anybody.) From the first it was evident that though the habiliments of woe still decked her, she had cast off the numb misery of the bereavement.

"So kind of you to invite us," she said to Olga, "and so good," she added in a whisper, "for my poor Peppino. I've been telling him he must face the world again and not mope. Daisy, dear! Sweet to see you, and Mr. Robert. Georgie! Well, I do think this is a delicious little party."

Peppino followed her: it was just like the arrival of Royal Personages, and Olga had to stiffen her knees so as not to curtsey.

Having greeted those who had the honour to meet her, Lucia became affable rather than gracious. Robert Quantock was between her and Olga at dinner, but then at dinner, everybody left Robert alone, for if disturbed over that function, he was apt to behave rather like a dog with a bone and growl. But if left alone, he was in an extremely good temper afterwards.

"And you're only here just for two days, Miss Olga," she said, "at least so Georgie tells me, and he usually knows your movements. And then London, I suppose, and you'll be busy rehearsing for the opera. I must certainly manage to be in London for a week or two this year, and come to *Siegfried,* and the *Valkyrie,* in which, so I see in the papers, you're singing. Georgie, you must take me up to London when the opera comes on. Or perhaps—"

She paused a moment.

"Peppino, shall I tell all our dear friends our little secret?" she said. "If you say 'no,' I shan't. But, please, Peppino—"

Peppino, however, had been instructed to say "yes," and accordingly did so.

"You see, dear Miss Olga," said Lucia, "that a little property has come to us through that grievous tragedy last week. A house has been left to Peppino in Brompton Square, all furnished, and with a beautiful music-room. So we're thinking, as there is no immediate hurry about selling it, of spending a few weeks there this season, very quietly of course, but still perhaps entertaining a few friends. Then we shall have time to look about us, and as the house is there, why not use it in the interval? We shall go there at the end of the month."

This little speech had been carefully prepared, for Lucia felt that if she announced the full extent of their plan, Riseholme would suffer a terrible blow. It must be broken to Riseholme by degrees: Riseholme must first be told that they were to be up in town for a week or two, pending the sale of the house. Subsequently Riseholme would hear that they were not going to sell the house.

She looked round to see how this section of Riseholme took it. A chorus of the emphatic "No" burst from Georgie, Mrs. Quantock and Olga, who, of course, had fully discussed this disclosure already; even Robert, very busy with his dinner, said "No" and went on gobbling.

"So sweet of you all to say 'No,'" said Lucia, who knew perfectly well that the emphatic interjection meant only surprise, and the desire to hear more, not the denial that such a thing was possible, "but there it is. Peppino and I have talked it over—*non e vero, carissimo*—and we feel that there is a sort of call to us to go to London. Dearest Aunt Amy, you know, and all her beautiful furniture! She never would have a stick of it sold, and that seems to point to the fact that she expected Peppino and me not to wholly desert the dear old family home. Aunt Amy was born there, eighty-three years ago."

"My dear! How it takes one back!" said Georgie.

"Doesn't it?" said Olga.

Lucia had now, so to speak, developed her full horsepower. Peppino's presence stoked her, Robert was stoking himself and might be disregarded, while Olga and Georgie were hanging on her words.

"But it isn't the past only that we are thinking of," she said, "but the present and the future. Of course our spiritual home is here—like Lord Haldane and Germany—and oh, how much we have learned at Riseholme, its lovely seriousness and its gaiety, its culture, its absorption in all that is worthy in art and literature, its old customs, its simplicity."

"Yes," said Olga. (She had meant long ago to tell Lucia that she had taken a house in Brompton Square exactly opposite Lucia's, but who could interrupt the splendour that was pouring out on them?)

Lucia fumbled for a moment at the brooch containing Beethoven's hair. She had a feeling that the pin had come undone. "Dear Miss Olga," she said, "how good of you to take an interest, you with your great mission of melody in the world, in our little affairs! I am encouraged. Well, Peppino and I feel— don't we? *sposo mio*—that now that this opportunity has come to us, of perhaps having a little salon in London, we ought to take it. There are modern movements in the world we really know nothing about. We want to educate ourselves. We want to know what the cosmopolitan mind is thinking about. Of course we're old, but it is never too late to learn. How we shall treasure all we are lucky enough to glean, and bring it back to our dear Riseholme."

There was a slight and muffled thud on the ground, and Lucia's fingers went back where the brooch should have been.

"Georgino, my brooch, the Beethoven brooch," she said; "it has fallen."

Georgie stooped rather stiffly to pick it up: that work with the garden roller had found out his lumbar muscles. Olga rose.

"Too thrilling, Mrs. Lucas!" she said. "You must tell me much more. Shall we go? And how lovely for me: I have just taken a house in Brompton Square for the season."

"No!" said Lucia. "Which?"

"Oh, one of the little ones," said Olga. "Just opposite yours. Forty-two A."

"Such dear little houses!" said Lucia. "I have a music-room. Always yours to practise in."

"Capital good dinner," said Robert, who had not spoken for a long time.

Lucia put an arm round Daisy Quantock's ample waist, and thus tactfully avoided the question of precedence. Daisy, of course, was far, far the elder, but then Lucia was Lucia.

"Delicious indeed," she said. "Georgie, bring the Beethoven with you."

"And don't be long," said Olga.

Georgie had no use for the society of his own sex unless they were young, which made him feel young too, or much older than himself, which had the same result. But Peppino had an unpleasant habit of saying to him "When we come to our age" (which was an unreasonable assumption of juvenility), and Robert of sipping port with the sound of many waters for an indefinite period. So when Georgie had let Robert have two good glasses, he broke up this symposium and trundled them away into the drawing-room, only pausing to snatch up his embroidery tambour, on which he was working at what had been originally intended for a bedspread, but was getting so lovely that he now thought of putting it when finished on the top of his piano. He noticed that Lucia had brought a portfolio of music, and peeping inside saw the morsel of Stravinski . . .

And then, as he came within range of the conversation of the ladies, he nearly fell down from sheer shock.

"Oh, but I adore it," Lucia was saying. "One of the most marvellous inventions of modern times. Were we not saying so last night, Peppino? And Miss Olga is telling me that everyone in London has a listening-in apparatus. Pray turn it on, Miss Olga; it will be a treat to hear it! Ah, the Beethoven brooch: thank you, Georgie—*mille grazie*."

Olga turned a handle or a screw or something, and there was a short pause: the next item presumably had already been announced. And then, wonder of wonders, there came from the trumpet the first bars of the "Moonlight Sonata."

Now the "Moonlight Sonata" (especially the first movement of it) had an almost sacred significance in Riseholme. It was Lucia's tune, much as "God Save the King" is the King's tune. Whatever musical entertainment had been going on, it was certain that if Lucia was present she would sooner or later be easily induced to play the first movement of the "Moonlight Sonata." Astonished as everybody already was at her not only countenancing but even allowing this mechanism, so lately abhorred by her, to be set to work at all, it was infinitely more amazing that she should permit it to play Her tune. But there she was composing her face to her well-known Beethoven expression, leaning a little forward, with her chin in her hand, and her eyes wearing the faraway look from which the last chord would recall her. At the end of the first movement everybody gave the little sigh which was its due, and the wistful sadness faded from their faces, and Lucia, with a gesture, hushing all attempt at comment or applause, gave a gay little smile to show she knew what was coming next. The smile broadened, as the Scherzo began, into a little ripple of laughter, the hand which had supported her chin once more sought the Beethoven brooch, and she sat eager and joyful and alert, sometimes just shaking her head in wordless criticism, and once saying "Tut-tut" when the clarity of a run did not come up to her standard, till the sonata was finished.

"A treat," she said at the end, "really most enjoyable. That dear old tune! I thought the first movement was a little hurried: Cortot, I remember, took it a little more slowly, and a little more *legato*, but it was very creditably played."

Olga, at the machine, was out of sight of Lucia, and during the performance Georgie noticed that she had glanced at the Sunday paper. And now when Lucia referred to Cortot, she hurriedly chucked it into a window seat and changed the subject.

"I ought to have stopped it," she said, "because we needn't

go to the wireless to hear that. Do show us what you mean, Mrs. Lucas, about the first movement."

Lucia glided to the piano.

"Just a bar or two, shall I?" she said.

Everybody gave a sympathetic murmur, and they had the first movement over again.

"Only just my impression of how Cortot plays it," she said. "It coincides with my own view of it."

"Don't move," said Olga, and everybody murmured "Don't," or "Please." Robert said "Please" long after the others, because he was drowsy. But he wanted more music, because he wished to doze a little and not to talk.

"How you all work me!" said Lucia, running her hands up and down the piano with a butterfly touch. "London will be quite a rest after Riseholme. *Peppino mio,* my portfolio on the top of my cloak; would you? . . . Peppino insisted on my bringing some music: he would not let me start without it." (This was a piece of picturesqueness during Peppino's absence: it would have been more accurate to say he was sent back for it, but less picturesque.) "Thank you, *carissimo.* A little morsel of Stravinski; Miss Olga, I am sure, knows it by heart, and I am terrified. Georgie, would you turn over?"

The morsel of Stravinski had improved immensely since Friday: it was still very odd, very modern, but not nearly so odd as when, a few days ago, Lucia had failed to observe the change of key. But it was strange to the true Riseholmite to hear the arch-priestess of Beethoven and the foe of all modern music, which she used to account sheer Bolshevism, producing these scrannel staccato tinklings that had so often made her wince. And yet it all fitted in with her approbation of the wireless and her borrowing of Georgie's manual on auction bridge. It was not the morsel of Stravinski alone that Lucia was practising (the performance though really improved might still be called practise): it was modern life, modern ideas on which she was engaged preparatory to her descent on London. Though still in harbour at Riseholme, so to speak, it was generally felt that Lucia had cast off her cable, and was preparing to put to sea.

"Very pretty: I call that very pretty. Honk!" said Robert when the morsel was finished, "I call that music."

"Dear Mr. Robert, how sweet of you," said Lucia, wheeling round on the music-stool. "Now positively, I will not touch another note. But may we, might we, have another little tune on your wonderful wireless, Miss Olga! Such a treat! I shall certainly have one installed at Brompton Square, and listen to it while Peppino is doing his crossword puzzles. Peppino can think of nothing else now but auction bridge and crossword puzzles, and interrupts me in the middle of my practise to ask for an Athenian sculptor whose name begins with P and is of ten letters."

"Ah, I've got it," said Peppino, "Praxiteles."

Lucia clapped her hands.

"Bravo," she said. "We shall not sit up till morning again."

There was a splendour in the ruthlessness with which Lucia bowled over, like ninepins, every article of her own Riseholme creed, which saw Bolshevism in all modern art, inanity in crossword puzzles and bridge, and aimless vacuity in London . . . Immediately after the fresh tune on the wireless began, and most unfortunately, they came in for the Funeral March of a Marionette. A spasm of pain crossed Lucia's face, and Olga abruptly turned off this sad reminder of unavailing woe.

"Go on: I like that tune!" said the drowsy and thoughtless Robert, and a hurried buzz of conversation covered this melancholy coincidence.

It was already late, and Lucia rose to go.

"Delicious evening!" she said. "And lovely to think that we

shall so soon be neighbours in London as well. My music-room always at your disposal. Are you coming, Georgie?"

"Not this minute," said Georgie firmly.

Lucia was not quite accustomed to this, for Georgie usually left any party when she left. She put her head in the air as she swept by him, but then relented again.

"Dine tomorrow, then? We won't have any music after this feast tonight," said she, forgetting that the feast had been almost completely of her own providing. "But perhaps a little game of cut-throat, you and Peppino and me."

"Delightful," said Georgie.

∞

Olga hurried back after seeing off her other guests.

"Oh, Georgie, what richness," she said. "By the way, of course it *was* Cortot who was playing the 'Moonlight' faster than Cortot plays it."

Georgie put down his tambour.

"I thought it probably would be," he said. "That's the kind of thing that happens to Lucia. And now we know where we are. She's going to make a circle in London and be its centre. Too thrilling! It's all as clear as it can be. All we don't know about yet is the pearls."

"I doubt the pearls," said Olga.

"No, I think there are pearls," said Georgie, after a moment's intense concentration. "Otherwise she wouldn't have told me they appeared in the Sargent portrait of the aunt."

Olga suddenly gave a wild hoot of laughter.

"Oh, why does one ever spend a single hour away from Riseholme?" she said.

"I wish you wouldn't," said Georgie. "But you go off tomorrow?"

"Yes, to Paris. My excuse is to meet my Georgie—"

"Here he is," said Georgie.

"Yes, bless him. But the one who happens to be my husband. Georgie, I think I'm going to change my name and become what I really am, Mrs. George Shuttleworth. Why should singers and actresses call themselves Madame Macaroni or Signora Semolina? Yes, that's my excuse, as I said when you interrupted me, and my reason is gowns. I'm going to have lots of new gowns."

"Tell me about them," said Georgie. He loved hearing about dress.

"I don't know about them yet; I'm going to Paris to find out. Georgie, you'll have to come and stay with me when I'm settled in London. And when I go to practise in Lucia's music-room you shall play my accompaniments. And shall I be shingled?"

Georgie's face was suddenly immersed in concentration.

"I wouldn't mind betting—" he began.

Olga again shouted with laughter.

"If you'll give me three to one that I don't know what you were going to say, I'll take it," she said.

"But you can't know," said Georgie.

"Yes I do. You wouldn't mind betting that Lucia will be shingled."

"Well, you are quick," said Georgie admiringly.

∞

It was known, of course, next morning, that Lucia and Peppino were intending to spend a few weeks in London before selling the house, and who knew what *that* was going to mean? Already it was time to begin rehearsing for the next May Day revels, and Foljambe, that paragon of all parlour-maids, had been overhauling Georgie's jerkin and hose and dainty little hunting boots with turn-down flaps in order to be ready. But when Georgie, dining at The Hurst next evening, said something about May Day revels (Lucia, of course, would be Queen again) as they played cut-throat with the manual on auction bridge handy for the settlement of such small disputes as might arise over the value of the different suits, she only said: "Those dear old customs! So quaint! And fifty to me above, Peppino, or is it a hundred? I will turn it up while you deal, Georgie!"

This complete apathy of Lucia to May Day revels indicated one of two things, that either mourning would prevent her being Queen, or absence. In consequence of which Georgie had his jerkin folded up again and put away, for he was determined that nobody except Lucia should drive him out to partake in such a day of purgatory as had been his last year . . . Still, there was nothing conclusive about that: it might be mourning. But evidence accumulated that Lucia meant to make a pretty solid stay in London, for she certainly had some cards printed at Ye Signe of Ye Daffodil on the village green where Peppino's poems were on sale, with the inscription

Mr. and Mrs. Philip Lucas

request the pleasure of the company of

at . . . . on . . . .

25 Brompton Square   R.S.V.P.

Daisy Quantock had found that out, for she saw the engraved copperplate lying on the counter, and while the shopman's back was turned, had very cleverly read it, though it was printed the wrong way round, and was very confusing. Still she managed to do so, and the purport was plain enough: that Lucia contemplated formally asking somebody to something some time at 25 Brompton Square. "And would she," demanded Daisy, with bitter irony, "have had cards printed like that, if they were only meaning to go up for a week or two?" And if that was not enough Georgie saw a postcard on Lucia's writing-table with "From Mrs. Philip Lucas, 25 Brompton Square, SW3" plainly printed on the top.

It was getting very clear then (and during this week Riseholme naturally thought of nothing else) that Lucia designed a longer residence in the garish metropolis than she had admitted. Since she chose to give no information on the subject, mere pride and scorn of vulgar curiosity forbade anyone to ask her, though of course it was quite proper (indeed a matter of duty) to probe the matter to the bottom by every other means in your power, and as these bits of evidence pieced themselves together, Riseholme began to take a very gloomy view of Lucia's real nature. On the whole it was felt that Mrs. Boucher, when she paused in her bath-chair as it was being wheeled round the green, nodding her head very emphatically, and bawling into Mrs. Antrobus's ear-trumpet, reflected public opinion.

"She's deserting Riseholme and all her friends," said Mrs. Boucher, "that's what she's doing. She means to cut a dash in London, and lead London by the nose. There'll be fashionable parties, you'll see, there'll be paragraphs, and then when the season's over she'll come back and swagger about them. For my part I shall take no interest in them. Perhaps she'll bring down some of her smart friends for a Saturday till Monday. There'll be dukes and duchesses at The Hurst. That's what she's meaning to do, I tell you, and I don't care who hears it."

That was lucky, as anyone within the radius of a quarter of a mile could have heard it.

"Well, never mind, my dear," said Colonel Boucher, who was pushing his wife's chair.

"Mind? I should hope not, Jacob," said Mrs. Boucher. "And now let us go home, or we'll be late for lunch and that would never do, for I expect the Prince of Wales and the Lord Chancellor, and we'll play bridge and crossword puzzles all afternoon."

Such fury and withering sarcasm, though possibly excessive, had, it was felt, a certain justification, for had not Lucia for years given little indulgent smiles when anyone referred to the cheap delights and restless apish chatterings of London? She had always come back from her visits to that truly provincial place which thought itself a centre, wearied with its false and foolish activity, its veneer of culture, its pseudo-Athenian rage for any new thing. They were all busy enough at Riseholme, but busy over worthy objects, over Beethoven and Shakespeare, over high thinking, over study of the true masterpieces. And now, the moment that Aunt Amy's death gave her and Peppino the means to live in the fiddling little ant-hill by the Thames they were turning their backs on all that hitherto had made existence so splendid and serious a reality, and were training, positively training for frivolity by exercises in Stravinski, auction bridge and crossword puzzles. Only the day before the fatal influx of fortune had come to them, Lucia, dropping in on Colonel and Mrs. Boucher about teatime, had found them very cosily puzzling out a children's crossword in the evening paper, having given up the adult conundrum as too difficult, had pretended that even this was far beyond her poor wits, and had gone home the moment she had swallowed her tea in order to finish a canto of Dante's *Purgatorio* . . . And it was no use Lucia's saying that they intended only to spend a week or two in Brompton Square before the house was sold: Daisy's quickness and cleverness about the copperplate at Ye Signe of Ye Daffodil had made short work of that. Lucia was evidently the prey of a guilty conscience too: she meant, so Mrs. Boucher was firmly convinced, to steal away, leaving the impression she was soon coming back.

Vigorous reflections like these came in fits and spurts from Mrs. Boucher as her husband wheeled her home for lunch.

"And as for the pearls, Jacob," she said, as she got out, hot with indignation, "if you asked me, actually asked me what I think about the pearls, I should have to tell you that I don't believe in the pearls. There may be half a dozen seed pearls in an old pillbox: I don't say there are not, but that's all the pearls we shall see. Pearls!"

Chapter Three

GEORGIE HAD ONLY JUST COME down to breakfast and had not yet opened his *Times,* one morning at the end of this hectic week, when the telephone bell rang. Lucia had not been seen at all the day before and he had a distinct premonition, though he had not time to write it down, that this was she. It was: and her voice sounded very brisk and playful.

"Is that Georgino?" she said. "Zat oo, Georgie?"

Georgie had another premonition, stronger than the first.

"Yes, it's me," he said.

"Georgie, is oo coming round to say 'Ta-ta' to poor Lucia and Peppino?" she said.

("I knew it," thought Georgie.)

"What, are you going away?" he asked.

"Yes, I told you the other night," said Lucia in a great hurry, "when you were doing crosswords, you and Peppino. Sure I did. Perhaps you weren't attending. But—"

"No, you never told me," said Georgie firmly.

"How cwoss oo sounds. But come round, Georgie, about eleven and have 'ickle chat. We're going to be very stravvy and motor up, and perhaps keep the motor for a day or two."

"And when are you coming back?" asked Georgie.

"Not quite settled," said Lucia brightly. "There's a lot of bizz-bizz for poor Peppino. Can't quite tell how long it will take. Eleven, then?"

Georgie had hardly replaced the receiver when there came a series of bangs and rings at his front door, and Foljambe coming from the kitchen with his dish of bacon in one hand, turned to open it. It was only de Vere with a copy of *The Times* in her hand.

"With Mrs. Quantock's compliments," said de Vere, "and would Mr. Pillson look at the paragraph she has marked, and send it back? Mrs. Quantock will see him whenever he comes round."

"That all?" said Foljambe rather crossly. "What did you want to knock the house down for then?"

De Vere vouchsafed no reply, but turned slowly in her high-heeled shoes and regarded the prospect.

Georgie also had come into the hall at this battering summons, and Foljambe gave him the paper. There were a large blue pencil mark and several notes of exclamation opposite a short paragraph.

"Mr. and Mrs. Philip Lucas will arrive today from The Hurst, Riseholme, at 25 Brompton Square."

"No!" said Georgie. "Tell Mrs. Quantock I'll look in after breakfast," and he hurried back, and opened his copy of *The Times* to see if it were the same there. It was: there was no misprint, nor could any other interpretation be attached to it. Though he knew the fact already, print seemed to bring it home. Print also disclosed the further fact that Lucia must have settled everything at least before the morning post yesterday, or this paragraph could never have appeared today. He gobbled up his breakfast, burning his tongue terribly with his tea . . .

"It isn't only deception," said Daisy the moment he appeared without even greeting him, "for that we knew already, but it's funk as well. She didn't dare tell us."

"She's going to motor up," said Georgie, "starting soon after eleven. She's just asked me to come and say goodbye."

"That's more deception then," said Daisy, "for naturally, having read that, we should have imagined she was going up by the afternoon train, and gone round to say goodbye after lunch, and found her gone. If I were you, I shouldn't dream of going to say goodbye to her after this. She's shaking the dust of Riseholme off her London shoes . . . But we'll have no May Day revels if I've got anything to do with it."

"Nor me," said Georgie. "But it's no use being cross with her. Besides, it's so terribly interesting. I shouldn't wonder if she was writing some invitations on the cards you saw—"

"No, I never saw the cards," said Daisy, scrupulously. "Only the plate."

"It's the same thing. She may be writing invitations now, to post in London."

"Go a little before eleven then, and see," said Daisy. "Even if she's not writing them then, there'll be envelopes lying about perhaps."

"Come too," said Georgie.

"Certainly not," said Daisy. "If Lucia doesn't choose to tell me she's going away, the only dignified thing to do is to behave as if I knew nothing whatever about it. I'm sure I hope she'll have a very pleasant drive. That's all I can say about it; I take no further interest in her movements. Besides, I'm very busy: I've got to finish weeding my garden, for I've not been able to touch it these last days, and then my planchette arrived this morning. And a ouija-board."

"What's that?" said Georgie.

"A sort of planchette, but much more—much more powerful. Only it takes longer, as it points at letters instead of writing," said Daisy. "I shall begin with planchette and take it up seriously, because I know I'm very psychic, and there'll be a little time for it now that we shan't be traipsing round all day in ruffs and stomachers over those May Day revels. Perhaps there'll be May Day revels in Brompton Square for a change. I shouldn't wonder: nothing would surprise me about Lucia now. And it's my opinion we shall get on very well without her."

Georgie felt he must stick up for her: she was catching it so frightfully hot all round.

"After all, it isn't criminal to spend a few weeks in London," he observed.

"Whoever said it was?" said Daisy. "I'm all for everybody doing exactly as they like. I just shrug my shoulders."

She heaved up her round little shoulders with an effort.

"Georgie, how do you think she'll begin up there?" she said. "There's that cousin of hers with whom she stayed sometimes, Aggie Sandeman, and then, of course, there's Olga Bracely. Will she just pick up acquaintances, and pick up more from them, like one of those charity snowballs? Will she be presented? Not that I take the slightest interest in it."

Georgie looked at his watch and rose.

"I do," he said. "I'm thrilled about it. I expect she'll manage. After all, we none of us wanted to have May Day revels last year but she got us to. She's got drive."

"I should call it push," said Daisy. "Come back and tell me exactly what's happened."

"Any message?" asked Georgie.

"Certainly not," said Daisy again, and began untying the string of the parcel that held the instruments of divination.

Georgie went quickly down the road (for he saw Lucia's motor already at the door) and up the paved walk that led past the sundial, round which was the circular flower-border known as Perdita's border, for it contained only the flowers that Perdita gathered. Today it was all a-bloom with daffodils and violets and primroses, and it was strange to think that Lucia would not go gassing on about Perdita's border, as she always did at this time of the year, but would have to be content with whatever flowers there happened to be in Brompton Square: a few sooty crocuses perhaps and a periwinkle . . . She was waiting for him, kissed her hand through the window, and opened the door.

"Now for little chat," she said, adjusting a very smart hat, which Georgie was sure he had never seen before. There was no trace of mourning about it: it looked in the highest spirits. So, too, did Lucia.

"Sit down, Georgie," she said, "and cheer me up. Poor Lucia feels ever so sad at going away."

"It is rather sudden," he said. "Nobody dreamed you were off today, at least until they saw *The Times* this morning."

Lucia gave a little sigh.

"I know," she said, "but Peppino thought that was the best plan. He said that if Riseholme knew when I was going, you'd all have had little dinners and lunches for us, and I should have been completely worn out with your kindness and hospitality. And there was so much to do, and we weren't feeling much like gaiety. Seen anybody this morning? Any news?"

"I saw Daisy," said Georgie.

"And told her?"

"No, it was she who saw it in *The Times* first, and sent it round to me," said Georgie. "She's got a ouija-board, by the way. It came this morning."

"That's nice," said Lucia. "I shall think of Riseholme as being ever so busy. And everybody must come up and stay with me, and you first of all. When will you be able to come?"

"Whenever you ask me," said Georgie.

"Then you must give me a day or two to settle down, and I'll write to you. You'll be popping across though every moment of the day to see Olga."

"She's in Paris," said Georgie.

"No! What a disappointment! I had already written her a card, asking her to dine with us the day after tomorrow, which I was taking up to London to post there."

"She may be back by then," said Georgie.

Lucia rose and went to her writing-table, on which, as Georgie was thrilled to observe, was a whole pile of stamped and directed envelopes.

"I think I won't chance it," said Lucia, "for I had enclosed another card for Signor Cortese which I wanted her to forward, asking him for the same night. He composed *Lucrezia* you know, which I see is coming out in London in the first week of the Opera Season, with her, of course, in the name-part. But it will be safer to ask them when I know she is back."

Georgie longed to know to whom all the other invitations were addressed. He saw that the top one was directed to an MP, and guessed that it was for the member for the Riseholme district, who had lunched at The Hurst during the last election.

"And what are you going to do tonight?" he asked.

"Dining with dear Aggie Sandeman. I threw myself on her mercy, for the servants won't have settled in, and I hoped we should have just a little quiet evening with her. But it seems that she's got a large dinner party on. Not what I should have chosen, but there's no help for it now. Oh, Georgie, to think of you in dear old quiet Riseholme and poor Peppino and me gabbling and gobbling at a huge dinner party."

She looked wistfully round the room.

"Goodbye, dear music-room," she said, kissing her hand in

all directions. "How glad I shall be to get back! Oh, Georgie, your manual on auction bridge got packed by mistake. So sorry. I'll send it back. Come in and play the piano sometimes, and then it won't feel lonely. We must be off, or Peppino will get fussing. Say goodbye to everyone for us, and explain. And Perdita's border! Will sweet Perdita forgive me for leaving all her lovely flowers and running away to London? After all, Georgie, Shakespeare wrote *The Winter's Tale* in London, did he not? Lovely daffies! And violets dim. Let me give you 'ickle violet, Georgie, to remind you of poor Lucia tramping about in long unlovely streets, as Tennyson said."

Lucia, so Georgie felt, wanted no more comments or questions about her departure, and went on drivelling like this till she was safely in the motor. She had expected Peppino to be waiting for her and beginning to fuss, but so far from his fussing he was not there at all. So she got in a fuss instead.

"Georgino, will you run back and shout for Peppino?" she said. "We shall be so late, and tell him that I am sitting in the motor waiting. Ah, there he is! Peppino, where have you been? Do get in and let us start, for there are Piggy and Goosie running across the green, and we shall never get off if we have to begin kissing everybody. Give them my love, Georgie, and say how sorry we were just to miss them. Shut the door quickly, Peppino, and tell him to drive on."

The motor purred and started. Lucia was gone. "She had a bad conscience too," thought Georgie, as Piggy and Goosie gambolled up rather out of breath with pretty playful cries, "and I'm sure I don't wonder."

The news that she had gone of course now spread rapidly, and by lunchtime Riseholme had made up its mind what to do, and that was hermetically to close its lips for ever on the subject of

Lucia. You might think what you pleased, for it was a free country, but silence was best. But this counsel of perfection was not
easy to practise next day when the evening paper came. There,
for all the world to read, were two quite long paragraphs, in "Five
o'clock Chit-Chat," over the renowned signature of Hermione,
entirely about Lucia and 25 Brompton Square, and there for all
the world to see was the reproduction of one of her most elegant photographs, in which she gazed dreamily outwards and
a little upwards, with her fingers still pressed on the last chord
of (probably) the "Moonlight Sonata" . . . She had come up, so
Hermione told countless readers, from her Elizabethan country seat at Riseholme (where she was a neighbour of Miss Olga
Bracely) and was settling for the season in the beautiful little
house in Brompton Square, which was the freehold property of
her husband, and had just come to him on the death of his aunt.
It was a veritable treasure house of exquisite furniture, with a
charming music-room where Lucia had given Hermione a cup of
tea from her marvellous Worcester tea service . . . (At this point
Daisy, whose hands were trembling with passion, exclaimed
in a loud and injured voice, "The very day she arrived!") Mrs.
Lucas (one of the Warwickshire Smythes by birth) was, as all the
world knew, a most accomplished musician and Shakespearian
scholar, and had made Riseholme a centre of culture and art. But
nobody would suspect the bluestocking in the brilliant, beautiful and witty hostess whose presence would lend an added gaiety
to the London season.

Daisy was beginning to feel physically unwell. She hurried
over the few remaining lines, and then ejaculating "Witty! Beautiful!" sent de Vere across to Georgie's with the paper, bidding
him to return it, as she hadn't finished with it. But she thought
he ought to know . . . Georgie read it through, and with admi-

rable self-restraint, sent Foljambe back with it and a message of thanks—nothing more—to Mrs. Quantock for the loan of it. Daisy, by this time feeling better, memorised the whole of it.

Life under the new conditions was not easy, for a mere glance at the paper might send any true Riseholmite into a paroxysm of chattering rage or a deep disgusted melancholy. *The Times* again recorded the fact that Mr. and Mrs. Philip Lucas had arrived at 25 Brompton Square, there was another terrible paragraph headed "Dinner," stating that Mrs. Sandeman entertained the following to dinner. There was an Ambassador, a Marquis, a Countess (dowager), two Viscounts with wives, a Baronet, a quantity of Honourables and Knights, and Mr. and Mrs. Philip Lucas. Every single person except Mr. and Mrs. Philip Lucas had a title. The list was too much for Mrs. Boucher, who, reading it at breakfast, suddenly exclaimed: "I didn't think it of them. And it's a poor consolation to know that they must have gone in last."

Then she hermetically sealed her lips again on this painful subject, and when she had finished her breakfast (her appetite had quite gone) she looked up every member of that degrading party in Colonel Boucher's *Who's Who*.

∽

The announcement that Mr. and Mrs. Philip Lucas had arrived at 25 Brompton Square was repeated once more, in case anybody had missed it (Riseholme had not), and Robert Quantock observed that at this rate the three thousand pounds a year would soon be gone, with nothing to show for it except a few press-cuttings. That was very clever and very withering, but anyone could be withering over such a subject. It roused, it is true, a faint and unexpressed hope that the arrival of Lucia in

London had not spontaneously produced the desired effect, or why should she cause it to be repeated so often? But that brought no real comfort, and a few days afterwards, there fell a further staggering blow. There was a Court, and Mrs. Agnes Sandeman presented Mrs. Philip Lucas. Worse yet, her gown was minutely described, and her ornaments were diamonds and pearls.

The vow of silence could no longer be observed: human nature was human nature, and Riseholme would have burst unless it had spoken. Georgie, sitting in his little back parlour overlooking the garden, and lost in exasperated meditation, was roused by his name being loudly called from Daisy's garden next door, and looking out, saw the unprecedented sight of Mrs. Boucher's bath-chair planted on Daisy's lawn.

"She must have come in along the gravel path by the back door," he thought to himself. "I shouldn't have thought it was wide enough." He looked to see if his tie was straight, and then leaned out to answer.

"Georgie, come round a minute," called Daisy. "Have you seen it?"

"Yes," said Georgie, "I have. And I'll come."

Mrs. Boucher was talking in her loud emphatic voice, when he arrived.

"As for pearls," she said, "I can't say anything about them, not having seen them. But as for diamonds, the only diamonds she ever had were two or three little chips on the back of her wristwatch. That I'll swear to."

The two ladies took no notice of him: Daisy referred to the description of Lucia's dress again.

"I believe it was her last dinner-gown with a train added," she said. "It was a sort of brocade."

"Yes, and plush is a sort of velvet," said Mrs. Boucher. "I've a good mind to write to *The Times,* and say they're mistaken. Brocade! Bunkum! It's pushing and shoving instead of diamonds and pearls. But I've had my say, and that's all. I shouldn't a bit wonder if we saw that the King and Queen had gone to lunch quite quietly at Brompton Square."

"That's all very well," said Daisy, "but what are we to do?"

"Do?" said Mrs. Boucher. "There's plenty to do in Riseholme, isn't there? I'm sure I never suffered from lack of employment, and I should be sorry to think that I had fewer interests now than I had before last Wednesday week. Wednesday, or was it Thursday, when they slipped away like that? Whichever it was, it makes no difference to me, and if you're both disengaged this evening, you and Mr. Georgie, the Colonel and I would be very glad if you would come and take your bit of dinner with us. And Mr. Quantock too, of course. But as for diamonds and pearls, well, let's leave that alone. I shall wear my emerald tiara tonight and my ruby necklace. My sapphires have gone to be cleaned."

But though Riseholme was justifiably incensed over Lucia's worldliness and all this pushing and shoving and this self-advertising publicity, it had seldom been so wildly interested. Also, after the first pangs of shame had lost their fierceness, a very different sort of emotion began to soothe the wounded hearts: it was possible to see Lucia in another light. She had stepped straight from the sheltered and cultured life of Riseholme into the great busy feverish world, and already she was making her splendid mark there. Though it might have been she who had told Hermione what to say in those fashionable paragraphs of hers (and those who knew Lucia best were surely best competent to form just conclusions about that), still Hermione had said it, and the public now knew how witty and beautiful Lucia was, and what a wonderful house she had. Then on the very night of her arrival she had been a guest at an obviously superb dinner party, and had since been presented at Court. All this, to look at it fairly, reflected glory on Riseholme, and if it was impossible in one mood not to be ashamed of her, it was even more impossible in other moods not to be proud of her. She had come, and almost before she had seen, she was conquering. She could be viewed as a sort of ambassadress, and her conquests in that light were Riseholme's conquests. But pride did not oust shame, nor shame pride, and shuddering anticipations as to what new enormity the daily papers might reveal were mingled with secret and delighted conjectures as to what Riseholme's next triumph would be.

It was not till the day after her presentation that any news came to Riseholme direct from the ambassadress's headquarters. Every day Georgie had been expecting to hear, and in anticipation of her summons to come up and stay in the bedroom with the bathroom and sitting-room attached, had been carefully through his wardrobe, and was satisfied that he would present a creditable appearance. His small portmanteau, Foljambe declared, would be ample to hold all that he wanted, including the suit with the Oxford trousers, and his cloth-topped boots. When the long-expected letter came, he therefore felt prepared to start that very afternoon, and tore it open with the most eager haste and propped it against his teapot.

GEORGINO MIO—Such a whirl ever since we left, that I haven't had a moment. But tonight (Oh such a relief) Peppino and I have dined alone quite *à la* Riseholme, and for the first time I have had half an hour's quiet practice in my music-room, and now sit down to write to you. (You'd have scolded me if you'd heard me play, so stiff and rusty have I become.)

Well, now for my little chronicles. The very first evening we were here, we went out to a big dinner at dearest Aggie's. Some interesting people: I enjoyed a pleasant talk with the Italian Ambassador, and called on them the day after, but I had no long conversation with anyone, for Aggie kept bringing up fresh people to introduce me to, and your poor Lucia got quite confused with so many, till Peppino and I sorted them out afterwards. Everyone seemed to have heard of our coming up to town, and I assure you that ever since the tiresome telephone has been a perfect nuisance, though all so kind. Would we go to lunch one day, or would we go to dinner another, and there was a private view here, and a little music in the afternoon there: I assure you I have never been so petted and made so much of.

We have done a little entertaining too, already, just a few old friends like our member of Parliament, Mr. Garroby-Ashton. ("She met him once," thought Georgie in parenthesis.) He insisted also on our going to tea with him at the House of Commons. I knew that would interest Peppino, for he's becoming quite a politician, and so we went. Tea on the terrace, and a pleasant little chat with the Prime Minister who came and sat at our table for ever so long. How I wanted you to be there and make a sketch of the Thames: just the sort of view you do, so beautifully! Wonderful river, and I repeated to myself, "Sweet Thames, run softly, till I end my song." Then such a scurry to get back to dine somewhere or other and go to a play. Then dearest Aggie (such a good soul) had set her heart on presenting me and I couldn't disappoint her. Did you see the description of my dress? How annoyed I was that it appeared in the papers! So vulgar, all that sort of thing, and you know how I hate publicity, but they tell me I must just put up with it and not mind.

The house is getting into order, but there are lots
of little changes and furbishings up to be done before I
venture to show it to anyone as critical as you, Georgino.
How you would scream at the carpet in the dining-room!
I know it would give you indigestion. But when I get the
house straight, I shall insist on your coming, whatever your
engagements are, and staying a long, long time. We will fix a
date when I come down for some weekend.

Your beloved Olga is back, but I haven't seen her yet.
I asked Signor Cortese to dine and meet her one night,
and I asked her to meet him. I thought that would make
a pleasant little party, but they were both engaged. I hope
they have not quarrelled. Her house, just opposite mine,
looks very tiny, but I dare say it is quite large enough for
her and her husband. She sings at the opening night of the
opera next week, in *Lucrezia*. I must manage to go even
if I can only look in for an act or two. Peppino (so extrava-
gant of him) has taken a box for two nights in the week.
It is his birthday present to me, so I couldn't scold the
dear! And after all, we shall give a great deal of pleasure
to friends, by letting them have it when we do not want it
ourselves.

Love to everybody at dear Riseholme. I feel quite like an
exile, and sometimes I long for its sweet peace and quietness. But there is no doubt that London suits Peppino very
well, and I must make the best of this incessant hustle. I
had hoped to get down for next Sunday, but Mrs. Garroby-
Ashton (I hear he will certainly be raised to the peerage
when the birthday honours come out) has made a point of
our spending it with them . . . Good-night, dear Georgino.
Me so so sleepy.

lucia

Georgie swallowed this letter at a gulp, and then, beginning again, took it in sips. At first it gave him an impression of someone wholly unlike her, but when sipped, every sentence seemed wonderfully characteristic. She was not adapting herself to new circumstances, she was adapting new circumstances to herself with all her old ingenuity and success, and with all her invincible energy. True, you had sometimes to read between the lines, and divide everything by about three in order to allow for exaggerations, and when Lucia spoke of not disappointing dearest Aggie, who had set her heart on presenting her at Court, or of Mrs. Garroby-Ashton making a point of her going down for the weekend which she had intended to spend at Riseholme, Georgie only had to remember how she had been forced (so she said) to be Queen at those May Day revels. By sheer power of will she had made each of them become a Robin Hood or a Maid Marian, or whatever it was, and then, when she had got them all at work she said it was she who was being worked to death over *their* May Day revels. They had forced her to organise them, they had insisted that she should be Queen, and lead the dances and sing louder than anybody, and be crowned and curtseyed to. They had been wax in her hands, and now in new circumstances, Georgie felt sure that dearest Aggie had been positively forced to present her, and no doubt Mrs. Garroby-Ashton, cornered on that terrace of the House of Commons, while sweet Thames flowed softly, had had no choice but to ask her down for a Sunday. Will-power, indomitable perseverance now, as always, was getting her just precisely what she had wanted: by it she had become Queen of Riseholme, and by it she was firmly climbing away in London, and already she was saying that everybody was insisting on her dining and lunching with them, whereas it was her moral force that made them powerless in her grip. Riseholme she had no use for now: she was busy with something else; she did not care to be bothered with Georgie, and so she said it was the dining-room carpet.

"Very well," said Georgie bitterly. "And if she doesn't want me, I won't want her. So that's that."

He briskly put the letter away, and began to consider what he should do with himself all day. It was warm enough to sit out and paint: in fact, he had already begun a sketch of the front of his house from the green opposite; there was his piano if he settled to have a morning of music; there was the paper to read, there was news to collect, there was Daisy Quantock next door who would be delighted to have a sitting with the planchette, which was really beginning to write whole words instead of making meaningless dashes and scribbles, and yet none of these things which, together with plenty of conversation and a little house-keeping and manicuring, had long made life such a busy and strenuous performance, seemed to offer an adequate stimulus. And he knew well enough what rendered them devoid of tonic: it was that Lucia was not here, and however much he told himself he did not want her, he like all the rest of Riseholme was begin-ning to miss her dreadfully. She aggravated and exasperated them: she was a hypocrite (all that pretence of not having read the Mozart duet, and desolation at Auntie's death), a poseuse, a sham and a snob, but there was something about her that stirred you into violent though protesting activity, and though she might infuriate you, she prevented your being dull. Georgie enjoyed painting, but he knew that the fact that he would show his sketch to Lucia gave spice to his enjoyment, and that she, though know-ing no more about it than a rhinoceros, would hold it at arm's length with her head a little on one side and her eyes slightly closed, and say:

"Yes, Georgie, very nice, very nice. But have you got the value of your middle-distance quite right? And a little more depth in your distance, do you think?"

Or if he played his piano, he knew that what inspired his nimbleness would be the prospect of playing his piece to her, and if he was practising on the sly a duet for performance with her, the knowledge that he was stealing a march on her and would astonish her (though she might suspect the cause of his facility). And as for conversation, it was useless to deny that conversation languished in Riseholme if the subject of Lucia, her feats and her frailties was tabooed.

"We've got to pull ourselves together," thought Georgie, "and start again. We must get going and learn to do without her, as she's getting on so nicely without us. I shall go and see how the planchette is progressing."

Daisy was already at it, and the pencil was getting up steam. A day or two ago it had written not once only but many times a strange sort of hieroglyphic, which might easily be interpreted to be the mystic word Abfou. Daisy had therefore settled (what could be more obvious?) that the name of the control who guided these strange gyrations was Abfou, which sounded very Egyptian and antique. Therefore, she powerfully reasoned, the scribbles which could not be made to fit any known configuration of English letters might easily be Arabic. Why Abfou should write his name in English characters and his communications in Arabic was not Daisy's concern, for who knew what were the conditions on the other side? A sheet was finished just as Georgie came in, and though it presented nothing but Arabic script, the movements of the planchette had been so swift and eager that Daisy quite forgot to ask if there was any news.

"Abfou is getting in more direct touch with me every time

I sit," said Daisy. "I feel sure we shall have something of great importance before long. Put your hand on the planchette too, Georgie, for I have always believed that you have mediumistic powers. Concentrate first: that means you must put everything else out of your head. Let us sit for a minute or two with our eyes shut. Breathe deeply. Relax. Sometimes slight hypnosis comes on, so the book says, which means you get very drowsy."

There was silence for a few moments: Georgie wanted to tell Daisy about Lucia's letter, but that would certainly interrupt Abfou, so he drew up a chair, and after laying his hand on Daisy's closed his eyes and breathed deeply. And then suddenly the most extraordinary things began to happen.

The planchette trembled: it vibrated like a kettle on the boil, and began to skate about the paper. He had no idea what its antic motions meant: he only knew that it was writing something, Arabic perhaps, but something firm and decided. It seemed to him that so far from aiding its movement, he almost, to be on the safe side, checked it. He opened his eyes, for it was impossible not to want to watch this manifestation of psychic force, and also he wished to be sure (though he had no real suspicions on the subject) that his collaborator was not, to put it coarsely, pushing. Exactly the same train of thought was passing in Daisy's mind, and she opened her eyes too.

"Georgie, my hand is positively being dragged about," she said excitedly. "If anything, I try to resist."

"Mine too; so do I," said Georgie. "It's too wonderful. Do you suppose it's Arabic still?"

The pencil gave a great dash, and stopped.

"It isn't Arabic," said Daisy as she examined the message, "at least, there's heaps of English too."

"No!" said Georgie, putting on his spectacles in his excitement, and not caring whether Daisy knew he wore them or not. "I can see it looks like English, but what a difficult handwriting! Look, that's 'Abfou,' isn't it? And that is 'Abfou' again there."

They bent their heads over the script.

"There's an 'L,' " cried Daisy, "and there it is again. And then there's 'L from L.' And then there's 'Dead' repeated twice. It can't mean that Abfou is dead, because this is positive proof that he's alive. And then I can see 'Mouse'?"

"Where?" said Georgie eagerly. "And what would 'dead mouse' mean?"

"There!" said Daisy, pointing. "No: it isn't 'dead mouse.' It's 'dead' and then a lot of Arabic, and then 'mouse.' "

"I don't believe it is 'Mouse,' " said Georgie, "though of course, you know Abfou's handwriting much better than I do. It looks to me far more like 'Museum.' "

"Perhaps he wants me to send all the Arabic he's written up to the British Museum," said Daisy with a flash of genius, "so that they can read it and say what it means."

"But then there's 'Museum' or 'Mouse' again there," said Georgie, "and surely that word in front of it—It is! It's Rise-holme! Riseholme Mouse or Riseholme Museum! I don't know what either would mean."

"You may depend upon it that it means something," said Daisy, "and there's another capital 'L.' Does it mean Lucia, do you think? But 'dead' . . ."

"No: dead's got nothing to do with the 'L,' " said Georgie. "Museum comes in between, and quantities of Arabic."

"I think I'll just record the exact time; it would be more sci-entific," said Daisy. "A quarter to eleven. No, that clock's three minutes fast by the church time."

"No, the church time is slow," said Georgie.

Suddenly he jumped up.

"I've got it," he said. "Look! 'L from L.' That means a letter from Lucia. And it's quite true. I heard this morning, and it's in my pocket now."

"No!" said Daisy. "That's just a sign Abfou is giving us, that he really is with us, and knows what is going on. Very evidential."

The absorption of them both in this script may be faintly appreciated by the fact that neither Daisy evinced the slightest curiosity as to what Lucia said, nor Georgie the least desire to communicate it.

"And then there's 'dead,'" said Georgie, looking out of the window. "I wonder what that means."

"I'm sure I hope it's not Lucia," said Daisy with stoical calmness, "but I can't think of anybody else."

Georgie's eyes wandered over the green; Mrs. Boucher was speeding round in her bath-chair, pushed by her husband, and there was the vicar walking very fast, and Mrs. Antrobus and Piggy and Goosie . . . nobody else seemed to be dead. Then his eye came back to the foreground of Daisy's front garden.

"What has happened to your mulberry tree?" he said parenthetically. "Its leaves are all drooping. You ought never to have pruned its roots without knowing how to do it."

Daisy jumped up.

"Georgie, you've got it!" she said. "It's the mulberry tree that's dead. Isn't that wonderful?"

Georgie was suitably impressed.

"That's very curious: very curious indeed," he said. "Letter from Lucia, and the dead mulberry tree. I do believe there's something in it. But let's go on studying the script. Now I look at it again I feel certain it is Riseholme Museum, not Riseholme

Mouse. The only difficulty is that there isn't a Museum in Riseholme."

"There are plenty of mice," observed Daisy, who had had some trouble with these little creatures. "Abfou may be wanting to give me advice about some kind of ancient Egyptian trap . . . But if you aren't very busy this morning, Georgie, we might have another sitting and see if we get anything more definite. Let us attain collectedness as the directions advise."

"What's collectedness?" asked Georgie.

Daisy gave him the directions. Collectedness seemed to be a sort of mixture of intense concentration and complete vacuity of mind.

"You seem to have to concentrate your mind upon nothing at all," said he after reading it.

"That's just it," said Daisy. "You put all thoughts out of your head, and then focus your mind. We have to be only the instrument through which Abfou functions."

They sat down again after a little deep breathing and relaxation, and almost immediately the planchette began to move across the paper with a firm and steady progression. It stopped sometimes for a few minutes, which was proof of the authenticity of the controlling force, for in spite of all efforts at collectedness, both Daisy's and Georgie's minds were full of things which they longed for Abfou to communicate, and if either of them was consciously directing those movements, there could have been no pause at all. When finally it gave that great dash across the paper again, indicating that the communication was finished, they found the most remarkable results.

Abfou had written two pages of foolscap in a tall upright hand, which was quite unlike either Daisy's or Georgie's ordinary script, and this was another proof (if proof were wanted) of authenticity. It was comparatively easy to read, and, except for a long passage at the end in Arabic, was written almost entirely in English.

"Look, there's Lucia written out in full four times," said Daisy eagerly. "And 'Pepper.' What's Pepper?"

Georgie gasped. "Why Peppino, of course," he said. "I do call that odd. And see how it goes on—'Muck company,' no, 'Much company, much grand company, higher and higher.'"

"Poor Lucia!" said Daisy. "How sarcastic! That's what Abfou thinks about it all. By the way, you haven't told me what she says yet; never mind, this is far more interesting . . . Then there's a little Arabic, at least I think it's Arabic, for I can't make anything out of it, and then—why, I believe those next words are 'From Olga.' Have you heard from Olga?"

"No," said Georgie, "but there's something about her in Lucia's letter. Perhaps that's it."

"Very likely. And then I can make out Riseholme, and it isn't 'mouse,' it's quite clearly 'Museum,' and then—I can't read that, but it looks English, and then 'opera,' that's Olga again, and 'dead,' which is the mulberry tree. And then 'It is better to work than to be idle. Think not—' something—"

"'Bark,'" said Georgie. "No, 'hard.'"

"Yes. 'Think not hard thoughts of any, but turn thy mind to improving work.'—Georgie, isn't that wonderful?—and then it goes off into Arabic, what a pity! It might have been more about the museum. I shall certainly send all the first Arabic scripts to the British Museum."

Georgie considered this.

"Somehow I don't believe that is what Abfou means," said he. "He says Riseholme Museum, not British Museum. You can't possibly get 'British' out of that word."

Georgie left Daisy still attempting to detect more English among Arabic passages and engaged himself to come in again after tea for fresh investigation. Within a minute of his departure Daisy's telephone rang.

"How tiresome these interruptions are," said Daisy to herself, as she hurried to the instrument. "Yes, yes. Who is it?"

Georgie's voice had the composure of terrific excitement.

"It's me," he said. "The second post has just come in, and a letter from Olga. 'From Olga,' you remember."

"No!" said Daisy. "Do tell me if she says anything about—"

But Georgie had already rung off. He wanted to read his letter from Olga, and Daisy sat down again quite awestruck at this further revelation. The future clearly was known to Abfou as well as the past, for Georgie knew nothing about Olga's letter when the words "From Olga" occurred in the script. And if in it she said anything about "opera" (which really was on the cards) it would be more wonderful still.

The morning was nearly over, so Daisy observed to her prodigious surprise, for it had really gone like a flash (a flash of the highest illuminative power), and she hurried out with a trowel and a rake to get half an hour in the garden before lunch. It was rather disconcerting to find that though she spent the entire day in the garden, often not sitting down to her planchette till dusk rendered it impossible to see the mazes of cotton threads she had stretched over newly sown beds, to keep off sparrows (she had on one occasion shattered with a couple of hasty steps the whole of those defensive fortifications), she seemed, in spite of blistered hands and aching back, to be falling more and more into arrears over her horticulture. Whereas that ruffian Simkinson, whom she had dismissed for laziness when she found him smoking a pipe in the potting-shed and doing a crossword puzzle when he ought to have been working, really kept her garden in very good order by slouching about it for three half-days in the week. To be sure, she had pruned the roots of the mulberry tree, which had taken a whole day (and so incidentally had killed the mulberry tree) and though the death of that antique vegetable had given Abfou a fine opportunity for proving himself, evidence now was getting so abundant that Daisy almost wished it hadn't happened. Then, too, she was beginning to have secret qualms that she had torn up as weeds a quantity of seedlings which the indolent Simkinson had just pricked out, for though the beds were now certainly weedless, there was no sign of any other growth there. And either Daisy's little wooden labels had got mixed, or she had sown Brussels sprouts in the circular bed just outside the dining-room window instead of Phlox Drummondi. She thought she had attached the appropriate label to the seed she had sown, but it was very dark at the time, and in the morning the label certainly said "Brussels sprouts." In which case there would be a bed of Phlox at the far end of the little strip of kitchen garden. The seeds in both places were sprouting now, so she would know the worst or the best before long.

Then, again, there was the rockery she had told Simkinson to build, which he had neglected for crossword puzzles, and though Daisy had been working six or eight hours a day in her garden ever since, she had not found time to touch a stone of it, and the fragments lying like a moraine on the path by the potting-shed still rendered any approach to the latter a mountaineering feat. They consisted of fragments of mediaeval masonry, from the site of the ancient abbey, finials and crockets and pieces of mullioned windows which had been turned up when a new siding of the railway had been made, and everyone almost had got some with the exception of Mrs. Boucher, who called them rubbish. Then there were some fossils, ammonites and spar and curious flints with holes in them and bits of talc, for Lucia one year had commandeered them all into the study of geology and they had got hammers and whacked away at the face of an old quarry, detaching these petrified relics and hitting themselves over the fingers in the process. It was that year that the Roman camp outside the village had been put under the plough and Riseholme had followed it like a bevy of rooks, and Georgie had got several trays full of fragments of iridescent glass, and Colonel Boucher had collected bits of Samian ware, and Mrs. Antrobus had found a bronze fibula or safety-pin. Daisy had got some chunks of Roman brickwork, and a section of Roman drain-pipe, which now figured among the materials for her rockery; and she had bought, for about their weight in gold, quite a dozen bronze coins. These, of course, would not be placed in the rockery, but she had put them somewhere very carefully, and had subsequently forgotten where that was. Now as these archaeological associations came into her mind from the contemplation of the materials for the rockery, she suddenly thought she remembered that she had put them at the back of the drawer in her card-table.

The sight of these antique fragments disgusted Daisy; they littered the path, and she could not imagine them built up into a rockery that should have the smallest claim to be an attractive object. How could the juxtaposition of a stone mullion, a drainpipe and an ammonite present a pleasant appearance? Besides, who was to juxtapose them? She could not keep pace with the other needs of the garden, let alone a rockery, and where, after all, was the rockery to stand? The asparagus-bed seemed the only place, and she preferred asparagus.

Robert was bawling out from the dining-room window that lunch was ready, and as she retraced her steps to the house, she thought that perhaps it would be better to eat humble pie and get Simkinson to return. It was clear to Daisy that if she was to do her duty as medium between ancient Egypt and the world of today, the garden would deteriorate even more rapidly than it was doing already, and no doubt Robert would consent to eat the humble pie for her, and tell Simkinson that they couldn't get on without him, and that when she had said he was lazy, she had meant industrious, or whatever else was necessary.

Robert was in a very good temper that day because Roumanian oils, which were the main source of his fortunes, had announced a higher dividend than usual, and he promised to seek out Simkinson and explain what lazy meant, and if he didn't understand, to soothe his injured feelings with a small tip.

"And tell him he needn't make a rockery at all," said Daisy. "He always hated the idea of a rockery. He can dig a pit and bury the fossils and the architectural fragments and everything. That will be the easiest way of disposing of them."

"And what is he to do with the earth he takes out of the pit, my dear?" asked Robert.

"Put it back, I suppose," said Daisy rather sharply. Robert was so pleased at having "caught" her, that he did not even explain that she had been caught . . .

∞

After lunch Daisy found the coins; it was odd that, having forgotten where she had put them for so long, she should suddenly remember, and she was inclined to attribute this inspiration to Abfou. The difficulty was to know what, having found them, to do with them next. Some of them obviously bore signs of once having had profiles of Roman emperors stamped on them, and she was sure she had heard that some Roman coins were of great value, and probably these were the ones. Perhaps when she sent the Arabic script to the British Museum she might send these too for identification . . . And then she dropped them all on the floor as the great idea struck her.

She flew into the garden, calling to Georgie, who was putting up croquet-hoops.

"Georgie, I've got it!" she cried. "It's as plain as plain. What Abfou wants us to do is to start a Riseholme Museum. He wrote Riseholme Museum quite distinctly. Think how it would pay too, when we're overrun with American tourists in the summer! They would all come to see it. A shilling admission I should put it at, and sixpence for the catalogue."

"I wonder if Abfou meant that," said Georgie.

"He said it," said Daisy. "You can't deny that!"

"But what should we put in the Museum?" asked he.

"My dear, we should fill it with antiquities and things which none of us want in our houses. There are those beautiful fragments of the Abbey which I've got, and which are simply wasted in my garden with no one to see them, and my drain-pipe. I would present them all to the Museum, and the fossils, and perhaps some of my coins. And my Roman brickwork."

Georgie paused with a hoop in his hand.

"That is an idea," he said. "And I've got all those lovely pieces of iridescent glass, which are always tumbling about. I would give them."

"And Colonel Boucher's Samian ware," cried Daisy. "He was saying only the other day how he hated it, but didn't quite want to throw it away. It will be a question of what we leave out, not of what we put in. Besides, I'm sure that's what Abfou meant. We must form a committee at once. You and Mrs. Boucher and I, I should think, would be enough. Large committees are a great mistake."

"Not Lucia?" asked Georgie, with lingering loyalty.

"No. Certainly not," said Daisy. "She would only send us orders from London, as to what we were to do and want us to undo all we had done when she came back, besides saying she had thought of it, and making herself President!"

"There's something in that," said Georgie.

"Of course there is, there's sense," said Daisy. "Now I shall go straight and see Mrs. Boucher."

Georgie dealt a few smart blows with his mallet to the hoop he was putting in place.

"I shall come too," he said. "Riseholme Museum! I believe Abfou did mean that. We *shall* be busy again."

Chapter Four

THE COMMITTEE MET THAT VERY afternoon, and the next morning and the next afternoon, and the scheme quickly took shape. Robert, rolling in golden billows of Roumanian oil, was called in as financial adviser, and after calculation, the scheme strongly recommended itself to him. All the summer the town was thronged with visitors, and enquiring American minds would hardly leave unvisited the Museum at so Elizabethan a place.

"I don't know what you'll have in your Museum," he said, "but I expect they'll go to look, and even if they don't find much they'll have paid their shillings. And if Mrs. Boucher thinks her husband will let you have that big tithe-barn of his, at a small rent, I dare say you'll have a paying proposition."

The question of funds therefore in order to convert the tithe-barn into a museum was instantly gone into. Robert professed himself perfectly ready to equip the tithe-barn with all necessary furniture and decoration, if he might collar the whole of the receipts, but his willingness to take all financial responsibilities made the committee think that they would like to have a share in them, since so shrewd a businessman clearly saw the probability of making something out of it. Up till then, the sordid question of money had not really occurred to them: there was to be a museum which would make them busy again, and the committee was to run it. They were quite willing to devote practically the whole of their time to it, for Riseholme was one of those happy places where the proverb that Time is money was a flat fallacy, for nobody had ever earned a penny with it. But since Robert's financial judgement argued that the Museum would be a profitable investment, the committee naturally wished to have a hand in it, and the three members each subscribed fifty pounds, and co-opted Robert to join the board and supply the rest. Profits (if any) would be divided up between the members of the committee in proportion to their subscriptions. The financial Robert would see to all that, and the rest of them could turn their attention to the provision of curiosities.

There was evidently to be no lack of them, for everyone in Riseholme had stores of miscellaneous antiquities and "specimens" of various kinds which encumbered their houses and required a deal of dusting, but which couldn't quite be thrown away. A very few striking objects were only lent: among these were Daisy's box of coins, and Mrs. Antrobus's fibula, but the most of them, like Georgie's glass and Colonel Boucher's pieces of Samian ware, were fervently bestowed. Objects of all sorts poured in, the greater portion of a spinning-wheel, an Elizabethan pestle and mortar, no end of Roman tiles, a large wooden post unhesitatingly called a whipping-post, some indecipherable documents on parchment with seals attached, belonging to the vicar, an ordnance map of the district, numerous collections of fossils and of carved stones from the site of the Abbey, ancient quilts, a baby's cradle, worm-eaten enough to be Anglo-Saxon, queer-shaped bottles, a tiger-ware jug, fire-irons too ponderous for use, and (by special vote of the Parish Council) the stocks which had hitherto stood at the edge of the pond on the green. All Riseholme was busy again, for fossils had to be sorted out (it was early realised that even a museum could have too many ammonites), curtains had to be stitched for the windows, labels to be written, Samian ware to be pieced together, cases arranged, a catalogue prepared. The period of flatness consequent on Lucia's desertion had passed off, and what had certainly added zest to industry was the thought that Lucia had nothing to do with the Museum. When next she deigned to visit her discarded kingdom, she would find how busily and successfully and originally they had got on without her, and that there was no place for her on the committee, and probably none in the Museum for the Elizabethan turnspit which so often made the chimney of her music-room to smoke.

Riseholme, indeed, was busier than ever, for not only had it the Museum feverishly to occupy it so that it might be open for the tourist season this year, and, if possible, before Lucia came down for one of her promised weekends, but it was immersed in a wave of psychical experiments. Daisy Quantock had been perfectly honest in acknowledging that the idea of the Museum was not hers at all, but Abfou's, her Egyptian guide. She had, it is true, been as ingenious as Joseph in interpreting Abfou's directions, but it was Abfou to whom all credit was due, and who evidently took such a deep interest in the affairs of Riseholme. She even offered to present the Museum with the sheet of foolscap on which the words "Riseholme Museum" (not mouse) were written, but the general feeling of the committee, while thanking her for her munificence, was that it would not be tactful to display it, since the same Sibylline sheet contained those sarcastic remarks about Lucia. It was proved also that Abfou had meant the Museum to be started, for subsequently he several times said, "Much pleased with your plans for the Museum. Abfou approves." So everybody else wanted to get into touch with Abfou too, and no less than four planchettes or ouija-boards were immediately ordered by various members of Riseholme society. At present Abfou did not manifest himself to any of them, except in what was possibly Arabic script (for it certainly bore a strong resemblance to his earlier efforts of communication with Daisy), and while she encouraged the scribes to persevere in the hope that he might soon regale them with English, she was not really very anxious that he should. With her he was getting Englisher and Englisher every day, and had not Simkinson, after having had the true meaning of the word "lazy" carefully explained to him, consented to manage her garden again, it certainly would have degenerated into primeval jungle, for she absolutely had not a minute to attend to it.

Simkinson, however, was quite genial.

"Oh yes, ma'am, very pleased to come back," he said. "I knew you wouldn't be able to get on long without me, and I want no explanations. Now let's have a look round and see what you've been doing. Why, whatever's happened to my mulberry tree?"

That was Simkinson's way: he always talked of "my flowers" and "my asparagus" when he meant hers.

"I've been pruning its roots," she said.

"Well, ma'am, you've done your best to do it in," said Simkinson. "I don't think it's dead though, I dare say it'll pull round."

Abfou had been understood to say it was dead, but perhaps he meant something else, thought Daisy, and they went on to the small circular bed below the dining-room windows.

"Phlox," said Daisy hopefully.

"Broccoli," said Simkinson, examining the young green sprouts. "And the long bed there. I sowed a lot of annuals there, and I don't see a sign of anything coming up."

He fixed her with a merry eye.

"I believe you've been weeding, ma'am," he said. "I shall have to get you a lot of young plants if you want a bit of colour there. It's too late for me to put my seeds in again."

Daisy rather wished she hadn't come out with him, and changed the subject to something more cheerful.

"Well, I shan't want the rockery," she said. "You needn't bother about that. All these stones will be carted away in a day or two."

"Glad of that, ma'am. I'll be able to get to my potting-shed again. Well, I'll try to put you to rights. I'd best pull up the broccoli first, you won't want it under your windows, will you? You stick to rolling the lawn, ma'am, if you want to garden. You won't do any harm then."

It was rather dreadful being put in one's place like this, but Daisy did not dare risk a second quarrel, and the sight of Georgie at the dining-room window (he had come across to "weedj," as the psychical processes, whether ouija or planchette, were now called) was rather a relief. Weeding, after all, was unimportant compared with weedjing.

"And I don't believe I ever told you what Olga wrote about," said Georgie, as soon as she was within range. "We've talked of nothing but museum. Oh, and Mrs. Boucher's planchette has come. But it broke in the post, and she's gumming it together."

"I doubt if it will act," said Daisy. "But what did Olga say? It quite went out of my head to ask you."

"It's too heavenly of her," said he. "She's asked me to go up and stay with her for the first night of the opera. She's singing Lucrezia, and has got a stall for me."

"No!" said Daisy, making a trial trip over the blotting-paper to see if the pencil was sharp. "That will be an event! I suppose you're going."

"Just about," said Georgie. "It's going to be broadcasted, too, and I shall be listening to the original."

"How interesting!" said Daisy. "And there you'll be in Brompton Square, just opposite Lucia. Oh, you heard from her? What did she say?"

"Apparently she's getting on marvellously," said Georgie. "Not a moment to spare. Just what she likes."

Daisy pushed the planchette aside. There would be time for that when she had had a little talk about Lucia.

"And are you going to stay with her too?" she asked.

Georgie was quite determined not to be ill-natured. He had taken no part (or very little) in this trampling on Lucia's majesty, which had been so merrily going on.

"I should love to, if she would ask me," he observed. "She only says she's going to. Of course, I shall go to see her."

"I wouldn't," said Daisy savagely. "If she asked me fifty times I should say 'no' fifty times. What's happened is that she's dropped us. I wouldn't have her on our museum committee if—if she gave her pearls to it and said they belonged to Queen Elizabeth. I wonder you haven't got more spirit."

"I've got plenty of spirit," said Georgie, "and I allow I did feel rather hurt at her letter. But then, after all, what does it matter?"

"Of course it doesn't if you're going to stay with Olga," said Daisy. "How she'll hate you for that!"

"Well, I can't help it," he said. "Lucia hasn't asked me and Olga has. She's twice reminded Olga that she may use her music-room to practise in whenever she likes. Isn't that kind? She would love to be able to say that Olga's always practising in her music-room. But aren't we ill-natured? Let's weedj instead."

∞

Georgie found, when he arrived next afternoon in Brompton Square, that Olga had already had her early dinner, and that he was to dine alone at seven and follow her to the opera house.

"I'm on the point of collapse from sheer nerves," she said. "I always am before I sing, and then out of desperation I pull myself together. If—I say 'if'—I survive till midnight, we're going to have a little party here. Cortese is coming, and Princess Isabel, and one or two other people. Georgie, it's very daring of you to come here, you know, because my husband's away, and I'm an unprotected female alone with Don Juan. How's Riseholme? Talk to me about Riseholme. Are you engaged to Piggy yet? And is it broccoli or phlox in Daisy's round bed? Your letter was so mysterious too. I know nothing about the Museum yet. What Museum? Are you going to kill and stuff Lucia and put her in the hall? You simply alluded to the Museum as if I knew all about it. If you don't talk to me, I shall scream."

Georgie flung himself into the task, delighted to be thought capable of doing anything for Olga. He described at great length and with much emphasis the whole of the history of Riseholme from the first epiphany of Arabic and Abfou on the planchette-board down to the return of Simkinson. Olga lost herself in these chronicles, and when her maid came in to tell her it was time to start, she got up quite cheerfully.

"And so it was broccoli," she said. "I was afraid it was going to be phlox after all. You're an angel, Georgie, for getting me through my bad hour. I'll give you anything you like for the Museum. Wait for me afterwards at the stage door. We'll drive back together."

From the moment Olga appeared, the success of the opera was secure. Cortese, who was conducting, had made his music well; it thoroughly suited her, and she was singing and looking and acting her best. Again and again after the first act the curtain had to go up, and not until the house was satisfied could Georgie turn his glances this way and that to observe the audience.

Then in the twilight of a small box on the second tier he espied a woman who was kissing her hand somewhere in his direction, and a man waving a programme, and then he suddenly focused them and saw who they were. He ran upstairs to visit them, and there was Lucia in an extraordinarily short skirt with her hair shingled, and round her neck three short rows of seed pearls.

"Georgino *mio*!" she cried. "This is a surprise! You came up to see our dear Olga's triumph. I do call that loyalty. Why did you not tell me you were coming?"

"I thought I would call tomorrow," said Georgie, with his eyes still going backwards and forwards between the shingle and the pearls and the legs.

"Ah, you are staying the night in town?" she asked. "Not going back by the midnight train? The dear old midnight train, and waking in Riseholme! At your club?"

"No, I'm staying with Olga," said Georgie.

Lucia seemed to become slightly cataleptic for a moment, but recovered.

"No! Are you really?" she said. "I think that is unkind of you, Georgie. You might have told me you were coming."

"But you said that the house wasn't ready," said he. "And she asked me."

Lucia put on a bright smile.

"Well, you're forgiven," she said. "We're all at sixes and sevens yet. And we've seen nothing of dearest Olga—or Mrs. Shuttleworth, I should say, for that's on the bills. Of course we'll drive you home, and you must come in for a chat, before Mrs. Shuttleworth gets home, and then no doubt she will be very tired and want to go to bed."

Lucia as she spoke had been surveying the house with occasional little smiles and wagglings of her hand in vague directions.

"Ah, there's Elsie Garroby-Ashton," she said, "and who is that with her, Peppino? Lord Shrivenham, surely. So come back with me and have 'ickle talk, Georgie. Oh, there's the Italian Ambassadress. Dearest Gioconda! Such a sweet. And look at the Royal Box. What a gathering! That's the Royal Box, Georgie, away to the left—that large one—in the tier below. Too near the stage for my taste: so little illusion—"

Lucia suddenly rose and made a profound curtsey.

"I think she saw us, Peppino," she said, "perhaps you had better bow. No, she's looking somewhere else now: you did not bow quick enough. And what a party in dearest Aggie's box. Who can that be? Oh yes, it's Toby Limpsfield. We met him at Aggie's, do you remember, on the first night we were up. So join us at the grand entrance, Georgie, and drive back with us. We shall be giving a lift to somebody else, I'll be bound, but if you have your motor, it is so ill-natured not to pick up friends. I always do it: they will be calling us the 'Lifts of London,' as Marcia Whitby said."

"I'm afraid I can't do that," said Georgie. "I'm waiting for Olga, and she's having a little party, I believe."

"No! Is she really?" asked Lucia, with all the old Riseholme vivacity. "Who is coming?"

"Cortese, I believe," said Georgie, thinking it might be too much for Lucia if he mentioned a princess, "and one or two of the singers."

Lucia's mouth watered, and she swallowed rapidly. That was the kind of party she longed to be asked to, for it would be so wonderful and glorious to be able casually to allude to Olga's tiny, tiny little party after the first night of the opera, not a party at all really, just a few *intimes,* herself and Cortese and so on. How could she manage it? she wondered. Could she pretend not to know that there was a party, and just drop in for a moment in neighbourly fashion with enthusiastic congratulations? Or should she pretend her motor had not come, and hang about the stage door with Georgie—Peppino could go home in the motor— and get a lift? Or should she hint very violently to Georgie how she would like to come in just for a minute. Or should she, now that she knew there was to be a party, merely assert that she had been to it? Perhaps a hint to Georgie was the best plan . . .

Her momentary indecision was put an end to by the appearance of Cortese threading his way among the orchestra, and the lowering of the lights. Georgie, without giving her any further opportunity, hurried back to his stall, feeling that he had had an escape, for Lucia's beady eye had been fixing him, just in the way it always used to do when she wanted something and, in consequence, meant to get it. He felt he had been quite wrong in ever supposing that Lucia had changed. She was just precisely the same, translated into a larger sphere. She had expanded: strange though it seemed, she had only been in bud at Riseholme. "I wonder what she'll do?" thought Georgie as he settled himself into his stall. "She wants dreadfully to come."

The opera came to an end in a blaze of bouquets and triumph and recalls, and curtseys. It was something of an occasion, for it was the first night of the opera, and the first performance of *Lucrezia* in London, and it was late when Olga came florally out. The party, which was originally meant to be no party at all, but just a little supper with Cortese and one or two of the singers, had marvellously increased during the evening, for friends had sent round messages and congratulations, and Olga had asked them to drop in, and when she and Georgie arrived at Brompton Square, the whole of the curve at the top was packed with motors.

"Heavens, what a lot of people I seem to have asked," she said, "but it will be great fun. There won't be nearly enough chairs, but we'll sit on the floor, and there won't be nearly enough supper, but I know there's a ham, and what can be better than a ham? Oh, Georgie, I am happy."

Now from opposite, across the narrow space of the square, Lucia had seen the arrival of all these cars. In order to see them better she had gone on to the balcony of her drawing-room, and noted their occupants with her opera-glasses. There was Lord Limpsfield, and the Italian Ambassadress, and Mr. Garroby-Ashton, and Cortese, and some woman to whom Mr. Garroby-Ashton bowed and Mrs. Garroby-Ashton curtseyed. Up they streamed. And there was the Duchess of Whitby (Marcia, for Lucia had heard her called that) coming up the steps, and curt-seying too, but as yet Olga and Georgie quite certainly had not come. It seemed strange that so many brilliant guests should arrive before their hostess, but Lucia saw at once that this was the most chic informality that it was possible to conceive. No doubt Mr. Shuttleworth was there to receive them, but how wonderful it all was! . . . And then the thought occurred to her that Olga would arrive, and with her would be Georgie, and she felt herself turning bright green all over with impotent jealousy. Georgie in that crowd! It was impossible that Georgie should be there, and not she, but that was certainly what would happen unless she thought of something. Georgie would go back to Rise-holme and describe this gathering, and he would say that Lucia was not there: he supposed she had not been asked.

Lucia thought of something; she hurried downstairs and let herself out. Motors were still arriving, but perhaps she was not too late. She took up her stand in the central shadow of a gas lamp close to Olga's door and waited.

Up the square came yet another car, and she could see it was full of flowers. Olga stepped out, and she darted forward.

"Oh, Mrs. Shuttleworth," she said. "Splendid! Glorious! Marvellous! If only Beethoven was alive! I could not think of going to bed, without just popping across to thank you for a revelation! Georgie, dear! Just to shake your hand: that is all. All! I won't detain you. I see you have a party! You wonderful Queen of Song."

Olga at all times was good-natured. Her eye met Georgie's for a moment.

"Oh, but come in," she said. "Do come in. It isn't a party: it's just anybody. Georgie, be a dear, and help to carry all those flowers in. How nice of you to come across, Mrs. Lucas! I know you'll excuse my running on ahead, because all—at least I hope all—my guests have come, and there's no one to look after them."

Lucia, following closely in her wake, and taking no further notice of Georgie, slipped into the little front drawing-room behind her. It was crammed, and it was such a little room. Why had she not foreseen this, why had she not sent a note across to Olga earlier in the day, asking her to treat Lucia's house precisely as her own, and have her party in the spacious music-room? It would have been only neighbourly. But the bitterness of such regrets soon vanished in the extraordinary sweetness of the present, and she was soon in conversation with Mrs. Garroby-Ashton, and distributing little smiles and nods to all the folk with whom she had the slightest acquaintance. By the fireplace was standing the Royal lady, and that for the moment was the only chagrin, for Lucia had not the vaguest idea who she was. Then Georgie came in, looking like a flower-stall, and then came a slight second chagrin, for Olga led him up to the Royal lady, and introduced him. But that would be all right, for she could easily get Georgie to tell her who she was, without exactly asking him, and then poor Georgie made a very awkward sort of bow, and dropped a large quantity of flowers, and said "tarsome."

Lucia glided away from Mrs. Garroby-Ashton and stood near the Duchess of Whitby. Marcia did not seem to recognise her at first, but that was quickly remedied, and after a little pleasant talk, Lucia asked her to lunch to meet Olga, and fixed in her mind that she must ask Olga to lunch on the same day to meet the Duchess of Whitby. Then edging a little nearer to the centre of attraction, she secured Lord Limpsfield by angling for him with the bait of dearest Aggie, to whom she must remember to telephone early next morning, to ask her to come and meet Lord Limpsfield.

That would do for the present, and Lucia abandoned herself to the joys of the moment. A move was made downstairs to supper, and Lucia, sticking like a limpet to Lord Limpsfield, was wafted in azure to Olga's little tiny dining-room, and saw at once that there were not nearly enough seats for everybody. There were two small round tables, and that was absolutely all: the rest would have to stand and forage at the narrow buffet which ran along the wall.

"It's musical chairs," said Olga cheerfully, "those who are quick get seats, and the others don't. Tony, go and sit next to the Princess, and Cortese, you go the other side. We shall all get something to eat sometime. Georgie, go and stand by the buffet, there's a dear, and make yourself wonderfully useful, and oh, rush upstairs first, and bring the cigarettes; they stay the pangs of hunger. Now we're getting on beautifully. Darling Marcia, there's just one chair left. Slip into it."

Lucia had lingered for a moment at the door to ask Olga to lunch the day after tomorrow, and Olga said she would be delighted, so there was a wonderful little party arranged for. To complete her content it was only needful to be presented to the hitherto anonymous Princess and learn her name. By dexterously picking up her fan for her and much admiring it, as she made a low curtsey, she secured a few precious words with her, but the name was still denied her. To ask anybody what it was would faintly indicate that she didn't know it, and that was not to be thought of.

∞

Georgie popped in, as they all said at Riseholme, to see Lucia next morning when Olga had gone to a rehearsal at Covent Garden, and found her in her music-room, busy over Stravinski. Olga's party had not been in *The Times*, which was annoying, and Lucia was still unaware what the Princess's name was. Though the previous evening had been far the most rewarding she had yet spent, it was wiser to let Georgie suppose that such an affair was a very ordinary occurrence, and not to allude to it for some time.

"Ah, Georgino!" she said. "How nice of you to pop in. By *buona fortuna* I have got a spare hour this morning, before Sophy Alingsby—dear Sophy, such a brain—fetches me to go to some private view or other, so we can have a good chat. Yes, this is the music-room, and before you go, I must trot you round to see the rest of our little establishment. Not a bad room—those are the famous Chippendale chairs—as soon as we get a little more settled, I shall give an evening party or two with some music. You must come."

"Should love to," said Georgie.

"Such a whirl it has been, and it gets worse every day," went on Lucia. "Sometimes Peppino and I go out together, but often he dines at one house and I at another—they do that in London, you know—and sometimes I hardly set eyes on him all day. I haven't seen him this morning, but just now they told me he had gone out. He enjoys it so much that I do not mind how tired I get. Ah! That telephone, it never ceases ringing. Sometimes I think I will have it taken out of the house altogether, for I get no peace. Somebody always seems to be wanting Peppino or me."

She hurried, all the same, with considerable alacrity to the machine, and really there was no thought in her mind of having the telephone taken out, for it had only just been installed. The call, however, was rather a disappointment, for it only concerned a pair of walking-shoes. There was no need, however, to tell Georgie that, and pressing her finger to her forehead she said, "Yes, I can manage half-past three" (which meant nothing), and quickly rang off.

"Not a moment's peace," said Lucia. "Ting-a-ting-a-ting from morning till night. Now tell me all about Riseholme, Georgie; that will give me such a delicious feeling of tranquillity. Dear me, who is this coming to interrupt us now?"

It was only Peppino. He seemed leisurely enough, and rather unnecessarily explained that he had only been out to get a toothbrush from the chemist's in Brompton Road. This he carried in a small paper parcel.

"And there's the man coming about the telephone this morning, Lucia," he said. "You want the extension to your bedroom, don't you?"

"Yes, dear, as we have got it in the house we may as well have it conveniently placed," she said. "I'm sure the miles I walk up and down stairs, as I was telling Georgie—"

Peppino chuckled.

"She woke them up, Georgie," he said. "None of their leisurely London ways for Lucia. She had the telephone put into the house in record time. Gave them no peace till she got it done."

"Very wise," said Georgie tactfully. "That's the way to get things. Well, about Riseholme. We've really been very busy indeed."

"Dear old place!" said Lucia. "Tell me all about it."

Georgie rapidly considered with himself whether he should mention the Museum. He decided against it, for, put it as you might, the Museum, apart from the convenience of getting rid of interesting rubbish, was of a conspiratorial nature, a policy of revenge against Lucia for her desertion, and a demonstration of how wonderfully well and truly they all got on without her. It was, then, the mark of a highly injudicious conspirator to give information to her against whom this plot was directed.

"Well, Daisy has been having some most remarkable experiences," he said. "She got a ouija-board and a planchette—we use the planchette most—and very soon it was quite clear that messages were coming through from a guide."

Lucia laughed with a shrill metallic note of rather hostile timbre.

"Dear Daisy," she said. "If only she would take common sense as her guide. I suppose the guide is a Chaldean astrologer or King Nebuchadnezzar."

"Not at all," said Georgie. "It's an Egyptian called Abfou."

A momentary pang of envy shot through Lucia. She could well imagine the quality of excitement which thrilled Riseholme, how Georgie would have popped in to tell her about it, and how she would have got a ouija-board too, and obtained twice as many messages as Daisy. She hated the thought of Daisy having Abfou all her own way, and gave another little shrill laugh.

"Daisy is priceless," she said. "And what has Abfou told her?"

"Well, it was very odd," said Georgie. "The morning I got

your letter Abfou wrote 'L from L,' and if that doesn't mean 'Letter from Lucia,' I don't know what else it could be."

"It might just as well mean 'Lozenges from Leamington,'" said Lucia witheringly. "And what else?"

Georgie felt the conversation was beginning to border rather dangerously on the Museum, and tried a light-hearted sortie into another subject.

"Oh, just things of that sort," he said. "And then she had a terrible time over her garden. She dismissed Simkinson for doing crossword puzzles instead of the lawn, and determined to do it all herself. She sowed sprouts in that round bed under the dining-room window."

"No!" said Peppino, who was listening with qualms of homesickness to these chronicles.

"Yes, and the phlox in the kitchen garden," said Georgie.

He looked at Lucia, and became aware that her gimlet-eye was on him, and was afraid he had made the transition from Abfou to horticulture rather too eagerly. He went volubly on.

"And she dug up all the seeds that Simkinson had planted, and pruned the roots of her mulberry tree and probably killed it," he said. "Then in that warm weather last week, no, the week before, I got out my painting things again, and am doing a sketch of my house from the green. Foljambe is very well, and, and . . ." He could think of nothing else except the Museum.

Lucia waited till he had quite run down.

"And what more did Abfou say?" she asked. "His message of 'L to L' would not have made you busy for very long."

Georgie had to reconsider the wisdom of silence. Lucia clearly suspected something, and when she came down for her weekend, and found the affairs of the Museum entirely engrossing the whole of Riseholme, his reticence, if he persisted in it, would wear a very suspicious aspect.

"Oh yes, the Museum," he said with feigned lightness. "Abfou told us to start a museum, and it's getting on splendidly. That tithe-barn of Colonel Boucher's. And Daisy's given all the things she was going to make into a rockery, and I'm giving my Roman glass and two sketches, and Colonel Boucher his Samian ware and an ordnance map, and there are lots of fossils and some coins."

"And a committee?" asked Lucia.

"Yes. Daisy and Mrs. Boucher and I, and we co-opted Robert," he said with affected carelessness.

Again some nameless pang shot through Lucia. Absent or present, she ought to have been the chairman of the committee and told them exactly what to do, and how to do it. But she felt no doubt that she could remedy all that when she came down to Riseholme for a weekend. In the meantime, it was sufficient to have pulled his secret out of Georgie, like a cork, with a loud pop, and an effusion of contents.

"Most interesting," she said. "I must think what I can give you for your museum. Well, that's a nice little gossip."

Georgie could not bring himself to tell her that the stocks had already been moved from the village green to the tithe-barn, for he seemed to remember that Lucia and Peppino had presented them to the Parish Council. Now the Parish Council had presented them to the Museum, but that was a reason the more why the Parish Council and not he should face the donors.

"A nice little gossip," said Lucia. "And what a pleasant party last night. I just popped over, to congratulate dear Olga on the favourable, indeed the very favourable reception of *Lucrezia*, for I thought she would be hurt—artists are so sensitive—if I did not add my little tribute, and then you saw how she refused to let me go, but insisted that I should come in. And I found it all most pleasant: one met many friends, and I was very glad to be able to look in."

This expressed very properly what Lucia meant to convey. She did not in the least want to put Olga in her place, but to put herself, in Georgie's eyes, in her own place. She had just, out of kindness, stepped across to congratulate Olga, and then had been dragged in. Unfortunately Georgie did not believe a single word of it: he had already made up his mind that Lucia had laid an ambush for Olga, so swiftly and punctually had she come out of the shadow of the gas lamp on her arrival. He answered her therefore precisely in the spirit in which she had spoken. Lucia would know very well . . .

"It was good of you," he said enthusiastically. "I'm sure Olga appreciated your coming immensely. How forgetful of her not to have asked you at first! And as for *Lucrezia* just having a favourable reception, I thought it was the most brilliant success it is possible to imagine."

Lucia felt that her attitude hadn't quite produced the impression she had intended. Though she did not want Georgie (and Riseholme) to think *she* joined in the uncritical adulation of Olga, she certainly did not want Georgie to tell Olga that she didn't. And she still wanted to hear the Princess's name.

"No doubt, dear Georgie," she said, "it was a great success. And she was in wonderful voice, and looked most charming. As you know, I am terribly critical, but I can certainly say that. Yes. And her party delicious. So many pleasant people. I saw you having great jokes with the Princess."

Peppino having been asleep when Lucia came back last night, and not having seen her this morning, had not heard about the Princess.

"Indeed, who was that?" he asked Lucia.

Very tiresome of Peppino. But Lucia's guide (better than

poor Daisy's Abfou) must have been very attentive to her needs that morning, for Peppino had hardly uttered these awkward words, when the telephone rang. She could easily therefore trip across to it, protesting at these tiresome interruptions, and leave Georgie to answer.

"Yes, Mrs. Lucas," said Lucia. "Covent Garden? Yes. Then please put me through . . . Dearest Olga is ringing up. No doubt about the *Valkyrie* next week . . ."

Georgie had a brainwave. He felt sure Lucia would have answered Peppino's question instantly if she had known what the Princess's name was. He had noticed that Lucia in spite of her hangings about had not been presented to the illustrious lady last night, and the brainwave that she did not know the illustrious lady's name swept over him. He also saw that Lucia was anxiously listening not to the telephone only, but to him. If Lucia (and there could be no doubt about that) wanted to know, she must eat her humble pie and ask him . . .

"Yes, dear Diva, it's me," said Lucia. "Couldn't sleep a wink: *Lucrezia* running in my head all night. Marvellous. You rang me up?"

Her face fell.

"Oh, I am disappointed you can't come," she said. "You are naughty. I shall have to give you a little engagement book to put things down in . . ."

Lucia's guide befriended her again, and her face brightened. It grew almost to an unearthly brightness as she listened to Olga's apologies and a further proposal.

"Sunday evening?" she said. "Now let me think a moment: yes, I am free on Sunday. So glad you said Sunday, because all other nights are full. Delightful. And how nice to see Princess Isabel again. Goodbye."

She snapped the receiver back in triumph.

"What was it you asked me, Peppino?" she said. "Oh, yes: it was Princess Isabel. Dear Olga insists on my dining with her on Sunday to meet her again. Such a nice woman."

"I thought we were going down to Riseholme for the Sunday," said Peppino.

Lucia made a little despairing gesture.

"My poor head!" she said. "It is I who ought to have an engagement book chained to me. What am I to do? I hardly like to disappoint dear Olga. But you go down, Peppino, just the same. I know you are longing to get a breath of country air. Georgie will give you dinner one night, I am sure, and the other he will dine with you. Won't you, Georgie? So dear of you. Now who shall I get to fill my Olga's place at lunch tomorrow? Mrs. Garroby-Ashton, I think. Dear me, it is close on twelve, and Sophy will scold me if I keep her waiting. How the morning flashes by! I had hardly begun my practise, when Georgie came, and I've hardly had a word with him before it is time to go out. What will happen to my morning's post I'm sure I don't know. But I insist on your getting your breath of country air on Sunday, Peppino. I shall have plenty to do here, with all my arrears."

There was one note Lucia found she had to write before she went out, and she sent Peppino to show Georgie the house while she scribbled it, and addressing it to Mr. Stephen Merriall at the office of the *Evening Gazette*, sent it off by hand. This was hardly done when Mrs. Alingsby arrived, and they went off together to the private view of the Post-Cubists, and revelled in the works of those remarkable artists. Some were portraits and some landscapes, and it was usually easy to tell which was which, because a careful scrutiny revealed an eye or a stray mouth in some, and a tree or a house in others. Lucia was specially enthusiastic over a picture of Waterloo Bridge, but she had mistaken the number in the catalogue, and it proved to be a portrait of the artist's wife. Luckily she had not actually read out to Sophy that it was Waterloo Bridge, though she had said something about the river, but this was easily covered up in appreciation.

"Too wonderful," she said. "How they get to the very soul of things! What is it that Wordsworth says? 'The very pulse of the machine.' Pulsating, is it not?"

Mrs. Alingsby was tall and weird and intense, dressed rather like a bird-of-paradise that had been out in a high gale, but very well connected. She had long straight hair which fell over her forehead, and sometimes got in her eyes, and she wore on her head a scarlet jockey-cap with an immense cameo in front of it. She hated all art that was earlier than 1923, and a considerable lot of what was later. In music, on the other hand, she was primitive, and thought Bach decadent; in literature her taste was for stories without a story, and poems without metre or meaning. But she had collected round her a group of interesting outlaws, of whom the men looked like women, and the women like nothing at all, and though nobody ever knew what they were talking about, they themselves were talked about. Lucia had been to a party of hers, where they all sat in a room with black walls, and listened to early Italian music on a spinet while a charcoal brazier on a blue hearth was fed with incense . . . Lucia's general opinion of her was that she might be useful up to a point, for she certainly excited interest.

"Wordsworth?" she asked. "Oh, yes, I remember who you mean. About the Westmoreland Lakes. Such a kill-joy."

She put on her large horn spectacles to look at the picture of the artist's wife, and her body began to sway with a lithe circular motion.

"Marvellous! What a rhythm!" she said. "Sigismund is the

most rhythmical of them all. You ought to be painted by him. He would make something wonderful of you. Something *andante, adagio* almost. He's coming to see me on Sunday. Come and meet him. Breakfast about half-past twelve. Vegetarian with cocktails."

Lucia accepted this remarkable invitation with avidity: it would be an interesting and progressive meal. In these first weeks, she was designedly experimental; she intended to sweep into her net all there was which could conceivably harbour distinction, and sort it out by degrees. She was no snob in the narrow sense of the word; she would have been very discontented if she had only the high-born on her visiting list. The high-born, of course, were safe—you could not make a mistake in having a duchess to tea, because in her own line a duchess had distinction—but it would not have been enough to have all the duchesses there were: it might even have been a disappointing tea-party if the whole room was packed with them. What she wanted was the foam of the wave, the topmost, the most sunlit of the billows that rode the sea. Anything that had proved itself billowish was her game, and anything which showed signs of being a billow, even if it entailed a vegetarian lunch with cocktails and the possible necessity of being painted like the artist's wife with an eyebrow in one corner of the picture and a substance like desiccated cauliflower in the centre. That had always been her way: whatever those dear funny folk at Riseholme had thought of, a juggler, a professor of Yoga, a geologist, a psychoanalyst, had been snapped up by her and exploited till he exploded.

But Peppino was not as nimble as she. The incense at Sophy's had made him sneeze, and the primitive tunes on the spinet had made him snore; that had been all the uplift they had held for him. Thus, though she did not mind tiring herself to death, because Peppino was having such an interesting time, she didn't mind his going down to Riseholme for the Sunday to rest, while she had a vegetarian lunch with Post-Cubists, and a dinner with a princess. Literally, she could scarcely tell which of the two she looked forward to most; the princess was safe, but the Post-Cubists might prove more perilously paying. It was impossible to make a corner in princesses for they were too independent, but already, in case of Post-Cubism turning out to be the rage, she could visualise her music-room and even the famous Chippendale chairs being painted black, and the Sargent picture of Auntie being banished to the attic. She could not make them the rage, for she was not (as yet) the supreme arbiter here that she had been at Riseholme, but should they become the rage, there was no one surely more capable than herself of giving the impression that she had discovered them.

Lucia spent a strenuous afternoon with correspondence and telephonings, and dropped into Mrs. Sandeman's for a cup of tea, of which she stood sorely in need. She found there was no need to tell dearest Aggie about the party last night at Olga's, for the *Evening Gazette* had come in, and there was an account of it, described in Hermione's matchless style. Hermione had found the bijou residence of the prima-donna in Brompton Square full of friends—*très intimes*—who had been invited to celebrate the huge success of *Lucrezia* and to congratulate Mrs. Shuttleworth. There was Princess Isabel, wearing her wonderful turquoises, chatting with the composer, Signor Cortese (Princess Isabel spoke Italian perfectly), and among other friends Hermione had noticed the Duchess of Whitby, Lord Limpsfield, Mrs. Garroby-Ashton, and Mrs. Philip Lucas.

Chapter Five

THE MYSTERY OF THAT FRIDAY evening in the last week in June became portentous on the ensuing Saturday morning . . .

A cab had certainly driven from the station to The Hurst late on Friday evening, but owing to the darkness it was not known who got out of it. Previously the windows of The Hurst had been very diligently cleaned all Friday afternoon. Of course the latter might be accounted for by the mere fact that they needed cleaning, but if it had been Peppino or Lucia herself who had arrived by the cab (if both of them, they would almost certainly have come by their motor), surely some sign of their presence would have manifested itself either to Riseholme's collective eye, or to Riseholme's ear. But the piano, Daisy felt certain, had not been heard, nor had the telephone tinkled for anybody. Also, when she looked out about half-past ten in the evening, and again when she went upstairs to bed, there were no lights in the house. But somebody had come, and as the servants' rooms looked out on to the back, it was probably a servant or servants. Daisy had felt so terribly interested in this that she came restlessly down, and had a quarter of an hour's weedjing to see if Abfou could tell her. She had been quite unable to form any satisfactory conjecture herself, and Abfou, after writing "Museum" once or twice, had relapsed into rapid and unintelligible Arabic. She did not ring up Georgie to ask his help in solving this conundrum, because she hoped to solve it unaided and be able to tell him the answer.

She went upstairs again, and after a little deep-breathing and bathing her feet in alternate applications of hot and cold water in order to produce somnolence, found herself more widely awake than ever. Her well-trained mind cantered about on scents that led nowhere, and she was unable to find any that seemed likely to lead anywhere. Of Lucia nothing whatever was known except what was accessible to anybody who spent a penny on the *Evening Gazette.* She had written to nobody, she had given no sign of any sort, and, but for the *Evening Gazette,* she might, as far as Riseholme was concerned, be dead. But the *Evening Gazette* showed that she was alive, painfully alive in fact, if Hermione could be trusted. She had been seen here, there and everywhere in London: Hermione had observed her chatting in the Park with friends, sitting with friends in her box at the opera, shopping in Bond Street, watching polo (why, she did not know a horse from a cow!) at Hurlingham, and even in a punt at Henley. She had been entertaining in her own house too: there had been dinner parties and musical parties, and she had dined at so many houses that Daisy had added them all up, hoping to prove that she had spent more evenings than there had been evenings to spend, but to her great regret they came out exactly right. Now she was having her portrait painted by Sigismund, and not a word had she written, not a glimpse of herself had she vouchsafed, to Riseholme . . . Of course Georgie had seen her, when he went up to stay with Olga, but his account of her had been far from reassuring. She had said that she did not care how tired she got while Peppino was enjoying London so tremendously. Why then, thought Daisy with a sense of incredulous indignation, had Peppino come down a few Sundays ago, all by himself, and looking a perfect wreck? . . . "Very odd, *I* call it," muttered Daisy, turning over to her other side.

It was odd, and Peppino had been odd. He had dined with Georgie one night, and on the other Georgie had dined with him, but he had said nothing about Lucia that Hermione had not trumpeted to the world. Otherwise, Peppino had not been seen at all on that Sunday except when Mrs. Antrobus, not feeling very well in the middle of the Psalms on Sunday morning, had come out, and observed him standing on tiptoe and peering into the window of the Museum that looked on to the Roman Antiquities. Mrs. Antrobus (feeling much better as soon as she got into the air) had come quite close up to him before he perceived her, and then with only the curtest word of greeting, just as if she was the Museum Committee, he had walked away so fast that she could not but conclude that he wished to be alone. It was odd too, and scarcely honourable, that he should have looked into the window like that, and clearly it was for that purpose that he had absented himself from church, thinking that he would be unobserved. Daisy had not the smallest doubt that he was spying for Lucia, and had been told merely to collect information and to say nothing, for though he knew that Georgie was on the committee, he had carefully kept off the subject of the Museum on both their tête-à-tête dinners. Probably he had begun his spying the moment church began, and if Mrs. Antrobus had not so providentially felt faint, no one would have known anything about it. As it was, it was quite likely that he had looked into every window by the time she saw him, and knew all that the Museum contained. Since then, the Museum had been formally opened by Lady Ambermere, who had lent (not presented) some mittens which she said belonged to Queen Charlotte (it was impossible to prove that they hadn't), and the committee had put up some very baffling casement curtains which would make an end to spying for ever.

Now this degrading espionage had happened three weeks ago (come Sunday), and therefore for three weeks (come Monday), Lucia must have known all about the Museum. But not a word had she transmitted on that or any other subject; she had not demanded a place on the committee, nor presented the Elizabethan spit which so often made the chimney of her music-room to smoke, nor written to say that they must arrange it all quite differently. That she had a plan, a policy about the Museum, no one who knew Lucia could possibly doubt, but her policy (which thus at present was wrapped in mystery) might be her complete and eternal ignoring of it. It would indeed be dreadful if she intended to remain unaware of it, but Daisy doubted if anyone in her position and of her domineering character could be capable of such inhuman self-control. No: she meant to do something when she came back, but nobody could guess what it was, or when she was coming.

Daisy tossed and turned as she revolved these knotty points. She was sure Lucia would punish them all for making a museum while she was away, and not asking her advice and begging her to be president, and she would be ill with chagrin when she learned how successful it was proving. The tourist season, when charabancs passed through Riseholme in endless procession, had begun, and whole parties after lunching at the Ambermere Arms went to see it. In the first week alone there had been a hundred and twenty-six visitors, and that meant a corresponding take of shillings without reckoning sixpenny catalogues. Even the committee paid their shillings when they went in to look at their own exhibits, and there had been quite a scene when Lady Ambermere with a party from The Hall tried to get in with-

out paying for any of them on the ground that she had lent the
Museum Queen Charlotte's mittens. Georgie, who was hanging
up another picture of his, had heard it all and hidden behind a
curtain. The small boy in charge of the turnstile (bought from
a bankrupt circus for a mere song) had, though trembling with
fright, absolutely refused to let the turnstile turn until the req-
uisite number of shillings had been paid, and didn't care whose
mittens they were which Lady Ambermere had lent, and when,
snatching up a catalogue without paying for it, she had threatened to report him to the committee, this intrepid lad had followed her, continuing to say "Sixpence, please, my lady," till one
of the party, in order to save brawling in a public place, had produced the insignificant sum. And if Lucia tried to get in without
paying, on the ground that she and Peppino had given the stocks
to the Parish Council, which had lent them to the Museum, she
would find her mistake. At length, in the effort to calculate what
would be the total receipts of the year if a hundred and twenty-
six people per week paid their shillings, Daisy lapsed into an
uneasy arithmetical slumber.

Next morning (Saturday), the mystery of that arrival at The
Hurst the evening before grew infinitely more intense. It was
believed that only one person had come, and yet there was no
doubt that several pounds of salmon, dozens ("Literally dozens,"
said Mrs. Boucher, "for I saw the basket") of eggs, two chickens,
a leg of lamb, as well as countless other provisions unidentified
were delivered at the back door of The Hurst; a positive frieze of
tradesmen's boys was strung across the green. Even if the mysterious arrival was Lucia herself, she could not, unless the whirl
and worldliness of her London life had strangely increased her
appetite, eat all that before Monday. And besides, why had she
not rung up Georgie, or somebody, or opened her bedroom win-

dow on this hot morning? Or could it be Peppino again, sent down here for a rest-cure and a stuffing of his emaciated frame? But then he would not have come down without some sort of attendant to look after him . . . Riseholme was completely baffled; never had its powers of inductive reasoning been so nonplussed, for though so much went into The Hurst, nobody but the tradesmen's boys with empty baskets came out. Georgie and Daisy stared at each other in blankness over the garden paling, and when, in despair of arriving at any solution, they sought the oracles of Abfou, he would give them nothing but hesitating Arabic.

"Which shows," said Daisy, as she put the planchette away in disgust, "that even he doesn't know, or doesn't wish to tell us." Lunchtime arrived, and there were very poor appetites in Riseholme (with the exception of that Gargantuan of whom nothing was known). But as for going to The Hurst and ringing the bell and asking if Mrs. Lucas was at home, all Riseholme would sooner have died lingering and painful deaths, rather than let Lucia know that they took the smallest interest in anything she had done, was doing or would do.

About three o'clock Georgie was sitting on the green opposite his house, finishing his sketch, which the affairs of the Museum had caused him sadly to neglect. He had got it upside down on his easel and was washing some more blue into the sky, when he heard the hoot of a motor. He just looked up, and what he saw caused his hand to twitch so violently that he put a large dab of cobalt on the middle of his red-brick house. For the motor had stopped at The Hurst, not a hundred yards away, and out of it got Lucia and Peppino. She gave some orders to her chauffeur, and then without noticing him (*perhaps* without seeing him) she followed Peppino into the house. Hardly waiting to wash the worst of the cobalt off his house, Georgie hurried into Daisy's, and told her exactly what had happened.

"No!" said Daisy, and out they came again, and stood in the shadow of her mulberry tree to see what would happen next. The mulberry tree had recovered from the pruning of its roots (so it wasn't it which Abfou had said was dead), and gave them good shelter.

Nothing happened next.

"But it's impossible," said Daisy, speaking in a sort of conspiratorial whisper. "It's queer enough her coming without telling any of us, but now she's here, she surely must ring somebody up."

Georgie was thinking intently.

"The next thing that will happen," he said, "will be that servants and luggage will arrive from the station. They'll be here any minute; I heard the three-twenty whistle just now. She and Peppino have driven down."

"I shouldn't wonder," said Daisy. "But even now, what about the chickens and all those eggs? Georgie, it must have been her cook who came last night—she and Peppino were dining out in London—and ordered all those provisions this morning. But there were enough to last them a week. And three pints of cream, so I've heard since, and enough ice for a skating rink and—"

It was then that Georgie had the flash of intuition that was for ever memorable. It soared above inductive reasoning.

"She's having a weekend party of some of her smart friends from London," he said slowly. "And she doesn't want any of us."

Daisy blinked at this amazing light. Then she cast one withering glance in the direction of The Hurst.

"She!" she said. "And her shingles. And her seed pearls! That's all."

A minute afterwards the station cab arrived pyramidal with luggage. Four figures disembarked, three female and one male.

"The major-domo," said Daisy, and without another word marched back into her house to ask Abfou about it all. He came through at once, and wrote "Snob" all over the paper.

There was no reason why Georgie should not finish his sketch, and he sat down again and began by taking out the rest of the misplaced cobalt. He felt so certain of the truth of his prophecy that he just let it alone to fulfil itself, and for the next hour he never worked with more absorbed attention. He knew that Daisy came out of her house, walking very fast, and he supposed she was on her way to spread the news and forecast the sequel. But beyond the fact that he was perfectly sure that a party from London was coming down for the weekend, he could form no idea of what would be the result of that. It might be that Lucia would ask him or Daisy, or some of her old friends to dine, but if she had intended to do that she would probably have done it already. The only alternative seemed to be that she meant to ignore Riseholme altogether. But shortly before the arrival of the fast train from London at half-past four, his prophetical calm began (for he was but human) to be violently agitated, and he took his tea in the window of his drawing-room, which commanded a good view of the front garden of The Hurst, and put his opera-glasses ready to hand. The window was a big bow, and he distinctly saw the end of Robert's brass telescope projecting from the corresponding window next door.

Once more a motor-horn sounded, and the Lucases' car drew up at the gate of The Hurst. There stepped out Mrs. Garroby-Ashton, followed by the weird bright thing which had called to take Lucia to the private view of the Post-Cubists. Georgie had not time for the moment to rack his brain as to the name he had forgotten, for observation was his primary concern, and next he saw Lord Limpsfield, whom he had met at Olga's party. Finally there emerged a tall, slim, middle-aged man in Oxford trousers, for whom Georgie instantly conceived a deep distrust. He had thick auburn hair, for he wore no hat, and he waved his hands about in a silly manner as he talked. Over his shoulder was a little cape. Then Lucia came tripping out of the house with her short skirts and her shingles, and they all chattered together, and kissed and squealed, and pointed in different directions, and moved up the garden into the house. The door was shut, and the end of Robert's brass telescope withdrawn.

∞

Hardly had these shameful events occurred when Georgie's telephone bell rang. It might be Daisy wanting to compare notes, but it might be Lucia asking him to tea. He felt torn in half at the idea: carnal curiosity urged him with clamour to go, dignity dissuaded him. Still halting between two opinions, he went towards the instrument, which continued ringing. He felt sure now that it was Lucia, and what on earth was he to say? He stood there so long that Foljambe came hurrying into the room, in case he had gone out.

"See who it is, Foljambe," he said.

Foljambe with amazing calm took off the receiver.

"Trunk call," she said.

He glued himself to the instrument, and soon there came a voice he knew.

"No! Is it you?" he asked. "What is it?"

"I'm motoring down tomorrow morning," said Olga, "and Princess Isabel is probably coming with me, though she is not absolutely certain. But expect her, unless I telephone tomorrow.

Be a darling and give us lunch, as we shall be late, and come and dine. Terrible hurry: goodbye."

"No, you must wait a minute," screamed Georgie. "Of course I'll do that, but I must tell you, Lucia's just come with a party from London and hasn't asked any of us."

"No!" said Olga. "Then don't tell her I'm coming. She's become such a bore. She asks me to lunch and dinner every day. How thrilling though, Georgie! Whom has she got?"

Suddenly the name of the weird bright female came back to Georgie.

"Mrs. Alingsby," he said.

"Lor!" said Olga. "Who else?"

"Mrs. Garroby-Ashton—"

"What?"

"Garr-o-by Ash-ton," said Georgie very distinctly; "and Lord Limpsfield. And a tall man in Oxford trousers with auburn hair."

"It sounds like your double, Georgie," said Olga. "And a little cape like yours?"

"Yes," said Georgie rather coldly.

"I think it must be Stephen Merriall," said Olga after a pause.

"And who's that?" asked he.

"Lucia's lover," said Olga quite distinctly.

"No!" said Georgie.

"Of course he isn't. I only meant he was always there. But I believe he's Hermione. I'm not sure, but I think so. Georgie, we shall have a hectic Sunday. Goodbye, tomorrow about two or three for lunch, and two or three *for* lunch. What a gossip you are."

He heard that delicious laugh, and the click of her receiver.

Georgie was far too thrilled to gasp. He sat quite quiet,

breathing gently. For the honour of Riseholme he was glad that a Princess was perhaps coming to lunch with him, but apart from that he would really have much preferred that Olga should be alone. The "affaire Lucia" was so much more thrilling than anything else, but Princess Isabel might feel no interest in it, and instead they would talk about all sorts of dull things like kings and courts . . . Then suddenly he sprang from his chair: there was a leg of lamb for Sunday lunch, and an apple tart, and nothing else at all. What was to be done? The shops by now would be shut.

He rang for Foljambe.

"Miss Olga's coming to lunch and possibly—possibly a friend of hers," he said. "What are we to do?"

"A leg of lamb and an apple tart's good enough for anybody, isn't it?" said Foljambe severely.

This really seemed true as soon as it was pointed out, and Georgie made an effort to dismiss the matter from his mind. But he could not stop still: it was all so exciting, and after having changed his Oxford trousers in order to minimise the likeness between him and that odious Mr. Merriall, he went out for a constitutional, round the green from all points of which he could see any important development at The Hurst. Riseholme generally was doing the same, and his stroll was interrupted by many agreeable stoppages. It was already known that Lucia and Peppino had arrived, and that servants and luggage had come by the three-twenty, and that Lucia's motor had met the half-past four and returned laden with exciting people. Georgie therefore was in high demand, for he might supply the names of the exciting people, and he had the further information to divulge that Olga was arriving tomorrow, and was lunching with him and dining at her own house. He said nothing about a possible Princess:

she might not come, and in that case he knew that there would be a faint suspicion in everybody's mind that he had invented it; whereas if she did, she would no doubt sign his visitors' book for everyone to see.

Feeling ran stormy high against Lucia, and as usual when Riseholme felt a thing deeply there was little said by way of public comment, though couples might have been observed with set and angry faces and gabbling mouths. But higher yet ran curiosity and surmise as to what Lucia would do, and what Olga would do. Not a sign had come for anyone from The Hurst, not a soul had been asked to lunch, dinner, or even tea, and if Lucia seemed to be ashamed of Riseholme society before her grand friends, there was no doubt that Riseholme society was ashamed of Lucia . . .

And then suddenly a deadly hush fell on these discussions, and even those who were walking fastest in their indignation came to a halt, for out of the front door of The Hurst streamed the "exciting people" and their hosts. There was Lucia, hatless and shingled and short-skirted, and the Bird-of-Paradise and Mrs. Garroby-Ashton, and Peppino and Lord Limpsfield and Mr. Merriall all talking shrilly together, with shrieks of hollow laughter. They came slowly across the green towards the little pond round which Riseholme stood, and passed within fifty yards of it, and if Lucia had been the Gorgon, Riseholme could not more effectually have been turned into stone. She too, appeared not to notice them, so absorbed was she in conversation, and on they went straight towards the Museum. Just as they passed Colonel Boucher's house, Mrs. Boucher came out in her bath-chair, and without pause was wheeled straight through the middle of them. She then drew up by the side of the green below the large elm.

The party passed into the Museum. The windows were

open, and from inside them came shrieks of laughter. This continued for about ten minutes, and then . . . they all came out again. Several of them carried catalogues, and Mr. Merriall was reading out of one in a loud voice.

"Pair of worsted mittens," he announced, "belonging to Queen Charlotte, and presented by the Lady Ambermere."

"Don't," said Lucia. "Don't make fun of our dear little Museum, Stephen."

As they retraced their way along the edge of the green, movement came back to Riseholme again. Lucia's policy with regard to the Museum had declared itself. Georgie strolled up to Mrs. Boucher's bath-chair. Mrs. Boucher was extremely red in the face, and her hands were trembling.

"Good-evening, Mr. Georgie," said she. "Another party of strangers, I see, visiting the Museum. They looked very odd people, and I hope we shan't find anything missing. Any news?"

That was a very dignified way of taking it, and Georgie responded in the same spirit.

"Not a scrap that I know of," he said, "except that Olga's coming down tomorrow."

"That will be nice," said Mrs. Boucher. "Riseholme is always glad to see *her*."

Daisy joined them.

"Good-evening, Mrs. Quantock," said Mrs. Boucher. "Any news?"

"Yes, indeed," said Daisy rather breathlessly. "Didn't you see them? Lucia and her party?"

"No," said Mrs. Boucher firmly. "She is in London surely. Anything else?"

Daisy took the cue. Complete ignorance that Lucia was in Riseholme at all was a noble manoeuvre.

"It must have been my mistake," she said. "Oh, my mulberry tree has quite come round."

"No!" said Mrs. Boucher in the Riseholme voice. "I am pleased. I dare say the pruning did it good. And Mr. Georgie's just told me that our dear Olga, or I should say Mrs. Shuttleworth, is coming down tomorrow, but he hasn't told me what time yet."

"Two or three, she said," answered Georgie. "She's motoring down, and is going to have lunch with me whenever she gets here."

"Indeed! Then I should advise you to have something cold that won't spoil by waiting. A bit of cold lamb, for instance. Nothing so good on a hot day."

"What an excellent idea!" said Georgie. "I was thinking of hot lamb. But the other's much better. I'll have it cooked tonight."

"And a nice tomato salad," said Mrs. Boucher, "and if you haven't got any, I can give you some. Send your Foljambe round, and she'll come back with half a dozen ripe tomatoes."

Georgie hurried off to see to these new arrangements, and Colonel Boucher having strolled away with Piggy, his wife could talk freely to Mrs. Quantock . . . She did.

∞

Lucia waking rather early next morning found she had rather an uneasy conscience as her bedfellow, and she used what seemed very reasonable arguments to quiet it. There would have been no point in writing to Georgie or any of them to say that she was bringing down some friends for the weekend and would be occupied with them all Sunday. She could not with all these guests play duets with Georgie, or get poor Daisy to give an exhibition of ouija, or have Mrs. Boucher in her bath-chair to tea, for she would give them all long histories of purely local interest, which could not conceivably amuse people like Lord Limpsfield or weird Sophy. She had been quite wise to keep Riseholme and Brompton Square apart, for they would not mix. Besides, her guests would go away on Monday morning, and she had determined to stop over till Tuesday and be extremely kind, and not the least condescending. She would have one or two of them to lunch, and one or two more to dinner, and give Georgie a full hour of duets as well. Naturally, if Olga had been here, she would have asked Olga on Sunday but Olga had been singing last night at the opera. Lucia had talked a good deal about her at dinner, and given the impression that they were never out of each other's houses either in town or here, and had lamented her absence.

"Such a pity," she had said. "For dearest Olga loves singing in my music-room. I shall never forget how she dropped in for some little garden-party and sang the awakening of Brünnhilde. Even you, dear Sophy, with your passion for the primitive, would have enjoyed that. She sang *Lucrezia* here, too, before anyone had heard it. Cortese brought the score down the moment he had finished it—ah, I think that was in her house—there was just Peppino and me, and perhaps one or two others. We would have had dearest Olga here all day tomorrow if only she had been here . . ."

So Lucia felt fairly easy, having planned these treats for Riseholme on Monday, as to her aloofness today, and then her conscience brought up the question of the Museum. Here she stoutly defended herself: she knew nothing about the Museum (except what Peppino had seen through the window a few Sundays before); she had not been consulted about the Museum, she was not on the committee, and it was perfectly proper for her to take her party to see it. She could not prevent them bursting into shrieks of laughter at Queen Charlotte's mittens and Daisy's drain-pipes, nor could she possibly prevent herself from joining in those shrieks of laughter herself, for surely this was the most ridiculous collection of rubbish ever brought together. A glass case for Queen Charlotte's mittens, a heap of fossils such as she had chipped out by the score from the old quarry, some fragments of glass (Georgie ought to have known better), some quilts, a dozen coins, lent, only lent, by poor Daisy! In fact the only object of the slightest interest was the pair of stocks which she and Peppino had bought and set up on the village green. She would see about that when she came down in August, and back they should go on to the village green. Then there was the catalogue: who could help laughing at the catalogue which described in most pompous language the contents of this dustbin? There was nothing to be uneasy about over that. And as for Mrs. Boucher having driven right through her party without a glance of recognition, what did that matter? On her own side also, Lucia had given no glance of recognition to Mrs. Boucher: if she had, Mrs. Boucher would have told them all about her asparagus or how her Elizabeth had broken a plate. It was odd, perhaps, that Mrs. Boucher hadn't stopped . . . and was it rather odd also that, though from the corner of her eye she had seen all Riseholme standing about on the green, no one had made the smallest sign of welcome? It was true that she had practically cut them (if a process conducted at the distance of fifty yards can be called a cut), but she was not quite sure that she enjoyed the same process herself. Probably it meant nothing; they saw she was engaged with her friends, and very properly had not thrust themselves forward.

Her guests mostly breakfasted upstairs, but by the middle of the morning they had all straggled down. Lucia had brought with her yesterday her portrait by Sigismund, which Sophy declared was a masterpiece of *adagio*. She was advising her to clear all other pictures out of the music-room and hang it there alone, like a wonderful slow movement, when Mr. Merriall came in with the Sunday paper.

"Ah, the paper has come," said Lucia. "Is not that Riseholm-ish of us? We never get the Sunday paper till midday."

"Better late than never," said Mr. Merriall, who was rather addicted to quoting proverbial sayings. "I see that Mrs. Shuttle-worth's coming down here today. Do ask her to dine and perhaps she'll sing to us."

Lucia paused for a single second, then clapped her hands.

"Oh, what fun that would be!" she said. "But I don't think it can be true. Dearest Olga popped in—or did I pop in—yesterday morning in town, and she said nothing about it. No doubt she had not made up her mind then whether she was coming or not. Of course I'll ring her up at once and scold her for not telling me."

Lucia found from Olga's caretaker that she and a friend were expected, but she knew they couldn't come to lunch with her, as they were lunching with Mr. Pillson. She "couldn't say, I'm sure" who the friend was, but promised to give the message that Mrs. Lucas hoped they would both come and dine . . . The next thing was to ring up Georgie and be wonderfully cordial.

"Georgino *mio*, is it 'oo?" she asked.

"Yes," said Georgie. He did not have to ask who it was, nor did he feel inclined for baby-talk.

"Georgino, I never caught a glimpse of you yesterday," she said. "Why didn't 'oo come round and see me?"

"Because you never asked me," said Georgie firmly, "and because you never told me you were coming."

"Me so sorry," said Lucia. "But me was so fussed and busy in town. Delicious to be in Riseholme again."

"Delicious," said Georgie.

Lucia paused a moment.

"Is Georgino cross with me?" she asked.

"Not a bit," said Georgie brightly. "Why?"

"I didn't know. And I hear my Olga and a friend are lunching with you. I am hoping they will come and dine with me tonight. And do come in afterwards. We shall be eight already, or of course I should ask you."

"Thanks so much, but I'm dining with her," said Georgie.

A pause.

"Well, all of you come and dine here," said Lucia. "Such amusing people, and I'll squeeze you in."

"I'm afraid I can't accept for Olga," said Georgie. "And I'm dining with her, you see."

"Well, will you come across after lunch and bring them?" said Lucia. "Or tea?"

"I don't know what they will feel inclined to do," said Georgie. "But I'll tell them."

"Do, and I'll ring up at lunchtime again, and have ickle talk to my Olga. Who is her friend?"

Georgie hesitated: he thought he would not give that away just yet. Lucia would know in heaps of time.

"Oh, just somebody whom she's possibly bringing down," he said, and rang off.

Lucia began to suspect a slight mystery, and she disliked mysteries, except when she made them herself. Olga's caretaker was "sure she couldn't say," and Georgie (Lucia was sure) wouldn't. So she went back to her guests, and very prudently said that Olga had not arrived at present, and then gave them a wonderful account of her little *intime* dinner with Olga and Princess Isabel. Such a delightful amusing woman: they must all come and meet Princess Isabel some day soon in town.

Lucia and her guests, with the exception of Sophy Alingsby, who continued to play primitive tunes with one finger on the piano, went for a stroll on the green before lunch. Mrs. Quantock hurried by with averted face, and naturally everybody wanted to know who the Red Queen from *Alice in Wonderland* was. Lucia amused them by a bright version of poor Daisy's ouija-board and the story of the mulberry tree.

"Such dears they all are," she said. "But too killing. And then she planted broccoli instead of phlox. It's only in Riseholme that such things happen. You must all come and stay with me in August, and we'll enter into the life of the place. I adore it, simply adore it. We are always wildly excited about something . . . And next door is Georgie Pillson's house. A lamb! I'm devoted to him. He does embroidery, and gave those broken bits of glass to the Museum. And that's dear Olga's house at the end of the road . . ."

Just as Lucia was kissing her hand to Olga's house, her eagle eye had seen a motor approaching, and it drew up at Georgie's house. Two women got out, and there was no doubt whatever who either of them were. They went in at the gate, and he came out of his front door like the cuckoo out of a clock and made a low bow. All this Lucia saw, and though for the moment petrified, she quickly recovered, and turned sharply round.

"Well, we must be getting home again," she said, in a rather strangled voice. "It is lunchtime."

Mr. Merriall did not turn so quickly, but watched the three figures at Georgie's door.

"Appearances are deceptive," he said. "But isn't that Olga Shuttleworth and Princess Isabel?"

"No! Where?" said Lucia, looking in the opposite direction.

"Just gone into that house; Georgie Pillson's, didn't you say?"

"No, really?" said Lucia. "How stupid of me not to have seen them. Shall I pop in now? No, I think I will ring them up presently, unless we find that they have already rung me up."

Lucia was putting a brave face on it, but she was far from easy. It looked like a plot: it did indeed, for Olga had never told her she was coming to Riseholme, and Georgie had never told her that Princess Isabel was the friend she was bringing with her. However, there was lunchtime in which to think over what was to be done. But though she talked incessantly and rather satirically about Riseholme, she said no more about the prima-donna and the Princess . . .

∞

Lucia might have been gratified (or again she might not) if she had known how vivacious a subject of conversation she afforded at Georgie's select little luncheon-party. Princess Isabel (with her mouth now full of Mrs. Boucher's tomatoes) had been subjected during this last week to an incessant bombardment from Lucia, and had heard on quite good authority that she alluded to her as "Isabel, dear Princess Isabel."

"And I will not go to her house," she said. "It is a free country, and I do not choose to go to her kind house. No doubt she is a very good woman. But I want to hear more of her, for she thrills me. So does your Riseholme. You were talking of the Museum."

"Georgie, go on about the Museum," said Olga.

"Well," said Georgie, "there it was. They all went in, and then they all came out again, and one of them was reading my catalogue—I made it—aloud, and they all screamed with laughter."

"But I dare say it was a very funny catalogue, Georgie," said Olga.

"I don't think so. Mr. Merriall read out about Queen Charlotte's mittens presented by Lady Ambermere."

"No!" said Olga.

"Most interesting!" said the Princess. "She was my aunt, big aunt, is it? No, great-aunt—that is it. Afterwards we will go to the Museum and see her mittens. Also, I must see the lady who kills mulberry trees. Olga, can't you ask her to bring her planchette and prophesy?"

"Georgie, ring up Daisy, and ask her to come to tea with me," said Olga. "We must have a weedj."

"And I must go for a drive, and I must walk on the green, and I must have some more delicious apple pie," began the Princess.

Georgie had just risen to ring up Daisy, when Foljambe entered with the news that Mrs. Lucas was on the telephone and would like to speak to Olga.

"Oh, say we're still at lunch, please, Foljambe," said she. "Can she send a message? And you say Stephen Merriall is there, Georgie?"

"No, you said he was there," said Georgie. "I only described him."

"Well, I'm pretty sure it is he, but you will have to go sometime this afternoon and find out. If it is, he's Hermione, who's always writing about Lucia in the *Evening Gazette*. Priceless! So you must go across for a few minutes, Georgie, and make certain."

Foljambe came back to ask if Mrs. Lucas might pop in to pay her respects to Princess Isabel.

"So kind of her, but she must not dream of troubling herself," said the Princess.

Foljambe retired and appeared for the third time with a faint, firm smile.

"Mrs. Lucas will ring up Mrs. Shuttleworth in a quarter of an hour," she said.

The Princess finished her apple tart.

"And now let us go and see the Museum," she said.

∞

Georgie remained behind to ring up Daisy, to explain when Lucia telephoned next that Olga had gone out, and to pay his visit to The Hurst. To pretend that he did not enjoy that, would be to misunderstand him altogether. Lucia had come down here with her smart party and had taken no notice of Riseholme, and now two people a million times smarter had by a clearly providential dealing come down at the same time and were taking no notice of her. Instead they were hobnobbing with people like himself and Daisy whom Lucia had slighted. Then she had laughed at the Museum, and especially at the catalogue and the mittens, and now the great-niece of the owner of the mittens had gone to see them. That was a stinger, in fact it was all a stinger, and well Lucia deserved it.

He was shown into the music-room, and he had just time to observe that there was a printed envelope on the writing-table addressed to the *Evening Gazette,* when Lucia and Mr. Merriall came hurrying in.

"Georgino *mio,*" said Lucia effusively. "How nice of you to come in. But you've not brought your ladies? Oh, this is Mr. Merriall."

(Hermione, of the *Evening Gazette,* it's proved, thought Georgie.)

"They thought they wouldn't add to your big party," said Georgie sumptuously. (That was another stinger.)

"And was it Princess Isabel I saw at your door?" asked Mr.

Merriall with an involuntary glance at the writing-table. (Lucia had not mentioned her since.)

"Oh yes. They just motored down and took pot luck with me."

"What did you give them?" asked Lucia, forgetting her anxieties for a moment.

"Oh, just cold lamb and apple tart," said Georgie.

"No!" said Lucia. "You ought to have brought them to lunch here. Oh, Georgie, my picture, look. By Sigismund."

"Oh yes," said Georgie. "What's it of?"

"*Cattivo!*" said Lucia. "Why, it's a portrait of me. Sigismund, you know, he's the great rage in London just now. Everyone is crazy to be painted by him."

"And they look crazy when they are. It's a mad world, my masters," said Mr. Merriall.

"Naughty," said Lucia. "Is it not wonderful, Georgie?"

"Yes. I expect it's very clever," said Georgie. "Very clever indeed."

"I should so like to show it dearest Olga," said Lucia, "and I'm sure the Princess would be interested in it. She was talking about modern art the other day when I dined with Olga. I wonder if they would look in at teatime, or indeed any other time."

"Not very likely, I'm afraid," said Georgie, "for Daisy Quantock's coming to tea, I know. We're going to weedj. And they're going out for a drive sometime."

"And where are they now?" asked Lucia. It was terrible to have to get news of her intimate friends from Georgie, but how else was she to find out?

"They went across to see the Museum," said he. "They were most interested in it."

Mr. Merriall waved his hands, just in the same way as Georgie did.

"Ah, that Museum!" he said. "Those mittens! Shall I ever get over those mittens? Lucia said she would give it the next shoe-lace she broke."

"Yes," said Georgie. "The Princess wanted to see those mittens. Queen Charlotte was her great-aunt. I told them how amused you all were at the mittens."

Lucia had been pressing her finger to her forehead, a sign of concentration. She rose as if going back to her other guests.

"Coming into the garden presently?" she asked, and glided from the room.

"And so you're going to have a sitting with the ouija-board," said Mr. Merriall. "I am intensely interested in ouija. Very odd phenomena certainly occur. Strange but true."

A fresh idea had come into Georgie's head. Lucia certainly had not appeared outside the window that looked into the garden, and so he walked across to the other one which commanded a view of the green. There she was heading straight for the Museum.

"It is marvellous," he said to Mr. Merriall. "We have had some curious results here, too."

Mr. Merriall was moving daintily about the room, and Georgie wondered if it would be possible to convert Oxford trousers into an ordinary pair. It was dreadful to think that Olga, even in fun, had suggested that such a man was his double. There was the little cape as well.

"I have quite fallen in love with your Riseholme," said Mr. Merriall.

"We all adore it," said Georgie, not attending very much because his whole mind was fixed on the progress of Lucia across the green. Would she catch them in the Museum, or had they already gone? Smaller and smaller grew her figure and her twinkling legs, and at last she crossed the road and vanished behind the belt of shrubs in front of the tithe-barn.

"All so homey and intimate. 'Home, Sweet Home,' in fact," said Mr. Merriall. "We have been hearing how Mrs. Shuttleworth loves singing in this room."

Georgie was instantly on his guard again. It was quite right and proper that Lucia should be punished, and of course Riseholme would know all about it, for indeed Riseholme was administering the punishment. But it was a very different thing to let her down before those who were not Riseholme.

"Oh yes, she sings here constantly," he said. "We are all in and out of each other's houses. But I must be getting back to mine now."

Mr. Merriall longed to be asked to this little ouija party at Olga's, and at present his hostess had been quite unsuccessful in capturing either of the two great stars. There was no harm in trying . . .

"You couldn't perhaps take me to Mrs. Shuttleworth's for tea?" he asked.

"No, I'm afraid I could hardly do that," said Georgie. "Goodbye. I hope we shall meet again."

∞

Nemesis meantime had been dogging Lucia's footsteps, with more success than Lucia was having in dogging Olga's. She had arrived, as Georgie had seen, at the Museum, and again paid a shilling to enter that despised exhibition. It was rather full, for visitors who had lunched at the Ambermere Arms had come in, and there was quite a crowd round Queen Charlotte's mittens, among whom was Lady Ambermere herself who had driven over from The Hall with two depressed guests whom she had forced to come with her. She put up her glasses and stared at Lucia.

"Ah, Mrs. Lucas!" she said with the singular directness for which she was famous. "For the moment I did not recognise you with your hair like that. It is a fashion that does not commend itself to me. You have come in, of course, to look at Her late Majesty's mittens, for really there is very little else to see."

As a rule, Lucia shamelessly truckled to Lady Ambermere, and schemed to get her to lunch or dinner. But today she didn't care two straws about her, and while these rather severe remarks were being addressed to her, her eyes darted eagerly round the room in search of those for whom she would have dropped Lady Ambermere without the smallest hesitation.

"Yes, dear Lady Ambermere," she said. "So interesting to think that Queen Charlotte wore them. Most good of you to have presented them to our little Museum."

"Lent," said Lady Ambermere. "They are heirlooms in my family. But I am glad to let others enjoy the sight of them. And by a remarkable coincidence I have just had the privilege of showing them to a relative of their late owner. Princess Isabel. I offered to have the case opened for her, and let her try them on. She said, most graciously, that it was not necessary."

"Yes, dear Princess Isabel," said Lucia, "I heard she had come down. Is she here still?"

"No. She and Mrs. Shuttleworth have just gone. A motor drive, I understand, before tea. I suggested, of course, a visit to The Hall, where I would have been delighted to entertain them. Where did they lunch?"

"At Georgie Pillson's," said Lucia bitterly.

"Indeed. I wonder why Mr. Pillson did not let me know. Did you lunch there too?"

"No. I have a party in my own house. Some friends from London, Lord Limpsfield, Mrs. Garroby-Ashton—"

"Indeed!" said Lady Ambermere. "I had meant to return to The Hall for tea, but I will change my plans and have a cup of tea with you, Mrs. Lucas. Perhaps you would ask Mrs. Shuttleworth and her distinguished guest to drop in. I will present you to her. You have a pretty little garden, I remember. Quaint. You are at liberty to say that I am taking tea with you. But stay! If they have gone out for a drive, they will not be back quite yet. It does not matter: we will sit in your garden."

Now in the ordinary way this would have been a most honourable event, but today, though Lady Ambermere had not changed, her value had. If only Olga had not come down bringing her whom Lucia could almost refer to as that infernal Princess, it would have been rich, it would have been glorious, to have Lady Ambermere dropping in to tea. Even now she would be better than nothing, thought Lucia, and after inspecting the visitors' book of the Museum, where Olga and the Princess had inscribed their names, and where now Lady Ambermere wrote hers, very close to the last one, so as to convey the impression that they were one party, they left the place.

Outside was drawn up Lady Ambermere's car, with her companion, the meek Miss Lyall, sitting on the front seat nursing Lady Ambermere's stertorous pug.

"Let me see," said she. "How had we best arrange? A walk would be good for Pug before he has his tea. Pug takes lukewarm milk with a biscuit broken up into it. Please put Pug on his leash, Miss Lyall, and we will all walk across the green to Mrs. Lucas's little house. The motor shall go round by the road and wait for us there. That is Mrs. Shuttleworth's little house, is it not? So you might kindly step in there, Mrs. Lucas, and leave a message for them about tea, stating that I shall be there. We will walk slowly and you will soon catch us up."

The speech was thoroughly Ambermerian: everybody in Riseholme had a "little house" compared with The Hall: everybody had a "little garden." Equally Ambermerian was her complete confidence that her wish was everybody else's pleasure, and Lucia dismally reflected that she, for her part, had never failed to indicate that it was. But just now, though Lady Ambermere was so conspicuously second-best, and though she was like a small luggage-engine with a Roman nose and a fat dog, the wretched Lucia badly wanted somebody to "drop in," and by so doing give her some sort of status—alas, that one so lately the Queen of Riseholme should desire it—in the sight of her guests. She could say what a bore Lady Ambermere was the moment she had gone.

Wretched also was her errand: she knew that Olga and the infernal Princess were to have a ouija with Daisy and Georgie, and that her invitation would be futile, and as for that foolish old woman's suggestion that her presence at The Hurst would prove an attraction to Olga, she was aware that if anything was needful to make Olga refuse to come, it would be that Lady Ambermere was there. Olga had dined at The Hall once, and had been induced to sing, while her hostess played Patience and talked to Pug.

Lucia had a thought: not a very bright one, but comparatively so. She might write her name in the Princess's book: that would be something. So, when her ring was answered, and she ascertained, as she already knew, that Olga was out, and left the hopeless invitation that she and her guest would come to tea, where they would meet Lady Ambermere, she asked for the Princess's book.

Olga's parlour-maid looked puzzled.

"Would that be the book of crossword puzzles, ma'am?" she asked. "I don't think her Highness brought any other book, and that she's taken with her for her drive."

Lucia trudged sadly away. Halfway across the green she saw Georgie and Daisy Quantock with a large sort of drawing-board under her arm coming briskly in her direction. She knew where they were going, and she pulled her shattered forces together.

"Dearest Daisy, not set eyes on you!" she said. "A few friends from London, how it ties one! But I shall pop in tomorrow, for I stop till Tuesday. Going to have a ouija party with dear Piggy and Goosie? Wish I could come, but Lady Ambermere has quartered herself on me for tea, and I must run on and catch her up. Just been to your delicious Museum. Wonderful mittens! Wonderful everything. Peppino and I will look out something for it!"

"Very kind," said Daisy. It was as if the North Pole had spoken.

Pug and Miss Lyall and Lady Ambermere and her two depressed guests had been admitted to The Hurst before Lucia caught them up, and she found them all seated stonily in the music-room, where Stephen Merriall had been finishing his official correspondence. Well Lucia knew what he had been writing about: there might perhaps be a line or two about The Hurst, and the party weekending there, but that, she was afraid, would form a mere little postscript to more exalted paragraphs. She hastily introduced him to Lady Ambermere and Miss Lyall, but she had no idea who Lady Ambermere's guests were, and suspected they were poor relations, for Lady Ambermere introduced them to nobody.

Pug gave a series of wheezy barks.

"Clever little man," said Lady Ambermere. "He is asking for his tea. He barks four times like that for his tea."

"And he shall have it," said Lucia. "Where are the others, Stephen?"

Mr. Merriall exerted himself a little on hearing Lady Ambermere's name: he would put in a sentence about her . . .

"Lord Limpsfield and Mrs. Garroby-Ashton have gone to play golf," he said. "Barbarously energetic of them, is it not, Lady Ambermere? What a sweet little dog."

"Pug does not like strangers," said Lady Ambermere. "And I am disappointed not to see Lord Limpsfield. Do we expect Mrs. Shuttleworth and the Princess?"

"I left the message," said Lucia.

Lady Ambermere's eyes finished looking at Mr. Merriall and proceeded slowly round the room.

"What is that curious picture?" she said. "I am completely puzzled."

Lucia gave her bright laugh: it was being an awful afternoon, but she had to keep her flag flying.

"Striking, is it not?" she said. "Dear Benjy Sigismund insisted on painting me. Such a lot of sittings."

Lady Ambermere looked from one to the other.

"I do not see any resemblance," she said. "It appears to me to resemble nothing. Ah, here is tea. A little lukewarm milk for Pug, Miss Lyall. Mix a little hot water with it, it does not suit him to have it quite cold. And I should like to see Mr. Georgie Pillson. No doubt he could be told that I am here."

This was really rather desperate: Lucia could not produce Olga or the Princess, or Lord Limpsfield or Mrs. Garroby-Ashton for Lady Ambermere, and she knew she could not produce Georgie, for by that time he would be at Olga's. All that was left for her was to be able to tell Lord Limpsfield and Mrs. Garroby-Ashton when they returned that they had missed Lady Ambermere. As for Riseholme . . . but it was better not to think how she stood with regard to Riseholme, which, yesterday, she had settled to be of no account at all. If only, before coming down, she had asked them all to lunch and tea and dinner . . .

The message came back that Mr. Pillson had gone to tea with Mrs. Shuttleworth. Five minutes later came regrets from Olga that she had friends with her, and could not come to tea. Lady Ambermere ate seed cake in silence. Mrs. Alingsby meantime had been spending the afternoon in her bedroom, and she now appeared in a chintz wrapper and morocco slippers. Her hair fell over her eyes like that of an Aberdeen terrier, and she gave a shrill scream when she saw Pug.

"I can't bear dogs," she said. "Take that dog away, dear Lucia. Burn it, drown it! You told me you hadn't got any dogs."

Lady Ambermere turned on her a face that should have instantly petrified her, if she had had any proper feeling. Never had Pug been so blasphemed. She rose as she swallowed the last mouthful of seed cake.

"We are inconveniencing your guests, Mrs. Lucas," she said. "Pug and I will be off. Miss Lyall, Pug's leash. We must be getting back to The Hall. I shall look in at Mrs. Shuttleworth's, and sign my name in the Princess's book. Goodbye, Mrs. Lucas. Thank you for my tea."

She pointedly ignored Mrs. Alingsby, and headed the gloomy frieze that defiled through the door. The sole bright spot was that she would find only a book of crossword puzzles to write her name in.

Chapter Six

LUCIA'S GUESTS WENT OFF BY the early train next morning and she was left, like Marius among the ruins of Carthage. But, unlike that weak-hearted senator, she had no intention of mourning: her first function was to rebuild, and presently she became aware that the work of rebuilding had to begin from its very foundations. There was as background the fact that her weekend party had not been a triumphant success, for she had been speaking in London of Riseholme being such a queer dear old-fashioned little place, where everybody adored her, and where Olga kept incessantly running in to sing acts and acts of the most renowned operas in her music-room; she had also represented Princess Isabel as being a dear and intimate friend, and these two cronies of hers had politely but firmly refused all invitations to pop in. Lady Ambermere, it is true, had popped in, but nobody had seemed the least impressed with her, and Lucia had really been very glad when after Sophy's painful remarks about Pug, she had popped out, leaving that astonished Post-Cubist free to enquire who that crashing old hag was. Of course all this could be quickly lived down again when she got to London, but it certainly did require obliteration.

What gave her more pause for thought was the effect that her weekend had produced on Riseholme. Lucia knew that all Riseholme knew that Olga and the Princess had lunched off cold

lamb with Georgie, and had never been near The Hurst, and
Riseholme, if she knew Riseholme at all, would have something
to talk about there. Riseholme knew also that Lucia and her party
had shrieked with laughter at the Museum, while the Princess
had politely signed her name in the visitors' book after reverently
viewing her great-aunt's mittens. But what else had been happening, whether Olga was here still, what Daisy and her ouija-board
had been up to, who had dined (if anyone except Georgie) at
Olga's last night, Lucia was at present ignorant, and all that she
had to find out, for she had a presentiment that nobody would
pop in and tell her. Above all, what was Riseholme saying about
her? How were they taking it all?

Lucia had determined to devote this day to her old friends,
and she rang up Daisy and asked her and Robert to lunch. Daisy
regretted that she was engaged, and rang off with such precipitation that (so it was easy to guess) she dropped the receiver on
the floor, said "Drat," and replaced it. Lucia then rang up Mrs.
Boucher and asked her and the Colonel to lunch. Mrs. Boucher
with great emphasis said that she had got friends to lunch. Of
course that might mean that Daisy Quantock was lunching
there; indeed it seemed a very natural explanation, but somehow
it was far from satisfying Lucia.

She sat down to think, and the unwelcome result of thought
was a faint suspicion that just as she had decided to ignore Riseholme while her smart party from London was with her, Riseholme was malignant enough to retaliate. It was very base, it was
very childish, but there was that possibility. She resolved to put
a playful face on it and rang up Georgie. From the extraordinary
celerity with which he answered, she wondered whether he was
expecting a call from her or another.

"Georgino *mio*!" she said.

The eagerness with which Georgie had said "Yes. Who is it?" seemed to die out of his voice.

"Oh, it's you, is it?" he said. "Good-morning."

Lucia was not discouraged.

"Me coming round to have good long chat," she said. "All my tiresome guests have gone, Georgie, and I'm staying till *domani*. So lovely to be here again."

"*Si*," said Georgie; just "*si*."

The faint suspicion became a shade more definite.

"Coming at once then," said Lucia.

Lucia set forth and emerging on to the green, was in time to see Daisy Quantock hurry out of Georgie's house and bolt into her own like a plump little red-faced rabbit. Somehow that was slightly disconcerting: it required very little inductive reasoning to form the theory that Daisy had popped in to tell Georgie that Lucia had asked her to lunch, and that she had refused. Daisy must have been present also when Lucia rang Georgie up and instead of waiting to join in the good long chat had scuttled home again. A slight effort therefore was needed to keep herself up to the gay playful level and be quite unconscious that anything unpropitious could possibly have occurred. She found Georgie with his sewing in the little room which he called his study because he did his embroidery there. He seemed somehow to Lucia to be encased in a thin covering of ice, and she directed her full effulgence to the task of melting it.

"Now that is nice!" she said. "And we'll have a good gossip. So lovely to be in Riseholme again. And isn't it naughty of me? I was almost glad when I saw the last of my guests off this morning, and promised myself a real Riseholme day. Such dears, all of them, too, and tremendously in the movement; such arguments and discussions as we had! All day yesterday I was occupied, talks with one, strolls with another, and all the time I was longing to trot round and see you and Daisy and all the rest. Any news, Georgie? What did you do with yourself yesterday?"

"Well, I was very busy too," said Georgie. "Quite a rush. I had two guests at lunch, and then I had tea at Olga's—"

"Is she here still?" asked Lucia. She did not intend to ask that, but she simply could not help it.

"Oh yes. She's going to stop here two or three days, as she doesn't sing in London again till Thursday."

Lucia longed to ask if the Princess was remaining as well, but she had self-control enough not to. Perhaps it would come out some other way . . .

"Dear Olga," said Lucia effusively. "I reckon her quite a Riseholmite."

"Oh quite," said Georgie, who was determined not to let his ice melt. "Yes: I had tea at Olga's, and we had the most wonderful weedj. Just she and the Princess and Daisy and I."

Lucia gave her silvery peal of laughter. It sounded as if it had "turned" a little in this hot weather, or got a little tarnished.

"Dear Daisy!" she said. "Is she not priceless? How she adores her conjuring tricks and hocus-pocuses! Tell me all about it. An Egyptian guide: Abfou, was it not?"

Georgie thought it might be wiser not to tell Lucia all that Abfou had vouchsafed, unless she really insisted, for Abfou had written the most sarcastic things about her in perfect English at top speed. He had called her a snob again, and said she was too grand now for her old friends, and had been really rude about her shingled hair.

"Yes, Abfou," he said. "Abfou was in great form, and Olga has telegraphed for a planchette. Abfou said she was most psychical, and had great mediumistic gifts. Well, that went on a long time."

"What else did Abfou say?" asked Lucia, fixing Georgie with her penetrating eye.

"Oh, he talked about Riseholme affairs," said Georgie. "He knew the Princess had been to the Museum, for he had seen her there. It was he, you know, who suggested the Museum. He kept writing Museum, though we thought it was Mouse at first."

Lucia felt perfectly certain in her own mind that Abfou had been saying things about her. But perhaps, as it was Daisy who had been operating, it was better not to ask what they were. Ignorance was not bliss, but knowledge might be even less blissful. And Georgie was not thawing: he was polite, he was reserved, but so far from chatting, he was talking with great care. She must get him in a more confidential mood.

"That reminds me," she said. "Peppino and I haven't given you anything for the Museum yet. I must send you the Elizabethan spit from my music-room. They say it is the most perfect spit in existence. I don't know what Peppino didn't pay for it."

"How kind of you," said Georgie. "I will tell the committee of your offer. Olga gave us a most magnificent present yesterday: the manuscript of *Lucrezia,* which Cortese had given her. I took it to the Museum directly after breakfast, and put it in the glass case opposite the door."

Again Lucia longed to be as sarcastic as Abfou, and ask whether a committee meeting had been held to settle if this should be accepted. Probably Georgie had some perception of that, for he went on in a great hurry.

"Well, the weedj lasted so long that I had only just time to get home to dress for dinner and go back to Olga's," he said.

"Who was there?" asked Lucia.

"Colonel and Mrs. Boucher, that's all," said Georgie. "And after dinner Olga sang too divinely. I played her accompaniments. A lot of Schubert songs."

Lucia was beginning to feel sick with envy. She pictured to herself the glory of having taken her party across to Olga's after dinner last night, of having played the accompaniments instead of Georgie (who was a miserable accompanist), of having been persuaded afterwards to give them the little morsel of Stravinski, which she had got by heart. How brilliant it would all have been; what a sumptuous paragraph Hermione would have written about her weekend! Instead of which Olga had sung to those old Bouchers, neither of whom knew one note from another, nor cared the least for the distinction of hearing the primadonna sing in her own house. The bitterness of it could not be suppressed.

"Dear old Schubert songs!" she said with extraordinary acidity. "Such sweet old-fashioned things. 'Widmung,' I suppose."

"No, that's by Schumann," said Georgie, who was nettled by her tone, though he guessed what she was suffering.

Lucia knew he was right, but had to uphold her own unfortunate mistake.

"Schubert, I think," she said. "Not that it matters. And so, as dear old Pepys said, and so to bed?"

Georgie was certainly enjoying himself.

"Oh no, we didn't go to bed till terribly late," he said. "But you would have hated to be there, for what we did next. We turned on the gramophone—"

Lucia gave a little wince. Her views about gramophones, as being a profane parody of music, were well known.

"Yes, I should have run away then," she said.

"We turned on the gramophone and danced!" said Georgie firmly.

This was the worst she had heard yet. Again she pictured what yesterday evening might have been. The idea of having popped in with her party after dinner, to hear Olga sing, and then dance impromptu with a prima-donna and a princess . . . It was agonising: it was intolerable.

She gave a dreadful little titter.

"How very droll!" she said. "I can hardly imagine it. Mrs. Boucher in her bath-chair must have been an unwieldy partner, Georgie. Are you not very stiff this morning?"

"No, Mrs. Boucher didn't dance," said Georgie with fearful literalness. "She looked on and wound up the gramophone. Just we four danced: Olga and the Princess and Colonel Boucher and I."

Lucia made a great effort with herself. She knew quite well that Georgie knew how she would have given anything to have brought her party across, and it only made matters worse (if they could be made worse) to be sarcastic about it and pretend to find it all ridiculous. Olga certainly had left her and her friends alone, just as she herself had left Riseholme alone, in this matter of her weekend party. Yet it was unwise to be withering about Colonel Boucher's dancing. She had made it clear that she was busy with her party, and but for this unfortunate accident of Olga's coming down, nothing else could have happened in Riseholme that day except by her dispensing. It was unfortunate, but it must be lived down, and if dear old Riseholme was offended with her, Riseholme must be propitiated.

"Great fun it must have been," she said. "How delicious a little impromptu thing like that is! And singing too: well, you had a nice evening, Georgie. And now let us make some delicious little plan for today. Pop in presently and have 'ickle music and bit of lunch."

"I'm afraid I've just promised to lunch with Daisy," said he.

This again was rather ominous, for there could be no doubt

that Daisy, having said she was engaged, had popped in here to effect an engagement.

"How gay!" said Lucia. "Come and dine this evening then! Really, Georgie, you are busier than any of us in London."

"Too tarsome," said Georgie, "because Olga's coming in here."

"And the Princess?" asked Lucia before she could stop herself.

"No, she went away this morning," said Georgie.

That was something, anyhow, thought Lucia. One distinguished person had gone away from Riseholme. She waited, in slowly diminishing confidence, for Georgie to ask her to dine with him instead. Perhaps he would ask Peppino too, but if not, Peppino would be quite happy with his telescope and his crosswords all by himself. But it was odd and distasteful to wait to be asked to dinner by anybody in Riseholme instead of everyone wanting to be asked by her.

"She went away by the ten-thirty," said Georgie, after an awful pause.

Lucia had already learned certain lessons in London. If you get a snub—and this seemed very like a snub—the only possible course was to be unaware of it. So, though the thought of being snubbed by Georgie nearly made her swoon, she was unaware of it.

"Such a good train," she said, magnificently disregarding the well-known fact that it stopped at every station, and crawled in between.

"Excellent," said Georgie with conviction. He had not the slightest intention of asking Lucia to dine, for he wanted his tête-à-tête with Olga. There would be such a lot to talk over, and besides it would be tiresome to have Lucia there, for she would be sure to gabble away about her wonderful life in London, and her music-room and her Chippendale chairs, and generally to lay down the law. She must be punished too, for her loathsome conduct in disregarding her old friends when she had her party from London, and be made to learn that her old friends were being much smarter than she was.

Lucia kept her end up nobly.

"Well, Georgie, I must trot away," she said. "Such a lot of people to see. Look in, if you've got a spare minute. I'm off again tomorrow. Such a whirl of things in London this week."

Lucia, instead of proceeding to see lots of people, went back to her house and saw Peppino. He was sitting in the garden in very old clothes, smoking a pipe, and thoroughly enjoying the complete absence of anything to do. He was aware that officially he loved the bustle of London, but it was extremely pleasant to sit in his garden and smoke a pipe, and above all to be rid of those rather hectic people who had talked quite incessantly from morning till night all Sunday. He had given up the crossword, and was thinking over the material for a sonnet on Tranquillity, when Lucia came out to him.

"I was wondering, Peppino," she said, "if it would not be pleasanter to go up to town this afternoon. We should get the cool of the evening for our drive, and really, now all our guests have gone, and we are going tomorrow, these hours will be rather tedious. We are spoilt, *caro,* you and I, by our full life up there, where any moment the telephone bell may ring with some delightful invitation. Of course in August we will be here, and settle down to our quaint old life again, but these little odds and ends of time, you know."

Peppino was reasonably astonished. Half an hour ago Lucia had set out, burning with enthusiasm to pick up the "old threads," and now all she seemed to want to do was to drop the old threads as quickly as possible. Though he knew himself to be incapable of following the swift and antic movements of Lucia's mind, he was capable of putting two and two together. He had been faintly conscious all yesterday that matters were not going precisely as Lucia wished, and knew that her efforts to entice Olga and her guest to the house had been as barren as a fig tree, but there must have been something more than that. Though not an imaginative man (except in thinking that words rhymed when they did not), it occurred to him that Riseholme was irritated with Lucia, and was indicating it in some unusual manner.

"Why, my dear, I thought you were going to have people in to lunch and dinner," he said, "and see about sending the spit to the Museum, and be tremendously busy all day."

Lucia pulled herself together. She had a momentary impulse to confide in Peppino and tell him all the ominous happenings of the last hour, how Daisy had said she was engaged for lunch and Mrs. Boucher had friends to lunch, and Georgie had Olga to dinner and had not asked her, and how the munificent gift of the spit was to be considered by the Museum Committee before they accepted it. But to have done that would be to acknowledge not one snub but many snubs, which was contrary to the whole principle of successful attainment. Never must she confess, even to Peppino, that the wheels of her chariot seemed to drive heavily, or that Riseholme was not at the moment agape to receive the signs of her favour. She must not even confess it to herself, and she made a rapid and complete *volte face*.

"It shall be as you like, *caro*," she said. "You would prefer to spend a quiet day here, so you shall. As for me, you've never known me yet otherwise than busy, have you? I have a stack of letters to write, and there's my piano looking, oh, so reproachfully at me, for I haven't touched the dear keys since I came, and I must just glance through *Henry VIII,* as we're going to see it tomorrow. I shall be busy enough, and you will have your day in the sun and the air. I only thought you might prefer to run up to town today, instead of waiting till tomorrow. Now don't keep me chatting here any longer."

Lucia proved her quality on that dismal day. She played her piano with all her usual concentration, she read *Henry VIII,* she wrote her letters, and it was not till the *Evening Gazette* came in that she allowed herself a moment's relaxation. Hurriedly she turned the pages, stopping neither for crossword nor record of international interests, till she came to Hermione's column. She had feared (and with a gasp of relief she saw how unfounded her fears had been) that Hermione would have devoted his picturesque pen to Olga and the Princess, and given her and her party only the fag-end of his last paragraph, but she had disquieted herself in vain. Olga had taken no notice of him, and now (what could be fairer?) he took no notice of Olga. He just mentioned that she had a "pretty little cottage" at Riseholme, where she came occasionally for weekends, and there were three long sumptuous paragraphs about The Hurst, and Mr. and Mrs. Philip Lucas who had Lord Limpsfield and the wife of the member, Mrs. Garroby-Ashton, and Mrs. Alingsby staying with them. Lady Ambermere and her party from The Hall had come to tea, and it was all glorious and distinguished. Hermione had proved himself a true friend, and there was not a word about Olga and the Princess going to lunch with Georgie, or about Daisy and her absurd weedj . . . Lucia read the luscious lines through twice, and then, as she often did, sent her copy across to Georgie, in order to help him to readjust values. Almost simultaneously Daisy sent de Vere across to him with her copy, and Mrs.

Boucher did the same, calling attention to the obnoxious paragraphs with blue and red pencil respectively, and a great many exclamation marks in both cases.

∞

Riseholme settled back into its strenuous life again when Lucia departed next morning to resume her vapid existence in London. It was not annoyed with her any more, because it had "larned" her, and was quite prepared to welcome her back if (and when) she returned in a proper spirit and behaved herself suitably. Moreover, even with its own perennial interests to attend to, it privately missed the old Lucia, who gave them a lead in everything, even though she domineered, and was absurd, and pretended to know all about everything, and put her finger into every pie within reach. But it did not miss the new shingled Lucia, the one who had come down with a party of fresh friends, and had laughed at the Museum, and had neglected her old friends altogether, till she found out that Olga and a Princess were in the place: the less seen of her the better. It was considered also that she had remained down here this extra day in order to propitiate those whom she had treated as pariahs, and condescend to take notice of them again, and if there was one thing that Riseholme could not stand, and did not mean to stand from anybody, it was condescension. It was therefore perfectly correct for Daisy and Mrs. Boucher to say they were engaged for lunch, and for Georgie to decline to ask her to dinner . . . These three formed the committee of the Museum, and they met that morning to audit the accounts for the week and discuss any other business connected or unconnected with their office. There was not, of course, with so small and intimate a body, any need to have a chairman, and they all rapped the table when they wanted to be listened to.

Mrs. Boucher was greedily counting the shillings which had been taken from the till, while Georgie counted the counterfoils of the tickets.

"A hundred and twenty-three," he said. "That's nearly the best week we've had yet."

"And fifteen and four is nineteen," said Mrs. Boucher, "and four is twenty-three, which makes exactly six pounds three shillings. Well, I do call that good. And I hear we've had a wonderful bequest made. Most generous of our dear Olga. I think she ought not only to be thanked, but asked to join the committee. I always said—"

Daisy rapped the table.

"Abfou said just the same," she interrupted. "I had a sitting this morning, and he kept writing 'committee.' I brought the paper along with me, because I was going to propose that myself. But there's another thing first, and that's about insurance. Robert told me he was insuring the building and its contents separately for a thousand pounds each. We shall have to pay a premium, of course. Oh, here's Abfou's message. 'Committee,' you see 'committee' written three times. I feel quite sure he meant Olga."

"He spells it with only one 'm,'" said Georgie, "but I expect he means that. There's one bit of business that comes before that, for I have been offered another object for the Museum, and I said I would refer the offer to the committee before I accepted it. Lucia came to see me yesterday morning and asked—"

"The Elizabethan spit," said Mrs. Boucher. "I don't see what we want with it, for my part, and if I had to say what I thought, I should thank her most politely, and beg that she would keep it herself. Most kind of her, I'm sure. Sorry to refuse, which was just what I said when she asked me to lunch yesterday. There'd have been legs of cold chickens of which her friends from London had eaten wings."

"She asked me too," said Daisy, "and I said 'no.' Did she leave this morning?"

"Yes, about half-past ten," said Georgie. "She wanted me to ask her to dinner last night."

Daisy had been writing "committee" again and again on her blotting-paper. It looked very odd with two "m"s and she would certainly have spelt it with one herself.

"I think Abfou is right about the way to spell 'committee,'" she said, "and even if he weren't the meaning is clear enough. But about the insurance. Robert only advises insurance against fire, for he says no burglar in his senses—"

Mrs. Boucher rapped the table.

"But there wasn't the manuscript of *Lucrezia* then," she said. "And I should think that any burglar whether in his senses or out of them would think *that* worth taking. If it was a question of insuring an Elizabethan spit—"

"Well, I want to know what the committee wishes me to say about that," said Georgie. "Oh, by the way, when we have a new edition of the catalogue, we must bring it up to date. There'll be the manuscript of *Lucrezia*."

"And if you ask me," said Mrs. Boucher, "she only wanted to get rid of the spit because it makes her chimney smoke. Tell her to get her chimney swept and keep the spit."

"There's a portrait of her in the music-room," said Georgie, "by Sigismund. It looks like nothing at all—"

"Of course everybody has a right to have their hair shingled," said Mrs. Boucher, "whatever their age, and there's no law to prevent you."

Daisy rapped the table.

"We were considering as to whether we should ask Mrs. Shuttleworth to join the committee," she said.

"She sang too, beautifully, on Sunday night," said Georgie, "and what fun we had dancing. Oh, and Lucia asked for the Princess's book to sign her name in, and the only book she had brought was a book of crossword puzzles."

"No!" said both ladies together.

"She did, because Olga's parlour-maid told Foljambe, and—"

"Well I never!" said Daisy. "That served her out. Did she write Lucia across, and Peppino down?"

"I'm sure I've nothing to say against her," said Mrs. Boucher, "but people usually get what they deserve. Certainly let us have the Museum insured if that's the right thing to do, and as for asking Olga to be on the committee, why we settled that hours ago, and I have nothing more to say about the spit. Have the spit if you like, but I would no more think of insuring it, than insuring a cold in the head. I've as much use for one as the other. All that stuff too about the gracious *châtelaine* at The Hurst in the *Evening Gazette*! My husband read it, and what he said was, 'Faugh!' Tush and faugh, was what he said."

Public opinion was beginning to boil up again about Lucia, and Georgie intervened.

"I think that's all the business before the meeting," he said, "and so we accept the manuscript of *Lucrezia* and decline the spit. I'm sure it was very kind of both the donors. And Olga's to be asked to join the committee. Well, we have got through a good morning's work."

∞

Lucia meanwhile was driving back to London, where she intended to make herself a busy week. There would be two nights at the opera, on the second of which Olga was singing in the *Valkyrie*, and so far from intending to depreciate her singing, or to refrain from going, by way of revenge for the slight she had suffered, she meant, even if Olga sang like a screech-owl and acted like a stick, to say there had never been so perfect a presentation of Brünnhilde. She could not conceive doing anything so stupid as snubbing Olga because she had not come to her house or permitted her to enter Old Place: that would have been the height of folly.

At present, she was (or hoped to be) on the upward road, and the upward road could only be climbed by industry and appreciation. When she got to the top, it would be a different matter, but just now it was an asset, a score to allude to dear Olga and the hoppings in and out that took place all day at Riseholme: she knew too, a good deal that Olga had done on Sunday and that would all be useful. "Always appreciate, always admire," thought Lucia to herself as she woke Peppino up from a profound nap on their arrival at Brompton Square. "Be busy: work, work, work."

She knew already that there would be hard work in front of her before she got where she wanted to get, and she whisked off like a disturbing fly which impeded concentration the slight disappointment which her weekend had brought. If you meant to progress, you must never look back (the awful example of Lot's wife!) and never, unless you are certain it is absolutely useless, kick down a ladder which has brought you anywhere, or might in the future bring you anywhere. Already she had learned a lesson about that, for if she had only told Georgie that she had been coming down for a weekend, and had bidden him to lunch and dinner and anything else he liked, he would certainly have got Olga to pop in at The Hurst, or have said that he couldn't dine with Olga on that fateful Sunday night because he was dining with her, and then no doubt Olga would have asked them all to come in afterwards. It had been a mistake to kick Riseholme down, a woeful mistake, and she would never do such a thing again. It was a mistake also to be sarcastic about anybody till you were sure they could not help you, and who could be sure of that? Even poor dear Daisy with her ridiculous Abfou had proved such an attraction at Old Place, that Georgie had barely time to get back and dress for dinner, and a benignant Daisy instead of a militant and malignant Daisy would have helped. Everything helps, thought Lucia, as she snatched up the tablets which stood by the telephone and recorded the ringings up that had taken place in her absence.

She fairly gasped at the amazing appropriateness of a message that had been received only ten minutes ago. Marcia Whitby hoped that she could dine that evening: the message was to be delivered as soon as she arrived. Obviously it was a last-moment invitation: somebody had thrown her over, and perhaps that made them thirteen. There was no great compliment in it, for Marcia, so Lucia conjectured, had already tried high and low to get another woman, and now in despair she tried Lucia . . . Of course there were the tickets for *Henry VIII,* and it was a first night, but perhaps she could get somebody to go with Peppino . . . Ah, she remembered Aggie Sanderson lamenting that she had not been able to secure a seat! Without a pause she rang up the Duchess of Whitby, and expressed her eager delight at coming to dine tonight. So lucky, so charmed. Then having committed herself, she rang up Aggie and hoped for the best, and Aggie jumped at the idea of a ticket for *Henry VIII,* and then she told Peppino all about it.

"*Caro,* I had to be kind," she said, tripping off into the music-room where he was at tea. "Poor Marcia Whitby in despair."

"Dear me, what has happened?" asked Peppino.

"One short, one woman short, evidently, for her dinner

tonight: besought me to go. But you shall have your play all the same, and a dear sweet woman to take to it. Guess! No. I'll tell you: Aggie. She was longing to go, and so it's a kindness all round. You will have somebody more exciting to talk to than your poor old *sposa,* and dearest Aggie will get her play, and Marcia will be ever so grateful to me. I shall miss the play, but I will go another night unless you tell me it is no good . . ."

Of course the *Evening Gazette* would contain no further news of the *châtelaine* at The Hurst, but Lucia turned to Hermione's column with a certain eagerness, for there might be something about the Duchess's dinner this evening. Hermione did not seem to have heard of it, but if Hermione came to lunch tomorrow, he would hear of it then. She rang him up . . .

∞

Lucia's kindness to Marcia Whitby met with all sorts of rewards. She got there, as was her custom in London, rather early, so that she could hear the names of all the guests as they arrived, and Marcia, feeling thoroughly warm-hearted to her, for she had tried dozens of women to turn her party from thirteen into fourteen, called her Lucia instead of Mrs. Lucas. It was no difficulty to Lucia to reciprocate this intimacy in a natural manner, for she had alluded to the Duchess as Marcia behind her back, for weeks, and now the syllables tripped to her tongue with the familiarity of custom.

"Sweet of you to ask me, dear Marcia," she said. "Peppino and I only arrived from Riseholme an hour or two ago, and he took Aggie Sandeman to the theatre instead of me. Such a lovely Sunday at Riseholme: you must spare a weekend and come down and vegetate. Olga Shuttleworth was there with Princess Isabel, and she sang too divinely on Sunday evening, and then, would you believe it, we turned on the gramophone and danced."

"What a coincidence!" said Marcia, "because I've got a small dance tonight, and Princess Isabel is coming. But not nearly so chic as your dance at Riseholme."

She moved towards the door to receive the guests who were beginning to arrive, and Lucia, with ears open for distinguished names, had just a moment's qualm for having given the impression which she meant to give, that she had been dancing to Olga's gramophone. It was no more than momentary, and presently the Princess arrived, and was led round by her hostess, to receive curtseys.

"And of course you know Mrs. Lucas," said Marcia. "She's been telling me about your dancing to the gramophone at her house on Sunday."

Lucia recovered from her curtsey.

"No, dear Marcia," she said. "It was at Olga's, in fact—"

The Princess fixed her with a Royal eye before she passed on, as if she seemed to understand.

But that was the only catastrophe, and how small a one! The Princess liked freaks, and so Marcia had asked a star of the movies and a distinguished novelist, and a woman with a skin like a kipper from having crossed the Sahara twice on foot, or having swum the Atlantic twice, or something of the sort, and a society caricaturist and a slim young gentleman with a soft voice, who turned out to be the bloodiest pugilist of the century, and the Prime Minister, two ambassadresses, and the great Mrs. Beaucourt who had just astounded the world by her scandalous volume of purely imaginary reminiscences. Each of these would furnish a brilliant centre for a dinner party, and the idea of spreading the butter as thick as that seemed to Lucia almost criminal: she herself, indeed, was the only bit of bread to be seen anywhere. Before dinner was over she had engaged both her neighbours, the pugilist and the cinema star, to dine with her on consecutive nights next week, and was mentally running through her list of friends to settle whom to group round them. Alf Watson, the pugilist, it appeared, when not engaged in knocking people out, spent his time in playing the flute to soothe his savage breast, while Marcelle Periscope, when not impersonating impassioned lovers, played with his moderately tame lion-cub. Lucia begged Alf to bring his flute, and they would have some music, but did not extend her invitation to the lion-cub, which sounded slightly Bolshevistic . . . Later in the evening she got hold of Herbert Alton, the social caricaturist, who promised to lunch on Sunday, but failed to do business with the lady from the Sahara, who was leaving next day to swim another sea, or cross another desert. Then the guests for the dance began to arrive, and Lucia, already half-intoxicated by celebrities, sank rapt in a chair at the top of the staircase and listened to the catalogue of sonorous names. Up trooped stars and garters and tiaras, and when she felt stronger, she clung firmly to Lord Limpsfield, who seemed to know everybody and raked in introductions.

Lucia did not get home till three o'clock (for having given up her play out of kindness to Marcia, she might as well do it thoroughly), but she was busy writing invitations for her two dinner parties next week by nine in the morning. Peppino was lunching at his club, where he might meet the Astronomer-Royal, and have a chat about the constellations, but he was to ring her up about a quarter past two and ascertain if she had made any engagement for him during the afternoon. The idea of this somehow occupied her brain as she filled up the cards of invitation in her small exquisite handwriting. There was a telephone in her dining-room, and she began to visualise to herself Peppino's ringing her up, while she and the two or three friends who were lunching with her would be still at table. It would be at the end of lunch: they would be drinking their coffee, which she always made herself in a glass machine with a spirit-lamp which, when it appeared to be on the point of exploding, indicated that coffee was ready. The servants would have left the room, and she would go to the telephone herself . . . She would hear Peppino's voice, but nobody else would. They would not know who was at the other end, and she might easily pretend that it was not Peppino, but . . . She would give a gabbling answer, audible to her guests, but she could divert her mouth a little away so that Peppino could not make anything out of it, and then hang up the receiver again . . . Peppino no doubt would think he had got hold of a wrong number, and presently call her up again, and she would then tell him anything there was to communicate. As she scribbled away the idea took shape and substance: there was an attraction about it, it smiled on her.

She came to the end of her dinner-invitations grouped round the cinema star and the fluting prizefighter, and she considered whom to ask to meet Herbert Alton on Sunday. He was working hard, he had told her, to finish his little gallery of caricatures with which he annually regaled London, and which was to open in a fortnight. He was a licensed satirist, and all London always flocked to his show to observe with glee what he made of them all, and what witty and pungent little remarks he affixed to their monstrous effigies. It was a distinct cachet, too, to be caricatured by him, a sign that you attracted attention and were a notable figure. He might (in fact, he always did) make you a perfect guy, and his captions invariably made fun of something characteristic, but it gave you publicity. She wondered whether he would take a commission: she wondered whether he might be induced to do a caricature of Peppino or herself or of them both, at a handsome price, with the proviso that it was to be on view at his exhibition. That could probably be ascertained, and then she might approach the subject on Sunday. Anyhow, she would ask one or two pleasant people to meet him, and hope for the best.

∞

Lucia's little lunch-party that day consisted only of four people. Lunch, Lucia considered, was for *intimes:* you sat with your elbows on the table, and all talked together, and learned the news, just as you did on the green at Riseholme. There was something unwieldy about a large lunch-party; it was a distracted affair, and in the effort to assimilate more news than you could really digest, you forgot half of it. Today, therefore, there was only Aggie Sandeman who had been to the play last night with Peppino, and was bringing her cousin Adele Brixton (whom Lucia had not yet met, but very much wanted to know), and Stephen Merriall. Lady Brixton was a lean, intelligent American of large fortune who found she got on better without her husband. But as Lord Brixton preferred living in America and she in England, satisfactory arrangements were easily made. Occasionally she had to go to see relatives in America, and he selected such periods for seeing relatives in England.

She explained the situation very good-naturedly to Lucia who rather rashly asked after her husband.

"In fact," she said, "we blow kisses to each other from the decks of Atlantic liners going in opposite directions, if it's calm, and if it's rough, we're sick into the same ocean."

Now that would never have been said at Riseholme, or if it was, it would have been very ill thought of, and a forced smile followed by a complete change of conversation would have given it a chilly welcome. Now, out of habit, Lucia smiled a forced smile, and then remembered that you could not judge London by the chaste standards of Riseholme. She turned the forced smile into a genial one.

"Too delicious!" she said. "I must tell Peppino that."

"Pep what?" asked Lady Brixton.

This was explained; it was also explained that Aggie had been with Peppino to the play last night; in fact there was rather too much explanation going on for social ease, and Lucia thought it was time to tell them all about what she had done last night. She did this in a characteristic manner.

"Dear Lady Brixton," she said, "ever since you came in I've been wondering where I have seen you. Of course it was last night, at our darling Marcia's dance."

This seemed to introduce the desirable topic, and though it was not in the least true, it was a wonderfully good shot.

"Yes, I was there," said Adele. "What a crush. Sheer Mormonism: one man to fifty women."

"How unkind of you! I dined there first; quite a small party. Princess Isabel, who had been down at our dear little Riseholme on Sunday, staying with Olga—such a coincidence—" Lucia stopped just in time; she was about to describe the impromptu dance at Olga's on Sunday night, but remembered that Stephen knew she had not been to it. So she left the coincidence alone, and went rapidly on:

"Dear Marcia insisted on my coming," she said, "and so, really, like a true friend I gave up the play and went. Such an amusing little dinner. Marcelle—Marcelle Periscope, the Prime Minister and the Italian Ambassadress, and Princess Isabel of course, and Alf, and a few more. There's nobody like Marcia for getting up a wonderful unexpected little party like that. Alf was too delicious."

"Not Alf Watson?" asked Lady Brixton.

"Yes, I sat next him at dinner, and he's coming to dine with me next week, and is bringing his flute. He adores playing the flute. Can't I persuade you to come, Lady Brixton? Thursday, let me see, is it Thursday? Yes, Thursday. No party at all, just a few old friends, and some music. I must find some duets for the piano and flute: Alf made me promise that I would play his accompaniments for him. And Dora: Dora Beaucourt. What a lurid life! And Sigismund: no, I don't think Sigismund was there; it was at Sophy's. Such a marvellous portrait he has done of me: is it not marvellous, Stephen? You remember it down at Riseholme. How amusing Sophy was, insisting that I should move every other picture out of my music-room. I must get her to come in after dinner on Thursday; there is something primitive about the flute." So Theocritan!

Lucia suddenly remembered that she mustn't kick ladders down, and turned to Aggie. Aggie had been very useful when first she came up to London, and she might quite easily be useful again, for she knew quantities of solid people, and if her parties lacked brilliance, they were highly respectable. The people whom Sophy called "the old crusted" went there.

"Aggie dear, as soon as you get home, put down Wednesday for dining with me," she said, "and if there's an engagement there already, as there's sure to be, cross it out and have pseudo-influenza. Marcelle—Marcelle Periscope is coming, but I didn't ask the lion-cub. A lion-cub: so quaint of him—and who else was there last night? Dear me, I get so mixed up with all the people one runs across."

Lucia, of course, never got mixed up at all: there was no one so clear-headed, but she had to spin things out a little, for Peppino was rather late ringing up. The coffee-equipage had been set before her, and she kept drawing away the spirit-lamp in an absent manner just before it boiled, for they must still be sitting in the dining-room when he rang up. But even as she lamented her muddled memory, the tinkle of the telephone bell sounded. She rapidly rehearsed in her mind what she was going to say.

"Ah, that telephone," she said, rising hastily, so as to get to it before one of the servants came back. "I often tell Peppino I shall cut it out of the house, for one never gets a moment's peace. Yes, yes, who is it?"

Lucia listened for a second, and then gave a curtsey.

"Oh, is it you, ma'am?" she said, holding the mouthpiece a little obliquely. "Yes, I'm Mrs. Lucas."

A rather gruff noise, clearly Peppino's voice, came from the instrument, but she trusted it was inaudible to the others, and she soon broke in again talking very rapidly.

"Oh, that is kind of you, your Highness," she said. "It would be too delightful. Tomorrow: charmed. Delighted."

She replaced the mouthpiece, and instantly began to talk again from the point at which she had left off.

"Yes, and of course Herbert Alton was there," she said. "His show opens in a fortnight, and how we shall all meet there at the private view and laugh at each other's caricatures! What is it that Rousseau—is it Rousseau?—says, about our not being wholly grieved at the misfortunes of our friends? So true! Bertie is rather wicked sometimes though, but still one forgives him everything. Ah, the coffee is boiling at last."

Peppino, as Lucia had foreseen, rang up again almost immediately, and she told him he had missed the most charming little lunch-party, because he would go to his club. Her guests, of course, were burning to know to whom she had curtseyed, but Lucia gave no information on the point. Adele Brixton and Aggie presently went off to a matinée, but Stephen remained behind. That looked rather well, Lucia thought, for she had noticed that often a handsome and tolerably young man lingered with the hostess when other guests had gone. There was something rather chic about it; if it happened very constantly, or if at another house they came together or went away together, people would begin to talk, quite pleasantly of course, about his devotion to her. Georgie had been just such a *cavaliere servente*. Stephen, for his part, was quite unconscious of any such scintillations in Lucia's mind: he merely knew that it was certainly convenient for an unattached man to have a very pleasant house always to go to, where he would be sure of hearing things that interested Hermione.

"Delicious little lunch-party," he said. "What a charming woman Lady Brixton is."

"Dear Adele," said Lucia dreamily. "Charming, isn't she? How pleased she was at the thought of meeting Alf! Do look in after dinner that night, Stephen. I wish I could ask you to dine, but I expect to be crammed as it is. Dine on Wednesday, though: let me see, Marcelle comes that night. What a rush next week will be!"

Stephen waited for her to allude to the voice to which she had curtseyed, but he waited in vain.

Chapter Seven

THIS DELICIOUS LITTLE LUNCHEON-PARTY had violently excited Adele Brixton: she was thrilled to the marrow at Lucia's curtsey to the telephone.

"My dear, she's marvellous," she said to Aggie. "She's a study. She's cosmic. The telephone, the curtsey! I've never seen the like. But why in the name of wonder didn't she tell us who the Highness was? She wasn't shy of talking about the other folk she'd met. Alf and Marcelle and Marcia and Bertie. But she made a mistake over Bertie. She shouldn't have said 'Bertie.' I've known Herbert Alton for years, and never has anybody called him anything but Herbert. 'Bertie' was a mistake, but don't tell her. I adore your Lucia. She'll go far, mark my words, and I bet you she's talking of me as Adele this moment. Don't you see how wonderful she is? I've been a climber myself and I know. But I was a snail compared to her."

Aggie Sandeman was rather vexed at not being asked to the Alf party.

"You needn't tell me how wonderful she is," she observed with some asperity. "It's not two months since she came to London first, and she didn't know a soul. She dined with me the first night she came up, and since then she has annexed every single person she met at my house."

"She would," said Adele appreciatively. "And who was the

man who looked as if he had been labelled 'Man' by mistake when he was born, and ought to have been labelled 'Lady'? I never saw such a perfect lady, though I only know him as Stephen at present. She just said, 'Stephen, do you know Lady Brixton?'"

"Stephen Merriall," said Aggie. "Just one of the men who go out to tea every day—one of the unattached."

"Well then, she's going to attach him," said Adele. "Dear me, aren't I poisonous, when I'm going to her house to meet Alf next week! But I don't feel poisonous; I feel wildly interested: I adore her. Here we are at the theatre: what a bore! And there's Tony Limpsfield. Tony, come and help me out. We've been lunching with the most marvellous—"

"I expect you mean Lucia," said Tony. "I spent Sunday with her at Riseholme."

"She curtseyed to the telephone," began Adele.

"Who was at the other end?" asked Tony eagerly.

"That's what she didn't say," said Adele.

"Why not?" asked Tony.

Adele stepped briskly out of her car, followed by Aggie.

"I can't make out," she said. "Oh, do you know Mrs. Sandeman?"

"Yes, of course," said Tony. "And it couldn't have been Princess Isabel."

"Why not? She met her at Marcia's last night."

"Yes, but the Princess fled from her. She fled from her at Riseholme too, and said she would never go to her house. It can't have been she. But she got hold of that boxer—"

"Alf Watson," said Adele. "She called him Alf, and I'm going to meet him at her house on Thursday."

"Then it's very unkind of you to crab her, Adele," said Tony.

"I'm not: I'm simply wildly interested. Anyhow, what about you? You spent a Sunday with her at Riseholme."

"And she calls you Tony," said Aggie vituperatively, still thinking about the Alf party.

"No, does she really?" said Tony. "But after all, I call her Lucia when she's not there. The bell's gone, by the way: the curtain will be up."

Adele hurried in.

"Come to my box, Tony," she said, "after the first act. I haven't been so interested in anything for years."

Adele paid no attention whatever to the gloomy play of Chekhov's. Her whole mind was concentrated on Lucia, and soon she leaned across to Aggie, and whispered: "I believe it was Peppino who rang her up."

Aggie knitted her brows for a moment.

"Couldn't have been," she said. "He rang her up directly afterwards."

Adele's face fell. Not being able to think as far ahead as Lucia she didn't see the answer to that, and relapsed into Lucian meditation, till the moment the curtain fell, when Tony Limpsfield slid into their box.

"I don't know what the play has been about," he said, "but I must tell you why she was at Marcia's last night. Some women chucked Marcia during the afternoon and made her thirteen—"

"Marcia would like that," said Aggie.

Tony took no notice of this silly joke.

"So she rang up everybody in town—" he continued.

"Except me," said Aggie bitterly.

"Oh, never mind that," said Tony. "She rang up everybody, and couldn't get hold of anyone. Then she rang up Lucia."

"Who instantly said she was disengaged, and rang me up to go to the theatre with Peppino," said Aggie. "I suspected something of the sort, but I wanted to see the play, and I wasn't going to cut off my nose to spite Lucia's face."

"Besides, she would have got someone else, or sent Peppino to the play alone," said Tony. "And you've got hold of the wrong end of the stick, Aggie. Nobody wants to spite Lucia. We all want her to have the most glorious time."

"Aggie's vexed because she thinks she invented Lucia," observed Adele. "That's the wrong attitude altogether. Tell me about Pep."

"Simply nothing to say about him," said Tony. "He has trousers and a hat, and a telescope on the roof at Riseholme, and when you talk to him you see he remembers what the leading articles in *The Times* said that morning. Don't introduce irrelevant matters, Adele."

"But husbands are relevant—all but mine," said Adele. "Part of the picture. And what about Stephen?"

"Oh, you always see him handing buns at tea-parties. He's irrelevant too."

"He might not be if her husband is," said Adele.

Tony exploded with laughter.

"You are off the track," he said. "You'll get nowhere if you attempt to smirch Lucia's character. How could she have time for a lover to begin with? And you misunderstand her altogether, if you think that."

"It would be frightfully picturesque," said Adele.

"No, it would spoil it altogether . . . Oh, there's this stupid play beginning again . . . Gracious heavens, look there!"

They followed his finger, and saw Lucia followed by Stephen coming up the central aisle of the stalls to two places in the front row. Just as she reached her place she turned round to survey the house, and caught sight of them. Then the lights were lowered, and her face slid into darkness.

∞

This little colloquy in Adele's box was really the foundation of the secret society of the Luciaphils, and the membership of the Luciaphils began swiftly to increase. Aggie Sandeman was scarcely eligible, for complete goodwill towards Lucia was a *sine qua non* of membership, and there was in her mind a certain asperity when she thought that it was she who had given Lucia her gambit, and that already she was beginning to be relegated to second circles in Lucia's scale of social precedence. It was true that she had been asked to dine to meet Marcelle Periscope, but the party to meet Alf and his flute was clearly the smarter of the two. Adele, however, and Tony Limpsfield were real members, so too, when she came up a few days later, was Olga. Marcia Whitby was another who greedily followed her career, and such as these, whenever they met, gave eager news to each other about it. There was, of course, another camp, consisting of those whom Lucia bombarded with pleasant invitations, but who (at present) firmly refused them. They professed not to know her and not to take the slightest interest in her, which showed, as Adele said, a deplorable narrowness of mind. Types and striking characters like Lucia, who pursued undaunted and indefatigable their aim in life, were rare, and when they occurred should be studied with reverent affection . . . Sometimes one of the old and original members of the Luciaphils discovered others, and if when Lucia's name was mentioned an eager and a kindly light shone in their eyes, and they said in a hushed whisper "Did you hear who was there on Thursday?" they thus disclosed themselves as Luciaphils . . . All this was gradual, but the movement went steadily on, keeping pace with her astonishing career, for the days were few on which some gratifying achievement was not recorded in the veracious columns of Hermione.

∞

Lucia was driving home one afternoon after a day passed in the Divorce Court. She had made the acquaintance of the President not long ago, and had asked him to dinner on the evening before this trial, which was the talk of the town, was to begin, and at the third attempt had got him to give her a seat in the court. The trial had already lasted three days, and really no one seemed to think about anything else, and the papers had been full of soulful and surprising evidence. Certainly, Babs Shyton, the lady whose husband wanted to get rid of her, had written very odd letters to Woof-dog, otherwise known as Lord Middlesex, and he to her: Lucia could not imagine writing to anybody like that, and she would have been very much surprised if anyone had written to her as Woof-dog wrote to Babs. But as the trial went on, Lucia found herself growing warm with sympathy for Babs. Her husband, Colonel Shyton, must have been an impossible person to live with, for sometimes he would lie in bed all day, get up in the evening, have breakfast at eight o'clock, lunch a little after midnight, and dine heavily at half-past eight in the morning. Surely with a husband like that, any woman would want some sort of a Woof-dog to take care of her. Both Babs and he, in the extracts from the remarkable correspondence between them which were read out in court, alluded to Colonel Shyton as the S. P., which Babs (amid loud laughter) frankly confessed meant Stinkpot; and Babs had certainly written to Woof-dog to say that she was in bed and very sleepy and cross, but wished that Woof-dog was thumping his tail on the hearthrug. That was indiscreet, but there was nothing incriminating about it, and as for the row of crosses which followed Babs's signature, she explained quite frankly that they indicated that she was cross. There were roars of laughter again at this, and even the judge wore a broad grin as he said that if there was any more disturbance he should clear the court. Babs had produced an excellent impression, in fact: she had looked so pretty and had answered so gaily, and the Woof-dog had been just as admirable, for he was a strong silent Englishman, and when he was asked whether he had ever kissed Babs he said "That's a lie" in such a loud fierce voice that you felt that the jury had better believe him unless they all wanted to be knocked down. The verdict was expected next day, and Lucia meant to lose no time in asking Babs to dinner if it was in her favour.

The court had been very hot and airless, and Lucia directed her chauffeur to drive round the Park before going home. She had asked one or two people to tea at five, and one or two more at half-past, but there was time for a turn first, and, diverting her mind from the special features of the case to the general features of such cases, she thought what an amazing and incomparable publicity they gave any woman. Of course, if the verdict went against her, such publicity would be extremely disagreeable, but, given that the jury decided that there was nothing against her, Lucia could imagine being almost envious of her. She did not actually want to be placed in such a situation herself, but certainly it would convey a notoriety that could scarcely be accomplished by years of patient effort. Babs would feel that there was not a single person in any gathering who did not know who she was, and all about her, and, if she was innocent, that would be a wholly delightful result. Naturally, Lucia only envied the outcome of such an experience, not the experience itself, for it would entail a miserable life with Peppino, and she felt sure that dinner at half-past eight in the morning would be highly indigestible, but it would be wonderful to be as well-known as Babs.

Another point that had struck her, both in the trial itself and in the torrents of talk that for the last few days had been poured out over the case, was the warm sympathy of the world in general with Babs, whether guilty or innocent. "The world always loves a lover," thought Lucia, and Woof-dog thumping his tail on the rug by her bedroom fire was a beautiful image.

Her thoughts took a more personal turn. The idea of having a real lover was, of course, absolutely abhorrent to her whole nature, and besides, she did not know whom she could get. But the reputation of having a lover was a wholly different matter, presenting no such objections or difficulties, and most decidedly it gave a woman a certain cachet, if a man was always seen about with her and was supposed to be deeply devoted to her. The idea had occurred to her vaguely before, but now it took more definite shape, and as to her choice of this sort of lover, there was no difficulty about that. Hitherto, she had done nothing to encourage the notion, beyond having Stephen at the house a good deal, but now she saw herself assuming an air of devoted proprietorship of him; she could see herself talking to him in a corner, and even laying her hand on his sleeve, arriving with him at an evening party, and going away with him, for Peppino hated going out after dinner . . .

But caution was necessary in the first steps, for it would be hard to explain to Stephen what the proposed relationship was, and she could not imagine herself saying "We are going to pretend to be lovers, but we aren't." It would be quite dreadful if he misunderstood, and unexpectedly imprinted on her lips or even her hand a hot lascivious kiss, but up till now he certainly had not shown the smallest desire to do anything of the sort. She would never be able to see him again if he did that, and the world would probably say that he had dropped her. But she knew she couldn't explain the proposed position to him and he would have to guess: she could only give him a lead and must trust to his intelligence, and to the absence in him of any unsuspected amorous proclivities. She would begin gently, anyhow, and have him to dinner every day that she was at home. And really it would be very pleasant for him, for she was entertaining a great deal during this next week or two, and if he only did not yield to one of those rash and turbulent impulses of the male, all would be well. Georgie, until (so Lucia put it to herself) Olga had come between them, had done it beautifully, and Stephen was rather like Georgie. As for herself, she knew she could trust her firm slow pulses never to beat wild measures for anybody.

∞

She reached home to find that Adele had already arrived, and pausing only to tell her servant to ring up Stephen and ask him to come round at once, she went upstairs.

"Dearest Adele," she said, "a million pardons. I have been in the Divorce Court all day. Too thrilled. Babs, dear Babs Shyton, was wonderful. They got nothing out of her at all—"

"No: Lord Middlesex has got everything out of her already," observed Adele.

"Ah, how can you say that?" said Lucia. "Lord Middlesex— Woof-dog, you know—was just as wonderful. I feel sure the jury will believe them. Dear Babs! I must get her to come here some night soon and have a friendly little party for her. Think of that horrid old man who had lunch in the middle of the night! How terrible for her to have to go back to him. Dear me, what is her address?"

"She may not have to go back to him," said Adele. "If so, 'care of Woof-dog' would probably find her."

Adele had been feeling rather cross. Her husband had announced his intention of visiting his friends and relations in

England, and she did not feel inclined to make a corresponding journey to America. But as Lucia went on, she forgot these minor troubles, and became enthralled. Though she was still talking about Babs and Woof-dog, Adele felt sure these were only symbols, like the dreams of psychoanalysts.

"My sympathy is entirely with dear Babs," she said. "Think of her position with that dreadful old wretch. A woman surely may be pardoned, even if the jury don't believe her for—"

"Of course she may," said Adele with a final spurt of ill-temper. "What she's not pardoned for is being found out."

"Now you're talking as everybody talked in that dreadful play I went to last night," said Lucia. "Dear Olga was there: she is singing tomorrow, is she not? And you are assuming that Babs is guilty. How glad I am, Adele, that you are not on the jury! I take quite the other view: a woman with a wretched home like that must have a man with whom she is friends. I think it was a pure and beautiful affection between Babs and Woof-dog, such as any woman, even if she was happily married, might be proud to enjoy. There can be no doubt of Lord Middlesex's devotion to her, and really—I hope this does not shock you—what their relations were concerns nobody but them. George Sands and Chopin, you know. Nelson and Lady Hamilton. Sir Andrew Moss—he was the judge, you know—dined here the other night; I'm sure he is broad-minded. He gave me an admission card to the court . . . Ah, Stephen, there you are. Come in, my dear. You know Lady Brixton, don't you? We were talking of Babs Shyton. Bring up your chair. Let me see, no sugar, isn't it? How you scolded me when I put sugar into your tea by mistake the other day!"

She held Stephen's hand for as long as anybody might, or, as Browning says, "so very little longer," and Adele saw a look of faint surprise on his face. It was not alarm, it was not rapture, it was just surprise.

"Were you there?" he said. "No verdict yet, I suppose."

"Not till tomorrow, but then you will see. Adele has been horrid about her, quite horrid, and I have been preaching to her. I shall certainly ask Babs to dine some night soon, and you shall come, if you can spare an evening, but we won't ask Adele. Tell me the news, Stephen. I've been in court all day."

"Lucia's quite misunderstood me," said Adele. "My sympathy is entirely with Babs: all I blame her for is being found out. If you and I had an affair, Mr. Merriall, we should receive the envious sympathy of everybody, until we were officially brought to book. But then we should acquiesce in even our darling Lucia's cutting us. And if you had an affair with anybody else—I'm sure you've got hundreds—I and everybody else would be ever so pleased and interested, until— Mark that word 'until.' Now I must go, and leave you two to talk me well over."

Lucia rose, making affectionate but rather half-hearted murmurs to induce her to stop.

"Must you really be going, Adele?" she said. "Let me see, what am I doing tomorrow—Stephen, what is tomorrow, and what am I doing? Ah yes, Bertie Alton's private view in the morning. We shall be sure to meet there, Adele. The wretch has done two caricatures of Peppino and me. I feel as if I was to be flayed in the sight of all London. *Au revoir,* then, dear Adele, if you're so tired of us. And then the opera in the evening: I shall hardly dare to show my face. Your motor's here, is it? Ring, Stephen, will you. Such a short visit, and I expect Olga will pop in presently. All sorts of messages to her, I suppose. Look in again, Adele: propose yourself."

∞

On the doorstep Adele met Tony Limpsfield. She hurried him into her motor, and told the chauffeur not to drive on.

"News!" she said. "Lucia's going to have a lover."

"No!" said Tony in the Riseholme manner.

"But I tell you she is. He's with her now."

"They won't want me then," said Tony. "And yet she asked me to come at half-past five."

"Nonsense, my dear. They will want you, both of them . . . Oh Tony, don't you see? It's a stunt."

Tony assumed the rapt expression of Luciaphils receiving intelligence.

"Tell me all about it," he said.

"I'm sure I'm right," said she. "Her poppet came in just now, and she held his hand as women do, and made him draw his chair up to her, and said he scolded her. I'm not sure that he knows yet. But I saw that he guessed something was up. I wonder if he's clever enough to do it properly . . . I wish she had chosen you, Tony, you'd have done it perfectly. They have got—don't you understand?—to have the appearance of being lovers, everyone must think they are lovers, while all the time there's nothing at all of any sort in it. It's a stunt; it's a play; it's a glory."

"But perhaps there is something in it," said Tony. "I really think I had better not go in."

"Tony, trust me. Lucia has no more idea of keeping a real lover than of keeping a chimpanzee. She's as chaste as snow, a kiss would scorch her. Besides, she hasn't time. She asked Stephen there in order to show him to me, and to show him to you. It's the most wonderful plan; and it's wonderful of me to have understood it so quickly. You must go in: there's nothing private of any kind: indeed, she thirsts for publicity."

Her confidence inspired confidence, and Tony was naturally consumed with curiosity. He got out, told Adele's chauffeur to drive on, and went upstairs. Stephen was no longer sitting in the chair next to Lucia, but on the sofa at the other side of the tea-table. This rather looked as if Adele was right: it was consistent anyhow with their being lovers in public, but certainly not lovers in private.

"Dear Lord Tony," said Lucia—this appellation was a half-way house between Lord Limpsfield and Tony, and she left out the "Lord" except to him—"how nice of you to drop in. You have just missed Adele. Stephen, you know Lord Limpsfield?"

Lucia gave him his tea, and presently getting up, reseated herself negligently on the sofa beside Stephen. She was a shade too close at first, and edged slightly away.

"Wonderful play of Chekhov's the other day," she said. "Such a strange, unhappy atmosphere. We came out, didn't we, Stephen, feeling as if we had been in some remote dream. I saw you there, Lord Tony, with Adele who had been lunching with me."

Tony knew that: was not that the birthday of the Luciaphils?

"It was a dream I wasn't sorry to wake from," he said. "I found it a boring dream."

"Ah, how can you say so? Such an experience! I felt as if the woe of a thousand years had come upon me, some old anguish which I had forgotten. With the effect, too, that I wanted to live more fully and vividly than ever, till the dusk closed round."

Stephen waved his hands, as he edged a little further away from Lucia. There was something strange about Lucia today. In those few minutes when they had been alone she had been quite normal, but both before, when Adele was here, and now after Lord Limpfield's entry, she seemed to be implying a certain intimacy, to which he felt he ought to respond.

"Morbid fancies, Lucia," he said, "I shan't let you go to a Chekhov play again."

"Horrid boy," said Lucia daringly. "But that's the way with

all you men. You want women to be gay and bright and thoughtless, and have no other ideas except to amuse you. I shan't ever
talk to either of you again about my real feelings. We will talk
about the trial today. My entire sympathies are with Babs, Lord
Tony. I'm sure yours are too."

Lord Limpsfield left Stephen there when he took his leave,
after a quarter of an hour's lighter conversation, and as nobody
else dropped in, Lucia only asked her lover to dine on two or
three nights the next week, to meet her at the private view of Herbert Alton's exhibition next morning, and let him go in a slightly
bewildered frame of mind.

∞

Stephen walked slowly up the Brompton Road, looking into the
shop windows, and puzzling this out. She had held his hand
oddly, she had sat close to him on the sofa, she had waved a
dozen of those little signals of intimacy which gave colour to a
supposition which, though it did not actually make his blood
run cold, certainly did not make it run hot . . . He and Lucia
were excellent friends, they had many tastes in common, but Stephen knew that he would sooner never see her again than have
an intrigue with her. He was no hand, to begin with, at amorous adventures, and even if he had been he could not conceive a
woman more ill-adapted to dally with than Lucia. "Galahad and
Artemis would make a better job of it than Lucia and me," he
muttered to himself, turning hastily away from a window full of
dainty underclothing for ladies. In vain he searched the blameless records of his intercourse with Lucia: he could not accuse
himself of thought, word or deed which could possibly have
given rise to any disordered fancy of hers that he observed her
with a lascivious eye.

"God knows I am innocent," he said to himself, and froze with horror at the sudden sight of a large news-board on which was printed in large capitals "Babs wants Woof-dog on the hearthrug."

He knew he had no taste for gallantry, and he felt morally certain that Lucia hadn't either . . . What then could she mean by those little tweaks and pressures? Conning them over for the second time, it struck him more forcibly than before that she had only indulged in these little licentiousnesses when there was someone else present. Little as he knew of the ways of lovers, he always imagined that they exchanged such tokens chiefly in private, and in public only when their passions had to find a small safety-valve. Again, if she had had designs on his virtue, she would surely, having got him alone, have given a message to her servants that she was out and not have had Lord Limpsfield admitted . . . He felt sure she was up to something, but to his dull male sense, it was at present wrapped in mystery. He did not want to give up all those charming hospitalities of hers, but he must need be very circumspect.

It was, however, without much misgiving that he awaited her next morning at the doors of the little Rutland Gallery, for he felt safe in so public a place as a private view. Only a few early visitors had come in when Lucia arrived, and as she passed the turnstile showing the two cards of invitation for herself and Peppino, impersonated by Stephen, she asked for hers back, saying that she was only going to make a short visit now and would return later. She had not yet seen the caricature of herself and Peppino, for which Bertie Alton (she still stuck to this little mistake) had accepted a commission, and she made her way at once to Numbers 39 and 40, which her catalogue told her were of Mr. and Mrs. Philip Lucas. Subjoined to their names were the captions, and she read with excitement that Peppino was supposed to be saying "At whatever personal inconvenience I must live up to Lucia," while below Number 40 was the enticing little legend "Oh, these duchesses! They give one no peace!" . . . And there was Peppino, in the knee-breeches of levee dress, tripping over his sword which had got entangled with his legs, and a cocked-hat on the back of his head, with his eyes very much apart, and no nose, and a small agonised hole in his face for a mouth . . . And there was she with a pile of opened letters on the floor, and a pile of unopened letters on the table. There was not much of her face to be seen, for she was talking into a telephone, but her skirt was very short, and so was her hair, and there was a wealth of weary resignation in the limpness of her carriage.

Lucia examined them both carefully, and then gave a long sigh of perfect happiness. That was her irrepressible comment: she could not have imagined anything more ideal. Then she gave a little peal of laughter.

"Look, Stephen," she said. "Bobbie—I mean Bertie—really is too wicked for anything! Really, outrageous! I am furious with him, and yet I can't help laughing. Poor Peppino, and poor me! Marcia will adore it. She always says she can never get hold of me nowadays."

Lucia gave a swift scrutiny to the rest of the collection, so as to be able to recognise them all without reference to her catalogue, when she came back, as she intended to do later in the morning. There was hardly anyone here at present, but the place would certainly be crowded an hour before lunchtime, and she proposed to make a *soi-disant* first visit then, and know at once whom all the caricatures represented (for Bertie in his enthusiasm for caricature sometimes omitted likenesses), and go into peals of laughter at those of herself and Peppino, and say she must buy them, which of course she had already done. Stephen remained behind, for Hermione was going to say a good deal about the exhibition, but promised to wait till Lucia came back. She had not shown the smallest sign of amorousness this morning. His apprehensions were considerably relieved, and it looked as if no storm of emotion was likely to be required of him.

"Hundreds of things to do!" she said. "Let me see, half-past eleven, twelve—yes, I shall be back soon after twelve, and we'll have a real look at them. And you'll lunch? Just a few people coming."

Before Lucia got back, the gallery had got thick with visitors, and Hermione was busy noting those whom he saw chatting with friends or looking lovely, or being very pleased with the new house in Park Lane, or receiving congratulations on the engagement of a daughter. There was no doubt which of the pictures excited most interest, and soon there was a regular queue waiting to look at Numbers 39 and 40. People stood in front of them regarding them gravely and consulting their catalogues and then bursting into loud cracks of laughter and looking again till the growing weight of the queue dislodged them. One of those who lingered longest and stood her ground best was Adele, who, when she was eventually shoved on, ran round to the tail of the queue and herself shoved till she got opposite again. She saw Stephen.

"Ah, then Lucia won't be far off," she observed archly. "Doesn't she adore it? Where is Lucia?"

"She's been, but she's coming back," he said. "I expect her every minute. Ah! There she is."

This was rather stupid of Stephen. He ought to have guessed that Lucia's second appearance was officially intended to be her first. He grasped that when she squeezed her way through the crowd and greeted him as if they had not met before that morning.

"And dearest Adele," she said. "What a crush! Tell me quickly, where are the caricatures of Peppino and me? I'm dying to see them; and when I see them no doubt I shall wish I was dead."

The light of Luciaphilism came into Adele's intelligent eyes.

"We'll look for them together," she said. "Ah, thirty-nine and forty. They must be somewhere just ahead."

Lucia exerted a steady indefatigable pressure on those in front, and presently came into range.

"Well, I never!" she said. "Oh, but so like Peppino! How could Bertie have told he got his sword entangled just like that? And look what he says . . . Oh, and then Me! Just because I met him at Marcia's party and people were wanting to know when I had an evening free! Of all the impertinences! How I shall scold him!"

Lucia did it quite admirably in blissful unconsciousness that Adele knew she had been here before. She laughed, she looked again and laughed again. ("Mrs. Lucas and Lady Brixton in fits of merriment over the cartoon of Mr. Lucas and herself," thought Hermione.)

"Ah, and there's Lord Hurtacombe," she said. "I'm sure that's Lord Hurtacombe, though you can't see much of him, and, look, Olga surely, is it not? How does he do it?"

That was a very clever identification for one who had not previously studied the catalogue, for Olga's face consisted entirely of a large open mouth and the tip of a chin; it might have been the face of anybody yawning. Her arms were stretched wide, and she towered above a small man in shorts.

"The last scene in *Siegfried*, I'm sure," said Lucia. "What does the catalogue say, Stephen? Yes, I am right. 'Siegfried! Brünnhilde!' How wicked, is it not? But killing! Who could be cross with him?"

This was all splendid stuff for Luciaphils; it was amazing how at a first glance she recognised everybody. The gallery, too, was full of dears and darlings of a few weeks' standing, and she completed a little dinner party for next Tuesday long before she had made the circuit. All the time she kept Stephen by her side, looked over his catalogue, put a hand on his arm to direct his attention to some picture, took a speck of alien material off his sleeve, and all the time the entranced Adele felt increasingly certain that she had plumbed the depth of the adorable situation. Her sole anxiety was as to whether Stephen would plumb it too. He might—though he didn't look like it—welcome these little tokens of intimacy as indicating something more, and when they were alone attempt to kiss her, and that would ruin the whole exquisite design. Luckily his demeanour was not that of a favoured swain; it was, on the other hand, more the demeanour of a swain who feared to be favoured, and if that shy thing took fright, the situation would be equally ruined . . . To think that the most perfect piece of Luciaphilism was dependent on the just perceptions of Stephen! As the three made their slow progress, listening to Lucia's brilliant identifications, Adele willed Stephen to understand; she projected a perfect torrent of suggestion towards his mind. He must, he should understand . . .

Fervent desire, so every psychist affirms, is never barren. It conveys something of its yearning to the consciousness to which it is directed, and there began to break on the dull male mind what had been so obvious to the finer feminine sense of Adele. Once again, and in the blaze of publicity, Lucia was full of touches and tweaks, and the significance of them dawned, like some pale, austere sunrise, on his darkened senses. The situation was revealed, and he saw it was one with which he could easily deal. His gloomy apprehensions brightened, and he perceived that there would be no need, when he went to stay at Riseholme next, to lock his bedroom door, a practice which was abhorrent to him, for fear of fire suddenly breaking out in the house. Last night he had had a miserable dream about what had happened when he failed to lock his door at The Hurst, but now he dismissed its haunting. These little intimacies of Lucia's were purely a public performance.

"Lucia, we must be off," he said loudly and confidently. "Peppino will wonder where we are."

Lucia sighed.

"He always bullies me like that, Adele," she said. "I must go: *au revoir*, dear. Tuesday next: just a few intimes."

Lucia's relief was hardly less than Stephen's. He would surely not have said anything so indiscreet if he had been contemplating an indiscretion, and she had no fear that his hurry to be off was due to any passionate desire to embrace her in the privacy of her car. She believed he understood, and her belief felt justified when he proposed that the car should be opened.

∞

Riseholme, in the last three weeks of social progress, had not occupied the front row of Lucia's thoughts, but the second row, so to speak, had been entirely filled with it, for, as far as the future dimly outlined itself behind the present, the plan was to go down there early in August, and remain there, with a few brilliant excursions, till autumn peopled London again. She had hoped for a dash to Aix, where there would be many pleasant people, but Peppino had told her summarily that the treasury would not stand it. Lucia had accepted that with the frankest good nature: she had made quite a gay little lament about it, when she was asked what she was going to do in August. "Ah, all you lucky rich people with money to throw about; we've got to go and live quietly at home," she used to say. "But I shall love it, though I shall miss you all dreadfully. Riseholme, dear Riseholme, you know, adorable, and all the delicious funny friends down there who spoil me so dreadfully. I shall have lovely tranquil days, with a trot across the green to order fish, and a chat on the way, and my books and my piano, and a chair in the garden, and an early bedtime instead of all these late hours. An anchorite life, but if you have a weekend to spare between your Aix and your yacht and your Scotland, ah, how nice it would be if you just sent a postcard!"

Before they became anchorites, however, there was a long weekend for her and Peppino over the August bank-holiday, and Lucia looked forward to that with unusual excitement. Adele was the hostess, and the scene that immense country-house of hers in Essex. The whole world, apparently, was to be there, for Adele had said the house would be full; and it was to be a final reunion of the choicest spirits before the annual dispersion. Mrs. Garroby-Ashton had longed to be bidden, but was not, and though Lucia was sorry for dear Millicent's disappointment, she could not but look down on it, as a sort of perch far below her that showed how dizzily she herself had gone upwards. But she had no intention of dropping good kind Millie who was hopping about below: she must certainly come to The Hurst for a Sunday: that would be nice for her, and she would learn all about Adele's party.

There were yet ten days before that, and the morning after the triumphant affair at the Rutland Gallery, Lucia heard a faint rumour, coming from nowhere in particular, that Marcia Whitby was going to give a very small and very wonderful dance to wind up the season. She had not seen much of Marcia lately, in other words she had seen nothing at all, and Lucia's last three invitations to her had been declined, one through a secretary, and two through a telephone. Lucia continued, however, to talk about her with unabated familiarity and affection. The next day the rumour became slightly more solid: Adele let slip some allusion to Marcia's ball, and hurriedly covered it up with talk of her own weekend. Lucia fixed her with a penetrating eye for a moment, but the eye failed apparently to penetrate: Adele went on gabbling about her own party, and took not the slightest notice of it.

But in truth Adele's gabble was a frenzied and feverish manoeuvre to get away from the subject of Marcia's ball. Marcia was no true Luciaphil; instead of feeling entranced pleasure in Lucia's successes and failures, her schemes and attainments and ambitions, she had lately been taking a high severe line about her.

"She's beyond a joke, Adele," she said. "I hear she's got a scrapbook, and puts in picture postcards and photographs of country-houses, with dates below them to indicate she has been there—"

"No!" said Adele. "How heavenly of her. I must see it, or did you make it up?"

"Indeed I didn't," said the injured Marcia. "And she's got in it a picture postcard of the moat-garden at Whitby with the date of the Sunday before last, when I had a party there and didn't ask her. Besides, she was in London at the time. And there's one of Buckingham Palace Garden, with the date of the last garden-party. Was she asked?"

"I haven't heard she was," said Adele.

"Then you may be sure she wasn't. She's beyond a joke, I tell you, and I'm not going to ask her to my dance. I won't, I won't—I will not. And she asked me to dine three times last week. It isn't fair: it's bullying. A weak-minded person would have submitted, but I'm not weak-minded, and I won't be bullied. I won't be forcibly fed, and I won't ask her to my dance. There!"

"Don't be so unkind," said Adele. "Besides, you'll meet her down at my house only a few days afterwards, and it will be awkward. Everybody else will have been."

"Well, then she can pretend she has been exclusive," said Marcia snappily, "and she'll like that . . ."

The rumours solidified into fact, and soon Lucia was forced to the dreadful conclusion that Marcia's ball was to take place without her. That was an intolerable thought, and she gave Marcia one more chance by ringing her up and inviting her to dinner on that night (so as to remind her she knew nothing about the ball), but Marcia's stony voice replied that most unfortunately she had a few people to dinner herself. Wherever she went (and where now did Lucia not go?) she heard talk of the ball, and the plethora of princes and princesses that were to attend it.

For a moment the thought of princesses lightened the depression of this topic. Princess Isabel was rather seriously ill with influenza, so Lucia, driving down Park Lane, thought it would not be amiss to call and enquire how she was, for she had noticed that sometimes the papers recorded the names of enquirers. She did not any longer care in the least how Princess Isabel was; whether she died or recovered was a matter of complete indifference to her in her present embittered frame of mind, for the princess had not taken the smallest notice of her all these weeks. However, there was the front door open, for there were other enquirers on the threshold, and Lucia joined them. She pre-

sented her card, and asked in a trembling voice what news there
was, and was told that the Princess was no better. Lucia bowed
her head in resignation, and then, after faltering a moment in her
walk, pulled herself together, and with a firmer step went back
to her motor.

After this interlude her mind returned to the terrible topic.
She was due at a drawing-room meeting at Sophy Alingsby's
house to hear a lecture on psychoanalysis, and she really hardly
felt up to it. But there would certainly be a quantity of interesting
people there, and the lecture itself might possibly be of interest,
and so before long she found herself in the black dining-room,
which had been cleared for the purpose. With the self-effacing
instincts of the English the audience had left the front-row chairs
completely unoccupied, and she got a very good place. The lecture had just begun, and so her entry was not unmarked. Stephen was there, and as she seated herself, she nodded to him,
and patted the empty chair by her side with a beckoning gesture.
Her lover, therefore, sidled up to her and took it.

Lucia whistled her thoughts away from such ephemeral and
frivolous subjects as dances, and tried to give Professor Bonstetter her attention. She felt that she had been living a very hectic
life lately; the world and its empty vanities had been too much
with her, and she needed some intellectual tonic. She had seen
no pictures lately, except Bobbie (or was it Bertie?) Alton's, she
had heard no music, she had not touched the piano herself for
weeks, she had read no books, and at the most had skimmed the
reviews of such as had lately appeared in order to be up to date
and be able to reproduce a short but striking criticism or two if
the talk became literary. She must not let the mere froth of living
entirely conceal by its winking headiness of foam the true bever-
age below it. There was Sophy, with her hair over her eyes and

her chin in her hand, dressed in a faded rainbow, weird beyond description, but rapt in concentration, while she herself was letting the notion of a dance to which she had not been asked and was clearly not to be asked, drive like a mist between her and these cosmic facts about dreams and the unconscious self. How curious that if you dreamed about boiled rabbit, it meant that sometime in early childhood you had been kissed by a poacher in a railway-carriage, and had forgotten all about it! What a magnificent subject for excited research psychoanalysis would have been in those keen intellectual days at Riseholme . . . She thought of them now with a vague yearning for their simplicity and absorbing earnestness; of the hours she had spent with Georgie over piano duets, of Daisy Quantock's ouija-board and planchette, of the Museum with its mittens. Riseholme presented itself now as an abode of sweet peace, where there were no disappointments or heartburnings, for sooner or later she had always managed to assert her will and constitute herself priestess of the current interests . . . Suddenly the solution of her present difficulty flashed upon her. Riseholme. She would go to Riseholme: that would explain her absence from Marcia's stupid ball.

The lecture came to an end, and with others she buzzed for a little while round Professor Bonstetter, and had a few words with her hostess.

"Too interesting: marvellous, was it not, dear Sophy? Boiled rabbit! How curious! And the outcropping of the unconscious in dreams. Explains so much about phobias: people who can't go in the tube. So pleased to have heard it. Ah, there's Aggie. Aggie darling! What a treat, wasn't it? Such a refreshment from our bustlings and runnings-about to get back into origins. I've got to fly, but I couldn't miss this. Dreadful overlapping all this afternoon, and poor Princess Isabel is no better. I just called on my way here, but I wasn't allowed to see her. Stephen, where is Stephen? See if my motor is there, dear. *Au revoir!* dear Sophy. We must meet again very soon. Are you going to Adele's next week? No? How tiresome! Wonderful lecture! Calming!"

Lucia edged herself out of the room with these very hurried greetings, for she was really eager to get home. She found Peppino there, having tea peacefully all by himself, and sank exhausted in a chair.

"Give me a cup of tea, strong tea, Peppino," she said. "I've been racketing about all day, and I feel done for. How I shall get through these next two or three days I really don't know. And London is stifling. You look worn out too, my dear."

Peppino acknowledged the truth of this. He had hardly had time even to go to his club this last day or two, and had been reflecting on the enormous strength of the weaker sex. But for Lucia to confess herself done for was a portentous thing: he could not remember such a thing happening before.

"Well, there are not many more days of it," he said. "Three more this week, and then Lady Brixton's party."

He gave several loud sneezes.

"Not a cold?" asked Lucia.

"Something extraordinarily like one," said he.

Lucia became suddenly alert again. She was sorry for Peppino's cold, but it gave her an admirable gambit for what she had made up her mind to do.

"My dear, that's enough," she said. "I won't have you flying about London with a bad cold coming on. I shall take you down to Riseholme tomorrow."

"Oh, but you can't, my dear," said he. "You've got your engagement book full for the next three days."

"Oh, a lot of stupid things," said she. "And really, I tell you quite honestly, I'm fairly worn out. It'll do us both good to have a rest for a day or two. Now don't make objections. Let us see what I've got to do."

The days were pretty full (though, alas, Thursday evening was deplorably empty) and Lucia had a brisk half-hour at the telephone. To those who had been bidden here, and to those to whom she had been bidden, she gave the same excuse, namely, that she had been advised (by herself) two or three days' complete rest.

She rang up The Hurst, to say that they were coming down tomorrow, and would bring the necessary attendants, she rang up Georgie (for she was not going to fall into *that* error again) and in a mixture of baby-language and Italian, which he found very hard to understand, asked him to dine tomorrow night, and finally she scribbled a short paragraph to the leading morning papers to say that Mrs. Philip Lucas had been ordered to leave London for two or three days' complete rest. She had hesitated a moment over the wording of that, for it was Peppino who was much more in need of rest than she, but it would have been rather ludicrous to say that Mr. and Mrs. Philip Lucas were in need of a complete rest . . . These announcements she sent by hand so that there might be no miscarriage in their appearance tomorrow morning. And then, as an afterthought, she rang up Daisy Quantock and asked her and Robert to lunch tomorrow.

She felt much happier. She would not be at the fell Marcia's ball, because she was resting in the country.

Chapter Eight

A FEW MINUTES BEFORE LUCIA and Peppino drove off next morning from Brompton Square, Marcia observed Lucia's announcement in the *Morning Post*. She was a good-natured woman, but she had been goaded, and now that Lucia could goad her no more for the present, she saw no objection to asking her to her ball. She thought of telephoning, but there was the chance that Lucia had not yet started, so she sent her a card instead, directing it to 25 Brompton Square, saying that she was At Home, dancing, to have the honour to meet a string of exalted personages. If she had telephoned, no one knows what would have happened, whether Daisy would have had any lunch that day or Georgie any dinner that night, and what excuse Lucia would have made to them . . . Adele and Tony Limpsfield, the most adept of all the Luciaphils, subsequently argued the matter out with much heat, but never arrived at a solution that they felt was satisfactory. But then Marcia did not telephone . . .

The news that the two were coming down was, of course, all over Riseholme a few minutes after Lucia had rung Georgie up. He was in his study when the telephone bell rang, in the fawn-coloured Oxford trousers, which had been cut down from their monstrous proportions and fitted quite nicely, though there had been a sad waste of stuff. Robert Quantock, the wag who had danced a hornpipe when Georgie had appeared in the original voluminousness, was waggish again, when he saw the abbreviated garments, and *à propos* of nothing in particular had said "Home is the sailor, home from sea," and that was the epitaph on the Oxford trousers.

Georgie had been busy indoors this afternoon, for he had been attending to his hair, and it was not quite dry yet, and the smell of the auburn mixture still clung to it. But the telephone was a trunk call, and, whether his hair was dry or not, it must be attended to. Since Lucia had disappeared after that weekend party, he had had a line from her once or twice, saying that they must really settle when he would come and spend a few days in London, but she had never descended to the sordid mention of dates.

A trunk call, as far as he knew, could only be Lucia or Olga, and one would be interesting and the other delightful. It proved to be the interesting one, and though rather difficult to understand because of the aforesaid mixture of baby-talk and Italian, it certainly conveyed the gist of the originator's intention.

"Me so tired," Lucia said, "and it will be divine to get to Riseholme again. So come to 'ickle quiet din-din with me and Peppino tomorrow, Georgino. Shall want to hear all *novelle*—"

"What?" said Georgie.

"All the news," said Lucia.

Georgie sat in the draught—it was very hot today—until the auburn mixture dried. He knew that Daisy Quantock and Robert were playing clock-golf on the other side of his garden paling, for their voices had been very audible. Daisy had not been weeding much lately but had taken to golf, and since all the authorities said that matches were entirely won or lost on the putting-green, she with her usual wisdom devoted herself to the winning factor in the game. Presently she would learn to drive and approach

and niblick and that sort of thing, and then they would see . . .
She wondered how good Miss Wethered really was.

Georgie, now dry, tripped out into the garden and shouted,
"May I come in?" That meant, of course, might he look over the
garden paling and talk.

Daisy missed a very short putt, owing to the interruption.

"Yes, do," she said icily. "I supposed you would give me that,
Robert."

"You supposed wrong," said Robert, who was now two up.

Georgie stepped on a beautiful pansy.

"Lucia's coming down tomorrow," he said.

Daisy dropped her putter.

"No!" she exclaimed.

"And Peppino," went on Georgie. "She says she's very tired."

"All those duchesses," said Daisy. Herbert Alton's cartoon
had been reproduced in an illustrated weekly, but Riseholme
up to this moment had been absolutely silent about it. It was
beneath notice.

"And she's asked me to dinner tomorrow," said Georgie.

"So she's not bringing down a party?" said Daisy.

"I don't know," remarked Robert, "if you are going on
putting, or if you give me the match."

"Pouf!" said Daisy, just like that. "But tired, Georgie? What
does that mean?"

"I don't know," said Georgie, "but that's what she said."

"It means something else," said Daisy, "I can't tell you what,
but it doesn't mean that. I suppose you've said you're engaged."

"No I haven't," said Georgie.

De Vere came out from the house. In this dry weather her
heels made no indentations on the lawn.

"Trunk call, ma'am," she said to Daisy.

"These tiresome interruptions," said Daisy, hurrying indoors with great alacrity.

Georgie lingered. He longed to know what the trunk call was, and was determined to remain with his head on the top of the paling till Daisy came back. So he made conversation.

"Your lawn is better than mine," he said pleasantly to Robert.

Robert was cross at this delay.

"That's not saying much," he observed.

"I can't say any more," said Georgie, rather nettled. "And there's the leather-jacket grub I see has begun on yours. I dare say there won't be a blade of grass left presently."

Robert changed the conversation: there were bare patches. "The Museum insurance," he said. "I got the fire-policy this morning. The contents are the property of the four trustees, me and you and Daisy and Mrs. Boucher. The building is Colonel Boucher's, and that's insured separately. If you had a spark of enterprise about you, you would take a match, set light to the mittens, and hope for the best."

"You're very tarsome and cross," said Georgie. "I should like to take a match and set light to you."

Georgie hated rude conversations like this, but when Robert was in such a mood, it was best to be playful. He did not mean, in any case, to cease leaning over the garden paling till Daisy came back from her trunk call.

"Beyond the mittens," began Robert, "and, of course, those three sketches of yours, which I dare say are masterpieces—"

Daisy bowled out of the dining-room and came with such speed down the steps that she nearly fell into the circular bed where the broccoli had been. (The mignonette there was poorish.)

"At half-past one or two," said she, bursting with the news

and at the same time unable to suppress her gift for withering sarcasm. "Lunch tomorrow. Just a picnic, you know, as soon as she happens to arrive. So kind of her. More notice than she took of me last time."

"Lucia?" asked Georgie.

"Yes. Let me see, I was putting, wasn't I?"

"If you call it putting," said Robert. He was not often two up and he made the most of it.

"So I suppose you said you were engaged," said Georgie.

Daisy did not trouble to reply at all. She merely went on putting. That was the way to deal with inquisitive questions.

This news, therefore, was very soon all over Riseholme, and next morning it was supplemented by the amazing announcement in *The Times, Morning Post, Daily Telegraph* and *Daily Mail* that Mrs. Philip Lucas had left London for two or three days' complete rest. It sounded incredible to Riseholme, but of course it might be true and, as Daisy had said, that the duchesses had been too much for her. (This was nearer the mark than the sarcastic Daisy had known, for it was absolutely and literally true that one Duchess had been too much for her . . .) In any case, Lucia was coming back to them again, and though Riseholme was still a little dignified and reticent, Georgie's acceptance of his dinner-invitation, and Daisy's of her lunch-invitation, were symptomatic of Riseholme's feelings. Lucia had foully deserted them, she had been down here only once since that fatal accession to fortune, and on that occasion had evidently intended to see nothing of her old friends while that Yahoo party ("Yahoo" was the only word for Mrs. Alingsby) was with her; she had laughed at their Museum, she had courted the vulgar publicity of the press to record her movements in London, but Riseholme was really perfectly willing to forget and forgive if she behaved properly now. For, though no one would have confessed it, they missed her more and more. In spite of all her bullying monarchical ways, she had initiative, and though the excitement of the Museum and the sagas from Abfou had kept them going for a while, it was really in relation to Lucia that these enterprises had been interesting. Since then, too, Abfou had been full of vain repetitions, and no one could go on being excited by his denunciation of Lucia as a snob, indefinitely. Lucia had personality, and if she had been here and had taken to golf Riseholme would have been thrilled at her skill, and have exulted over her want of it, whereas Daisy's wonderful scores at clock-golf (she was off her game today) produced no real interest. Degrading, too, as were the records of Lucia's movements in the columns of Hermione, Riseholme had been thrilled (though disgusted) by them, because they were about Lucia, and though she was coming down now for complete rest (whatever that might mean), the mere fact of her being here would make things hum. This time too she had behaved properly (perhaps she had learned wisdom) and had announced her coming, and asked old friends in.

Forgiveness, therefore, and excitement were the prevalent emotions in the morning parliament on the green next day. Mrs. Boucher alone expressed grave doubts on the situation.

"I don't believe she's ill," she said. "If she's ill, I shall be very sorry, but I don't believe it. If she is, Mr. Georgie, I'm all for accepting her gift of the spit to the Museum, for it would be unkind not to. You can write and say that the committee have reconsidered it and would be very glad to have it. But let's wait to see if she's ill first. In fact, wait to see if she's coming at all, first."

Piggy came whizzing up with news, while Goosie shouted it into her mother's ear-trumpet. Before Piggy could come out with it, Goosie's announcement was audible everywhere.

"A cab from the station has arrived at The Hurst, mamma," she yelled, "with the cook and the housemaid, and a quantity of luggage."

"Oh, Mrs. Boucher, have you heard the news?" panted Piggy.

"Yes, my dear, I've just heard it," said Mrs. Boucher, "and it looks as if they were coming. That's all I can say. And if the cook's come by half-past eleven, I don't see why you shouldn't get a proper lunch, Daisy. No need for a cup of strong soup or a sandwich which I should have recommended if there had been no further news since you were asked to a picnic lunch. But if the cook's here now . . ."

Daisy was too excited to go home and have any serious putting and went off to the Museum. Mr. Rushbold, the vicar, had just presented his unique collection of walking-sticks to it, and though the committee felt it would be unkind not to accept them, it was difficult to know how to deal with them. They could not all be stacked together in one immense stick-stand, for then they could not be appreciated. The handles of many were curiously carved, some with gargoyle-heads of monsters putting out their tongues and leering, some with images of birds and fish, and there was one rather indelicate one, of a young man and a girl passionately embracing . . . On the other hand, if they were spaced and leaned against the wall, some slight disturbance upset the equilibrium of one and it fell against the next, and the whole lot went down like ninepins. In fact, the boy at the turnstile said his entire time was occupied with picking them up. Daisy had a scheme of stretching an old lawn-tennis net against the wall, and tastefully entangling them in its meshes . . .

Riseholme lingered on the green that morning long after one o'clock, which was its usual lunchtime, and at precisely twenty-five minutes past they were rewarded. Out of the motor stepped Peppino in a very thick coat and a large muffler. He sneezed twice as he held out his arm to assist Lucia to alight. She clung to it, and leaning heavily on it went with faltering steps past Perdita's garden into the house. So she was ill.

Ten minutes later, Daisy and Robert Quantock were seated at lunch with them. Lucia certainly looked very well and she ate her lunch very properly, but she spoke in a slightly faded voice, as befitted one who had come here for complete rest. "But Riseholme, dear Riseholme will soon put me all right again," she said. "Such a joy to be here! Any news, Daisy?"

Really there was very little. Daisy ran through such topics as had interested Riseholme during those last weeks, and felt that the only thing which had attracted true, feverish, Riseholme-attention was the record of Lucia's own movements. Apart from this there was only her own putting, and the embarrassing gift of walking-sticks to the Museum . . . But then she remembered that the committee had authorised the acceptance of the Elizabethan spit, if Lucia seemed ill, and she rather precipitately decided that she was ill enough.

"Well, we've been busy over the Museum," she began.

"Ah, the dear Museum," said Lucia wistfully.

That quite settled it.

"We should so like to accept the Elizabethan spit, if we may," said Daisy. "It would be a great acquisition."

"Of course; delighted," said Lucia. "I will have it sent over. Any other gifts?"

Daisy went on to the walking-sticks, omitting all mention of the indelicate one in the presence of gentlemen, and described the difficulty of placing them satisfactorily. They were eighty-one (including the indelicacy) and a lawn-tennis net would barely hold them. The invalid took but a wan interest in this, and Daisy's putting did not rouse much keener enthusiasm. But soon she recovered a greater animation and was more herself. Indeed, before the end of lunch it had struck Daisy that Peppino was really the invalid of the two. He certainly had a prodigious cold, and spoke in a throaty wheeze that was scarcely audible. She wondered if she had been a little hasty about accepting the spit, for that gave Lucia a sort of footing in the Museum.

∞

Lucia recovered still further when her guests had gone, and her habitual energy began to assert itself. She had made her impressive invalid entry into Riseholme, which justified the announcement in the papers, and now, quietly, she must be on the move again. She might begin by getting rid, without delay, of that tiresome spit.

"I think I shall go out for a little drive, Peppino," she said, "though if I were you I would nurse my cold and get it all right before Saturday when we go to Adele's. The gardener, I think, could take the spit out of the chimney for me, and put it in the motor, and I would drop it at the Museum. I thought they would want it before long . . . And that clock-golf of Daisy's; it sounds amusing; the sort of thing for Sunday afternoon if we have guests with us. I think she said that you could get the apparatus at the Stores. Little tournaments might be rather fun."

The spit was easily removed, and Lucia, having written to the Stores for a set of clock-golf, had it loaded up on the motor, and conveyed to the Museum. So that was done. She waved and fluttered a hand of greeting to Piggy and Goosie who were gambolling on the green, and set forth into the country, satisfied that she had behaved wisely in leaving London rather than being left out in London. Apart from that, too, it had been politic to come down to Riseholme again like this, to give them a taste of her quality before she resumed, in August, as she entirely meant to do, her ancient sway. She guessed from the paucity of news which that arch-gossip, dear Daisy, had to give, that things had been remarkably dull in her absence, and though she had made a sad mistake over her weekend party, a little propitiation would soon put that right. And Daisy had had nothing to say about Abfou: they seemed to have got a little tired of Abfou. But Abfou might be revived: clock-golf and a revival of ouija would start August very pleasantly. She would have liked Aix better, but Peppino was quite clear about that . . .

Georgie was agreeably surprised to find her so much herself when he came over for dinner. Peppino, whose cold was still extremely heavy, went to bed very soon after, and he and Lucia settled themselves in the music-room.

"First a little chat, Georgie," she said, "and then I insist on our having some music. I've played nothing lately, you will find me terribly out of practice, but you mustn't scold me. Yes, the spit has gone: dear Daisy said the Museum was most anxious to get it, and I took it across myself this afternoon. I must see what else I can find worthy of it."

This was all rather splendid. Lucia had a glorious way of completely disregarding the past, and pushing on ahead into the future.

"And have you been playing much lately?" she asked.

"Hardly a note," said Georgie, "there is nobody to play with. Piggy wanted to do some duets, but I said 'No, thanks.'"

"Georgie, you've been lazy," she said, "there's been nobody to keep you up to the mark. And Olga? Has Olga been down?"

"Not since—not since that Sunday when you were both down together," said he.

"Very wrong of her to have deserted Riseholme. But just

as wrong of me, you will say. But now we must put our heads together and make great plans for August. I shall be here to bully you all August. Just one visit, which Peppino and I are paying to dear Adele Brixton on Saturday, and then you will have me here solidly. London? Yes, it has been great fun, though you and I never managed to arrange a date for your stay with us. That must come in the autumn when we go up in November. But, oh, how tired I was when we settled to leave town yesterday. Not a kick left in me. Lots of engagements, too, and I just scrapped them. But people must be kind to me and forgive me. And sometimes I feel that I've been wasting time terribly. I've done nothing but see people, people, people. All sorts, from Alf Watson the pugilist—"

"No!" said Georgie, beginning to feel the thrill of Lucia again.

"Yes, he came to dine with me, such a little duck, and brought his flute. There was a great deal of talk about my party for Alf, and how the women buzzed round him!"

"Who else?" said Georgie greedily.

"My dear, who *not* else? Marcelle—Marcelle Periscope came another night, Adele, Sophy Alingsby, Bertie Alton, Aggie—I must ask dear Aggie down here; Tony—Tony Limpsfield; a thousand others. And then of course dear Marcia Whitby often. She is giving a ball tomorrow night. I should like to have been there, but I was just *finito*. Ah, and your friend Princess Isabel. Very bad influenza. You should ring up her house, Georgie, and ask how she is. I called there yesterday. So sad! But let us talk of more cheerful things. Daisy's clock-golf: I must pop in and see her at it tomorrow. She is wonderful, I suppose. I have ordered a set from the Stores, and we will have great games."

"She's been doing nothing else for weeks," said Georgie.

"I dare say she's very good, but nobody takes any interest in it. She's rather a bore about it—"

"Georgie, don't be unkind about poor Daisy," said Lucia. "We must start little competitions, with prizes. Do you have partners? You and I will be partners at mixed putting. And what about Abfou?"

It seemed to Georgie that this was just the old Lucia, and so no doubt it was. She was intending to bag any employments that happened to be going about and claim them as her own. It was larceny, intellectual and physical larceny, no doubt, but Lucia breathed life into those dead bones and made them interesting. It was weary work to watch Daisy dabbing away with her putter and then trying to beat her score without caring the least whether you beat it or not. And Daisy even telephoned her more marvellous feats, and nobody cared how marvellous they were. But it would be altogether different if Lucia was the goddess of putting . . .

"I haven't Abfou'd for ages," said Georgie. "I fancy she has dropped it."

"Well, we must pick everything up again," said Lucia briskly, "and you shan't be lazy any more, Georgie. Come and play duets. My dear piano! What shall we do?"

They did quantities of things, and then Lucia played the slow movement of the "Moonlight Sonata," and Georgie sighed as usual, and eventually Lucia let him out and walked with him to the garden-gate. There were quantities of stars, and as usual she quoted "See how the floor of heaven is thick inlaid . . ." and said she must ring him up in the morning, after a good night's rest.

There was a light in Daisy's drawing-room, and just as he came opposite it she heard his step, for which she had long been listening, and looked out.

"Is it Georgie?" she said, knowing perfectly well that it must be.

"Yes," said Georgie. "How late you are."

"And how is Lucia?" asked Daisy.

Georgie quite forgot for the moment that Lucia was having complete rest.

"Excellent form," he said. "Such a talk, and such a music."

"There you are, then!" said Daisy. "There's nothing the matter with her. She doesn't want rest any more—than the moon. What does it mean, Georgie? Mark my words: it means something."

∞

Lucia, indeed, seemed in no need whatever of complete rest the next day. She popped into Daisy's very soon after breakfast, and asked to be taught how to putt. Daisy gave her a demonstration, and told her how to hold the putter and where to place her feet, and said it was absolutely essential to stand like a rock and to concentrate. Nobody could putt if anyone spoke. Eventually Lucia was allowed to try, and she stood all wrong and grasped her putter like an umbrella, and holed out of the longest of putts in the middle of an uninterrupted sentence. Then they had a match, Daisy proposing to give her four strokes in the round, which Lucia refused, and Daisy, dithering with excitement and superiority, couldn't putt at all. Lucia won easily, with Robert looking on, and she praised Daisy's putter, and said it was beautifully balanced, though where she picked that up Daisy couldn't imagine.

"And now I must fly," said Lucia, "and we must have a return match sometime. So amusing! I have sent for a set, and you will have to give me lessons. Goodbye, dear Daisy, I'm away for the

Sunday at dear Adele Brixton's, but after that how lovely to settle down at Riseholme again! You must show me your ouija-board too. I feel quite rested this morning. Shall I help you with the walking-sticks later on?"

Daisy went uneasily back to her putting: it was too awful that Lucia in that amateurish manner should have beaten a serious exponent of the art, and already, in dark anticipation, she saw Lucia as the impresario of clock-golf, popularising it in Riseholme. She herself would have to learn to drive and approach without delay, and make Riseholme take up real golf, instead of merely putting.

Lucia visited the Museum next, and arranged the spit in an empty and prominent place between Daisy's fossils and Colonel Boucher's fragments of Samian ware. She attended the morning parliament on the green, and walked beside Mrs. Boucher's bath-chair. She shouted into Mrs. Antrobus's ear-trumpet, she dallied with Piggy and Goosie, and never so much as mentioned a duchess. All her thoughts seemed wrapped up in Riseholme; just one tiresome visit lay in front of her, and then, oh, the joy of settling down here again! Even Mrs. Boucher felt disarmed; little as she would have thought it, there was something in Lucia beyond mere snobbery.

Georgie popped in that afternoon about teatime. The afternoon was rather chilly, and Lucia had a fire lit in the grate of the music-room, which, now that the spit had been removed, burned beautifully. Peppino, drowsy with his cold, sat by it, while the other two played duets. Already Lucia had taken down Sigismund's portrait and installed Georgie's watercolours again by the piano. They had had a fine tussle over the Mozart duet, and Georgie had promised to practise it, and Lucia had promised to practise it, and she had called him an idle boy, and he had called her a lazy girl, quite in the old style, while Peppino dozed. Just then the evening post came in, with the evening paper, and Lucia picked up the latter to see what Hermione had said about her departure from London. Even as she turned back the page her eye fell on two or three letters which had been forwarded from Brompton Square. The top one was a large square envelope, the sort of fine thick envelope that contained a rich card of invitation, and she opened it. Next moment she sprang from her seat.

"Peppino, dear," she cried. "Marcia! Her ball. Marcia's ball tonight!"

Peppino roused himself a little.

"Ball? What ball?" he said. "No ball. Riseholme."

Lucia pushed by Georgie on the treble music-stool, without seeming to notice that he was there.

"No dear, of course you won't go," she said. "But do you know, I think I shall go up and pop in for an hour. Georgie will come to dine with you, won't you, Georgie, and you'll go to bed early. Half-past six! Yes, I can be in town by ten. That will be heaps of time. I shall dress at Brompton Square. Just a sandwich to take with me and eat it in the car."

She wheeled round to Georgie, pressing the bell in her circumvolution.

"Marcia Whitby," she said. "Winding up the season. So easy to pop up there, and dear Marcia would be hurt if I didn't come. Let me see, shall I come back tomorrow, Peppino? Perhaps it would be simpler if I stayed up there and sent the car back. Then you could come up in comfort next day, and we would go on to Adele's together. I have a host of things to do in London tomorrow. That party at Aggie's. I will telephone to Aggie to say that I can come after all. My maid, my chauffeur," she said to the

butler, rather in the style of Shylock. "I want my maid and my
chauffeur and my car. Let him have his dinner quickly—no, he
can get his dinner at Brompton Square. Tell him to come round
at once."

Georgie sat positively aghast, for Lucia ran on like a thing
demented. Mozart, ouija, putting, the Elizabethan spit, all the
simple joys of Riseholme fizzled out like damp fireworks. Gone,
too, utterly gone was her need of complete rest; she had never
been so full of raw, blatant, savage vitality.

"Dear Marcia," she said. "I felt it must be an oversight from
the first, but naturally, Georgie, though she and I are such
friends, I could not dream of reminding her. What a blessing that
my delicious day at Riseholme has so rested me: I feel I could
go to fifty balls without fatigue. Such a wonderful house, Georgie; when you come up to stay with us in the autumn, I must
take you there. Peppino, is it not lucky that I only brought down
here just enough for a couple of nights, and left everything in
London to pick up as we came through to go to Adele's? What
a sight it will be, all the Royal Family almost I believe, and the
whole of the Diplomatic corps: my Gioconda, I know, is going.
Not a large ball though at all: not one of those great promiscuous
affairs, which I hate so. How dear Marcia was besieged for invitations! How vulgar people are and how pushing! Goody-bye,
mind you practise your Mozart, Georgie. Oh, and tell Daisy that
I shan't be able to have another of those delicious puttings with
her tomorrow. Back on Tuesday after the weekend at Adele's,
and then weeks and weeks of dear Riseholme. How long they
are! I will just go and hurry my maid up."

Georgie tripped off, as soon as she had gone, to see Daisy,
and narrated to her open-mouthed disgust this amazing scene.

"And the question is," he said, "about the complete rest that was ordered her. I don't believe she was ordered any rest at all. I believe—"

Daisy gave a triumphant crow: inductive reasoning had led her to precisely the same point at precisely the same moment.

"Why, of course!" she said. "I always felt there was something behind that complete rest. I told you it meant something different. She wasn't asked, and so—"

"And so she came down here for rest," said Georgie in a loud voice. He was determined to bring that out first. "Because she wasn't asked—"

"And the moment she was asked she flew," said Daisy. "Nothing could be plainer. No more rest, thank you."

"She's wonderful," said Georgie. "Too interesting!"

∞

Lucia sped through the summer evening on this errand of her own reprieve, too excited to eat, and too happy to wonder how it had happened like this. How wise, too, she had been to hold her tongue and give way to no passionate laments at her exclusion from the paradise towards which she was now hastening. Not one word of abuse had she uttered against Marcia: she had asked nobody to intercede: she had joined in all the talk about the ball as if she was going, and finally had made it impossible for herself to go by announcing that she had been ordered a few days of complete rest. She could (and would) explain her appearance perfectly: she had felt much better—doctors were such fussers— and at the last moment had made just a little effort, and here she was.

A loud explosion interrupted these agreeable reflections and the car drew up. A tyre had burst, but they carried an extra wheel, and though the delay seemed terribly long they were soon on their way again. They traversed another ten miles, and now in the north-east the smouldering glow of London reddened the toneless hue of the summer night. The stars burned bright, and she pictured Peppino at his telescope—no, Peppino had a really bad cold, and would not be at his telescope. Then there came another explosion—was it those disgusting stars in their courses that were fighting against her?—and again the car drew up by the side of the empty road.

"What has happened?" asked Lucia in a strangled voice.

"Another tyre gone, ma'am," said the chauffeur. "Never knew such a thing."

Lucia looked at her clock. It was ten already, and she ought now to be in Brompton Square. There was no further wheel that could be put on, and the tyre had to be taken off and mended. The minutes passed like seconds . . . Lucia, outwardly composed, sat on a rug at the edge of the road, and tried unsuccessfully not to curse Almighty Providence. The moon rose, like a gelatine lozenge.

She began to count the hours that intervened between the tragic present and, say, four o'clock in the morning, and she determined that whatever further disasters might befall, she would go to Whitby House, even if it was in a dustman's cart, so long as there was a chance of a single guest being left there. She would go . . .

And all the time, if she had only known it, the stars were fighting not against her but for her. The tyre was mended, and she got to Brompton Square at exactly a quarter past eleven. Cupboards were torn open, drawers ransacked, her goaded maid burst into tears. Aunt Amy's pearls were clasped round her neck, Peppino's hair in the shrine of gold sausage that had once been Beethoven's was pinned on, and at five minutes past twelve she hurried up the

great stairs at Whitby House. Precisely as she came to the door
of the ballroom there emerged the head of the procession going
down to supper. Marcia for a moment stared at her as if she was a
ghost, but Lucia was so busy curtseying that she gave no thought
to that. Seven times in rapid succession did she curtsey. It almost
became a habit, and she nearly curtseyed to Adele who (so like
Adele) followed immediately after.

"Just up from Riseholme, dearest Adele," she said. "I felt
quite rested—How are you, Lord Tony?—and so I made a little
effort. Peppino urged me to come. How nice to see your Excellency! Millie! Dearest Olga! What a lot of friends! How is poor
Princess Isabel? Marcia looked so handsome. Brilliant! Such a
delicious drive: I felt I had to pop in . . ."

Chapter Nine

POOR PEPPINO'S COLD NEXT DAY, instead of being better, was a good deal worse. He had aches and pains, and felt feverish, and sent for the doctor, who peremptorily ordered him to go to bed. There was nothing in the least to cause alarm, but it would be the height of folly to go to any weekend party at all. Bed.

Peppino telegraphed to Lady Brixton with many regrets for the unavoidable, and rang up Lucia. The state of his voice made it difficult to catch what he said, but she quite understood that there was nothing to be anxious about, and that he hoped she would go to Adele's without him. Her voice on the other hand was marvellously distinct, and he heard a great deal about the misfortunes which had come to so brilliant a conclusion last night. There followed a string of seven Christian names, and Lucia said a flashlight photograph had been permitted during supper. She thought she was in it, though rather in the background.

Lucia was very sorry for Peppino's indisposition, but, as ordered, had no anxiety about him. She felt too that he wouldn't personally miss very much by being prevented from coming to Adele's party, for it was to be a very large party, and Peppino— bless him—occasionally got a little dazed at these brilliant gatherings. He did not grasp who people were with the speed and certainty which were needful, and he had been known to grasp the hand of an eminent author and tell him how much he had admired his fine picture at the Academy. (Lucia constantly did that sort of thing herself, but then she got herself out of the holes she had herself digged with so brilliant a manoeuvre that it didn't matter, whereas Peppino was only dazed the more by his misfortunes.) Moreover she knew that Peppino's presence somehow hampered her style: she could not be the brilliant *mondaine* when his patient but proud eye was on her, with quite the dash that was hers when he was not there. There was always the sense that he knew her best in her Riseholme incarnation, in her duets with Georgie, and her rendering of the slow movement of the "Moonlight Sonata," and her grabbing of all Daisy's little stunts. She electrified him as the superb butterfly, but the electrification was accompanied by slight shocks and surprises. When she referred by her Christian name to some woman with whom her only bond was that she had refused to dine at Brompton Square, that puzzled Peppino . . . In the autumn she must be a little more serious, have some quiet dinner parties of ordinary people, for really up till now there had scarcely been an "ordinary" person at Brompton Square at all, such noble lions of every species had been entrapped there. And Adele's party was to be of a very leonine kind; the smart world was to be there, and some highbrows and some politicians, and she was aware that she herself would have to do her very best, and be allusive, and pretend to know what she didn't know, and seem to swim in very distinguished currents. Dear Peppino wasn't up to that sort of thing, he couldn't grapple with it, and she grappled with it best without him . . . At the moment of that vainglorious thought, it is probable that Nemesis fixed her inexorable eye on Lucia.

Lucia, unconscious of this deadly scrutiny, turned to her immediate affairs. Her engagement book pleasantly informed her that she had many things to do on the day when the need for complete rest overtook her, and now she heralded through the telephone the glad tidings that she could lunch here and drop in there, and dine with Aggie. All went well with these restorations, and the day would be full, and tomorrow also, down to the hour of her departure for Adele's. Having despatched this agreeable business, she was on the point of ringing up Stephen, to fit him in for the spare three-quarters of an hour that was left, when she was rung up and it was Stephen's voice that greeted her.

"Stephano *mio*," she said. "How did you guess I was back?"

"Because I rang up Riseholme first," said he, "and heard you had gone to town. Were you there last night?"

There was no cause to ask where "there" was. There had only been one place in London last night.

"Yes; delicious dance," said Lucia. "I was just going to ring you up and see if you could come round for a chat at a quarter to five. I am free till half-past five. Such fun it was. A flashlight photograph."

"No!" said Stephen in the Riseholme manner. "I long to hear about it. And were there really seven of them?"

"Quite," said Lucia magnificently.

"Wonderful! But quarter to five is no use for me. Can't you give me another time?"

"My dear, impossible," said Lucia. "You know what London is in these last days. Such a scrimmage."

"Well, we shall meet tomorrow then," said he.

"But, alas, I go to Adele's tomorrow," she said.

"Yes, but so do I," said Stephen. "She asked me this morning. I was wondering if you would drive me down, if you're going in your car. Would there be room for you and Peppino and me?"

Lucia rapidly reviewed the situation. It was perfectly clear to her that Adele had asked Stephen, at the last moment, to fill Peppino's place. But naturally she had not told him that, and Lucia determined not to do so either. It would spoil his pleasure (at least it would have spoiled hers) to know that . . . And what a wonderful entry it would make for her—rather daring—to drive down alone with her lover. She could tell him about Peppino's indisposition tomorrow, as if it had just occurred.

"Yes, Stephano, heaps of room," she said. "Delighted. I'll call for you, shall I, on my way down, soon after three."

"Angelic," he said. "What fun we shall have."

And it is probable that Nemesis at that precise moment licked her dry lips. "Fun!" thought Nemesis.

∞

Marcia Whitby was of the party. She went down in the morning, and lunched alone with Adele. Their main topic of conversation was obvious.

"I saw her announcement in the *Morning Post*," said the infuriated Marcia, "that she had gone for a few days' complete rest into the country, and naturally I thought I was safe. I was determined she shouldn't come to my ball, and when I saw that, I thought she couldn't. So out of sheer good nature I sent her a card, so that she could tell everybody she had been asked. Never did I dream that there was a possibility of her coming. Instead of which, she made the most conspicuous entry that she could have made. I believe she timed it: I believe she waited on the stairs till she saw we were going down to supper."

"I wonder!" said Adele. "Genius, if it was that. She curtseyed seven times, too. I can't do that without loud cracks from my aged knees."

"And she stopped till the very end," said Marcia. "She was positively the last to go. I shall never do a kind thing again."

"You're horrid about her," said Adele. "Besides, what has she done? You asked her and she came. You don't rave at your guests for coming when they're asked. You wouldn't like it if none of them came."

"That's different," said Marcia. "I shouldn't wonder if she announced she was ordered complete rest in order that I should fall into her trap."

Adele sighed, but shook her head.

"Oh, my dear, that *would* have been magnificent," she said. "But I'm afraid I can't hope to believe that. I dare say she went into the country because you hadn't asked her, and that was pretty good. But the other: no. However, we'll ask Tony what he thinks."

"What's Tony got to do with it?" said Marcia.

"Why, he's even more wrapped up in her than I am," said Adele. "He thinks of nothing else."

Marcia was silent a moment. Then a sort of softer gleam came into her angry eye.

"Tell me some more about her," she said.

Adele clapped her hands.

"Ah, that's splendid," she said. "You're beginning to feel kinder. What we would do without our Lucia I can't imagine. I don't know what there would be to talk about."

"She's ridiculous!" said Marcia, relapsing a little.

"No, you mustn't feel that," said Adele. "You mustn't laugh at her ever. You must just richly enjoy her."

"She's a snob!" said Marcia, as if this was a tremendous discovery.

"So am I: so are you: so are we all," said Adele. "We all run after distinguished people like—like Alf and Marcelle. The difference between you and Lucia is entirely in her favour, for you pretend you're not a snob, and she is perfectly frank and open about it. Besides, what is a duchess like you for except to give pleasure to snobs? That's your work in the world, darling; that's why you were sent here. Don't shirk it, or when you're old you will suffer agonies of remorse. And you're a snob too. You liked having seven—or was it seventy?—Royals at your dance."

"Well, tell me some more about Lucia," said Marcia, rather struck by this ingenious presentation of the case.

"Indeed I will: I long for your conversion to Luciaphilism. Now today there are going to be marvellous happenings. You see Lucia has got a lover—"

"Quite absolutely impossible!" said Marcia firmly.

"Oh, don't interrupt. Of course he is only an official lover, a public lover, and his name is Stephen Merriall. A perfect lady. Now Peppino, Lucia's husband, was coming down with her today, but he's got a very bad cold and has put me off. I'm rather glad: Lucia has got more—more dash when he's not there. So I've asked her lover instead—"

"No!" said Marcia. "Go on."

"My dear, they are much better than any play I have ever seen. They do it beautifully: they give each other little glances and smiles, and then begin to talk hurriedly to someone else. Of course, they're both as chaste as snow, chaster if possible. I think poor Babs's case put it into Lucia's head that in this naughty world it gave a cachet to a woman to have the reputation of having a lover. So safe too: there's nothing to expose. They only behave like lovers strictly in public. I was terrified when it began that Mr. Merriall would think she meant something, and try to kiss her when they were alone, and so rub the delicate bloom completely off, but I'm sure he's tumbled to it."

"How perfect!" said Marcia.

"Isn't it? Aren't you feeling more Luciaphil? I'm sure you are. You must enjoy her: it shows such a want of humour to be annoyed with her. And really I've taken a great deal of trouble to get people she will revel in. There's the Prime Minister, there's you, there's Greatorex the pianist who's the only person who can play Stravinski, there's Professor Bonstetter the psychoanalyst, there's the Italian Ambassador, there's her lover, there's Tony . . . I can't go on. Oh, and I must remember to tell her that Archie Singleton is Babs's brother, or she may say something dreadful. And then there are lots who will revel in Lucia, and I the foremost. I'm devoted to her; I am really, Marcia. She's got character, she's got an iron will, and I like strong talkative women so much better than strong silent men."

"Yes, she's got will," said Marcia. "She determined to come to my ball, and she came. I allow I gave her the chance."

"Those are the chances that come to gifted people," said Adele. "They don't come to ordinary people."

"Suppose I flirted violently with her lover?" said Marcia.

Adele's eyes grew bright with thought.

"I can't imagine what she would do," she said. "But I'm sure she would do something that scored. Otherwise she wouldn't be Lucia. But you mustn't do it."

"Just one evening," said Marcia. "Just for an hour or two. It's not poaching, you see, because her lover isn't her lover. He's just a stunt."

Adele wavered.

"It would be wonderful to know what she would do," she said. "And it's true that he's only a stunt. Perhaps for an hour or two tomorrow, and then give him back."

∞

Adele did not expect any of her guests till teatime, and Marcia and she both retired for after-lunch siestas. Adele had been down here for the last four or five days, driving up to Marcia's ball and

back in the very early morning, and had three days before settled everything in connection with her party, assigning rooms,
discussing questions of high importance with her chef, and
arranging to meet as many trains as possible. It so happened,
therefore, that Stephen Merriall, since the house was full, was
to occupy the spacious dressing-room, furnished as a bedroom,
next Lucia's room, which had been originally allotted to Peppino. Adele had told her butler that Mr. Lucas was not coming,
but that his room would be occupied by Mr. Merriall, thought
no more about it, and omitted to substitute a new card on his
door. These two rooms were halfway down a long corridor of
bedrooms and bathrooms that ran the whole length of the house,
a spacious oak-boarded corridor, rather dark, with the broad
staircase coming up at the end of it. Below was the suite of public
rooms, a library at the end, a big music-room, a long gallery of
a drawing-room, and the dining-room. These all opened on to a
paved terrace overlooking the gardens and tennis-courts, and it
was here, with the shadow of the house lying coolly across it, that
her guests began to assemble. In ones and twos they gathered,
some motoring down from London, others arriving by train, and
it was not till there were some dozen of them, among whom were
the most fervent Luciaphils, that the object of their devotion,
attended by her lover, made her appearance, evidently at the top
of her form.

"Dearest Adele," she said. "How delicious to get into the cool
country again. Marcia dear! Such adventures I had on my way
up to your ball: two burst tyres: I thought I should never get
there. How are you, your Excellency? I saw you at the Duchess's,
but couldn't get a word with you. Aggie darling! Ah, Lord Tony!
Yes, a cup of tea would be delicious; no sugar, Stephen, thanks."

Lucia had not noticed quite everybody. There were one or

two people rather retired from the tea-table, but they did not seem to be of much importance, and certainly the Prime Minister was not among them. Stephen hovered, loverlike, just behind her chair, and she turned to the Italian Ambassador.

"I was afraid of a motor accident all the way down," she said, "because last night I dreamed I broke a looking-glass. Quaint things dreams are, though really the psychoanalysts who interpret them are quainter. I went to a meeting at Sophy's, dear Sophy Alingsby, the other day—your Excellency I am sure knows Sophy Alingsby—and heard a lecture on it. Let me see: boiled rabbit, if you dream of boiled rabbit—"

Lucia suddenly became aware of a sort of tension. Just a tension. She looked quickly round, and recognised one of the men she had not paid much attention to. She sprang from her chair.

"Professor Bonstetter," she said. "How are you? I know you won't remember me, but I did have the honour of shaking hands with you after your enthralling lecture the other day. Do come and tell his Excellency and me a little more about it. There were so many questions I longed to ask you."

Adele wanted to applaud, but she had to be content with catching Marcia's eye. Was Lucia great, or was she not? Stephen too: how exactly right she was to hand him her empty cup when she had finished with it, without a word, and how perfectly he took it! "More?" he said, and Lucia just shook her head without withdrawing her attention from Professor Bonstetter. Then the Prime Minister arrived, and she said how lovely Chequers must be looking. She did not annex him, she just hovered and hinted, and made no direct suggestion, and sure enough, within five minutes he had asked her if she knew Chequers. Of course she did, but only as a tourist—and so one thing led on to another. It would be a nice break in her long drive down to Riseholme on

Tuesday to lunch at Chequers, and not more than forty miles out of her way.

People dispersed and strolled on the terrace, and gathered again, and some went off to their rooms. Lucia had one little turn up and down with the Ambassador, and spoke with great tact of Mussolini, and another with Lord Tony, and not for a long time did she let Stephen join her. But then they wandered off into the garden, and were seen standing very close together and arguing publicly about a flower, and Lucia, seeing they were observed, called to Adele to know if it wasn't Dropmore Borage. They came back very soon, and Stephen went up to his room while Lucia remained downstairs. Adele showed her the library and the music-room, and the long drawing-room, and then vanished. Lucia gravitated to the music-room, opened the piano, and began the slow movement of the "Moonlight Sonata."

About halfway through it, she became aware that somebody had come into the room. But her eyes were fixed dreamily on the usual point at the edge of the ceiling, and her fingers faultlessly doled out the slow triplets. She gave a little sigh when she had finished, pressed her fingers to her eyes, and slowly awoke, as from some melodious anaesthetic.

It was a man who had come in and who had seated himself not far from the keyboard.

"Charming!" he said. "Thank you."

Lucia didn't remember seeing him on the terrace: perhaps he had only just arrived. She had a vague idea, however, that whether on the terrace or elsewhere, she had seen him before. She gave a pretty little start. "Ah, had no idea I had an audience," she said. "I should never have ventured to go on playing. So dreadfully out of practice."

"Please have a little more practice then," said the polite stranger.

She ran her hands, butterfly fashion, over the keys.

"A little morsel of Stravinski?" she said.

It was in the middle of the morsel that Adele came in and found Lucia playing Stravinski to Mr. Greatorex. The position seemed to be away, away beyond her orbit altogether, and she merely waited with undiminished faith in Lucia, to see what would happen when Lucia became aware to whom she was playing . . . It was a longish morsel, too: more like a meal than a morsel, and it was also remarkably like a muddle. Finally, Lucia made an optimistic attempt at the double chromatic scale in divergent directions which brought it to an end, and laughed gaily.

"My poor fingers," she said. "Delicious piano, dear Adele. I love a Bechstein; that was a little morsel of Stravinski. Hectic perhaps, do you think? But so true to the modern idea: little feverish excursions: little bits of tunes, and nothing worked out. But I always say that there is something in Stravinski, if you study him. How I worked at that little piece, and I'm afraid it's far from perfect yet."

Lucia played one more little run with her right hand, while she cudgelled her brain to remember where she had seen this man before, and turned round on the music-stool. She felt sure he was an artist of some kind, and she did not want to ask Adele to introduce him, for that would look as if she did not know everybody. She tried pictures next.

"In art I always think that the Stravinski school is represented by the Post-Cubists," she said. "They give us pattern in lines, just as Stravinski gives us patterns in notes, and the modern poet patterns in words. At Sophy Alingsby's the other night we had a feast of patterns. Dear Sophy—what a curious mixture of tastes! She cares only for the ultra-primitive in music, and the ultra-modern in art. Just before you came in, Adele, I was trying to remember the first movement of Beethoven's 'Moonlight';

those triplets though they look easy have to be kept so level. And yet Sophy considers Beethoven a positive decadent. I ought to have taken her to Diva's little concert—Diva Dalrymple—for I assure you really that Stravinski sounded classical compared to the rest of the programme. It was very creditably played, too. Mr.—" what was his name?—"Mr. Greatorex."

She had actually said the word before her brain made the connection. She gave her little peal of laughter.

"Ah, you wicked people," she cried. "A plot: clearly a plot. Mr. Greatorex, how could you? Adele told you to come in here when she heard me begin my little strummings, and told you to sit down and encourage me. Don't deny it, Adele! I know it was like that. I shall tell everybody how unkind you've been, unless Mr. Greatorex sits down instantly and magically restores to life what I have just murdered."

Adele denied nothing. In fact there was no time to deny anything, for Lucia positively thrust Mr. Greatorex on to the music-stool, and instantly put on her rapt musical face, chin in hand, and eyes looking dreamily upwards. There was Nemesis, you would have thought, dealing thrusts at her, but Nemesis was no match for her amazing quickness. She parried and thrust again, and here—what richness of future reminiscence—was Mr. Greatorex playing Stravinski to her, before no audience but herself and Adele, who really didn't count, for the only tune she liked was "Land of Hope and Glory" . . . Great was Lucia!

Adele left the two, warning them that it was getting on for dressing time, but there was some more Stravinski first, for Lucia's sole ear. Adele had told her the direction of her room, and said her name was on the door, and Lucia found it at once. A beautiful room it was, with a bathroom on one side, and a magnificent Charles II bed draped at the back with wool-work tapestry. It was a little late for Lucia's Elizabethan taste, and she noticed that the big wardrobe was Chippendale, which was later still. There was a Chinese paper on the wall, and fine Persian rugs on the floor, and though she could have criticised it was easy to admire. And there for herself was a very smart dress, and for decoration Aunt Amy's pearls, and the Beethoven brooch. But she decided to avoid all possible chance of competition, and put the pearls back into her jewel-case. The Beethoven brooch, she was sure, need fear no rival.

Lucia felt that dinner, as far as she went, was a huge success. Stephen was seated just opposite her, and now and then she exchanged little distant smiles with him. Next her on one side was Lord Tony, who adored her story about Stravinski and Greatorex. She told him also what the Italian Ambassador had said about Mussolini, and the Prime Minister about Chequers: she was going to pop in to lunch on her way down to Riseholme after this delicious party. Then conversation shifted, and she turned left, and talked to the only man whose identity she had not grasped. But, as matter of public knowledge, she began about poor Babs, and her own admiration of her demeanour at that wicked trial, which had ended so disastrously. And once again there was slight tension.

Bridge and mah-jong followed, and rich allusive conversation and the sense, so dear to Lucia, of being in the very centre of everything that was distinguished. When the women went upstairs she hurried to her room, made a swift change into greater simplicity, and, by invitation, sought out Marcia's room, at the far end of the passage, for a chat. Adele was there, and dear (rather common) Aggie was there, and Aggie was being just a shade sycophantic over the six rows of Whitby pearls. Lucia was glad she had limited her splendours to the Beethoven brooch.

"But why didn't you wear your pearls, Lucia?" asked Adele. "I was hoping to see them." (She had heard talk of Aunt Amy's pearls, but had not noticed them on the night of Marcia's ball.)

"My little seedlings!" said Lucia. "Just seedlings, compared to Marcia's marbles. Little trumperies!"

Aggie had seen them, and she knew Lucia did not overstate their minuteness. Like a true Luciaphil, she changed a subject that might prove embarrassing.

"Take away your baubles, Marcia," said Aggie. "They are only diseases of a common shellfish which you eat when it's healthy and wear when it's got a tumour . . . How wretched it is to think that all of us aren't going to meet day after day as we have been doing! There's Adele going to America, and there's Marcia going to Scotland—what a foul spot, Marcia, come to Marienbad instead with me. And what are you going to do, Lucia?"

"Oh, my dear, how I wanted to go to Aix or Marienbad," she said. "But my Peppino says it's impossible. We've got to stop quiet at Riseholme. Shekels, tiresome shekels."

"There she goes, talking about Riseholme as if it was some dreadful penance to go there," said Adele. "You adore Riseholme, Lucia, at least if you don't, you ought to. Olga raves about it. She says she's never really happy away from it. When are you going to ask me there?"

"Adele, as if you didn't know that you weren't always welcome," said Lucia.

"Me, too," said Marcia.

"A standing invitation to both of you always," said Lucia. "Dear Marcia, how sweet of you to want to come! I go there on Tuesday, and there I remain. But it's true, I do adore it. No balls, no parties, and such dear Arcadians. You couldn't believe in them without seeing them. Life at its very simplest, dears."

"It can't be simpler than Scotland," said Marcia. "In Scotland you kill birds and fish all day, and eat them at night. That's all."

Lucia through these months of strenuous effort had never perhaps felt herself so amply rewarded as she was at this moment. All evening she had talked in an effortless deshabille of mind to the great ones of the country, the noble, the distinguished, the accomplished, and now here she was in a duchess's bedroom having a good-night talk. This was nearer Nirvana than even Marcia's ball. And the three women there seemed to be grouped round her: they waited—there was no mistaking it—listening for something from her, just as Riseholme used to wait for her lead. She felt that she was truly attaining, and put her chin in her hand and looked a little upwards.

"I shall get tremendously put in my place when I go back to Riseholme again," she said. "I'm sure Riseholme thinks I have been wasting my time in idle frivolities. It sees perhaps in an evening paper that I have been to Aggie's party, or Adele's house or Marcia's ball, and I assure you it will be very suspicious of me. Just as if I didn't know that all these delightful things were symbols."

Adele had got the cataleptic look of a figure in a stained-glass window, so rapt she was. But she wanted to grasp this with full appreciation.

"Lucia, don't be so dreadfully clever," she said. "You're talking high over my head: you're like the whirr of an aeroplane. Explain what you mean by symbols."

Lucia was toying with the string of Whitby pearls, which Marcia still held, with one hand. The other she laid on Adele's knee. She felt that a high line was expected of her.

"My dear, you know," she said. "All our runnings-about, all

our gaieties are symbols of affection: we love to see each other because we partake of each other. Interesting people, distinguished people, obscure people, ordinary people, we long to bring them all into our lives in order to widen our horizons. We learn, or we try to learn, of other interests beside our own. I shall have to make Riseholme understand that dear little Alf, playing the flute at my house, or half a dozen princes eating quails at Marcia's mansion, it's all the same, isn't it? We get to know the point of view of prizefighters and princes. And it seems to me, it seems to me—"

Lucia's gaze grew a shade more lost and aloof.

"It seems to me that we extend our very souls," she said, "by letting them flow into other lives. How badly I put it! But when Eric Greatorex—so charming of him—played those delicious pieces of Stravinski to me before dinner, I felt I was stepping over some sort of frontier *into* Stravinski. Eric made out my passport. A multiplication of experience: I think that is what I mean."

None of those present could have said with any precision what Lucia had meant, but the general drift seemed to be that an hour with a burglar or a cannibal was valuable for the amplification of the soul.

"Odd types too," she said. "How good for one to be put into touch with something quite remote. Marcelle—Marcelle Periscope—you met him at my house, didn't you, Aggie—"

"Why wasn't I asked?" said Marcia.

Lucia gave a little quick smile, as at some sweet child's interruption.

"Darling Marcia, why didn't you propose yourself? Surely you know me well enough to do that. Yes, Marcelle, a cinema artist. A fresh horizon, a fresh attitude towards life. So good for me: it helps me not to be narrow. *Dio mio!* How I pray I shall never be narrow. To be shocked, too! How shocking to be shocked. If you all had fifty lovers apiece, I should merely think it a privilege to know about them all."

Marcia longed, with almost the imperativeness of a longing to sneeze, to allude directly to Stephen. She raised her eyes for a half second to Adele, the priestess of this cult in which she knew she was rapidly becoming a worshipper, but if ever an emphatic negative was wordlessly bawled at a tentative enquirer, it was bawled now. If Lucia chose to say anything about Stephen it would indeed be manna, but to ask—never! Aggie, seated sideways to them, had not seen this telegraphy, and spoke unwisely with her lips.

"If an ordinary good-looking woman," she said, "tells me that she hasn't got a lover or a man who wants to be her lover, I always say 'You lie!' So she does. You shall begin, Lucia, about your lovers."

Nothing could have been more unfortunate. Adele could have hurled the entire six rows of the Whitby pearls at Aggie's face. Lucia had no lover, but only the wraith of a lover, on whom direct light must never be flashed. Such a little reflection should have shown Aggie that. The effect of her carelessness was that Lucia became visibly embarrassed, looked at the clock, and got up in a violent hurry.

"Good gracious me!" she said. "What a time of night! Who could have thought that our little chat had lasted so long? Yes, dear Adele, I know my room, on the left with my name on the door. Don't dream of coming to show it me."

∞

Lucia distributed little pressures and kisses and clingings, and holding her very smart pale blue wrapper close about her, slid

noiselessly out in her slippers into the corridor. It was late, the
house was quite quiet, for a quarter of an hour ago they had heard
the creaking of men's footsteps going to their rooms. The main
lights had been put out, only here and there down the long silent
aisle there burned a single small illumination. Past half a dozen
doors Lucia tiptoed, until she came to one on which she could
just see the name Philip Lucas preceded by a dim hieroglyph
which of course was "Mrs." She turned the handle and went in.

Two yards in front of her, by the side of the bed, was standing
Stephen, voluptuous in honey-coloured pyjamas. For one awful
second—for she felt sure this was her room (*and so did he*)—they
stared at each other in dead silence.

"How dare you?" said Stephen, so agitated that he could
scarcely form the syllables.

"And how dare *you*?" hissed Lucia. "Go out of my room
instantly."

"Go out of mine!" said Stephen.

Lucia's indignant eye left his horror-stricken face and swept
round the room. There was no Chinese paper on the wall, but a
pretty Morris paper: there was no Charles II bed with tapestry,
but a brass-testered couch; there was no Chippendale wardrobe,
but something useful from Tottenham Court Road. She gave one
little squeal, of a pitch between the music of the slate-pencil and
of the bat, and closed his door again. She staggered on to the
next room where again the legend "Philip Lucas" was legible,
popped in, and locked the door. She hurried to the door of communication between this and the fatal chamber next it, and as
she locked that also she heard from the other side of it the bolt
violently pulled forward.

She sat down on her bed in a state of painful agitation. Her
excursion into the fatal chamber had been an awful, a hideous

mistake: none knew that better than herself, but how was she to explain that to her lover? For weeks they had been advertising the guilt of their blameless relationship, and now it seemed to her impossible ever to resume it. Every time she gave Stephen one of those little smiles or glances, at which she had become so perfect an adept, there would start into her mind that moment of speechless horror, and her smile would turn to a tragic grimace, and her sick glance recoil from him. Worse than that, how was she ever to speak of it to him, or passionately protest her innocence? He had thought that she had come to his room (indeed she had) when the house was quiet, on the sinister errand of love, and though, when he had repudiated her, she had followed suit, she saw the recoiling indignation of her lover. If only, just now, she had kept her head, if only she had said at once, "I beg your pardon, I mistook my room," all might have been well, but how nerve herself to say it afterwards? And in spite of the entire integrity of her moral nature, which was puritanical to the verge of prudishness, she had not liked (no woman could) his unfeigned horror at her irruption.

Stephen next door was in little better plight. He had had a severe shock. For weeks Lucia had encouraged him to play the lover, and had (so he awfully asked himself) this pleasant public stunt become a reality to her, a need of her nature? She had made it appear, when he so rightly repulsed her, that she had come to his room by mistake, but was that pretence? Had she really come with a terrible motive? It was her business, anyhow, to explain, and insist on her innocence, if she was innocent, and he would only be too thankful to believe her. But at present and without that, the idea of resuming the public loverlike demeanour was frankly beyond him. She might be encouraged again . . . Though now he was safe with locked and bolted doors, he knew he would not be able to sleep, and he took a large dose of aspirin.

Lucia was far more thorough: she never shelved difficulties, but faced them. She still sat on the edge of her bed, long after Stephen's nerves were quieted, and as she herself calmed down, thought it all out. For the present, loverlike relations in public were impossible, and it was lucky that in a couple of days more she would be interned at Riseholme. Then with a flash of genius there occurred to her the interesting attitude to adopt in the interval. She would give the impression that there had been a lovers' quarrel. The more she thought of that, the more it commended itself to her. People would notice it, and wonder what it was all about, and their curiosity would never be gratified, for Lucia felt sure, from the horror depicted on Stephen's face, that he as well as she would be for ever dumb on the subject of that midnight encounter. She must not look unhappy: she must on the other hand be more vivid and eager than ever, and just completely ignore Stephen. But there would be no lift for him in her car back to London: he would have to go by train.

∞

The ex-lovers both came down very late next day, for fear of meeting each other alone, and thus they sat in adjoining rooms half the morning. Stephen had some Hermione-work on hand, for this party would run to several paragraphs, but, however many it ran to, Hermione was utterly determined not to mention Lucia in any of them. Hermione knew, however, that Mr. Stephen Merriall was there, and said so . . . By one of those malignant strokes which are rained on those whom Nemesis desires to chastise, they came out of their rooms at precisely the same moment, and had to walk downstairs together, coldly congratulating each other on the beauty of the morning. Luckily there were people on the terrace, among whom was Marcia. She thought this was an excellent opportunity for beginning her flirtation with Stephen, and instantly carried him off to the kitchen garden, for unless she ate gooseberries on Sunday morning she died. Lucia seemed sublimely unaware of their departure, and joined a select little group round the Prime Minister. Between a discussion on the housing problem with him, a stroll with Lord Tony, who begged her to drop the "lord," and a little more Stravinski alone with Greatorex, the short morning passed very agreeably. But she saw when she went into lunch rather late that Marcia and Stephen had not returned from their gooseberrying. There was a gap of just three places at the table, and it thus became a certainty that Stephen would sit next her.

Lunch was fully half over before they appeared, Marcia profusely apologetic.

"Wretchedly rude of me, dear Adele," she said, "but we had no idea it was so late, did we, Mr. Merriall? We went to the gooseberries, and—and I suppose we must have stopped there. Your fault, Mr. Merriall; you men have no idea of time."

"Who could, Duchess, when he was with you?" said Stephen most adroitly.

"Sweet of you," said she. "Now do go on. You were in the middle of telling me something quite thrilling. And please, Adele, let nobody wait for us. I see you are all at the end of lunch, and I haven't begun, and gooseberries, as usual, have given me an enormous appetite. Yes, Mr. Merriall?"

Adele looked in vain, when throughout the afternoon Marcia continued in possession of Lucia's lover, for the smallest sign of resentment or uneasiness on her part. There was simply none; it was impossible to detect a thing that had no existence. Lucia seemed completely unconscious of any annexation, or indeed of Stephen's existence. There she sat, just now with Tony and herself, talking of Marcia's ball, and the last volume of risky memoirs, of which she had read a review in the Sunday paper, and Sophy's black room and Alf: never had she been more equipped at all points, more prosperously central. Marcia, thought Adele, was being wonderfully worsted, if she imagined she could produce any sign of emotion on Lucia's part. The lovers understood each other too well . . . Or, she suddenly conjectured, had they quarrelled? It really looked rather like it. Though she and Tony were having a good Luciaphil meeting, she almost wanted Lucia to go away, in order to go into committee over this entrancing possibility. And how naturally she Tony'd him: she must have been practising on her maid.

Somewhere in the house a telephone bell rang, and a footman came out on to the terrace.

"Lucia, I know that's for you," said Adele. "Wherever you are, somebody wants you on the telephone. If you were in the middle of the Sahara, a telephone would ring for you from the sands of the desert. Yes? Who is it for?" she said to the footman.

"Mrs. Lucas, my lady," he said.

Lucia got up, quite delighted.

"You're always chaffing me, Adele," she said. "What a nuisance the telephone is. One never gets a rest from it. But I won't be a moment."

She tripped off.

"Tony, there's a great deal to talk about," said Adele quickly. "Now what's the situation between the lovers? Perfect understanding or a quarrel? And who has been ringing her up? What would you bet that it was—"

"Alf," said Tony.

"I wonder, Tony, about the lovers. There's something. I never saw such superb indifference. How I shall laugh at Marcia. She's producing no effect at all. Lucia doesn't take the slightest notice. I knew she would be great. Last night we had a wonderful talk in Marcia's room, till Aggie was an ass. There she is again. Now we shall know."

Lucia came quickly along the terrace.

"Adele dear," she said. "Would it be dreadful of me if I left this afternoon? They've rung me up from Riseholme. Georgie rang me up. My Peppino is very far from well. Nothing really anxious, but he's in bed and he's alone. I think I had better go."

"Oh my dear," said Adele, "of course you shall do precisely as you wish. I'm dreadfully sorry: so shall we all be if you go. But if you feel you would be easier in your mind—"

Lucia looked round on all the brilliant little groups. She was leaving the most wonderful party: it was the highest perch she had reached yet. On the other hand she was leaving her lover, which was a compensation. But she truly didn't think of any of these things.

"My poor old Peppino," she said. "I must go, Adele."

Chapter Ten

TODAY, THE LAST OF AUGUST, Peppino had been allowed for the first time to go out and have a half-hour's quiet strolling in the garden and sit in the sun. His illness which had caused Lucia to recall herself had been serious, and for a few days he had been dangerously ill with pneumonia. After turning a bad corner he had made satisfactory progress.

Lucia, who for these weeks had been wholly admirable, would have gone out with him now, but the doctor, after his visit, had said he wanted to have a talk with her, and for twenty minutes or so they had held colloquy in the music-room. Then, on his departure, she sat there a few minutes more, arranged her ideas, and went out to join Peppino.

"Such a good cheering talk, *caro*," she said. "There never was such a perfect convalescer—my dear, what a word—as you. You're a prize patient. All you've got to do is to go on exactly as you're going, doing a little more, and a little more every day, and in a month's time you'll be ever so strong again. Such a good constitution."

"And no sea-voyage?" asked Peppino. The dread prospect had been dangled before him at one time.

"Not unless they think a month or two on the Riviera in the winter might be advisable. Then the sea-voyage from Dover to Calais, but no more than that. Now I know what you're thinking about. You told me that we couldn't manage Aix this August because of expense, so how are we to manage two months of Cannes?"

Lucia paused a moment.

"That delicious story of dear Marcia's," she said, "about those cousins of hers who had to retrench. After talking everything over they decided that all the retrenchment they could possibly make was to have no coffee after lunch. But we can manage better than that . . ."

Lucia paused again. Peppino had had enough of movement under his own steam, and they had seated themselves in the sunny little arbour by the sundial, which had so many appropriate mottoes carved on it.

"The doctor told me too that it would be most unwise of you to attempt to live in London for any solid period," she said. "Fogs, sunlessness, damp darkness: all bad. And I know again what's in your kind head. You think I adore London, and can spend a month or two there in the autumn, and in the spring, coming down here for weekends. But I haven't the slightest intention of doing anything of the kind. I'm not going to be up there alone. Besides, where are the dibs, as that sweet little Alf said, where are the dibs to come from for our Riviera?"

"Let the house for the winter then?" said Peppino.

"Excellent idea, if we could be certain of letting it. But we can't be certain of letting it, and all the time a stream of rates and taxes, and caretakers. It would be wretched to be always anxious about it, and always counting the dibs. I've been going into what we spent there this summer, *caro,* and it staggered me. What I vote for is to sell it. I'm not going to use it without you, and you're not going to use it at all. You know how I looked forward to being there for your sake, your club, the Reading Room at the British Museum, the Astronomer-Royal, but now that's all kaput, as Tony says. We'll bring down here anything that's particularly connected with dear Auntie: her portrait by Sargent, of course, though Sargents are fetching immense prices; or the walnut bureau, or the Chippendale chairs or that little worsted rug in her bedroom; but I vote for selling it all, freehold, furniture, everything. As if I couldn't go up to Claridge's now and then, when I want to have a luncheon-party or two of all our friends! And then we shall have no more anxieties, and if they say you must get away from the cold and the damp, we shall know we're doing nothing on the margin of our means. That would be hateful: we mustn't do that."

"But you'll never be able to be content with Riseholme again," said Peppino. "After your balls and your parties and all that, what will you find to do here?"

Lucia turned her gimlet-eye on him.

"I shall be a great fool if I don't find something to do," she said. "Was I so idle and unoccupied before we went to London? Good gracious, I was always worked to death here. Don't you bother your head about that, Peppino, for if you do it will show you don't understand me at all. And our dear Riseholme, let me tell you, has got very slack and inert in our absence, and I feel very guilty about that. There's nothing going on: there's none of the old fizz and bubble and Excelsior there used to be. They're vegetating, they're dry-rotting, and Georgie's getting fat. There's never any news. All that happens is that Daisy slashes a golf-ball about the green for practice in the morning, and then goes down to the links in the afternoon, and positively the only news next day is whether she has been round under a thousand strokes, whatever that means."

Lucia gave a little indulgent sigh.

"Dear Daisy has ideas sometimes," she said, "and I don't deny that. She had the idea of ouija, she had the idea of the Museum, and though she said that came from Abfou, she had the idea of Abfou. Also she had the idea of golf. But she doesn't carry her ideas out in a vivid manner that excites interest and keeps people on the boil. On the boil! That's what we all ought to be, with a thousand things to do that seem immensely important and which are important because they seem so. You want a certain touch to give importance to things, which dear Daisy hasn't got. Whatever poor Daisy does seems trivial. But they shall see that I've come home. What does it matter to me whether it's Marcia's ball, or playing Alf's accompaniments, or playing golf with Daisy, or playing duets with poor dear Georgie, whose fingers have all become thumbs, so long as I find it thrilling? If I find it dull, *caro*, I shall be, as Adele once said, a bloody fool. Dear Adele, she has always that little vein of coarseness."

Lucia encountered more opposition from Peppino than she anticipated, for he had taken a huge pride in her triumphant summer campaign in London, and though at times he had felt bewildered and buffeted in this high gale of social activity, and had, so to speak, to close his streaming eyes and hold his hat on, he gloried in the incessant and tireless blowing of it, which stripped the choicest fruits from the trees. He thought they could manage, without encroaching on financial margins, to keep the house open for another year yet, anyhow: he acknowledged that he had been unduly pessimistic about going to Aix, he even alluded to the memories of Aunt Amy which were twined about 25 Brompton Square, and which he would be so sorry to sever. But Lucia, in that talk with his doctor, had made up her mind: she rejected at once the idea of pursuing her victorious career in London if all the time she would have to be careful and thrifty, and if, far more importantly, she would be leaving Peppino down at Riseholme. That was not to be thought of: affection no less than decency made it impossible, and so having made up her mind, she set about the attainment of her object with all her usual energy. She knew, too, the value of incessant attack: smash little Alf, for instance, when he had landed a useful blow on his opponent's face, did not wait for him to recover, but instantly followed it up with another and yet another till his victim collapsed and was counted out. Lucia behaved in precisely the same way with Peppino: she produced rows of figures to show they were living beyond their means: she quoted (or invented) something the Prime Minister had said about the probability of an increase in income-tax: she assumed that they would go to the Riviera for certain, and was appalled at the price of tickets in the Blue Train, and of the tariff at hotels.

"And with all our friends in London, Peppino," she said in the decisive round of these combats, "who are longing to come down to Riseholme and spend a week with us, our expenses here will go up. You mustn't forget that. We shall be having a succession of visitors in October, and indeed till we go south. Then there's the meadow at the bottom of the garden: you've not bought that yet, and on that I really have set my heart. A spring garden there. A profusion of daffodils, and a paved walk. You promised me that. I described what it would be like to Tony, and he is wildly jealous. I'm sure I don't wonder. Your new telescope too. I insist on that telescope, and I'm sure I don't know where the money's to come from. My dear old piano also: it's on its very last legs, and won't last much longer, and I know you don't expect me to live, literally keep alive, without a good piano in the house."

Peppino was weakening. Even when he was perfectly well

and strong he was no match for her, and this rain of blows was visibly staggering him.

"I don't want to urge you, *caro*," she continued. "You know I never urge you to do what you don't feel is best."

"But you are urging me," said Peppino.

"Only to do what you feel is best. As for the memories of Aunt Amy in Brompton Square, you must not allow false sentiment to come in. You never saw her there since you were a boy, and if you brought down here her portrait, and the wool-work rug which you remember her putting over her knees, I should say, without urging you, mind, that that was ample . . . What a sweet morning! Come to the end of the garden and imagine what the meadow will look like with a paved walk and a blaze of daffodils . . . The Chippendale chairs, I think I should sell."

Lucia did not really want Aunt Amy's portrait either, for she was aware she had said a good deal from time to time about Aunt Amy's pearls, which were there, a little collar of very little seeds, faultlessly portrayed. But then Georgie had seen them on that night at the opera, and Lucia felt that she knew Riseholme very poorly if it was not perfectly acquainted by now with the nature and minuteness of Aunt Amy's pearls. The pearls had better be sold too, and also, she thought, her own portrait by Sigismund, for the Post-Cubists were not making much of a mark.

The determining factor in her mind, over this abandonment of her London career, to which in a few days, by incessant battering, she had got Peppino to consent, was Peppino himself. He could not be with her in London, and she could not leave him week after week (for nothing less than that, if you were to make any solid progress in London, was any good) alone in Riseholme. But a large factor, also, was the discovery of how little at present she counted for in Riseholme, and that could not be tolerated.

Riseholme had deposed her, Riseholme was not intending to be managed by her from Brompton Square. The throne was vacant, for poor Daisy, and for the matter of that poor Georgie were not the sort of people who could occupy thrones at all. She longed to queen it there again, and though she was aware that her utmost energies would be required, what were energies for except to get you what you wanted?

Just now she was nothing in Riseholme: they had been sorry for her because Peppino had been so ill, but as his steady convalescence proceeded, and she began to ring people up, and pop in, and make plans for them, she became aware that she mattered no more than Piggy and Goosie . . . There on the green, as she saw from the window of her hall, was Daisy, whirling her arms madly, and hitting a ball with a stick which had a steel blade at the end, and Georgie, she was rather horrified to observe, was there too, trying to do the same. Was Daisy reaping the reward of her persistence, and getting somebody interested in golf? And, good heavens, there were Piggy and Goosie also smacking away. Riseholme was clearly devoting itself to golf.

"I shall have to take to golf," thought Lucia. "What a bore! Such a foolish game."

At this moment a small white ball bounded over her yew-hedge, and tapped smartly against the front door.

"What an immense distance to have hit a ball," she thought. "I wonder which of them did that?"

It was soon clear, for Daisy came tripping through the garden after it, and Lucia, all smiles, went out to meet her.

"Good-morning, dear Daisy," she said. "Did you hit that ball that immense distance? How wonderful! No harm done at all. But what a splendid player you must be!"

"So sorry," panted Daisy, "but I thought I would have a hit

with a driver. Very wrong of me; I had no idea it would go so far or so crooked."

"A marvellous shot," said Lucia. "I remember how beautifully you putted. And this is all part of golf too? Do let me see you do it again."

Daisy could not reproduce that particular masterpiece, but she sent the ball high in the air, or skimming along the ground, and explained that one was a lofted shot, and the other a windcheater.

"I like the windcheater best," said Lucia. "Do let me see if I can do that."

She missed the ball once or twice, and then made a lovely windcheater, only this time Daisy called it a top. Daisy had three clubs, two of which she put down when she used the third, and then forgot about them, so that they had to go back for them . . . And up came Georgie, who was making windcheaters too.

"Good-morning, Lucia," he said. "It's so tarsome not to be able to hit the ball, but it's great fun if you do. Have you put down your clock-golf yet? There, didn't that go?"

Lucia had forgotten all about the clock-golf. It was somewhere in what was called the "game-cupboard," which contained bowls (as being Elizabethan) and some old tennis rackets, and a cricket bat Peppino had used at school.

"I'll put it down this afternoon," she said. "Come in after lunch, Georgie, and play a game with me. You too, Daisy."

"Thanks, but Georgie and I were going to have a real round on the links," said Daisy, in a rather superior manner.

"What fun!" said Lucia sycophantically. "I shall walk down and look at you. I think I must learn. I never saw anything so interesting as golf."

This was gratifying: Daisy was by no means reluctant to

show Lucia the way to do anything, but behind that, she was
not quite sure whether she liked this sudden interest in golf.
Now that practically the whole of Riseholme was taking to it,
and she herself could beat them all, having had a good start,
she was hoping that Lucia would despise it, and find herself left
quite alone on these lovely afternoons. Everybody went down to
the little nine-hole course now after lunch, the vicar (Mr. Rushbold) and his wife, the curate, Colonel Boucher, Georgie, Mrs.
Antrobus (who discarded her ear-trumpet for these athletics
and never could hear you call "Fore") and Piggy and Goosie, and
often Mrs. Boucher was wheeled down in her bath-chair, and
applauded the beautiful putts made on the last green. Indeed,
Daisy had started instruction classes in her garden, and Riseholme stood in rows and practised swinging and keeping its
eye on a particular blade of grass: golf in fact promised to make
Riseholme busy and happy again just as the establishment of the
Museum had done. Of course, if Lucia was wanting to learn (and
not learn too much) Daisy would be very happy to instruct her,
but at the back of Daisy's mind was a strange uneasiness. She
consoled herself, however, by supposing that Lucia would go
back to London again in the autumn, and by giving Georgie an
awful drubbing.

Lucia did not accompany them far on their round, but turned
back to the little shed of a clubhouse, where she gathered information about the club. It was quite new, having been started
only last spring by the tradesmen and townspeople of Riseholme
and the neighbouring little town of Blitton. She then entered
into pleasant conversation with the landlord of the Ambermere
Arms, who had just finished his round and said how pleased
they all were that the gentry had taken to golf.

"There's Mrs. Quantock, ma'am," said he. "She comes down

every afternoon and practises on the green every morning. Walking over the green now of a morning, is to take your life in your hand. Such keenness I never saw, and she'll never be able to hit the ball at all."

"Oh, but you mustn't discourage us, Mr. Stratton," said Lucia. "I'm going to devote myself to golf this autumn."

"You'll make a better hand at it, I'll be bound," said Mr. Stratton obsequiously. "They say Mrs. Quantock putts very nicely when she gets near the hole, but it takes her so many strokes to get there. She's lost the hole, in a manner of speaking, before she has a chance of winning it."

Lucia thought hard for a minute.

"I must see about joining at once," she said. "Who—who are the committee?"

"Well, we are going to reconstitute it next October," he said, "seeing that the ladies and gentlemen of Riseholme are joining. We should like to have one of you ladies as President, and one of the gentlemen on the committee."

Lucia made no hesitation about this.

"I should be delighted," she said, "if the present committee did me the honour to ask me. And how about Mr. Pillson? I would sound him if you like. But we must say nothing about it, till your committee meets."

That was beautifully settled then; Mr. Stratton knew how gratified the committee would be, and Lucia, long before Georgie and Daisy returned, had bought four clubs, and was having a lesson from a small wiry caddie.

Every morning while Daisy was swanking away on the green, teaching Georgie and Piggy and Goosie how to play, Lucia went surreptitiously down the hill and learned, while after tea she humbly took her place in Daisy's class and observed Daisy doing everything all wrong. She putted away at her clock-golf, she bought a beautiful book with pictures and studied them, and all the time she said nothing whatever about it. In her heart she utterly despised golf, but golf just now was the stunt, and she had to get hold of Riseholme again . . .

Georgie popped in one morning after she had come back from her lesson, and found her in the act of holing out from the very longest of the stations.

"My dear, what a beautiful putt!" he said. "I believe you're getting quite keen on it."

"Indeed I am," said she. "It's great fun. I go down sometimes to the links and knock the ball about. Be very kind to me this afternoon and come round with me."

Georgie readily promised to do so.

"Of course I will," he said, "and I should be delighted to give you a hint or two, if I can. I won two holes from Daisy yesterday."

"How clever of you, Georgie! Any news?"

Georgie said the sound that is spelt "tut."

"I quite forgot," he said. "I came round to tell you. Neither Mrs. Boucher nor Daisy nor I know *what* to do."

("That's the Museum Committee," thought Lucia.)

"What is it, Georgie?" she said. "See if poor Lucia can help."

"Well," said Georgie, "you know Pug?"

"That mangy little thing of Lady Ambermere's?" asked Lucia.

"Yes. Pug died, I don't know what of—"

"Cream, I should think," said Lucia. "And cake."

"Well, it may have been. Anyhow, Lady Ambermere had him stuffed, and while I was out this morning, she left him in a glass case at my house, as a present for the Museum. There he is lying on a blue cushion, with one ear cocked, and a great watery eye, and the end of his horrid tongue between his lips."

"No!" said Lucia.

"I assure you. And we don't know what to do. We can't put him in the Museum, can we? And we're afraid she'll take the mittens away if we don't. But, how can we refuse? She wrote me a note about 'her precious Pug.'"

Lucia remembered how they had refused an Elizabethan spit, though they had subsequently accepted it. But she was not going to remind Georgie of that. She wanted to get a better footing in the Museum than an Elizabethan spit had given her.

"What a dreadful thing!" she said. "And so you came to see if your poor old Lucia could help you."

"Well, we all wondered if you might be able to think of something," said he.

Lucia enjoyed this: the Museum was wanting her . . . She fixed Georgie with her eye.

"Perhaps I can get you out of your hole," she said. "What I imagine is, Georgie, that you want *me* to take that awful Pug back to her. I see what's happened. She had him stuffed, and then found he was too dreadful an object to keep, and so thought she'd be generous to the Museum. We—I should say 'you,' for I've got nothing to do with it—you don't care about the Museum being made a dump for all the rubbish that people don't want in their houses. Do you?"

"No, certainly not," said Georgie. (Did Lucia mean anything by that? Apparently she did.) She became brisk and voluble.

"Of course, if you asked my opinion," said Lucia, "I should say that there has been a little too much dumping done already. But that is not the point, is it? And it's not my business either. Anyhow, you don't want any more rubbish to be dumped. As for withdrawing the mittens—only lent, are they?—she won't do anything of the kind. She likes taking people over and showing them. Yes, Georgie, I'll help you: tell Mrs. Boucher and Daisy that I'll help you. I'll drive over this afternoon—no, I won't, for I'm going to have a lovely game of golf with you—I'll drive over tomorrow and take Pug back, with the committee's regrets that they are not taxidermists. Or, if you like, I'll do it on my own authority. How odd to be afraid of poor old Lady Ambermere! Never mind: I'm not. How all you people bully me into doing just what you want! I always was Riseholme's slave. Put Pug's case in a nice piece of brown paper, Georgie, for I don't want to see the horrid little abortion, and don't think anything more about it. Now let's have a good little putting match till lunchtime."

Georgie was nowhere in the good little putting match, and he was even less anywhere when it came to their game in the afternoon. Lucia made magnificent swipes from the tee, the least of which, if she happened to hit it, must have gone well over a hundred yards, whereas Daisy considered eighty yards from the tee a most respectable shot, and was positively pleased if she went into a bunker at a greater distance than that, and said the bunker ought to be put further off for the sake of the longer hit-ters. And when Lucia came near the green, she gave a smart little dig with her mashie, and, when this remarkable stroke came off, though she certainly hit the ground, the ball went beauti-fully, whereas when Daisy hit the ground the ball didn't go at all. All the time she was light-hearted and talkative, and even up to the moment of striking, would be saying "Now oo naughty ickle ball: Lucia's going to give you such a spank!" whereas when Daisy was playing, her opponent and the caddies had all to be dumb and turned to stone, while she drew a long breath and waved her club with a pendulum-like movement over the ball.

"But you're marvellous," said Georgie as, three down, he stood on the fourth tee, and watched Lucia's ball sail away over a sheep that looked quite small in the distance. "It's only three weeks or so since you began to play at all. You are clever! I believe you'd nearly beat Daisy."

"Georgie, I'm afraid you're a flatterer," said Lucia. "Now give your ball a good bang, and then there's something I want to talk to you about."

"Let's see; it's slow back, isn't it?" said Georgie. "Or is it quick back? I believe Daisy says sometimes one and sometimes the other."

Daisy and Piggy, starting before them, were playing in a parallel and opposite direction. Daisy had no luck with her first shot, and very little with her second. Lucia just got out of the way of her third and Daisy hurried by them.

"Such a slice!" she said. "How are you getting on, Lucia? How many have you played to get there?"

"One at present, dear," said Lucia. "But isn't it difficult?"

Daisy's face fell.

"One?" she said.

Lucia kissed her hand.

"That's all," she said. "And has Georgie told you that I'll manage about Pug for you?"

Daisy looked round severely. She had begun to address her ball and nobody must talk.

Lucia watched Daisy do it again, and rejoined Georgie who was in a "tarsome" place, and tufts of grass flew in the air.

"Georgie, I had a little talk with Mr. Stratton the other day," she said. "There's a new golf-committee being elected in October, and they would so like to have you on it. Now be good-natured and say you will."

Georgie had no intention of saying anything else.

"And they want poor little me to be President," said Lucia.

"So shall I send Mr. Stratton a line and say we will? It would be kind, Georgie. Oh, by the way, do come and dine tonight. Peppino—so much better, thanks—Peppino told me to ask you. He would enjoy it. Just one of our dear little evenings again."

Lucia, in fact, was bringing her batteries into action, and Georgie was the immediate though not the ultimate objective. He longed to be on the golf-committee, he was intensely grateful for the promised removal of Pug, and it was much more amusing to play golf with Lucia than to be dragooned round by Daisy who told him after every stroke what he ought to have done and could never do it herself. A game should not be a lecture.

Lucia thought it was time to confide in him about the abandoning of Brompton Square. Georgie would love knowing what nobody else knew yet. She waited till he had failed to hole a short putt, and gave him the subsequent one, which Daisy never did.

"I hope we shall have many of our little evenings, Georgie," she said. "We shall be here till Christmas. No, no more London for us, though it's a secret at present."

"What?" said Georgie.

"Wait a moment," said Lucia, teeing up for the last hole. "Now ickle ballie, fly away home. There! . . ." and ickle ballie flew at about right angles to home, but ever such a long way.

She walked with him to cover-point, where he had gone too.

"Peppino must never live in London again," she said. "All going to be sold, Georgie. The house and the furniture and the pearls. You must put up with your poor old Lucia at Riseholme again. Nobody knows yet but you, but now it is all settled. Am I sorry? Yes, Georgie, 'course I am. So many dear friends in London. But then there are dear friends in Riseholme. Oh, what a beautiful bang, Georgie. You nearly hit Daisy. Call 'Five!' Isn't that what they do?"

Lucia was feeling much surer of her ground. Georgie, bribed by a place on the golf-committee and by her admiration of his golf, and by her nobility with regard to Pug, was trotting back quick to her, and that was something. Next morning she had a hectic interview with Lady Ambermere . . .

Lady Ambermere was said to be not at home, though Lucia had seen her majestic face at the window of the pink saloon. So she asked for Miss Lyall, the downtrodden companion, and waited in the hall. Her chauffeur had deposited the large brown-paper parcel with Pug inside on the much-admired tessellated pavement.

"Oh, Miss Lyall," said Lucia. "So sad that dear Lady Amber-mere is out, for I wanted to convey the grateful thanks of the Museum Committee to her for her beautiful gift of poor Pug. But they feel they can't . . . Yes, that's Pug in the brown-paper parcel. So sweet. But will you, on Lady Ambermere's return, make it quite clear?"

Miss Lyall, looking like a mouse, considered what her duty was in this difficult situation. She felt that Lady Ambermere ought to know Lucia's mission and deal with it in person.

"I'll see if Lady Ambermere has come in, Mrs. Lucas," she said. "She may have come in. Just out in the garden, you know. Might like to know what you've brought. Oh dear me!"

Poor Miss Lyall scuttled away, and presently the door of the pink saloon was thrown open. After an impressive pause Lady Ambermere appeared, looking vexed. The purport of this astounding mission had evidently been conveyed to her.

"Mrs. Lucas, I believe," she said, just as if she wasn't sure.

Now Lucia after all her duchesses was not going to stand that. Lady Ambermere might have a Roman nose, but she hadn't any manners.

"Lady Ambermere, I presume," she retorted. So there they were.

Lady Ambermere glared at her in a way that should have turned her to stone. It made no impression.

"You have come, I believe, with a message from the committee of your little Museum at Riseholme, which I may have misunderstood."

Lucia knew she was doing what neither Mrs. Boucher nor Daisy in their most courageous moments would have dared to do. As for Georgie . . .

"No, Lady Ambermere," she said. "I don't think you've misunderstood it. A stuffed dog on a cushion. They felt that the Museum was not quite the place for it. I have brought it back to you with their thanks and regrets. So kind of you and—and so sorry of them. This is the parcel. That is all, I think."

It wasn't quite all . . .

"Are you aware, Mrs. Lucas," said Lady Ambermere, "that the mittens of the late Queen Charlotte are my loan to your little Museum?"

Lucia put her finger to her forehead.

"Mittens?" she said. "Yes, I believe there are some mittens. I think I have seen them. No doubt those are the ones. Yes?"

That was brilliant: it implied complete indifference on the part of the committee (to which Lucia felt sure she would presently belong) as to what Lady Ambermere might think fit to do about mittens.

"The committee shall hear from me," said Lady Ambermere, and walked majestically back to the pink saloon.

Lucia felt sorry for Miss Lyall: Miss Lyall would probably not have a very pleasant day, but she had no real apprehensions, so she explained to the committee, who were anxiously awaiting her return on the green, about the withdrawal of these worsted relics.

"Bluff, just bluff," she said. "And even if it wasn't— Surely, dear Daisy, it's better to have no mittens and no Pug than both. Pug—I caught a peep of him through a hole in the brown paper— Pug would have made your Museum a laughing-stock."

"Was she very dreadful?" asked Georgie.

Lucia gave a little silvery laugh.

"Yes, dear Georgie, quite dreadful. You would have collapsed if she had said to you 'Mr. Pillson, I believe.' Wouldn't you, Georgie? Don't pretend to be braver than you are."

"Well, I think we ought all to be much obliged to you, Mrs. Lucas," said Mrs. Boucher. "And I'm sure we are. I should never have stood up to her like that! And if she takes the mittens away, I should be much inclined to put another pair in the case, for the case belongs to us and not to her, with just the label 'These mittens did not belong to Queen Charlotte, and were not presented by Lady Ambermere.' That would serve her out."

Lucia laughed gaily again. "So glad to have been of use," she said. "And now, dear Daisy, will you be as kind to me as Georgie was yesterday and give me a little game of golf this afternoon? Not much fun for you, but so good for me."

Daisy had observed some of Lucia's powerful strokes yesterday, and she was rather dreading this invitation for fear it should not be, as Lucia said, much fun for her. Luckily, she and Georgie had already arranged to play today, and she had, in anticipation of the dread event, engaged Piggy, Goosie, Mrs. Antrobus and Colonel Boucher to play with her on all the remaining days of that week. She meant to practise like anything in the interval. And then, like a raven croaking disaster, the infamous Georgie let her down.

"I'd sooner not play this afternoon," he said. "I'd sooner just stroll out with you."

"Sure, Georgie?" said Lucia. "That will be nice then. Oh, how nervous I shall be."

Daisy made one final effort to avert her downfall, by offering, as they went out that afternoon, to give Lucia a stroke a hole. Lucia said she knew she could do it, but might they, just for fun, play level? And as the round proceeded, Lucia's kindness was almost intolerable. She could see, she said, that Daisy was completely off her game, when Daisy wasn't in the least off her game: she said, "Oh, that was bad luck!" when Daisy missed short putts: she begged her to pick her ball out of bushes and not count it . . . At half-past four Riseholme knew that Daisy had halved four holes and lost the other five. Her short reign as Queen of Golf had come to an end.

∞

The Museum Committee met after tea at Mrs. Boucher's (Daisy did not hold her golfing-class in the garden that day) and tact, Georgie felt, seemed to indicate that Lucia's name should not be suggested as a new member of the committee so swiftly on the heels of Daisy's disaster. Mrs. Boucher, privately consulted, concurred, though with some rather stinging remarks as to Daisy's having deceived them all about her golf, and the business of the meeting was chiefly concerned with the proposed closing down of the Museum for the winter. The tourist season was over, no charabancs came anymore with visitors, and for three days not a soul had passed the turnstile.

"So where's the use," asked Mrs. Boucher, "of paying a boy to let people into the Museum when nobody wants to be let in? I call it throwing money away. Far better close it till the spring, and have no more expense, except to pay him a shilling a week to open the windows and air it, say on Tuesday and Friday, or Wednesday and Saturday."

"I should suggest Monday and Thursday," said Daisy, very decisively. If she couldn't have it all her own way on the links, she could make herself felt on committees.

"Very well, Monday and Thursday," said Mrs. Boucher. "And then there's another thing. It's getting so damp in there, that if you wanted a cold bath, you might undress and stand there. The water's pouring off the walls. A couple of oil-stoves, I suggest, every day except when it's being aired. The boy will attend to them, and make it half a crown instead of a shilling. I'm going to Blitton tomorrow, and if that's your wish I'll order them. No: I'll bring them back with me, and I'll have them lit tomorrow morning. But unless you want to have nothing to show next spring but mildew, don't let us delay about it. A crop of mildew won't be sufficient attraction to visitors, and there'll be nothing else."

Georgie rapped the table.

"And I vote we take the manuscript of *Lucrezia* out, and that one of us keeps it till we open again," he said.

"I should be happy to keep it," said Daisy.

Georgie wanted it himself, but it was better not to thwart Daisy today. Besides, he was in a hurry, as Lucia had asked him to bring round his planchette and see if Abfou would not like a little attention. Nobody had talked to Abfou for weeks.

"Very well," he said, "and if that's all—"

"I'm not sure I shouldn't feel happier if it was at the bank," said Mrs. Boucher. "Supposing it was stolen."

Georgie magnanimously took Daisy's side: he knew how Daisy was feeling. Mrs. Boucher was outvoted, and he got up.

"If that's all then, I'll be off," he said.

Daisy had a sort of conviction that he was going to do something with Lucia, perhaps have a lesson at golf.

"Come in presently?" she said.

"I can't, I'm afraid," he said. "I'm busy till dinner."

And of course, on her way home, she saw him hurrying across to The Hurst with his planchette.

Chapter Eleven

LUCIA MADE NO ALLUSION WHATEVER to her athletic triumph in the afternoon when Georgie appeared. That was not her way: she just triumphed, and left other people to talk about it. But her principles did not prevent her speaking about golf in the abstract.

"We must get more businesslike when you and I are on the committee, Georgie," she said. "We must have competitions and handicaps, and I will give a small silver cup, the President's Cup, to be competed for. There's no organisation at present, you see: great fun, but no organisation. We shall have to put our heads together over that. And foursomes: I have been reading about foursomes, when two people on one side hit the ball in turn. Peppino, I'm sure, would give a little cup for foursomes, the Lucas Cup . . . And you've brought the planchette? You must teach me how to use it. What a good employment for winter evenings, Georgie. And we must have some bridge tournaments. Wet afternoons, you know, and then tea, and then some more bridge. But we will talk about all that presently, only I warn you I shall expect you to get up all sorts of diversions for Peppino."

Lucia gave a little sigh.

"Peppino adored London," she said, "and we must cheer him up, Georgie, and not let him feel dull. You must think of lots of little diversions: little pleasant bustling things for these long evenings: music, and bridge, and some planchette. Then I shall get up some Shakespeare readings, selections from plays, with a small part for Peppino and another for poor Daisy. I foresee already that I shall have a very busy autumn. But you must all be very kind and come here for our little entertainments. Madness for Peppino to go out after sunset. Now let us get to our planchette. How I do chatter, Georgie!"

Georgie explained the technique of planchette, how important it was not to push, but on the other hand not to resist its independent motions. As he spoke Lucia glanced over the directions for planchette which he had brought with him.

"We may not get anything," he said. "Abfou was very disappointing sometimes. We can go on talking: indeed, it is better not to attend to what it does."

"I see," said Lucia, "let us go on talking then. How late you are, Georgie. I expected you half an hour ago. Oh, you said you might be detained by a Museum Committee meeting."

"Yes, we settled to shut the Museum up for the winter," he said. "Just an oil-stove or two to keep it dry. I wanted—and so did Mrs. Boucher, I know—to ask you—"

He stopped, for planchette had already begun to throb in a very extraordinary manner.

"I believe something is going to happen," he said.

"No! How interesting!" said Lucia. "What do we do?"

"Nothing," said Georgie. "Just let it do what it likes. Let's concentrate: that means thinking of nothing at all."

Georgie of course had noticed and inwardly applauded the lofty reticence which Lucia had shown about Daisy's disaster this afternoon. But he had the strongest suspicion of her wish to weedj, and he fully expected that if Abfou "came through" and talked anything but Arabic, he would express his scorn of Daisy's golf. There would be scathing remarks, corresponding to "snob" and those rude things about Lucia's shingling of her hair, and then he would feel that Lucia had pushed. She might say she hadn't, just as Daisy said she hadn't, but it would be very unconvincing if Abfou talked about golf. He hoped it wouldn't happen, for the very appositeness of Abfou's remarks before had strangely shaken his faith in Abfou. He had been willing to believe that it was Daisy's subconscious self that had inspired Abfou—or at any rate he tried to believe it—but it had been impossible to dissociate the complete Daisy from these violent criticisms.

Planchette began to move.

"Probably it's Arabic," said Georgie. "You never quite know. Empty your mind of everything, Lucia."

She did not answer, and he looked up at her. She had that faraway expression which he associated with renderings of the "Moonlight Sonata." Then her eyes closed.

Planchette was moving quietly and steadily along. When it came near the edge of the paper, it ran back and began again, and Georgie felt quite sure he wasn't pushing: he only wanted it not to waste its energy on the tablecloth. Once he felt almost certain that it traced out the word "drive," but one couldn't be sure. And was that "committee"? His heart rather sank: it would be such a pity if Abfou was only talking about the golf club which no doubt was filling Lucia's subconscious as well as conscious mind . . . Then suddenly he got rather alarmed, for Lucia's head was sunk forward, and she breathed with strange rapidity.

"Lucia!" he said sharply.

Lucia lifted her head, and planchette stopped.

"Dear me, I felt quite dreamy," she said. "Let us go on talking, Georgie. Lady Ambermere this morning: I wish you could have seen her."

"Planchette has been writing," said Georgie.

"No!" said Lucia. "Has it? May we look?"

Georgie lifted the machine. There was no Arabic at all, nor was it Abfou's writing, which in quaint little ways resembled Daisy's when he wrote quickly.

"Vittoria," he read. "I am Vittoria."

"Georgie, how silly," said Lucia, "or is it the Queen?"

"Let's see what she says," said Georgie. "I am Vittoria. I come to Riseholme. For proof, there is a dog and a Vecchia—"

"That's Italian," said Lucia excitedly. "You see, Vittoria is Italian. Vecchia means—let me see; yes, of course, it means 'old woman.' 'A dog, and an old woman who is angry.' Oh Georgie, you did that! You were thinking about Pug and Lady Ambermere."

"I swear I wasn't," said Georgie. "It never entered my head. Let's see what else. 'And Vittoria comes to tell you of fire and water, of fire and water. The strong elements that burn and soak. Fire and water and moonlight.'"

"Oh Georgie, what gibberish," said Lucia. "It's as silly as Abfou. What does it mean? Moonlight! I suppose you would say I pushed and was thinking of the 'Moonlight Sonata.'"

That base thought had occurred to Georgie's mind, but where did fire and water come in? Suddenly a stupendous interpretation struck him.

"It's most extraordinary!" he said. "We had a Museum Committee meeting just now, and Mrs. Boucher said the place was streaming wet. We settled to get some oil-stoves to keep it dry. There's fire and water for you!" Georgie had mentioned this fact about the Museum Committee, but so casually that he had quite forgotten he had done so. Lucia did not remind him of it.

"Well, I do call that remarkable!" she said. "But I dare say it's only a coincidence."

"I don't think so at all," said Georgie. "I think it's most curious, for I wasn't thinking about that a bit. What else does it say? 'Vittoria bids you keep love and loyalty alive in your hearts. Vittoria has suffered, and bids you be kind to the suffering.' "

"That's curious!" said Lucia. "That might apply to Peppino, mightn't it? . . . Oh Georgie, why, of course, that was in both of our minds: we had just been talking about it. I don't say you pushed intentionally, and you mustn't say I did, but that might easily have come from us."

"I think it's very strange," said Georgie. "And then, what came over you, Lucia? You looked only half-conscious. I believe it was what the planchette directions call light hypnosis."

"No!" said Lucia. "Light hypnosis, that means half-asleep, doesn't it? I did feel drowsy."

"It's a condition of trance," said Georgie. "Let's try again."

Lucia seemed reluctant.

"I think I won't, Georgie," she said. "It is so strange. I'm not sure that I like it."

"It can't hurt you if you approach it in the right spirit," said Georgie, quoting from the directions.

"Not again this evening, Georgie," said she. "Tomorrow perhaps. It is interesting, it is curious, and somehow I don't think Vittoria would hurt us. She seems kind. There's something noble, indeed, about her message."

"Much nobler than Abfou," said Georgie, "and much more powerful. Why, she came through at once, without pages of scribbles first! I never felt quite certain that Abfou's scribbles were Arabic."

Lucia gave a little indulgent smile.

"There didn't seem much evidence for it from what you told me," she said. "All you could be certain of was that they weren't English."

Georgie left his planchette with Lucia, in case she would

consent to sit again tomorrow, and hurried back, it is unnecessary to state, not to his own house, but to Daisy's. Vittoria was worth two of Abfou, he thought . . . that communication about fire and water, that kindness to the suffering, and, hardly less, the keeping of loyalty alive. That made him feel rather guilty, for certainly loyalty to Lucia had flickered somewhat in consequence of her behaviour during the summer.

He gave a short account of these remarkable proceedings (omitting the loyalty) to Daisy, who took a superior and scornful attitude.

"Vittoria, indeed!" she said, "and Vecchia. Isn't that Lucia all over, lugging in easy Italian like that? And Pug and the angry old lady. Glorifying herself, I call it. Why, that wasn't even subconscious: her mind was full of it."

"But how about the fire and water?" asked Georgie. "It does apply to the damp in the Museum and the oil-stoves."

Daisy knew that her position as priestess of Abfou was tottering. It was true that she had not celebrated the mysteries of late, for Riseholme (and she) had got rather tired of Abfou, but it was gall and wormwood to think that Lucia should steal (steal was the word) her invention and bring it out under the patronage of Vittoria as something quite new.

"A pure fluke," said Daisy. "If she'd written mutton and music, you would have found some interpretation for it. Such far-fetched nonsense!"

Georgie was getting rather heated. He remembered how when Abfou had written "death" it was held to apply to the mulberry tree which Daisy believed she had killed by amateur root-pruning, so if it came to talking about far-fetched nonsense, he could have something to say. Besides, the mulberry tree hadn't died at all, so that if Abfou meant that, he was wrong. But there was no good in indulging in recriminations with Daisy, not only for the sake of peace and quietness, but because Georgie could guess very well all she was feeling.

"But she didn't write about mutton and music," he observed, "so we needn't discuss that. Then there was moonlight. I don't know what that means."

"I should call it moonshine," said Daisy brightly.

"Well, it wrote moonlight," said Georgie. "Of course there's the 'Moonlight Sonata' which might have been in Lucia's mind, but it's all curious. And I believe Lucia was in a condition of light hypnosis—"

"Light fiddlesticks!" said Daisy . . . (Why hadn't she thought of going into a condition of light hypnosis when she was Abfou-ing? So much more impressive!) "We can all shut our eyes and droop our heads."

"Well, I think it was light hypnosis," said Georgie firmly. "It was very curious to see. I hope she'll consent to sit again. She didn't much want to."

Daisy profoundly hoped that Lucia would not consent to sit again, for she felt Abfouism slipping out of her fingers. In any case, she would instantly resuscitate Abfou, for Vittoria shouldn't have it all her own way. She got up.

"Georgie, why shouldn't we see if Abfou has anything to say about it?" she asked. "After all, Abfou told us to make a museum, and that hasn't turned out so badly. Abfou was practical; what he suggested led to something."

Though the notion that Daisy had thought of the Museum and pushed flitted through Georgie's mind, there was something in what she said, for certainly Abfou had written museum (if it wasn't "mouse") and there was the Museum which had turned out so profitably for the committee.

"We might try," he said.

Daisy instantly got out her planchette, which sadly wanted dusting, and it began to move almost as soon as they laid their hands on it: Abfou was in a rather inartistic hurry. And it really wasn't very wise of Daisy to close her eyes and snort: it was indeed light fiddlesticks to do that. It was a sheer unconvincing plagiarism from Lucia, and his distrust of Daisy and of Abfou immeasurably deepened. Furiously the pencil scribbled, going off the paper occasionally and writing on the table till Georgie could insert the paper under it: it was evident that Abfou was very indignant about something, and there was no need to enquire what that was. For some time the writing seemed to feel to Georgie like Arabic, but presently the pencil slowed down, and he thought some English was coming through. Finally Abfou gave a great scrawl, as he usually did when the message was complete, and Daisy looked dreamily up. "Anything?" she said.

"It's been writing hard," said Georgie.

They examined the script. It began, as he had expected, with quantities of Arabic, and then (as he had expected) dropped into English, which was quite legible.

"Beware of charlatans," wrote Abfou, "beware of southern charlatans. All spirits are not true and faithful like Abfou, who instituted your Museum. False guides deceive. A warning from Abfou."

"Well, if that isn't convincing, I don't know what is," said Daisy.

Georgie thought it convincing too.

The din of battle began to rise. It was known that very evening, for Colonel and Mrs. Boucher dined with Georgie, that he and Lucia (for Georgie did not give all the credit to Lucia) had received that remarkable message from Vittoria about fire and water and the dog and the angry old woman, and it was agreed that Abfou cut a very poor figure, and had a jealous temper. Why hadn't Abfou done something better than merely warn them against southern charlatans?

"If it comes to that," said Mrs. Boucher, "Egypt is in the south, and charlatans can come from Egypt as much as from Italy. Fire and water! Very remarkable. There's the water there now, plenty of it, and the fire will be there tomorrow. I must get out my planchette again, for I put it away. I got sick of writing nothing but Arabic, even if it was Arabic. I call it very strange. And not a word about golf from Vittoria. I consider that's most important. If Lucia had been pushing, she'd have written about her golf with Daisy. Abfou and Vittoria! I wonder which will win."

That summed it up pretty well, for it was felt that Abfou and Vittoria could not both direct the affairs of Riseholme from the other world, unless they acted jointly; and Abfou's remarks about the southern charlatan and false spirits put the idea of a coalition out of the question. All the time, firm in the consciousness of Riseholme, but never under any circumstances spoken of, was the feeling that Abfou and Vittoria (as well as standing for themselves) were pseudonyms: they stood also for Daisy and Lucia. And how much finer and bigger, how much more gifted of the two in every way was Vittoria-Lucia. Lucia quickly got over her disinclination to weedj, and messages, not very definite, but of high moral significance came from this exalted spirit. There was never a word about golf, and there was never a word about Abfou, nor any ravings concerning inferior and untrustworthy spirits. Vittoria was clearly above all that (indeed, she was probably in some sphere miles away above Abfou), whereas Abfou's pages (Daisy sat with her planchette morning after morning and obtained sheets of the most voluble English) were blistered with denunciations of low and earth-born intelligences and dark with awful warnings for those who trusted them.

Riseholme, in fact, had never been at a higher pitch of excited activity; even the arrival of the *Evening Gazette* during those weeks when Hermione had recorded so much about Mrs. Philip Lucas hadn't roused such emotions as the reception of a new message from Abfou or Vittoria. And it was Lucia again who was the cause of it all: no one for months had cared what Abfou said, till Lucia became the recipient of Vittoria's messages. She had invested planchette with the interest that attached to all she did. On the other hand it was felt that Abfou (though certainly he lowered himself by these pointed recriminations) had done something. Abfou-Daisy had invented the Museum, whereas Vittoria-Lucia, apart from giving utterance to high moral sentiments, had invented nothing (high moral sentiments couldn't count as an invention). To be sure there was the remarkable piece about Pug and angry Lady Ambermere, but the facts of that were already known to Lucia, and as for the communication about fire, water and moonlight, though there were new oil-stoves in the damp Museum, that was not as remarkable as inventing the Museum, and moonlight unless it meant the Sonata was quite unexplained. Over this cavilling objection, rather timidly put forward by Georgie, who longed for some striking vindication of Vittoria, Lucia was superb.

"Yes, Georgie, I can't tell you what it means," she said. "I am only the humble scribe. It is quite mysterious to me. For myself, I am content to be Vittoria's medium. I feel it a high honour. Perhaps some day it will be explained, and we shall see."

They saw.

Meanwhile, since no one can live entirely on messages from the unseen, other interests were not neglected. There were bridge parties at The Hurst, there was much music, there was a reading of *Hamlet* at which Lucia doubled several of the principal parts and Daisy declined to be the Ghost. The new committee of the golf club was formed, and at the first meeting Lucia announced her gift of the President's Cup, and Peppino's of the Lucas Cup for foursomes. Notice of these was duly put up in the clubhouse, and Daisy's face was of such a grimness when she read them that something very savage from Abfou might be confidently expected. She went out for a round soon after with Colonel Boucher, who wore a scared and worried look when he returned. Daisy had got into a bunker, and had simply hewed her ball to pieces . . . Peppino's convalescence proceeded well; Lucia laid down the law a good deal at auction bridge, and the oil-stoves at the Museum were satisfactory. They were certainly making headway against the large patches of damp on the walls, and Daisy, one evening, recollecting that she had not made a personal inspection of them, went in just before dinner to look at them. The boy in charge of them had put them out, for they only burned during the day, and certainly they were doing their work well. Daisy felt she would not be able to bring forward any objection to them at the next committee meeting, as she had rather hoped to do. In order to hurry on the drying process, she filled them both up and lit them so that they should burn all night. She spilt a little paraffin, but that would soon evaporate. Georgie was tripping back across the green from a visit to Mrs. Boucher, and they walked homeward together.

∞

Georgie had dined at home that night, and working at a crossword puzzle was amazed to see how late it was. He had pored long over a map of South America, trying to find a river of seven letters with "pt" in the middle, but he determined to do no more at it tonight.

"The tarsome thing," he said, "if I could get that, I'm sure it would give me thirty-one across."

He strolled to the window and pushed aside the blind. It was a moonlight night with a high wind and a few scudding clouds. Just as he was about to let the blind drop again he saw a reddish light in the sky, immediately above his tall yew-hedge, and wondered what it was. His curiosity combined with the fact that a breath of air was always pleasant before going to bed, led him to open the front door and look out. He gave a wild gasp of dismay and horror.

The windows of the Museum were vividly illuminated by a red glow. Smoke poured out of one which apparently was broken, and across the smoke shot tongues of flame. He bounded to his telephone, and with great presence of mind rang up the fire-station at Blitton. "Riseholme," he called. "House on fire: send engine at once." He ran into his garden again, and seeing a light still in the drawing-room next door (Daisy was getting some sulphurous expressions from Abfou) tapped at the pane. "The Museum's burning," he cried, and set off across the green to the scene of the fire.

By this time others had seen it too, and were coming out of their houses, looking like little black ants on a red tablecloth. The fire had evidently caught strong hold, and now a piece of the roof fell in, and the flames roared upwards. In the building itself there was no apparatus for extinguishing fire, nor, if there had been, could anyone have reached it. A hose was fetched from the Ambermere Arms, but that was not long enough, and there was nothing to be done except wait for the arrival of the fire-engine from Blitton. Luckily the Museum stood well apart from other houses, and there seemed little danger of the fire spreading.

Soon the bell of the approaching engine was heard, but

already it was clear that nothing could be saved. The rest of the roof crashed in, a wall tottered and fell. The longer hose was adjusted, and the stream of water directed through the windows, now here, now there, where the fire was fiercest, and clouds of steam mingled with the smoke. But all efforts to save anything were absolutely vain: all that could be done, as the fire burned itself out, was to quench the glowing embers of the conflagration . . . As he watched, three words suddenly repeated themselves in Georgie's mind. "Fire, water, moonlight," he said aloud in an awed tone . . . Victorious Vittoria!

The committee, of course, met next morning, and Robert as financial adviser was specially asked to attend. Georgie arrived at Mrs. Boucher's house where the meeting was held before Daisy and Robert got there, and Mrs. Boucher could hardly greet him, so excited was she.

"I call it most remarkable," she said. "Dog and angry old woman never convinced me, but this is beyond anything. Fire, water, moonlight! It's prophecy, nothing less than prophecy. I shall believe anything Vittoria says, for the future. As for Abfou—well—"

She tactfully broke off at Daisy's and Robert's entrance.

"Good-morning," she said. "And good-morning, Mr. Robert. This is a disaster, indeed. All Mr. Georgie's sketches, and the walking-sticks, and the mittens and the spit. Nothing left at all."

Robert seemed amazingly cheerful.

"I don't see it as such a disaster," he said. "Lucky I had those insurances executed. We get two thousand pounds from the company, of which five hundred goes to Colonel Boucher for his barn—I mean the Museum."

"Well, that's something," said Mrs. Boucher. "And the rest? I never could understand about insurances. They've always been a sealed book to me."

"Well, the rest belongs to those who put the money up to equip the Museum," he said. "In proportion, of course, to the sums they advanced. Altogether four hundred and fifty pounds was put up; you and Daisy and Georgie each put in fifty. The rest, well, I advanced the rest."

There were some rapid and silent calculations made. It seemed rather hard that Robert should get such a lot. Business always seemed to favour the rich. But Robert didn't seem the least ashamed of that. He treated it as a perfect matter of course.

"The—the treasures in the Museum almost all belonged to the committee," he went on. "They were given to the Museum, which was the property of the committee. Quite simple. If it had been a loan collection now—well, we shouldn't be finding quite such a bright lining to our cloud. I'll manage the insurance business for you, and pay you pleasant little cheques all round. The company, no doubt, will ask a few questions as to the origin of the fire."

"Ah, there's a mystery for you," said Mrs. Boucher. "The oil-stoves were always put out in the evening, after burning all day, and how a fire broke out in the middle of the night beats me."

Daisy's mouth twitched. Then she pulled herself together.

"Most mysterious," she said, and looked carelessly out of the window to where the debris of the Museum was still steaming. Simultaneously, Georgie gave a little start, and instantly changed the subject, rapping on the table.

"There's one thing we've forgotten," said he. "It wasn't entirely our property. Queen Charlotte's mittens were only on loan."

The faces of the committee fell slightly.

"A shilling or two," said Mrs. Boucher hopefully. "I'm only glad we didn't have Pug as well. Lucia got us out of that!"

Instantly the words of Vittoria about the dog and the angry old woman, and fire and water and moonlight occurred to everybody. Most of all they occurred to Daisy, and there was a slight pause, which might have become awkward if it had continued. It was broken by the entry of Mrs. Boucher's parlour-maid, who carried a letter in a large square envelope with a deep mourning border, and a huge coronet on the flap.

"Addressed to the Museum Committee, ma'am," she said.

Mrs. Boucher opened it, and her face flushed.

"Well, she's lost no time," she said. "Lady Ambermere. I think I had better read it."

"Please," said everybody in rather strained voices.

Mrs. Boucher read:

"Ladies and Gentlemen of the Committee of Riseholme Museum

Your little Museum, I hear, has been totally destroyed with all its contents by fire. I have to remind you therefore that the mittens of her late Majesty Queen Charlotte were there on loan, as lent by me. No equivalent in money can really make up for the loss of so irreplaceable a relic, but I should be glad to know, as soon as possible, what compensation you propose to offer me.

The figure that has been suggested to me is £50, and an early cheque would oblige.

Faithfully yours,
CORNELIA AMBERMERE."

A dead silence succeeded, broken by Mrs. Boucher as soon as her indignation allowed her to speak.

"I would sooner," she said, "go to law about it, and appeal if it went against us, and carry it up to the House of Lords, than pay fifty pounds for those rubbishy things. Why, the whole contents of the Museum weren't worth more than—well, leave it at that."

The figure at which the contents of the Museum had been insured floated into everybody's mind, and it was more dignified to "leave it at that," and not let the imagination play over the probable end of Mrs. Boucher's sentence.

The meeting entirely concurred, but nobody, not even Robert, knew what to do next.

"I propose offering her ten pounds," said Georgie at last, "and I call that handsome."

"Five," said Daisy, like an auction reversed.

Robert rubbed the top of his head, as was his custom in perplexity.

"Difficult to know what to do," he said. "I don't know of any standard of valuation for the old clothes of deceased queens."

"Two," said Mrs. Boucher, continuing the auction, "and that's a fancy price. What would Pug have been, I wonder, if we're asked fifty pounds for two old mittens. A pound each, I say, and that's a monstrous price. And if you want to know who suggested to Lady Ambermere to ask fifty, I can tell you, and her name was Cornelia Ambermere."

This proposal of Lady Ambermere's rather damped the secret exaltation of the committee, though it stirred a pleasant feeling of rage. Fifty pounds was a paltry sum compared to what they would receive from the insurance company, but the sense of the attempt to impose on them caused laudable resentment. They broke up, to consider separately what was to be done, and to poke about the ashes of the Museum, all feeling very rich. The rest of Riseholme were there, of course, also poking about, Piggy and Goosie skipping over smouldering heaps of ash, and Mrs. Antrobus, and the vicar and the curate, and Mr. Stratton. Only Lucia was absent, and Georgie, after satisfying himself that nothing whatever remained of his sketches, popped in to The Hurst.

Lucia was in the music-room reading the paper. She had heard, of course, about the total destruction of the Museum, that ridiculous invention of Daisy and Abfou, but not a shadow of exultation betrayed itself.

"My dear, too sad about the Museum," she said. "All your beautiful things. Poor Daisy, too, her idea."

Georgie explained about the silver lining to the cloud.

"But what's so marvellous," he said, "is Vittoria. Fire, water, moonlight. I never heard of anything so extraordinary, and I thought it only meant the damp on the walls, and the new oil-stoves. It was prophetical, Lucia, and Mrs. Boucher thinks so too."

Lucia still showed no elation. Oddly enough, she had thought it meant damp and oil-stoves, too, for she did remember what Georgie had forgotten that he had told her just before the epiphany of Vittoria. But now this stupendous fulfilment of Vittoria's communication of which she had never dreamed, had happened. As for Abfou, it was a mere waste of time to give another thought to poor dear malicious Abfou. She sighed.

"Yes, Georgie, it was strange," she said. "That was our first sitting, wasn't it? When I got so drowsy and felt so queer. Very strange indeed: convincing, I think. But whether I shall go on sitting now, I hardly know."

"Oh, but you must," said Georgie. "After all the rubbish—"

Lucia held up a finger.

"Now, Georgie, don't be unkind," she said. "Let us say, 'Poor Daisy,' and leave it there. That's all. Any other news?"

Georgie retailed the monstrous demand of Lady Ambermere.

"And, as Robert says, it's so hard to know what to offer her," he concluded.

Lucia gave the gayest of laughs.

"Georgie, what would poor Riseholme do without me?" she said. "I seem to be made to pull you all out of difficulties. That mismanaged golf club, Pug, and now there's this. Well, shall I be kind and help you once more?"

She turned over the leaves of her paper.

"Ah, that's it," she said. "Listen, Georgie. Sale at Pemberton's auction-rooms in Knightsbridge yesterday. Various items. Autograph of Crippen the murderer. Dear me, what horrid minds people have! Mother-of-pearl brooch belonging to the wife of the poet Mr. Robert Montgomery; a pair of razors belonging to Carlyle, all odds and ends of trumpery, you see . . . Ah yes, here it is. Pair of riding gaiters, in good condition, belonging to His Majesty King George IV. That seems a sort of guide, doesn't it, to the value of Queen Charlotte's mittens. And what do you think they fetched? A terrific sum, Georgie; fifty pounds is nowhere near it. They fetched ten shillings and sixpence."

"No!" said Georgie. "And Lady Ambermere asked fifty pounds!"

Lucia laughed again.

"Well, Georgie, I suppose I must be good-natured," she said. "I'll draft a little letter for your committee to Lady Ambermere. How you all bully me and work me to death! Why, only yesterday I said to Peppino that those months we spent in London seemed a holiday compared to what I have to do here. Dear old Riseholme! I'm sure I'm very glad to help it out of its little holes."

Georgie gave a gasp of admiration. It was but a month or two ago that all Riseholme rejoiced when Abfou called her a snob, and now here they all were again (with the exception of Daisy) going to her for help and guidance in all those employments and excitements in which Riseholme revelled. Golf competitions and bridge tournaments, and duets, and real séances, and deliverance from Lady Ambermere, and above all, the excitement supplied by her personality.

"You're too wonderful," he said, "indeed, I don't know what we should do without you."

Lucia got up.

"Well, I'll scribble a little letter for you," she said, "bringing in the price of George IV's gaiters in good condition. What shall we—I mean what shall you offer? I think you must be generous, Georgie, and not calculate the exact difference between the value of a pair of gaiters in good condition belonging to a king, and that of a pair of moth-eaten mittens belonging to a queen consort. Offer her the same; in fact, I think I should enclose a treasury note for ten shillings and six stamps. That will be more than generous, it will be munificent."

Lucia sat down at her writing-table, and after a few minutes' thought, scribbled a couple of sides of notepaper in that neat handwriting that bore no resemblance to Vittoria's. She read them through, and approved.

"I think that will settle it," she said. "If there is any further bother with the Vecchia, let me know. There's one more thing, Georgie, and then let us have a little music. How do you think the fire broke out?"

Georgie felt her penetrating eye was on him. She had not asked that question quite idly. He tried to answer it quite idly.

"It's most mysterious," he said. "The oil-stoves are always

put out quite early in the evening, and lit again next morning. The boy says he put them out as usual."

Lucia's eye was still on him.

"Georgie, how do you think the fire broke out?" she repeated.

This time Georgie felt thoroughly uncomfortable. Had Lucia the power of divination? . . .

"I don't know," he said. "Have you any idea about it?"

"Yes," said Lucia. "And so have you. I'll tell you my idea if you like. I saw our poor misguided Daisy coming out of the Museum close on seven o'clock last night."

"So did I," said Georgie in a whisper.

"Well, the oil-stoves must have been put out long before that," said Lucia. "Mustn't they?"

"Yes," said Georgie.

"Then how was it that there was a light coming out of the Museum windows? Not much of a light, but a little light; I saw it. What do you make of that?"

"I don't know," said Georgie.

Lucia held up a censuring finger.

"Georgie, you must be very dull this morning," she said. "What I make of it is that our poor Daisy lit the oil-stoves again. And then probably in her fumbling way, she spilt some oil. Something of the sort, anyhow. In fact, I'm afraid Daisy burned down the Museum."

There was a terrible pause.

"What are we to do?" said Georgie.

Lucia laughed.

"Do?" she said. "Nothing, except never know anything about it. We know quite well that poor Daisy didn't do it on purpose. She hasn't got the pluck or the invention to be an incendiary. It was only her muddling, meddling ways."

"But the insurance money?" said Georgie.

"What about it? The fire was an accident, whether Daisy confessed what she had done or not. Poor Daisy! We must be nice to Daisy, Georgie. Her golf, her Abfou! Such disappointments. I think I will ask her to be my partner in the foursome for the Lucas Cup. And perhaps if there was another place on the golf-committee, we might propose her for it."

Lucia sighed, smiling wistfully.

"A pity she is not a little wiser," she said.

Lucia sat looking wistful for a moment. Then to Georgie's immense surprise she burst out into peals of laughter.

"My dear, what is the matter?" said Georgie.

Lucia was helpless for a little, but she gasped and recovered and wiped her eyes.

"Georgie, you *are* dull this morning!" she said. "Don't you see? Poor Daisy's meddling has made the reputation of Vittoria and crumpled up Abfou. Fire, water, moonlight: Vittoria's prophecy. Vittoria owes it all to poor dear Daisy!"

Georgie's laughter set Lucia off again, and Peppino coming in found both at it.

"Good-morning, Georgie," he said. "Terrible about the Museum. A sad loss. What are you laughing at?"

"Nothing, *caro,*" said Lucia. "Just a little joke of Daisy's. Not worth repeating, but it amused Georgie and me. Come, Georgie, half an hour's good practice of celestial Mozartino. We have been lazy lately."

MAPP AND LUCIA

Chapter One

THOUGH IT WAS NEARLY A year since her husband's death, Emmeline Lucas (universally known to her friends as Lucia) still wore the deepest and most uncompromising mourning. Black certainly suited her very well, but that had nothing to do with this continued use of it, whatever anybody said. Peppino and she had been the most devoted couple for over twenty-five years, and her grief at his loss was heart-felt: she missed him constantly and keenly. But months ago now, she, with her very vital and active personality, had felt a most natural craving to immerse herself again in all those thrilling interests which made life in this Elizabethan village of Riseholme so exciting a business, and she had not yet been able to make up her mind to take the plunge she longed for. Though she had not made a luxury out of the tokens of grief, she had perhaps made, ever so slightly, a stunt of them.

For instance. There was that bookshop on the green, Ye Signe of Ye Daffodil, under the imprint of which Peppino had published his severely limited edition of *Fugitive Lyrics* and *Pensieri Persi*. A full six months after his death Lucia had been walking past it with Georgie Pillson, and had seen in the window a book she would have liked to purchase. But next to it, on the shelf, was the thin volume of Peppino's *Pensieri Persi*, and, frankly, it had been rather stuntish of her to falter on the threshold and, with eyes that were doing their best to swim, to say to Georgie: "I can't quite face going in, Georgie. Weak of me, I know, but there it is. Will you please just pop in, *caro,* and ask them to send me *Beethoven's Days of Boyhood?* I will stroll on."

So Georgie had pressed her hand and done this errand for her, and of course he had repeated this pathetic little incident to others. Tasteful embroideries had been tacked on to it, and it was soon known all over Riseholme that poor Lucia had gone into Ye Signe of Ye Daffodil to buy the book about Beethoven's boyhood, and had been so sadly affected by the sight of Peppino's poems in their rough brown linen cover with dark-green tape to tie them up with (although she constantly saw the same volume in her own house), that she had quite broken down. Some said that sal volatile had been administered.

Similarly, she had never been able to bring herself to have a game of golf, or to resume her Dante-readings, and having thus established the impression that her life had been completely smashed up it had been hard to decide that on Tuesday or Wednesday next she would begin to glue it together again. In consequence she had remained in as many pieces as before. Like a sensible woman she was very careful of her physical health, and since this stunt of mourning made it impossible for her to play golf or take brisk walks, she sent for a very illuminating little book, called *An Ideal System of Callisthenics for Those No Longer Young,* and in a secluded glade of her garden she exposed as much of herself as was proper to the invigorating action of the sun, when there was any, and had long bouts of skipping, and kicked, and jerked, and swayed her trunk, gracefully and vigorously, in accordance with the instructions laid down. The effect was most satisfactory, and at the very, very back of her mind she conceived it possible that some day she might conduct callisthenic classes for those ladies of Riseholme who were no longer young.

Then there was the greater matter of the Elizabethan fête to be held in August next, when Riseholme would be swarming with tourists. The idea of it had been entirely Lucia's, and there had been several meetings of the fête-committee (of which, naturally, she was President) before Peppino's death. She had planned the great scene in it: this was to be Queen Elizabeth's visit to the *Golden Hind*, when, on the completion of Francis Drake's circumnavigation of the world, Her Majesty went to dine with him on board his ship at Deptford and knighted him. The *Golden Hind* was to be moored in the pond on the village green; or, more accurately, a platform on piles was to be built there, in the shape of a ship's deck, with masts and rudder and cannons and bulwarks, and banners and ancients, particularly ancients. The pond would be an admirable stage, for rows of benches would be put up all round it, and everybody would see beautifully. The Queen's procession with trumpeters and men-at-arms and ladies of the Court was planned to start from The Hurst, which was Lucia's house, and make its glittering and melodious way across the green to Deptford to the sound of madrigals and mediaeval marches. Lucia would impersonate the Queen, Peppino following her as Raleigh, and Georgie would be Francis Drake. But at an early stage of these incubations Peppino had died, and Lucia had involved herself in this inextricable widowhood. Since then the reins of government had fallen into Daisy Quantock's podgy little hands, and she, in this as in all other matters, had come to consider herself quite the Queen of Riseholme, until Lucia could get a move on again and teach her better.

One morning in June, some seven weeks before the date fixed for the fête, Mrs. Quantock telephoned from her house a hundred yards away to say that she particularly wanted to see Lucia, if she might pop over for a little talk. Lucia had heard nothing lately about the preparations for the fête, for the last time that it had

been mentioned in her presence, she had gulped and sat with her
hand over her eyes for a moment overcome with the memory of
how gaily she had planned it. But she knew that the preparations
for it must by this time be well in hand, and now she instantly
guessed that it was on this subject that Daisy wanted to see her.
She had premonitions of that kind sometimes, and she was sure
that this was one of them. Probably Daisy wanted to address a
moving appeal to her that, for the sake of Riseholme generally,
she should make this fête the occasion of her emerging from her
hermetic widowhood. The idea recommended itself to Lucia, for
before the date fixed for it, she would have been a widow for over
a year, and she reflected that her dear Peppino would never have
wished her to make this permanent suttee of herself: also there
was the prestige of Riseholme to be considered. Besides, she was
really itching to get back into the saddle again, and depose Daisy
from her awkward, clumsy seat there, and this would be an admirable opportunity. So, as was usual now with her, she first sighed
into the telephone, said rather faintly that she would be delighted
to see dear Daisy, and then sighed again. Daisy, very stupidly,
hoped she had not got a cough, and was reassured on that point.

Lucia gave a few moments' thought as to whether she would be
found at the piano, playing the funeral march from Beethoven's
Sonata in A flat which she now knew by heart, or be sitting out
in Perdita's garden, reading Peppino's poems. She decided on
the latter, and putting on a shady straw hat with a crêpe bow on
it, and taking a copy of the poems from the shelf, hurried out
into Perdita's garden. She also carried with her a copy of today's
Times, which she had not yet read.

Perdita's garden requires a few words of explanation. It was a
charming little square plot in front of the timbered façade of The
Hurst, surrounded by yew-hedges and intersected with paths of
crazy pavement, carefully smothered in stone-crop, which led to

the Elizabethan sundial from Wardour Street in the centre. It was gay in spring with those flowers (and no others) on which Perdita doted. There were "violets dim," and primroses and daffodils, which came before the swallow dared and took the winds (usually of April) with beauty. But now in June the swallow had dared long ago, and when spring and the daffodils were over, Lucia always allowed Perdita's garden a wider, though still strictly Shakespearian scope. There was eglantine (Penzance briar) in full flower now, and honeysuckle and gillyflowers and plenty of pansies for thoughts, and yards of rue (more than usual this year), and so Perdita's garden was gay all the summer.

Here then, this morning, Lucia seated herself by the sundial, all in black, on a stone bench on which was carved the motto "Come thou north wind, and blow thou south, that my garden spices may flow forth." Sitting there with Peppino's poems and *The Times* she obscured about one-third of this text, and fat little Daisy would obscure the rest . . . It was rather annoying that the tapes which tied the covers of Peppino's poems had got into a hard knot, which she was quite unable to unravel, for she had meant that Daisy should come up, unheard by her, in her absorption, and find her reading Peppino's lyric called "Loneliness." But she could not untie the tapes, and as soon as she heard Daisy's footsteps she became lost in reverie with the book lying shut on her lap, and the famous faraway look in her eyes.

It was a very hot morning. Daisy, like many middle-aged women who enjoyed perfect health, was always practising some medical regime of a hygienic nature, and just now she was a devoted slave to the eliminative processes of the body. The pores of the skin were the most important of these agencies, and, after her drill of physical jerks by the open window of her bedroom, she had trotted in all this heat across the green to keep up the elimination. She mopped and panted for a little.

"Made quite a new woman of me," she said. "You should try it, dear Lucia. But so good of you to see me, and I'll come to the point at once. The Elizabethan fête, you know. You see it won't be till August. Can't we persuade you, as they say, to come amongst us again? We all want you: such a fillip you'd give it."

Lucia made no doubt that this request implied the hope that she might be induced to take the part of Queen Elizabeth, and under the spell of the exuberant sunshine that poured in upon Perdita's garden, she felt the thrill and the pulse of life bound in her veins. The fête would be an admirable occasion for entering the arena of activities again, and, as Daisy had hinted (delicately for Daisy), more than a year of her widowhood would have elapsed by August. It was self-sacrificing, too, of Daisy to have suggested this herself, for she knew that according to present arrangements Daisy was to take the part of the Virgin Queen, and Georgie had told her weeks ago (when the subject of the fête had been last alluded to) that she was already busy pricking her fingers by sewing a ruff to go round her fat little neck, and that she had bought a most sumptuous string of Woolworth pearls. Perhaps dear Daisy had realised what a very ridiculous figure she would present as Queen, and was anxious for the sake of the fête to retire from so laughable a role. But, however that might be, it was nice of her to volunteer abdication.

Lucia felt that it was only proper that Daisy should press her a little. She was being asked to sacrifice her personal feelings which so recoiled from publicity, and for the sake of Riseholme to rescue the fête from being a farce. She was most eager to do so, and a very little pressing would be sufficient. So she sighed again, she stroked the cover of Peppino's poems, but she spoke quite briskly.

"Dear Daisy," she said, "I don't think I could face it. I cannot imagine myself coming out of my house in silks and jewels to take my place in the procession without my Peppino. He was to have been Raleigh, you remember, and to have walked immediately behind me. The welcome, the shouting, the rejoicing, the madrigals, the Morris-dances and me with my poor desolate heart! But perhaps I ought to make an effort. My dear Peppino, I know, would have wished me to. You think so, too, and I have always respected the soundness of your judgement."

A slight change came over Daisy's round red face. Lucia was getting on rather too fast and too far.

"My dear, none of us ever thought of asking you to be Queen Elizabeth," she said. "We are not so unsympathetic, for of course that would be far too great a strain on you. You must not think of it. All that I was going to suggest was that you might take the part of Drake's wife. She only comes forward just for a moment, and makes her curtsey to me—I mean to the Queen—and then walks backwards again into the chorus of ladies-in-waiting and halberdiers and things."

Lucia's beady eyes dwelt for a moment on Daisy's rather anxious face with a glance of singular disdain. What a fool poor Daisy was to think that she, Lucia, could possibly consent to take any subordinate part in tableaux or processions or anything else at Riseholme where she had been Queen so long! She had decided in her own mind that with a very little judicious pressing she would take the part of the Queen, and thus make her superb entry into Riseholme life again, but all the pressure in the world would not induce her to impersonate anyone else, unless she could double it with the Queen. Was there ever anything so tactless as Daisy's tact? . . .

She gave a wintry smile, and stroked the cover of Peppino's poems again.

"Sweet of you to suggest it, dear," she said, "but indeed it would be quite too much for me. I was wrong to entertain the idea even for a moment. Naturally I shall take the greatest, the *very* greatest interest in it all, and I am sure you will understand if I do not even feel equal to coming to it, and read about it instead in the *Worcestershire Herald*."

She paused. Perhaps it would be more in keeping with her empty heart to say nothing more about the fête. On the other hand, she felt a devouring curiosity to know how they were getting on. She sighed.

"I must begin to interest myself in things again," she said. "So tell me about it all, Daisy, if you would like to."

Daisy was much relieved to know that even the part of Drake's wife was too much for Lucia. She was safe now from any risk of having the far more arduous part of the Queen snatched from her.

"All going splendidly," she said. "Revels on the green to open with, and madrigals and Morris-dances. Then comes the scene on the *Golden Hind* which was entirely your idea. We've only elaborated it a little. There will be a fire on the poop of the ship, or is it the prow?"

"It depends, dear, which end of the ship you mean," said Lucia.

"The behind part, the stern. Poop, is it? Well, there will be a fire on the poop for cooking. Quite safe, they say, if the logs are laid on a sheet of iron. Over the fire we shall have an Elizabethan spit, and roast a sheep on it."

"I wouldn't," said Lucia, feeling the glamour of these schemes glowing in her. "Half of it will be cinders and the rest blood."

"No, dear," said Daisy. "It will really be roasted first at the Ambermere Arms, and then just hung over the fire on the *Golden Hind*."

"Oh, yes: just to get a little kippered in the smoke," said Lucia.

"Not to matter. Of course I shan't really eat any, because I never touch meat of any sort now: I shall only pretend to. But there'll be the scene of cooking going on for the Queen's dinner on the deck of the *Golden Hind*, just to fill up, while the Queen's procession is forming. Oh, I wonder if you would let us start the procession from your house rather than mine. The route would be so much more in the open: everyone will see it better. I would come across to dress, if you would let me, half an hour before."

Lucia of course knew perfectly well that Daisy was to be the Queen, but she wanted to make her say so.

"Certainly start from here," said Lucia. "I am only too happy to help. And dress here yourself. Let me see: what are you going to be?"

"They've all insisted that I should be Queen Elizabeth," said Daisy hurriedly. "Where had we got to? Oh yes: as the procession is forming, the cooking will be going on. Songs of course, a chorus of cooks. Then the procession will cross the green to the *Golden Hind*, then dinner, and then I knight Drake. Such a lovely sword. Then Elizabethan games, running, jumping, wrestling and so on. We thought of baiting a bear, one out of some menagerie that could be trusted not to get angry, but we've given that up. If it didn't get angry, it wouldn't be baited, and if it did get angry it would be awful."

"Very prudent," said Lucia.

"Then I steal away into the Ambermere Arms which is quite close, and change into a riding-dress. There'll be a white palfrey at the door, the one that draws the milk-cart. Oh, I forgot. While I'm dressing, before the palfrey comes round, a rider gallops in from Plymouth on a horse covered with soapsuds to say that the Spanish Armada has been sighted. I think we must have a megaphone for that, or no one will hear. So I come out, and mount my palfrey, and make my speech to my troops at Tilbury. A large board, you know, with Tilbury written up on it like a station. That's quite in the Shakespearian style. I shall have to learn it all by heart, and just have Raleigh standing by the palfrey with a copy of my speech to prompt me if I forget."

The old familiar glamour glowed brighter and brighter to Lucia as Daisy spoke. She wondered if she had made a mistake in not accepting the ludicrous part of Drake's wife, just in order to get a footing in these affairs again and attend committees, and, gradually ousting Daisy from her supremacy, take the part of the Queen herself. She felt that she must think it all over, and settle whether, in so advanced a stage of the proceedings, it could be done. At present, till she had made up her mind, it was wiser, in order to rouse no suspicions, to pretend that these things were all very remote. She would take a faint though kindly interest in them, as if some elderly person was watching children at play, and smiling pensively at their pretty gambols. But as for watching the fête when the date arrived, that was unthinkable. She would either be Queen Elizabeth herself, or not be at Riseholme at all. That was that.

"Well, you have got your work cut out for you, dear Daisy," she said, giving a surreptitious tug at the knotted tape of Peppino's poems. "What fun you will have, and, dear me, how far away it all seems!"

Daisy wrenched her mind away from the thought of the fête.

"It won't always, dear," she said, making a sympathetic little dab at Lucia's wrist. "Your joy in life will revive again. I see you've got Peppino's poems there. Won't you read me one?"

Lucia responded to this gesture with another dab.

"Do you remember the last one he wrote?" she said. "He

called it 'Loneliness.' I was away in London at the time. Beginning:

> 'The spavined storm-clouds limp down the ruinous sky,
>> While I sit alone.
> Thick through the acid air the dumb leaves fly . . .'

But I won't read it you now. Another time."

Daisy gave one more sympathetic poke at her wrist, and rose to go.

"Must be off," she said. "Won't you come round and dine quietly tonight?"

"I can't, many thanks. Georgie is dining with me. Any news in Riseholme this morning?"

Daisy reflected for a moment.

"Oh, yes," she said. "Mrs. Antrobus's got a wonderful new apparatus. Not an ear-trumpet at all. She just bites on a small leather pad, and hears everything perfectly. Then she takes it out of her mouth and answers you, and puts it back again to listen."

"No!" said Lucia excitedly. "All wet?"

"Quite dry. Just between her teeth. No wetter anyhow than a pen you put in your mouth, I assure you."

Daisy hurried away to do some more exercises and drink pints and pints of hot water before lunch. She felt that she had emerged safely from a situation which might easily have become menacing, for without question Lucia, in spite of her sighs and her wistful stroking of the covers of Peppino's poems, and her great crêpe bow, was beginning to show signs of her old animation. She had given Daisy a glance or two from that beady eye which had the qualities of a gimlet about it, she had shown eager interest in such topics as the roasting of the sheep and

Mrs. Antrobus's gadget, which a few weeks ago would not have aroused the slightest response from her stricken mind, and it was lucky, Daisy thought, that Lucia had given her the definite assurance that even the part of Drake's wife in the fête would be too much for her. For goodness only knew, when once Lucia settled to be on the mend, how swift her recuperation might be, or what mental horsepower in the way of schemings and domination she might not develop after this fallow period of quiescence. There was a new atmosphere about her today: she was like some spring morning when, though winds might still be chilly and the sun still of tepid and watery beams, the air was pregnant with the imminent birth of new life. But evidently she meant to take no hand in the fête, which at present completely filled Daisy's horizon. "She may do what she likes afterwards," thought Daisy, breaking into a trot, "but I will be Queen Elizabeth."

Her house, with its mulberry tree in front and its garden at the back, stood next to Georgie Pillson's on the edge of the green, and as she passed through it and out on to the lawn behind, she heard from the other side of the paling that tap-tap of croquet-mallet and ball which now almost without cessation punctuated the hours of any fine morning. Georgie had developed a craze for solitary croquet: he spent half the day practising all by himself, to the great neglect of his watercolour painting and his piano-playing. He seemed indeed, apart from croquet, to be losing his zest for life; he took none of his old interest in the thrilling topics of Riseholme. He had not been a bit excited at Daisy's description of Mrs. Antrobus's new apparatus, and the prospect of impersonating Francis Drake at the forthcoming fête aroused only the most tepid enthusiasm in him. A book of Elizabethan costumes, full of sumptuous coloured plates, had roused him for a while from his lethargy, and he had chosen a white

satin tunic with puffed sleeves slashed with crimson, and a cloak
of rose-coloured silk, on the reproduction of which his peerless
parlour-maid Foljambe was at work, but he didn't seem to have
any keenness about him. Of course he had had some rather cruel
blows of Fate to contend against lately: Miss Olga Bracely the
prima-donna to whom he had been so devoted had left Riseholme a month ago for a year's operatic tour in the United States
and Australia, and that was a desolate bereavement for him,
while Lucia's determination not to do any of all these things
which she had once enjoyed so much had deprived him of all
the duets they used to play together. Moreover, it was believed
in Riseholme (though only whispered at present) that Foljambe,
that paragon of parlour-maids, in whom the smoothness and
comfort of his domestic life was centred, was walking out with
Cadman, Lucia's chauffeur. It might not mean anything, but if
it did, if Foljambe and he intended to get married and Foljambe
left Georgie, and if Georgie had got wind of this, then indeed
there would be good cause for that lack of zest, that air of gloom
and apprehension which was now so often noticeable in him. All
these causes, the blows Fate had already rained on him, and the
anxiety concerning this possible catastrophe in the future, probably contributed to the eclipsed condition of his energies.

Daisy sat down on a garden-bench, and began to do a little
deep-breathing, which was a relic of the days when she had
studied Yoga. It was important to concentrate (otherwise the
deep-breathing did no good at all), or rather to attain a complete blankness of mind and exclude from it all mundane interests which were Maya, or illusion. But this morning she found it
difficult: regiments of topics grew up like mushrooms. Now she
congratulated herself on having made certain that Lucia was not
intending to butt into the fête, now she began to have doubts—

these were disconcerting mushrooms—as to whether that was so certain, for Lucia was much brisker today than she had been since Peppino's death, and if that continued, her reawakened interest in life would surely seek for some outlet. Then the thought of her own speech to her troops at Tilbury began to leak into her mind: would she ever get it so thoroughly by heart that she could feel sure that no attack of nervousness or movement on the part of her palfrey would put it out of her head? Above all there was that disturbing tap-tap going on from Georgie's garden, and however much she tried to attain blankness of mind, she found herself listening for the next tap . . . It was no use and she got up.

"Georgie, are you there?" she called out.

"Yes," came his voice, trembling with excitement. "Wait a minute. I've gone through nine hoops and— Oh, how tarsome, I missed quite an easy one. What is it? I rather wish you hadn't called me just then."

Georgie was tall, and he could look over the paling. Daisy pulled her chair up to it, and mounted on it, so that they could converse with level heads.

"So sorry, Georgie," she said, "I didn't know you were making such a break. Fancy! Nine! I wanted to tell you I've been to see Lucia."

"Is that all? I knew that because I saw you," said Georgie. "I was polishing my bibelots in the drawing-room. And you sat in Perdita's garden."

"And there's a change," continued Daisy, who had kept her mouth open, in order to go on again as soon as Georgie stopped. "She's better. Distinctly. More interested, and not so faint and die-away. Sarcastic about the roast sheep for instance."

"What? Did she talk about the fête again?" asked Georgie. "That is an improvement."

"That was what I went to talk about. I asked her if she wouldn't make an effort to be Drake's wife. But she said it would be too great a strain."

"My dear, you didn't ask her to be Drake's wife?" said Georgie incredulously. "You might as well have asked her to be a confused noise within. What can you have been thinking of?"

"Anyhow, she said she couldn't be anything at all," said Daisy. "I have her word for that. But if she is recovering, and I'm sure she is, her head will be full of plans again. I'm not quite happy about it."

"What you mean is that you're afraid she may want to be the Queen," observed Georgie acutely.

"I won't give it up," said Daisy very firmly, not troubling to confirm so obvious an interpretation. "I've had all the trouble of it, and very nearly learnt the speech to the troops, and made my ruff and bought a rope of pearls. It wouldn't be fair, Georgie. So don't encourage her, will you? I know you're dining with her tonight."

"No, I won't encourage her," said he. "But you know what Lucia is, when she's in working order. If she wants a thing, she gets it somehow. It happens. That's all you can say about it."

"Well, this one shan't happen," said Daisy, dismounting from her basket chair which was beginning to sag. "It would be too mean. And I wish you would come across now and let us practise that scene where I knight you. We must get it very slick."

"Not this morning," said Georgie. "I know my bit: I've only got to kneel down. You can practise on the end of a sofa. Besides, if Lucia is really waking up, I shall take some duets across this evening, and I must have a go at some of them. I've not touched my piano for weeks. And my shoulder's sore where you knighted me so hard the other day. Quite a bruise."

Daisy suddenly remembered something more.

"And Lucia repeated me several lines out of one of Peppino's last poems," she said. "She couldn't possibly have done that a month ago without breaking down. And I believe she would have read one to me when I asked her to, but I'm pretty sure she couldn't undo one of those tapes that the book is tied up with. A hard knot. She was picking at it . . ."

"Oh, she must be better," said he. "Ever so much."

So Georgie went in to practise some of the old duets in case Lucia felt equal to evoking the memories of happier days at the piano, and Daisy hit the end of her sofa some half-dozen times with her umbrella bidding it rise Sir Francis Drake. She still wondered if Lucia had some foul scheme in her head, but though there had ticked by some minutes, directly after their talk in Perdita's garden, which might have proved exceedingly dangerous to her own chance of being the Queen, these, by the time that she was knighting the sofa, had passed. For Lucia, still meditating whether she should not lay plots for ousting Daisy, had, in default of getting that knotted tape undone, turned to her unread *Times*, and scanned its columns with a rather absent eye. There was no news that could interest anybody, and her glance wandered up and down the lists of situations vacant and wanted, of the sailings of steamers, and finally of houses to be let for summer months. There was a picture of one with a plain pleasant Queen Anne front looking on to a cobbled street. It was highly attractive, and below it she read that Miss Mapp sought a tenant for her house in Tilling, called Mallards, for the months of August and September. Seven bedrooms, four sitting-rooms, h. & c., and an old-world garden. At that precise psychological moment Daisy's prospects of being Queen Elizabeth became vastly rosier, for this house to let started an idea in Lucia's mind which instantly took precedence of other schemes. She must talk to Georgie about it this evening: till then it should simmer. Surely also the name of Miss Mapp aroused faint echoes of memory in her mind: she seemed to remember a large woman with a wide smile who had stayed at the Ambermere Arms a few years ago, and had been very agreeable but slightly superior. Georgie would probably remember her . . . But the sun had become extremely powerful, and Lucia picked up her *Times* and her book of poems and went indoors to the cool lattice-paned parlour where her piano stood. By it was a bookcase with volumes of bound-up music, and she drew from it one which contained the duets over which Georgie and she used to be so gay and so industrious. These were Mozart quartets arranged for four hands, delicious, rippling airs: it was months since she had touched them, or since the music-room had resounded to anything but the most sombre and pensive strains. Now she opened the book and put it on the music rest. "*Uno, due, tre,*" she said to herself and began practising the treble part which was the more amusing to play.

∞

Georgie saw the difference in her at once when he arrived for dinner that evening. She was sitting outside in Perdita's garden and for the first time hailed him as of old in brilliant Italian.

"*Buona sera, caro,*" she said. "*Come sta?*"

"*Molto bene,*" he answered, "and what a *caldo* day. I've brought a little music across with me in case you felt inclined. Mozartino."

"What a good idea! We will have *un po' di musica* afterwards, but I've got *tanto, tanto* to talk to you about. Come in: dinner will be ready. Any news?"

"Let me think," he said. "No, I don't think there's much. I've

got rather a bruised shoulder where Daisy knighted me the other
day—"

"Dear Daisy!" said Lucia. "A little heavy-handed sometimes,
don't you find? Not a light touch. She was in here this morning
talking about the fête. She urged me to take part in it. What part
do you think she suggested, Georgie? You'll never guess."

"I never should have, if she hadn't told me," he said. "The
most ludicrous thing I ever heard."

Lucia sighed.

"I'm afraid not much more ludicrous than her being Queen
Elizabeth," she said. "Daisy on a palfrey addressing her troops!
Georgie dear, think of it! It sounds like that rather vulgar game
called 'Consequences.' Daisy, I am afraid, has got tipsy with
excitement at the thought of being a queen. She is running
amok, and she will make a deplorable exhibition of herself, and
Riseholme will become the laughing-stock of all those American tourists who come here in August to see our lovely Elizabethan village. The village will be all right, but what of Elizabeth?
Tacete un momento, Georgie. *Le domestiche*."

Georgie's Italian was rusty after so much disuse, but he managed to translate this sentence to himself, and unerringly inferred
that Lucia did not want to pursue the subject while Grosvenor,
the parlour-maid, and her colleague were in the room.

"*Sicuro*," he said, and made haste to help himself to his fish.
The *domestiche* thereupon left the room again, to be summoned
back by the stroke of a silver bell in the shape of a pomander
which nestled among pepper- and mustard-pots beside Lucia.
Almost before the door had closed on their exit, Lucia began to
speak again.

"Of course after poor Daisy's suggestion I shall take no part
myself in this fête," she said; "and even if she besought me on
her knees to play Queen Elizabeth, I could not dream of doing

so. She cannot deprive me of what I may call a proper pride, and since she has thought good to offer me the role of Drake's wife, who, she hastened to explain, only came on for one moment and curtseyed to her, and then retired into the ranks of men-at-arms and ladies-in-waiting again, my sense of dignity, of which I have still some small fragments left, would naturally prevent me from taking any part in the performance, even at the end of a barge-pole. But I am sorry for Daisy, since she knows her own deficien-cies so little, and I shall mourn for Riseholme if the poor thing makes such a mess of the whole affair as she most indubitably will if she is left to organise it herself. That's all."

It appeared, however, that there was a little more, for Lucia quickly finished her fish, and continued at once.

"So after what she said to me this morning, I cannot myself offer to help her, but if you like to do so, Georgie, you can tell her—not from me, mind, but from your own impression—that you think I should be perfectly willing to coach her and make the best I can of her as the embodiment of great Queen Bess. Something might be done with her. She is short, but so was the Queen. She has rather bad teeth, but that doesn't matter, for the Queen had the same. Again she is not quite a lady, but the Queen also had a marked strain of vulgarity and bourgeoisie. There was a coarse fibre in the Tudors, as I have always maintained. All this, dear Georgie, is to the good. If dear Daisy will only not try to look tall, and if she will smile a good deal, and behave naturally, these are advantages, real advantages. But in spite of them Daisy will merely make herself and Riseholme silly if she does not manage to get hold of some semblance of dignity and queenship. Little gestures, little turnings of the head, little gra-ciousnesses; all that acting means. I thought it out in those dear old days when we began to plan it, and, as I say, I shall be happy to give poor Daisy all the hints I can, if she will come and ask me to do so. But mind, Georgie, the suggestion must not come from me. You are at liberty to say that you think I possibly might help her, but nothing more than that. *Capite?*"

This Italian word, not understood of the people, came rather late, for already Lucia had struck the bell, as, unconsciously, she was emphasising her generous proposal, and Grosvenor and her satellite had been in the room quite a long time. Concealment from *le domestiche* was therefore no longer possible. In fact both Georgie and Lucia had forgotten about the *domestiche* altogether.

"That's most kind of you, Lucia," said Georgie. "But you know what Daisy is. As obstinate as—"

"As a palfrey," interrupted Lucia.

"Yes, quite. Certainly I'll tell her what you say, or rather suggest what you might say if she asked you to coach her, but I don't believe it will be any use. The whole fête has become an awful bore. There are six weeks yet before it's held, and she wants to practise knighting me every day, and has processions up and down her garden, and she gets all the tradesmen in the place to walk before her as halberdiers and sea-captains, when they ought to be attending to their businesses and chopping meat and milking cows. Everyone's sick of it. I wish you would take it over, and be Queen yourself. Oh, I forgot, I promised Daisy I wouldn't encourage you. Dear me, how awful!"

Lucia laughed, positively laughed. This was an enormous improvement on the pensive smiles.

"Not awful at all, *Georgino mio*," she said. "I can well imagine poor Daisy's feverish fear that I should try to save her from being ridiculous. She loves being ridiculous, dear thing; it's a complex with her—that wonderful new book of Freud's which I must read—and subconsciously she pines to be ridiculous on as large a scale as possible. But as for my taking it over, that's quite out of the question. To begin with, I don't suppose I shall be here. Twelfth of August isn't it? Grouse-shooting opens in Scotland and bear-baiting at Riseholme."

"No, that was given up," said Georgie. "I opposed it through-out on the committee. I said that even if we could get a bear at all, it wouldn't be baited if it didn't get angry—"

Lucia interrupted.

"And that if it did get angry it would be awful," she put in.

"Yes. How did you know I said that?" asked Georgie. "Rather neat, wasn't it?"

"Very neat indeed, *caro*," said she. "I knew you said it because Daisy told me she had said it herself."

"What a cheat!" said Georgie indignantly.

Lucia looked at him wistfully.

"Ah, you mustn't think hardly of poor dear Daisy," she said. "Cheat is too strong a word. Just a little envious, perhaps, of bright clever things that other people say, not being very quick herself."

"Anyhow, I shall tell her that I know she has bagged my joke," said he.

"My dear, not worth while. You'll make quantities of others. All so trivial, Georgie, not worth noticing. Beneath you."

Lucia leaned forward with her elbows on the table, quite in the old braced way, instead of drooping.

"But we've got far more important things to talk about than Daisy's little pilferings," she said. "Where shall I begin?"

"From the beginning," said Georgie greedily. He had not felt so keen about the affairs of daily life since Lucia had buried her-self in her bereavement.

"Well, the real beginning was this morning," she said, "when I saw something in *The Times*."

"More than I did," said Georgie. "Was it about Riseholme or

the fête? Daisy said she was going to write a letter to *The Times* about it."

"I must have missed that," said Lucia, "unless by any chance they didn't put it in. No, not about the fête, nor about Riseholme. Very much not about Riseholme. Georgie, do you remember a woman who stayed at the Ambermere Arms one summer called Miss Mapp?"

Georgie concentrated.

"I remember the name, because she was rather globular, like a map of the world," he said. "Oh, wait a moment: something's coming back to me. Large, with a great smile. Teeth."

"Yes, that's the one," cried Lucia. "There's telepathy going on, Georgie. We're suggesting to each other . . . Rather like a hyena, a handsome hyena. Not hungry now but might be."

"Yes. And talked about a place called Tilling, where she had a Queen Anne house. We rather despised her for that. Oh, yes, and she came to a garden-party of mine. And I know when it was too. It was that summer when you invented saying '*Au reservoir*' instead of '*Au revoir.*' We all said it for about a week and then got tired of it. Miss Mapp came here just about then, because she picked it up at my garden-party. She stopped quite to the end, eating quantities of redcurrant fool, and saying that she had inherited a recipe from her grandmother which she would send me. She did, too, and my cook said it was rubbish. Yes: it was the *au reservoir* year, because she said *au reservoir* to everyone as they left, and told me she would take it back to Tilling. That's the one. Why?"

"Georgie, your memory's marvellous," said Lucia. "Now about the advertisement I saw in *The Times*. Miss Mapp is letting her Queen Anne house called Mallards, h. & c. and old-world garden, for August and September. I want you to drive over with me tomorrow and see it. I think that very likely, if it's at all what I hope, I shall take it."

"No!" cried Georgie. "Why of course I'll drive there with you tomorrow. What fun! But it will be too awful if you go away for two months. What shall I do? First there's Olga not coming back for a year, and now you're thinking of going away, and there'll be nothing left for me except my croquet and being Drake."

Lucia gave him one of those glances behind which lurked so much purpose, which no doubt would be disclosed at the proper time. The bees were astir once more in the hive, and presently they would stream out for swarmings or stingings or honey-harvesting . . . It was delightful to see her looking like that again.

"Georgie, I want change," she said, "and though I'm much touched at the idea of your missing me, I think I must have it. I want to get roused up again and shaken and made to tick. Change of air, change of scene, change of people. I don't suppose anyone alive has been more immersed than I in the spacious days of Elizabeth, or more devoted to Shakespearian tradition and environment—perhaps I ought to except Sir Sidney Lee, isn't it?—than I, but I want for the present anyhow to get away from it, especially when poor Daisy is intending to make this deplorable public parody of all that I have held sacred so long."

Lucia swallowed three or four strawberries as if they had been pills and took a gulp of water.

"I don't think I could bear to be here for all the rehearsals," she said; "to look out from the rue and honeysuckle of my sweet garden and see her on her palfrey addressing her lieges of Rise-holme, and making them walk in procession in front of her. It did occur to me this morning that I might intervene, take the part of the Queen myself, and make a pageant such as I had planned in those happy days, which would have done honour to the great age and credit to Riseholme, but it would spoil the dream of Daisy's life, and one must be kind. I wash my hands of it all, though of course I shall allow her to dress here, and the procession to start from my house. She wanted that, and she shall have it, but of course she must state on the programmes that the procession starts from Mrs. Philip Lucas's house. It would be too much that the visitors, if there are any, should think that my beautiful Hurst belongs to Daisy. And, as I said, I shall be happy to coach her, and see if I can do anything with her. But I won't be here for the fête, and I must be somewhere and that's why I'm thinking of Tilling."

They had moved into the music-room where the bust of Shakespeare stood among its vases of flowers, and the picture of Lucia by Tancred Sigismund, looking like a chessboard with some arms and legs and eyes sticking out of it, hung on the wall. There were Georgie's sketches there, and the piano was open, and *Beethoven's Days of Boyhood* was lying on the table with the paperknife stuck between its leaves, and there was animation about the room once more.

Lucia seated herself in the chair that might so easily have come from Anne Hathaway's cottage, though there was no particular reason for supposing that it did.

"Georgie, I am beginning to feel alive again," she said. "Do you remember what wonderful Alfred says in *Maud*? 'My life hath crept so long on a broken wing.' That's what my life has been doing, but now I'm not going to creep any more. And just for the time, as I say, I'm 'off' the age of Elizabeth, partly poor Daisy's fault, no doubt. But there were other ages, Georgie, the age of Pericles, for instance. Fancy sitting at Socrates's feet or Plato's, and hearing them talk while the sun set over Salamis or Pentelicus. I must rub up my Greek, Georgie. I used to know a little Greek at one time, and if I ever manage any tableaux again, we must have the death of Agamemnon. And then there's the age of Anne. What a wonderful time, Pope and Addison! So civilised, so cultivated. Their routs and their tea-parties and rapes of the lock. With all the greatness and splendour of the Elizabethan age, there must have been a certain coarseness and crudity about them. No one reveres it more than I, but it is a mistake to remain in the same waters too long. There comes a tide in the affairs of men, which, if you don't nip it in the bud, leads on to boredom."

"My dear, is that yours?" said Georgie. "And absolutely impromptu like that! You're too brilliant."

It was not quite impromptu, for Lucia had thought of it in her bath. But it would be meticulous to explain that.

"Wicked of me, I'm afraid," she said. "But it expresses my feelings just now. I do want a change, and my happening to see this notice of Miss Mapp's in *The Times* seems a very remarkable coincidence. Almost as if it was sent: what they call a leading. Anyhow, you and I will drive over to Tilling tomorrow and see it. Let us make a jaunt of it, Georgie, for it's a long way, and stay the night at an inn there. Then we shall have plenty of time to see the place."

This was rather a daring project, and Georgie was not quite sure if it was proper. But he knew himself well enough to be certain that no passionate impulse of his would cause Lucia to regret that she had made so intimate a proposal.

"That'll be the greatest fun," he said. "I shall take my painting things. I haven't sketched for weeks."

"*Cattivo ragazzo!*" said Lucia. "What have you been doing with yourself?"

"Nothing. There's been no one to play the piano with, and no one, who knows, to show my sketches to. Hours of croquet, just killing the time. Being Drake. How that fête bores me!"

"'Oo poor thing!" said Lucia, using again the baby-talk in which she and Georgie used so often to indulge. "But me's back again now, and me will scold 'oo vewy vewy much if 'oo does not do your lessons."

"And me vewy glad to be scolded again," said Georgie. "Me idle boy! Dear me, how nice it all is!" he exclaimed enthusiastically.

The clock on the old oak dresser struck ten, and Lucia jumped up.

"Georgie, ten o'clock already," she cried. "How time has flown. Now I'll write out a telegram to be sent to Miss Mapp first thing tomorrow to say we'll get to Tilling in the afternoon, to see her house, and then ickle *musica*. There was a Mozart duet we used to play. We might wrestle with it again."

She opened the book that stood on the piano. Luckily that was the very one Georgie had been practising this morning. (So too had Lucia.)

"That will be lovely," he said. "But you mustn't scold me if I play vewy badly. Months since I looked at it."

"Me too," said Lucia. "Here we are! Shall I take the treble? It's a little easier for my poor fingers. Now: *Uno, due, tre!* Off we go!"

Chapter Two

THEY ARRIVED AT TILLING IN the middle of the afternoon, entering it from the long level road that ran across the reclaimed marshland to the west. Blue was the sky overhead, complete with larks and small white clouds; the town lay basking in the hot June sunshine, and its narrow streets abounded in red-brick houses with tiled roofs, that shouted Queen Anne and George I in Lucia's enraptured ears, and made Georgie's fingers itch for his sketching-tools.

"Dear Georgie, perfectly enchanting!" exclaimed Lucia. "I declare I feel at home already. Look, there's another lovely house. We must just drive to the end of this street, and then we'll enquire where Mallards is. The people, too, I like their looks. Faces full of interest. It's as if they expected us."

The car had stopped to allow a dray to turn into the High Street from a steep cobbled way leading to the top of the hill. On the pavement at the corner was standing quite a group of Tillingites: there was a clergyman, there was a little round bustling woman dressed in a purple frock covered with pink roses which looked as if they were made of chintz, there was a large military-looking man with a couple of golf clubs in his hand, and there was a hatless girl with hair closely cropped, dressed in a fisherman's jersey and knickerbockers, who spat very neatly in the roadway.

"We must ask where the house is," said Lucia, leaning out of the window of her Rolls-Royce. "I wonder if you would be so good as to tell me—"

The clergyman sprang forward.

"It'll be Miss Mapp's house you're seeking," he said in a broad Scotch accent. "Straight up the street, to yon corner, and it's right there is Mistress Mapp's house."

The odd-looking girl gave a short hoot of laughter, and they all stared at Lucia. The car turned with difficulty and danced slowly up the steep narrow street.

"Georgie, he told me where it was before I asked," said Lucia. "It must be known in Tilling that I was coming. What a strange accent that clergyman had! A little tipsy, do you think, or only Scotch? The others too! All most interesting and unusual. Gracious, here's an enormous car coming down. Can we pass, do you think?"

By means of both cars driving on to the pavement on each side of the cobbled roadway, the passage was effected, and Lucia caught sight of a large woman inside the other, who in spite of the heat of the day wore a magnificent sable cloak. A small man with a monocle sat eclipsed by her side. Then, with glimpses of more red-brick houses to right and left, the car stopped at the top of the street opposite a very dignified door. Straight in front where the street turned at a right angle, a room with a large bow-window faced them; this, though slightly separate from the house, seemed to belong to it. Georgie thought he saw a woman's face peering out between half-drawn curtains, but it whisked itself away.

"Georgie, a dream," whispered Lucia, as they stood on the doorstep waiting for their ring to be answered. "That wonderful chimney, do you see, all crooked. The church, the cobbles, the grass and dandelions growing in between them . . . Oh, is Miss Mapp in? Mrs. Lucas. She expects me."

They had hardly stepped inside, when Miss Mapp came hurrying in from a door in the direction of the bow-window where Georgie had thought he had seen a face peeping out.

"Dear Mrs. Lucas," she said. "No need for introductions, which makes it all so happy, for how well I remember you at Riseholme, your lovely Riseholme. And Mr. Pillson! Your wonderful garden-party! All so vivid still. Red-letter days! Fancy your having driven all this way to see my little cottage! Tea at once, Withers, please. In the garden-room. Such a long drive but what a heavenly day for it. I got your telegram at breakfast-time this morning. I could have clapped my hands for joy at the thought of possibly having such a tenant as Mrs. Lucas of Riseholme. But let us have a cup of tea first. Your chauffeur? Of course he will have his tea here, too. Withers: Mrs. Lucas's chauffeur. Mind you take care of him."

Miss Mapp took Lucia's cloak from her, and still keeping up an effortless flow of hospitable monologue, led them through a small panelled parlour which opened on to the garden. A flight of eight steps with a canopy of wistaria overhead led to the garden-room.

"My little plot," said Miss Mapp. "Very modest, as you see, three-quarters of an acre at the most, but well screened. My flower-beds: sweet roses, tortoiseshell butterflies. Rather a nice clematis. My Little Eden I call it, so small, but so well beloved."

"Enchanting!" said Lucia, looking round the garden before mounting the steps up to the garden-room door. There was a very green and well-kept lawn, set in bright flower-beds. A trellis at one end separated it from a kitchen garden beyond, and round the rest ran high brick walls, over which peered the roofs of other houses. In one of these walls was cut a curved archway with a Della Robbia head above it.

"Shall we just pop across the lawn," said Miss Mapp, pointing to this, "and peep in there while Withers brings our tea? Just to stretch the—the limbs, Mrs. Lucas, after your long drive. There's a wee little plot beyond there which is quite a pet of mine. And here's sweet Puss-Cat come to welcome my friends. Lamb! Lovebird!"

Lovebird's welcome was to dab rather crossly at the caressing hand which its mistress extended, and to trot away to ambush itself beneath some fine hollyhocks, where it regarded them with singular disfavour.

"My little secret garden," continued Miss Mapp as they came to the archway. "When I am in here and shut the door, I mustn't be disturbed for anything less than a telegram. A rule of the house: I am very strict about it. The tower of the church keeping watch, as I always say over my little nook, and taking care of me. Otherwise not overlooked at all. A little paved walk round it, you see, flower-beds, a pocket-handkerchief of a lawn, and in the middle a pillar with a bust of good Queen Anne. Picked it up in a shop here for a song. One of my lucky days."

"Oh Georgie, isn't it too sweet?" cried Lucia. "*Un giardino segreto. Molto bello!*"

Miss Mapp gave a little purr of ecstasy.

"How lovely to be able to talk Italian like that," she said. "So pleased you like my little . . . *giardino segreto,* was it? Now shall we have our tea, for I'm sure you want refreshment, and see the house afterwards? Or would you prefer a little whisky and soda, Mr. Pillson? I shan't be shocked. Major Benjy—I should say Major Flint—often prefers a small whisky and soda to tea on a hot day after his game of golf, when he pops in to see me and tell me all about it."

The intense interest in humankind, so strenuously cultivated at Riseholme, obliterated for a moment Lucia's appreciation of the secret garden.

"I wonder if it was he whom we saw at the corner of the High Street," she said. "A big soldier-like man, with a couple of golf clubs."

"How you hit him off in a few words," said Miss Mapp admiringly. "That can be nobody else but Major Benjy. Going off no doubt by the steam-tram (most convenient, lands you close to the links) for a round of golf after tea. I told him it would be far too hot to play earlier. I said I should scold him if he was naughty and played after lunch. He served for many years in India. Hindustani is quite a second language to him. Calls '*Quai-hai*' when he wants his breakfast. Volumes of wonderful diaries, which we all hope to see published some day. His house is next to mine down the street. Lots of tiger-skins. A rather impetuous bridge-player: quite wicked sometimes. You play bridge of course, Mrs. Lucas. Plenty of that in Tilling. Some good players."

They had strolled back over the lawn to the garden-room where Withers was laying tea. It was cool and spacious, one window was shaded with the big leaves of a fig tree, through which, unseen, Miss Mapp so often peered out to see whether her gardener was idling. Over the big bow-window looking on to the street one curtain was half-drawn, a grand piano stood near it, bookcases half-lined the walls, and above them hung many watercolour sketches of the sort that proclaims a domestic origin. Their subjects also betrayed them, for there was one of the front of Miss Mapp's house, and one of the secret garden, another of the crooked chimney, and several of the church tower looking over the house-roofs on to Miss Mapp's lawn.

Though she continued to spray on her visitors a perpetual shower of flattering and agreeable trifles, Miss Mapp's inner attention was wrestling with the problem of how much a week, when it came to the delicate question of terms for the rent of her house, she should ask Lucia. The price had not been mentioned in her advertisement in *The Times,* and though she had told the local house-agent to name twelve guineas a week, Lucia was clearly more than delighted with what she had seen already, and it would be a senseless Quixotism to let her have the house for twelve, if she might, all the time, be willing to pay fifteen. Moreover, Miss Mapp (from behind the curtain where Georgie had seen her) was aware that Lucia had a Rolls-Royce car, so that a few additional guineas a week would probably be of no significance to her. Of course, if Lucia was not enthusiastic about the house as well as the garden, it might be unwise to ask fifteen, for she might think that a good deal, and would say something tiresome about letting Miss Mapp hear from her when she got safe away back to Riseholme, and then it was sure to be a refusal. But if she continued to rave and talk Italian about the house when she saw over it, fifteen guineas should be the price. And not a penny of that should Messrs. Woolgar & Pipstow, the house-agents, get for commission, since Lucia had said definitely that she saw the advertisement in *The Times.* That was Miss Mapp's affair: nothing to do with Woolgar & Pipstow. Meantime she begged Georgie not to look at those watercolours on the walls.

"Little daubs of my own," she said, most anxious that this should be known. "I should sink into the ground with shame, dear Mr. Pillson, if you looked at them, for I know what a great artist you are yourself. And Withers has brought us our tea . . . You like the one of my little *giardino segreto*? (I must remember that beautiful phrase.) How kind of you to say so! Perhaps it isn't quite so bad as the others, for the subject inspired me, and it's so important, isn't it, to love your subject? Major Benjy likes it too.

Cream, Mrs. Lucas? I see Withers has picked some strawberries for us from my little plot. Such a year for strawberries! And Major Benjy was chatting with friends I'll be bound, when you passed him."

"Yes, a clergyman," said Lucia, "who kindly directed us to your house. In fact he seemed to know we were going there before I said so, didn't he, Georgie? A broad Scotch accent."

"Dear Padre!" said Miss Mapp. "It's one of his little ways to talk Scotch, though he came from Birmingham. A very good bridge-player when he can spare time as he usually can. Reverend Kenneth Bartlett. Was there a teeny little thin woman with him like a mouse? It would be his wife."

"No, not thin, at all," said Lucia, thoroughly interested. "Quite the other way round: in fact round. A purple coat and a skirt covered with pink roses that looked as if they were made of chintz."

Miss Mapp nearly choked over her first sip of tea, but just saved herself.

"I declare I'm quite frightened of you, Mrs. Lucas," she said. "What an eye you've got. Dear Diva Plaistow, whom we're all devoted to. Christened Godiva! Such a handicap! And they *were* chintz roses, which she cut out of an old pair of curtains and tacked them on. She's full of absurd delicious fancies like that. Keeps us all in fits of laughter. Anyone else?"

"Yes, a girl with no hat and an Eton crop. She was dressed in a fisherman's jersey and knickerbockers."

Miss Mapp looked pensive.

"Quaint Irene," she said. "Irene Coles. Just a touch of unconventionality, which sometimes is very refreshing, but can be rather embarrassing. Devoted to her art. She paints strange pictures, men and women with no clothes on. One has to be careful to knock when one goes to see quaint Irene in her studio. But a great original."

"And then when we turned up out of the High Street," said Georgie eagerly, "we met another Rolls-Royce. I was afraid we shouldn't be able to pass it."

"So was I," said Miss Mapp, unintentionally betraying the fact that she had been watching from the garden-room. "That car is always up and down this street here."

"A large woman in it," said Lucia. "Wrapped in sables on this broiling day. A little man beside her."

"Mr. and Mrs. Wyse," said Miss Mapp. "Lately married. She was Mrs. Poppit, MBE. Very worthy, and such a crashing snob."

As soon as tea was over and the inhabitants of Tilling thus plucked and roasted, the tour of the house was made. There were charming little panelled parlours with big windows letting in a flood of air and sunshine and vases of fresh flowers on the tables. There was a broad staircase with shallow treads, and every moment Lucia became more and more enamoured of the plain well-shaped rooms. It all looked so white and comfortable, and, for one wanting a change, so different from The Hurst with its small latticed windows, its steep irregular stairs, its single steps, up or down, at the threshold of every room. People of the age of Anne seemed to have a much better idea of domestic convenience, and Lucia's Italian exclamations grew gratifyingly frequent. Into Miss Mapp's own bedroom she went alone with the owner, leaving Georgie on the landing outside, for delicacy would not permit his looking on the scene where Miss Mapp nightly disrobed herself, and the bed where she nightly disposed herself. Besides, it would be easier for Lucia to ask that important point-blank question of terms, and for herself to answer it if they were alone.

"I'm charmed with the house," said Lucia. "And what exactly, how much I mean, for a period of two months—"

"Fifteen guineas a week," said Miss Mapp without pause. "That would include the use of my piano. A sweet instrument by Blumenfelt."

"I will take it for August and September," said Lucia.

"And I'm sure I hope you'll be as pleased with it," said Miss Mapp, "as I'm sure I shall be with my tenant."

A bright idea struck her, and she smiled more widely than ever.

"That would not include, of course, the wages of my gardener, such a nice steady man," she said, "or garden-produce. Flowers for the house by all means, but not fruit or vegetables."

At that moment Lucia, blinded by passion for Mallards, Tilling and the Tillingites, would have willingly agreed to pay the water-rate as well. If Miss Mapp had guessed that, she would certainly have named this unusual condition.

Miss Mapp, as requested by Lucia, had engaged rooms for her and Georgie at a pleasant hostelry near by, called the Trader's Arms, and she accompanied them there with Lucia's car following, like an empty carriage at a funeral, to see that all was ready for them. There must have been some misunderstanding of the message, for Georgie found that a double bedroom had been provided for them. Luckily Lucia had lingered outside with Miss Mapp, looking at the view over the marsh, and Georgie with embarrassed blushes explained at the bureau that this would not do at all, and the palms of his hands got cold and wet until the mistake was erased and remedied. Then Miss Mapp left them and they went out to wander about the town. But Mallards was the magnet for Lucia's enamoured eye, and presently they stole back towards it. Many houses apparently were to be let furnished in Tilling just now, and Georgie too grew infected with the desire to have one. Riseholme would be very dismal without Lucia, for the moment the fête was over he felt sure that an appalling reaction after the excitement would settle on it; he might even miss being knighted. He had sketched everything sketchable, there would be nobody to play duets with, and the whole place would stagnate again until Lucia's return, just as it had stagnated during her impenetrable widowhood. Whereas here there were innumerable subjects for his brush, and Lucia would be installed in Mallards with a Blumenfelt in the garden-room, and, as was already obvious, a maelstrom of activities whirling in her brain. Major Benjy interested her, so did quaint Irene and the Padre, all the group, in fact, which had seen them drive up with such pre-knowledge, so it seemed, of their destination.

The wall of Miss Mapp's garden, now known to them from inside, ran up to where they now stood, regarding the front of Mallards, and Georgie suddenly observed that just beside them was the sweetest little gabled cottage with the board announcing that it was to be let furnished.

"Look, Lucia," he said. "How perfectly fascinating! If it wasn't for that blasted fête, I believe I should be tempted to take it, if I could get it for the couple of months when you are here."

Lucia had been waiting just for that. She was intending to hint something of the sort before long unless he did, and had made up her mind to stand treat for a bottle of champagne at dinner, so that when they strolled about again afterwards, as she was quite determined to do, Georgie, adventurous with wine, might find the light of the late sunset glowing on Georgian fronts in the town and on the levels of the surrounding country, quite irresistible. But how wise to have waited, so that Georgie should make the suggestion himself.

"My dear, what a delicious idea!" she said. "Are you really

thinking of it? Heavenly for me to have a friend here instead of being planted among strangers. And certainly it is a darling little house. It doesn't seem to be occupied, no smoke from any of the chimneys. I think we might really peep in through the windows and get some idea of what it's like."

They had to stand on tiptoe to do this, but by shading their eyes from the westerly sun they could get a very decent idea of the interior.

"This must be the dining-room," said Georgie, peering in.

"A lovely open fireplace," said Lucia. "So cosy."

They moved on sideways like crabs.

"A little hall," said Lucia. "Pretty staircase going up out of it." More crab-like movements.

"The sitting-room," said Georgie. "Quite charming, and if you press your nose close you can see out of the other window into a tiny garden beyond. The wooden paling must be that of your kitchen garden."

They stepped back into the street to get a better idea of the topography, and at this moment Miss Mapp looked out of the bow-window of her garden-room and saw them there. She was as intensely interested in this as they in the house.

"And three bedrooms I should think upstairs," said Lucia, "and two attics above. Heaps."

"I shall go and see the agent tomorrow morning," said Georgie. "I can imagine myself being very comfortable there!"

They strolled off into the disused graveyard round the church. Lucia turned to have one more look at the front of Mallards, and Miss Mapp made a low swift curtsey, remaining down so that she disappeared completely.

"About that old fête," said Georgie, "I don't want to throw Daisy over, because she'll never get another Drake."

"But you can go down there for the week," said Lucia, who had thought it all out, "and come back as soon as it's over. You know how to be knighted by now. You needn't go to all those endless rehearsals. Georgie, look at that wonderful clock on the church."

"Lovely," said Georgie absently. "I told Daisy I simply would not be knighted every day. I shall have no shoulder left."

"And I think that must be the Town Hall," said Lucia. "Quite right about not being knighted so often. What a perfect sketch you could do of that."

"Heaps of room for us all in the cottage," said Georgie. "I hope there's a servants' sitting-room."

"They'll be in and out of Mallards all day," said Lucia. "A lovely servants' hall there."

"If I can get it, I will," said Georgie. "I shall try to let my house at Riseholme, though I shall take my bibelots away. I've often had applications for it in other years. I hope Foljambe will like Tilling. She will make me miserable if she doesn't. Tepid water, fluff on my clothes."

It was time to get back to their inn to unpack, but Georgie longed for one more look at his cottage, and Lucia for one at Mallards. Just as they turned the corner that brought them in sight of these there was thrust out of the window of Miss Mapp's garden-room a hand that waved a white handkerchief. It might have been samite.

"Georgie, what can that be?" whispered Lucia. "It must be a signal of some sort. Or was it Miss Mapp waving us good-night?"

"Not very likely," said he. "Let's wait one second."

He had hardly spoken when Miss Coles, followed by the breathless Mrs. Plaistow, hurried up the three steps leading to the front door of Mallards and entered.

"Diva and quaint Irene," said Lucia. "It must have been a signal."

"It might be a coincidence," said Georgie. To which puerile suggestion Lucia felt it was not worth while to reply.

Of course it was a signal and one long prearranged, for it was a matter of the deepest concern to several householders in Tilling, whether Miss Mapp found a tenant for Mallards, and she had promised Diva and quaint Irene to wave a handkerchief from the window of the garden-room at six o'clock precisely, by which hour it was reasonable to suppose that her visitors would have left her. These two ladies, who would be prowling about the street below, on the look-out, would then hasten to hear the best or the worst.

Their interest in the business was vivid, for if Miss Mapp succeeded in letting Mallards, she had promised to take Diva's house, Wasters, for two months at eight guineas a week (the house being much smaller) and Diva would take Irene's house, Taormina (smaller still) at five guineas a week, and Irene would take a four-roomed labourer's cottage (unnamed) just outside the town at two guineas a week, and the labourer, who, with his family, would be harvesting in August and hop-picking in September, would live in some sort of shanty and pay no rent at all. Thus from top to bottom of this ladder of lessors and lessees they all scored, for they all received more than they paid, and all would enjoy the benefit of a change without the worry and expense of travel and hotels. Each of these ladies would wake in the morning in an unfamiliar room, would sit in unaccustomed chairs, read each other's books (and possibly letters), look at each other's pictures, imbibe all the stimulus of new surroundings, without the wrench of leaving Tilling at all. No true Tillingite was ever really happy away from her town; foreigners were very queer untrustworthy people, and if you did not like the food it was impossible to engage another cook for an hotel of which you were not the proprietor. Annually in the summer this sort of ladder of house-letting was set up in Tilling and was justly popular. But it all depended on a successful letting of Mallards, for if Elizabeth Mapp did not let Mallards, she would not take Diva's Wasters nor Diva Irene's Taormina.

Diva and Irene therefore hurried to the garden-room where they would hear their fate; Irene forging on ahead with that long masculine stride that easily kept pace with Major Benjy's, the short-legged Diva with that twinkle of feet that was like the scudding of a thrush over the lawn.

"Well, Mapp, what luck?" asked Irene.

Miss Mapp waited till Diva had shot in.

"I think I shall tease you both," said she playfully with her widest smile.

"Oh, hurry up," said Irene. "I know perfectly well from your face that you've let it. Otherwise it would be all screwed up."

Miss Mapp, though there was no question about her being the social queen of Tilling, sometimes felt that there were ugly Bolshevistic symptoms in the air, when quaint Irene spoke to her like that. And Irene had a dreadful gift of mimicry, which was a very low weapon, but formidable. It was always wise to be polite to mimics.

"Patience, a little patience, dear," said Miss Mapp soothingly. "If you know I've let it, why wait?"

"Because I should like a cocktail," said Irene. "If you'll just send for one, you can go on teasing."

"Well, I've let it for August and September," said Miss Mapp, preferring to abandon her teasing than give Irene a cocktail. "And I'm lucky in my tenant. I never met a sweeter woman than dear Mrs. Lucas."

"Thank God," said Diva, drawing up her chair to the still-uncleared table. "Give me a cup of tea, Elizabeth. I could eat nothing till I knew."

"How much did you stick her for it?" asked Irene.

"Beg your pardon, dear?" asked Miss Mapp, who could not be expected to understand such a vulgar expression.

"What price did you screw her up to? What's she got to pay you?" said Irene impatiently. "Damage: dibs."

"She instantly closed with the price I suggested," said Miss Mapp. "I'm not sure, quaint one, that anything beyond that is what might be called your business."

"I disagree about that," said the quaint one. "There ought to be a sliding-scale. If you've made her pay through the nose, Diva ought to make you pay through the nose for her house, and I ought to make her pay through the nose for mine. Equality, Fraternity, Nosality."

Miss Mapp bubbled with disarming laughter and rang the bell for Irene's cocktail, which might stop her pursuing this subject, for the sliding-scale of twelve, eight and five guineas a week had been the basis of previous calculations. Yet if Lucia so willingly consented to pay more, surely that was nobody's affair but that of the high contracting parties. Irene, soothed by the prospect of her cocktail, pursued the dangerous topic no further, but sat down at Miss Mapp's piano and picked out "God Save the King," with one uncertain finger. Her cocktail arrived just as she finished it.

"Thank you, dear," said Miss Mapp. "Sweet music."

"Cheerio!" said Irene. "Are you charging Lucas anything extra for use of a fine old instrument?"

Miss Mapp was goaded into a direct and emphatic reply.

"No, darling, I am not," she said, "as you are so interested in matters that don't concern you."

"Well, well, no offence meant," said Irene. "Thanks for the cocktail. Look in tomorrow between twelve and one at my studio, if you want to see far the greater part of a well-made man. I'll be off now to cook my supper. *Au reservoir.*"

Miss Mapp finished the few strawberries that Diva had spared and sighed.

"Our dear Irene has a very coarse side to her nature, Diva," she said. "No harm in her, but just common. Sad! Such a contrast to dear Mrs. Lucas. So refined: scraps of Italian beautifully pronounced. And so delighted with everything."

"Ought we to call on her?" asked Diva. "Widow's mourning, you know."

Miss Mapp considered this. One plan would be that she should take Lucia under her wing (provided she was willing to go there), another to let it be known in Tilling (if she wasn't) that she did not want to be called upon. That would set Tilling's back up, for if there was one thing it hated it was anything that (in spite of widow's weeds) might be interpreted into superiority. Though Lucia would only be two months in Tilling, Miss Mapp did not want her to be too popular on her own account, independently. She wanted . . . she wanted to have Lucia in her pocket, to take her by the hand and show her to Tilling, but to be in control. It all had to be thought out.

"I'll find out when she comes," she said. "I'll ask her, for indeed I feel quite an old friend already."

"And who's the man?" asked Diva.

"Dear Mr. Georgie Pillson. He entertained me so charmingly when I was at Riseholme for a night or two some years ago. They are staying at the Trader's Arms, and off again tomorrow."

"What? Staying there together?" asked Diva.

Miss Mapp turned her head slightly aside as if to avoid some faint unpleasant smell.

"Diva dear," she said. "Old friends as we are, I should be sorry to have a mind like yours. Horrid. You've been reading too many novels. If widow's weeds are not a sufficient protection against such innuendoes, a baby girl in its christening-robe wouldn't be safe."

"Gracious me, I made no innuendo," said the astonished Diva. "I only meant it was rather a daring thing to do. So it is. Anything more came from your mind, Elizabeth, not mine. I merely ask you not to put it on to me, and then say I'm horrid."

Miss Mapp smiled her widest.

"Of course I accept your apology, dear Diva," she said. "Fully, without back-thought of any kind."

"But I haven't apologised and I won't," cried Diva. "It's for you to do that."

To those not acquainted with the usage of the ladies of Tilling, such bitter plain-speaking might seem to denote a serious friction between old friends. But neither Elizabeth nor Diva had any such feeling: they would both have been highly surprised if an impartial listener had imagined anything so absurd. Such breezes, even if they grew far stronger than this, were no more than bracing airs that disposed to energy, or exercises to keep the mind fit. No malice.

"Another cup of tea, dear?" said Miss Mapp earnestly.

That was so like her, thought Diva: that was Elizabeth all over. When logic and good feeling alike had produced an irresistible case against her, she swept it all away, and asked you if you would have some more cold tea or cold mutton, or whatever it was.

Diva gave up. She knew she was no match for her and had more tea.

"About our own affairs then," she said, "if that's all settled—"

"Yes, dear: so sweetly so harmoniously," said Elizabeth.

Diva swallowed a regurgitation of resentment, and went on as if she had not been interrupted.

"—Mrs. Lucas takes possession on the first of August," she said. "That's to say, you would like to get into Wasters that day."

"Early that day, Diva, if you can manage it," said Elizabeth, "as I want to give my servants time to clean and tidy up. I would pop across in the morning, and my servants follow later. All so easy to manage."

"Then there's another thing," said Diva. "Garden-produce. You're leaving yours, I suppose."

Miss Mapp gave a little trill of laughter.

"I shan't be digging up all my potatoes and stripping the beans and the fruit trees," she said. "And I thought—correct me if I am wrong—that my eight guineas a week for your little house included garden-produce, which is all that really concerns you and me. I think we agreed as to that."

Miss Mapp leaned forward with an air of imparting luscious secret information, as that was settled.

"Diva: something thrilling," she said. "I happened to be glancing out of my window just by chance a few minutes before I waved to you, and there were Mrs. Lucas and Mr. Pillson peering, positively peering into the windows of Mallards Cottage. I couldn't help wondering if Mr. Pillson is thinking of taking it. They seemed to be so absorbed in it. It is to let, for Isabel Poppit has taken that little brown bungalow with no proper plumbing out by the golf links."

"Thrilling!" said Diva. "There's a door in the paling between that little back-yard at Mallards Cottage and your garden. They could unlock it—"

She stopped, for this was a development of the trend of ideas for which neither of them had apologised.

"But even if Mr. Pillson is thinking of taking it, what next, Elizabeth?" she asked.

Miss Mapp bent to kiss the roses in that beautiful vase of flowers which she had cut this morning in preparation for Lucia's visit.

"Nothing particular, dear," she said. "Just one of my madcap notions. You and I might take Mallards Cottage between us, if it appealed to you. Sweet Isabel is only asking four guineas a week for it. If Mr. Pillson happens—it's only a speculation—to want it, we might ask, say, six. So cheap at six."

Diva rose.

"Shan't touch it," she said. "What if Mr. Pillson doesn't want it? A pure speculation."

"Perhaps it would be rather risky," said Miss Mapp. "And now I come to think of it, possibly, possibly rather stealing a march—don't they call it—on my friends."

"Oh, decidedly," said Diva. "No 'possibly possibly' about it."

Miss Mapp winced for a moment under this smart rap, and changed the subject.

"I shall have little more than a month, then, in my dear house," she said, "before I'm turned out of it. I must make the most of it, and have a quantity of little gaieties for you all."

∞

Georgie and Lucia had another long stroll through the town after their dinner. The great celestial signs behaved admirably; it was as if the spirit of Tilling had arranged that sun, moon and stars alike should put forth their utmost arts of advertisement on its behalf, for scarcely had the fires of sunset ceased to blaze on its red walls and roofs and to incarnadine the thin skeins of mist that hung over the marsh, than a large punctual moon arose in the east and executed the most wonderful nocturnes in black and silver.

They found a great grey Norman tower keeping watch seaward, an Edwardian gate with drum towers looking out landward: they found a belvedere platform built out on a steep slope to the east of the town, and the odour of the flowering hawthorns that grew there was wafted to them as they gazed at a lighthouse winking in the distance. In another street there stood Elizabethan cottages of brick and timber, very picturesque, but of no interest to those who were at home in Riseholme. Then there were human interests as well: quaint Irene was sitting, while the sunset flamed, on a camp-stool in the middle of a street, hatless and trousered, painting a most remarkable picture, apparently of the Day of Judgement, for the whole world was enveloped in fire. Just as they passed her, her easel fell down, and in a loud angry voice she said, "Damn the beastly thing." Then they saw Diva scuttling along the High Street carrying a birdcage. She called up to an open window very lamentably, "Oh, Dr. Dobbie, please! My canary's had a fit!" From another window, also open and unblinded, positively inviting scrutiny, there came a baritone voice singing "Will ye no' come back again?" and there, sure enough, was the Padre from Birmingham, with the little grey mouse tinkling on the piano. They could not tear themselves away (indeed there was quite a lot of people listening) till the song was over, and then they stole up the street, at the head of which stood Mallards, and from the house just below it came a muffled cry of "*Quai-hai,*" and Lucia's lips formed the syllables "Major Benjy. At his diaries." They tiptoed on past Mallards itself, for the garden-room window was open wide, and so past Mallards Cottage, till they were out of sight.

"Georgie, entrancing," said Lucia. "They're all being themselves, and all so human and busy—"

"If I don't get Mallards Cottage," said Georgie, "I shall die."

"But you must. You shall. Now it's time to go to bed, though I could wander about for ever. We must be up early in order to get to the house-agents' as soon as it's open. Woggles & Pickstick, isn't it?"

"Now you've confused me," said Georgie. "Rather like it, but not quite."

They went upstairs to bed: their rooms were next each other, with a communicating door. There was a bolt on Georgie's side of it, and he went swiftly across to this and fastened it. Even as he did so, he heard a key quietly turned from the other side of it. He undressed with the stealth of a burglar prowling about a house, for somehow it was shy work that he and Lucia should be going to bed so close to each other; he brushed his teeth with infinite precaution and bent low over the basin to eject (spitting would be too noisy a word) the water with which he had rinsed his mouth, for it would never do to let a sound of these intimate manoeuvres penetrate next door. When half-undressed he remembered that the house-agents' name was Woolgar & Pipstow, and he longed to tap at Lucia's door and proclaim it, but the silence of the grave reigned next door, and perhaps Lucia was asleep already. Or was she, too, being as stealthy as he? Whichever it was (particularly if it was the last) he must not let a betrayal of his presence reach her.

He got into bed and clicked out his light. That could be done quite boldly: she might hear that, for it only betokened that all was over. Then, in spite of this long day in the open air, which should have conduced to drowsiness, he felt terribly wide-awake, for the subject which had intermittently occupied his mind, shadowing it with dim apprehension, ever since Peppino's death, presented itself in the most garish colours. For years, by a pretty Riseholme fantasy, it had always been supposed that he was the implacably

Platonic but devout lover of Lucia: somehow that interesting fiction had grown up, and Lucia had certainly abetted it as well as himself. She had let it be supposed that he was, and that she accepted this chaste fervour. But now that her year of widowhood was nearly over, there loomed in front of Georgie the awful fact that very soon there could be no earthly reason why he should not claim his reward for these years of devotion and exchange his passionate celibacy for an even more passionate matrimony. It was an unnerving thought that he might have the right before the summer was over, to tap at some door of communication like that which he had so carefully bolted (and she locked) and say, "May I come in, darling?" He felt that the words would freeze on his tongue before he could utter them.

Did Lucia expect him to ask to marry her? There was the crux and his imagination proceeded to crucify him upon it. They had posed for years as cherishing for each other a stainless devotion, but what if, with her, it had been no pose at all, but a dreadful reality? Had he been encouraging her to hope, by coming down to stay at this hotel in this very compromising manner? In his ghastly midnight musing, it seemed terribly likely. He had been very rash to come, and all this afternoon he had been pursuing his foolhardy career. He had said that life wasn't worth living if he could not get hold of Mallards Cottage, which was less than a stone's throw (even he could throw a stone as far as that) from the house she was to inhabit alone. Really it looked as if it was the proximity to her that made the cottage so desirable. If she only knew how embarrassing her proximity had been just now when he prepared himself for bed! . . .

And Lucia always got what she wanted. There was a force about her he supposed (so different from poor Daisy's violent yappings and scufflings), which caused things to happen in the way she wished. He had fallen in with all her plans with a zest which it was only reasonable she should interpret favourably: only an hour or two ago he had solemnly affirmed that he must take Mallards Cottage, and the thing already was as good as done, for they were to breakfast tomorrow morning at eight, in order to be at the house-agents' (Woggle & Pipsqueak, was it? He had forgotten again), as soon as it opened. Things happened like that for her: she got what she wanted. "But never, never," thought Georgie, "shall she get me. I couldn't possibly marry her, and I won't. I want to live quietly and do my sewing and my sketching, and see lots of Lucia, and play any amount of duets with her, but not marry her. Pray God, she doesn't want me to!"

Lucia was lying awake, too, next door, and if either of them could have known what the other was thinking about, they would both instantly have fallen into a refreshing sleep, instead of tossing and turning as they were doing. She, too, knew that for years she and Georgie had let it be taken for granted that they were mutually devoted, and had both about equally encouraged that impression. There had been an interlude, it is true, when that wonderful Olga Bracely had shone (like evening stars singing) over Riseholme, but she was to be absent from England for a year; besides she was married, and even if she had not been would certainly not have married Georgie. "So we needn't consider Olga," thought Lucia. "It's all about Georgie and me. Dear Georgie: he was so terribly glad when I began to be myself again, and how he jumped at the plan of coming to Tilling and spending the night here! And how he froze on to the idea of taking Mallards Cottage as soon as he knew I had got Mallards! I'm afraid I've been encouraging him to hope. He knows that my year of widowhood is almost over, and on the very eve of its accomplishment, I take him off on this solitary expedition with me. Dear me: it looks as if I was positively asking for it. How perfectly horrible!"

Though it was quite dark, Lucia felt herself blushing.

"What on earth am I to do?" continued these disconcerting reflections. "If he asks me to marry him, I must certainly refuse, for I couldn't do so: quite impossible. And then when I say no, he has every right to turn on me, and say I've been leading him on. I've been taking moonlight walks with him, I'm at this moment staying alone with him in an hotel. Oh dear! Oh dear!"

Lucia sat up in bed and listened. She longed to hear sounds of snoring from the next room, for that would show that the thought of the fulfilment of his long devotion was not keeping him awake, but there was no sound of any kind.

"I must do something about it tomorrow," she said to herself, "for if I allow things to go on like this, these two months here with him will be one series of agitating apprehensions. I must make it quite clear that I won't before he asks me. I can't bear to think of hurting Georgie, but it will hurt him less if I show him beforehand he's got no chance. Something about the beauty of a friendship untroubled with passion. Something about the tranquillity that comes with age . . . There's that eternal old church clock striking three. Surely it must be fast."

Lucia lay down again: at last she was getting sleepy.

"Mallards," she said to herself. "Quaint Irene . . . Woffles and . . . Georgie will know. Certainly Tilling is fascinating . . . Intriguing, too . . . characters of strong individuality to be dealt with . . . A great variety, but I think I can manage them . . . And what about Miss Mapp? . . . Those wide grins . . . We shall see about that . . ."

Lucia awoke herself from a doze by giving a loud snore, and for one agonised moment thought it was Georgie, whom she had hoped to hear snoring, in alarming proximity to herself. That nightmare-spasm was quickly over, and she recognised that it was she that had done it. After all her trouble in not letting a sound of any sort penetrate through that door!

Georgie heard it. He was getting sleepy, too, in spite of his uneasy musings, but he was just wide-awake enough to realise where that noise had come from.

"And if she snores as well . . ." he thought, and dozed off.

Chapter Three

IT WAS HARDLY NINE O'CLOCK in the morning when they set out for the house-agents', and the upper circles of Tilling were not yet fully astir. But there was a town-crier in a blue frock-coat ringing a bell in the High Street and proclaiming that the water-supply would be cut off that day from twelve noon till three in the afternoon. It was difficult to get to the house-agents', for the street where it was situated was being extensively excavated and they had chosen the wrong side of the road, and though they saw it opposite them when halfway down the street, a long detour must be made to reach it.

"But so characteristic, so charming," said Lucia. "Naturally there is a town-crier in Tilling, and naturally the streets are up. Do not be so impatient, Georgie. Ah, we can cross here."

There was a further period of suspense.

"The occupier of Mallards Cottage," said Mr. Woolgar (or it might have been Mr. Pipstow), "is wanting to let for three months, July, August and September. I'm not so sure that she would entertain—"

"Then will you please ring her up," interrupted Georgie, "and say you've had a firm offer for two months."

Mr. Woolgar turned round a crank like that used for starting rather old-fashioned motor cars, and when a bell rang, he gave a number, and got into communication with the brown bungalow without proper plumbing.

"Very sorry, sir," he said, "but Miss Poppit has gone out for her sun-bath among the sand-dunes. She usually takes about three hours if fine."

"But we're leaving again this morning," said Georgie. "Can't her servant, or whoever it is, search the sand-dunes and ask her?"

"I'll enquire, sir," said Mr. Woolgar sympathetically. "But there are about two miles of sand-dunes, and she may be anywhere."

"Please enquire," said Georgie.

There was an awful period, during which Mr. Woolgar kept on saying "Quite," "Just so," "I see," "Yes, dear," with the most tedious monotony, in answer to unintelligible quacking noises from the other end.

"Quite impossible, I am afraid," he said at length. "Miss Poppit only keeps one servant, and she's got to look after the house. Besides, Miss Poppit likes . . . likes to be private when she's enjoying the sun."

"But how tarsome," said Georgie. "What am I to do?"

"Well, sir, there's Miss Poppit's mother you might get hold of. She is Mrs. Wyse now. Lately married. A beautiful wedding. The house you want is her property."

"I know," broke in Lucia. "Sables and a Rolls-Royce. Mr. Wyse has a monocle."

"Ah, if you know the lady, madam, that will be all right, and I can give you her address. Starling Cottage, Porpoise Street. I will write it down for you."

"Georgie, Porpoise Street!" whispered Lucia in an entranced aside. "*Com' e bello e molto characteristuoso!*"

While this was being done, Diva suddenly blew in, beginning to speak before she was wholly inside the office. A short tempestuous interlude ensued.

"—morning, Mr. Woolgar," said Diva, "and I've let Wasters, so you can cross it off your books; such a fine morning."

"Indeed, madam," said Mr. Woolgar. "Very satisfactory. And I hope your dear little canary is better."

"Still alive and in less pain, thank you, pip," said Diva, and plunged through the excavations outside sooner than waste time in going round.

Mr. Woolgar apparently understood that "pip" was not a salutation but a disease of canaries, and did not say "So long" or "Pip pip." Calm returned again.

"I'll ring up Mrs. Wyse to say you will call, madam," he said. "Let me see: what name? It has escaped me for the moment."

As he had never known it, it was difficult to see how it could have escaped.

"Mrs. Lucas and Mr. Pillson," said Lucia. "Where is Porpoise Street?"

"Two minutes' walk from here, madam. As if you were going up to Mallards, but first turning to the right just short of it."

"Many thanks," said Lucia, "I know Mallards."

"The best house in Tilling, madam," said Mr. Woolgar, "if you were wanting something larger than Mallards Cottage. It is on our books, too."

The pride of proprietorship tempted Lucia for a moment to say "I've got it already," but she refrained. The complications which might have ensued, had she asked the price of it, were endless . . .

"A great many houses to let in Tilling," she said.

"Yes, madam, a rare lot of letting goes on about this time of year," said Mr. Woolgar, "but they're all snapped up very quickly. Many ladies in Tilling like a little change in the summer."

It was impossible (since time was so precious, and Georgie

so feverishly apprehensive, after this warning, that somebody else would secure Mallards Cottage before him, although the owner was safe in the sand-dunes for the present) to walk round the excavations in the street, and like Diva they made an intrepid short cut among gas-pipes and water-mains and braziers and bricks to the other side. A sad splash of mud hurled itself against Georgie's fawn-coloured trousers as he stepped in a puddle, which was very tarsome, but it was useless to attempt to brush it off till it was dry. As they went up the now familiar street towards Mallards they saw quaint Irene leaning out of the upper window of a small house, trying to take down a board that hung outside it which advertised that this house, too, was to let: the fact of her removing it seemed to indicate that from this moment it was to let no longer. Just as they passed, the board, which was painted in the most amazing colours, slipped from her hand and crashed on to the pavement, narrowly missing Diva who simultaneously popped out of the front door. It broke into splinters at her feet, and she gave a shrill cry of dismay. Then perceiving Irene she called up, "No harm done, dear," and Irene, in a voice of fury, cried, "No harm? My beautiful board's broken to smithereens. Why didn't you catch it, silly?"

A snort of infinite contempt was the only proper reply, and Diva trundled swiftly away into the High Street again.

"But it's like a game of general post, Georgie," said Lucia excitedly, "and we're playing too. Are they all letting their houses to each other? Is that it?"

"I don't care whom they're letting them to," said Georgie, "so long as I get Mallards Cottage. Look at this tarsome mud on my trousers, and I daren't try to brush it off. What will Mrs. Wyse think? Here's Porpoise Street anyhow, and there's Starling Cottage. Elizabethan again."

The door was of old oak, without a handle, but with a bobbin in the strictest style, and there was a thickly patinated green
bronze chain hanging close by, which Georgie rightly guessed
to be the bell-pull, and so he pulled it. A large bronze bell,
which he had not perceived, hanging close to his head, thereupon broke into a clamour that might have been heard not only
in the house but all over Tilling, and startled him terribly. Then
bobbins and gadgets were manipulated from within and they
were shown into a room in which two very diverse tastes were
clearly exhibited. Oak beams crossed the ceiling, oak beams
made a criss-cross on the walls: there was a large open fireplace
of grey Dutch bricks, and on each side of the grate an ingle-
nook with a section of another oak beam to sit down upon. The
windows were latticed and had antique levers for their control:
there was a refectory-table and a spice-chest and some pewter
mugs and a Bible-box and a coffin-stool. All this was one taste,
and then came in another, for the room was full of beautiful
objects of a very different sort. The refectory-table was covered
with photographs in silver frames: one was of a man in uniform
and many decorations signed "Cecco Faraglione," another of
a lady in Court dress with a quantity of plumes on her head
signed "Amelia Faraglione." Another was of the King of Italy,
another of a man in a frock-coat signed "Wyse." In front of these,
rather prominent, was an open purple morocco box in which
reposed the riband and cross of a Member of the Order of the
British Empire. There was a cabinet of china in one corner with
a malachite vase above it: there was an occasional table with a
marble mosaic top: there was a satinwood piano draped with
a piece of embroidery: a palm tree: a green velvet sofa over the
end of which lay a sable coat, and all these things spoke of post-
Elizabethan refinements.

Long before Lucia had time to admire them all, there came a jingling from a door over which hung a curtain of reeds and beads, and Mrs. Wyse entered.

"So sorry to keep you waiting, Mrs. Lucas," she said, "but they thought I was in the garden, and I was in my boudoir all the time. And you must excuse my deshabille, just my shopping-frock. And Mr. Pillson, isn't it? So pleased. Pray be seated."

She heaved the sable coat off the end of the sofa on to the window seat.

"We've just been to see the house-agent," said Georgie in a great hurry, as he turned his muddied leg away from the light, "and he told us that you might help me."

"Most happy I am sure, if I can. Pray tell me," said Mrs. Wyse, in apparent unconsciousness of what she could possibly help him about.

"Mallards Cottage," said Georgie. "There seems to be no chance of getting hold of Miss Poppit and we've got to leave before she comes back from her sun-bath. I so much want to take it for August and September."

Mrs. Wyse made a little cooing sound.

"Dear Isabel!" she said. "My daughter. Out in the sand-dunes all morning! What if a tramp came along? I say to her. But no use: she calls it the Browning Society, and she must not miss a meeting. So quick and clever! Browning, not the poet but the action of the sun."

"Most amusing!" said Georgie. "With regard to Mallards Cottage—"

"The little house is mine, as no doubt Mr. Woolgar told you," said Mrs. Wyse, forgetting she had been in complete ignorance of these manoeuvres, "but you must certainly come and see over it, before anything is settled . . . Ah, here is Mr. Wyse. Algernon:

Mrs. Lucas and Mr. Pillson. Mr. Pillson wants to take Mallards Cottage."

Lucia thought she had never seen anyone so perfectly correct and polite as Mr. Wyse. He gave little bows and smiles to each as he spoke to them, and that in no condescending manner, nor yet cringingly, but as one consorting with his high-bred equals.

"From your beautiful Riseholme, I understand," he said to Lucia (bowing to Riseholme as well). "And we are all encouraging ourselves to hope that for two months at the least the charm of our picturesque—do you not find it so?—little Tilling will give Susan and myself the inestimable pleasure of being your neighbours. We shall look forward to August with keen anticipation. Remind me, dear Susan, to tell Amelia what is in store for us." He bowed to August, Susan and Amelia and continued—"And now I hear that Mr. Pillson" (he bowed to Georgie and observed the drying spot of mud) "is 'after' as they say, after Mallards Cottage. This will indeed be a summer for Tilling."

Georgie, during this pretty speech which Mr. Wyse delivered in the most finished manner, was taking notes of his costume and appearance. His clean-shaven face, with abundant grey hair brushed back from his forehead, was that of an actor who has seen his best days, but who has given command performances at Windsor. He wore a brown velveteen coat, a Byronic collar and a tie strictured with a cameo-ring: he wore brown knickerbockers and stockings to match, he wore neat golfing shoes. He looked as if he might be going to play golf, but somehow it didn't seem likely . . .

Georgie and Lucia made polite deprecating murmurs.

"I was telling Mr. Pillson he must certainly see over it first," said Mrs. Wyse. "There are the keys of the cottage in my boudoir, if you'll kindly fetch them, Algernon. And the Royce is at the door, I see, so if Mrs. Lucas will allow us, we will all drive up there together, and show her and Mr. Pillson what there is."

While Algernon was gone, Mrs. Wyse picked up the photograph signed Amelia Faraglione.

"You recognise, no doubt, the family likeness," she said to Lucia. "My husband's sister Amelia who married the Conte di Faraglione, of the old Neapolitan nobility. That is he."

"Charming," said Lucia. "And so like Mr. Wyse. And that Order? What is that?"

Mrs. Wyse hastily shut the morocco box.

"So like servants to leave that about," she said. "But they seem proud of it. Graciously bestowed upon me. Member of the British Empire. Ah, here is Algernon with the keys. I was showing Mrs. Lucas, dear, the photograph of Amelia. She recognised the likeness at once. Now let us all pack in. A warm morning, is it not? I don't think I shall need my furs."

The total distance to be traversed was not more than a hundred yards, but Porpoise Street was very steep, and the cobbles which must be crossed very unpleasant to walk on, so Mrs. Wyse explained. They had to wait some little while at the corner, twenty yards away from where they started, for a van was coming down the street from the direction of Mallards, and the Royce could not possibly pass it, and then they came under fire of the windows of Miss Mapp's garden-room. As usual at this hour she was sitting there with the morning paper in her hand in which she could immerse herself if anybody passed whom she did not wish to see, but was otherwise intent on the movements of the street.

Diva Plaistow had looked in with the news that she had seen Lucia and Georgie at the house-agents', and that her canary still lived. Miss Mapp professed her delight to hear about the canary, but was secretly distrustful of whether Diva had seen the visitors or not. Diva was so imaginative; to have seen a man and a woman who were strangers was quite enough to make her believe she had seen Them. Then the Royce heaved into sight round the corner below, and Miss Mapp became much excited.

"I think, Diva," she said, "that this is Mrs. Lucas's beautiful car coming. Probably she is going to call on me about something she wants to know. If you sit at the piano you will see her as she gets out. Then we shall know whether you really—"

The car came slowly up, barked loudly and instead of stopping at the front door of Mallards, turned up the street in the direction of Mallards Cottage. Simultaneously Miss Mapp caught sight of that odious chauffeur of Mrs. Wyse's. She could not see more than people's knees in the car itself (that was the one disadvantage of the garden-room window being so high above the street), but there were several pairs of them.

"No, it's only Susan's great lumbering bus," she said, "filling up the street as usual. Probably she has found out that Mrs. Lucas is staying at the Trader's Arms, and has gone to leave cards. Such a woman to shove herself in where she's not wanted I never saw. Luckily I told Mrs. Lucas what a dreadful snob she was."

"A disappointment to you, dear, when you thought Mrs. Lucas was coming to call," said Diva. "But I did see them this morning at Woolgar's and it's no use saying I didn't!"

Miss Mapp uttered a shrill cry.

"Diva, they've stopped at Mallards Cottage. They're getting out. Susan first—so like her—and . . . it's Them. She's got hold of them somehow . . . There's Mr. Wyse with the keys, bowing . . . They're going in . . . I was right, then, when I saw them peering in through the windows yesterday. Mr. Pillson's come to see the house, and the Wyses have got hold of them. You may wager they know by now about the Count and Countess Faradiddleone, and the Order of the British Empire. I really didn't think Mrs. Lucas would be so easily taken in. However, it's no business of mine."

There could not have been a better reason for Miss Mapp being violently interested in all that happened. Then an idea struck her and the agitated creases in her face faded out.

"Let us pop in to Mallards Cottage, Diva, while they are still there," she said. "I should hate to think that Mrs. Lucas should get her ideas of the society she will meet in Tilling from poor common Susan. Probably they would like a little lunch before their long drive back to Riseholme."

The inspection of the cottage had taken very little time. The main point in Georgie's mind was that Foljambe should be pleased, and there was an excellent bedroom for Foljambe, where she could sit when unoccupied. The rooms that concerned him had been viewed through the windows from the street the evening before. Consequently Miss Mapp had hardly had time to put on her garden-hat, and trip up the street with Diva, when the inspecting party came out.

"Sweet Susan!" she said. "I saw your car go by . . . Dear Mrs. Lucas, good-morning, I just popped across—this is Mrs. Plaistow—to see if you would not come and have an early lunch with me before you drive back to your lovely Riseholme. Any time would suit me, for I never have any breakfast. Twelve, half-past twelve? A little something?"

"So kind of you," said Lucia, "but Mrs. Wyse has just asked us to lunch with her."

"I see," said Miss Mapp, grinning frightfully. "Such a pity. I had hoped—but there it is."

Clearly it was incumbent on sweet Susan to ask her to join them at this early lunch, but sweet Susan showed no signs of doing anything of the sort. Off went Lucia and Georgie to the Trader's Arms to pack their belongings and leave the rest of the morning free, and the Wyses, after vainly trying to persuade them to drive there in the Royce, got into it themselves and backed down the street till it could turn in the slightly wider space opposite Miss Mapp's garden-room. This took a long time, and she was not able to get to her own front door till the manoeuvre was executed, for as often as she tried to get round the front of the car it took a short run forward, and it threatened to squash her flat against the wall of her own room if she tried to squeeze round behind it.

But there were topics to gloat over which consoled her for this act of social piracy on the part of the Wyses. It was a noble stroke to have let Mallards for fifteen guineas a week without garden-produce, and an equally brilliant act to have got Diva's house for eight with garden-produce, for Diva had some remarkably fine plum trees, the fruit of which would be ripe during her tenancy, not to mention apples: Miss Mapp foresaw a kitchen-cupboard the doors of which could not close because of the jam-pots within. Such reflections made a happy mental background as she hurried out into the town, for there were businesses to be transacted without delay. She first went to the house-agents' and had rather a job to convince Mr. Woolgar that the letting of Mallards was due to her own advertisement in *The Times,* and that therefore she owed no commission to his firm, but her logic proved irresistible. Heated but refreshed by that encounter, she paid a visit to her greengrocer and made a pleasant arrangement for the sale of the produce of her own kitchen garden at Mallards during the months of August and September. This errand brought her to the east end of the High Street, and there was Georgie already established on the belvedere busy sketching the

Landgate, before he went to breakfast (as those Wyses always called lunch) in Porpoise Street. Miss Mapp did not yet know whether he had taken Mallards Cottage or not, and that must be instantly ascertained.

She leaned on the railing close beside him, and moved a little, rustled a little, till he looked up.

"Oh, Mr. Pillson, how ashamed of myself I am!" she said. "But I couldn't help taking a peep at your lovely little sketch. So rude of me: just like an inquisitive stranger in the street. Never meant to interrupt you, but to steal away again when I'd had my peep. Every moment's precious to you, I know, as you're off this afternoon after your early lunch. But I must ask you whether your hotel was comfortable. I should be miserable if I thought that I had recommended it, and that you didn't like it."

"Very comfortable indeed, thank you," said Georgie.

Miss Mapp sidled up to the bench where he sat.

"I will just perch here for a moment before I flit off again," she said, "if you'll promise not to take any notice of me, but go on with your picky, as if I was not here. How well you've got the perspective! I always sit here for two or three minutes every morning to feast my eyes on the beauty of the outlook. What a pity you can't stay longer here! You've only had a glimpse of our sweet Tilling."

Georgie held up his drawing.

"Have I got the perspective right, do you think?" he said. "Isn't it tarsome when you mean to make a road go downhill and it will go up instead?"

"No fear of that with you!" ejaculated Miss Mapp. "If I was a little bolder I should ask you to send your drawing to our Art Society here. We have a little exhibition every summer. Could I persuade you?"

"I'm afraid I shan't be able to finish it this morning," said Georgie.

"No chance then of your coming back?" she asked.

"In August, I hope," said he, "for I've taken Mallards Cottage for two months."

"Oh, Mr. Pillson, that is good news!" cried Miss Mapp. "Lovely! All August and September. Fancy!"

"I've got to be away for a week in August," said Georgie, "as we've got an Elizabethan fête at Riseholme. I'm Francis Drake."

That was a trove for Miss Mapp and must be published at once. She prepared to flit off.

"Oh how wonderful!" she said. "Dear me, I can quite see you. The *Golden Hind*! Spanish treasure! All the pomp and majesty. I wonder if I could manage to pop down to see it. But I won't interrupt you anymore. So pleased to think it's only *au reservoir* and not goodbye."

She walked up the street again, bursting with her budget of news. Only the Wyses could possibly know that Georgie had taken Mallards Cottage, and nobody that he was going to impersonate Francis Drake . . . There was the Padre talking to Major Benjy, no doubt on his way to the steam-tram, and there were Diva and Irene a little farther on.

"Good-morning, Padre; good-morning, Major Benjy," said she.

"Good-morrow, Mistress Mapp," said the Padre. "An' hoo's the time o' day wi' ye? 'Tis said you've a fair tenant for yon Mallards."

Miss Mapp fired off her news in a broadside.

"Indeed, I have, Padre," she said. "And there's Mallards Cottage, too, about which you won't have heard. Mr. Pillson has taken that, though he won't be here all the time as he's playing Francis Drake in a fête at Riseholme for a week."

Major Benjy was not in a very good temper. It was porridge-morning with him, and his porridge had been burned. Miss Mapp already suspected something of the sort, for there had been loud angry sounds from within as she passed his dining-room window.

"That fellow whom I saw with Mrs. Lucas this morning with a cape over his arm?" he said scornfully. "Not much of a hand against the Spaniards, I should think. Ridiculous! Tea-parties with a lot of old cats more in his line. Pshaw!" And away he went to the tram, shovelling passengers off the pavement.

"Porridge burned, I expect," said Miss Mapp, thoughtfully, "though I couldn't say for certain. Morning, dear Irene. Another artist is coming to Tilling for August and September."

"Hoot awa', woman," said Irene, in recognition of the Padre's presence. "I ken that fine, for Mistress Wyse told me half an hour agone."

"But he'll be away for a week, though of course you know that, too," said Miss Mapp, slightly nettled. "Acting Francis Drake in a fête at Riseholme."

Diva trundled up.

"I don't suppose you've heard, Elizabeth," she said in a great hurry, "that Mr. Pillson has taken Mallards Cottage."

Miss Mapp smiled pityingly.

"Quite correct, dear Diva," she said. "Mr. Pillson told me himself hours ago. He's sketching the Landgate now—a sweet picky—and insisted that I should sit down and chat to him while he worked."

"Lor! How you draw them all in, Mapp," said quaint Irene. "He looks a promising young man for his age, but it's time he had his hair dyed again. Grey at the roots."

The Padre tore himself away; he had to hurry home and tell wee wifie.

"Aweel, I mustn't stand daffing here," he said, "I've got my sermon to think on."

Miss Mapp did a little more shopping, hung about on the chance of seeing Lucia again, and then went back to Mallards, to attend to her sweet flowers. Some of the beds wanted weeding, and now as she busied herself with that useful work and eradicated groundsel, each plant as she tore it up and flung it into her basket might have been Mr. and Mrs. Wyse. It was very annoying that they had stuck their hooks (so the process represented itself to her vigorous imagery) into Lucia, for Miss Mapp had intended to have no one's hook there but her own. She wanted to run her, to sponsor her, to arrange little parties for her, and cause Lucia to arrange little parties at her dictation, and, while keeping her in her place, show her off to Tilling. Providence, or whatever less beneficent power ruled the world, had not been considerate of her clear right to do this, for it was she who had been put to the expense of advertising Mallards in *The Times,* and it was entirely owing to that that Lucia had come down here, and wound up that pleasant machine of sub-letting houses, so that everybody scored financially as well as got a change. But there was nothing to be done about that for the present: she must wait till Lucia arrived here, and then be both benignant and queenly. A very sweet woman, up till now, was her verdict, though possibly lacking in fine discernment, as witnessed by her having made friends with the Wyses. Then there was Georgie: she was equally well disposed towards him for the present, but he, like Lucia, must be good, and recognise that she was the arbiter of all things social in Tilling. If he behaved properly in that regard she would propose him as an honorary member of the Tilling Art Society, and, as member of the hanging committee, see that his work had a conspicuous place on the walls of the exhibition, but it was worth remembering (in case he was not good) that quaint Irene had said that his hair was dyed, and that Major Benjy thought that he would have been very little use against the Spaniards.

But thinking was hungry work, and weeding was dirty work, and she went indoors to wash her hands for lunch after this exciting morning.

There was a dreadful block in Porpoise Street when Lucia's car came to pick up her and Georgie after their breakfast at Starling Cottage, for Mrs. Wyse's Royce was already drawn up there. The two purred and backed and advanced foot by foot, they sidled and stood on pavements meant for pedestrians, and it was not till Lucia's car had gone backwards again round the corner below Miss Mapp's garden-room, and Mrs. Wyse's forward towards the High Street, that Lucia's could come to the door, and the way down Porpoise Street lie open for their departure to Riseholme. As long as they were in sight, Susan stood waving her hand, and Algernon bowing.

Often during the drive Lucia tried, but always in vain, to start the subject which had kept them both awake last night, and tell Georgie that never would she marry again, but the moment she got near the topic of friendship, or even wondered how long Mrs. Plaistow had been a widow or whether Major Benjy would ever marry, Georgie saw a cow or a rainbow or something out of the window and violently directed attention to it. She could not quite make out what was going on in his mind. He shied away from such topics as friendship and widowhood, and she wondered if that was because he was not feeling quite ready yet, but was screwing himself up. If he only would let her develop those topics she could spare him the pain of a direct refusal, and thus soften the blow. But she had to give it up, determining, however, that when he came to dine with her that evening, she would not be silenced by his irrelevances: she would make it quite clear to him, before he embarked on his passionate declaration that, with all her affection for him, she could never marry him . . . Poor Georgie!

She dropped him at his house, and as soon as he had told Foljambe about his having taken the house at Tilling (for that must be done at once), he would come across to The Hurst.

"I hope she will like the idea," said Georgie very gravely, as he got out, "and there is an excellent room for her, isn't there?"

Foljambe opened the door to him.

"A pleasant outing, I hope, sir," said she.

"Very indeed, thank you, Foljambe," said Georgie. "And I've got great news. Mrs. Lucas has taken a house at Tilling for August and September, and so have I. Quite close to hers. You could throw a stone."

"That'll be an agreeable change," said Foljambe.

"I think you'll like it. A beautiful bedroom for you."

"I'm sure I shall," said Foljambe.

Georgie was immensely relieved, and, as he went gaily across to The Hurst, he quite forgot for the time about this menace of matrimony.

"She likes the idea," he said before he had opened the gate into Perdita's garden, where Lucia was sitting.

"Georgie, the most wonderful thing," cried she. "Oh, Foljambe's pleased, is she? So glad. An excellent bedroom. I knew she would. But I've found a letter from Adele Brixton; you know, Lady Brixton who always goes to America when her husband comes to England, and the other way about, so that they only pass each other on the Atlantic; she wants to take The Hurst for three months. She came down here for a Sunday, don't you remember, and adored it. I instantly telephoned to say I would let it."

"Well, that is luck for you," said Georgie. "But three months; what will you do for the third?"

"Georgie, I don't know, and I'm not going to think," she said. "Something will happen: it's sure to. My dear, it's perfect rapture to feel the great tide of life flowing again. How I'm going to set to work on all the old interests and the new ones as well. Tilling, the age of Anne, and I shall get a translation of Pope's *Iliad* and of Plato's *Symposium* till I can rub up my Greek again. I have been getting lazy, and I have been getting—let us go into dinner—narrow. I think you have been doing the same. We must open out, and receive new impressions, and adjust ourselves to new conditions!"

This last sentence startled Georgie very much, though it might only apply to Tilling, but Lucia did not seem to notice his faltering step as he followed her into the panelled dining-room with the refectory-table, below which it was so hard to adjust the feet with any comfort, owing to the foot-rail.

"Those people at Tilling," she said, "how interesting it will all be. They seemed to me very much alive, especially the women, who appear to have got their majors and their padres completely under their thumbs. Delicious, isn't it, to think of the new interchange of experience which awaits us. Here, nothing happens. Our dear Daisy gets a little rounder and Mrs. Antrobus a little deafer. We're in a rut: Riseholme is in a rut. We want, both of us, to get out of it, and now we're going to. Fresh fields and pastures new, Georgie . . . Nothing on your mind, my dear? You were so *distrait* as we drove home."

Some frightful revivification, thought poor Georgie, had happened to Lucia. It had been delightful, only a couple of days ago, to see her returning to her normal interests, but this repudiation of Riseholme and the craving for the *Iliad* and Tilling and the *Symposium* indicated an almost dangerous appetite for novelty. Or was it only that having bottled herself up for a year, it was natural that, the cork being now out, she should overflow in these ebullitions? She seemed to be lashing her tail, goading herself to some further revelation of her mental or spiritual needs. He shuddered at the thought of what further novelty might be popping out next. The question perhaps.

"I'm sorry I was *distrait,*" said he. "Of course I was anxious about how Foljambe might take the idea of Tilling."

Lucia struck the pomander, and it was a relief to Georgie to know that Grosvenor would at once glide in . . . She laughed and laid her hand affectionately on his.

"Georgie, dear, you are"—she took refuge in Italian as Grosvenor appeared—"you are *una vecchia signorina.*" (That means "old maid," thought Georgie.) "Wider horizons, Georgie: that is what you want. Put the rest of the food on the table, Grosvenor, and we'll help ourselves. Coffee in the music-room when I ring."

This was ghastly: Lucia, with all this talk of his being an old maid and needing to adapt himself to new conditions, was truly alarming. He almost wondered if she had been taking monkey-gland during her seclusion. Was she going to propose to him in the middle of dinner? Never, in all the years of his friendship with her, had he felt himself so strangely alien. But he was still the master of his fate (at least he hoped so), and it should not be that.

"Shall I give you some strawberry fool?" he asked miserably.

Lucia did not seem to hear him.

"Georgie, we must have ickle talk, before I ring for coffee," she said. "How long have you and I been dear friends? Longer than either of us care to think."

"But all so pleasant," said Georgie, rubbing his cold moist hands on his napkin . . . He wondered if drowning was anything like this.

"My dear, what do the years matter, if they have only deepened and broadened our friendship? Happy years, Georgie, bringing their sheaves with them. That lovely scene in Esmondi; Winchester Cathedral! And now we're both getting on. You're rather alone in the world, and so am I, but people like us with this dear strong bond of friendship between us can look forward to old age—can't we?—without any qualms. Tranquillity comes with years, and that horrid thing which Freud calls sex is expunged. We must read some Freud, I think; I have read none at present. That was one of the things I wanted to say all the time that you would show me cows out of the window. Our friendship is just perfect as it is."

Georgie's relief when he found that Foljambe liked the idea of Tilling was nothing, positively nothing, to the relief he felt now.

"My dear, how sweet of you to say that," he said. "I, too, find the quality of our friendship perfect in every way. Quite impossible, in fact, to think of—I mean, I quite agree with you. As you say, we're getting on in years, I mean I am. You're right a thousand times."

Lucia saw the sunlit dawn of relief in Georgie's face, and though she had been quite sincere in hoping that he would not be terribly hurt when she hinted to him that he must give up all hopes of being more to her than he was, she had not quite expected this effulgence. It was as if instead of pronouncing his sentence, she had taken from him some secret burden of terrible anxiety. For the moment her own satisfaction at having brought this off without paining him was swallowed up in surprise that he was so far from being pained. Was it possible that all his concern to interest her in cows and rainbows was due to apprehension that she might be leading up, *via* the topics of friendship and marriage, to something exceedingly different from the disclosure which had evidently gratified him rather than the reverse?

She struck the pomander quite a sharp blow.

"Let us go and have our coffee then," she said. "It is lovely that we are of one mind. Lovely! And there's another subject we haven't spoken about at all. Miss Mapp. What do you make of Miss Mapp? There was a look in her eye when she heard we were going to lunch with Mrs. Wyse that amazed me. She would have liked to bite her or scratch her. What did it mean? It was as if Mrs. Wyse—she asked me to call her Susan by the way, but I'm not sure that I can manage it just yet without practising—as if Mrs. Wyse had pocketed something of hers. Most extraordinary. I don't belong to Miss Mapp. Of course it's easy to see that she thinks herself very much superior to all the rest of Tilling. She says that all her friends are angels and lambs, and then just crabs them a little. *Marcate mie parole, Georgino!* I believe she wants to run me. I believe Tilling is seething with intrigue. But we shall see. How I hate all that sort of thing! We have had a touch of it now and then in Riseholme. As if it mattered who took the lead! We should aim at being equal citizens of a noble republic, where art and literature and all the manifold interests of the world are our concern. Now let us have a little music."

∞

Whatever might be the state of affairs at Tilling, Riseholme during this month of July boiled and seethed with excitements. It was just like old times, and all circled, as of old, round Lucia. She had taken the plunge; she had come back (though just now for so brief a space before her entering upon Mallards) into her native centrality. Gradually, and in increasing areas, grey and white and violet invaded the unrelieved black in which she had spent the year of her widowhood; one day she wore a white belt, another there were grey panels in her skirt, another her garden-hat had a violet riband on it. Even Georgie, who had a great eye for female attire, could not accurately follow these cumulative changes: he could not be sure whether she had worn a grey cloak before, or whether she had had white gloves in church last Sunday. Then, instead of letting her hair droop in slack and mournful braids over her ears, it resumed its old polished and corrugated appearance, and on her pale cheeks (ashen with grief) there bloomed a little brown rouge, which made her look as if she had been playing golf again, and her lips certainly were ruddier. It was all intensely exciting, a series of subtle changes at the end of which, by the middle of July, her epiphany in church without anything black about her, and with the bloom of her vitality quite restored, passed almost unremarked.

These outward and visible signs were duly representative of what had taken place within. Time, the great healer, had visited her sickroom, laid his hand on her languid brow, and the results were truly astonishing. Lucia became as good as new, or as good as old. Mrs. Antrobus and her tall daughters, Piggy and Goosie, Georgie and Daisy and her husband, greedy Robert, Colonel Boucher and his wife, and the rest were all bidden to dinner at The Hurst once more, and sometimes Lucia played to them the slow movement of the "Moonlight Sonata," and sometimes she instructed them in such elements of contract bridge as she had mastered during the day. She sketched, she played the organ in church in the absence of the organist who had measles, she sang a solo, "O for the Wings of a Dove" when he recovered and the leading chorister got chickenpox, she had lessons in bookbinding at Ye Signe of Ye Daffodil, she sat in Perdita's garden, not reading Shakespeare, but Pope's *Iliad,* and murmured half-forgotten fragments of Greek irregular verbs as she went to sleep. She had a plan for visiting Athens in the spring

("'the violet-crowned,' is not that a lovely epithet, Georgie?")
and in compliment to Queen Anne regaled her guests with rich
thick chocolate. The hounds of spring were on the winter traces
of her widowhood, and snapped up every fragment of it, and
indeed spring seemed truly to have returned to her, so various
and so multi-coloured were the blossoms that were unfolding.
Never at all had Riseholme seen Lucia in finer artistic and intellectual fettle, and it was a long time since she had looked so gay.
The world, or at any rate Riseholme, which at Riseholme came
to much the same thing, had become her parish again.

Georgie, worked to the bone with playing duets, with
consulting Foljambe as to questions of linen and plate (for it
appeared that Isabel Poppit, in pursuance of the simple life, slept
between blankets in the back-yard, and ate uncooked vegetables
out of a wooden bowl like a dog), with learning Vanderbilt con-
ventions, with taking part in Royal processions across the green,
with packing his bibelots and sending them to the bank, with
sketching, so that he might be in good form when he began to
paint at Tilling with a view to exhibiting in the Art Society, wondered what was the true source of these stupendous activities
of Lucia's, whether she was getting fit, getting in training, so
to speak, for a campaign at Tilling. Somehow it seemed likely,
for she would hardly think it worth while to run the affairs of
Riseholme with such energy, when she was about to disappear
from it for three months. Or was she intending to let Riseholme
see how dreadfully flat everything would become when she left
them? Very likely both these purposes were at work; it was like
her to kill two birds with one stone. Indeed, she was perhaps
killing three birds with one stone, for multifarious as were the
interests in which she was engaged there was one, now looming
large in Riseholme, namely the Elizabethan fête, of which she
seemed strangely unconscious. Her drive, her powers of instill-

ing her friends with her own fervour, never touched that: she did not seem to know that a fête was being contemplated at all, though now a day seldom passed without a procession of some sort crossing the green or a Morris-dance getting entangled with the choristers practising madrigals, or a crowd of soldiers and courtiers being assembled near the front entrance of the Ambermere Arms, while Daisy harangued them from a chair put on the top of a table, pausing occasionally because she forgot her words, or in order to allow them to throw up their hats and cry "God Save the Queen's Grace," "To hell with Spain," and other suitable ejaculations. Daisy, occasionally now in full dress, ruff and pearls and all, came across to the gate of The Hurst, to wait for the procession to join her, and Lucia sitting in Perdita's garden would talk to her about Tilling or the importance of being prudent if you were vulnerable at contract, apparently unaware that Daisy was dressed up at all. Once Lucia came out of the Ambermere Arms when Daisy was actually mounting the palfrey that drew the milk-cart for a full-dress rehearsal, and she seemed to be positively palfrey-blind. She merely said "Don't forget that you and Robert are dining with me tonight. Half-past seven, so that we shall get a good evening's bridge," and went on her way . . . Or she would be passing the pond on which the framework of the *Golden Hind* was already constructed, and on which Georgie was even then kneeling down to receive the accolade amid the faint cheers of Piggy and Goosie, and she just waved her hand to Georgie and said: "*Musica* after lunch, Georgie?" She made no sarcastic comments to anybody, and did not know that they were doing anything out of the ordinary.

Under this pointed unconsciousness of hers, a species of blight spread over the scheme to which Riseholme ought to have been devoting its most enthusiastic energies. The courtiers were late for rehearsals, they did not even remove their cigarettes when they bent to kiss the Queen's hand, Piggy and Goosie made steps of Morris-dances when they ought to have been holding up Elizabeth's train, and Georgie snatched up a cushion, when the accolade was imminent, to protect his shoulder. The choir-boys droned their way through madrigals, sucking peppermints, there was no life, no keenness about it all, because Lucia, who was used to inspire all Riseholme's activities, was unaware that anything was going on.

One morning when only a fortnight of July was still to run, Drake was engaged on his croquet-lawn tapping the balls about and trying to tame his white satin shoes which hurt terribly. From the garden next door came the familiar accents of the Queen's speech to her troops.

"And though I am only a weak woman," declaimed Daisy, who was determined to go through the speech without referring to her book. "Though I am only a weak woman, a weak woman—" she repeated.

"Yet I have the heart of a Prince," shouted Drake with the friendly intention of prompting her.

"Thank you, Georgie. Or ought it to be Princess, do you think?"

"No: Prince," said Georgie.

"Prince," cried Daisy. "Though I am only a weak woman, yet I have the heart of a Prince . . . Let me see . . . Prince."

There was silence.

"Georgie," said Daisy in her ordinary voice. "Do stop your croquet a minute and come to the paling. I want to talk."

"I'm trying to get used to these shoes," said Georgie. "They hurt frightfully. I shall have to take them to Tilling and wear them there. Oh, I haven't told you, Lady Brixton came down yesterday evening—"

"I know that," said Daisy.

"—and she thinks that her brother will take my house for a couple of months, as long as I don't leave any servants. He'll be here for the fête, if he does, so I wonder if you could put me up. How's Robert's cold?"

"Worse," she said. "I'm worse too. I can't remember half of what I knew by heart a week ago. Isn't there some memory-system?"

"Lots, I believe," said Georgie. "But it's rather late. They don't improve your memory all in a minute. I really think you had better read your speech to the troops, as if it was the opening of Parliament."

"I won't," said Daisy, taking off her ruff. "I'll learn it if it costs me the last breath of blood in my body—I mean drop."

"Well, it will be very awkward if you forget it all," said Georgie. "We can't cheer nothing at all. Such a pity, because your voice carries perfectly now. I could hear you while I was breakfasting."

"And it's not only that," said Daisy. "There's no life in the thing. It doesn't look as if it was happening."

"No, that's true," said Georgie. "These tarsome shoes of mine are real enough, though!"

"I begin to think we ought to have had a producer," said Daisy. "But it was so much finer to do it all ourselves, like—like Oberammergau. Does Lucia ever say anything about it? I think it's too mean for words of her to take no interest in it."

"Well, you must remember that you asked her only to be my wife," said Georgie. "Naturally she wouldn't like that."

"She ought to help us instead of going about as if we were all invisible," exclaimed Daisy.

"My dear, she did offer to help you. At least, I told you ages ago, that I felt sure she would if you asked her to."

"I feel inclined to chuck the whole thing," said Daisy.

"But you can't. Masses of tickets have been sold. And who's to pay for the *Golden Hind* and the roast sheep and all the costumes?" asked Georgie. "Not to mention all our trouble. Why not ask her to help, if you want her to?"

"Georgie, will you ask her?" said Daisy.

"Certainly not," said Georgie very firmly. "You've been managing it from the first. It's your show. If I were you, I would ask her at once. She'll be over here in a few minutes, as we're going to have a music. Pop in."

A melodious cry of "*Georgino mio!*" resounded from the open window of Georgie's drawing-room, and he hobbled away down the garden walk. Ever since that beautiful understanding they had arrived at, that both of them shrank, as from a cup of hemlock, from the idea of marriage, they had talked Italian or baby-language to a surprising extent from mere lightness of heart.

"Me tummin'," he called. "'Oo very good girl, Lucia. 'oo *molto punctuale.*"

(He was not sure about that last word, nor was Lucia, but she understood it.)

"*Georgino! Che curiose scalpe!*" said Lucia, leaning out of the window.

"Don't be so *cattiva*. They are *cattivo* enough," said Georgie. "But Drake did have shoes exactly like these."

The mere mention of Drake naturally caused Lucia to talk about something else. She did not understand any allusion to Drake.

"Now for a good practise," she said, as Georgie limped into the drawing-room. "Foljambe beamed at me. How happy it all is! I hope you said you were at home to nobody. Let us begin at once. Can you manage the *sostenuto* pedal in those odd shoes?"

Foljambe entered.

"Mrs. Quantock, sir," she said.

"Daisy darling," said Lucia effusively. "Come to hear our little practise? We must play our best, Georgino."

Daisy was still in queenly costume, except for the ruff. Lucia seemed as usual to be quite unconscious of it.

"Lucia, before you begin—" said Daisy.

"So much better than interrupting," said Lucia. "Thank you, dear. Yes?"

"About this fête. Oh, for gracious' sake don't go on seeming to know nothing about it. I tell you there is to be one. And it's all nohow. Can't you help us?"

Lucia sprang from the music-stool. She had been waiting for this moment, not impatiently, but ready for it if it came, as she knew it must, without any scheming on her part. She had been watching from Perdita's garden the straggling procession smoking cigarettes, the listless halberdiers not walking in step, the courtiers yawning in Her Majesty's face, the languor and the looseness arising from the lack of an inspiring mind. The scene on the *Golden Hind,* and that of Elizabeth's speech to her troops were equally familiar to her, for though she could not observe them from under her garden-hat close at hand, her husband had been fond of astronomy and there were telescopes great and small, which brought these scenes quite close. Moreover, she had that speech which poor Daisy found so elusive by heart. So easy to learn, just the sort of cheap bombast that Elizabeth would indulge in: she had found it in a small history of England, and had committed it to memory, just in case . . .

"But I'll willingly help you, dear Daisy," she said. "I seem to remember you told me something about it. You as Queen Elizabeth, was it not, a roast sheep on the *Golden Hind,* a speech to the troops, Morris-dances, bear-baiting, no, not bear-baiting. Isn't it all going beautifully?"

"No! It isn't," said Daisy in a lamentable voice. "I want you to help us, will you? It's all like dough."

Great was Lucia. There was no rubbing in: there was no hesitation, there was nothing but helpful sunny cordiality in response to this SOS.

"How you all work me!" she said, "but I'll try to help you if I can. Georgie, we must put off our practise, and get to grips with all this, if the fête is to be a credit to Riseholme. *Addio, caro Mozartino* for the present. Now begin, Daisy, and tell me all the trouble."

For the next week Mozartino and the *Symposium* and contract bridge were non-existent and rehearsals went on all day. Lucia demonstrated to Daisy how to make her first appearance, and, when the trumpeters blew a fanfare, she came out of the door of The Hurst, and without the slightest hurry majestically marched down the crazy pavement. She did not fumble at the gate as Daisy always did, but with a swift imperious nod to Robert Quantock, which made him pause in the middle of a sneeze, she caused him to fly forward, open it, and kneel as she passed through. She made a wonderful curtsey to her lieges and motioned them to close up in front of her. And all this was done in the clothes of today, without a ruff or a pearl to help her.

"Something like that, do you think, dear Daisy, for the start of the procession?" she said to her. "Will you try it like that and see how it goes? And a little more briskness, gentlemen, from the halberdiers. Would you form in front of me now, while Mrs. Quantock goes into the house . . . Ah, that has more snap, hasn't it? Excellent. Quite like guardsmen. Piggy and Goosie, my dears, you must remember that you are Elizabethan Countesses.

Very stately, please, and Countesses never giggle. Sweep two low curtseys, and while still down pick up the Queen's train. You opened the gate very properly, Robert. Very nice indeed. Now may we have that all over again. Queen, please," she called to Daisy.

Daisy came out of the house in all the panoply of Majesty, and with the idea of not hurrying came so slowly that her progress resembled that of a queen following a hearse. ("A little quicker, dear," called Lucia encouragingly. "We're all ready.") Then she tripped over a piece of loose crazy pavement. Then she sneezed, for she had certainly caught Robert's cold. Then she forgot to bow to her lieges, until they had closed up in procession in front of her, and then bobbed to their backs.

"Hey ho, nonny, nonny," sang Lucia to start the chorus. "Off we go! Right, left—I beg your pardon, how stupid of me—left, right. Crescendo, choir. Sing out, please. We're being Merrie England. Capital!"

Lucia walked by the side of the procession across the green, beating time with her parasol, full of encouragement and enthusiasm. Sometimes she ran on in front and observed their progress, sometimes she stood still to watch them go by.

"Open out a little, halberdiers," she cried, "so that we can get a glimpse of the Queen from in front. Hey nonny! Hold that top G, choirboys! Queen, dear, don't attempt to keep step with the halberdiers. Much more royal to walk as you choose. The train a little higher, Piggy and Goosie. Hey nonny, nonny HEY!"

She looked round as they got near the *Golden Hind,* to see if the cooks were basting the bolster that did duty for the sheep, and that Drake's sailors were dancing their hornpipes.

"Dance, please, sailors," she shrieked. "Go on basting, cooks, until the procession stops, and then begins the chorus of sailors on the last 'nonny Hey.' Cooks must join in, too, or we shan't get enough body of sound. Open out, halberdiers, leave plenty of room for the Queen to come between you. Slowly, Elizabeth! 'When the storm winds blow and the surges sweep.' Louder! Are you ready, Georgie? No; don't come off the *Golden Hind*. You receive the Queen on the deck. A little faster, Elizabeth, the chorus will be over before you get here."

Lucia clapped her hands.

"A moment, please," she said. "A wonderful scene. But just one suggestion. May I be Queen for a minute and show you the effect I want to get, dear Daisy? Let us go back, procession, please, twenty yards. Halberdiers still walking in front of Queen. Sailors' chorus all over again. Off we go! Now, halberdiers, open out. Half right and left turn respectively. Two more steps and halt, making an avenue."

It was perfectly timed. Lucia moved forward up the avenue of halberdiers, and just as the last "Yo ho" was yelled by cooks, courtiers and sailors, she stepped with indescribable majesty on to the deck of the *Golden Hind*. She stood there a moment quite still, and whispered to Georgie, "Kneel and kiss my hand, Georgie. Now, everybody together! 'God save the Queen.' 'Hurrah.' Hats in the air. Louder, louder! Now die away! There!"

Lucia had been waving her own hat, and shrilly cheering herself, and now she again clapped her hands for attention, as she scrutinised the deck of the *Golden Hind*.

"But I don't see Drake's wife," she said. "Drake's wife, please."

Drake's wife was certainly missing. She was also the grocer's wife, and as she had only to come forward for one moment, curtsey and disappear, she was rather slack at her attendance of rehearsals.

"It doesn't matter," said Lucia. "I'll take Drake's wife, just for this rehearsal. Now we must have that over again. It's one of the most important moments, this Queen's entry on to the *Golden Hind*. We must make it rich in romance, in majesty, in spaciousness. Will the procession, please, go back, and do it over again?"

This time poor Daisy was much too early. She got to the *Golden Hind* long before the cooks and the chorus were ready for her. But there was a murmur of applause when Mrs. Drake (so soon to be Lady Drake) ran forward and threw herself at the Queen's feet in an ecstasy of loyalty, and having kissed her hand walked backwards from the Presence with head bent low, as if in adoration.

"Now step to the Queen's left, Georgie," said Lucia, "and take her left hand, holding it high and lead her to the banquet. Daisy dear, you *must* mind your train. Piggy and Goosie will lay it down as you reach the deck, and then you must look after it yourself. If you're not careful you'll tread on it and fall into the Thames. You've got to move so that it follows you when you turn round."

"May I kick it?" asked Daisy.

"No, it can be done without. You must practise that."

The whole company now, sailors, soldiers, courtiers and all were eager as dogs are to be taken out for a walk by their mistress, and Lucia reluctantly consented to come and look at the scene of the review at Tilbury. Possibly some little idea, she diffidently said, might occur to her; fresh eyes sometimes saw something, and if they all really wanted her she was at their disposal. So off they went to the rendezvous in front of the Ambermere Arms, and the fresh eyes perceived that according to the present grouping of soldiers and populace no spectator would see anything of the Queen at all. So that was rectified, and the mob was drilled to run into its proper places with due eagerness, and Lucia sat where the front row of spectators would be to hear the great speech. When it was over she warmly congratulated the Queen.

"Oh, I'm so glad you liked it," said the Queen. "Is there anything that strikes you?"

Lucia sat for a while in pensive silence.

"Just one or two little tiny things, dear," she said, thoughtfully. "I couldn't hear very well. I wondered sometimes what the mob was cheering about. And would it perhaps be safer to read the speech? There was a good deal of prompting that was quite audible. Of course there are disadvantages in reading it. It won't seem so spontaneous and inspiring if you consult a paper all the time. Still, I dare say you'll get it quite by heart before the time comes. Indeed, the only real criticism I have to make is about your gestures, your movements. Not quite, quite majestic enough, not inspiring enough. Too much as if you were whisking flies away. More breadth!"

Lucia sighed, she appeared to be lost in meditation.

"What kind of breadth?" asked Daisy.

"So difficult to explain," said Lucia. "You must get more variety, more force, both in your gestures and your voice. You must be fierce sometimes, the great foe of Spain, you must be tender, the mother of your people. You must be a Tudor. The daughter of that glorious cad, King Hal. Coarse and kingly. Shall I show you for a moment the sort of thing I mean? So much easier to show than to explain."

Daisy's heart sank: she was full of vague apprehensions. But having asked for help, she could hardly refuse this generous granting of it, for indeed Lucia was giving up her whole morning.

"Very good of you," she said.

"Lend me your copy of the speech, then," said Lucia, "and might I borrow your ruff, just to encourage myself. Now let me read through the speech to myself. Yes . . . yes . . . crescendo, and flare up then . . . pause again; a touch of tenderness . . . Well, as you insist on it I'll try to show you what I mean. Terribly nervous, though."

Lucia advanced and spoke in the most ingratiating tones to her army and the mob.

"Please have patience with me, ladies and gentlemen," she said, "while I go through the speech once more. Wonderful words, aren't they? I know I shan't do them justice. Let me see: the palfrey with the Queen will come out from the garden of the Ambermere Arms, will it not? Then will the whole mob, please, hurry into the garden and then come out romping and cheering and that sort of thing in front of me. When I get to where the table is, that is to say, where the palfrey will stand as I make my speech, some of the mob must fall back, and the rest sit on the grass, so that the spectators may see. Now, please."

Lucia stalked in from the garden, joining the mob now and then to show them how to gambol, and nimbly vaulted (thanks to callisthenics) on to the table on which was the chair where she sat on horseback.

Then with a great sweep of her arm she began to speak. The copy of the speech which she carried flew out of her hand, but that made no difference, for she had it all by heart, and without pause, except for the bursts of cheering from the mob, when she pointed at them, she declaimed it all, her voice now rising, now falling, now full of fire, now tender and motherly. Then she got down from the table, and passed along the line of her troops, beckoned to the mob—which in the previous scene had been cooks and sailors and all sorts of things—to close up behind her with shouts and cheers and gambollings, and went off down the garden path again.

"That sort of thing, dear Daisy, don't you think?" she said to

the Queen, returning her ruff. "So crude and awkwardly done
I know, but perhaps that may be the way to put a little life into
it. Ah, there's your copy of the speech. Quite familiar to me, I
found. I dare say I learned it when I was at school. Now, I really
must be off. I wish I could think that I had been any use."

Next morning Lucia was too busy to superintend the
rehearsal: she was sure that Daisy would manage it beautifully,
and she was indeed very busy watching through a field-glass in
the music-room the muddled and anaemic performance. The
halberdiers strolled along with their hands in their pockets.
Piggy and Goosie sat down on the grass, and Daisy knew less
of her speech than ever. The collective consciousness of Riseholme began to be aware that nothing could be done without
Lucia, and conspiratorial groups conferred stealthily, dispers-
ing or dropping their voices as Queen Elizabeth approached
and forming again when she had gone by. The choir which had
sung so convincingly when Lucia was there with her loud "Hey
nonny nonny," never bothered about the high G at all, but simply left it out; the young Elizabethans who had gambolled like
intoxicated lambkins under her stimulating eye sat down and
chewed daisies; the cooks never attempted to baste the bolster;
and the Queen's speech to her troops was received with the most
respectful tranquillity.

Georgie, in Drake's shoes which were becoming less agonising with use, lunched with Colonel and Mrs. Boucher. Mrs.
Boucher was practically the only Riseholmite who was taking
no part in the fête, because her locomotion was confined to the
wheels of a bath-chair. But she attended every rehearsal and had
views which were as strong as her voice.

"You may like it or not," she said very emphatically, "but the
only person who can pull you through is Lucia."

"Nobody can pull poor Daisy through," said Georgie. "Hopeless!"

"That's what I mean," said she. "If Lucia isn't the Queen, I say give it all up. Poor Daisy's bitten off, if you won't misunderstand me, as we're all such friends of hers, more than she can chew. My kitchen-cat, and I don't care who knows it, would make a better Queen."

"But Lucia's going off to Tilling, next week," said Georgie. "She won't be here even."

"Well, beg and implore her not to desert Riseholme," said Mrs. Boucher. "Why, everybody was muttering about it this morning, army and navy and all. It was like a revolution. There was Mrs. Antrobus; she said to me, 'Oh dear, oh dear, it will never do at all,' and there was poor Daisy standing close beside her; and we all turned red. Most awkward. And it's up to you, Georgie, to go down on your knees to Lucia and say 'Save Riseholme!' There!"

"But she refused to have anything to do with it, after Daisy asked her to be my wife," said Georgie Drake.

"Naturally she would be most indignant. An insult. But you and Daisy must implore her. Perhaps she could go to Tilling and settle herself in and then come back for the fête, for she doesn't need any rehearsals. She could act every part herself if she could be a crowd."

"Marvellous woman!" said Colonel Boucher. "Every word of the Queen's speech by heart, singing with the choir, basting with the cooks, dancing with the sailors. That's what I call instinct, eh? You'd have thought she had been studying it all the time. I agree with my wife, Georgie. The difficulty is Daisy. *Would* she give it up?"

Georgie brightened.

"She did say that she felt inclined to chuck the whole thing, a few days ago," he said.

"There you are, then," said Mrs. Boucher. "Remind her of what she said. You and she go to Lucia before you waste time over another rehearsal without her, and implore her. Implore! I shouldn't a bit wonder if she said yes. Indeed, if you ask me, I believe that she's been keeping out of it all until you saw you couldn't do without her. Then she came to help at a rehearsal, and you all saw what you could do when she was there. Why, I burst out cheering myself when she said she had the heart of a Prince. Then she retires again as she did this morning, and more than ever you see you can't do without her. I say she's waiting to be asked. It would be like her, you know."

That was an illuminating thought; it certainly seemed tremendously like Lucia at her very best.

"I believe you're right. She's cleverer than all of us put together," said Georgie. "I shall go over to Daisy at once and sound her. Thank God, my shoes are better."

It was a gloomy queen that Georgie found, a Queen of Sheba with no spirit left in her, but only a calmness of despair.

"It went worse than ever this morning," she remarked. "And I dare say we've not touched bottom yet. Georgie, what is to be done?"

It was more delicate to give Daisy the chance of abdicating herself.

"I'm sure I don't know," said he. "But something's got to be done. I wish I could think what."

Daisy was rent with pangs of jealousy and of consciousness of her supreme impotence. She took half a glass of port, which her regime told her was deadly poison.

"Georgie! Do you think there's the slightest chance of getting Lucia to be the Queen and managing the whole affair?" she asked quaveringly.

"We might try," said Georgie. "The Bouchers are for it, and everybody else as well, I think."

"Well, come quick then, or I may repent," said Daisy.

∞

Lucia had seen them coming, and sat down at her piano. She had not time to open her music, and so began the first movement of the "Moonlight Sonata."

"Ah, how nice!" she said. "Georgie, I'm going to practise all afternoon. Poor fingers so rusty! And did you have a lovely rehearsal this morning? Speech going well, Daisy? I'm sure it is."

"Couldn't remember a word," said Daisy. "Lucia, we all want to turn the whole thing over to you, Queen and all. Will you—"

"Please, Lucia," said Georgie.

Lucia looked from one to the other in amazement.

"But, dear things, how can I?" she said. "I shan't be here to begin with, I shall be at Tilling. And then all the trouble you've been taking, Daisy. I couldn't. Impossible. Cruel."

"We can't do it at all without you," said Daisy firmly. "So that's impossible too. Please, Lucia."

Lucia seemed quite bewildered by these earnest entreaties.

"Can't you come back for the fête?" said Georgie. "Rehearse all day, every day, till the end of the month. Then go to Tilling, and you and I will return just for the week of the fête."

Lucia seemed to be experiencing a dreadful struggle with herself.

"Dear Georgie, dear Daisy, you're asking a great sacrifice of me," she said. "I had planned my days here so carefully. My music, my Dante: all my lessons! I shall have to give them all up, you know, if I'm to get this fête into any sort of shape. No time for anything else."

A miserable two-part fugue of "Please, Lucia. It's the only chance. We can't do it unless you're Queen" suddenly burst into the happy strains of "It *is* good of you. Oh, thank you, Lucia," and the day was won.

Instantly she became extremely businesslike.

"No time to waste then," she said. "Let us have a full rehearsal at three, and after that I'll take the Morris-dancers and the halberdiers. You and Georgie must be my lieutenants, dear Daisy. We shall all have to pull together. By the way, what will you be now?"

"Whatever you like," said Daisy recklessly.

Lucia looked at her fixedly with that gimlet-eye, as if appraising, at their highest, her possibilities.

"Then let us see, dear Daisy," she said, "what you can make of Drake's wife. Quite a short part, I know, but so important. You have to get into that one moment all the loyalty, all the devotion of the women of England to the Queen."

She rose. "Let us begin working at once," she said. "This is the *Golden Hind*: I have just stepped on to it. Now go behind the piano, and then come tripping out, full of awe, full of reverence . . . Oh, dear me, that will never do. Shall I act it for you once more?" . . .

Chapter Four

LUCIA HAD COME BACK TO Tilling last night from the fêteful week at Riseholme, and she was sitting next morning after breakfast at the window of the garden-room in Miss Mapp's house. It was a magic casement to anyone who was interested in life, as Lucia certainly was, and there was a tide every morning in the affairs of Tilling which must be taken at the flood. Mrs. Wyse's Royce had lurched down the street, Diva had come out with her market basket from quaint Irene's house, of which she was now the tenant, Miss Mapp's (she was already by special request "Elizabeth") gardener had wheeled off to the greengrocer his daily barrowful of garden-produce. Elizabeth had popped in to welcome her on her return from Riseholme and congratulate her on the fête of which the daily illustrated papers had been so full, and, strolling about the garden with her, had absently picked a few roses (Diva's had greenfly); the Padre passing by the magic casement had wished her, "Good-morrow, Mistress Lucas," and finally Major Benjy had come out of his house on the way to catch the tram to the golf links. Lucia called "*Quai-hai*" to him in silvery tones, for they had made great friends in the days she had already spent at Tilling, and reminded him that he was dining with her that night. With great gallantry he had taken off his cap, and bawled out that this wasn't the sort of engagement he was in any danger of forgetting, *au reservoir*.

The tide had ebbed now, and Lucia left the window. There was so much to think about that she hardly knew where to begin. First her eyes fell on the piano which was no longer the remarkable Blumenfelt belonging to Elizabeth on which she had been granted the privilege to play, but one which she had hired from Brighton. No doubt it was quite true that, as Elizabeth had said, her Blumenfelt had been considered a very fine instrument, but nobody, for the last twenty years or so, could have considered it anything but a remarkable curiosity. Some notes sounded like the chirping of canaries (Diva's canary was quite well again after its pip), others did not sound at all, and the *sostenuto* pedal was a thing of naught. So Lucia had hired a new piano, and had put the canary-piano in the little telephone-room off the hall. It filled it up, but it was still possible to telephone if you went in sideways. Elizabeth had shown traces of acidity about this when she discovered the substitution, and had rather pensively remarked that her piano had belonged to her dearest mamma, and she hoped the telephone-room wasn't damp. It seemed highly probable that it had been her mother's if not her grandmother's, but after all Lucia had not promised to play on it.

So much for the piano. There lay on it now a china bowl full of press-cuttings, and Lucia glanced at a few, recalling the triumphs of the past week. The fête, favoured by brilliant weather and special trains from Worcester and Gloucester and Birmingham, had been a colossal success. The procession had been cinematographed, so too had the scene on the *Golden Hind* and the click of cameras throughout the whole performance had been like the noise of cicadas in the south. The Hurst had been the target for innumerable lenses (Lucia was most indulgent) and she was photographed at her piano and in Perdita's garden and musing in an arbour, as Queen Elizabeth and as herself, and she had got one of those artists to take (rather reluctantly) a special photograph of Drake's poor wife. That had not been a success, for Daisy had moved, but Lucia's intention was of the kindest. And throughout, to photographers and interviewers alike, Lucia (knowing that nobody would believe it) had insisted that all the credit was due to Drake's wife, who had planned everything (or nearly) and had done all the spadework.

There had nearly been one dreadful disaster. In fact there had been the disaster, but the amazing Lucia, quite impromptu, had wrung a fresh personal triumph out of it. It was on the last day of the fête, when the green would hardly contain the influx of visitors, and another tier of benches had been put up round the pond where the *Golden Hind* lay, that this excruciating moment had occurred. Queen Elizabeth had just left the deck where she had feasted on a plateful of kippered cinders, and the procession was escorting her away, when the whole of the stern of the *Golden Hind,* on which was the fire and the previously roasted sheep and a mast, streaming with ancients and the crowd of cheering cooks, broke off, and with a fearful splash and hiss fell into the water. Before anyone could laugh, Lucia (remembering that the water was only three feet deep at the most and so there was no danger of anyone drowning) broke into a ringing cry. "Zounds and Zooks," she shouted. "Thus will I serve the damned galleons of Spain," and with a magnificent gesture of disdain at the cooks standing waist-high in the water, she swept on with her procession. The reporters singled out for special notice this wonderful piece of symbolism. A few of the most highbrow deemed it not quite legitimate business, but none questioned the superb dramatic effect of the device, for it led on with such perfect fitness to the next topic, namely the coming of the Armada. The cooks waded ashore, rushed home to change

their clothes, and were in time to take their places in the mob
that escorted her white palfrey. Who would mind a ducking in
the service of such a resourceful Queen? Of all Lucia's triumphs
during the week, that inspired moment was the crown, and she
could not help wondering what poor Daisy would have done, if
she had been on the throne that day. Probably she would have
said: "Oh dear, oh dear, they've all fallen into the water. We must
stop."

No wonder Riseholme was proud of Lucia, and Tilling which
had been greedily devouring the picture papers was proud too.
There was one possible exception, she thought, and that was
Elizabeth, who in her visit of welcome just now had said, "How
dreadful all this publicity must be for you, dear! How you must
shrink from it!"

But Lucia, as usual, had been quite up to the mark.

"Sweet of you to be so sympathetic, Elizabeth," she had said.
"But it was my duty to help dear Riseholme, and I mustn't regard
the consequences to myself."

That put the lid on Elizabeth: she said no more about the
fête.

∞

Lucia, as these random thoughts suggested by that stack of press-
cuttings flitted through her brain, felt that she would have soon
to bring it to bear on Elizabeth, for she was becoming something
of a problem. But first, for this was an immediate concern, she
must concentrate on Georgie. Georgie at the present moment,
unconscious of his doom, and in a state of the highest approbation with life generally, was still at Riseholme, for Adele Brixton's
brother, Colonel Cresswell, had taken his house for two months
and there were many bits of things, embroidery and sketches and

little bottles with labels, "For outward application only," which he must put away. He had been staying with Daisy for the fête, for Foljambe and the rest of his staff had come to Tilling at the beginning of August and it was not worth while taking them all back, though it would be difficult to get on without Foljambe for a week. Then he had stopped on for this extra day with Daisy after the fête was over, to see that everything was tidy and discreet and Lucia expected him back this morning.

She had very upsetting news for him: ghastly in fact. The vague rumours which had been rife at Riseholme were all too true, and Cadman, her chauffeur, had come to Lucia last night with the bombshell that he and Foljambe were thinking of getting married. She had seen Foljambe as well, and Foljambe had begged her to break the news to Georgie.

"I should take it very kind of you, ma'am, if you would," Foljambe had said, "for I know I could never bring myself to do it, and he wouldn't like to feel that I had made up my mind without telling him. We're in no hurry, me and Cadman, we shouldn't think of being married till after we got back to Riseholme in the autumn, and that'll give Mr. Georgie several months to get suited. I'm sure you'll make him see it the right way, if anybody can."

This handsome tribute to her tact had had its due weight, and Lucia had promised to be the messenger of these dismal tidings. Georgie would arrive in time for lunch today, and she was determined to tell him at once. But it was dreadful to think of poor Georgie on his way now, full of the pleasantest anticipations for the future (since Foljambe had expressed herself more than pleased with her bedroom) and rosy with the remarkable success of his Drake, and the very substantial rent for which he had let his house for two months, with this frightful blow so soon to be dealt him by her hand. Lucia had no idea how he would take it, except that he was certain to be terribly upset. So, leaving the garden-room and establishing herself in the pleasant shade on the lawn outside, she thought out quite a quantity of bracing and valuable reflections.

She turned her thoughts towards Elizabeth Mapp. During those ten days before Lucia had gone to Riseholme for the fête, she had popped in every single day: it was quite obvious that Elizabeth was keeping her eye on her. She always had some glib excuse: she wanted a hot-water bottle, or a thimble or a screwdriver that she had forgotten to take away, and declining all assistance would go to look for them herself, feeling sure that she could put her hand on them instantly without troubling anybody. She would go into the kitchen wreathed in smiles and pleasant observations for Lucia's cook, she would pop into the servants' hall and say something agreeable to Cadman, and pry into cupboards to find what she was in search of. (It was during one of these expeditions that she had discovered her dearest mamma's piano in the telephone-room.) Often she came in without knocking or ringing the bell, and then if Lucia or Grosvenor heard her clandestine entry, and came to see who it was, she scolded herself for her stupidity in not remembering that for the present, this was not her house. So forgetful of her.

On one of these occasions she had popped out into the garden, and found Lucia eating a fig from the tree that grew against the garden-room, and was covered with fruit.

"Oh you dear thief!" she said. "What about garden-produce?"

Then seeing Lucia's look of blank amazement, she had given a pretty peal of laughter.

"Lulu, dear! Only my joke," she cried. "Poking a little fun at

Queen Elizabeth. You may eat every fig in my garden, and I wish there were more of them."

On another occasion Elizabeth had found Major Benjy having tea with Lucia, and she had said, "Oh, how disappointed I am! I had so hoped to introduce you to each other, and now someone else has taken that treat from me. Who was the naughty person?" But perhaps that was a joke too. Lucia was not quite sure that she liked Elizabeth's jokes, any more than she liked her informal visits.

This morning, Lucia cast an eye over her garden. The lawn badly wanted cutting, the flower-beds wanted weeding, the box-edgings to them wanted clipping, and it struck her that the gardener, whose wages she paid, could not have done an hour's work here since she left. He was never in this part of the garden at all, she seemed to remember, but was always picking fruit and vegetables in the kitchen garden, or digging over the asparagus-bed, or potting chrysanthemums, or doing other jobs that did not concern her own interests but Elizabeth's. There he was now, a nice genial man, preparing a second basketful of garden-produce to take to the greengrocer's, from whom eventually Lucia bought it. An enquiry must instantly be held.

"Good-morning, Coplen," she said. "I want you to cut the lawn today. It's got dreadfully long."

"Very sorry, ma'am," said he. "I don't think I can find time today myself. I could get a man in perhaps to do it."

"I should prefer that you should," said Lucia. "You can get a man in to pick those vegetables."

"It's not only them," he said. "Miss Mapp she told me to manure the strawberry-beds today."

"But what has Miss Mapp got to do with it?" said she. "You're in my employment."

"Well, that does only seem fair," said the impartial Coplen. "But you see, ma'am, my orders are to go to Miss Mapp every morning and she tells me what she wants done."

"Then for the future please come to me every morning and see what I want done," she said. "Finish what you're at now, and then start on the lawn at once. Tell Miss Mapp by all means that I've given you these instructions. And no strawberry-bed shall be manured today, nor indeed until my garden looks less like a tramp who hasn't shaved for a week."

Supported by an impregnable sense of justice but still dangerously fuming, Lucia went back to her garden-room, to tranquillise herself with an hour's practice on the new piano. Very nice tone; she and Georgie would be able to start their musical hours again now. This afternoon, perhaps, if he felt up to it after the tragic news, a duet might prove tonic. Not a note had she played during that triumphant week at Riseholme. Scales first then, and presently she was working away at a new Mozart, which she and Georgie would subsequently read over together.

There came a tap at the door of the garden-room. It opened a chink, and Elizabeth in her sweetest voice said: "May I pop in once more, dear?"

Elizabeth was out of breath. She had hurried up from the High Street.

"So sorry to interrupt your sweet music, *Lucia mia*," she said. "What a pretty tune! What fingers you have! But my good Coplen has come to me in great perplexity. So much better to clear it up at once, I thought, so I came instantly though rather rushed today. A little misunderstanding, no doubt. Coplen is not clever."

Elizabeth seemed to be labouring under some excitement which might account for this loss of wind. So Lucia waited till she was more controlled.

"—And your new piano, dear?" asked Elizabeth. "You like it? It sounded so sweet, though not quite the tone of dearest mamma's. About Coplen then?"

"Yes, about Coplen," said Lucia.

"He misunderstood, I am sure, what you said to him just now. So distressed he was. Afraid I should be vexed with him. I said I would come to see you and make it all right."

"Nothing easier, dear," said Lucia. "We can put it all right in a minute. He told me he had not time to cut the lawn today because he had to manure your strawberry-beds, and I said 'The lawn please, at once,' or words to that effect. He didn't quite grasp, I think, that he's in my employment, so naturally I reminded him of it. He understands now, I hope."

Elizabeth looked rather rattled at these energetic remarks, and Lucia saw at once that this was the stuff to give her.

"But my garden-produce, you know, dear Lulu," said Elizabeth. "It is not much use to me if all those beautiful pears are left to rot on the trees till the wasps eat them."

"No doubt that is so," said Lucia; "but Coplen, whose wages I pay, is no use to me if he spends his entire time in looking after your garden-produce. I pay for his time, dear Elizabeth, and I intend to have it. He also told me he took his orders every morning from you. That won't do at all. I shan't permit that for a moment. If I had engaged your cook as well as your gardener, I should not allow her to spend her day in roasting mutton for you. So that's all settled."

It was borne in upon Elizabeth that she hadn't got a leg to stand upon and she sat down.

"Lulu," she said, "anything would be better than that I should have a misunderstanding with such a dear as you are. I won't argue, I won't put my point of view at all. I yield. There! If you can spare Coplen for an hour in the morning to take my little fruits and vegetables to the greengrocer's I should be glad."

"Quite impossible, I'm afraid, dear Elizabeth," said Lucia with the greatest cordiality. "Coplen has been neglecting the flower-garden dreadfully, and for the present it will take him all his time to get it tidy again. You must get someone else to do that."

Elizabeth looked quite awful for a moment: then her face was wreathed in smiles again.

"Precious one!" she said. "It shall be exactly as you wish. Now I must run away. *Au reservoir.* You're not free, I suppose, this evening to have a little dinner with me? I would ask Major Benjy to join us, and our beloved Diva, who has a passion, positively a passion for you. Major Benjy indeed too. He raves about you. Wicked woman, stealing all the hearts of Tilling."

Lucia felt positively sorry for the poor thing. Before she left for Riseholme last week, she had engaged Diva and Major Benjy to dine with her tonight, and it was quite incredible that Elizabeth, by this time, should not have known that.

"Sweet of you," she said, "but I have a tiny little party myself tonight. Just one or two, dropping in."

Elizabeth lingered a moment yet, and Lucia said to herself that the thumbscrew and the rack would not induce her to ask Elizabeth, however long she lingered.

Lucia and she exchanged kissings of the hand as Elizabeth emerged from the front door, and tripped down the street. "I see I must be a little firm with her," thought Lucia, "and when I've taught her her place, then it will be time to be kind. But I won't ask her to dinner just yet. She must learn not to ask me when she knows I'm engaged. And she shall not pop in without ringing. I must tell Grosvenor to put the door on the chain."

Lucia returned to her practice, but shovelled the new Mozart out of sight, when, in one of her glances out of the open window, she observed Georgie coming up the street, on his way from the station. He had a light and airy step, evidently he was in the best of spirits and he waved to her as he caught sight of her.

"Just going to look in at the cottage one second," he called out, "to see that everything's all right, and then I'll come and have a chat before lunch. Heaps to tell you."

"So have I," said Lucia, ruefully thinking what one of those things was. "Hurry up, Georgie."

He tripped along up to the cottage, and Lucia's heart was wrung for him, for all that gaiety would soon suffer a total eclipse, and she was to be the darkener of his day. Had she better tell him instantly, she wondered, or hear his news first, and outline the recent Manoeuvres of Mapp. These exciting topics might prove tonic, something to fall back on afterwards. Whereas, if she stabbed him straight away, they would be of no service as restoratives. Also there was stewed lobster for lunch, and Georgie who adored it would probably not care a bit about it if the blow fell first.

Georgie began to speak almost before he opened the door.

"All quite happy at the cottage," he said, "and Foljambe ever so pleased with Tilling. Everything in spick-and-span order and my paintbox cleaned up and the hole in the carpet mended quite beautifully. She must have been busy while I was away."

("Dear, oh dear, she has," thought Lucia.)

"And everything settled at Riseholme," continued poor Georgie. "Colonel Cresswell wants my house for three months, so I said yes, and now we're both homeless for October, unless we keep on our houses here. I had to put on my Drake clothes again yesterday, for the *Birmingham Gazette* wanted to photograph me. My dear, what a huge success it all was, but I'm glad to get away, for everything will be as flat as ditch-water now, all except Daisy. She began to buck up at once the moment you left, and I positively heard her say how quickly you picked up the part of the Queen after watching her once or twice."

"No! Poor thing!" said Lucia with deep compassion.

"Now tell me all about Tilling," said Georgie, feeling he must play fair.

"Things are beginning to move, Georgie," said she, forgetting for the time the impending tragedy. "Night-marches, Georgie, manoeuvres. Elizabeth, of course. I'm sure I was right, she wants to run me, and if she can't (if!) she'll try to fight me. I can see glimpses of hatred and malice in her."

"And you'll fight her?" asked Georgie eagerly.

"Nothing of the kind, my dear," said Lucia. "What do you take me for? Every now and then, when necessary, I shall just give her two or three hard slaps. I gave her one this morning: I did indeed. Not a very hard one, but it stung."

"No! Do tell me," said Georgie.

Lucia gave a short but perfectly accurate description of the gardener-crisis.

"So I stopped that," she said, "and there are several other things I shall stop. I won't have her, for instance, walking into my house without ringing. So I've told Grosvenor to put up the chain. And she calls me Lulu which makes me sick. Nobody's ever called me Lulu and they shan't begin now. I must see if calling her Liblib will do the trick. And then she asked me to dinner tonight, when she must have known perfectly well that Major Benjy and Diva are dining with me. You're dining too, by the way."

"I'm not sure if I'd better," said Georgie. "I think Foljambe might expect me to dine at home the first night I get back. I know she wants to go through the linen and plate with me."

"No, Georgie, quite unnecessary," said she. "I want you to help me to give the others a jolly comfortable evening. We'll play bridge and let Major Benjy lay down the law. We'll have a genial evening, make them enjoy it. And tomorrow I shall ask the Wyses and talk about Countesses. And the day after I shall ask the Padre and his wife and talk Scotch. I want you to come every night. It's new in Tilling I find, to give little dinners. Tea is the usual entertainment. And I shan't ask Liblib at all till next week."

"But my dear, isn't that war?" asked Georgie. (It did look rather like it.)

"Not the least. It's benevolent neutrality. We shall see if she learns sense. If she does, I shall be very nice to her again and ask her to several pleasant little parties. I am giving her every chance. Also Georgie . . ." Lucia's eyes assumed that gimlet-like expression which betokened an earnest purpose, "I want to understand her and be fair to her. At present I can't understand her. The idea of her giving orders to a gardener to whom I give wages! But that's all done with. I can hear the click of the mowing-machine on the lawn now. Just two or three things I won't stand. I won't be patronised by Liblib, and I won't be called Lulu, and I won't have her popping in and out of my house like a cuckoo clock."

Lunch drew to an end. There was Georgie looking so prosperous and plump, with his chestnut-coloured hair no longer in the least need of a touch of dye, and his beautiful clothes. Already Major Benjy, who had quickly seen that if he wanted to be friends with Lucia he must be friends with Georgie too, had pronounced him to be the best-dressed man in Tilling, and Lucia, who invariably passed on dewdrops of this kind, had caused Georgie the deepest gratification by repeating this. And now she was about to plunge a dagger in his heart. She put her elbows on the table, so as to be ready to lay a hand of sympathy on his.

"Georgie, I've got something to tell you," she said.

"I'm sure I shall like it," said he. "Go on."

"No, you won't like it at all," she said.

It flashed through his mind that Lucia had changed her mind about marrying him, but it could not be that, for she would never have said he wouldn't like it at all. Then he had a flash of intuition.

"Something about Foljambe," he said in a quavering voice.

"Yes. She and Cadman are going to marry."

Georgie turned on her a face from which all other expression except hopeless despair had vanished, and her hand of sympathy descended on his, firmly pressing it.

"When?" he said, after moistening his dry lips.

"Not for the present. Not till we get back to Riseholme."

Georgie pushed away his untasted coffee.

"It's the most dreadful thing that's ever happened to me," he said. "It's quite spoiled all my pleasure. I didn't think Foljambe was so selfish. She's been with me fifteen years, and now she goes and breaks up my home like this."

"My dear, that's rather an excessive statement," said Lucia. "You can get another parlour-maid. There are others."

"If you come to that, Cadman could get another wife," said Georgie, "and there isn't another parlour-maid like Foljambe. I have suspected something now and then, but I never thought it would come to this. What a fool I was to leave her here when I went back to Riseholme for the fête! Or if only we had driven back there with Cadman instead of going by train. It was madness. Here they were with nothing to do but make plans behind our backs. No one will ever look after my clothes as she does. And the silver. You'll miss Cadman, too."

"Oh, but I don't think he means to leave me," said Lucia in some alarm. "What makes you think that? He said nothing about it."

"Then perhaps Foljambe doesn't mean to leave me," said Georgie, seeing a possible dawn on the wreck of his home.

"That's rather different," said Lucia. "She'll have to look after his house, you see, by day, and then at night he'd—he'd like her to be there."

"Horrible to think of," said Georgie bitterly. "I wonder what she can see in him. I've got a good mind to go and live in an hotel. And I had left her five hundred pounds in my will."

"Georgie, that was very generous of you. Very," put in Lucia, though Georgie would not feel the loss of that large sum after he was dead.

"But now I shall certainly add a codicil to say 'if still in my service,'" said Georgie rather less generously. "I didn't think it of her."

Lucia was silent a moment. Georgie was taking it very much to heart indeed, and she racked her ingenious brain.

"I've got an idea," she said at length. "I don't know if it can be worked, but we might see. Would you feel less miserable about it if Foljambe would consent to come over to your house say at nine in the morning and be there till after dinner? If you were dining out as you so often are, she could go home earlier. You see Cadman's at The Hurst all day, for he does odd jobs as well, and his cottage at Riseholme is quite close to your house. You would have to give them a charwoman to do the housework."

"Oh, that is a good idea," said Georgie, cheering up a little.

"Of course I'll give her a charwoman or anything else she wants if she'll only look after me as before. She can sleep wherever she likes. Of course there may be periods when she'll have to be away, but I shan't mind that as long as I know she's coming back. Besides, she's rather old for that, isn't she?"

It was no use counting the babies before they were born, and Lucia glided along past this slightly indelicate subject with Victorian eyes.

"It's worth while seeing if she'll stay with you on these terms," she said.

"Rather. I shall suggest it at once," said Georgie. "I think I shall congratulate her very warmly, and say how pleased I am, and then ask her. Or would it be better to be very cold and preoccupied and not talk to her at all? She'd hate that, and then when I ask her after some days whether she'll stop on with me, she might promise anything to see me less unhappy again."

Lucia did not quite approve of this Machiavellian policy.

"On the other hand, it might make her marry Cadman instantly, in order to have done with you," she suggested. "You'd better be careful."

"I'll think it over," said Georgie. "Perhaps it would be safer to be very nice to her about it and appeal to her better nature, if she's got one. But I know I shall never manage to call her Cadman. She must keep her maiden name, like an actress."

∞

Lucia duly put in force her disciplinary measures for the reduction of Elizabeth. Major Benjy, Diva and Georgie dined with her that night, and there was a plate of nougat chocolates for Diva, whose inordinate passion for them was known all over Tilling, and a fiery curry for the Major to remind him of India, and a dish of purple figs bought at the greengrocer's but plucked from the tree outside the garden-room. She could not resist giving Elizabeth ever so gentle a little slap over this, and said that it was rather a roundabout process to go down to the High Street to buy the figs which Coplen plucked from the tree in the garden, and took down with other garden-produce to the shop: she must ask dear Elizabeth to allow her to buy them, so to speak, at the pit-mouth. But she was genuinely astonished at the effect this little joke had on Diva. Hastily she swallowed a nougat chocolate entire and turned bright red.

"But doesn't Elizabeth give you garden-produce?" she asked in an incredulous voice.

"Oh no," said Lucia. "Just flowers for the house. Nothing else."

"Well, I never!" said Diva. "I fully understood, at least I thought I did—"

Lucia got up. She must be magnanimous and encourage no public exposure, whatever it might be, of Elizabeth's conduct, but for the pickling of the rod of discipline she would like to hear about it quietly.

"Let's go into the garden-room and have a chat," she said. "Look after Major Benjy, Georgie, and don't sit too long in bachelordom, for I must have a little game of bridge with him. I'm terribly frightened of him, but he and Mrs. Plaistow must be kind to beginners like you and me."

The indignant Diva poured out her tale of Elizabeth's iniquities in a turgid flood.

"So like Elizabeth," she said. "I asked her if she gave you garden-produce, and she said she wasn't going to dig up her potatoes and carry them away. Well, of course I thought that meant she did give it you. So like her. Bismarck, wasn't it, who told the truth in order to deceive? And so of course I gave her my garden-produce and she's selling one and eating the other. I wish I'd known I ought to have distrusted her."

Lucia smiled that indulgent Sunday-evening smile which meant she was thinking hard on weekday subjects.

"I like Elizabeth so much," she said, "and what do a few figs matter?"

"No, but she always scores," said Diva, "and sometimes it's hard to bear. She got my house with garden-produce thrown in for eight guineas a week and she lets her own without garden-produce for twelve."

"No dear, I pay fifteen," said Lucia.

Diva stared at her open-mouthed.

"But it was down in Woolgar's books at twelve," she said. "I saw it myself. She is a one: isn't she?"

Lucia maintained her attitude of high nobility, but this information added a little more pickling.

"Dear Elizabeth!" she said. "So glad that she was sharp enough to get a few more guineas. I expect she's very clever, isn't she? And here come the gentlemen. Now for a jolly little game of bridge."

Georgie was astonished at Lucia. She was accustomed to lay down the law with considerable firmness, and instruct partners and opponents alike, but tonight a most unusual humility possessed her. She was full of diffidence about her own skill and of praise for her partner's: she sought advice, even once asking Georgie what she ought to have played, though that was clearly a mistake, for next moment she rated him. But for the other two she had nothing but admiring envy at their declarations and their management of the hand, and when Diva revoked she took all the blame on herself for not having asked her whether her hand was bare of the suit. Rubber after rubber they played in an amity hitherto unknown in the higher gambling circles of Tilling; and when, long after the incredible hour of twelve had struck, it was found on the adjustment of accounts that Lucia was the universal loser, she said she had never bought experience so cheaply and pleasantly.

Major Benjy wiped the foam of his third (surreptitious and hastily consumed) whisky and soda from his walrus-moustache.

"Most agreeable evening of bridge I've ever spent in Tilling," he said. "Bless me, when I think of the scoldings I've had in this room for some little slip, and the friction there's been . . . Mrs. Plaistow knows what I mean."

"I should think I did," said Diva, beginning to simmer again at the thought of garden-produce. "Poor Elizabeth! Lessons in self-control are what she wants and after that a few lessons on the elements of the game wouldn't be amiss. Then it would be time to think about telling other people how to play."

This very pleasant party broke up, and Georgie, hurrying home to Mallards Cottage, thought he could discern in these comments the key to Lucia's unwonted humility at the card-table. For herself she had only kind words on the subject of Elizabeth as befitted a large-hearted woman, but Diva and Major Benjy could hardly help contrasting brilliantly to her advantage, the charming evening they had spent with the vituperative scenes which usually took place when they played bridge in the garden-room. "I think Lucia has begun," thought Georgie to himself as he went noiselessly upstairs so as not to disturb the slumbers of Foljambe.

It was known, of course, all over Tilling the next morning that there had been a series of most harmonious rubbers of bridge last night at Mallards till goodness knew what hour, for Diva spent half the morning in telling everybody about it, and the other half in advising them not to get their fruit and vegetables at the shop which dealt in the garden-produce of the Bismarckian Elizabeth. Equally well known was it that the Wyses were dining at Mallards tonight, for Mrs. Wyse took care of that, and at eight o'clock that evening the Royce started from Porpoise Street, and arrived at Mallards at precisely one minute past. Georgie came on foot from the Cottage thirty yards away in the other direction, in the highest spirits, for Foljambe after consultation with her Cadman had settled to continue on day-duty after the return to Riseholme. So Georgie did not intend at present to execute that vindictive codicil to his will. He told the Wyses whom he met on the doorstep of Mallards about the happy termination of this domestic crisis, while Mrs. Wyse took off her sables and disclosed the fact that she was wearing the order of the MBE on her ample bosom; and he observed that Mr. Wyse had a soft crinkly shirt with a low collar, and velveteen dress clothes: this pretty costume caused him to look rather like a conjurer. There followed very polite conversations at dinner, full of bows from Mr. Wyse; first he talked to his hostess, and when Lucia tried to produce general talk and spoke to Georgie, he instantly turned his head to the right, and talked most politely to his wife about the weather and the news in the evening paper till Lucia was ready for him again.

"I hear from our friend Miss Mapp," he said to her, "that you speak the most beautiful and fluent Italian."

Lucia was quite ready to oblige.

"*Ah, che bella lingua!*" said she. "*Ma ho dimenticato tutto, non parla nessuno* in Riseholme."

"But I hope you will have the opportunity of speaking it before long in Tilling," said Mr. Wyse. "My sister Amelia, Contessa Faraglione, may possibly be with us before long and I shall look forward to hearing you and she talk together. A lovely language to listen to, though Amelia laughs at my poor efforts when I attempt it."

Lucia smelled danger here. There had been a terrible occasion once at Riseholme when her bilingual reputation had been shattered by her being exposed to the full tempest of Italian volleyed at her by a native, and she had been unable to understand anything that he said. But Amelia's arrival was doubtful and at present remote, and it would be humiliating to confess that her knowledge was confined to a chosen though singularly limited vocabulary.

"Georgie, we must rub up our Italian again," she said. "Mr. Wyse's sister may be coming here before long. What an opportunity for us to practise!"

"I do not imagine that you have much need of practise," said Mr. Wyse, bowing to Lucia. "And I hear your Elizabethan fête" (he bowed to Queen Elizabeth) "was an immense success. We so much want somebody at Tilling who can organise and carry through schemes like that. My wife does all she can, but she sadly needs someone to help, or indeed direct her. The hospital for instance, terribly in need of funds. She and I were talking as to whether we could not get up a garden fête with some tableaux or something of the sort to raise money. She has designs on you, I know, when she can get you alone, for indeed there is no one in Tilling with ability and initiative."

Suddenly it struck Lucia that though this was very gratifying to herself, it had another purpose, namely to depreciate somebody else, and surely that could only be one person. But that name must not escape her lips.

"My services, such as they are, are completely at Mrs. Wyse's disposal," she said, "as long as I am in Tilling. This garden for instance. Would that be a suitable place for something of the sort?"

Mr. Wyse bowed to the garden.

"The ideal spot," said he. "All Tilling would flock here at your bidding. Never yet in my memory has the use of it been granted for such a purpose; we have often lamented it."

There could no longer be much doubt as to the sub-current in such remarks, but the beautiful smooth surface must not be broken.

"I quite feel with you," said Lucia. "If one is fortunate enough, even for a short time, to possess a pretty little garden like this, it should be used for the benefit of charitable entertainment. The hospital: what more deserving object could we have? Some tableaux, you suggested. I'm sure Mr. Pillson and I would be only too glad to repeat a scene or two from our fête at Riseholme."

Mr. Wyse bowed so low that his large loose tie nearly dipped itself in an ice-pudding.

"I was trying to summon my courage to suggest exactly that," he said. "Susan, Mrs. Lucas encourages us to hope that she will give you a favourable audience about the project we talked over."

The favourable audience began as soon as the ladies rose, and was continued when Georgie and Mr. Wyse followed them. Already it had been agreed that the Padre might contribute an item to the entertainment, and that was very convenient, for he was to dine with Lucia the next night.

"His Scotch stories," said Susan. "I can never hear them too often, for though I've not got a drop of Scotch blood myself, I can appreciate them. Not a feature of course, Mrs. Lucas, but just to fill up pauses. And then there's Mrs. Plaistow. How I laugh when she does the seasick passenger with an orange, though I doubt if you can get oranges now. And Miss Coles. A wonderful mimic. And then there's Major Benjy. Perhaps he would read us portions of his diary."

A pause followed. Lucia had one of those infallible presentiments that a certain name hitherto omitted would follow. It did.

"And if Miss Mapp would supply the refreshment department with fruit from her garden here, that would be a great help," said Mrs. Wyse.

Lucia caught in rapid succession the respective eyes of all her guests, each of whom in turn looked away. "So Tilling knows all about the garden-produce already," she thought to herself.

Bridge followed, and here she could not be as humble as she had been last night, for both the Wyses abased themselves before she had time to begin.

"We know already," said Algernon, "of the class of player that you are, Mrs. Lucas. Any hints you will give Susan and me will be so much appreciated. We shall give you no game at all I am afraid, but we shall have a lesson. There is no one in Tilling who has any pretensions of being a player. Major Benjy and Mrs. Plaistow and we sometimes have a well-fought rubber on our own level, and the Padre does not always play a bad game. But otherwise the less said about our bridge the better. Susan, my dear, we must do our best."

Here indeed was a reward for Lucia's humility last night. The winners had evidently proclaimed her consummate skill, and was that, too, a reflection on somebody else, only once hitherto named, and that in connection with garden-produce? Tonight Lucia's hands dripped with aces and kings: she denuded her adversaries of all their trumps, and then led one more for safety's sake, after which she poured forth a galaxy of winners. Whoever was her partner was in luck, and tonight it was Georgie who had to beg for change for a ten-shilling note and leave the others to adjust their portions. He recked nothing of this financial disaster, for Foljambe was not lost to him. When the party broke up Mrs. Wyse begged him to allow her to give him a lift in the Royce, but as this would entail a turning of that majestic car, which would take at least five minutes followed by a long drive for them round the church square and down into the High Street and up again to Porpoise Street, he adventured forth on foot for his walk of thirty yards and arrived without undue fatigue.

∞

Georgie and Lucia started their sketching next morning. Like charity, they began at home, and their first subjects were each other's houses. They put their camp-stools side by side, but facing in opposite directions, in the middle of the street halfway between Mallards and Mallards Cottage; and thus, by their having different objects to portray, they avoided any sort of rivalry, and secured each other's companionship.

"So good for our drawing," said Georgie. "We were getting to do nothing but trees and clouds which needn't be straight."

"I've got the crooked chimney," said Lucia proudly. "That one beyond your house. I think I shall put it straight. People might think I had done it crooked by accident. What do you advise?"

"I think I wouldn't," said he. "There's character in its crookedness. Or you might make it rather more crooked than it is: then there won't be any doubt . . . Here comes the Wyses' car. We shall have to move on to the pavement. Tarsome."

A loud hoot warned them that that was the safer course, and the car lurched towards them. As it passed, Mr. Wyse saw whom he had disturbed, stopped the Royce (which had so much better a right to the road than the artists) and sprang out, hat in hand.

"A thousand apologies," he cried. "I had no idea who it was, and for what artistic purpose, occupying the roadway. I am indeed distressed, I would instantly have retreated and gone round the other way had I perceived in time. May I glance? Exquisite! The crooked chimney! Mallards Cottage! The west front of the church!" He bowed to them all.

There followed that evening the third dinner party when the Padre and wee wifie made the quartet. The Royce had called for him that day to take him to lunch in Porpoise Street (Lucia had seen it go by), and it was he who now introduced the subject of the proposed entertainment on behalf of the hospital, for he knew all about it and was ready to help in any way that Mistress Lucas might command. There were some Scottish stories which he would be happy to narrate, in order to fill up intervals between the tableaux, and he had ascertained that Miss Coles (dressed as usual as a boy) would give her most amusing parody of "The boy stood on the burning deck," and that Mistress Diva said she thought that an orange or two might be procured. If not, a ripe tomato would serve the purpose. He would personally pledge himself for the services of the church choir to sing catches and glees and madrigals, whenever required. He suggested also that such members of the workhouse as were not bedridden might be entertained to tea, in which case the choir would sing grace before and after buns.

"As to the expense of that, if you approve," he said, "put another baubee on the price of admission, and there'll be none in Tilling to grudge the extra expense wi' such entertainment as you and the other leddies will offer them."

"Dear me, how quickly it is all taking shape," said Lucia,

finding that almost without effort on her part she had been drawn into the place of prime mover in all this, and that still a sort of conspiracy of silence prevailed with regard to Miss Mapp's name, which hitherto had only been mentioned as a suitable provider of fruit for the refreshment department. "You must form a little committee, Padre, for putting all the arrangements in hand at once. There's Mr. Wyse who really thought of the idea, and you—"

"And with yourself," broke in the Padre, "that will make three. That's sufficient for any committee that is going to do its work without any argle-bargle."

There flashed across Lucia's mind a fleeting vision of what Elizabeth's face would be like when she picked up, as she would no doubt do next morning, the news of all that was becoming so solid.

"I think I had better not be on the committee," she said, quite convinced that they would insist on it. "It should consist of real Tillingites who take the lead among you in such things. I am only a visitor here. They will all say I want to push myself in."

"Ah, but we can't get on wi'out ye, Mistress Lucas," said the Padre. "You must consent to join us. An' three, as I say, makes the perfect committee."

Mrs. Bartlett had been listening to all this with a look of ecstatic attention on her sharp but timid little face. Here she gave vent to a series of shrill minute squeaks which expressed a mouse-like merriment, quite unexplained by anything that had been actually said, but easily accounted for by what had not been said. She hastily drank a sip of water and assured Lucia that a crumb of something (she was eating a peach) had stuck in her throat and made her cough. Lucia rose when the peach was finished.

"Tomorrow we must start working in earnest," she said.

"And to think that I planned to have a little holiday in Tilling! You and Mr. Wyse are regular slave-drivers, Padre."

Georgie waited behind that night after the others had gone, and bustled back to the garden-room after seeing them off.

"My dear, it's getting too exciting," he said. "But I wonder if you're wise to join the committee."

"I know what you mean," said Lucia, "but there really is no reason why I should refuse, because they won't have Elizabeth. It's not me, Georgie, who is keeping her out. But perhaps you're right, and I think tomorrow I'll send a line to the Padre and say that I am really too busy to be on the committee, and beg him to ask Elizabeth instead. It would be kinder. I can manage the whole thing just as well without being on the committee. She'll hear all about the entertainment tomorrow morning, and know that she's not going to be asked to do anything, except supply some fruit."

"She knows a good deal about it now," said Georgie. "She came to tea with me today."

"No! I didn't know you had asked her."

"I didn't," said Georgie. "She came."

"And what did she say about it?"

"Not very much, but she's thinking hard what to do. I could see that. I gave her the little sketch I made of the Landgate when we first came down here, and she wants me to send in another picture for the Tilling Art Exhibition. She wants you to send something too."

"Certainly she shall have my sketch of Mallards Cottage and the crooked chimney," said Lucia. "That will show goodwill. What else did she say?"

"She's getting up a jumble sale in aid of the hospital," said Georgie. "She's busy, too."

"Georgie, that's copied from us."

"Of course it is; she wants to have a show of her own, and I'm sure I don't wonder. And she knows all about your three dinner parties."

Lucia nodded. "That's all right then," she said. "I'll ask her to the next. We'll have some duets that night, Georgie. Not bridge I think, for they all say she's a perfect terror at cards. But it's time to be kind to her."

Lucia rose.

"Georgie, it's becoming a frightful rush already," she said. "This entertainment which they insist on my managing will make me very busy, but when one is appealed to like that, one can't refuse. Then there's my music, and sketching, and I haven't begun to rub up my Greek . . . And don't forget to send for your Drake clothes. Good-night, my dear. I'll call to you over the garden paling tomorrow if anything happens."

"I feel as if it's sure to," said Georgie with enthusiasm.

Chapter Five

LUCIA WAS WRITING LETTERS IN the window of the garden-room next morning. One, already finished, was to Adele Brixton asking her to send to Mallards the Queen Elizabeth costume for the tableaux: a second, also finished, was to the Padre, saying that she found she would not have time to attend committees for the hospital fête, and begging him to co-opt Miss Mapp. She would, however, do all in her power to help the scheme, and make any little suggestions that occurred to her. She added that the chance of getting fruit gratis for the refreshment department would be far brighter if the owner of it was on the board.

The third letter, firmly beginning "Dearest Liblib" (and to be signed very large, LUCIA), asking her to dine in two days' time, was not quite done when she saw dearest Liblib, with a fixed and awful smile, coming swiftly up the street. Lucia, sitting sideways to the window, could easily appear absorbed in her letter and unconscious of Elizabeth's approach, but from beneath half-lowered eyelids she watched her with the intensest interest. She was slanting across the street now, making a beeline for the door of Mallards ("And if she tries to get in without ringing the bell, she'll find the chain on the door," thought Lucia).

The abandoned woman, disdaining the bell, turned the handle and pushed. It did not yield to her intrusion, and she pushed more strongly. There was the sound of jingling metal, audible even in the garden-room, as the hasp that held the end of the chain gave way; the door flew open wide, and with a few swift and nimble steps she just saved herself from falling flat on the floor of the hall.

Lucia, pale with fury, laid down her pen and waited for the situation to develop. She hoped she would behave like a lady, but was quite sure it would be a firm sort of lady. Presently up the steps to the garden-room came that fairy tread, the door was opened an inch, and that odious voice said: "May I come in, dear?"

"Certainly," said Lucia brightly.

"Lulu dear," said Elizabeth, tripping across the room with little brisk steps. "First I must apologise: so humbly. Such a stupid accident. I tried to open your front door, and gave it a teeny little push and your servants had forgotten to take the chain down. I am afraid I broke something. The hasp must have been rusty."

Lucia looked puzzled. "But didn't Grosvenor come to open the door when you rang?" she asked.

"That was just what I forgot to do, dear," said Elizabeth. "I thought I would pop in to see you without troubling Grosvenor. You and I such friends, and so difficult to remember that my dear little Mallards— Several things to talk about!"

Lucia got up.

"Let us first see what damage you have done," she said with an icy calmness, and marched straight out of the room, followed by Elizabeth. The sound of the explosion had brought Grosvenor out of the dining-room, and Lucia picked up the dangling hasp and examined it.

"No, no sign of rust," she said. "Grosvenor, you must go down to the ironmonger and get them to come up and repair this at once. The chain must be made safer and you must remember always to put it on, day and night. If I am out, I will ring."

"So awfully sorry, dear Lulu," said Elizabeth, slightly cowed by this firm treatment. "I had no idea the chain could be up. We all keep our doors on the latch in Tilling. Quite a habit."

"I always used to in Riseholme," said Lucia. "Let us go back to the garden-room, and you will tell me what you came to talk about."

"Several things," said Elizabeth when they had settled themselves. "First, I am starting a little jumble sale for the hospital, and I wanted to look out some old curtains and rugs, laid away in cupboards, to give to it. May I just go upstairs and downstairs and poke about to find them?"

"By all means," said Lucia. "Grosvenor shall go round with you as soon as she has come back from the ironmonger's."

"Thank you, dear," said Elizabeth, "though there's no need to trouble Grosvenor. Then another thing. I persuaded Mr. Georgie to send me a sketch for our picky exhibition. Promise me that you'll send me one too. Wouldn't be complete without something by you. How you get all you do into the day is beyond me: your sweet music, your sketching, and your dinner parties every evening."

Lucia readily promised, and Elizabeth then appeared to lose herself in reverie.

"There *is* one more thing," she said at last. "I have heard a little gossip in the town both today and yesterday about a fête which it is proposed to give in my garden. I feel sure it is mere tittle-tattle, but I thought it would be better to come up here to know from you that there is no foundation for it."

"But I hope there is a great deal," said Lucia. "Some tableaux, some singing, in order to raise funds for the hospital. It would be so kind of you if you would supply the fruit for the refreshment booth from your garden. Apropos I should be so pleased to buy some of it every day myself. It would be fresher than if, as at present, it is taken down to the greengrocer and brought up again."

"Anything to oblige you, dear Lulu," said Elizabeth. "But that would be difficult to arrange. I have contracted to send all my garden-produce to Twistevant's—such a quaint name, is it not?—for these months, and for the same reason I should be unable to supply this fête which I have heard spoken of. The fruit is no longer mine."

Lucia had already made up her mind that, after this affair of the chain, nothing would induce her to propose that Elizabeth should take her place on the committee. She would cling to it through storm and tempest.

"I see," she said. "Perhaps then you could let us have some fruit from Diva's garden, unless you have sold that also."

Elizabeth came to the point, disregarding so futile a suggestion.

"The fête itself, dear one," she said, "is what I must speak about. I cannot possibly permit it to take place in my garden. The ragtag and bobtail of Tilling passing through my hall and my sweet little sitting-room and spending the afternoon in my garden! All my carpets soiled and my flower-beds trampled on! And how do I know that they will not steal upstairs and filch what they can find?"

Lucia's blood had begun to boil: nobody could say that she was preserving a benevolent neutrality. In consequence she presented an icy demeanour, and if her voice trembled at all, it was from excessive cold.

"There will be no admission to the rooms in the house," she said. "I will lock all the doors, and I am sure that nobody in Tilling will be so ill bred as to attempt to force them open."

That was a nasty one. Elizabeth recoiled for a moment from the shock, but rallied. She opened her mouth very wide to begin again, but Lucia got in first.

"They will pass straight from the front door into the garden," she said, "where we undertake to entertain them, presenting their tickets of admission or paying at the door. As for the carpet in your sweet little sitting-room, there isn't one. And I have too high an opinion of the manners of Tilling in general to suppose that they will trample on your flower-beds."

"Perhaps you would like to hire a menagerie," said Elizabeth, completely losing her self-control, "and have an exhibition of tigers and sharks in the garden-room."

"No: I should particularly dislike it," said Lucia earnestly. "Half of the garden-room would have to be turned into a sea-water tank for the sharks and my piano would be flooded. And the rest would have to be full of horseflesh for the tigers. A most ridiculous proposal, and I cannot entertain it."

Elizabeth gave a dreadful gasp as if she was one of the sharks and the water had been forgotten. She adroitly changed the subject.

"Then again, there's the rumour—of course it's only rumour—that there is some idea of entertaining such inmates of the workhouse as are not bedridden. Impossible."

"I fancy the Padre is arranging that," said Lucia. "For my part, I'm delighted to give them a little treat."

"And for my part," said Miss Mapp, rising (she had become Miss Mapp again in Lucia's mind), "I will not have my little home-sanctuary invaded by the ragtag—"

"The tickets will be half a crown," interposed Lucia.

"—and bobtail of Tilling," continued Miss Mapp.

"As long as I am tenant here," said Lucia, "I shall ask here whom I please, and when I please, and—and how I please. Or do you wish me to send you a list of the friends I ask to dinner for your sanction?"

Miss Mapp, trembling very much, forced her lips to form the syllables: "But, dear Lulu—"

"Dear Elizabeth, I must beg you not to call me Lulu," she said. "Such a detestable abbreviation—"

Grosvenor had appeared at the door of the garden-room.

"Yes, Grosvenor, what is it?" asked Lucia in precisely the same voice.

"The ironmonger is here, ma'am," she said, "and he says that he'll have to put in some rather large screws, as they're pulled out—"

"Whatever is necessary to make the door safe," said Lucia. "And Miss Mapp wants to look into cupboards and take some things of her own away. Go with her, please, and give her every facility."

Lucia, quite in the grand style, turned to look out of the window in the direction of Mallards Cottage, in order to give Miss Mapp the opportunity of a discreet exit. She threw the window open.

"Georgino! Georgino!" she called, and Georgie's face appeared above the paling.

"Come round and have ickle talk, Georgie," she said. "Sumfin' I want to tell you. *Presto!*"

She kissed her hand to Georgie and turned back into the room. Miss Mapp was still there, but now invisible to Lucia's eye. She hummed a gay bar of Mozartino, and went back to her table in the bow-window where she tore up the letter of resignation and recommendation she had written to the Padre, and the half-finished note to Miss Mapp, which so cordially asked her to dinner, saying that it was so long since they had met, for they had met again now. When she looked up she was alone, and there was Georgie tripping up the steps by the front door. Though it was standing open (for the ironmonger was already engaged on the firm restoration of the chain) he very properly rang the bell and was admitted.

"There you are," said Lucia brightly as he came in. "Another lovely day."

"Perfect. What has happened to your front door?"

Lucia laughed.

"Elizabeth came to see me," she said gaily. "The chain was on the door, as I have ordered it always shall be. But she gave the door such a biff that the hasp pulled out. It's being repaired."

"No!" said Georgie, "and did you give her what for?"

"She had several things she wanted to see me about," said Lucia, keeping an intermittent eye on the front door. "She wanted to get out of her cupboards some stuff for the jumble sale she is getting up in aid of the hospital, and she is at it now under Grosvenor's superintendence. Then she wanted me to send a sketch for the picture exhibition, I said I would be delighted. Then she said she could not manage to send any fruit for our fête here. She did not approve of the fête at all, Georgie. In fact, she forbade me to give it. We had a little chat about that."

"But what's to be done then?" asked Georgie.

"Nothing that I know of, except to give the fête," said Lucia. "But it would be no use asking her to be on the committee for an object of which she disapproved, so I tore up the letter I had written to the Padre about it."

Lucia suddenly focused her eyes and her attention on the front door, and a tone of warm human interest melted the deadly chill of her voice.

"Georgie, there she goes," she said. "What a quantity of

things! There's an old kettle and a boot-jack, and a rug with a hole in it, and one stair-rod. And there's a shaving from the front door where they are putting in bigger screws, stuck to her skirt . . . And she's dropped the stair-rod . . . Major Benjy's picking it up for her."

Georgie hurried to the window to see these exciting happenings, but Miss Mapp, having recovered the stair-rod, was already disappearing.

"I wish I hadn't given her my picture of the Landgate," said he. "It was one of my best. But aren't you going to tell me all about your interview? Properly, I mean: everything."

"Not worth speaking of," said Lucia. "She asked me if I would like to have a menagerie and keep tigers and sharks in the garden-room. That sort of thing. Mere raving. Come out, Georgie. I want to do a little shopping. Coplen told me there were some excellent greengages from the garden which he was taking down to Twistevant's."

It was the hour when the collective social life of Tilling was at its briskest. The events of the evening before, tea-parties and games of bridge had become known and were under discussion, as the ladies of the place with their baskets on their arms collided with each other as they popped in and out of shops and obstructed the pavements. Many parcels were being left at Wasters which Miss Mapp now occupied, for jumble sales on behalf of deserving objects were justly popular, since everybody had a lot of junk in their houses, which they could not bear to throw away, but for which they had no earthly use. Diva had already been back from Taormina to her own house (as Elizabeth to hers) and had disinterred from a cupboard of rubbish a pair of tongs, the claws of which twisted round if you tried to pick up a lump of coal and dropped it on the carpet, but which were otherwise perfect. Then there was a scuttle which had a hole in the bottom, through which coal dust softly dribbled, and a candlestick which had lost one of its feet, and a glass inkstand once handsome, but now cracked. These treasures, handsome donations to a jumble sale, but otherwise of no particular value, she carried to her own hall, where donors were requested to leave their offerings, and she learned from Withers, Miss Mapp's parlour-maid, the disagreeable news that the jumble sale was to be held here. The thought revolted her; all the ragtag and bobtail of Tilling would come wandering about her house, soiling her carpets and smudging her walls. At this moment Miss Mapp herself came in carrying the tea kettle and the boot-jack and the other things. She had already thought of half a dozen withering retorts she might have made to Lucia.

"Elizabeth, this will never do," said Diva. "I can't have the jumble sale held here. They'll make a dreadful mess of the place."

"Oh no, dear," said Miss Mapp, with searing memories of a recent interview in her mind. "The people will only come into your hall where you see there's no carpet, and make their purchases. What a beautiful pair of tongs! For my sale? Fancy! Thank you, dear Diva."

"But I forbid the jumble sale to be held here," said Diva. "You'll be wanting to have a menagerie here next."

This was amazing luck.

"No, dear, I couldn't dream of it," said Miss Mapp. "I should hate to have tigers and sharks all over the place. Ridiculous!"

"I shall put up a merry-go-round in quaint Irene's studio at Taormina," said Diva.

"I doubt if there's room, dear," said Miss Mapp, scoring heavily again, "but you might measure. Perfectly legitimate, of course, for if my house may be given over to parties for paupers, you can surely have a merry-go-round in quaint Irene's and I a jumble sale in yours."

"It's not the same thing," said Diva. "Providing beautiful tableaux in your garden is quite different from using my panelled hall to sell kettles and coal-scuttles with holes in them."

"I dare say I could find a good many holes in the tableaux," said Miss Mapp.

Diva could think of no adequate verbal retort to such coruscations, so for answer she merely picked up the tongs, the coal-scuttle, the candlestick and the inkstand, and put them back in the cupboard from which she had just taken them, and left her tenant to sparkle by herself.

∞

Most of the damaged objects for the jumble sale must have arrived by now, and after arranging them in tasteful groups Miss Mapp sat down in a rickety basket chair presented by the Padre for fell meditation. Certainly it was not pretty of Diva (no one could say that Diva was pretty) to have withdrawn her treasures, but that was not worth thinking about. What did demand her highest mental activities was Lucia's conduct. How grievously different she had turned out to be from that sweet woman for whom she had originally felt so warm an affection, whom she had planned to take so cosily under her wing, and administer in small doses as treats to Tilling society! Lucia had turned upon her and positively bitten the caressing hand. By means of showy little dinners and odious flatteries, she had quite certainly made Major Benjy and the Padre and the Wyses and poor Diva think that she was a very remarkable and delightful person and in these manoeuvres Miss Mapp saw a shocking and sinister attempt to set herself up as the Queen of Tilling society. Lucia had given dinner parties on three consecutive nights since her return, she had put herself on the committee for this fête, which (however much Miss Mapp might say she could not possibly permit it) she had not the slightest idea how to stop, and though Lucia was only a temporary resident here, these weeks would be quite intolerable if she continued to inflate herself in this presumptuous manner. It was certainly time for Miss Mapp to reassert herself before this rebel made more progress, and though dinner-giving was unusual in Tilling, she determined to give one or two most amusing ones herself, to none of which, of course, she would invite Lucia. But that was not nearly enough: she must administer some frightful snub (or snubs) to the woman. Georgie was in the same boat and must suffer too, for Lucia would not like that. So she sat in this web of crippled fire-irons and napless rugs like a spider, meditating reprisals. Perhaps it was a pity, when she needed allies, to have quarrelled with Diva, but a dinner would set that right. Before long she got up with a pleased expression. "That will do to begin with: she won't like that at all," she said to herself and went out to do her belated marketing.

She passed Lucia and Georgie, but decided not to see them, and, energetically waving her hand to Mrs. Bartlett, she popped into Twistevant's, from the door of which they had just come out. At that moment quaint Irene, after a few words with the Padre, caught sight of Lucia, and hurried across the street to her. She was hatless, as usual, and wore a collarless shirt and knickerbockers unlike any other lady of Tilling, but as she approached Lucia her face assumed an acid and awful smile, just like somebody else's, and then she spoke in a cooing velvety voice that was quite unmistakable.

"The boy stood on the burning deck, Lulu," she said. "Whence all but he had fled, dear. The flames that lit the battle-wreck, sweet one, shone round him—"

Quaint Irene broke off suddenly, for within a yard of her at the door of Twistevant's appeared Miss Mapp. She looked clean over all their heads, and darted across the street to Wasters, carrying a small straw basket of her own delicious greengages.

"Oh, lor!" said Irene. "The Mapp's in the fire, so that's done. Yes. I'll recite for you at your fête. Georgie, what a saucy hat! I was just going to Taormina to rout out some old sketches of mine for the Art Show, and then this happens. I wouldn't have had it not happen for a hundred pounds."

"Come and dine tonight," said Lucia warmly, breaking all records in the way of hospitality.

"Yes, if I needn't dress, and you'll send me home afterwards. I'm half a mile out of the town and I may be tipsy, for Major Benjy says you've got jolly good booze, '*quai-hai*,' the King, God bless him! Goodbye."

∞

"Most original!" said Lucia. "To go on with what I was telling you, Georgie, Liblib said she would not have her little home-sanctuary— Good-morning, Padre. Miss Mapp shoved her way into Mallards this morning without ringing, and broke the chain which was on the door, such a hurry was she in to tell me that she will not have her little home-sanctuary, as I was just saying to Georgie, invaded by the ragtag and bobtail of Tilling."

"Hoots awa!" said the Padre. "What in the world has Mistress Mapp got to do with it? An' who's holding a jumble sale in Mistress Plaistow's? I keeked in just now wi' my bit o' rubbish and never did I see such a mess. Na, na! Fair play's a jool, an' we'll go richt ahead. Excuse me, there's wee wifie wanting me."

"It's war," said Georgie as the Padre darted across to the Mouse, who was on the other side of the street, to tell her what had happened.

"No, I'm just defending myself," said Lucia. "It's right that people should know she burst my door-chain."

"Well, I feel like the fourth of August, 1914," said Georgie. "What do you suppose she'll do next?"

"You may depend upon it, Georgie, that I shall be ready for her whatever it is," said Lucia. "I shan't raise a finger against her, if she behaves. But she *shall* ring the bell and I *won't* be dictated to and I *won't* be called Lulu. However, there's no immediate danger of that. Come, Georgie, let us go home and finish our sketches. Then we'll have them framed and send them to Liblib for the picture exhibition. Perhaps that will convince her of my general goodwill, which I assure you is quite sincere."

∞

The jumble sale opened next day, and Georgie, having taken his picture of Lucia's house and her picture of his to be framed in a very handsome manner, went on to Wasters with the idea of buying anything that could be of the smallest use for any purpose, and thus showing more goodwill towards the patroness. Miss Mapp was darting to and fro with lures for purchasers, holding the kettle away from the light so that the hole in its bottom should not be noticed, and she gave him a smile that looked rather like a snarl, but after all very like the smile she had for others. Georgie selected a hearth-brush, some curtain-rings and a kettle-holder.

Then in a dark corner he came across a large cardboard tray, holding miscellaneous objects with the label "All 6*d*. Each." There were thimbles, there were photographs with slightly damaged frames, there were chipped china ornaments and cork-screws, and there was the picture of the Landgate which he had painted himself and given Miss Mapp. Withers, Miss Mapp's parlour-maid, was at a desk for the exchange of custom by the door, and he exhibited his purchases for her inspection.

"Ninepence for the hearth-brush and threepence for the curtain-rings," said Georgie in a trembling voice, "and sixpence for the kettle-holder. Then there's this little picture out of the sixpenny tray, which makes just two shillings."

Laden with these miscellaneous purchases he went swiftly up the street to Mallards. Lucia was at the window of the garden-room, and her gimlet-eye saw that something had happened. She threw the sash up.

"I'm afraid the chain is on the door, Georgie," she called out. "You'll have to ring. What is it?"

"I'll show you," said Georgie.

He deposited the hearth-brush, the curtain-rings and the kettle-holder in the hall, and hurried out to the garden-room with the picture.

"The sketch I gave her," he said. "In the sixpenny tray. Why, the frame cost a shilling."

Lucia's face became a flint.

"I never heard of such a thing, Georgie," said she. "The monstrous woman!"

"It may have got there by mistake," said Georgie, frightened at this Medusa countenance.

"Rubbish, Georgie," said Lucia.

∞

Pictures for the annual exhibition of the Art Society of which Miss Mapp was President had been arriving in considerable numbers at Wasters, and stood stacked round the walls of the hall where the jumble sale had been held a few days before, awaiting the judgment of the hanging committee which consisted of the

President, the Treasurer and the Secretary: the two latter were Mr. and Mrs. Wyse. Miss Mapp had sent in half a dozen water-colours, the Treasurer a study in still-life of a tea-cup, an orange and a wallflower, the Secretary a pastel portrait of the King of Italy, whom she had seen at a distance in Rome last spring. She had reinforced the vivid impression he had made on her by pho-tographs. All these, following the precedent of the pictures of Royal Academicians at Burlington House, would be hung on the line without dispute, and there could not be any friction con-cerning them. But quaint Irene had sent some at which Miss Mapp felt lines must be drawn. They were, as usual, very strange and modern: there was one, harmless but insane, that purported to be Tilling church by moonlight: a bright green pinnacle all crooked (she supposed it was a pinnacle) rose up against a strip of purple sky and the whole of the rest of the canvas was black. There was the back of somebody with no clothes on lying on an emerald-green sofa: and, worst of all, there was a picture called "Women Wrestlers," from which Miss Mapp hurriedly averted her eyes. A proper regard for decency alone, even if Irene had not mimicked her reciting "The boy stood on the burning deck," would have made her resolve to oppose, tooth and nail, the exhi-bition of these shameless athletes. Unfortunately Mr. Wyse had the most unbounded admiration for quaint Irene's work, and if she had sent in a picture of mixed wrestlers he would prob-ably have said, "Dear me, very powerful!" He was a hard man to resist, for if he and Miss Mapp had a very strong difference of opinion concerning any particular canvas he broke off and fell into fresh transports of admiration at her own pictures and this rather disarmed opposition.

The meeting of the hanging committee was to take place this morning at noon. Half an hour before that time, an errand-boy arrived at Wasters from the frame-maker's bringing, according to the order he had received, two parcels which contained Georgie's picture of Mallards and Lucia's picture of Mallards Cottage: they had the cards of their perpetrators attached. "Rubbishy little daubs," thought Miss Mapp to herself, "but I suppose those two Wyses will insist." Then an imprudent demon of revenge suddenly took complete possession of her, and she called back the boy, and said she had a further errand for him.

At a quarter before twelve the boy arrived at Mallards and rang the bell. Grosvenor took down the chain and received from him a thin square parcel labelled "With care." One minute afterwards he delivered a similar parcel to Foljambe at Mallards Cottage, and had discharged Miss Mapp's further errand. The two maids conveyed these to their employers, and Georgie and Lucia, tearing off the wrappers, found themselves simultaneously confronted with their own pictures. A typewritten slip accompanied each, conveying to them the cordial thanks of the hanging committee and its regrets that the limited wall-space at its disposal would not permit of these works of art being exhibited.

Georgie ran out into his little yard and looked over the paling of Lucia's garden. At the same moment Lucia threw open the window of the garden-room which faced towards the paling.

"Georgie, have you received—" she called.

"Yes," said Georgie.

"So have I."

"What are you going to do?" he asked.

Lucia's face assumed an expression eager and pensive, the faraway look with which she listened to Beethoven. She thought intently for a moment.

"I shall take a season ticket for the exhibition," she said, "and constantly—"

"I can't quite hear you," said Georgie.

Lucia raised her voice.

"I shall buy a season ticket for the exhibition," she shouted, "and go there every day. Believe me, that's the only way to take it. They don't want our pictures, but we mustn't be small about it. Dignity, Georgie."

There was nothing to add to so sublime a declaration and Lucia went across to the bow-window, looking down the street. At that moment the Wyses' Royce lurched out of Porpoise Street, and turned down towards the High Street. Lucia knew they were both on the hanging committee which had just rejected one of her own most successful sketches (for the crooked chimney had turned out beautifully), but she felt not the smallest resentment towards them. No doubt they had acted quite conscientiously and she waved her hand in answer to a flutter of sables from the interior of the car. Presently she went down herself to the High Street to hear the news of the morning, and there was the Wyses' car drawn up in front of Wasters. She remembered then that the hanging committee met this morning, and a suspicion, too awful to be credible, flashed through her mind. But she thrust it out, as being unworthy of entertainment by a clean mind. She did her shopping and on her return took down a pale straw-coloured sketch by Miss Mapp that hung in the garden-room, and put in its place her picture of Mallards Cottage and the crooked chimney. Then she called to mind that powerful platitude, and said to herself that time would show . . .

∞

Miss Mapp had not intended to be present at the desecration of her garden by paupers from the workhouse and such low haunts. She had consulted her solicitor, about her power to stop the entertainment, but he assured her that there was no known statute in English law, which enabled her to prevent her tenant giving a party. So she determined, in the manner of Lucia and the Elizabethan fête at Riseholme, to be unaware of it, not to know that any fête was contemplated, and never afterwards to ask a single question about it. But as the day approached she suspected that the hot tide of curiosity, rapidly rising in her, would probably end by swamping and submerging her principles. She had seen the Padre dressed in a long black cloak, and carrying an axe of enormous size, entering Mallards; she had seen Diva come out in a white satin gown and scuttle down the street to Taormina, and those two prodigies taken together suggested that the execution of Mary Queen of Scots was in hand. (Diva as the Queen!) She had seen boards and posts carried in by the garden door and quantities of red cloth, so there was perhaps to be a stage for these tableaux. More intriguing yet was the apparition of Major Benjy carrying a cardboard crown glittering with gold paper. What on earth did that portend? Then there was her fruit to give an eye to: those choirboys, scampering all over the garden in the intervals between their glees, would probably pick every pear from the tree. She starved to know what was going on, but since she avoided all mention of the fête herself, others were most amazingly respectful to her reticence. She knew nothing, she could only make these delirious guesses, and there was *that* Lucia, being the centre of executioners and queens and choirboys, instead of in her proper place, made much of by kind Miss Mapp, and enjoying such glimpses of Tilling society as she chose to give her. "A fortnight ago," thought kind Miss Mapp, "I was popping in and out of the house, and she was Lulu. Anyhow, that was a nasty one she got over her picture, and I must bear her no grudge. I shall go to the fête because I can't help it, and I shall be very cordial to her and admire her tableaux. We're all Christians together, and I despise smallness."

It was distressing to be asked to pay half a crown for admittance to her own Mallards, but there seemed positively no other way to get past Grosvenor. Very distressing, too, it was, to see Lucia in full fig as Queen Elizabeth, graciously receiving newcomers on the edge of the lawn, precisely as if this was her party and these people who had paid half a crown to come in, her invited guests. It was a bitter thought that it ought to be herself who (though not dressed in all that flummery, so unconvincing by daylight) welcomed the crowd; for to whom, pray, did Mallards belong, and who had allowed it (since she could not stop it) to be thrown open? At the bottom of the steps into the garden-room was a large placard "Private," but of course that would not apply to her. Through the half-opened door, as she passed, she caught a glimpse of a familiar figure, though sadly travestied, sitting in a robe and a golden crown and pouring something into a glass: no doubt then the garden-room was the green-room of performers in the tableaux, who, less greedy of publicity than Lulu, hid themselves here till the time of their exposure brought them out. She would go in there presently, but her immediate duty, bitter but necessary, was to greet her hostess. With a very happy inspiration she tripped up to Lucia and dropped a low curtsey.

"Your Majesty's most obedient humble servant," she said, and then trusting that Lucia had seen that this obeisance was made in a mocking spirit, abounded in geniality.

"My dear, what a love of a costume!" she said. "And what a lovely day for your fête! And what a crowd! How the half-crowns have been pouring in! All Tilling seems to be here, and I'm sure I don't wonder."

Lucia rivalled these cordialities with equal fervour and about as much sincerity.

"Elizabeth! How nice of you to look in!" she said. *"Ecco, le due Elizabethe!* And you like my frock? Sweet of you! Yes. Tilling has indeed come to the aid of the hospital! And your jumble sale too was a wonderful success, was it not? Nothing left, I am told."

Miss Mapp had a moment's hesitation as to whether she should not continue to stand by Lucia and shake hands with new arrivals and give them a word of welcome, but she decided she could do more effective work if she made herself independent and played hostess by herself. Also this mention of the jumble sale made her slightly uneasy. Withers had told her that Georgie had bought his own picture of the Landgate from the sixpenny tray, and Lucia (for all her cordiality) might be about to spring some horrid trap on her about it.

"Yes, indeed," she said. "My little sale-room was soon as bare as Mother Hubbard's cupboard. But I mustn't monopolise you, dear, or I shall be lynched. There's a whole *queue* of people waiting to get a word with you. How I shall enjoy the tableaux! Looking forward to them so!"

She sidled off into the crowd. There were those dreadful old wretches from the workhouse, snuffy old things, some of them smoking pipes on her lawn and scattering matches, and being served with tea by Irene and the Padre's curate.

"So pleased to see you all here," she said, "sitting in my garden and enjoying your tea. I must pick a nice nosegay for you to take back home. How de do, Mr. Sturgis. Delighted you could come and help to entertain the old folks for us. Good-afternoon, Mr. Wyse; yes, my little garden is looking nice, isn't it? Susan, dear! Have you noticed my bed of delphiniums? I must give you some seed. Oh, there is the town-crier ringing his bell! I suppose that means we must take our places for the tableaux. What a good stage! I hope the posts will not have made very big holes in my lawn. Oh, one of those naughty choirboys is hovering about my fig tree. I cannot allow that."

She hurried off to stop any possibility of such depredation, and had made some telling allusions to the eighth commandment when on a second peal of the town-crier's bell, the procession of mummers came down the steps of the garden-room and advancing across the lawn disappeared behind the stage. Poor Major Benjy (so weak of him to allow himself to be dragged into this sort of thing) looked a perfect guy in his crown (who could he be meant for?) and as for Diva— Then there was Georgie (Drake indeed!), and last of all Queen Elizabeth with her train held up by two choirboys. Poor Lucia! Not content with a week of mumming at Riseholme she had to go on with her processions and dressings-up here. Some people lived on limelight.

Miss Mapp could not bring herself to take a seat close to the stage, and be seen applauding—there seemed to be some hitch with the curtain: no, it righted itself, what a pity!—and she hung about on the outskirts of the audience. Glees were interposed between the tableaux; how thin were the voices of those little boys out of doors! Then Irene, dressed like a sailor, recited that ludicrous parody. Roars of laughter. Then Major Benjy was King Cophetua: that was why he had a crown. Oh dear, oh dear! It was sad to reflect that an elderly, sensible man (for when at his best, he was that) could be got hold of by a pushing woman. The final tableau, of course (anyone might have guessed that), was the knighting of Drake by Queen Elizabeth. Then amid sycophantic applause the procession of guys returned and went back into the garden-room. Mr. and Mrs. Wyse followed them, and it seemed pretty clear that they were going to have a private tea there. Doubtless she would be soon sought for among the crowd with a message from Lucia to hope that she would join them in her own garden-room, but as nothing of the sort came, she presently thought that it would be only kind to Lucia to do so, and add her voice to the general chorus of congratulation that was no doubt going on. So with a brisk little tap on the door, and the enquiry "May I come in?" she entered.

There they all were, as pleased as children with dressing-up. King Cophetua still wore his crown, tilted slightly to one side like a forage cap, and he and Queen Elizabeth and Queen Mary were seated round the tea-table and calling each other your Majesty. King Cophetua had a large whisky and soda in front of him and Miss Mapp felt quite certain it was not his first. But though sick in soul at these puerilities she pulled herself together and made a beautiful curtsey to the silly creatures. And the worst of it was that there was no one left of her own intimate circle to whom she could in private express her disdain, for they were all in it, either actively or, like the Wyses, truckling to Lucia.

Lucia for the moment seemed rather surprised to see her, but she welcomed her and poured her out a cup of rather tepid tea, nasty to the taste. She must truckle, too, to the whole lot of them, though that tasted nastier than the tea.

"How I congratulate you all," she cried. "Padre, you looked too cruel as executioner, your mouth so fixed and stern. It was quite a relief when the curtain came down. Irene, quaint one, how you made them laugh! Diva, Mr. Georgie, and above all our wonderful Queen Lucia. What a treat it has all been! The choir! Those beautiful glees. A thousand pities, Mr. Wyse, that the Contessa was not here."

There was still Susan to whom she ought to say something

pleasant, but positively she could not go on, until she had eaten something solid. But Lucia chimed in.

"And your garden, Elizabeth," she said. "How they are enjoying it. I believe if the truth was known they are all glad that our little tableaux are over, so that they can wander about and admire the flowers. I must give a little party some night soon with Chinese lanterns and fairy-lights in the beds."

"Upon my word, your Majesty is spoiling us all," said Major Benjy. "Tilling's never had a month with so much pleasure provided for it. Glorious."

Miss Mapp had resolved to stop here if it was anyhow possible, till these sycophants had dispersed, and then have one private word with Lucia to indicate how ready she was to overlook all the little frictions that had undoubtedly arisen. She fully meant, without eating a morsel of humble pie herself, to allow Lucia to eat proud pie, for she saw that just for the present she herself was nowhere and Lucia everywhere. So Lucia should glut herself into a sense of complete superiority, and then it would be time to begin fresh manoeuvres. Major Benjy and Diva soon took themselves off: she saw them from the garden-window going very slowly down the street, ever so pleased to have people staring at them, and Irene, at the Padre's request, went out to dance a hornpipe on the lawn in her sailor clothes. But the two Wyses (always famous for sticking) remained and Georgie.

Mr. Wyse got up from the tea-table and passed round behind Miss Mapp's chair. Out of the corner of her eye she could see he was looking at the wall where a straw-coloured picture of her own hung. He always used to admire it, and it was pleasant to feel that he was giving it so careful and so respectful a scrutiny. Then he spoke to Lucia.

"How well I remember seeing you painting that," he said,

"and how long I took to forgive myself for having disturbed you in my blundering car. A perfect little masterpiece, Mallards Cottage and the crooked chimney. To the life."

Susan heaved herself up from the sofa and joined in the admiration.

"Perfectly delightful," she said. "The lights, the shadows. Beautiful! What a touch!"

Miss Mapp turned her head slowly as if she had a stiff neck, and verified her awful conjecture that it was no longer a picture of her own that hung there, but the very picture of Lucia's which had been rejected for the Art Exhibition. She felt as if no picture but a bomb hung there, which might explode at some chance word, and blow her into a thousand fragments. It was best to hurry from this perilous neighbourhood.

"Dear Lucia," she said, "I must be off. Just one little stroll, if I may, round my garden, before I go home. My roses will never forgive me, if I go away without noticing them."

She was too late.

"How I wish I had known it was finished!" said Mr. Wyse. "I should have begged you to allow us to have it for our Art Exhibition. It would have been the gem of it. Cruel of you, Mrs. Lucas!"

"But I sent it in to the hanging committee," said Lucia. "Georgie sent his, too, of Mallards. They were both sent back to us."

Mr. Wyse turned from the picture to Lucia with an expression of incredulous horror, and Miss Mapp quietly turned to stone.

"But impossible," he said. "I am on the hanging committee myself, and I hope you cannot think I should have been such an imbecile. Susan is on the committee too: so is Miss Mapp. In fact, we are the hanging committee. Susan, that gem, that little masterpiece never came before us."

"Never," said Susan. "Never. Never, never."

Mr. Wyse's eye transferred itself to Miss Mapp. She was still stone and her face was as white as the wall of Mallards Cottage in the masterpiece. Then for the first time in the collective memory of Tilling Mr. Wyse allowed himself to use slang.

"There has been some hanky-panky," he said. "That picture never came before the hanging committee."

The stone image could just move its eyes and they looked, in a glassy manner, at Lucia. Lucia's met them with one short gimlet thrust, and she whisked round to Georgie. Her face was turned away from the others, and she gave him a prodigious wink, as he sat there palpitating with excitement.

"*Georgino mio,*" she said. "Let us recall exactly what happened. The morning, I mean, when the hanging committee met. Let me see: let me see. Don't interrupt me: I will get it all clear."

Lucia pressed her hands to her forehead. "I have it," she said. "It is perfectly vivid to me now. You had taken our little pictures down to the framer's, Georgie, and told him to send them in to Elizabeth's house direct. That was it. The errand-boy from the framer's came up here that very morning, and delivered mine to Grosvenor, and yours to Foljambe. Let me think exactly when that was. What time was it, Mr. Wyse, that the hanging committee met?"

"At twelve, precisely," said Mr. Wyse.

"That fits in perfectly," said Lucia. "I called to Georgie out of the window here, and we told each other that our pictures had been rejected. A moment later, I saw your car go down to the High Street and when I went down there soon afterwards, it was standing in front of Miss—I mean Elizabeth's house. Clearly what happened was that the framer misunderstood Georgie's instructions, and returned the pictures to us before the hanging committee sat at all. So you never saw them, and we imagined all the time—did we not, Georgie?—that you had simply sent them back."

"But what must you have thought of us?" said Mr. Wyse, with a gesture of despair.

"Why, that you did not conscientiously think very much of our art," said Lucia. "We were perfectly satisfied with your decision. I felt sure that my little picture had a hundred faults and feeblenesses."

Miss Mapp had become unpetrified. Could it be that by some miraculous oversight she had not put into those parcels the formal, typewritten rejection of the committee? It did not seem likely, for she had a very vivid remembrance of the gratification it gave her to do so, but the only alternative theory was to suppose a magnanimity on Lucia's part which seemed even more miraculous. She burst into speech.

"How we all congratulate ourselves," she cried, "that it has all been cleared up! Such a stupid errand-boy! What are we to do next, Mr. Wyse? Our exhibition must secure Lucia's sweet picture, and of course Mr. Pillson's too. But how are we to find room for them? Everything is hung."

"Nothing easier," said Mr. Wyse. "I shall instantly withdraw my paltry little piece of still-life, and I am sure that Susan—"

"No, that would never do," said Miss Mapp, currying favour all round. "That beautiful wallflower, I could almost smell it: that King of Italy. Mine shall go: two or three of mine. I insist on it."

Mr. Wyse bowed to Lucia and then to Georgie.

"I have a plan better yet," he said. "Let us put—if we may have the privilege of securing what was so nearly lost to our exhibition—let us put these two pictures on easels as showing how deeply we appreciate our good fortune in getting them."

He bowed to his wife, he bowed—was it quite a bow?—to Miss Mapp, and had there been a mirror, he would no doubt have bowed to himself.

"Besides," he said, "our little sketches will not thus suffer so much from their proximity to—" and he bowed to Lucia. "And if Mr. Pillson will similarly allow us—" He bowed to Georgie.

Georgie, following Lucia's lead, graciously offered to go round to the Cottage and bring back his picture of Mallards, but Mr. Wyse would not hear of such a thing. He and Susan would go off in the Royce now, with Lucia's masterpiece, and fetch Georgie's from Mallards Cottage, and the sun should not set before they both stood on their distinguished easels in the enriched exhibition. So off they went in a great hurry to procure the easels before the sun went down and Miss Mapp, unable alone to face the reinstated victims of her fraud, scurried after them in a tumult of mixed emotions. Outside in the garden Irene, dancing hornpipes, was surrounded by both sexes of the enraptured youth of Tilling, for the boys knew she was a girl, and the girls thought she looked so like a boy. She shouted out "Come and dance, Mapp," and Elizabeth fled from her own sweet garden as if it had been a plague-stricken area, and never spoke to her roses at all.

The Queen and Drake were left alone in the garden-room.

"Well, I never!" said Georgie. "Did you? She sent them back all by herself."

"I'm not the least surprised," said Lucia. "It's like her."

"But why did you let her off?" he asked. "You ought to have exposed her and have done with her."

Lucia showed a momentary exultation, and executed a few steps from a Morris-dance.

"No, Georgie, that would have been a mistake," she said.

"She knows that we know, and I can't wish her worse than that. And I rather think, though he makes me giddy with so much bowing, that Mr. Wyse has guessed. He certainly suspects something of the sort."

"Yes, he said there had been some hanky-panky," said Georgie. "That was a strong thing for him to say. All the same—"

Lucia shook her head.

"No, I'm right," she said. "Don't you see I've taken the moral stuffing out of that woman far more completely than if I had exposed her?"

"But she's a cheat," cried Georgie. "She's a liar, for she sent back our pictures with a formal notice that the committee had rejected them. She hasn't got any moral stuffing to take out."

Lucia pondered this.

"That's true, there doesn't seem to be much," she said. "But even then, think of the moral stuffing that I've put into myself. A far greater score, Georgie, than to have exposed her, and it must be quite agonising for her to have that hanging over her head. Besides, she can't help being deeply grateful to me if there are any depths in that poor shallow nature. There may be: we must try to discover them. Take a broader view of it all, Georgie . . . Oh, and I've thought of something fresh! Send round to Mr. Wyse for the exhibition your picture of the Landgate, which poor Elizabeth sold. He will certainly hang it and she will see it there. That will round everything off nicely."

Lucia moved across to the piano and sat down on the treble music-stool.

"Let us forget all about these *piccoli disturbi*, Georgie," she said, "and have some music to put us in tune with beauty again. No, you needn't shut the door: it is so hot, and I am sure that no one else will dream of passing that notice of 'Private,' or come in here unasked. Ickle bit of divine Mozartino?"

Lucia found the duet at which she had worked quietly at odd moments.

"Let us try this," she said, "though it looks rather diffy. Oh, one thing more, Georgie. I think you and I had better keep those formal notices of rejection from the hanging committee just in case. We might need them some day, though I'm sure I hope we shan't. But one must be careful in dealing with that sort of woman. That's all I think. Now let us breathe harmony and loveliness again. *Uno, due . . .* pom."

Chapter Six

IT WAS A MELLOW MORNING of October, the season, as Lucia reflected, of mists and mellow fruitfulness, wonderful John Keats. There was no doubt about the mists, for there had been several sea-fogs in the English Channel, and the mellow fruitfulness of the garden at Mallards was equally indisputable. But now the fruitfulness of that sunny plot concerned Lucia far more than it had done during August and September, for she had taken Mallards for another month (Adele Brixton having taken The Hurst, Riseholme, for three), not on those original Shylock terms of fifteen guineas a week, and no garden-produce—but of twelve guineas a week, and all the garden-produce. It was a wonderful year for tomatoes: there were far more than a single widow could possibly eat, and Lucia, instead of selling them, constantly sent little presents of them to Georgie and Major Benjy. She had sent one basket of them to Miss Mapp, but these had been returned and Miss Mapp had written an effusive note saying that they would be wasted on her. Lucia had applauded that; it showed a very proper spirit.

The chain of consequences, therefore, of Lucia's remaining at Mallards was far-reaching. Miss Mapp took Wasters for another month at a slightly lower rent, Diva extended her lease of Taormina, and Irene still occupied the four-roomed labourer's cottage outside Tilling, which suited her so well, and the labourer and his family remained in the hop-picker's shanty. It was getting chilly of nights in the shanty, and he looked forward to the time when, Adele having left The Hurst, his cottage could be restored to him. Nor did the chain of consequences end here, for Georgie could not go back to Riseholme without Foljambe, and Foljambe would not go back there and leave her Cadman, while Lucia remained at Mallards. So Isabel Poppit continued to inhabit her bungalow by the sea, and Georgie remained in Mallards Cottage. With her skin turned black with all those sun-baths, and her hair spiky and wiry with so many sea-baths, Isabel resembled a cross between a kipper and a sea-urchin.

September had been full of events. The Art Exhibition had been a great success, and quantities of the pictures had been sold. Lucia had bought Georgie's picture of Mallards, Georgie had bought Lucia's picture of Mallards Cottage, Mr. Wyse had bought his wife's pastel of the King of Italy, and sent it as a birthday present to Amelia, and Susan Wyse had bought her husband's tea-cup and wallflower and kept them herself. But the greatest gesture of all had been Lucia's purchase of one of Miss Mapp's six exhibits, and this had practically forced Miss Mapp, so powerful was the suggestion hidden in it, to buy Georgie's picture of the Landgate, which he had given her, and which she had sold (not even for her own benefit but for that of the hospital) for sixpence at her jumble sale. She had had to pay a guinea to regain what had once been hers, so that in the end the revengeful impulse which had prompted her to put it in the sixpenny tray had been cruelly expensive. But she had still felt herself to be under Lucia's thumb in the whole matter of the exhibition (as indeed she was) and this purchase was of the nature of a propitiatory act. They had met one morning at the show, and Lucia had looked long at this sketch of Georgie's and then, looking long at Elizabeth, she had said it was one of the most charming and exquisite of his watercolours. Inwardly raging, yet somehow impotent to resist, Elizabeth had forked up. But she was now busily persuading herself that this purchase had something to do with the hospital, and that she need not make any further contributions to its funds this year: she felt there was a very good chance of persuading herself about this. No one had bought quaint Irene's pictures, and she had turned the women wrestlers into men.

Since then Miss Mapp had been very busy with the conversion of the marvellous crop of apples, plums and redcurrants in Diva's garden into jam and jelly. Her cook could not tackle so big a job alone, and she herself spent hours a day in the kitchen, and the most delicious odours of boiling preserves were wafted out of the windows into the High Street. It could not be supposed that they would escape Diva's sharp nose, and there had been words about it. But garden-produce (Miss Mapp believed) meant what it said, or would dear Diva prefer that she let the crop rot on the trees, and be a portion for wasps. Diva acknowledged that she would. And when the fruit was finished Miss Mapp proposed to turn her attention to the vegetable marrows, which, with a little ginger, made a very useful preserve for the household. She would leave a dozen of these pots for Diva.

But the jam-making was over now and Miss Mapp was glad of that, for she had scalded her thumb: quite a blister. She was even gladder that the Art Exhibition was over. All the important works of the Tilling school (except the pastel of the King of Italy) remained in Tilling, she had made her propitiatory sacrifice about Georgie's sketch of the Landgate, and she had no reason to suppose that Lucia had ever repented of that moment of superb magnanimity in the garden-room, which had averted an exposure of which she still occasionally trembled to think. Lucia could not go back on that now, it was all over and done with like the jam-making (though, like the jam-making, it had left a certain seared and sensitive place behind), and having held her tongue then, Lucia could not blab afterwards. Like the banns in church, she must for ever hold her peace. Miss Mapp had been deeply grateful for that clemency at the time, but no one could go on being grateful indefinitely. You were grateful until you had paid your debt of gratitude, and then you were free. She would certainly be grateful again, when this month was over and Lucia and Georgie left Tilling, never, she hoped, to return, but for the last week or two she had felt that she had discharged in full every groat of gratitude she owed Lucia, and her mind had been busier than usual over plots and plans and libels and inductions with regard to her tenant who, with those cheese-paring ways so justly abhorred by Miss Mapp, had knocked down the rent to twelve guineas a week and grabbed the tomatoes.

But Miss Mapp did not yet despair of dealing Lucia some nasty blow, for the fact of the matter was (she felt sure of it) that Tilling generally was growing a little restive under Lucia's autocratic ways. She had been taking them in hand, she had been patronising them, which Tilling never could stand, she had been giving them treats, just like that! She had sent out cards for an evening party (not dinner at all) with *"un po' di musica"* written in the left-hand corner. Even Mr. Wyse, that notorious syco-phant, had raised his eyebrows over this, and had allowed that this was rather an unusual inscription: *"musica"* (he thought) would have been more ordinary, and he would ask Amelia when she came. That had confirmed a secret suspicion which Miss Mapp had long entertained that Lucia's Italian (and, of course, Georgie's too) was really confined to such words as *"ecco"* and "*bon giorno*" and "*bello*" and she was earnestly hoping that Amelia would come before October was over, and they would all see what these great talks in Italian, to which Mr. Wyse was so looking forward, would amount to.

And what an evening that "po-di-mu" (as it was already referred to with faint little smiles) had been! It was a wet night and in obedience to her command (for at that time Lucia was at the height of the ascendancy she had acquired at the hospital fête), they had all put mackintoshes over their evening clothes, and galoshes over their evening shoes, and slopped up to Mallards through the pouring rain. A couple of journeys of Lucia's car could have brought them all in comfort and dryness, but she had not offered so obvious a convenience. Mrs. Wyse's Royce was being overhauled, so they had to walk too, and a bedraggled and discontented company had assembled. They had gone into the garden-room dripped on by the wistaria, and an interminable po-di-mu ensued. Lucia turned off all the lights in the room except one on the piano, so that they saw her profile against a black background, like the head on a postage stamp, and first she played the slow movement out of the "Moonlight Sonata." She stopped once, just after she had begun, because Diva coughed, and when she had finished there was a long silence. Lucia sighed and Georgie sighed, and everyone said "Thank you" simultaneously. Major Benjy said he was devoted to Chopin and Lucia playfully told him that she would take his musical education in hand.

Then she had allowed the lights to be turned up again, and there was a few minutes' pause to enable them to conquer the poignancy of emotion aroused by that exquisite rendering of the "Moonlight Sonata," to disinfect it so to speak with cigarettes, or drown it, as Major Benjy did, in rapid whiskies and sodas, and when they felt braver the po-di-mu began again, with a duet, between her and Georgie, of innumerable movements by Mozart, who must indeed have been a most prolific composer if he wrote all that. Diva fell quietly asleep, and presently there were indications that she would soon be noisily asleep. Miss Mapp hoped that she would begin to snore properly, for that would be a good set-down for Lucia, but Major Benjy poked her stealthily on the knee to rouse her. Mr. Wyse began to stifle yawns, though he sat as upright as ever, with his eyes fixed rather glassily on the ceiling, and ejaculated "Charming" at the end of every movement. When it was all over there were some faintly murmured requests that Lucia would play to them again, and without any further pressing, she sat down. Her obtuseness was really astounding.

"How you all work me!" she said. "A fugue by Bach then, if you insist on it, and if Georgie will promise not to scold me if I break down."

Luckily amid suppressed sighs of relief, she did break down, and though she was still perfectly willing to try again, there was a general chorus of unwillingness to take advantage of her great good nature, and after a wretched supper, consisting largely of tomato-salad, they trooped out into the rain, cheered by the promise of another musical evening next week when she would have that beautiful fugue by heart.

It was not the next week but the same week that they had all been bidden to a further evening of harmony, and symptoms of revolt, skilfully fomented by Miss Mapp, were observable. She had just received her note of invitation one morning, when Diva trundled in to Wasters.

"Another po-di-mu already," said she sarcastically. "What are you—"

"Isn't it unfortunate?" interrupted Elizabeth, "for I hope,

dear Diva, you have not forgotten that you promised to come in that very night—Thursday, isn't it—and play piquet with me."

Diva returned Elizabeth's elaborate wink. "So I did," she said. "Anyhow, I do."

"Consequently we shall have to refuse dear Lucia's invitation," said Elizabeth regretfully. "Lovely, wasn't it, the other night? And so many movements of Mozart. I began to think he must have discovered the secret of perpetual motion, and that we should be stuck there till Doomsday."

Diva was fidgeting about the room in her restless manner. ("Rather like a spinning top," thought Miss Mapp, "bumping into everything. I wish it would die.")

"I don't think she plays bridge very well," said Diva. "She began, you know, by saying she was so anxious to learn, and that we all played marvellously, but now she lays down the law like anything, telling us what we ought to have declared, and how we ought to have played. It's quite like—"

She was going to say "It's quite like playing with you," but luckily stopped in time.

"I haven't had the privilege of playing with her. Evidently I'm not up to her form," said Elizabeth, "but I hear, only report, mind, that she doesn't know the elements of the game."

"Well, not much more," said Diva. "And she says she will start a bridge class if we like."

"She spoils us! And who will the pupils be?" asked Elizabeth.

"I know one who won't," said Diva darkly.

"And one and one make two," observed Elizabeth. "A pity that she sets herself up like that. Saying the other night that she would take Major Benjy's musical education in hand! I always thought education began at home, and I'm sure I never heard so many wrong notes in my life."

Diva ruminated a moment, and began spinning again. "She offered to take the choir-practises in church, only the Padre wouldn't hear of it," she said. "And there's talk of a class to read Homer in Pope's translation."

"She has every accomplishment," said Elizabeth, "including push."

Diva bumped into another topic.

"I met Mr. Wyse just now," she said. "Countess Amelia Faraglione is coming tomorrow."

Miss Mapp sprang up.

"Not really?" she cried. "Why, she'll be here for Lucia's po-di-mu on Thursday. And the Wyses will be going, that's certain, and they are sure to ask if they may bring the Faradiddleone with them. Diva, dear, we must have our piquet another night. I wouldn't miss that for anything."

"Why?" asked Diva.

"Just think what will happen! She'll be forced to talk Italian, for Mr. Wyse has often said what a treat it will be to hear them talk it together, and I'm sure Lucia doesn't know any. I must be there."

"But if she does know it, it will be rather a sell," said Diva. "We shall have gone there for nothing except to hear all that Mozart over again and to eat tomatoes. I had heartburn half the night afterwards."

"Trust me, Diva," said Elizabeth. "I swear she doesn't know any Italian. And how on earth will she be able to wriggle out of talking it? With all her ingeniousness, it can't be done. She can't help being exposed."

"Well, that would be rather amusing," said Diva. "Being put down a peg or two certainly wouldn't hurt her. All right. I'll say I'll come."

Miss Mapp's policy was now of course the exact reverse of

what she had first planned. Instead of scheming to get all Tilling to refuse Lucia's invitation to listen to another po-di-mu, her
object was to encourage everyone to go, in order that they might
listen not so much to Mozart as to her rich silences or faltering
replies when challenged to converse in the Italian language. She
found that the Padre and Mrs. Bartlett had hurriedly arranged
a choir-practise and a meeting of the girl-guides respectively to
take place at the unusual hour of half-past nine in the evening in
order to be able to decline the po-di-mu, but Elizabeth, throwing
economy to the winds, asked them both to dine with her on the
fatal night, and come on to Lucia's delicious music afterwards.
This added inducement prevailed, and off they scurried to tell
choirboys and girl-guides that the meetings were cancelled and
would be held at the usual hour the day after. The curate needed
no persuasion, for he thought that Lucia had a wonderful touch
on the piano, and was already looking forward to more; Irene
similarly had developed a violent *schwärm* for Lucia and had
accepted, so that Tilling, thanks to Elizabeth's friendly offices,
would now muster in force to hear Lucia play duets and fugues
and not speak Italian. And when, in casual conversation with
Mr. Wyse, Elizabeth learned that he had (as she had anticipated)
ventured to ask Lucia if she would excuse the presumption of
one of her greatest admirers, and allow him to bring his sister
Amelia to her *soirée* and that Lucia had sent him her most cordial permission to do so, it seemed that nothing could stand in
the way of the fulfilment of Elizabeth's romantic revenge on that
upstart visitor for presuming to set herself up as Queen of the
social life of Tilling.

It was, as need hardly be explained, this aspect of the affair
which so strongly appealed to the sporting instincts of the place.
Miss Mapp had long been considered by others as well as her-

self the first social citizen of Tilling, and though she had often
been obliged to fight desperately for her position, and had suffered from time to time manifold reverses, she had managed to
maintain it, because there was no one else of so commanding
and unscrupulous a character. Then, this alien from Riseholme
had appeared and had not so much challenged her as just taken
her sceptre and her crown and worn them now for a couple of
months. At present all attempts to recapture them had failed,
but Lucia had grown a little arrogant, she had offered to take
choir-practise, she had issued her invitations (so thought Tilling) rather as if they had been commands, and Tilling would not
have been sorry to see her suffer some set-back. Nobody wanted
to turn out in the evening to hear her play Mozart (except the
curate), no one intended to listen to her read Pope's translation
of Homer's *Iliad,* or to be instructed how to play bridge, and
though Miss Mapp was no favourite, they would have liked to
see her score. But there was little partisanship; it was the sporting instinct which looked forward to witnessing an engagement
between two well-equipped Queens, and seeing whether one
really could speak Italian or not, even if they had to listen to all
the fugues of Bach first. Everyone, finally, except Miss Mapp,
wherever their private sympathies might lie, regretted that now
in less than a month, Lucia would have gone back to her own
kingdom of Riseholme, where it appeared she had no rival of any
sort, for these encounters were highly stimulating to students of
human nature and haters of Miss Mapp. Never before had Tilling known so exciting a season.

∞

On this mellow morning, then, of October, Lucia, after practising
her fugue for the coming po-di-mu, and observing Coplen bring

into the house a wonderful supply of tomatoes, had received that appalling note from Mr. Wyse, conveyed by the Royce, asking if he might bring Contessa Amelia di Faraglione to the musical party to which he so much looked forward. The gravity of the issue was instantly clear to Lucia, for Mr. Wyse had made no secret about the pleasure it would give him to hear his sister and herself mellifluously converse in the Italian tongue, but without hesitation she sent back a note by the chauffeur and the Royce, that she would be charmed to see the Contessa. There was no getting out of that, and she must accept the inevitable before proceeding irresistibly to deal with it. From the window she observed the Royce backing and advancing and backing till it managed to turn and went round the corner to Porpoise Street.

Lucia closed the piano, for she had more cosmic concerns to think about than the fingerings of a fugue. Her party of course (that required no consideration) would have to be cancelled, but that was only one point in the problem that confronted her. For that baleful bilinguist the Contessa di Faraglione was not coming to Tilling (all the way from Italy) for one night but she was to stay here, so Mr. Wyse's note had mentioned, for "about a week," after which she would pay visits to her relations the Wyses of Whitchurch and others. So for a whole week (or about) Lucia would be in perpetual danger of being called upon to talk Italian. Indeed, the danger was more than mere danger, for if anything in this world was certain, it was that Mr. Wyse would ask her to dinner during this week, and exposure would follow. Complete disappearance from Tilling during the Contessa's sojourn here was the only possible plan, yet how was that to be accomplished? Her house at Riseholme was let, but even if it had not been, she could not leave Tilling tomorrow, when she had invited everybody to a party in the evening.

The clock struck noon: she had meditated for a full half-hour, and now she rose.

"I can only think of influenza," she said to herself. "But I shall consult Georgie. A man might see it from another angle."

He came at once to her SOS.

"*Georgino mio,*" began Lucia, but then suddenly corrected herself. "Georgie," she said. "Something very disagreeable. The Contessa Thingummy is coming to the Wyses tomorrow, and he's asked me if he may bring her to our *musica*. I had to say yes; no way out of it."

Georgie was often very perceptive. He saw what this meant at once.

"Good Lord," he said. "Can't you put it off? Sprain your thumb."

The man's angle was not being of much use so far.

"Not a bit of good," she said. "She'll be here about a week, and naturally I have to avoid meeting her altogether. The only thing I can think of is influenza."

Georgie never smoked in the morning, but the situation seemed to call for a cigarette.

"That would do it," he said. "Rather a bore for you, but you could live in the secret garden a good deal. It's not overlooked."

He stopped: the unusual tobacco had stimulated his perceptive powers.

"But what about me?" he said.

"I'm sure I don't know," said Lucia.

"You're not looking far enough," said Georgie. "You're not taking the long view which you so often talk to me about. I can't have influenza too, it would be too suspicious. So I'm bound to meet the Faraglione and she'll see in a minute I can't talk Italian."

"Well?" said Lucia in a very selfish manner, as if he didn't matter at all.

"Oh, I'm not thinking about myself only," said Georgie in self-defence. "Not so at all. It'll react on you. You and I are supposed to talk Italian together, and when it's obvious I can't say more than three things in it, the fat's in the fire, however much influenza you have. How are you going to be supposed to jabber away in Italian to me when it's seen that I can't understand a word of it?"

Here indeed was the male angle, and an extremely awkward angle it was. For a moment Lucia covered her face with her hands.

"Georgie, what are we to do?" she asked in a stricken voice.

Georgie was a little ruffled at having been considered of such absolute unimportance until he pointed out to Lucia that her fate was involved with his, and it pleased him to echo her words.

"I'm sure I don't know," he said stiffly.

Lucia hastened to smooth his smart.

"My dear, I'm so glad I thought of consulting you," she said. "I knew it would take a man's mind to see all round the question, and how right you are! I never thought of that."

"Quite," said Georgie. "It's evident you haven't grasped the situation at all."

She paced up and down the garden-room in silence, recoiling once from the window, as she saw Elizabeth go by and kiss her hand with that awful hyena grin of hers.

"Georgie, 'oo not cross with poor Lucia?" she said, resorting to the less dangerous lingo which they used in happier days. This softened Georgie.

"I was rather," said Georgie, "but never mind that now. What am I to do? *Che faro,* in fact."

Lucia shuddered.

"Oh, for goodness' sake, don't talk Italian," she said. "It's that we've got to avoid. It's odd that we have to break ourselves of the habit of doing something we can't do . . . And you can't have influenza too. It would be too suspicious if you began simultaneously with me tomorrow. I've often wondered, now I come to think of it, if that woman, that Mapp, hasn't suspected that our Italian was a fake, and if we both had influenza exactly as the Faraglione arrived, she might easily put two and two together. Her mind is horrid enough for anything."

"I know she suspects," said Georgie. "She said some word in Italian to me the other day, which meant paperknife, and she looked surprised when I didn't understand, and said it in English. Of course, she had looked it out in a dictionary: it was a trap."

A flood of horrid light burst in on Lucia. "Georgie," she cried. "She tried me with the same word. I've forgotten it again, but it did mean paperknife. I didn't know it either, though I pretended it was her pronunciation that puzzled me. There's no end to her craftiness. But I'll get the better of her yet. I think you'll have to go away, while the Faraglione is here and I have influenza."

"But I don't want to go away," began Georgie. "Surely we can think of—"

Lucia paid no heed to this attempt at protest: it is doubtful if she even heard it, for the spark was lit now, and it went roaring through her fertile brain like a prairie fire in a high gale.

"You must go away tomorrow," she said. "Far better than influenza, and you must stop away till I send you a telegram, that the Faraglione has left. It will be very dull for me because I shall be entirely confined to the house and garden all the time you are gone. I think the garden will be safe. I cannot remember that it is overlooked from any other house and I shall do a lot of reading, though even the piano won't be possible . . . Georgie, I see it all. You have not been looking very well lately (my dear, you're the picture of health really, I have never seen you looking younger or better) and so you will have gone off to have a week at Folkestone or Littlestone, whichever you prefer. Sea air; you needn't bathe. And you can take my car, for I shan't be able to use it, and why not take Foljambe as well to valet you, as you often do when you go for a jaunt? She'll have her Cadman: we may as well make other people happy, Georgie, as it all seems to fit in so beautifully. And one thing more: this little jaunt of yours is entirely undertaken for my sake, and I must insist on paying it all. Go to a nice hotel and make yourself thoroughly comfortable; half a bottle of champagne whenever you want it in the evening, and what extras you like, and I will telephone to you to say when you can come back. You must start tomorrow morning before the Faraglione gets here."

Georgie knew it was useless to protest when Lucia got that loud, inspired, gabbling ring in her voice; she would cut through any opposition, as a steam saw buzzes through the most solid oak board till, amid a fountain of flying sawdust, it has sliced its way. He did not want to go away, but when Lucia exhibited that calibre of determination that he should, it was better to yield at once than to collapse later in a state of wretched exhaustion. Besides, there were bright points in her scheme. Foljambe would be delighted at the plan, for it would give her and Cadman leisure to enjoy each other's society; and it would not be disagreeable to stay for a week at some hotel in Folkestone and observe the cargoes of travellers from abroad arriving at the port after a billowy passage. Then he might find some bibelots in the shops, and he would listen to a municipal band, and have a bathroom next his bedroom, and do some sketches, and sit in a lounge in a series of those suits which had so justly earned him the title of the best-dressed man in Tilling. He would have a fine Rolls-

Royce in the hotel garage, and a smart chauffeur coming to ask for orders every morning, and he would be seen, an interesting and opulent figure, drinking his half-bottle of champagne every evening and he would possibly pick up an agreeable aquaintance or two. He had no hesitation whatever in accepting Lucia's proposal to stand the charges of this expedition, for, as she had most truly said, it was undertaken in her interests, and naturally she paid (besides, she was quite rich) for its equipment.

The main lines of this defensive campaign being thus laid down, Lucia, with her Napoleonic eye for detail, plunged into minor matters. She did not, of course, credit "that Mapp" with having procured the visit of the Faraglione, but a child could see that if she herself met the Faraglione during her stay here the grimmest exposure of her ignorance of the language she talked in such admired snippets must inevitably follow. "That Mapp" would pounce on this, and it was idle to deny that she would score heavily and horribly. But Georgie's absence (cheap at the cost) and her own invisibility by reason of influenza made a seemingly unassailable position, and it was with a keen sense of exhilaration in the coming contest that she surveyed the arena.

Lucia sent for the trusty Grosvenor and confided in her sufficiently to make her a conspirator. She told her that she had a great mass of arrears to do in reading and writing, and that for the next week she intended to devote herself to them, and lead the life of a hermit. She wanted no callers, and did not mean to see anyone, and the easiest excuse was to say that she had influenza. No doubt there would be many enquiries, and so day by day she would issue to Grosvenor her own official bulletin. Then she told Cadman that Mr. Georgie was far from well, and she had bundled him off with the car to Folkestone for about a week: he and Foljambe would accompany him. Then she made a care-

ful survey of the house and garden to ascertain what freedom of
movement she could have during her illness. Playing the piano,
except very carefully with the soft pedal down, would be risky,
but by a judicious adjustment of the curtains in the garden-room
window, she could refresh herself with very satisfactory glances
at the world outside. The garden, she was pleased to notice,
was quite safe, thanks to its encompassing walls, from any pry-
ing eyes in the houses round: the top of the church tower alone
overlooked it, and that might be disregarded, for only tourists
ascended it.

Then forth she went for the usual shoppings and chats in the
High Street and put in some further fine work. The morning tide
was already on the ebb, but by swift flirtings this way and that
she managed to have a word with most of those who were coming
to her po-di-mu tomorrow, and interlarded all she said to them
with brilliant scraps of Italian. She just caught the Wyses as they
were getting back into the Royce and said how *molto amabile*
it was of them to give her the *gran' piacere* of seeing the Contessa next evening: indeed she would be a welcome guest, and
it would be another *gran' piacere* to talk *la bella lingua* again.
Georgie, alas, would not be there for he was *un po' ammalato,*
and was going to spend a *settimana* by the *mare per stabilirsi.*
Never had she been so fluent and idiomatic, and she accepted
with *mille grazie* Susan's invitation to dine the evening after
her music and renew the conversations to which she so much
looked forward. She got almost tipsy with Italian . . . Then she
flew across the street to tell the curate that she was going to shut
herself up all afternoon in order to get the Bach fugue more worthy of his critical ear, she told Diva to come early to her party in
order that they might have a little chat first, and she just managed
by a flutelike "Cooee" to arrest Elizabeth as she was on the very

doorstep of Wasters. With glee she learned that Elizabeth was entertaining the Padre and his wife and Major Benjy to dinner before she brought them on to her party, and then, remembering the trap which that woman had laid for her and Georgie over the Italian paperknife, she could not refrain from asking her to dine and play bridge on the third night of her coming illness. Of course she would be obliged to put her off, and that would be about square . . . This half-hour's active work produced the impression that, however little pleasure Tilling anticipated from tomorrow's po-di-mu, the musician herself looked forward to it enormously, and was thirsting to talk Italian.

From the window of her bedroom next morning Lucia saw Georgie and Cadman and Foljambe set off for Folkestone, and it was with a Lucretian sense of pleasure in her own coming tranquillity that she contemplated the commotion and general upset of plans which was shortly to descend on Tilling. She went to the garden-room, adjusted the curtains and brewed the tempest which she now sent forth in the shape of a series of notes charged with the bitterest regrets. They were written in pencil (the consummate artist) as if from bed, and were traced in a feeble hand not like her usual firm script. "What a disappointment!" she wrote to Mrs. Wyse. "How cruel to have got the influenza—where could she have caught it?—on the very morning of her party, and what a blow not to be able to welcome the Contessa today or to dine with dear Susan tomorrow!" There was another note to Major Benjy, and others to Diva and quaint Irene and the curate and the Padre and Elizabeth. She still hoped that possibly she might be well enough for bridge and dinner the day after tomorrow, but Elizabeth must remember how infectious influenza was, and again she herself might not be well enough. That seemed pretty safe, for Elizabeth had a frantic phobia of infection, and Wasters had reeked of carbolic all the time the jumble sale was being held, for fear of some bit of rubbish having come in contact with tainted hands. Lucia gave these notes to Grosvenor for immediate delivery and told her that the bulletin for the day in answer to callers was that there was no anxiety, for the attack though sharp was not serious, and only demanded warmth and complete quiet. She then proceeded to get both by sitting in this warm October sun in her garden, reading Pope's translation of the *Iliad* and seeing what the Greek for it was.

Three impregnable days passed thus. From behind the adjusted curtains of the garden-room she observed the coming of many callers and Grosvenor's admirable demeanour to them. The Royce lurched up the street, and there was Susan in her sables, and, sitting next her, a vivacious gesticulating woman with a monocle, who looked the sort of person who could talk at the most appalling rate. This without doubt was the fatal Contessa, and Lucia felt that to see her thus was like observing a lion at large from behind the bars of a comfortable cage. Miss Mapp on the second day came twice, and each time she glanced piercingly at the curtains, as if she knew that trick, and listened as if hoping to hear the sound of the piano. The Padre sent a note almost entirely in Highland dialect, the curate turned away from the door with evident relief in his face at the news he had received, and whistled the Bach fugue rather out of tune.

On the fifth day of her illness new interests sprang up for Lucia that led her to neglect Pope's *Iliad* altogether. By the first post there came a letter from Georgie, containing an enclosure which Lucia saw (with a slight misgiving) was written in Italian. She turned first to Georgie's letter.

The most wonderful thing has happened [wrote Georgie] and you will be pleased . . . There's a family here with whom I've made friends, an English father, an Italian mother and a girl with a pigtail. Listen! The mother teaches the girl Italian, and sets her little themes to write on some subject or other, and then corrects them and writes a fair copy. Well, I was sitting in the lounge this morning while the girl was having her lesson, and Mrs. Brocklebank (that's her name) asked me to suggest a subject for the theme, and I had the most marvellous idea. I said "Let her write a letter to an Italian Countess whom she has never seen before, and say how she regretted having been obliged to put off her musical party to which she had asked the Countess and her brother, because she had caught influenza. She was so sorry not to meet her, and she was afraid that as the Countess was only staying a week in the place, she would not have the pleasure of seeing her at all." Mrs. B. thought that would do beautifully for a theme, and I repeated it over again to make sure. Then the girl wrote it, and Mrs. B. corrected it and made a fair copy. I begged her to give it me, because I adored Italian (though I couldn't speak it) and it was so beautifully expressed. I haven't told this very well, because I'm in a hurry to catch the post, but I enclose Mrs. B.'s Italian letter, and you just see whether it doesn't do the trick too marvellously. I'm having quite a gay time, music and drives and seeing the Channel boat come in, and aren't I clever?

> Your devoted,
> *Georgie*

Foljambe and Cadman have had a row, but I'm afraid they've made it up.

∞

Lucia, with her misgivings turned to joyful expectation, seized and read the enclosure. Indeed it was a miraculous piece of manna to one whom the very sight of it made hungry. It might have been the result of telepathy between Mrs. Brocklebank and her own subconscious self, so aptly did that lady grasp her particular unspoken need. It expressed in the most elegant idiom precisely what met the situation, and she would copy out and send it today, without altering a single word. And how clever of Georgie to have thought of it. He deserved all the champagne he could drink.

Lucia used her highest art in making a copy (on Mallard paper) of this document, as if writing hastily in a familiar medium. Occasionally she wrote a word (it did not matter what), erased it so as to render it illegible to the closest scrutiny, and then went on with Mrs. Brocklebank's manuscript; occasionally she omitted a word of it and then inserted it with suitable curves of direction above. No one receiving her transcript could imagine that it was other than her own extempore scribble. Mrs. Brocklebank had said that in two or three days she hoped to be able to see her friends again, and that fitted beautifully, because in two or three days now the Contessa's visit would have come to an end, and Lucia could get quite well at once.

The second post arrived before Lucia had finished this thoughtful copy. There was a letter in Lady Brixton's handwriting, and hastily scribbling the final florid salutations to the Contessa, she opened this, and thereupon forgot Georgie and Mrs. Brocklebank and everything else in the presence of the tremendous question which was brought for her decision. Adele had simply fallen in love with Riseholme; she affirmed that life was no longer worth living without a house there, and, of all houses, she would like best to purchase, unfurnished, The Hurst. Failing that there was another that would do, belonging to round red little Mrs. Quantock, who, she had ascertained, might consider selling it. Could darling Lucia therefore let her know with the shortest possible delay whether she would be prepared to sell The Hurst? If she had no thought of doing so Adele would begin tempting Mrs. Quantock at once. But if she had, let genteel indications about price be outlined at once.

There are certain processes of mental solidification which take place with extraordinary rapidity, because the system is already soaked and super-saturated with the issues involved. It was so now with Lucia. Instantly, on the perusal of Adele's enquiries her own mind solidified. She had long been obliquely contemplating some such step as Adele's letter thrust in front of her, and she was surprised to find that her decision was already made. Riseholme, once so vivid and significant, had during these weeks at Tilling been fading like an ancient photograph exposed to the sun, and all its features, foregrounds and backgrounds had grown blurred and dim. If she went back to Riseholme at the end of the month, she would find there nothing to occupy her energies, or call out her unique powers of self-assertion. She had so swept the board with her management of the Elizabethan fête that no further progress was possible. Poor dear Daisy might occasionally make some minute mutinies, but after being Drake's wife (what a lesson for her!) there would be no real fighting spirit left in her. It was far better, while her own energies still bubbled within her, to conquer this fresh world of Tilling than to smoulder at Riseholme. Her work there was done, whereas here, as this week of influenza testified, there was a very great deal to do. Elizabeth Mapp was still in action and capable of delivering broadsides; innumerable crises might still arise, volcanoes smoked, thunderclouds threatened, there were hostile and malignant forces to be thwarted. She had never been better occupied and diverted, the place suited her, and it bristled with opportunities. She wrote to Adele at once saying that dear as Riseholme (and especially The Hurst) was to her, she was prepared to be tempted, and indicated a sum before which she was likely to fall.

∽

Miss Mapp by this fifth day of Lucia's illness was completely baffled. She did not yet allow herself to despair of becoming unbaffled, for she was certain that there was a mystery here, and every mystery had an explanation if you only worked at it enough. The coincidence of Lucia's illness with the arrival of the Contessa and Georgie's departure, supported by the trap she had laid about the paperknife, was far too glaring to be overlooked by any constructive mind, and there must be something behind it. Only a foolish ingenuous child (and Elizabeth was anything but that) could have considered these as isolated phenomena. With a faith that would have removed mountains, she believed that Lucia was perfectly well, but all she had been able to do at present was to recite her creed to Major Benjy and Diva and others, and eagerly wait for any shred of evidence to support it. Attempts to pump Grosvenor and lynxlike glances at the window of the garden-room had yielded nothing, and her anxious enquiry addressed to Dr. Dobbie, the leading physician of Tilling, had yielded a snub. She did not know who Lucia's doctor was, so with a view to ascertaining that, and possibly getting other information, she had approached him with her most winning smile, and asked how the dear patient at Mallards was.

"I am not attending any dear patient at Mallards," had been his unpromising reply, "and if I was I need hardly remind you that, as a professional man, I should not dream of answering any enquiry about my patients without their express permission to do so. Good-morning."

"A very rude man," thought Miss Mapp, "but perhaps I had better not try to get at it that way."

She looked up at the church, wondering if she would find inspiration in that beautiful grey tower, which she had so often sketched, outlined against the pellucid blue of the October sky. She found it instantly, for she remembered that the leads at the top of it which commanded so broad a view of the surrounding country commanded also a perfectly wonderful view of her own little secret garden. It was a small chance, but no chance however small must be neglected in this famine of evidence, and it came to her in a flash that there could be no more pleasant way of spending the morning than making a sketch of the green, green marsh and the line of the blue, blue sea beyond. She hurried back to Wasters, pausing only at Mallards to glance at the garden-room where the curtains were adjusted in the most exasperatingly skilful manner, and to receive Grosvenor's assurance that the patient's temperature was quite normal today.

"Oh, that is good news," said Miss Mapp. "Then tomorrow perhaps she will be about again."

"I couldn't say, miss," said Grosvenor, holding on to the door.

"Give her my fondest love," said Miss Mapp, "and tell her how rejoiced I am, please, Grosvenor."

"Yes, miss," said Grosvenor, and before Miss Mapp could step from the threshold, she heard the rattle of the chain behind the closed door.

She was going to lunch that day with the Wyses, a meal which Mr. Wyse, in his absurd affected fashion, always alluded to as breakfast, especially when the Contessa was staying with

them. Breakfast was at one, but there was time for an hour at the
top of the church tower first. In order to see the features of the
landscape better, she took up an opera-glass with her sketching
things. She first put a blue watery wash on her block for the sky
and sea, and a green one for the marsh, and while these were drying she examined every nook of her garden with the opera-glass.
No luck, and she picked up her sketch again on which the sky
was rapidly inundating the land.

Lucia had learned this morning *via* Grosvenor and her cook
and Figgis, Mr. Wyse's butler, that the week of the Contessa's
stay here was to be curtailed by one day and that the Royce
would convey her to Whitchurch next morning on her visit to the
younger but ennobled branch of the family. Further intelligence
from the same source made known that the breakfast today to
which Miss Mapp was bidden was a Belshazzar breakfast, eight
if not ten. This was good news: the period of Lucia's danger
of detection would be over in less than twenty-four hours, and
about the time that Miss Mapp at the top of the tower of Tilling
Church was hastily separating the firmament from the dry land,
Lucia wrote out a telegram to Georgie that he might return the
following day and find all clear. Together with that she sent a
request to Messrs Woolgar & Pipstow that they should furnish
her with an order to view a certain house she had seen just outside Tilling, near quaint Irene's cottage, which she had observed
was for sale.

She hesitated about giving Grosvenor the envelope addressed
to Contessa di Faraglione, which contained the transcript, duly
signed, of Mrs. Brocklebank's letter to a Countess, and decided,
on the score of dramatic fitness, to have it delivered shortly after
one o'clock when Mrs. Wyse's breakfast would be in progress,
with orders that it should be presented to the Contessa at once.

Lucia was feeling the want of vigorous exercise, and bethought herself of the *Ideal System of Callisthenics for Those No Longer Young*. For five days she had been confined to house and garden, and the craving to skip took possession of her. Skipping was an exercise highly recommended by the ideal system, and she told Grosvenor to bring back for her, with the order to view from Messrs Woolgar & Pipstow, a simple skipping-rope from the toyshop in the High Street. While Grosvenor was gone this desire for free active movement in the open air awoke a kindred passion for the healthful action of the sun on the skin, and she hurried up to her sick-room, changed into a dazzling bathing-suit of black and yellow, and, putting on a very smart dressing-gown gay with ribands, was waiting in the garden-room when Grosvenor returned, recalling to her mind the jerks and swayings which had kept her in such excellent health when grief forbade her to play golf.

The hour was a quarter to one when Lucia tripped into the secret garden, shed her dressing-gown and began skipping on the little lawn with the utmost vigour. The sound of the church clock immediately below Miss Mapp's eyrie on the tower warned her that it was time to put her sketching things away, deposit them at Wasters and go out to breakfast. During the last half-hour she had cast periodical but fruitless glances at her garden, and had really given it up as a bad job. Now she looked down once more, and there close beside the bust of good Queen Anne was a gay striped figure of waspish colours skipping away like mad. She dropped her sketch, she reached out a trembling hand for her opera-glasses, the focus of which was already adjusted to a nicety, and by their aid she saw that this athletic wasp who was skipping with such exuberant activity was none other than the invalid.

Miss Mapp gave a shrill crow of triumph. All came to him who waited, and if she had known Greek she would undoubtedly have exclaimed "Eureka": as it was she only crowed. It was all too good to be true, but it was all too distinct not to be. "Now I've got her," she thought. "The whole thing is as clear as daylight. I was right all the time. She has not had influenza anymore than I, and I'll tell everybody at breakfast what I have seen." But the sight still fascinated her. What shameless vigour, when she should have been languid with fever! What abysses of falsehood, all because she could not talk Italian! What expense to herself in that unnecessary dinner to the Padre and Major Benjy! There was no end to it . . .

Lucia stalked about the lawn with a high prancing motion when she had finished her skipping. Then she skipped again, and then she made some odd jerks, as if she was being electrocuted. She took long deep breaths, she lifted her arms high above her head as if to dive, she lay down on the grass and kicked, she walked on tiptoe like a ballerina, she swung her body round from the hips. All this had for Miss Mapp the fascination that flavours strong disgust and contempt. Eventually, just as the clock struck one, she wrapped herself in her dressing-gown, the best was clearly over. Miss Mapp was already late, and she must hurry straight from the tower to her breakfast, for there was no time to go back to Wasters first. She would be profuse in pretty apologies for her lateness; the view from the church tower had been so entrancing (this was perfectly true) that she had lost all count of time. She could not show her sketch to the general company, because the firmament had got dreadfully muddled up with the waters which were below it, but instead she would tell them something which would muddle up Lucia.

The breakfast party was all assembled in Mrs. Wyse's

drawing-room with its dark oak beams and its silver-framed photographs and its morocco case containing the order of the MBE, still negligently open. Everybody had been waiting, everybody was rather grumpy at the delay, and on her entry the Contessa had clearly said "*Ecco*! Now at last!"

They would soon forgive her when they learned what had really made her late, but it was better to wait for a little before imparting her news, until breakfast had put them all in a more appreciative mood. She hastened on this desired moment by little compliments all round: what a wonderful sermon the Padre had preached last Sunday; how well dear Susan looked; what a delicious dish these eggs *à la Capri* were, she must really be greedy and take a teeny bit more. But these dewdrops were only interjected, for the Contessa talked in a loud continuous voice as usual, addressing the entire table, and speaking with equal fluency whether her mouth was full or empty.

At last the opportunity arrived. Figgis brought in a note on an immense silver (probably plated) salver, and presented it to the Contessa: it was to be delivered at once. Amelia said "*Scusi*" which everybody understood—even Lucia might have understood that—and was silent for a space as she tore it open and began reading it.

Miss Mapp decided to tantalise and excite them all before actually making her revelation.

"I will give anybody three guesses as to what I have seen this morning," she said. "Mr. Wyse, Major Benjy, Padre, you must all guess. It is about someone whom we all know, who is still an invalid. I was sketching this morning at the top of the tower, and happened to glance down into my pet little secret garden. And there was Lucia in the middle of the lawn. How was she dressed, and what was she doing? Three guesses each, shall it be?"

Alas! The introductory tantalisation had been too long, for before anybody could guess anything the Contessa broke in again.

"But never have I read such a letter!" she cried. "It is from Mrs. Lucas. All in Italian, and such Italian! Perfect. I should not have thought that any foreigner could have had such command of idiom and elegance. I have lived in Italy for ten years, but my Italian is a bungle compared to this. I have always said that no foreigner ever can learn Italian perfectly, and Cecco too, but we were wrong. This Mrs. Lucas proves it. It is composed by the ear, the spoken word on paper. *Dio mio!* What an escape I have had, Algernon! You had a plan to bring me and your Mrs. Lucas together to hear us talk. But she would smile to herself, and I should know what she was thinking, for she would be thinking how very poorly I talk Italian compared with herself. I will read her letter to you all, and though you do not know what it means you will recognise a fluency, a music . . ."

The Contessa proceeded to do so, with renewed exclamations of amazement, and all that bright edifice of suspicion, so carefully reared by the unfortunate Elizabeth, that Lucia knew no Italian, collapsed like a house built of cards when the table is shaken. Elizabeth had induced everybody to accept invitations to the second po-di-mu in order that all Tilling might hear Lucia's ignorance exposed by the Contessa, and when she had wriggled out of that, Elizabeth's industrious efforts had caused the gravest suspicions to be entertained that Lucia's illness was feigned in order to avoid any encounter with one who did know Italian, and now not only was not one pane of that Crystal Palace left unshattered, but the Contessa was congratulating herself on her own escape.

Elizabeth stirred feebly below the ruins: she was not quite crushed.

"I'm sure it sounds lovely," she said when the recitation was over. "But did not you yourself, dear Mr. Wyse, think it odd that anyone who knew Italian should put *un po' di musica* on her invitation-card?"

"Then he was wrong," said the Contessa. "No doubt that phrase is a little humorous quotation from something I do not know. Rather like you ladies of Tilling who so constantly say '*au reservoir.*' It is not a mistake: it is a joke."

Elizabeth made a final effort.

"I wonder if dear Lucia wrote that note herself," she said pensively.

"Pish! Her parlour-maid, doubtless," said the Contessa. "For me, I must spend an hour this afternoon to see if I can answer that letter in a way that will not disgrace me."

There seemed little more to be said on that subject and Elizabeth hastily resumed her tantalisation.

"Nobody has tried to guess yet what I saw from the church tower," she said. "Major Benjy, you try! It was Lucia, but how was she dressed and what was she doing?"

There was a coldness about Major Benjy. He had allowed himself to suspect, owing to Elizabeth's delicate hints, that there was perhaps some Italian mystery behind Lucia's influenza, and now he must make amends.

"Couldn't say, I'm sure," he said. "She was sure to have been very nicely dressed from what I know of her."

"I'll give you a hint then," said she. "I've never seen her dressed like that before."

Major Benjy's attention completely wandered. He made no attempt to guess but sipped his coffee.

"You then, Mr. Wyse, if Major Benjy gives up," said Elizabeth, getting anxious. Though the suspected cause of Lucia's illness was disproved, it still looked as if she had never had influenza at all, and that was something.

"My ingenuity, I am sure, will not be equal to the occasion," said Mr. Wyse very politely. "You will be obliged to tell me. I give up."

Elizabeth emitted a shrill little titter.

"A dressing-gown," she said. "A bathing-costume. And she was skipping! Fancy! With influenza!"

There was a dreadful pause. No babble of excited enquiry and comment took place at all. The Contessa put up her monocle, focused Elizabeth for a moment, and this pause somehow was like the hush that succeeds some slight *gaffe,* some small indelicacy that had better have been left unsaid. Her host came to her rescue.

"That is indeed good news," said Mr. Wyse. "We may encourage ourselves to hope that our friend is well on the road to convalescence. Thank you for telling us that, Miss Mapp."

Mrs. Bartlett gave one of her little mouse-like squeals, and Irene said: "Hurrah! I shall try to see her this afternoon. I am glad."

That again was an awful thought. Irene no doubt, if admitted, would give an account of the luncheon-party which would lose nothing in the telling, and she was such a ruthless mimic. Elizabeth felt a sinking feeling.

"Would that be wise, dear?" she said. "Lucia is probably not yet free from infection, and we mustn't have you down with it. I wonder where she caught it, by the way?"

"But your point is that she's never had influenza at all," said Irene with that dismal directness of hers.

Choking with this monstrous dose of fiasco, Elizabeth made for the present no further attempt to cause her friends to recoil from the idea of Lucia's skippings, for they only rejoiced that she was sufficiently recovered to do so. The party presently dispersed, and she walked away with her sketching things and Diva, and glanced up the street towards her house. Irene was already standing by the door, and Elizabeth turned away with a shudder, for Irene waved her hand to them and was admitted.

"It's all very strange, dear Diva, isn't it?" she said. "It's impossible to believe that Lucia's been ill, and it's useless to try to do so. Then there's Mr. Georgie's disappearance. I never thought of that before."

Diva interrupted.

"If I were you, Elizabeth," she said, "I should hold my tongue about it all. Much wiser."

"Indeed?" said Elizabeth, beginning to tremble.

"Yes. I tell you so as a friend," continued Diva firmly. "You got hold of a false scent. You made us think that Lucia was avoiding the Faraglione. All wrong from beginning to end. One of your worst shots. Give it up."

"But there is something queer," said Elizabeth wildly. "Skipping—"

"If there is," said Diva, "you're not clever enough to find it out. That's my advice. Take it or leave it. I don't care. *Au reservoir.*"

Chapter Seven

HAD MISS MAPP BEEN ABLE to hear what went on in the garden-room that afternoon, as well as she had been able to see what had gone on that morning in the garden, she would never have found Irene more cruelly quaint. Her account of this luncheon-party was more than graphic, for so well did she reproduce the Contessa's fervid monologue and poor Elizabeth's teasings over what she wanted them all to guess, that it positively seemed to be illustrated. Almost more exasperating to Miss Mapp would have been Lucia's pitiful contempt for the impotence of her malicious efforts.

"Poor thing!" she said. "Sometimes I think she is a little mad. *Una pazza: un po' pazza* . . . But I regret not seeing the Contessa. Nice of her to have approved of my scribbled note, and I dare say I should have found that she talked Italian very well indeed. Tomorrow—for after my delicious exercise on the lawn this morning, I do not feel up to more today—tomorrow I should certainly have hoped to call—in the afternoon—and have had a chat with her. But she is leaving in the morning, I understand."

Lucia, looking the picture of vigour and vitality, swept across to the curtained window and threw back those screenings with a movement that made the curtain-rings chime together.

"Poor Elizabeth!" she repeated. "My heart aches for her, for I am sure all that carping bitterness makes her wretched. I dare say it is only physical: liver perhaps, or acidity. The ideal system of callisthenics might do wonders for her. I cannot, as you will readily understand, dear Irene, make the first approaches to her after her conduct to me, and the dreadful innuendoes she has made, but I should like her to know that I bear her no malice at all. Do convey that to her sometime. Tactfully, of course. Women like her who do all they can on every possible occasion to hurt and injure others are usually very sensitive themselves, and I would not add to the poor creature's other chagrins. You must all be kind to her."

"My dear, you're too wonderful!" said Irene, in a sort of ecstasy. "What a joy you are! But, alas, you're leaving us so soon. It's too unkind of you to desert us."

Lucia had dropped on to the music-stool by the piano which had so long been dumb, except for a few timorous chords muffled by the *unsustenuto* pedal, and dreamily recalled the first bars of the famous slow movement.

Irene sat down on the cold hot-water pipes and yearned at her.

"You can do everything," she said. "You play like an angel, and you can knock out Mapp with your little finger, and you can skip and play bridge, and you've got such a lovely nature that you don't bear Mapp the slightest grudge for her foul plots. You are adorable! Won't you ask me to come and stay with you at Riseholme sometime?"

Lucia, still keeping perfect time with her triplets while this recital of her perfections was going on, considered whether she should not tell Irene at once that she had practically determined not to desert them. She had intended to tell Georgie first, but she would do that when he came back tomorrow, and she wanted to see about getting a house here without delay. She played a nimble arpeggio on the chord of C sharp minor and closed the piano.

"Too sweet of you to like me, dear," she said, "but as for your staying with me at Riseholme, I don't think I shall ever go back there myself. I have fallen in love with this dear Tilling, and I fully expect I shall settle here for good."

"Angel!" said Irene.

"I've been looking about for a house that might suit me," she continued when Irene had finished kissing her, "and the house-agents have just sent me the order to view one which particularly attracts me. It's that white house on the road that skirts the marsh, half a mile away. A nice garden sheltered from the north wind. Right down on the level, it is true, but such a divine view. Broad, tranquil! A dyke and a bank just across the road, keeping back the high tides in the river."

"But of course I know it; you mean Grebe," cried Irene. "The cottage I am in now adjoins the garden. Oh, do take it! While you're settling in, I'll let Diva have Taormina, and Diva will let Mapp have Wasters, and Mapp will let you have Mallards till Grebe's ready for you. And I shall be at your disposal all day to help you with your furniture."

Lucia decided that there was no real danger of meeting the Contessa if she drove out there: besides the Contessa now wanted to avoid her for fear of showing how inferior was her Italian.

"It's such a lovely afternoon," she said, "that I think a little drive would not hurt me. Unfortunately Georgie, who comes back tomorrow, has got my car. I lent it him for his week by the sea."

"Oh, how like you!" cried Irene. "Always unselfish!"

"Dear Georgie! So pleased to give him a little treat," said Lucia. "I'll ring up the garage and get them to send me something closed. Come with me, dear, if you have nothing particular to do, and we'll look over the house."

Lucia found much to attract her in Grebe. Though it was close to the road it was not overlooked, for a thick hedge of horn-beam made a fine screen: besides, the road did not lead anywhere particular. The rooms were of good dimensions, there was a hall and dining-room on the ground floor, with a broad staircase lead-ing up to the first floor where there were two or three bedrooms and a long admirable sitting-room with four windows looking across the road to the meadows and the high bank bounding the river. Beyond that lay the great empty levels of the marsh, with the hill of Tilling rising out of it half a mile away to the west. Close behind the house was the cliff which had once been the coastline before the marshes were drained and reclaimed, and this would be a rare protection against northerly and easterly winds. All these pleasant rooms looked south, and all had this open view away seawards; they had character and dignity, and at once Lucia began to see herself living here. The kitchen and offices were in a wing by themselves, and here again there was character, for the kitchen had evidently been a coach-house, and still retained the big double doors appropriate to such. There had once been a road from it to the end of the kitchen garden, but with its disuse as a coach-house, the road had been replaced by a broad cinder path now bordered with beds of useful vegetables.

"*Ma molto conveniente,*" said Lucia more than once, for it was now perfectly safe to talk Italian again, since the Contessa, no less than she, was determined to avoid a duet in that language. "*Mi piace molto. E un bel giardino.*"

"How I love hearing you talk Italian," ejaculated Irene, "especially since I know it's the very best. Will you teach it me? Oh, I am so pleased you like the house."

"But I am charmed with it," said Lucia. "And there's a garage with a very nice cottage attached which will do beautifully for Cadman and Foljambe."

She broke off suddenly, for in the fervour of her enthusiasm for the house, she had not thought about the awful catastrophe which must descend on Georgie, if she decided to live at Tilling. She had given no direct thought to him, and now for the first time she realised the cruel blow that would await him, when he came back tomorrow, all bronzed from his week at Folkestone. He had been a real *Deus ex machina* to her: his stroke of genius had turned a very hazardous moment into a blaze of triumph, and now she was going to plunge a dagger into his domestic heart by the news that she and therefore Cadman and therefore Foljambe were not coming back to Riseholme at all . . .

"Oh, are they going to marry?" asked Irene. "Or do you mean they just live together? How interesting!"

"Dear Irene, do not be so modern," said Lucia, quite sharply. "Marriage of course, and banns first. But never mind that for the present. I like those great double doors to the kitchen. I shall certainly keep them."

"How ripping that you're thinking about kitchen-doors already," said Irene. "That really sounds as if you did mean to buy the house. Won't Mapp have a fit when she hears it! I must be there when she's told. She'll say 'Darling Lulu, what a joy,' and then fall down and foam at the mouth."

Lucia gazed out over the marsh where the level rays of sunset turned a few low-lying skeins of mist to rose and gold. The tide was high and the broad channel of the river running out to sea was brimming from edge to edge. Here and there, where the banks were low, the water had overflowed on to adjacent margins of land; here and there, spread into broad lakes, it lapped the confining dykes. There were sheep cropping the meadows, there were seagulls floating in the water, and half a mile away to the west the red roofs of Tilling glowed as if molten not only with the soft brilliance of the evening light, but (to the discerning eye) with the intensity of the interests that burned beneath them . . . Lucia hardly knew what gave her the most satisfaction, the magic of the marsh, her resolve to live here, or the recollection of the complete discomfiture of Elizabeth.

Then again the less happy thought of Georgie recurred, and she wondered what arguments she could use to induce him to leave Riseholme and settle here. Tilling with all its manifold interests would be incomplete without him, and how dismally incomplete Riseholme would be to him without herself and Foljambe. Georgie had of late taken his painting much more seriously than ever before, and he had often during the summer put off dinner to an unheard-of lateness in order to catch a sunset, and had risen at most inconvenient hours to catch a sunrise. Lucia had strongly encouraged this zeal, she had told him that if he was to make a real career as an artist he had no time to waste. Appreciation and spurring-on was what he needed: perhaps Irene could help.

She pointed to the glowing landscape. "Irene, what would life be without sunsets?" she asked. "And to think that this miracle happens every day, except when it's very cloudy!"

Irene looked critically at the view. "Generally speaking, I don't like sunsets," she said. "The composition of the sky is usually childish. But good colouring about this one."

"There are practically no sunsets at Riseholme," said Lucia. "I suppose the sun goes down, but there's a row of hills in the way. I often think that Georgie's development as an artist is starved there. If he goes back there he will find no one to make him work. What do you think of his painting, dear?"

"I don't think of it at all," said Irene.

"No? I am astonished. Of course your own is so different in character. Those wrestlers! Such movement! But personally I find very great perception in Georgie's work. A spaciousness, a calmness! I wish you would take an interest in it and encourage him. You can find beauty anywhere if you look for it."

"Of course I'll do my best if you want me to," said Irene. "But it will be hard work to find beauty in Georgie's little valentines."

"Do try. Give him some hints. Make him see what you see. All that boldness and freedom. That's what he wants . . . Ah, the sunset is fading. *Buona notte, bel sole!* We must be getting home too. *Addio, mia bella casa.* But Georgie must be the first to know, Irene, do not speak of it until I have told him. Poor Georgie: I hope it will not be a terrible blow to him."

∞

Georgie came straight to Mallards on his arrival next morning from Folkestone with Cadman and Foljambe. His recall, he knew, meant that the highly dangerous Contessa had gone, and his admission by Grosvenor, after the door had been taken off the chain, that Lucia's influenza was officially over. He looked quite bronzed, and she gave him the warmest welcome.

"It all worked without a hitch," she said as she told him of the plots and counter-plots which had woven so brilliant a tapestry of events. "And it was that letter of Mrs. Brocklebank's which you sent me that clapped the lid on Elizabeth. I saw at once what I could make of it. Really, Georgie, I turned it into a stroke of genius."

"But it was a stroke of genius already," said Georgie. "You only had to copy it out and send it to the Contessa."

Lucia was slightly ashamed of having taken the supreme credit for herself: the habit was hard to get rid of.

"My dear, all the credit shall be yours then," she said handsomely. "It was your stroke of genius. I copied it out very carelessly as if I had scribbled it off without thought. That was a nice touch, don't you think? The effect? Colossal, so Irene tells me, for I could not be there myself. That was only yesterday. A few desperate wriggles from Elizabeth, but of course no good. I do not suppose there was a more thoroughly thwarted woman in all Sussex than she."

Georgie gave a discreet little giggle.

"And what's so terribly amusing is that she was right all the time about your influenza and your Italian and everything," he said. "Perfectly maddening for her."

Lucia sighed pensively.

"Georgie, she was malicious," she observed, "and that never pays."

"Besides, it serves her right for spying on you," Georgie continued.

"Yes, poor thing. But I shall begin now at once to be kind to her again. She shall come to lunch tomorrow, and you of course. By the way, Georgie, Irene takes so much interest in your painting. It was news to me, for her style is so different from your beautiful, careful work."

"No! That's news to me too," said Georgie. "She never seemed to see my sketches before: they might have been blank sheets of paper. Does she mean it? She's not pulling my leg?"

"Nothing of the sort. And I couldn't help thinking it was a great opportunity for you to learn something about more modern methods. There is something you know in those fierce canvases of hers."

"I wish she had told me sooner," said Georgie. "We've only got a fortnight more here. I shall be very sorry when it's over, for

I felt terribly pleased to be getting back to Tilling this morning. It'll be dull going back to Riseholme. Don't you feel that too? I'm sure you must. No plots: no competition."

Lucia had just received a telegram from Adele concerning the purchase of The Hurst, and it was no use putting off the staggering moment. She felt as if she was Zeus about to discharge a thunderbolt on some unhappy mortal.

"Georgie, I'm not going back to Riseholme at all," she said. "I have sold The Hurst: Adele Brixton has bought it. And, practically, I've bought that white house with the beautiful garden, which we admired so much, and that view over the marsh (how I thought of you at sunset yesterday), and really charming rooms with character."

Georgie sat open-mouthed, and all expression vanished from his face. It became as blank as a piece of sunburnt paper. Then slowly, as if he was coming round from an anaesthetic while the surgeon was still carving dexterously at living tissue, a look of intolerable anguish came into his face.

"But Foljambe, Cadman!" he cried. "Foljambe can't come back here every night from Riseholme. What am I to do? Is it all irrevocable?"

Lucia bridled. She was quite aware that this parting (if there was to be one) between him and Foljambe would be a dagger; but it was surprising, to say the least, that the thought of the parting between herself and him should not have administered him the first shock. However, there it was. Foljambe first by all means.

"I knew parting from Foljambe would be a great blow to you," she said, with an acidity that Georgie could hardly fail to notice. "What a pity that row you told me about came to nothing! But I am afraid that I can't promise to live in Riseholme for ever in order that you may not lose your parlour-maid."

"But it's not only that," said Georgie, aware of this acidity and hastening to sweeten it. "There's you as well. It will be ditch-water at Riseholme without you."

"Thank you, Georgie," said Lucia. "I wondered if and when, as the lawyers say, you would think of that. No reason why you should, of course."

Georgie felt that this was an unjust reproach.

"Well, after all, you settled to live in Tilling," he retorted, "and said nothing about how dull it would be without me. And I've got to do without Foljambe as well."

Lucia had recourse to the lowest artifice.

"Georgie-orgie, 'oo not cwoss with me?" she asked in an innocent, childish voice.

Georgie was not knocked out by this sentimental stroke below the belt. It was like Lucia to settle everything in exactly the way that suited her best, and then expect her poor pawns to be stricken at the thought of losing their queen. Besides, the loss of Foljambe *had* occurred to him first. Comfort, like charity, began at home.

"No, I'm not cross," he said, utterly refusing to adopt baby-talk which implied surrender. "But I've got every right to be hurt with you for settling to live in Tilling and not saying a word about how you would miss me."

"My dear, I knew you would take that for granted," began Lucia.

"Then why shouldn't you take it for granted about me?" he observed.

"I ought to have," she said. "I confess it, so that's all right. But why don't you leave Riseholme too and settle here, Georgie? Foljambe, me, your career, now that Irene is so keen about your pictures, and this marvellous sense of not knowing what's going to happen next. Such stimulus, such stuff to keep the soul awake. And you don't want to go back to Riseholme: you said so yourself. You'd moulder and vegetate there."

"It's different for you," said Georgie. "You've sold your house and I haven't sold mine. But there it is: I shall go back, I suppose, without Foljambe or you—I mean you or Foljambe. I wish I had never come here at all. It was that week when we went back for the fête, leaving Cadman and her here, which did all the mischief."

There was no use in saying anything more at present, and Georgie, feeling himself the victim of an imperious friend and of a faithless parlour-maid, went sadly back to Mallards Cottage. Lucia had settled to leave Riseholme without the least thought of what injury she inflicted on him by depriving him at one fell blow of Foljambe and her own companionship. He was almost sorry he had sent her that wonderful Brocklebank letter, for she had been in a very tight place, especially when Miss Mapp had actually seen her stripped and skipping in the garden as a cure for influenza; and had he not, by his stroke of genius, come to her rescue, her reputation here might have suffered an irretrievable eclipse, and they might all have gone back to Riseholme together. As it was, he had established her on the most exalted pinnacle and her thanks for that boon were expressed by dealing this beastly blow at him.

He threw himself down, in deep dejection, on the sofa in the little parlour of Mallards Cottage, in which he had been so comfortable. Life at Tilling had been full of congenial pleasures, and what a spice all these excitements had added to it! He had done a lot of painting, endless subjects still awaited his brush, and it had given him a thrill of delight to know that quaint Irene, with all her modern notions about art, thought highly of his work. Then there was the diversion of observing and nobly assisting in Lucia's campaign for the sovereignty, and her wars, as he knew, were far from won yet, for Tilling certainly had grown restive under her patronisings and acts of autocracy, and there was probably life in the old dog (meaning Elizabeth Mapp) yet. It was dreadful to think that he would not witness the campaign that was now being planned in those Napoleonic brains. These few weeks that remained to him here would be blackened by the thought of the wretched future that awaited him, and there would be no savour in them, for in so short a time now he would go back to Rise-holme in a state of the most pitiable widowerhood, deprived of the ministering care of Foljambe, who all these years had made him so free from household anxieties, and of the companion who had spurred him on to ambitions and activities. Though he had lain awake shuddering at the thought that perhaps Lucia expected him to marry her, he felt he would almost sooner have done that than lose her altogether. "It may be better to have loved and lost," thought Georgie, "than never to have loved at all, but it's very poor work not having loved and also to have lost" . . .

There was Foljambe singing in a high buzzing voice as she unpacked his luggage in his room upstairs, and though it was a rancid noise, how often had it filled him with the liveliest satis-faction, for Foljambe seldom sang, and when she did, it meant that she was delighted with her lot in life and was planning fresh efforts for his comfort. Now, no doubt, she was planning all sorts of pleasures for Cadman, and not thinking of him at all. Then there was Lucia: through his open window he could already hear the piano in the garden-room, and that showed a horrid cal-lousness to his miserable plight. She didn't care; she was roll-ing on like the moon or the car of Juggernaut. It was heartless of her to occupy herself with those gay tinkling tunes, but the fact was that she was odiously selfish, and cared about nothing but her own successes . . . He abstracted himself from those painful reflections for a moment and listened more attentively. It was clearly Mozart that she was practising, but the melody was new to him. "I bet," thought Georgie, "that this evening or tomorrow, she'll ask me to read over a new Mozart, and it'll be that very piece that she's practising now."

His bitterness welled up within him again, as that pleasing reflection faded from his mind, and almost involuntarily he began to revolve how he could pay her back for her indifference to him. A dark but brilliant thought (like a black pearl) occurred to him. What if he dismissed his own chauffeur, Dickie, at present in the employment of his tenant at Riseholme, and, by a prospect of a rise in wages, seduced Cadman from Lucia's service, and took him and Foljambe back to Riseholme? He would put into practise the plan that Lucia herself had suggested, of establishing them in a cottage of their own, with a charwoman, so that Foljambe's days should be his, and her nights Cadman's. That would be a nasty one for Lucia, and the idea was feasible, for Cadman didn't think much of Tilling, and might easily fall in with it. But hardly had this devilish device occurred to him than his better nature rose in revolt against it. It would serve Lucia right, it is true, but it was unworthy of him. "I should be descending to her level," thought Georgie very nobly, "if I did such a thing. Besides, how awful it would be if Cadman said no, and then told her that I had tempted him. She would despise me for doing it, as much as I despise her, and she would gloat over me for having failed. It won't do. I must be more manly about it all somehow. I must be like Major Benjy and say 'Damn the woman! Faugh!' and have a drink. But I feel sick at the idea of going back to Riseholme alone . . . I wish I had eyebrows like a paste-brush, and could say damn properly."

With a view to being more manly he poured himself out a very small whisky and soda, and his eye fell on a few letters lying for him on the table, which must have come that morning. There was one with the Riseholme postmark, and the envelope was of that very bright blue which he always used. His own stationery evidently, of which he had left a supply, without charge, for the use of his tenant. He opened it, and behold there was dawn breaking on his dark life, for Colonel Cresswell wanted to know if he had any thoughts of selling his house. He was much taken by Riseholme, his sister had bought The Hurst, and he would like to be near her. Would Georgie therefore let him have a line about this as soon as possible, for there was another house, Mrs. Quantock's, about which he would enter into negotiations, if there was no chance of getting Georgie's . . .

The revulsion of feeling was almost painful. Georgie had another whisky and soda at once, not because he was depressed, but because he was so happy. "But I mustn't make a habit of it," he thought, as he seized his pen.

Georgie's first impulse when he had written his letter to Colonel Cresswell was to fly round to Mallards with this wonderful news, but now he hesitated. Some hitch might arise, the price Colonel Cresswell proposed might not come up to his expectations, though—God knew—he would not dream of haggling over any reasonable offer. Lucia would rejoice at the chance of his staying in Tilling but she did not deserve to have such a treat of pleasurable expectation for the present. Besides, though he had been manly enough to reject with scorn the wiles of the devil who had suggested the seduction of Cadman, he thought he would tease her a little even if his dream came true. He had often told her that if he was rich enough he would have a flat in London, and now, if this sale of his house came off, he would pretend that he was not meaning to live in Tilling at all, but would live in town, and he would see how she would take that. It would be her turn to be hurt, and serve her right. So instead of interrupting the roulades of Mozart that were pouring from the window of the garden-room, he walked briskly down to the High Street to see how Tilling was taking the news that it would have Lucia always with it, if her purchase of Grebe had become public property. If not, he would have the pleasure of disseminating it.

There was a hint of seafaring about Georgie's costume as befitted one who had lately spent so much time on the pier at Folkestone. He had a very nautical-looking cap, with a black shining brim, a dark-blue double-breasted coat, white trousers and smart canvas shoes: really he might have been supposed to have come up to Tilling in his yacht, and have landed to see the town . . . A piercing whistle from the other side of the street showed him that his appearance had at once attracted attention, and there was Irene planted with her easel in the middle of the pavement, and painting a row of flayed carcasses that hung in the butcher's shop. Rembrandt had better look out . . .

"Avast there, Georgie," she cried. "Home is the sailor, home from sea. Come and talk."

This was rather more attention than Georgie had anticipated, but as Irene was quite capable of shouting nautical remarks after him if he pretended not to hear, he tripped across the street to her.

"Have you seen Lucia, Commodore?" she said. "And has she told you?"

"About her buying Grebe?" asked Georgie. "Oh, yes."

"That's all right then. She told me not to mention it till she'd seen you. Mapp's popping in and out of the shops, and I simply must be the first to tell her. Don't cut in in front of me, will you? Oh, by the way, have you done any sketching at Folkestone?"

"One or two," said Georgie. "Nothing very much."

"Nonsense. Do let me come and see them. I love your han-dling. Just cast your eye over this and tell me what's wrong with— There she is. Hi! Mapp!"

Elizabeth, like Georgie, apparently thought it more prudent to answer that summons and avoid further public proclamation of her name, and came hurrying across the street.

"Good-morning, Irene mine," she said. "What a beautiful picture! All the poor skinned piggies in a row, or are they sheep? Back again, Mr. Georgie? How we've missed you. And how do you think dear Lulu is looking after her illness?"

"Mapp, there's news for you," said Irene, remembering the luncheon-party yesterday. "You must guess: I shall tease you. It's about your Lulu. Three guesses."

"Not a relapse, I hope?" said Elizabeth brightly.

"Quite wrong. Something much nicer. You'll enjoy it tremen-dously."

"Another of those beautiful musical parties?" asked Eliza-beth. "Or has she skipped a hundred times before breakfast?"

"No, much nicer," said Irene. "Heavenly for us all."

A look of apprehension had come over Elizabeth's face, as an awful idea occurred to her.

"Dear one, give over teasing," she said. "Tell me."

"She's not going away at the end of the month," said Irene. "She's bought Grebe."

Blank dismay spread over Elizabeth's face.

"Oh, what a joy!" she said. "Lovely news."

She hurried off to Wasters, too much upset even to make Diva, who was coming out of Twistevant's, a partner in her joy. Only this morning she had been consulting her calendar and observing that there were only fifteen days more before Tilling was quit of Lulu, and now at a moderate estimate there might be at least fifteen years of her. Then she found she could not bear the weight of her joy alone and sped back after Diva.

"Diva dear, come in for a minute," she said. "I've heard something."

Diva looked with concern at that lined and agitated face.

"What's the matter?" she said. "Nothing serious?"

"Oh no, lovely news," she said with bitter sarcasm. "Tilling will rejoice. *She's* not going away. *She's* going to stop here for ever."

There was no need to ask who "she" was. For weeks Lucia had been "she." If you meant Susan Wyse, or Diva or Irene, you said so. But "she" was Lucia.

"I suspected as much," said Diva. "I know she had an order to view Grebe."

Elizabeth, in a spasm of exasperation, banged the door of Wasters so violently after she and Diva had entered, that the house shook and a note leaped from the wire letter-box on to the floor.

"Steady on with my front door," said Diva, "or there'll be some dilapidations to settle."

Elizabeth took no notice of this petty remark, and picked up the note. The handwriting was unmistakable, for Lucia's study of Homer had caused her (subconsciously or not) to adopt a modified form of Greek script, and she made her "a" like alpha and her "e" like epsilon. At the sight of it Elizabeth suffered a complete loss of self-control, she held the note on high as if exposing a relic to the gaze of pious worshippers, and made a low curtsey to it.

"And this is from Her," she said. "Oh, how kind of Her Majesty to write to me in her own hand with all those ridiculous twiddles. Not content with speaking Italian quite perfectly, she must also write in Greek. I dare say she talks it beautifully too."

"Come, pull yourself together, Elizabeth," said Diva.

"I am not aware that I am coming to bits, dear," said Elizabeth, opening the note with the very tips of her fingers, as if it had been written by someone infected with plague or at least influenza. "But let me see what Her Majesty says . . . 'Dearest Liblib' . . . the impertinence of it! Or is it Riseholme humour?"

"Well, you call her Lulu," said Diva. "Do get on."

Elizabeth frowned with the difficulty of deciphering this crabbed handwriting.

"'Now that I am quite free of infection,'" she read— (Infection indeed. She never had flu at all)—"'of infection, I can receive my friends again, and hope so much you will lunch with me tomorrow. I hasten also to tell you of my change of plans, for I have so fallen in love with your delicious Tilling that I have bought a house here—(Stale news!)—and shall settle into it next month. An awful wrench, as you may imagine, to leave my dear Riseholme—(Then why wrench yourself?)— . . . and poor Georgie is in despair, but Tilling and all you dear people have wrapped yourselves round my heart—(Have we? The same to you!)—and it is no use my struggling to get free. I wonder therefore if you would consider letting me take your beautiful Mallards at the same rent for another month, while Grebe is being done up, and my furniture being installed? I should be so grateful if this is possible, otherwise I shall try to get Mallards Cottage when my Georgie—(My!)—goes back to Riseholme. Could you, do you think, let me know about this tomorrow, if, as I hope, you will send me *un amabile "si"*—(What in the world is an *amabile si*?)—and come to lunch? *Tanti saluti*, Lucia.'"

"I understand," said Diva. "It means 'an amiable yes,' about going to lunch."

"Thank you, Diva. You are quite an Italian scholar too," said Elizabeth. "I call that a thoroughly heartless letter. And all of us, mark you, must serve her convenience. I can't get back into Mallards, because She wants it, and even if I refused, She would be next door at Mallards Cottage. I've never been so long out of my own house before."

Both ladies felt that it would be impossible to keep up any semblance of indignation that Lucia was wanting to take Mallards for another month, for it suited them both so marvellously well.

"You are in luck," said Diva, "getting another month's let at that price. So am I too, if you want to stop here, for Irene is certain to let me stay on at her house, because her cottage is next to Grebe and she'll be in and out all day—"

"Poor Irene seems to be under a sort of spell," said Elizabeth in parenthesis. "She can think about nothing except that woman. Her painting has fallen off terribly. Coarsened . . . Yes, dear, I think I will give the Queen of the Italian language an *amabile si* about Mallards. I don't know if you would consider taking rather a smaller rent for November. Winter prices are always lower."

"Certainly not," said Diva. "You're going to get the same as before for Mallards."

"That's my affair, dear," said Elizabeth.

"And this is mine," said Diva firmly. "And will you go to lunch with her tomorrow?"

Elizabeth, now comparatively calm, sank down in the window seat, which commanded so good a view of the High Street.

"I suppose I shall have to," she said. "One must be civil, whatever has happened. Oh, there's Major Benjy. I wonder if he's heard."

She tapped at the window and threw it open. He came hurrying across the street and began to speak in a loud voice before she could get in a word.

"That amusing guessing game of yours, Miss Elizabeth," he said, just like Irene. "About Mrs. Lucas. I'll give you three—"

"One's enough: we all know," said Elizabeth. "Joyful news, isn't it?"

"Indeed, it is delightful to know that we are not going to lose one who—who has endeared herself to us all so much," said he very handsomely.

He stopped. His tone lacked sincerity; there seemed to be something in his mind which he left unsaid. Elizabeth gave him a piercing and confidential look.

"Yes, Major Benjy?" she suggested.

He glanced round like a conspirator to see there was no one eavesdropping.

"Those parties, you know," he said. "Those entertainments which we've all enjoyed so much. Beautiful music. But Grebe's a long way off on a wet winter night. Not just round the corner. Now if she was settling in Mallards—"

He saw at once what an appalling interpretation might be put on this, and went on in a great hurry.

"You'll have to come to our rescue, Miss Elizabeth," he said, dropping his voice so that even Diva could not hear. "When you're back in your own house again, you'll have to look after us all as you always used to. Charming woman, Mrs. Lucas, and most hospitable, I'm sure, but in the winter, as I was saying, that long way out of Tilling, just to hear a bit of music, and have a tomato, if you see what I mean."

"Why, of course I see what you mean," murmured Elizabeth. "The dear thing, as you say, is so hospitable. Lovely music and tomatoes, but we must make a stand."

"Well, you can have too much of a good thing," said Major Benjy, "and for my part a little Mozart lasts me a long time, especially if it's a long way on a wet night. Then I'm told there's an idea of callisthenic classes, though no doubt they would be for ladies only—"

"I wouldn't be too sure about that," said Elizabeth. "Our dear friend has got enough—shall we call it self-confidence?—to think herself capable of teaching anybody anything. If you aren't careful, Major Benjy, you'll find yourself in a skipping-match on the lawn at Grebe, before you know what you're doing. You've been King Cophetua already, which I, for one, never thought to see."

"That was just once in a way," said he. "But when it comes to callisthenic classes—"

Diva, in an agony at not being able to hear what was going on, had crept up behind Elizabeth, and now crouched close to her as she stood leaning out of the window. At this moment, Lucia, having finished her piano-practise, came round the corner from Mallards into the High Street. Elizabeth hastily withdrew from the window and bumped into Diva.

"So sorry: didn't know you were there, dear," she said. "We must put our heads together another time, Major Benjy. *Au reservoir.*"

She closed the window.

"Oh, do tell me what you're going to put your heads together about," said Diva. "I only heard just the end."

It was important to get allies: otherwise Elizabeth would have made a few well-chosen remarks about eavesdroppers.

"It is sad to find that just when Lucia has settled never to leave us anymore," she said, "that there should be so much feeling in Tilling about being told to do this and being made to listen to that. Major Benjy—I don't know if you heard that part, dear—spoke very firmly, and I thought sensibly about it. The question really is if England is a free country or not, and whether we're going to be trampled upon. We've been very happy in Tilling all these years, going our own way, and living in sweet harmony together, and I for one, and Major Benjy for another, don't intend to put our necks under the yoke. I don't know how you feel about it. Perhaps you like it, for after all you were Mary Queen of Scots just as much as Major Benjy was King Cophetua."

"I won't go to any po-di-mus, after dinner at Grebe," said Diva. "I shouldn't have gone to the last, but you persuaded us all to go. Where was your neck then, Elizabeth? Be fair."

"Be fair yourself, Diva," said Elizabeth with some heat. "You know perfectly well that I wanted you to go in order that you might all get your necks from under her yoke, and hear that she couldn't speak a word of Italian."

"And a nice mess you made of that," said Diva. "But never mind. She's established now as a perfect Italian linguist, and there it is. Don't meddle with that again, or you'll only prove that she can talk Greek too."

Elizabeth rose and pointed at her like one of Raphael's Sibyls.

"Diva, to this day I don't believe she can talk Italian. It was a conjuring trick, and I'm no conjurer but a plain woman, and I can't tell you how it was done. But I will swear it was a trick. Besides, answer me this! Why doesn't she offer to give us Italian lessons if she knows it? She has offered to teach us bridge and Homer and callisthenics and take choir-practises and arranged tableaux. Why not Italian?"

"That's curious," said Diva thoughtfully.

"Not the least curious. The reason is obvious. Everyone

snubbed me and scolded me, you among others, at that dreadful luncheon-party, but I know I'm right, and some day the truth will come out. I can wait. Meantime what she means to do is to take us all in hand, and I won't be taken in hand. What is needed from us all is a little firmness."

Diva went home thrilled to the marrow of her bones at the thought of the rich entertainment that these next months promised to provide. Naturally she saw through Elizabeth's rodomontade about yokes and free countries: what she meant was that she intended to assert herself again, and topple Lucia over. Two could not reign in Tilling, as everybody could see by this time. "All most interesting," said Diva to herself. "Elizabeth's got hold of Major Benjy for the present, and Lucia's going to lose Georgie, but then men don't count for much in Tilling: it's brains that do it. There'll be more bridge parties and teas this winter than ever before. Really, I don't know which of them I would back. Hello, there's a note from her. Lunch tomorrow, I expect . . . I thought so."

Lucia's luncheon-party next day was to be of the nature of a banquet to celebrate the double event of her recovery and of the fact that Tilling, instead of mourning her approaching departure, was privileged to retain her, as Elizabeth had said, for ever and ever. The whole circle of her joyful friends would be there, and she meant to give them to eat of the famous dish of lobster *à la Riseholme,* which she had provided for Georgie, a few weeks ago, to act as a buffer to break the shock of Foljambe's engagement. It had already produced a great deal of wild surmise in the minds of the housewives at Tilling, for no one could conjecture how it was made, and Lucia had been deaf to all requests for the recipe: Elizabeth had asked her twice to give it her, but Lucia had merely changed the subject without attempt at transition: she had merely talked about something quite different. This secretiveness was considered unamiable, for the use of Tilling was to impart its culinary mysteries to friends, so that they might enjoy their favourite dishes at each other's houses, and lobster *à la Riseholme* had long been an agonising problem to Elizabeth. She had made an attempt at it herself, but the result was not encouraging. She had told Diva and the Padre that she felt sure she had "guessed it," and, when bidden to come to lunch and partake of it, they had both anticipated a great treat. But Elizabeth had clearly guessed wrong, for lobster *à la Riseholme à la Mapp* had been found to consist of something resembling lumps of india-rubber (so tough that the teeth positively bounced away from them on contact) swimming in a dubious pink gruel, and both of them left a great deal on their plates, concealed as far as possible under their knives and forks, though their hostess continued manfully to chew, till her jaw-muscles gave out. Then Elizabeth had had recourse to underhand methods. Lucia had observed her more than once in the High Street, making herself suspiciously pleasant to her cook, and from the window of the garden-room just before her influenza, she had seen her at the back door of Mallards again in conversation with the lady of the kitchen. On this occasion, with an unerring conviction in her mind, she had sent for her cook and asked her what Miss Mapp wanted. It was even so: Elizabeth's ostensible enquiry was for an egg-whisk, which she had left by mistake at Mallards three months ago, but then she had unmasked her batteries, and, actually fingering a bright half-crown, had asked point-blank for the recipe of this lobster *à la Riseholme*. The cook had given her a polite but firm refusal, and Lucia was now more determined than ever that Elizabeth should never know the exquisite secret. She naturally felt that it was beneath her to take the slightest notice of this low and paltry attempt to obtain by naked bribery a piece of private knowledge, and she never let Elizabeth know that she was cognisant of it.

During the morning before Lucia's luncheon-party a telegram
had come for Georgie from Colonel Cresswell making a firm and
very satisfactory offer for his house at Riseholme, unfurnished.
That had made him really busy: first he had to see Foljambe and
tell her (under seal of secrecy, for he had his little plot of teasing
Lucia in mind) that he was proposing to settle in Tilling. Foljambe was very pleased to hear it, and in a burst of most unusual
feeling, had said that it would have gone to her heart to leave his
service, after so many harmonious years, when he went back to
Riseholme, and that she was very glad to adopt the plan, which
she had agreed to, when it was supposed that they would all go
back to Riseholme together. She would do her work all day in
Georgie's house, and retire in the evening to the connubialities
of the garage at Grebe. When this affecting interview was over,
she went back to her jobs, and again Georgie heard her singing
as she cleaned the silver. "So that's beautiful," he said to himself, "and the cloud has passed for ever. Now I must instantly see
about getting a house here."

He hurried out. There was still an hour before he was due
at the lobster lunch. Though he had left the seaside twenty-four
hours ago, he put on his yachtsman's cap and, walking on air, set
off for the house-agents'. Of all the houses in the place which he
had seen, he was sure that none would suit him as well as this
dear little Mallards Cottage which he now occupied; he liked it,
Foljambe liked it, they all liked it, but he had no idea whether he
could get a lease from kippered Isabel. As he crossed the High
Street, a wild hoot from a motor-horn just behind him gave him a
dreadful fright, but he jumped nimbly for the pavement, reached
it unhurt, and though his cap fell off and landed in a puddle,
he was only thankful to have escaped being run down by Isabel
Poppit on her motorcycle. Her hair was like a twisted mop, her
skin incredibly tanned, and mounted on her cycle she looked

like a sort of modernised Valkyrie in rather bad repair . . . Meeting her just at this moment, when he was on his way to enquire about Mallards Cottage, seemed a good omen to Georgie, and he picked up his cap and ran back across the street, for in her natural anxiety to avoid killing him she had swerved into a baker's cart, and had got messed up in the wheels.

"I do apologise, Miss Poppit," he said. "Entirely my fault for not looking both ways before I crossed."

"No harm done," said she. "Oh, your beautiful cap. I am sorry. But after all the wonderful emptiness and silence among the sand-dunes, a place like a town seems to me a positive nightmare."

"Well, the emptiness and silence does seem to suit you," said Georgie, gazing in astonishment at her mahogany face. "I never saw anybody looking so well."

Isabel, with a tug of her powerful arms, disentangled her cycle.

"It's the simple life," said she, shaking her hair out of her eyes. "Never again will I live in a town. I have taken the bungalow I am in now for six months more, and I only came in to Tilling to tell the house-agent to get another tenant for Mallards Cottage, as I understand that you're going back to Riseholme at the end of this month."

Georgie had never felt more firmly convinced that a wise and beneficent Providence looked after him with the most amiable care.

"And I was also on my way to the house-agents'," he said, "to see if I could get a lease of it."

"Gracious! What a good thing I didn't run over you just now," said Isabel, with all the simplicity derived from the emptiness and silence of sand-dunes. "Come on to the agents'."

Within half an hour the whole business was as good as settled. Isabel held a lease from her mother of Mallards Cottage, which had five years yet to run, and she agreed to transfer this to Georgie, and store her furniture. He had just time to change into his new mustard-coloured suit with its orange tie and its topaz tie-pin, and arrived at the luncheon-party in the very highest spirits. Besides, there was his talk with Lucia when other guests had gone, to look forward to. How he would tease her about settling in London!

Though Tilling regarded the joyful prospect of Lucia's never going away again with certain reservations, and, in the case of Elizabeth, with nothing but reservations, her guests vied with each other in the fervency of their self-congratulations, and Elizabeth outdid them all, as she took into her mouth small fragments of lobster, in the manner of a wine-taster, appraising subtle flavours. There was cheese, there were shrimps, there was cream: there were so many things that she felt like Adam giving names to the innumerable procession of different animals. She had helped herself so largely that when the dish came to Georgie there was nothing left but a little pink juice, but he hardly minded at all, so happy had the events of the morning made him. Then when Elizabeth felt that she would choke if she said anything more in praise of Lucia, Mr. Wyse took it up, and Georgie broke in and said it was cruel of them all to talk about the delicious busy winter they would have, when they all knew that he would not be here any longer but back at Riseholme. In fact, he rather overdid his lamentations, and Lucia, whose acute mind detected the grossest insincerity in Elizabeth's raptures, began to wonder whether Georgie for some unknown reason was quite as woeful as he professed to be. Never had he looked more radiant, not a shadow of disappointment had come over his face when he inspected the casserole that had once contained his favourite dish, and found nothing left for him. There was something up—

what on earth could it be? Had Foljambe jilted Cadman?—and just as Elizabeth was detecting flavours in the mysterious dish, so Lucia was trying to arrive at an analysis of the gay glad tones in which Georgie expressed his misery.

"It's too tarsome of you all to go on about the lovely things you're going to do," he said. "Callisthenic classes and Homer and bridge, and poor me far away. I shall tell myself every morning that I hate Tilling; I shall say like Coué, 'Day by day in every way, I dislike it more and more,' until I've convinced myself that I shall be glad to go."

Mr. Wyse made him a beautiful bow.

"We too shall miss you very sadly, Mr. Pillson," he said, "and for my part I shall be tempted to hate Riseholme for taking from us one who has so endeared himself to us."

"I ask to be allowed to associate myself with those sentiments," said Major Benjy, whose contempt for Georgie and his sketches and his needlework had been intensified by the sight of his yachting cap, which he had pronounced to be only fit for a popinjay. It had been best to keep on good terms with him while Lucia was at Mallards, for he might poison her mind about himself, and now that he was going, there was no harm in these handsome remarks. Then the Padre said something Scotch and sympathetic and regretful, and Georgie found himself, slightly to his embarrassment, making bows and saying "thank you" right and left in acknowledgement of these universal expressions of regret that he was so soon about to leave them. It was rather awkward, for within a few hours they would all know that he had taken Mallards Cottage unfurnished for five years, which did not look like an immediate departure. But this little deception was necessary if he was to bring off his joke against Lucia, and make her think that he meant to settle in London. And after all, since everybody seemed so sorry that (as they imagined) he was soon to leave Tilling, they ought to be very much pleased to find that he was doing nothing of the kind.

The guests dispersed soon after lunch and Georgie, full of mischief and naughtiness, lingered with his hostess in the garden-room. All her gimlet glances during lunch had failed to fathom his high good-humour: here was he on the eve of parting with his Foljambe and herself, and yet his face beamed with content. Lucia was in very good spirits also, for she had seen Elizabeth's brow grow more and more furrowed as she strove to find a formula for the lobster.

"What a lovely luncheon-party, although I got no lobster at all," said Georgie, as he settled himself for his teasing. "I did enjoy it. And Elizabeth's rapture at your stopping here! She must have an awful blister on her tongue."

Lucia sighed.

"Sapphira must look to her laurels, poor thing," she observed pensively. "And how sorry they all were that you are going away."

"Wasn't it nice of them?" said Georgie. "But never mind that now: I've got something wonderful to tell you. I've never felt happier in my life, for the thing I've wanted for so many years can be managed at last. You will be pleased for my sake."

Lucia laid a sympathetic hand on his. She felt that she had shown too little sympathy with one who was to lose his parlourmaid and his oldest friend so soon. But the gaiety with which he bore his double stroke was puzzling . . .

"Dear Georgie," she said, "anything that makes you happy makes me happy. I am rejoiced that something of the sort has occurred. Really rejoiced. Tell me what it is instantly."

Georgie drew a long breath. He wanted to give it out all in a burst of triumph like a fanfare.

"Too lovely," he said. "Colonel Cresswell has bought my

house at Riseholme—such a good price—and now at last I shall be able to settle in London. I was just as tired of Riseholme as you, and now I shall never see it again or Tilling either. Isn't it a dream? Riseholme, stuffy little Mallards Cottage, all things of the past! I shall have a nice little home in London, and you must promise to come up and stay with me sometimes. How I looked forward to telling you! Orchestral concerts at Queen's Hall, instead of our fumbling little arrangements of Mozartino for four hands. Pictures, a club if I can afford it, and how nice to think of you so happy down at Tilling! As for all the fuss I made yesterday about losing Foljambe, I can't think why it seemed to me so terrible."

Lucia gave him one more gimlet glance, and found she did not believe a single word he was saying except as regards the sale of his house at Riseholme. All the rest must be lies, for the Foljambe-wound could not possibly have healed so soon. But she instantly made up her mind to pretend to believe him, and clapped her hands for pleasure.

"Dear Georgie! What splendid news!" she said. "I am pleased. I've always felt that you, with all your keenness and multifarious interests in life, were throwing your life away in these little backwaters like Riseholme and Tilling. London is the only place for you! Now, tell me: Are you going to get a flat or a house? And where is it to be? If I were you I should have a house!"

This was not quite what Georgie had expected. He had thought that Lucia would suggest that now that he was quit of Riseholme he positively must come to Tilling, but not only did she fail to do that, but she seemed delighted that no such thought had entered into his head.

"I haven't really thought about that yet," he said. "There's something to be said for a flat."

"No doubt. It's more compact, and then there's no bother about rates and taxes. And you'll have your car, I suppose. And will your cook go with you? What does she say to it all?"

"I haven't told her yet," said Georgie, beginning to get a little pensive.

"Really? I should have thought you would have done that at once. And isn't Foljambe pleased that you are so happy again?"

"She doesn't know yet," said Georgie. "I thought I would tell you first."

"Dear Georgie, how sweet of you," said Lucia. "I'm sure Foljambe will be as pleased as I am. You'll be going up to London, I suppose, constantly now till the end of this month, so that you can get your house or your flat, whichever it is, ready as soon as possible. How busy you and I will be, you settling into London and I into Tilling. Do you know, supposing you had thought of living permanently here, now that you've got rid of your house at Riseholme, I should have done my best to persuade you not to, though I know in my selfishness that I did suggest that yesterday. But it would never do, Georgie. It's all very well for elderly women like me, who just want a little peace and quietness, or for retired men like Major Benjy or for dilettantes like Mr. Wyse, but for you, a thousand times no. I am sure of it."

Georgie got thoughtfuller and thoughtfuller. It had been rather a mistake to try to tease Lucia, for so far from being teased she was simply pleased. The longer she went on like this, and there seemed no end to her expressions of approval, the harder it would be to tell her.

"Do you really think that?" he said.

"Indeed I do. You would soon be terribly bored with Tilling. Oh, Georgie, I am so pleased with your good fortune and your good sense. I wonder if the agents here have got any houses or flats in London on their books. Let's go down there at once and see. We might find something. I'll run and put on my hat."

Georgie threw in his hand. As usual Lucia had come out on top.

"You're too tarsome," he said. "You don't believe a single word I've been telling you of my plans."

"My dear, of course I don't," said Lucia brightly. "I never heard such a pack of rubbish. Ananias is not in it. But it is true about selling your Riseholme house, I hope?"

"Yes, that part is," said Georgie.

"Then of course you're going to live here," said she. "I meant you to do that all along. Now how about Mallards Cottage? I saw that Yahoo in the High Street this morning, and she told me she wanted to let it for the winter. Let's go down to the agents' as I suggested, and see."

"I've done that already," said Georgie, "for I met her too, and she nearly knocked me down. I've got a five years' lease of it."

It was not in Lucia's nature to crow over anybody. She proved her quality and passed on to something else.

"Perfect!" she said. "It has all come out just as I planned, so that's all right. Now, if you've got nothing to do, let us have some music."

She got out the new Mozart which she had been practising.

"This looks a lovely duet," she said, "and we haven't tried it yet. I shall be terribly rusty, for all the time I had influenza, I hardly dared to play the piano at all."

Georgie looked at the new Mozart.

"It does look nice," he said. "Tum-ti-tum. Why, that's the one I heard you practising so busily yesterday morning."

Lucia took not the slightest notice of this.

"We begin together," she said, "on the third beat. Now . . . *Uno, due, TRE!*"

Chapter Eight

THE PAINTING AND DECORATING OF Grebe began at once. Irene offered to do all the painting with her own hands, and recommended as a scheme for the music-room, a black ceiling and four walls of different colours, vermilion, emerald green, ultramarine and yellow. It would take a couple of months or so to execute, and the cost would be considerable as lapis lazuli must certainly be used for the ultramarine wall, but she assured Lucia that the result would be unique and marvellously stimulating to the eye, especially if she would add a magenta carpet and a nickel-plated mantelpiece.

"It sounds too lovely, dear," said Lucia, contemplating the sample of colours which Irene submitted to her, "but I feel sure I shan't be able to afford it. Such a pity! Those beautiful hues!"

Then Irene besought her to introduce a little variety into the shape of the windows. It would be amusing to have one window egg-shaped, and another triangular, and another with five or six or seven irregular sides, so that it looked as if it was a hole in the wall made by a shell. Or how about a front door that, instead of opening sideways, let down like a portcullis?

Irene rose to more daring conceptions yet. One night she had dined on a pot of strawberry jam and half a pint of very potent cocktails, because she wanted her eye for colour to be at its keenest round about eleven o'clock when the moon would rise over the marsh, and she hoped to put the lid for ever on Whistler's naïve old-fashioned attempts to paint moonlight. After this salubrious meal she had come round to Mallards, waiting for the moon to rise and sat for half an hour at Lucia's piano, striking random chords, and asking Lucia what colour they were. These musical rainbows suggested a wonderful idea, and she shut down the piano with a splendid purple bang.

"Darling, I've got a new scheme for Grebe," she said. "I want you to furnish a room sideways, if you understand what I mean."

"I don't think I do," said Lucia.

"Why, like this," said Irene very thoughtfully. "You would open the door of the room and find you were walking about on wallpaper with pictures hanging on it. (I'll do the pictures for you.) Then one side of the room where the window is would be whitewashed as if it was a ceiling and the window would be the skylight. The opposite side would be the floor; and you would have the furniture screwed on to it. The other walls, including the one which would be the ceiling in an ordinary room, would be covered with wallpaper and more pictures and a bookcase. It would all be sideways, you see: you'd enter through the wall, and the room would be at right angles to you; ceiling on the left, floor on the right, or vice versa. It would give you a perfectly new perception of the world. You would see everything from a new angle, which is what we want so much in life nowadays. Don't you think so?"

Irene's speech was distinct and clear cut, she walked up and down the garden-room with a firm unwavering step, and Lucia put from her the uneasy suspicion that her dinner had gone to her head.

"It would be most delightful," she said, "but slightly too experimental for me."

"And then, you see," continued Irene, "how useful it would be if somebody tipsy came in. It would make him sober at once, for tipsy people see everything crooked, and so your sideways-room, being crooked, would appear to him straight, and so he would be himself again. Just like that."

"That would be splendid," said Lucia, "but I can't provide a room where tipsy people could feel sober again. The house isn't big enough."

Irene sat down by her, and passionately clasped one of her hands.

"Lucia, you're too adorable," she said. "Nothing defeats you. I've been talking the most abject nonsense, though I do think that there may be something in it, and you remain as calm as the moon which I hope will rise over the marsh before long, unless the almanac in which I looked it out is last year's. Don't tell anybody else about the sideways-room, will you, or they might think I was drunk. Let it be our secret, darling."

Lucia wondered for a moment if she ought to allow Irene to spend the night on the marsh, but she was perfectly capable of coherent speech and controlled movements, and possibly the open air might do her good.

"Not a soul shall know, dear," she said. "And now if you're really going to paint the moon, you had better start. You feel quite sure you can manage it, don't you?"

"Of course I can manage the moon," said Irene stoutly. "I've managed it lots of times. I wish you would come with me. I always hate leaving you. Or shall I stop here, and paint you instead? Or do you think Georgie would come? What a lamb, isn't he? Pass the mint-sauce please, or shall I go home?"

"Perhaps that would be best," said Lucia. "Paint the moon another night."

∞

Lucia next day hurried up the firm to which she had entrusted the decoration of Grebe, in case Irene had some new schemes, and halfway through November, the house was ready to receive her furniture from Riseholme. Georgie simultaneously was settling into Mallards Cottage, and in the course of it went through a crisis of the most agitating kind. Isabel had assured him that by noon on a certain day men would arrive to take her furniture to the repository where it was to be stored, and as the vans with his effects from Riseholme had arrived in Tilling the night before, he induced the foreman to begin moving everything out of the house at nine next morning and bring his furniture in. This was done, and by noon all Isabel's tables and chairs and beds and crockery were standing out in the street ready for her van. They completely blocked it for wheeled traffic, though pedestrians could manage to squeeze by in single file. Tilling did not mind this little inconvenience in the least, for it was all so interesting, and tradesmen's carts coming down the street were cheerfully backed into the churchyard again and turned round in order to make a more circuitous route, and those coming up were equally obliging, while foot-passengers, thrilled with having the entire contents of a house exposed for their inspection, were unable to tear themselves away from so intimate an exhibition. Then Georgie's furniture was moved in, and there were dazzling and fascinating objects for inspection, pictures that he had painted, screens and bedspreads that he had worked, very pretty woollen pyjamas for the winter and embroidered covers for hot-water bottles. These millineries roused Major Benjy's manliest indignation, and he was nearly late for the tram to take him out to play golf, for he could not tear himself away from the revolting sight.

In a few hours Georgie's effects had passed into the house, but still there was no sign of anyone coming to remove Isabel's from the street, and, by dint of telephoning, it was discovered that she had forgotten to give any order at all about them, and the men from the repository were out on other jobs. It then began to rain rather heavily, and though Georgie called heaven and earth to witness that all this muddle was not his fault he felt compelled, out of mere human compassion, to have Isabel's furniture moved back into his house again. In consequence the rooms and passages on the ground floor were completely blocked with stacks of cupboards and tables piled high with books and crockery and saucepans, the front door would not shut, and Foljambe, caught upstairs by the rising tide, could not come down. The climax of intensity arrived when she let down a string from an upper window, and Georgie's cook attached a small basket of nourishing food to it. Diva was terribly late for lunch at the Wyses, for she was rooted to the spot, though it was raining heavily, till she was sure that Foljambe would not be starved.

But by the time that the month of November was over, the houses of the newcomers were ready to receive them, and a general post of owners back to their homes took place after a remunerative let of four months. Elizabeth returned to Mallards from Wasters, bringing with her, in addition to what she had taken there, a cargo of preserves made from Diva's garden of such bulk that Coplen had to make two journeys with her large wheelbarrow. Diva returned to Wasters from Taormina, quaint Irene came back to Taormina from the labourer's cottage with a handcart laden with striking canvases including that of the women wrestlers who had become men, and the labourer and his family were free to trek to their own abode from the hop-picker's shanty which they had inhabited so much longer than they had intended.

There followed several extremely busy days for most of the returning emigrants. Elizabeth in particular was occupied from morning till night in scrutinising every corner of Mallards and making out a list of dilapidations against Lucia. There was a tea-cup missing, the men who removed Lucia's hired piano from the garden-room had scraped a large piece of paint off the wall, Lucia had forgotten to replace dearest mamma's piano which still stood in the telephone-room, and there was no sign of a certain egg-whisk. Simultaneously Diva was preparing a similar list for Elizabeth which would astonish her, but was pleased to find that the tenant had left an egg-whisk behind; while the wife of the labourer, not being instructed in dilapidations, was removing from the whitewashed wall of her cottage the fresco which Irene had painted there in her spare moments. It wasn't fit to be seen, that it wasn't, but a scrubbing-brush and some hot water made short work of all those naked people. Irene, for her part, was frantically searching among her canvases for a picture of Adam and Eve with quantities of the sons of God shouting for joy: an important work. Perhaps she had left it at the cottage, and then remembering that she had painted it on the wall, she hurried off there in order to varnish it against the inclemencies of weather. But it was already too late, for the last of the sons of God was even then disappearing under the strokes of the scrubbing-brush.

Gradually, though not at once, these claims and counter-claims were (with the exception of the fresco) adjusted to the general dissatisfaction. Lucia acknowledged the charge for the re-establishment of dearest mamma's piano in the garden-room, but her cook very distinctly remembered that on the day when Miss Mapp tried to bribe her to impart the secret of lobster *à la Riseholme,* she took away the egg-whisk, which had formed the gambit of Miss Mapp's vain attempt to corrupt her. So Lucia reminded Elizabeth that not very long ago she had called at the back door of Mallards and had taken it away herself. Her cook believed that it was in two if not three pieces. So Miss Mapp, having made certain it had not got put by mistake among the pots of preserves she had brought from Wasters, went to see if she had left it there, and found not it alone, but a preposterous list of claims against her from Diva. But by degrees these billows, which were of annual occurrence, subsided, and apart from Elizabeth's chronic grievance against Lucia for her hoarding the secret of the lobster, they and other differences in the past faded away and Tilling was at leisure to turn its attention again to the hardly more important problems and perplexities of life and the menaces that might have to be met in the future.

∽

Elizabeth, on this morning of mid-December, was quite settled into Mallards again, egg-whisk and all, and the window of her garden-room was being once more used by the rightful owner for the purpose of taking observations. It had always been a highly strategic position; it commanded, for instance, a perfect view of the front door of Taormina, which at the present moment quaint Irene was painting in stripes of salmon pink and azure. She had tried to reproduce the lost fresco on it, but there had been earnest remonstrances from the Padre, and also the panels on the door broke it up and made it an unsuitable surface for such a cartoon. She therefore was contenting herself with brightening it up. Then Elizabeth could see the mouth of Porpoise Street and register all the journeys of the Royce. These, after a fortnight's intermission, had become frequent again, for the Wyses had just come back from "visiting friends in Devonshire," and though Elizabeth had strong reason to suspect that friends in Devonshire denoted nothing more than an hotel in Torquay, they had certainly taken the Royce with them, and during its absence the streets of Tilling had been far more convenient for traffic. Then there was Major Benjy's house as before, under her very eye, and now Mallards Cottage as well was a point that demanded frequent scrutiny. She had never cared what that distraught Isabel Poppit did, but with Georgie there it was different, and neither Major Benjy nor he (nor anybody else visiting them) could go in or out of either house without instant detection. The two most important men in Tilling, in fact, were powerless to evade her observation.

Nothing particular was happening at the moment, and Elizabeth was making a mental retrospect rather as if she was the King preparing his speech for the opening of Parliament. Her relations with foreign powers were excellent, and though during the last six months there had been disquieting incidents, there was nothing immediately threatening . . . Then round the corner of the High Street came Lucia's car and the King's speech was put aside.

The car stopped at Taormina. Quaint Irene instantly put down her painting paraphernalia on the pavement, and stood talking into the window of the car for quite a long time. Clearly therefore Lucia, though invisible, was inside it. Eventually Irene leaned her head forward into the car, exactly as if she was kissing something, and stepping back again upset one of her paint-pots. This was pleasant, but not of first-rate importance compared with what the car would do next. It turned down into Porpoise Street: naturally there was no telling for certain what happened to it there, for it was out of sight, but a tyro could conjecture that it had business at the Wyses', even if he had been so deaf as not to hear the clanging of that front-door bell. Then it came backing out again, went through the usual manoeuvres of turning, and next stopped at Major Benjy's. Lucia was still invisible, but Cadman got down and delivered a note. The tyro could therefore conjecture by this time that invitations were coming from Grebe.

She slid her chair a little farther back behind the curtain, feeling sure that the car would stop next at her own door. But it turned the corner below the window without drawing up, and Elizabeth got a fleeting glance into the interior, where Lucia was sitting with a large book open in her lap. Next it stopped at Mallards Cottage: no note was delivered there, but Cadman rang the bell, and presently Georgie came out. Like Irene, he talked for quite a long time into the window of the car, but, unlike her, did not kiss anything at the conclusion of the interview. The situation was therefore perfectly clear: Lucia had asked Irene and Major Benjy and Georgie and probably the Wyses to some entertainment, no doubt the house-warming of which there had been rumours, but had not asked her. Very well. The relations with foreign powers therefore had suddenly become far from satisfactory.

Elizabeth quitted her seat in the window, for she had observed enough to supply her with plenty of food for thought, and went back, in perfect self-control, to the inspection of her household books; adding up figures was a purely mechanical matter, which allowed the intenser emotions full play. Georgie would be coming in here presently, for he was painting a sketch of the interior of the garden-room; this was to be his Christmas present to Lucia (a surprise, about which she was to know nothing), to remind her of the happy days she had spent in it. He usually left his sketch here, for it was not worth while to take it backwards and forwards, and there it stood, propped up on the bookcase. He had first tried an Irene-ish technique, but he had been obliged to abandon that, since the garden-room with this handling persisted in looking like Paddington Station in a fog, and he had gone back to the style he knew, in which bookcases, chairs and curtains were easily recognisable. It needed a few mornings' work yet, and now the idea of destroying it, and, when he arrived, of telling him that she was quite sure he had taken it back with him yesterday darted unbidden into Elizabeth's mind. But she rejected it, though it would have been pleasant to deprive Lucia of her Christmas present . . . and she did not believe for a moment that she had ordered a dozen eggs on Tuesday and a dozen more on Thursday. The butcher's bill seemed to be correct, though extortionate, and she must find out as soon as possible whether the Padre and his wife and Diva were asked to Grebe too. If they were—but she banished the thought of what was to be done if they were: it was difficult enough to know what to do even if they weren't.

The books were quickly done, and Elizabeth went back to finish reading the morning paper in the window. Just as she got there Georgie, with his little cape over his shoulders and his paintbox in his hand, came stepping briskly along from Mallards Cottage. Simultaneously Lucia's great bumping car returned round the corner by the churchyard, in the direction of Mallards.

An inspiration of purest ray serene seized Elizabeth. She waited till Georgie had rung the front-door bell, at which psychological moment Lucia's car was straight below the window. Without a second's hesitation Elizabeth threw up the sash, and, without appearing to see Lucia at all, called out to Georgie in a high cheerful voice, using baby-language.

" 'Oo is very naughty boy, Georgie!" she cried. "Never ring Elizabeth's belly-pelly. 'Oo walk straight in always, and sing out for her. There's no chain up."

Georgie looked round in amazement. Never had Elizabeth called him Georgie before, or talked to him in the language consecrated for his use and Lucia's. And there was Lucia's car close to him. She must have heard this affectionate welcome, and what would she think? But there was nothing to do but to go in.

Still without seeing (far less cutting) Lucia, Elizabeth closed the window again, positively dazzled by her own brilliance. An hour's concentrated thought could not have suggested to her anything that Lucia would dislike more thoroughly than hearing that gay little speech, which parodied her and revealed such playful intimacy with Georgie. Georgie came straight out to the garden-room, saying "Elizabeth, Elizabeth" to himself below his breath, in order to get used to it, for he must return this token of friendship in kind.

"Good-morning, Elizabeth," he said firmly (and the worst was over until such time as he had to say it again in Lucia's presence).

"Good-morning, Georgie," she said by way of confirmation. "What a lovely light for your painting this morning. Here it is ready for you, and Withers will bring you out your glass of water. How you've caught the feel of my dear little room!"

Another glance out of the window as she brought him his sketch was necessary, and she gasped. There was Cadman on the doorstep just handing Withers a note. In another minute she came into the garden-room.

"From Mrs. Lucas," she said. "She forgot to leave it when she went by before."

"That's about the house-warming, I'm sure," said Georgie, getting his paintbox ready.

What was done, was done, and there was no use in thinking about that. Elizabeth tore the note open.

"A house-warming?" she said. "Dear Lucia! What a treat that will be. Yes, you're quite right."

"She's sending her car up for the Padre and his wife and Irene and Mrs. Plaistow," said Georgie, "and asked me just now if I would bring you and Major Benjy. Naturally I will."

Elizabeth's brilliant speech out of the window had assumed the aspect of a gratuitous act of war. But she could not have guessed that Lucia had merely forgotten to leave her invitation. The most charitable would have assumed that there was no invitation to leave.

"How kind of you!" she said. "Tomorrow night, isn't it? Rather short notice. I must see if I'm disengaged."

As Lucia had asked the whole of the élite of Tilling, this proved to be the case. But Elizabeth still pondered as to whether she should accept or not. She had committed one unfriendly act in talking baby-language to Georgie, with a pointed allusion to the door-chain, literally over Lucia's head, and it was a question whether, having done that, it would not be wise to commit another (while Lucia, it might be guessed, was still staggering) by refusing to go to the house-warming. She did not doubt that there would be war before long: the only question was if she was ready now.

As she was pondering Withers came in to say that Major Benjy had called. He would not come out into the garden-room, but he would like to speak to her a minute.

"Evidently he has heard that Georgie is here," thought Elizabeth to herself as she hurried into the house. "Dear me, how men quarrel with each other, and I only want to be on good terms with everybody. No doubt he wants to know if I'm going to the house-warming— Good-morning, Major Benjy."

"Thought I wouldn't come out," said this bluff fellow, "as I heard your Miss Milliner Michael-Angelo, ha, was with you—"

"Oh Major Benjy, fie!" said Elizabeth. "Cruel of you."

"Well, leave it at that. Now about this party tomorrow. I think I shall make a stand straight away, for I'm not going to spend the whole of the winter evenings tramping through the mud to Grebe. To be sure it's dinner this time, which makes a difference."

Elizabeth found that she longed to see what Lucia had made of Grebe, and what she had made of her speech from the window.

"I quite agree in principle," she said, "but a house-warming, you know. Perhaps it wouldn't be kind to refuse. Besides, Georgie—"

"Eh?" said the Major.

"Mr. Pillson, I mean," said Elizabeth, hastily correcting herself, "has offered to drive us both down."

"And back?" asked he suspiciously.

"Of course. So just for once, shall we?"

"Very good. But none of those after-dinner musicals, or lessons in bridge for me."

"Oh, Major Benjy!" said Elizabeth. "How can you talk so? As if poor Lucia would attempt to teach *you* bridge."

This could be taken in two ways, one interpretation would read that he was incapable of learning, the other that Lucia was incapable of teaching. He took the more obvious one.

"Upon my soul she did, at the last game I had with her," said he. "Laid out the last three tricks and told me how to play them. Beyond a joke. Well, I won't keep you from your dressmaker."

"O fie!" said Elizabeth again. *"Au reservoir."*

∞

Lucia, meantime, had driven back to Grebe with that mocking voice still ringing in her ears, and a series of most unpleasant images, like some diabolical film, displaying themselves before her inward eye. Most probably Elizabeth had seen her when she called out to Georgie like that, and was intentionally insulting her. Such conduct called for immediate reprisals and she must presently begin to think these out. But the alternative, possible though not probable, that Elizabeth had not seen her, was infinitely more wounding, for it implied that Georgie was guilty of treacheries too black to bear looking at. Privately, when she herself was not present, he was on Christian-name terms with that woman, and permitted and enjoyed her obvious mimicry of herself. And what was Georgie doing popping in to Mallards like this, and being scolded in baby-voice for ringing the bell instead of letting himself in, with allusions of an absolutely unmistakable kind to that episode about the chain? Did they laugh over that together: did Georgie poke fun at his oldest friend behind her back? Lucia positively writhed at the thought. In any case, whether or not he was guilty of this monstrous infidelity, he must be in the habit of going into Mallards, and now she remembered that he had his paintbox in his hand. Clearly then he was going there to paint, and in all their talks when he so constantly told her what he had been doing, he had never breathed a word of that. Perhaps he was painting Elizabeth, for in this winter weather he could never be painting in the garden. Just now too, when she called at Mallards Cottage, and they had had a talk together, he had refused to go out and drive with her, because he had some little jobs to do indoors, and the moment he had got rid of her—no less than that—he had hurried off to Mallards with his paintbox. With all this evidence, things looked very dark indeed, and the worst and most wounding of these two alternatives began to assume probability.

Georgie was coming to tea with her that afternoon, and she must find out what the truth of the matter was. But she could not imagine herself saying to him: "Does she really call you Georgie, and does she imitate me behind my back, and are you painting her?" Pride absolutely forbade that: such humiliating enquiries would choke her. Should she show him an icy aloof demeanour, until he asked her if anything was the matter? But that wouldn't do, for either she must say that nothing was the matter, which would not help, or she must tell him what the matter was, which was impossible. She must behave to him exactly as usual, and he would probably do the same. "So how am I to find out?" said the bewildered Lucia quite aloud.

Another extremely uncomfortable person in tranquil Tilling that morning was Georgie himself. As he painted this sketch of the garden-room for Lucia, with Elizabeth busying herself with dusting her piano and bringing in chrysanthemums from her greenhouse, and making bright little sarcasms about Diva who was in ill odour just now, there painted itself in his mind, in colours growing ever more vivid, a most ominous picture of Lucia. If he knew her at all, and he was sure he did, she would say nothing whatever about that disconcerting scene on the door-step. Awkward as it would be, he would be obliged to protest his innocence, and denounce Elizabeth. Most disagreeable, and who could foresee the consequences? For Lucia (if he knew her) would see red, and there would be war. Bloody war of the most devastating sort. "But it will be rather exciting too," thought he, "and I back Lucia."

Georgie could not wait for tea-time, but set forth on his uncomfortable errand soon after lunch. Lucia had seen him coming up the garden, and abandoned her musings and sat down hastily at the piano. Instantly on his entry she sprang up again, and plunged into mixed Italian and baby-talk.

"*Ben arrivato, Georgino,*" she cried. "How early you are, and so we can have cosy ickle chat-chat before tea. Any newsy-pewsy?"

Georgie took the plunge.

"Yes," he said.

"Tell Lucia, *presto*. 'Oo think me like it?"

"It'll interest you," said Georgie guardedly. "Now! When I was standing on Mallards doorstep this morning, did you hear what that old witch called to me out of the garden-room window?"

Lucia could not repress a sigh of relief. The worst could not be true. Then she became herself again.

"Let me see now!" she said. "Yes. I think I did. She called you Georgie, didn't she: she scolded you for ringing. Something of that sort."

"Yes. And she talked baby-talk like you and me," interrupted Georgie, "and she said the door wasn't on the chain. I want to tell you straight off that she never called me Georgie before, and that we've never talked baby-talk together in my life. I owe it to myself to tell you that."

Lucia turned her piercing eye on to Georgie. There seemed to be a sparkle in it that boded ill for somebody.

"And you think she saw me, Georgie?" she asked.

"Of course she did. Your car was directly below her window."

"I am afraid there is no doubt about it," said Lucia. "Her remarks, therefore, seem to have been directed at me. A singularly ill-bred person. There's one thing more. You were taking your paintbox with you—"

"Oh, that's all right," said he. "I'm doing a sketch of the garden-room. You'll know about that in time. And what are you going to do?" he asked greedily.

Lucia laughed in her most musical manner.

"Well, first of all I shall give her a very good dinner tomorrow, as she has not had the decency to say she was engaged. She telephoned to me just now telling me what a joy it would be, and how she was looking forward to it. And mind you call her Elizabeth."

"I've done that already," said Georgie proudly. "I practised saying it to myself."

"Good. She dines here then tomorrow night, and I shall be her hostess and shall make the evening as pleasant as I can to all my guests. But apart from that, Georgie, I shall take steps to teach her manners if she's not too old to learn. She will be sorry; she will wish she had not been so rude. And I can't see any objection to our other friends in Tilling knowing what occurred this morning, if you feel inclined to speak of it. I shan't, but there's no reason why you shouldn't."

"Hurrah, I'm dining with the Wyses tonight," said Georgie. "They'll soon know."

Lucia knitted her brows in profound thought.

"And then there's that incident about our pictures, yours and mine, being rejected by the hanging committee of the Art Club," said she. "We have both kept the forms we received saying that they regretted having to return them, and I think, Georgie, that while you are on the subject of Elizabeth Mapp, you might show yours to Mr. Wyse. He is a member, so is Susan, of the committee, and I think they have a right to know that our pictures were rejected on official forms without ever coming before the committee at all. I behaved towards our poor friend with a magnanimity that now appears to me excessive, and since she does not appreciate magnanimity we will try her with something else. That would not be amiss." Lucia rose.

"And now let us leave this very disagreeable subject for the present," she said, "and take the taste of it out of our mouths with a little music. Beethoven, noble Beethoven, don't you think? The fifth symphony, Georgie, for four hands. Fate knocking at the door."

Georgie rather thought that Lucia smacked her lips as she said, "this very disagreeable subject," but he was not certain, and presently Fate was knocking at the door with Lucia's firm fingers, for she took the treble.

They had a nice long practise, and when it was time to go home Lucia detained him.

"I've got one thing to say to you, Georgie," she said, "though not about that paltry subject. I've sold The Hurst, I've bought this new property, and so I've made a new will. I've left Grebe and all it contains to you, and also, well, a little sum of money. I should like you to know that."

Georgie was much touched.

"My dear, how wonderful of you," he said. "But I hope it will be ages and ages before—"

"So do I, Georgie," she said in her most sincere manner.

∞

Tilling had known tensions before and would doubtless know them again. Often it had been on a very agreeable rack of suspense, as when, for instance, it had believed (or striven to believe) that Major Benjy might be fighting a duel with that old crony of his, Captain Puffin, lately deceased. Now there was a suspense of a more intimate quality (for nobody would have cared at all if Captain Puffin had been killed, nor much, if Major Benjy), for it was as if the innermost social guts of Tilling were attached to some relentless windlass, which, at any moment now, might be wound, but not relaxed. The High Street next morning, therefore, was the scene of almost painful excitement. The Wyses'

Royce, with Susan smothered in sables, went up and down, until she was practically certain that she had told everybody that she and Algernon had retired from the hanging committee of the Art Club, pending explanations which they had requested Miss (no longer Elizabeth) Mapp to furnish, but which they had no hope of receiving. Susan was perfectly explicit about the cause of this step, and Algernon who, at a very early hour, had interviewed the errand-boy at the frame-shop, was by her side, to corroborate all she said. His high-bred reticence, indeed, had been even more weighty than Susan's volubility. "I am afraid it is all too true," was all that could be got out of him. Two hours had now elapsed since their resignations had been sent in, and still no reply had come from Mallards.

But that situation was but an insignificant fraction of the prevalent suspense, for the exhibition had been open and closed months before, and if Tilling was to make a practise of listening to such posthumous revelations, life would cease to have any poignant interest, but be wholly occupied in retrospective retributions. Thrilling therefore as was the past, as revealed by the stern occupants of the Royce, what had happened only yesterday on the doorstep of Mallards was far more engrossing. The story of that, by 11:30 a.m., already contained several remarkable variants. The Padre affirmed that Georgie had essayed to enter Mallards without knocking, and that Miss Mapp (the tendency to call her Miss Mapp was spreading) had seen Lucia in her motor just below the window of the garden-room, and had called out, "Turn in, *Georgino mio,* no tarsome chains now that Elizabeth has got back to her own housie-pousie." Diva had reason to believe that Elizabeth (she still stuck to that) had not seen Lucia in her motor, and had called out of the window to Georgie "Ring the belly-pelly, dear, for I'm afraid the chain is on the door." Mrs.

Bartlett (she was no use at all) said, "All so distressing and exciting and Christmas Day next week, and very little goodwill, oh dear me!" Irene had said, "That old witch will get what for."

Again, it was known that Major Benjy had called at Mallards soon after the scene, whatever it was, had taken place, and had refused to go into the garden-room, when he heard that Georgie was painting Elizabeth's portrait. Withers was witness (she had brought several pots of jam to Diva's house that morning, not vegetable marrow at all, but raspberry, which looked like a bribe) that the Major had said "Faugh!" when she told him that Georgie was there. Major Benjy himself could not be cross-examined because he had gone out by the eleven o'clock tram to play golf. Lucia had not been seen in the High Street at all, nor had Miss Mapp, and Georgie had only passed through it in his car, quite early, going in the direction of Grebe. This absence of the principals, in these earlier stages of development, was felt to be in accordance with the highest rules of dramatic technique, and everybody, as far as was known, was to meet that very night at Lucia's house-warming. Opinion as to what would happen then was as divergent as the rumours of what had happened already. Some said that Miss Mapp had declined the invitation on the plea that she was engaged to dine with Major Benjy. This was unlikely, because he never had anybody to dinner. Some said that she had accepted, and that Lucia no doubt intended to send out a message that she was not expected, but that Georgie's car would take her home again. So sorry. All this, however, was a matter of pure conjecture, and it was work enough to sift out what had happened, without wasting time (for time was precious) in guessing what would happen.

The church clock had hardly struck half-past eleven (winter time) before the first of the principals appeared on the stage of the High Street. This was Miss Mapp, wreathed in smiles, and occupied in her usual shopping errands. She trotted about from grocer to butcher, and butcher to general stores, where she bought a mousetrap, and was exceedingly affable to tradespeople. She nodded to her friends, she patted Mr. Woolgar's dog on the head, she gave a penny to a ragged individual with a lugubrious baritone voice who was singing "The Last Rose of Summer," and said "Thank you for your sweet music." Then after pausing for a moment on the pavement in front of Wasters, she rang the bell. Diva, who had seen her from the window, flew to open it.

"Good-morning, Diva dear," she said. "I just looked in. Any news?"

"Good gracious, it's I who ought to ask you that," said Diva. "What *did* happen really?"

Elizabeth looked very much surprised.

"How? When? Where?" she asked.

"As if you didn't know," said Diva, fizzing with impatience. "Mr. Georgie, Lucia, paintboxes, no chain on the door, you at the garden-room window, belly-pelly. Etcetera. Yesterday morning."

Elizabeth put her finger to her forehead, as if trying to recall some dim impression. She appeared to succeed.

"Dear gossipy one," she said, "I believe I know what you mean. Georgie came to paint in the garden-room, as he so often does—"

"Do you call him Georgie?" asked Diva in an eager parenthesis.

"Yes, I fancy that's his name, and he calls me Elizabeth."

"No!" said Diva.

"Yes," said Elizabeth. "Do not interrupt me, dear . . . I happened to be at the window as he rang the bell, and I just popped my head out, and told him he was a naughty boy not to walk straight in."

"In baby-talk?" asked Diva. "Like Lucia?"

"Like any baby you chance to mention," said Elizabeth. "Why not?"

"But with her sitting in her car just below?"

"Yes, dear, it so happened that she was just coming to leave an invitation on me for her house-warming tonight. Are you going?"

"Yes, of course, everybody is. But how could you do it?"

Elizabeth sat wrapped in thought.

"I'm beginning to see what you mean," she said at length. "But what an absurd notion. You mean, don't you, that dear Lulu thinks—goodness, how ridiculous—that I was mimicking her."

"Nobody knows what she thinks," said Diva. "She's not been seen this morning."

"But gracious goodness me, what have I done?" asked Elizabeth. "Why this excitement? Is there a law that only Mrs. Lucas of Grebe may call Georgie, Georgie? So ignorant of me if there is. Ought I to call him Frederick? And pray, why shouldn't I talk baby-talk? Another law perhaps. I must get a book of the laws of England."

"But you knew she was in the car just below you and must have heard."

Elizabeth was now in possession of what she wanted to know. Diva was quite a decent barometer of Tilling weather, and the weather was stormy.

"Rubbish, darling," she said. "You are making mountains out of molehills. If Lulu heard—and I don't know that she did, mind—what cause of complaint has she? Mayn't I say Georgie? Mayn't I say 'vewy naughty boy'? Let us hear no more about it.

You will see this evening how wrong you all are. Lulu will be just as sweet and cordial as ever. And you will hear with your own ears how Georgie calls me Elizabeth."

These were brave words, and they very fitly represented the stout heart that inspired them. Tilling had taken her conduct to be equivalent to an act of war, exactly as she had meant it to be, and if anyone thought that E. M. was afraid, they were wrong . . . Then there was that matter of Mr. Wyse's letter, resigning from the hanging committee. She must tap the barometer again.

"I think everybody is a shade mad this morning," she observed, "and I should call Mr. Wyse, if anybody asked me to be candid, a raving lunatic. There was a little misunderstanding months and months ago—I am vague about it—concerning two pictures that Lulu and Georgie sent in to the art exhibition in the summer. I thought it was all settled and done with. But I did act a little irregularly. Technically I was wrong, and when I have been wrong about a thing, as you very well know, dear Diva, I am not ashamed to confess it."

"Of course you were wrong," said Diva cordially, "if Mr. Wyse's account of it is correct. You sent the pictures back, such beauties, too, with a formal rejection from the hanging committee when they had never seen them at all. So rash, too: I wonder at you."

These unfavourable comments did not make the transaction appear any the less irregular.

"I said I was wrong, Diva," remarked Elizabeth with some asperity, "and I should have thought that was enough. And now Mr. Wyse, raking bygones up again in the way he has, has written to me to say that he and Susan resign their places on the hanging committee."

"I know: they told everybody," said Diva. "Awkward. What are you going to do?"

The barometer had jerked alarmingly downwards on this renewed tapping.

"I shall cry *peccavi*," said Elizabeth, with the air of doing something exceedingly noble. "I shall myself resign. That will show that whatever anybody else does, I am doing the best in my power to put right a technical error. I hope Mr. Wyse will appreciate that, and be ashamed of the letter he wrote me. More than that, I shall regard his letter as having been written in a fit of temporary insanity, which I trust will not recur."

"Yes; I suppose that's the best thing you can do," said Diva. "It will show him that you regret what you did, now that it's all found out."

"That is not generous of you, Diva," cried Elizabeth, "I am sorry you said that."

"More than I am," said Diva. "It's a very fair statement. Isn't it now? What's wrong with it?"

Elizabeth suddenly perceived that at this crisis it was unwise to indulge in her usual tiffs with Diva. She wanted allies.

"Diva, dear, we mustn't quarrel," she said. "That would never do. I felt I had to pop in to consult you as to the right course to take with Mr. Wyse, and I'm so glad you agree with me. How I trust your judgement! I must be going. What a delightful evening we have in store for us. Major Benjy was thinking of declining, but I persuaded him it would not be kind. A house-warming, you know. Such a special occasion."

The evening to which everybody had looked forward so much was, in the main, a disappointment to bellicose spirits. Nothing could exceed Lucia's cordiality to Elizabeth unless it was Elizabeth's to Lucia: they left the dining-room at the end of dinner with arms and waists intertwined, a very bitter sight. They then played bridge at the same table, and so loaded each other with compliments while deploring their own errors, that

Diva began to entertain the most serious fears that they had been mean enough to make it up on the sly, or that Lucia in a spirit of Christian forbearance, positively unnatural, had decided to overlook all the attacks and insults with which Elizabeth had tried to provoke her. Or did Lucia think that this degrading display of magnanimity was a weapon by which she would secure victory, by enlisting for her the sympathy and applause of Tilling? If so, that was a great mistake; Tilling did not want to witness a demonstration of forgiveness or white feathers but a combat without quarter. Again, if she thought that such nobility would soften the malevolent heart of Mapp, she showed a distressing ignorance of Mapp's nature, for she would quite properly construe this as not being nobility at all but the most ignoble cowardice. There was Georgie under Lucia's very nose, interlarding his conversation with far more "Elizabeths" than was in the least necessary to show that he was talking to her, and she volleyed "Georgies" at him in return. Every now and then, when these discharges of Christian names had been particularly resonant, Elizabeth caught Diva's eye with a glance of triumph as if to remind her that she had prophesied that Lulu would be all sweetness and cordiality, and Diva turned away sick at heart.

On the other hand, there were still grounds for hope, and, as the evening went on, these became more promising: they were like small caps of foam and cats'-paws of wind upon a tranquil sea. To begin with, it was only this morning that the baseness of Elizabeth in that matter concerning the art committee had come to light. Georgie, not Lucia, had been directly responsible for that damning disclosure, but it must be supposed that he had acted with her connivance, if not with her express wish, and this certainly did not look so much like forgiveness as a nasty one for Elizabeth. That was hopeful, and Diva's eagle eye espied other signs of bad weather. Elizabeth, encouraged by Lucia's compliments and humilities throughout a long rubber, began to come out more in her true colours, and to explain to her partner that she had lost a few tricks (no matter) by not taking a finesse, or a whole game by not supporting her declaration, and Diva thought she detected a certain dangerous glitter in Lucia's eye as she bent to these chastisements. Surely, too, she bit her lip when Elizabeth suddenly began to call her Lulu again. Then there was Irene's conduct to consider: Irene was fizzing and fidgeting in her chair, she cast glances of black hatred at Elizabeth, and once Diva distinctly saw Lucia frown and shake her head at her. Again, at the voluptuous supper which succeeded many rubbers of bridge, there was the famous lobster *à la Riseholme.* It had become, as all Tilling knew, a positive obsession with Elizabeth to get the secret of that delicious dish, and now, flushed with continuous victories at bridge and with Lucia's persevering pleasantness, she made another direct request for it.

"Lulu dear," she said, "it would be sweet of you to give me the recipe for your lobster. So good . . ."

Diva felt this to be a crucial moment: Lucia had often refused it before, but now if she was wholly Christian and cowardly she would consent. But once more she gave no reply, and asked the Padre on what day of the week Christmas fell. So Diva heaved a sigh of relief, for there was still hope.

In spite of this rebuff, it was hardly to be wondered at that Elizabeth felt in a high state of elation when the evening was over. The returning revellers changed the order of their going, and Georgie took back her and Diva. He went outside with Diva, for, during the last half-hour, Mapp (as he now mentally termed her in order to be done with Elizabeth) had grown like a mushroom in complaisance and self-confidence, and he could not trust himself, if she went on, as she would no doubt do, in the same strain, not to rap out something very sharp. "Let her just wait," he thought, "she'll soon be singing a different tune."

Georgie's precautions in going outside, well wrapped up in his cap and his fur tippet and his fur rug, were well founded, for hardly had Mapp kissed her hand for the last time to Lulu (who would come to the door to see them off), and counted over the money she had won, than she burst into staves of intolerable triumph and condescension.

"So that's that!" she said, pulling up the window. "And if I was to ask you, dear Diva, which of us was right about how this evening would go off, I don't think there would be very much doubt about the answer. Did you ever see Lulu so terribly anxious to please me? And did you happen to hear me say Georgie and him say Elizabeth? Lulu didn't like it, I am sure, but she had to swallow her medicine, and she did so with a very good grace, I am bound to say. She just wanted a little lesson, and I think I may say I've given it her. I had no idea, I will confess, that she would take it lying down like that. I just had to lean out of the window, pretend not to see her, and talk to Georgie in that silly voice and language and the thing was done."

Diva had been talking simultaneously for some time, but Elizabeth only paused to take breath, and went on in a slightly louder tone. So Diva talked louder too, until Georgie turned round to see what was happening. They both broke off, and smiled at him, and then both began again.

"If you would allow me to get a word in edgeways," said Diva, who had some solid arguments to produce, and, had she not been a lady, could have slapped Mapp's face in impotent rage—

"I don't think," said Elizabeth, "that we shall have much more trouble with her and her queenly airs. Quite a pleasant house-warming, and there was no doubt that the house wanted it, for it was bitterly cold in the dining-room, and I strongly suspect that chicken-cream of being rabbit. She only had to be shown that whatever Riseholme may have stood from her in the way of condescensions and graces, she had better not try them on at Tilling. She was looking forward to teaching us, and ruling us and guiding us. Pop! Elizabeth (that's me, dear!) has a little lamb, which lives at Grebe and gives a house-warming, so you may guess who *that* is. The way she flattered and sued tonight over our cards when but a few weeks ago she was thinking of holding bridge classes—"

"You were just as bad," shouted Diva. "You told her she played beauti—"

"She was 'all over me,' to use that dreadful slang expression of Major Benjy's," continued Mapp. "She was like a dog that has had a scolding and begs—so prettily—to be forgiven. Mind, dear, I do not say that she is a bad sort of woman by any means, but she required to be put in her place, and Tilling ought to thank me for having done so. Dear me, here we are already at your house. How short the drive has seemed!"

"Anyhow, you didn't get the recipe for the lobster *à la Rise-holme*," said Diva, for this was one of the things she most wanted to say.

"A little final wriggle," said Mapp. "I have not the least doubt that she will think it over and send it me tomorrow. Good-night, darling. I shall be sending out invitations for a cosy evening of bridge some time at the end of this week."

The baffled Diva let herself into Wasters in low spirits, so convinced and lucid had been Mapp's comments on the evening. It was such a dismal conclusion to so much excitement; and all that thrilling tension, instead of snapping, had relaxed into the most depressing slackness. But she did not quite give up hope, for there had been cats'-paws and caps of foam on the tranquil sea. She fell asleep visualising these.

Chapter Nine

THOUGH GEORGIE HAD THOUGHT THAT the garden-room would have to give him at least two more sittings before his sketch arrived at that high state of finish which he, like the Pre-Raphaelites, regarded as necessary to any work of art, he decided that he would leave it in a more impressionist state, and sent it next morning to be framed. In consequence the glass of water which Elizabeth had brought out for him in anticipation of his now usual visit at eleven o'clock remained unsullied by washings from his brush, and at twelve, Elizabeth, being rather thirsty in consequence of so late a supper the night before, drank it herself. On the second morning, a very wet one, Major Benjy did not go out for his usual round of golf, and again Georgie did not come to paint. But at a few minutes to one she observed that his car was at the door of Mallards Cottage; it passed her window, it stopped at Major Benjy's, and he got in. It was impossible not to remember that Lucia always lunched at one in the winter because a later hour for *colazione* made the afternoon so short. But it was a surprise to see Major Benjy driving away with Miss Milliner Michael-Angelo, and difficult to conjecture where else it was at all likely that they could have gone.

There was half an hour yet to her own luncheon, and she wrote seven postcards inviting seven friends to tea on Saturday, with bridge to follow. The Wyses, the Padres, Diva, Major Benjy and Georgie were the *destinataires* of these missives; these, with herself, made eight, and there would thus be two tables of agreeable gamblers. Lucia was not to be favoured: it would be salutary for her to be left out every now and then, just to impress upon her the lesson of which she had stood so sadly in need. She must learn to go to heel, to come when called, and to produce recipes when desired, which at present she had not done.

There had been several days of heavy rain, but early in the afternoon it cleared up, and Elizabeth set out for a brisk healthy walk. The field-paths would certainly make very miry going, for she saw from the end of the High Street that there was much water lying in the marsh, and she therefore kept to that excellent road, which, having passed Grebe, went nowhere particular. She was prepared to go in and thank Lucia for her lovely house-warming, in order to make sure whether Georgie and Major Benjy had gone to lunch with her, but no such humiliating need occurred, for there in front of the house was drawn up Georgie's motor car, so (whether she liked it or not, and she didn't) *that* problem was solved. The house stood quite close to the road: a flagged pathway of half a dozen yards, flanked at the entrance-gate by thick hornbeam hedges on which the leaf still lingered, separated it from the road, and just as Elizabeth passed Georgie's car drawn up there, the front door opened, and she saw Lucia and her two guests on the threshold. Major Benjy was laughing in that fat voice of his, and Georgie was giving forth his shrill little neighs like a colt with a half-cracked voice.

The temptation to know what they were laughing at was irresistible. Elizabeth moved a few steps on and, screened by the hornbeam hedge, held her breath.

Major Benjy gave another great haw-haw and spoke.

" 'Pon my word, did she really?" he said. "Do it again, Mrs.

Lucas. Never laughed so much in my life. Infernal impertinence!"

There was no mistaking the voice and the words that followed.

"'Oo is vewy naughty boy, Georgie," said Lucia. "Never ring Elizabeth's belly-pelly—"

Elizabeth hurried on, as she heard steps coming down that short flagged pathway. But hurry as she might, she heard a little more.

"'Oo walk straight in always and sing out for her," continued the voice, repeating word for word the speech of which she had been so proud. "There's no chain up"—and then came loathsome parody—"now that Liblib has *ritornata* to *Mallardino*."

It was in a scared mood, as if she had heard or seen a ghost, that Elizabeth hastened along up the road that led nowhere in particular, before Lucia's guests could emerge from the gate. Luckily at the end of the kitchen garden the hornbeam hedge turned at right angles, and behind this bastion she hid herself till she heard the motor move away in the direction of Tilling, the prey of the most agitated misgivings. Was it possible that her own speech, which she had thought had scarified Lucia's pride, was being turned into a mockery and a derision against herself? It seemed not only possible but probable. And how dare Mrs. Lucas invent and repeat as if spoken by herself that rubbish about *ritornata* and *Mallardino*? Never in her life had she said such a thing.

When the coast was clear, she took the road again, and walked quickly on away from Tilling. The tide was very high, for the river was swollen with rain, and the waters overbrimmed its channel and extended in a great lake up to the foot of the bank and dyke which bounded the road. Perturbed as she was, Miss Mapp could not help admiring that broad expanse of water, now lit by a gleam of sun, in front of which to the westward, the hill of Tilling rose dark against a sky already growing red with the winter sunset. She had just turned a corner in the road, and now she perceived that close ahead of her somebody else was admiring it too in a more practical manner, for there by the roadside within twenty yards of her sat quaint Irene, with her mouth full of paintbrushes and an easel set up in front of her. She had not seen Irene since the night of the house-warming, when the quaint one had not been very cordial, and so, thinking she had walked far enough, she turned back. But Irene had quite evidently seen her, for she shaded her eyes for a moment against the glare, took some of the paintbrushes out of her mouth and called to her with words that seemed to have what might be termed a dangerous undertow.

"Hello, Mapp," she said. "Been lunching with Lulu?"

"What a lovely sketch, dear," said Mapp. "No, just a brisk little walk. Not been lunching at Grebe today."

Irene laughed hoarsely.

"I didn't think it was very likely, but thought I would ask," she said. "Yes; I'm rather pleased with my sketch. A bloody look about the sunlight, isn't there, as if the Day of Judgement was coming. I'm going to send it to the winter exhibition of the Art Club."

"Dear girlie, what do you mean?" asked Mapp. "We don't have winter exhibitions."

"No, but we're going to," said girlie. "A new hanging committee, you see, full of pep and pop and vim. Haven't they asked you to send them something . . . Of course the space at their disposal is very limited."

Mapp laughed, but not with any great exuberance. This undertow was tweaking at her disagreeably.

"That's news to me," she said. "Most enterprising of Mr. Wyse and dear Susan."

"Sweet Lulu's idea," said Irene. "As soon as you sent in your resignation, of course they asked her to be President."

"That is nice for her," said Mapp enthusiastically. "She will like that. I must get to work on some little picky to send them."

"There's that one you did from the church tower when Lucia had influenza," said this awful Irene. "That would be nice . . . Oh, I forgot. Stupid of me. It's by invitation: the committee are asking a few people to send pickies. No doubt they'll beg you for one. Such a good plan. There won't be any mistakes in the future about rejecting what is sent in."

Mapp gave a gulp but rallied.

"I see. They'll be all Academicians together, and be hung on the line," said she unflinchingly.

"Yes. On the line or be put on easels," said Irene. "Curse the light! It's fading. I must pack up. Hold these brushes, will you?"

"And then we'll walk back home together, shall we? A cup of tea with me, dear?" asked Mapp, anxious to conciliate and to know more.

"I'm going into Lucia's, I'm afraid. Wyses tummin' to play bridgey and hold a committee meeting," said Irene.

"You are a cruel thing to imitate poor Lulu," said Mapp. "How well you've caught that silly baby-talk of hers. Just her voice. Bye-bye."

"Same to you," said Irene.

∞

There was undoubtedly, thought Mapp, as she scudded swiftly homewards alone, a sort of mocking note about quaint Irene's conversation, which she did not relish. It was full of hints and awkward allusions; it bristled with hidden menace, and even her imitation of Lucia's baby-talk was not wholly satisfactory, for quaint Irene might be mimicking her imitation of Lucia, even as Lucia herself had done, and there was very little humour in that. Presently she passed the Wyses' Royce going to Grebe. She kissed her hand to a mound of sables inside, but it was too dark to see if the salute was returned. Her brisk afternoon's walk had not freshened her up; she was aware of a feeling of fatigue, of a vague depression and anxiety. And mixed with that was a hunger not only for tea but for more information. There seemed to be things going on of which she was sadly ignorant, and even when her ignorance was enlightened, they remained rather sad. But Diva (such a gossip) might know more about this winter exhibition, and she popped into Wasters. Diva was in, and begged her to wait for tea: she would be down in a few minutes.

It was a cosy little room, looking out on to the garden which had yielded her so many pots of excellent preserves during the summer, but dreadfully untidy, as Diva's house always was. There was a litter of papers on the table, notes half-thrust back into their envelopes, crossword puzzles cut out from the *Evening Standard* and partially solved: there was her own postcard to Diva sent off that morning and already delivered, and there was a sheet of paper with the stamp of Grebe upon it and Lucia's monogram, which seemed to force itself on Elizabeth's eye. The most cursory glance revealed that this was a request from the Art Committee that Mrs. Plaistow would do them the honour to send them a couple of her sketches for the forthcoming winter exhibition. All the time there came from Diva's bedroom, directly overhead, the sound of rhythmical steps or thumps, most difficult to explain. In a few minutes these ceased, and Diva's tread on the stairs gave Elizabeth sufficient warning to enable her to snatch up the first book that came to hand, and sink into a chair by the fire. She saw, with some feeling of apprehension similar to those which had haunted her all afternoon, that this was a copy of *An Ideal System of Callisthenics for Those No Longer Young,* of which she seemed to have heard. On the title page was an inscription "Diva from Lucia," and in brackets, like a prescription, "Ten minutes at the exercises in Chapter I, twice a day for the present."

Diva entered very briskly. She was redder in the face than usual, and, so Elizabeth instantly noticed, lifted her feet very high as she walked, and held her head well back and her breast out like a fat little pigeon. This time there was to be no question about getting a word in edgeways, for she began to talk before the door was fully open.

"Glad to see you, Elizabeth," she said, "and I shall be very pleased to play bridge on Saturday. I've never felt so well in my life, do you know, and I've only been doing them two days. Oh, I see you've got the book."

"I heard you stamping and thumping, dear," said Elizabeth. "Was that them?"

"Yes, twice a day, ten minutes each time. It clears the head, too. If you sit down to a crossword puzzle afterwards you find you're much brighter than usual."

"Callisthenics *à la Lucia*?" asked Elizabeth.

"Yes. Irene and Mrs. Bartlett and I all do them, and Mrs. Wyse is going to begin, but rather more gently. Hasn't Lucia told you about them?"

Here was another revelation of things happening. Elizabeth met it bravely.

"No. Dear Lulu knows my feelings about that sort of fad. A brisk walk such as I've had this afternoon is all I require. Such lovely lights of sunset and a very high tide. Quaint Irene was sketching on the road just beyond Grebe."

"Yes. She's going to send it in and three more for the winter exhibition. Oh, perhaps you haven't heard. There's to be an exhibition directly after Christmas."

"Such a good idea: I've been discussing it," said Elizabeth.

Diva's eye travelled swiftly and suspiciously to the table where this flattering request to her lay on the top of the litter. Elizabeth did not fail to catch the significance of this.

"Irene told me," she said hastily. "I must see if I can find time to do them something."

"Oh, then they have asked you," said Diva with a shade of disappointment in her voice. "They've asked me too—"

"No! Really?" said Elizabeth.

"—so of course I said yes, but I'm afraid I'm rather out of practise. Lucia is going to give an address on modern art at the opening, and then we shall all go round and look at each other's pictures."

"What fun!" said Elizabeth cordially.

Tea had been brought in. There was a pot of greenish jam and Elizabeth loaded her buttered toast with it, and put it into her mouth. She gave a choking cry and washed it down with a gulp of tea.

"Anything wrong?" asked Diva.

"Yes, dear. I'm afraid it's fermenting," said Elizabeth, laying down the rest of her toast. "And I can't conceive what it's made of."

Diva looked at the pot.

"You ought to know," she said. "It's one of the pots you gave me. Labelled vegetable marrow. So sorry it's not eatable. By the way, talking of food, did Lucia send you the recipe for the lobster?"

Elizabeth smiled her sweetest.

"Dear Lucia," she said. "She's been so busy with art and callisthenics. She must have forgotten. I shall jog her memory."

∞

The afternoon had been full of rather unpleasant surprises, thought Elizabeth to herself, as she went up to Mallards that evening. They were concerned with local activities, art and gymnastics, of which she had hitherto heard nothing, and they all seemed to show a common origin: there was a hidden hand directing them. This was disconcerting, especially since, only a few nights ago, she had felt so sure that that hand had been upraised to her, beseeching pardon. Now it rather looked as if that hand had spirited itself away and was very busy and energetic on its own account.

She paused on her doorstep. There was a light shining out through chinks behind the curtains in Mallards Cottage, and she thought it would be a good thing to pop in on Georgie and see if she could gather some further gleanings. She would make herself extremely pleasant: she would admire his needlework if he was at it, she would praise the beautiful specklessness of his room, for Georgie always appreciated any compliment to Foljambe, she would sing the praises of Lucia, though they blistered her tongue.

Foljambe admitted her. The door of the sitting-room was ajar, and as she put down her umbrella, she heard Georgie's voice talking to the telephone.

"Saturday, half-past four," he said. "I've just found a postcard. Hasn't she asked you?"

Georgie, as Elizabeth had often observed, was deafer than he knew (which accounted for his not hearing all the wrong notes she played in his duets with Lucia) and he had not heard her entry, though Foljambe spoke her name quite loud. He was listening with rapt attention to what was coming through and saying "My dear!" or "No!" at intervals. Now, however, he turned and saw her, and with a scared expression hung up the receiver.

"Dear me, I never heard you come in!" he said. "How nice! I was just going to tell Foljambe to bring up tea. Two cups, Foljambe."

"I'm interrupting you," said Elizabeth. "I can see you were just settling down to your sewing and a cosy bachelor evening."

"Not a bit," said Georgie. "Do have a chair near the fire." It was not necessary to explain that she had already had tea with Diva, even if one mouthful of fermenting vegetable could properly be called tea, and she took the chair he pulled up for her.

"Such beautiful work," she said, looking at Georgie's tambour of *petit point,* which lay near by. "What eyes you must have to be able to do it."

"Yes, they're pretty good yet," said Georgie, slipping his spectacle-case into his pocket. "And I shall be delighted to come to tea and bridge on Saturday. Thanks so much. Just got your invitation."

Miss Mapp knew that already.

"That's charming," she said. "And how I envy you your Foljambe. Not a speck of dust anywhere. You could eat your tea off the floor, as they say."

Georgie noticed that she did not use his Christian name. This confirmed his belief that the employment of it was reserved for Lucia's presence as an annoyance to her. Then the telephone bell rang again.

"May I?" said Georgie.

He went across to it, rather nervous. It was as he thought: Lucia was at it again, explaining that somebody had cut her off.

Listen as she might, Miss Mapp, from where she sat, could only hear a confused quacking noise. So to show how indifferent she was as to the conversation, she put her fingers close to her ears ready to stop them when Georgie turned round again, and listened hard to what he said.

"Yes . . . yes," said Georgie. "Thanks so much—lovely. I'll pick him up then, shall I? Quarter to eight, is it? Yes, her too. Yes, I've done them once today: not a bit giddy . . . I can't stop now, Lucia. Miss Ma—Elizabeth's just come in for a cup of tea . . . I'll tell her."

Elizabeth felt she understood all this; she was an adept at telephonic reconstruction. There was evidently another party at Grebe. "Him" and "her" no doubt were Major Benjy and herself, whom Georgie would pick up as before. "Them" were exercises, and Georgie's promise to tell "her" clearly meant that he should convey an invitation. This was satisfactory: evidently Lucia was hoping to propitiate. Then Georgie turned round and saw Elizabeth smiling gaily at the fire with her hands over her ears. He moved into her field of vision and she uncorked herself.

"Finished?" she said. "Hope you did not cut it short because of me."

"Not at all," said Georgie, for she couldn't (unless she was pretending) have heard him say that he had done precisely that. "It was Lucia ringing up. She sends you her love."

"Sweet of her, such a pet," said Elizabeth, and waited for more about picking up and that invitation. But Lucia's love appeared to be all, and Georgie asked her if she took sugar. She did, and tried if he in turn would take another sort of sugar, both for himself and Lucia.

"Such a lovely house-warming," she said, "and how we all enjoyed ourselves. Lucia seems to have time for everything, bridge, those lovely duets with you, Italian, Greek (though we haven't heard much about that lately), a winter art exhibition, and an address (how I shall look forward to it!) on modern art, callisthenics—"

"Oh, you ought to try those," said Georgie. "You stretch and stamp and feel ever so young afterwards. We're all doing them."

"And does she take classes as she threat—promised to do?" asked Elizabeth.

"She will when we've mastered the elements," said Georgie. "We shall march round the kitchen garden at Grebe—cinder paths you know, so good in wet weather—keeping time, and then skip and flex and jerk. And if it's raining we shall do them in the kitchen. You can throw open those double doors, and have plenty of fresh air which is so important. There's that enormous kitchen table too, to hold on to, when we're doing that swimming movement. It's like a great raft."

Elizabeth had not the nerve to ask if Major Benjy was to be of that company. It would be too bitter to know that he, who had so sternly set his face against Lucia's domination, was in process of being sucked down in that infernal whirlpool of her energetic grabbings. Almost she wished that she had asked her to be one of her bridge party tomorrow: but it was too late now. Her seven invitations—seven against Lucia—had gone forth, and not till she got home would she know whether her two bridge-tables were full.

"And this winter exhibition," she asked. "What a good idea! We're all so idle in the winter at dear old Tilling, and now there's another thing to work for. Are you sending that delicious picture of the garden-room? How I enjoyed our lovely chatty mornings when you were painting it!"

By the ordinary rules of polite conversation, Georgie ought

to have asked her what she was sending. He did nothing of the kind, but looked a little uncomfortable. Probably then, as Irene had told her, the exhibition was to consist of pictures sent by request of the committee, and at present they had not requested her. She felt that she must make sure about that, and determined to send in a picture without being asked. That would show for certain what was going on.

"Weren't those mornings pleasant?" said the evasive Georgie. "I was quite sorry when my picture was finished."

Georgie appeared unusually reticent: he did not volunteer any more information about the winter exhibition, nor about Lucia's telephoning, nor had he mentioned that he and Major Benjy had lunched with her today. She would lead him in the direction of that topic . . .

"How happy dear Lucia is in her pretty Grebe," she said. "I took my walk along the road there today. Her garden, so pleasant! A high tide this afternoon. The beautiful river flowing down to the sea, and the tide coming up to meet it. Did you notice it?"

Georgie easily saw through that: he would talk about tides with pleasure, but not lunch.

"It looked lovely," he said, "but they tell me that in ten days' time the spring tides are on, and they will be much higher. The water has been over the road in front of Lucia's house sometimes."

Elizabeth went back to Mallards more uneasy than ever. Lucia was indeed busy arranging callisthenic classes and winter exhibitions and, clearly, some party at Grebe, but not a word had she said to her about any of these things, nor had she sent the recipe for lobster *à la Riseholme.* But there was nothing more to be done tonight except to take steps concerning the picture exhibition to which she had not been asked to contribute. The house was full of her sketches, and she selected quite the best of them and directed Withers to pack it up and send it, with her card, to the Committee of the Art Club, Grebe.

∞

The winter bridge parties in Tilling were in their main features of a fixed and invariable pattern. An exceedingly substantial tea, including potted-meat sandwiches, was served at half-past four, and, after that was disposed of, at least three hours of bridge followed. After such a tea, nobody, as was perfectly well known, dreamed of having dinner: and though round about eight o'clock, the party broke up, with cries of astonishment at the lateness of the hour, and said it must fly back home to dress, this was a mere fashion of speech. "A tray" was the utmost refreshment that anyone could require, and nobody dressed for a solitary tray. Elizabeth was a great upholder of the dress-and-dinner fiction, and she had been known to leave a bridge party at nine, saying that Withers would scold her for being so late, and that her cook would be furious.

So on this Saturday afternoon the party of eight (for all seven had accepted) assembled at Mallards. They were exceedingly cordial: it was as if they desired to propitiate their hostess for something presently to emerge. Also it struck that powerful observer that there was not nearly so much eaten as usual. She had provided the caviare sandwiches of which Mrs. Wyse had been known absentmindedly to eat nine, she had provided the nougat chocolates of which Diva had been known to have eaten all, but though the chocolates were in front of Diva, and the caviare in front of Susan, neither of them exhibited anything resembling their usual greed. There was Scotch shortbread for the Padre, who, though he came from Birmingham, was insatiable with regard to that national form of biscuit, and there was whisky and soda for Major Benjy, who had no use for tea, and both of them, too, were mysteriously abstemious. Perhaps this wet muggy weather, thought Elizabeth, had made them all a trifle liverish, or very likely those callisthenics had taken away their appetites. It was noticeable, moreover, that throughout tea nobody mentioned the name of Lucia.

They adjourned to the garden-room where two tables were set out for bridge, and till half-past six nothing momentous occurred. At that hour Elizabeth was partner to Major Benjy, and she observed with dark misgivings that when she had secured the play of the hand (at a staggering sacrifice, as it was soon to prove) he did not as usual watch her play, but got up, and standing by the fireplace indulged in some very antic movements. He bent down, apparently trying to touch his toes with his fingers, and a perfect fusillade of small crackling noises from his joints (knee or hip it was impossible to tell) accompanied these athletic flexings. Then he whisked himself round to right and left as if trying to look down his back, like a parrot. This was odd and ominous conduct, this strongly suggested that he had been sucked into the callisthenic whirlpool, and what was more ominous yet was that when he sat down again he whispered to Georgie, who was at the same table, "That makes my ten minutes, old boy." Elizabeth did not like that at all. She knew now what the ten minutes must refer to, and that endearing form of address to Miss Milliner Michael-Angelo was a little worrying. The only consolation was that Georgie's attention was diverted from the game, and that he trumped his partner's best card. At the conclusion of the hand, Elizabeth was three tricks short of her contract, and another very puzzling surprise awaited her, for instead of Major Benjy taking her failure in very ill part, he was more than pleasant about it. What could be the matter with him?

"Very well played, Miss Elizabeth," he said. "I was afraid that after my inexcusable declaration we should lose more than that."

Elizabeth began to feel more keenly puzzled as to why none of them had any appetites, and why they were all so pleasant to her. Were they rallying round her again, was their silence about Lucia a tactful approval of her absence? Or was there some hidden connection between their abstemiousness, their reticence and their unwontedly propitiatory attitude? If there was, it quite eluded her. Then as Diva dealt in her sloppy manner Lucia's name came up for the first time.

"Mr. Georgie, you ought not to have led trumps," she said. "Lucia always says— Oh, dear me, I believe I've misdealt. Oh no, I haven't. That's all right."

Elizabeth pondered this as she sorted her cards. Nobody enquired what Lucia said, and Diva's swift changing of the subject as if that name had slipped out by accident, looked as if possibly they none of them desired any allusion to be made to her. Had they done with her? she wondered. But if so, what about the callisthenics?

She was dummy now and was absorbed in watching Major Benjy's tragical mismanagement of the hand, for he was getting into a sadder bungle than anyone, except perhaps Lucia, could have involved himself in. Withers entered while this was going on, and gave Elizabeth a parcel. With her eye and her mind still glued to the cards, she absently unwrapped it, and took its contents from its coverings just as the last trick was being played. It was the picture she had sent to the Art Committee the day before and with it was a typewritten form to convey its regrets that the limited wall-space at its disposal would not permit of Miss Mapp's picture being exhibited. This slip floated out on to the floor, and Georgie bent down and returned it to her. She handed it and the picture and the wrappings to Withers, and told her to put them in the cupboard. Then she leaned over the table to her partner, livid with mixed and uncontrollable emotions.

"Dear Major Benjy, what a hash!" she said. "If you had pulled out your cards at random from your hand, you could not, bar revokes, have done worse. I think you must have been having lessons from dear Lulu. Never mind: live and unlearn."

There was an awful pause. Even the players at the other table were stricken into immobility and looked at each other with imbecile eyes. Then the most surprising thing of all happened.

" 'Pon my word, partner," said Major Benjy, "I deserve all the scoldings you can give me. I played it like a baby. I deserve to pay all our losings. A thousand apologies."

Elizabeth, though she did not feel like it, had to show that she was generous too. But why didn't he answer her back in the usual manner?

"Naughty Major Benjy!" she said. "But what does it matter? It's only a game, and we all have our ups and downs. I have them myself. That's the rubber, isn't it? Not very expensive after all. Now let us have another and forget all about this one."

Diva drew a long breath, as if making up her mind to something, and glanced at the watch set with false pearls (Elizabeth was sure) on her wrist.

"Rather late to begin again," she said. "I make it ten minutes to seven. I think I ought to be going to dress."

"Nonsense, dear," said Elizabeth. "Much too early to leave off. Cut, Major Benjy."

He also appeared to take his courage in his hands, not very successfully.

"Well, upon my word, do you know, really Miss Elizabeth," he babbled, "a rubber goes on sometimes for a very long while, and if it's close on seven now, if, you know what I mean . . . What do you say, Pillson?"

It was Georgie's turn.

"Too tarsome," he said, "but I'm afraid personally that I must stop. Such a delightful evening. Such good rubbers . . ."

They all got up together, as if some common mechanism controlled their movements. Diva scuttled away to the other table, without even waiting to be paid the sum of one and threepence which she had won from Elizabeth.

"I'll see how they're getting on here," she said. "Why they're just adding up, too."

Elizabeth sat where she was and counted out fifteen pennies. That would serve Diva right for going at ten minutes to seven. Then she saw that the others had got up in a hurry, for Susan Wyse said to Mrs. Bartlett, "I'll pay you later on," and her husband held up her sable coat for her.

"Diva, your winnings," said Elizabeth, piling up the coppers.

Diva whisked round, and instead of resenting this ponderous discharge of the debt, received it with enthusiasm.

"Thank you, Elizabeth," she said. "All coppers: how nice! So useful for change. Good-night, dear. Thanks ever so much."

She paused a moment by the door, already open, by which Georgie was standing.

"Then you'll call for me at twenty minutes to eight," she said to him in the most audible whisper, and Georgie with a nervous glance in Elizabeth's direction gave a silent assent. Diva vanished into the night where Major Benjy had gone. Elizabeth rose from her deserted table.

"But you're not all going too?" she said to the others. "So early yet."

Mr. Wyse made a profound bow.

"I regret that my wife and I must get home to dress," he said. "But one of the most charming evenings of bridge I have ever spent, Miss Mapp. So many thanks. Come along, Susan."

"Delicious bridge," said Susan. "And those caviare sandwiches. Good-night, dear. You must come round and play with us some night soon."

"A grand game of bridge, Mistress Mapp," said the Padre. "Ah, wee wifie's callin' for me. *Au reservoir.*"

Next moment Elizabeth was alone. Georgie had followed on the heels of the others, closing the door very carefully, as if she had fallen asleep. Instead of that she hurried to the window and peeped out between the curtains. There were three or four of them standing on the steps while the Wyses got into the Royce, and they dispersed in different directions like detected conspirators, as no doubt they were.

The odd disconnected little incidents of the evening, the lack of appetites, the propitiatory conduct to herself, culminating in this unexampled departure a full hour before bridge parties had ever been known to break up, now grouped themselves together in Elizabeth's constructive mind. They fitted on to other facts that had hitherto seemed unrelated, but now were charged with significance. Georgie, for instance, had telephoned the day and the hour of this bridge party to Lucia, he had accepted an invitation to something at a quarter to eight: he had promised to call for "him" and "her." There could be no reasonable doubt that Lucia had purposely broken up Elizabeth's party at this early hour by bidding to dinner the seven guests who had just slunk away to dress . . . And her picture had been returned by the Art Committee, two of whom (though she did them the justice to admit that they were but the cats'-paws of a baleful intelligence) had hardly eaten any caviare sandwiches at all, for fear that they should not have good appetites for dinner. Hence also Diva's abstention from nougat chocolate, Major Benjy's from whisky, and the Padre's from shortbread. Nothing could be clearer.

Elizabeth was far from feeling unhappy or deserted, and very very far from feeling beaten. Defiance and hatred warmed her blood most pleasantly, and she spent half an hour sitting by the window, thoroughly enjoying herself. She meant to wait here till twenty minutes to eight, and if by that time she had not seen the Royce turning the corner of Porpoise Street, and Georgie's car calling at the perfidious Major Benjy's house, she would be ready to go barefoot to Grebe, and beg Lucia's pardon for having attributed to her so devilish a device. But no such humiliating pilgrimage awaited her, for all happened exactly as she knew it would. The great glaring headlights of the Royce blazed on the house opposite the turning to Porpoise Street, its raucous fog-horn sounded, and the porpoise car lurched into view scaring everybody by its lights and its odious voice, and by its size mak-ing foot-passengers flatten themselves against the walls. Hardly had it cleared the corner into the High Street when Georgie's gay bugle piped out and his car came under the window of the garden-room, and stopped at Major Benjy's. Elizabeth's intellect, unaided by any direct outside information, except that which she had overheard on the telephone, had penetrated this hole-and-corner business, and ringing the bell for her tray, she ate the large remainder of caviare sandwiches and nougat chocolate and fed her soul with schemes of reprisals. She could not offhand think of any definite plan of sufficiently withering a nature, and presently, tired with mental activity, she fell into a fireside doze and had a happy dream that Dr. Dobbie had popped in to tell her that Lucia had developed undoubted symptoms of leprosy.

∞

During the positively voluptuous week that followed Elizabeth's brief bridge party, no fresh development occurred of the drama on which Tilling was concentrated, except that Lucia asked Elizabeth to tea and that Elizabeth refused. The rivals therefore did not meet, and neither of them seemed aware of the existence of the other. But both Grebe and Mallards had been inordinately gay; at Grebe there had been many lunches with bridge afterwards, and the guests on several occasions had hurried back for tea and more bridge at Mallards. Indeed, Tilling had never had so much lunch and tea in its life or enjoyed so brilliant a winter season, for Diva and the Wyses and Mrs. Padre followed suit in lavish hospitality, and Georgie on one notable morning remembered that he had not had lunch or tea at home for five days; this was a record that beat Riseholme all to fits.

In addition to these gaieties there were celebrated the nuptials of Foljambe and Cadman, conducted from the bride's home, and the disposition of Foljambe's time between days with Georgie and nights with Cadman was working to admiration: everybody was pleased. At Grebe there had been other entertainments as well; the callisthenic class met on alternate days and Lucia in a tunic rather like Artemis, but with a supplementary skirt and scarlet stockings, headed a remarkable procession, consisting of Diva and the Wyses and Georgie and Major Benjy and the Padres and quaint Irene, out on to the cinder path of the kitchen garden, and there they copied her jerks and flexings and whirlings of the arms and touchings of the toes to the great amazement of errand-boys who came legitimately to the kitchen-door, and others who peered through the hornbeam hedge. On wet days the athletes assembled in the kitchen with doors flung wide to the open air, and astonished the cook with their swimming movements, an arm and leg together, while they held on with the other hand to the great kitchen table. "*Uno, due, tre,*" counted Lucia, and they all kicked out like frogs. And quaint Irene in her knickerbockers sometimes stood on her head, but nobody else attempted that. Lucia played them soothing music as they rested afterwards in her drawing-room; she encouraged Major Benjy to learn his notes on the piano, for she would willingly teach him: she persuaded Susan to take up her singing again, and played "*La ci darem*" for her, while Susan sang it in a thin shrill voice, and Mr. Wyse said "*Brava!* How I wish Amelia was here." Sometimes Lucia read them Pope's translation of the *Iliad* as they drank their lemonade and Major Benjy his whisky and soda, and not content with these diversions (the wonderful creature) she was composing the address on modern art which she was to deliver at the opening of the exhibition on the day following Boxing Day. She made notes for it and then dictated to her secretary (Elizabeth Mapp's face was something awful to behold when Diva told her that Lucia had a secretary) who took down what she said on a typewriter. Indeed, Elizabeth's face had never been more awful than when she heard that, except when Diva informed her that she was quite certain that Lucia would be delighted to let her join the callisthenic class.

But though, during these days, no act of direct aggression like that of Lucia's dinner party causing Elizabeth's bridge party to break up had been committed on either side, it was generally believed that Elizabeth was not done for yet, and Tilling was on tiptoe, expectant of some "view halloo" call to show that the chase was astir. She had refused Lucia's invitation to tea, and if she had been done for or gone to earth she would surely have accepted. Probably she took the view that the invitation was merely a test

question to see how she was getting on, and her refusal showed
that she was getting on very nicely. It would be absolutely unlike
Elizabeth (to adopt a further metaphor) to throw up the sponge
like that, for she had not yet been seriously hurt, and the bridge-
party-round had certainly been won by Lucia; there would be
fierce boxing in the next. It seemed likely that, in this absence of
aggressive acts, both antagonists were waiting till the season of
peace and goodwill was comfortably over and then they would
begin again. Elizabeth would have a God-sent opportunity at
the opening of the exhibition, when Lucia delivered her address.
She could sit in the front row and pretend to go to sleep or suppress an obvious inclination to laugh. Tilling felt that she must
have thought of that and of many other acts of reprisal unless she
was no longer the Elizabeth they all knew and (within limits)
respected, and (on numerous occasions) detested.

The pleasant custom of sending Christmas cards prevailed
in Tilling, and most of the world met in the stationer's shop on
Christmas Eve, selecting suitable salutations from the threepenny, the sixpenny and the shilling trays. Elizabeth came in
rather early and had almost completed her purchases when some
of her friends arrived, and she hung about looking at the backs
of volumes in the lending library, but keeping an eye on what
they purchased. Diva, she observed, selected nothing from the
shilling tray any more than she had herself; in fact, she thought
that Diva's purchases this year were made entirely from the
threepenny tray. Susan, on the other hand, ignored the threepenny tray and hovered between the sixpennies and the shillings and expressed an odiously opulent regret that there were
not some "choicer" cards to be obtained. The Padre and Mrs.
Bartlett were certainly exclusively threepenny, but that was
always the case. However they, like everybody else, studied the
other trays, so that when, next morning, they all received season-

able coloured greetings from their friends, a person must have a shocking memory if he did not know what had been the precise cost of all that were sent him. But Georgie and Lucia as was universally noticed, though without comment, had not been in at all, in spite of the fact that they had been seen about in the High Street together and going into other shops. Elizabeth therefore decided that they did not intend to send any Christmas cards and before paying for what she had chosen, she replaced in the threepenny tray a pretty picture of a robin sitting on a sprig of mistletoe which she had meant to send Georgie. There was no need to put back what she had chosen for Lucia, since the case did not arise.

Christmas Day dawned, a stormy morning with a strong gale from the south-west, and on Elizabeth's breakfast-table was a pile of letters, which she tore open. Most of them were threepenny Christmas cards, a sixpenny from Susan, smelling of musk, and none from Lucia or Georgie. She had anticipated that, and it was pleasant to think that she had put back into the threepenny tray the one she had selected for him, before purchasing it.

The rest of her post was bills, some of which must be stoutly disputed when Christmas was over, and she found it difficult to realise the jollity appropriate to the day. Last evening various choirs of amateur riff-raffs and shrill bobtails had rendered the night hideous by repetitions of "Good King Wenceslas" and "The First Noël," church-bells borne on squalls of wind and rain had awakened her while it was still dark and now sprigs of holly kept falling down from the picture-frames where Withers had perched them. Bacon made her feel rather better, and she went to church, with a mackintosh against these driving gusts of rain, and a slightly blue nose against this boisterous wind. Diva was coming to a dinner-lunch: this was an annual institution held at Wasters and Mallards alternately.

Elizabeth hurried out of church at the conclusion of the service by a side door, not feeling equal to joining in the gay group of her friends who with Lucia as their centre were gathered at the main entrance. The wind was stronger than ever, but the rain had ceased, and she battled her way round the square surrounding the church before she went home. Close to Mallards Cottage she met Georgie holding his hat on against the gale. He wished her a merry Christmas, but then his hat had been whisked off his head; something very strange happened to his hair, which seemed to have been blown off his skull, leaving a quite bare place there, and he vanished in frenzied pursuit of his hat with long tresses growing from the side of his head streaming in the wind. A violent draught eddying round the corner by the garden-room propelled her into Mallards holding on to the knocker, and it was with difficulty that she closed the door. On the table in the hall stood a substantial package, which had certainly not been there when she left. Within its wrappings was a *terrine* of *pâté de foie gras* with a most distinguished label on it, and a card fluttered on to the floor, proclaiming that wishes for a merry Christmas from Lucia and Georgie accompanied it. Elizabeth instantly conquered the feeble temptation of sending this gift back again in the manner in which she had returned that basket of tomatoes from her own garden. Tomatoes were not *pâté*. But what a treat for Diva!

Diva arrived, and they went straight in to the banquet. The *terrine* was wrapped in a napkin, and Withers handed it to Diva. She helped herself handsomely to the truffles and the liver.

"How delicious!" she said. "And such a monster!"

"I hope it's good," said Elizabeth, not mentioning the donors. "It ought to be. Paris."

Diva suddenly caught sight of a small label pasted below the distinguished one. It was that of the Tilling grocer, and a flood of light poured in upon her.

"Lucia and Mr. Georgie have sent such lovely Christmas presents to everybody," she said. "I felt quite ashamed of myself for only having given them threepenny cards."

"How sweet of them," said Elizabeth. "What were they?"

"A beautiful box of hard chocolates for me," said Diva. "And a great pot of caviare for Susan, and an umbrella for the Padre—his blew inside out in the wind yesterday—and—"

"And this beautiful *pâté* for me," interrupted Elizabeth, grasping the nettle, for it was obvious that Diva had guessed. "I was just going to tell you."

Diva knew that was a lie, but it was no use telling Elizabeth so, because she knew it too, and she tactfully changed the subject.

"I shall have to do my exercises three times today after such a lovely lunch," she said, as Elizabeth began slicing the turkey. But that was not a well-chosen topic, for subjects connected with Lucia might easily give rise to discord and she tried again and again and again, bumping, in her spinning-top manner, from one impediment to another.

"Major Benjy can play the scale of C with his right hand"—(No, that wouldn't do). "What an odd voice Susan's got: she sang an Italian song the other day at"—(Worse and worse). "I sent two pictures to the winter exhibition"—(Worse if possible: there seemed to be no safe topic under the sun). "A terrific gale, isn't it? There'll be three days of tremendous high tides for the wind is heaping them up. I should not wonder if the road by Grebe—" (she gave it up: it was no use) "—isn't flooded tomorrow."

Elizabeth behaved like a perfect lady. She saw that Diva was doing her best to keep off disagreeable subjects on Christmas Day, but there were really no others. All topics led to Lucia.

"I hope not," she said, "for with all the field-paths soaked from the rain it is my regular walk just now. But not very likely, dear, for after the last time that the road was flooded, they built the bank opposite—opposite that house much higher."

They talked for quite a long while about gales and tides and dykes in complete tranquillity. Then the proletarian diversions of Boxing Day seemed safe.

"There's a new film tomorrow at the Picture Palace about tadpoles," said Elizabeth. "So strange to think they become toads: or is it frogs? I think I must go."

"Lucia's giving a Christmas tree for the choirboys in the evening, in that great kitchen of hers," said Diva.

"How kind!" said Elizabeth hastily, to show she took no offence.

"And in the afternoon there's a whist drive at the Institute," said Diva. "I'm letting both my servants go, and Lucia's sending all hers too. I'm not sure I should like to be quite alone in a house along that lonely road. We in the town could scream from a top window if burglars got into our houses and raise the alarm."

"It would be a very horrid burglar who was so wicked on Boxing Day," observed Elizabeth sententiously. "Ah, here's the plum-pudding! Blazing beautifully, Withers! So pretty!"

Diva became justifiably somnolent when lunch was over, and after half an hour's careful conversation she went off home to have a nice long nap, which she expressed by the word exercises. Elizabeth wrote two notes of gratitude to the donors of the *pâté* and sat herself down to think seriously of what she could do. She had refused Lucia's invitation to tea a few days before, thus declaring her attitude, and now it seemed to her that that was a mistake, for she had cut herself off from the opportunities of reprisals which intercourse with her might have provided.

She had been unable, severed like this, to devise anything at all effective; all she could do was to lie awake at night hating Lucia, and this seemed to be quite barren of results. It might be better (though bitter) to join that callisthenic class in order to get a foot in the enemy's territory. Her note of thanks for the *pâté* would have paved the way towards such a step, and though it would certainly be eating humble pie to ask to join an affair that she had openly derided, it would be pie with a purpose. As it was, for a whole week she had had no opportunities, she had surrounded herself with a smoke-cloud, she heard nothing about Lucia any more, except when clumsy Diva let out things by accident. All she knew was that Lucia, busier than any bee known to science, was undoubtedly supreme in all the social activities which she herself had been accustomed to direct, and to remain, like Achilles in his tent, did not lead to anything. Also she had an idea that Tilling expected of her some exhibition of spirit and defiance, and no one was more anxious than she to fulfil those expectations to the utmost. So she settled she would go to Grebe tomorrow, and, after thanking her in person for the *pâté,* ask to join the callisthenic class. Tilling, and Lucia too, no doubt would take that as a sign of surrender, but let them wait a while, and they should see.

"I can't fight her unless I get in touch with her," reflected Elizabeth; "at least I don't see how, and I'm sure I've thought enough."

Chapter Ten

IN PURSUANCE OF THIS POLICY Elizabeth set out early in the afternoon next day to walk out to Grebe, and there eat pie with a purpose. The streets were full of holiday folk, and by the railings at the end of the High Street, where the steep steps went down to the levels below, there was a crowd of people looking at the immense expanse of water that lay spread over the marsh. The south-westerly gale had piled up the spring tides, the continuous rains had caused the river to come down in flood, and the meeting of the two, the tide now being at its height, formed a huge lake, a mile and more wide, which stretched seawards. The gale had now quite ceased, the sun shone brilliantly from the pale blue of the winter sky, and this enormous estuary sparkled in the gleam. Far away to the south a great bank of very thick vapour lay over the horizon, showing that out in the Channel there was thick fog, but over Tilling and the flooded marsh the heavens overhead were of a dazzling radiance.

Many of Elizabeth's friends were there, the Padre and his wife (who kept exclaiming in little squeaks, "Oh dear me, what a quantity of water!"), the Wyses who had dismounted from the Royce, which stood waiting, to look at the great sight, before they proceeded on their afternoon drive. Major Benjy was saying that it was nothing to the Jumna in flood, but then he always held up India as being far ahead of England in every way (he had even once said on an extremely frosty morning, that this was nothing to the bitterness of Bombay): Georgie was there and Diva. With them all Elizabeth exchanged the friendliest greetings, and afterwards, when the great catastrophe had happened, everyone agreed that they had never known her more cordial and pleasant, poor thing. She did not of course tell them what her errand was, for it would be rash to do that till she saw how Lucia received her, but merely said that she was going for her usual brisk walk on this lovely afternoon, and should probably pop into the Picture Palace to learn about tadpoles. With many flutterings of her hand and enough *au reservoir*s to provide water for the world, she tripped down the hill, through the Landgate, and out on to the road that led to Grebe and nowhere else particular.

She passed, as she neared Grebe, Lucia's four indoor servants and Cadman coming into the town, and, remembering that they were going to a whist drive at the Institute, wished them a merry Christmas and hoped that they would all win. (Little kindly remarks like that always pleased servants, thought Elizabeth; they showed a human sympathy with their pleasures, and cost nothing; so much better than Christmas boxes.) Her brisk pace made short work of the distance, and within quite a few minutes of her leaving her friends, she had come to the thick hornbeam hedge which shielded Grebe from the road. She stopped opposite it for a moment: there was that prodigious sheet of dazzling water now close to the top of the restraining bank to admire: there was herself to screw up to the humility required for asking Lucia if she might join her silly callisthenic class. Finally, coming from nowhere, there flashed into her mind the thought of lobster *à la Riseholme,* the recipe for which Lucia had so meanly withheld from her. Instantly that thought fructified into apples of Desire.

She gave one glance at the hornbeam hedge to make sure that she was not visible from the windows of Grebe. (Lucia used often to be seen spying from the windows of the garden-room during her tenancy of Mallards, and she might be doing the same thing here.) But the hedge was quite impenetrable to human eye, as Elizabeth had often regretfully observed already, and now instead of going in at the high wooden gate which led to the front door, she passed quickly along till she came to the far corner of the hedge bordering the kitchen garden. So swift was thought to a constructive mind like hers already stung with desire, that, brisk though was her physical movement, her mind easily out-stripped it, and her plan was laid before she got to the corner.

Viz.: The servants were all out—of that she had received ocu-lar evidence but a few moments before—and the kitchen would certainly be empty. She would therefore go round to the gate at the end of the kitchen garden and approach the house that way. The cinder path, used for the prancing of the callisthenic class in fine weather, led straight to the big coach-house doors of the kitchen, and she would ascertain by the simple device of trying the handle if these were unlocked. If they were locked, there was an end to her scheme, but if they were unlocked, she would qui-etly pop in, and see whether the cook's book of recipes was not somewhere about. If it was she would surely find in it the recipe for lobster *à la Riseholme*. A few minutes would suffice to copy it, and then tiptoeing out of the kitchen again, with the key to the mystery in her pocket, she would go round to the front door as cool as a cucumber, and ring the bell. Should Lucia (alone in the house and possibly practising for more po-di-mus) not hear the bell, she would simply postpone the eating of her humble pie till the next day. If, by ill chance, Lucia was in the garden and saw her approaching by this unusual route, nothing was easier than to explain that, returning from her walk, she thought she would look in to thank her for the *pâté* and ask if she might join her callisthenic class. Knowing that the servants were all out (she would glibly explain) she felt sure that the main gate on to the road would be locked, and therefore she tried the back way . . . The whole formation of the scheme was instantaneous; it was as if she had switched on the lights at the door of a long gallery, and found it lit from end to end.

Without hurrying at all she walked down the cinder path and tested the kitchen-door. It was unlocked, and she slipped in, closing it quietly behind her. In the centre of the kitchen, decked and ready for illumination, stood the Christmas tree designed for the delectation of the choirboys that evening, and the great kitchen table, with its broad skirting of board halfway down the legs, had been moved away and stood on its side against the dresser in order to give more room for the tree. Elizabeth hardly paused a second to admire the tapers, the reflecting glass balls, the bright tinselly decorations, for she saw a small shelf of books on the wall opposite, and swooped like a merlin on it. There were a few trashy novels, there was a hymn-book and a prayer-book, and there was a thick volume, with no title on the back, bound in American cloth. She opened it and saw at once that her claws had at last gripped the prey, for on one page was pasted a cutting from the daily press concerning *oeufs à l'aurore,* on the next was a recipe in manuscript for cheese straws. Rapidly she turned the leaves, and there manifest at last was the pearl of great price, lobster *à la Riseholme.* It began with the luscious words, "Take two hen lobsters."

Out came her pencil; that and a piece of paper in which had been wrapped a present for a choirboy was all she needed. In a couple of minutes she had copied out the mystic spell, replaced the sacred volume on its shelf, and put in her pocket the information for which she had pined so long. "How odd," she cynically reflected, "that only yesterday I should have said to Diva that it must be a very horrid burglar who was so wicked as to steal things on Boxing Day. Now I'll go round to the front door."

At the moment when this Mephistophelian thought came into her mind, she heard with a sudden stoppage of her heartbeat, a step on the crisp path outside, and the handle of the kitchen-door was turned. Elizabeth took one sideways stride behind the gaudy tree and, peering through its branches, saw Lucia standing at the entrance. Lucia came straight towards her, not yet perceiving that there was a Boxing Day burglar in her own kitchen, and stood admiring her tree. Then with a startled exclamation she called out, "Who's that?" and Elizabeth knew that she was discovered. Further dodging behind the decorated fir would be both undignified and ineffectual, however skilful her footwork.

"It's me, dear Lucia," she said. "I came to thank you in person for that delicious *pâté* and to ask if—"

From somewhere close outside there came a terrific roar and rush as of great water-floods released. Reunited for the moment by a startled curiosity, they ran together to the open door, and saw, already leaping across the road and over the hornbeam hedge, a solid wall of water.

"The bank has given way," cried Lucia. "Quick, into the house through the door in the kitchen, and up the stairs."

They fled back past the Christmas tree, and tried the door into the house. It was locked: the servants had evidently taken this precaution before going out on their pleasuring.

"We shall be drowned," wailed Elizabeth, as the flood came foaming into the kitchen.

"Rubbish," cried Lucia. "The kitchen table! We must turn it upside down and get on to it."

It was but the work of a moment to do this, for the table was already on its side, and the two stepped over the high boarding that ran round it. Would their weight be too great to allow it to float on the rushing water that now deepened rapidly in the kitchen? That anxiety was short-lived, for it rose free from the floor and bumped gently into the Christmas tree.

"We must get out of this," cried Lucia. "One doesn't know how much the water will rise. We may be drowned yet if the table-legs come against the ceiling. Catch hold of the dresser and pull."

But there was no need for such exertion, for the flood, eddying fiercely round the submerged kitchen, took them out of the doors that it had flung wide, and in a few minutes they were floating away over the garden and the hornbeam hedge. The tide had evidently begun to ebb before the bank gave way, and now the kitchen table, occasionally turning round in an eddy, moved off in the direction of Tilling and of the sea. Luckily it had not got into the main stream of the river but floated smoothly and swiftly along, with the tide and the torrent of the flood to carry it. Its two occupants, of course, had no control whatever over its direction, but soon, with an upspring of hope, they saw that the current was carrying it straight towards the steep slope above the Landgate, where not more than a quarter of an hour ago Elizabeth had interchanged greetings and *au reservoir*s with her friends who had been looking at the widespread waters. Little had she thought that so soon she would be involved in literal reservoirs of the most gigantic sort—but this was no time for light conceits.

The company of Tillingites was still there when the bank opposite Grebe gave way. All but Georgie had heard the rush and roar of the released waters, but his eyes were sharper than others, and he had been the first to see where the disaster had occurred.

"Look, the bank opposite Grebe has burst!" he cried. "The road's under water, her garden's under water: the rooms downstairs must be flooded. I hope Lucia's upstairs, or she'll get dreadfully wet."

"And that road is Elizabeth's favourite walk," cried Diva. "She'll be on it now."

"But she walks so fast," said the Padre, forgetting to speak Scotch. "She'll be past Grebe by now, and above where the bank has burst."

"Oh dear, oh dear, and on Boxing Day!" wailed Mrs. Bartlett.

The huge flood was fast advancing on the town, but with this outlet over the fields, it was evident that it would get no deeper at Grebe, and that, given Lucia was upstairs and that Elizabeth had walked as fast as usual, there was no real anxiety for them. All eyes now watched the progress of the water. It rose like a wave over a rock when it came to the railway line that crossed the marsh and in a couple of minutes more it was foaming over the fields immediately below the town.

Again Georgie uttered woe like Cassandra.

"There's something coming," he cried. "It looks like a raft with its legs in the air. And there are two people on it. Now it's spinning round and round; now it's coming straight here ever so fast. There are two women, one without a hat. It's Them! It's Lucia and Miss Mapp! What *has* happened?"

The raft, with legs sometimes madly waltzing, sometimes floating smoothly along, was borne swiftly towards the bottom of the cliff, below which the flood was pouring by. The Padre, with his new umbrella, ran down the steps that led to the road below in order to hook it in, if it approached within umbrella-distance. On and on it came, now clearly recognisable as Lucia's great kitchen table upside down, until it was within a yard or two of the bank. To attempt to wade out to it, for any effective purpose, was useless: the strongest would be swept away in such a headlong torrent, and even if he reached the raft there would be three helpless people on it instead of two and it would probably sink. To hook it with the umbrella was the only chance, for there was no time to get a boat hook or a rope to throw out to the passengers. The Padre made a desperate lunge at it, slipped and fell flat into the water, and was only saved from being carried away by clutching at the iron railing alongside the lowest of the submerged steps. Then some fresh current tweaked the table and, still moving in the general direction of the flood water, it sheered off across the fields. As it receded Lucia showed the real stuff of which she was made. She waved her hand and her clear voice rang out gaily across the waste of water.

"*Au reservoir,* all of you," she cried. "We'll come back: just wait till we come back," and she was seen to put her arm round the huddled form of Mapp, and comfort her.

The kitchen table was observed by the watchers to get into the main channel of the river, where the water was swifter yet. It twirled round once or twice as if waving a farewell, and then shot off towards the sea and that great bank of thick mist which hung over the horizon.

There was not yet any reason to despair. A telephone-message was instantly sent to the fishermen at the port, another to the coastguards, another to the lifeboat, that a kitchen table with a cargo of ladies on it was coming rapidly down the river, and no effort must be spared to arrest its passage out to sea. But, one after the other, as the short winter afternoon waned, came discouraging messages from the coast. The flood had swept from their moorings all the fishing boats anchored at the port or drawn up on the shore above high-water mark, and a coastguardsman had seen an unintelligible object go swiftly past the mouth of the river before the telephone-message was received. He could not distinguish what it was, for the fog out in the Channel had spread to the coastline, and it had seemed to him more like the heads and necks of four sea-serpents playing together than anything else. But when interrogated as to whether it might be the legs of a kitchen table upside down he acknowledged that the short glimpse which he obtained of it before it got lost in the fog would suit a kitchen table as well as sea-serpents. He had said sea-serpents because it was in the sea, but it was just as like the legs of a kitchen table, which had never occurred to him as possible. His missus had just such a kitchen table—but as he seemed to be diverging into domestic reminiscences, the Mayor of Tilling, who himself conducted enquiries instead of opening the whist drive at the Institute with a short speech on the sin of gambling, cut him off. It was only too clear that this imaginative naturalist had seen—too late—the kitchen table going out to sea.

The lifeboat had instantly responded to the SOS call on its services, and the great torrent of the flood having now gone by, the crew had been able to launch the boat and had set off to search the English Channel, in the blinding fog, for the table. The tide was setting west down the coast, the flood pouring out from the river mouth was discharged east, but they had gone off to row about in every direction, where the kitchen table might have been carried. Rockets had been sent up from the station in case the ladies didn't know where they were. That, so the Mayor reflected, might conceivably show the ladies where they were, but it didn't really enable them to get anywhere else.

Dusk drew on and the friends of the missing went back to their respective houses, for there was no good in standing about in this dreadful cold fog which had now crept up from the marsh.

Pneumonia wouldn't help matters. Four of them, Georgie and Major Benjy and Diva and quaint Irene, lived solitary and celibate, and the prospect of a lonely evening with only suspense and faint hopes to feed upon was perfectly ghastly. In consequence, when each of them in turn was rung up by Mr. Wyse, who hoped, in a broken voice, that he might find them disengaged and willing to come round to his house for supper (not dinner), they all gladly accepted. Mr. Wyse requested them not to dress as for dinner, and this was felt to show a great delicacy: not dressing would be a sort of symbol of their common anxiety. Supper would be at half-past eight, and Mr. Wyse trusted that there would be encouraging news before that hour.

The Padre and Mrs. Bartlett had been bidden as well, so that there was a supper party of eight. Supper began with the most delicious caviare, and on the black oak mantelpiece were two threepenny Christmas cards. Susan helped herself plentifully to the caviare. There was no use in not eating.

"Dear Lucia's Christmas present to me," she said. "Hers and yours I should say, Mr. Georgie."

"Lucia sent me a wonderful box of nougat chocolates," said Diva. "She and you, I mean, Mr. Georgie."

Major Benjy audibly gulped.

"Mrs. Lucia," he said, "if I may call her so, sent me half a dozen bottles of pre-war whisky."

The Padre had pulled himself together by this time, and spoke Scotch.

"I had a wee mischance wi' my umbrella two days agone," he said, "and Mistress Lucia, such a menseful woman, sent me a new one. An' now that's gone bobbin' out to sea."

"You're too pessimistic, Kenneth," said Mrs. Bartlett. "An umbrella soon gets waterlogged and sinks, I tell you. The chances are it will be picked up in the marsh tomorrow, and it'll find its way back to you, for there's that beautiful silver band on the handle with your name engraved on it."

"Eh, 'twould be a bonnie thing to recover it," said her husband.

Mr. Wyse thought that the conversation was getting a little too much concerned with minor matters; the recovery of an umbrella, though new, was a loss that might be lamented later. Besides, the other missing lady had not been mentioned yet. He pointed to the two threepenny Christmas cards on the mantel-piece.

"Our friend Elizabeth Mapp sent those to my wife and me yesterday," he said. "We shall keep them always among our most cherished possessions in case—I mean in any case. Pretty designs. Roofs covered with snow. Holly. Robins. She had a very fine artistic taste. Her pictures had always something striking and original about them."

Everybody cudgelled their brains for something appropri-ate to say about Elizabeth's connection with Art. The effort was quite hopeless, for her ignoble trick in rejecting Lucia's and Georgie's pictures for the last exhibition, and the rejection by the new committee of her own for the forthcoming exhibition were all that could occur to the most nimble brain, and while the artist was in direst peril on the sea, or possibly now at rest beneath it, it would be in the worst taste to recall those discordant incidents. A very long pause of silence followed, broken only by the crash-ing of toast in the mouths of those who had not yet finished their caviare.

Irene had eaten no caviare, nor hitherto had she contrib-uted anything to the conversation. Now she suddenly burst into shrieks of hysterical laughter and sobs.

"What rubbish you're all talking," she cried, wiping her eyes. "How can you be so silly? I'm sure I beg your pardons, but there it is. I'll go home, please."

She fled from the room and banged the front door so loudly that the house shook, and one of Miss Mapp's cards fell into the fireplace.

"Poor thing. Very excitable and uncontrolled," said Susan. "But I think she's better alone."

There was a general feeling of relief that Irene had gone, and as Mrs. Wyse's excellent supper progressed, with its cold turkey and its fried slices of plum-pudding, its toasted cheese and its figs stuffed with almonds sent by Amelia from Capri, the general numbness caused by the catastrophe began to pass off. Consumed with anxiety as all were for the two (especially one of them) who had vanished into the Channel fogs on so unusual a vehicle, they could not fail to recognise what problems of unparalleled perplexity and interest were involved in what all still hoped might not turn out to be a tragedy. But whether it proved so or not, the whole manner of these happenings, the cause, the conditions, the circumstances which led to the two unhappy ladies whisking by on the flood must be discussed, and presently Major Benjy broke into this unnatural reticence.

"I've seen many floods on the Jumna," he said, refilling his glass of port, "but I never saw one so sudden and so—so fraught with enigmas. They must have been in the kitchen. Now we all know there was a Christmas tree there—"

A conversational flood equal to the largest ever seen on the Jumna was unloosed; a torrent of conjectures, and reconstruction after reconstruction of what could have occurred to produce what they had all seen, was examined and rejected as containing some inherent impossibility. And then what did the gallant

Lucia's final words mean, when she said, "Just wait till we come back"? By now discussion had become absolutely untrammelled, the rivalry between the two, Miss Mapp's tricks and pointless meannesses, Lucia's scornful victories, and, no less, her domineering ways were openly alluded to.

"But 'Just wait till we come back' is what we're talking about," cried Diva. "We must keep to the point, Major Benjy. I believe she simply meant 'Don't give up hope. We *shall* come back.' And I'm sure they will."

"No, there's more in it than that," said Georgie, interrupting. "I know Lucia better than any of you. She meant that she had something frightfully interesting to tell us when she did come back, as of course she will, and I'd bet it was something about Elizabeth. Some new thing she'd found her out in."

"But at such a solemn moment," said the Padre, again forgetting his pseudo-Highland origin, "when they were being whirled out to sea with death staring them in the face, I hardly think that such trivialities as those which had undoubtedly before caused between those dear ladies the frictions which we all deplored—"

"Nonsense, Kenneth," said his wife, rather to his relief, for he did not know how he was to get out of this sentence, "you enjoyed those rows as much as anybody."

"I don't agree with you, Padre," said Georgie. "To begin with, I'm sure Lucia didn't think she was facing death and even if she did, she'd still have been terribly interested in life till she went phut."

"Thank God I live on a hill," exclaimed Major Benjy, thinking, as usual, of himself.

Mr. Wyse held up his hand. As he was the host, it was only kind to give him a chance, for he had had none as yet. "Your pardon," he said, "if I may venture to suggest what may combine the ideas of our reverend friend and of Mr. Pillson"—he made them two bows—"I think Mrs. Lucas felt she was facing death—who wouldn't?—but she was of that vital quality which never gives up interest in life, until, in fact (which we trust with her is not the case), all is over. But like a true Christian, she was, as we all saw, employed in comforting the weak. She could not have been using her last moments, which we hope are nothing of the sort, better. And if there had been frictions, they arose only from the contact of two highly vitalised—"

"She kissed Elizabeth too," cried Mrs. Bartlett. "I saw her. She hasn't done that for ages. Fancy!"

"I want to get back to the kitchen," said Diva. "What could have taken Elizabeth to the kitchen? I've got a brilliant idea, though I don't know what you'll think of it. She knew Lucia was giving a Christmas tree to the choirboys, because I told her so yesterday—"

"I wonder what's happened to that," said the Padre. "If it wasn't carried away by the flood, and I think we should have seen it go by, it might be dried."

Diva, as usual when interrupted, had held her mouth open, and went straight on.

"—and she knew the servants were out, because I'd told her that too, and she very likely wanted to see the Christmas tree. So I suggest that she went round the back way into the kitchen—that would be extremely like her, you know—in order to have a look at it, without asking a favour of—"

"Well, I do call that clever," interrupted Georgie admiringly. "Go on. What happened next?"

Diva had not got further than that yet, but now a blinding brilliance illuminated her and she clapped her hands.

"I see, I see," she cried. "In she went into the kitchen and while she was looking at it, Lucia came in too, and then the flood came in too. All three of them. That would explain what was behind her words, 'Just wait till we come back.' She meant that she wanted to tell us that she'd found Elizabeth in her kitchen."

It was universally felt that Diva had hit it, and after such a stroke of reconstructive genius, any further discussion must be bathos. Instantly a sad reaction set in, and they all looked at each other much shocked to find how wildly interested they had become in these trivial affairs, while their two friends were, to put the most hopeful view of the case, on a kitchen table somewhere in the English Channel. But still Lucia had said that she and her companion were coming back, and though no news had arrived of the castaways, every one of her friends, at the bottom of their hearts, felt that these were not idle words, and that they must keep alive their confidence in Lucia. Miss Mapp alone would certainly have been drowned long ago, but Lucia, whose power of resource all knew to be unlimited, was with her. No one could suggest what she could possibly do in such difficult circumstances, but never yet had she been floored, nor failed to emerge triumphant from the most menacing situations.

Mrs. Wyse's cuckoo clock struck the portentous hour of one o'clock. They all sighed, they all got up, they all said good-night with melancholy faces, and groped their ways home in the cold fog. Above Georgie's head as he turned the corner by Mallards there loomed the gable of the garden-room, where so often a chink of welcoming light had shone between the curtains, as the sound of Mozartino came from within. Dark and full of suspense as was the present, he could still, without the sense of something forever past from his life, imagine himself sitting at the piano again with Lucia, waiting for her *Uno, due, TRE* as they tried over for the first time the secretly familiar duets.

The whole of the next day this thick fog continued both on land and water, but no news came from seawards save the bleating and hooting of fog-horns, and as the hours passed, anxiety grew more acute. Mrs. Wyse opened the picture exhibition on behalf of Lucia, for it was felt that in any case she would have wished that, but owing to the extreme inclemency of the weather only Mr. Wyse and Georgie attended this inaugural ceremony. Mrs. Wyse in the lamented absence of the authoress read Lucia's lecture on modern art from the typewritten copy which she had sent Georgie to look through and criticise. It lasted an hour and twenty minutes, and after Georgie's applause had died away at the end, Mr. Wyse read the speech he had composed to propose a vote of thanks to Lucia for her most enthralling address. This also was rather long, but written in the most classical and urbane style. Georgie seconded this in a shorter speech, and Mrs. Wyse (*vice* Lucia) read another longer speech of Lucia's which was appended in manuscript to her lecture, in which she thanked them for thanking her, and told them how diffident she had felt in thus appearing before them. There was more applause, and then the three of them wandered round the room and peered at each other's pictures through the dense fog. Evening drew in again, without news, and Tilling began to fear the worst.

Next morning there came a mute and terrible message from the sea. The fog had cleared, the day was of crystalline brightness, and since air and exercise would be desirable after sitting at home all the day before, and drinking that wonderful pre-war whisky, Major Benjy set off by the eleven o'clock tram to play a round of golf with the Padre. Though hope was fast expiring, neither of them said anything definitely indicating that they no longer really expected to see their friends again, but there had been talk indirectly bearing on the catastrophe; the Major had asked casually whether Mallards was a freehold, and the Padre replied that both it and Grebe were the property of their occupiers and not held on lease; he also made a distant allusion to memorial services, saying he had been to one lately, very affecting. Then Major Benjy lost his temper with the caddie, and their game assumed a more normal aspect.

They had now come to the eighth hole, the tee of which was perched high like a pulpit on the sand-dunes and overlooked the sea. The match was most exciting: hole after hole had been halved in brilliant sixes and sevens, the players were both on the top of their form, and in their keenness had quite banished from their minds the overshadowing anxiety. Here Major Benjy topped his ball into a clump of bents immediately in front of the tee, and when he had finished swearing at his caddie for moving on the stroke, the Padre put his iron shot on to the green.

"A glorious day," he exclaimed, and, turning to pick up his clubs, gazed out seawards. The tide was low, and an immense stretch of "shining sands" as in Charles Kingsley's poem was spread in front of him. Then he gave a gasp.

"What's that?" he said to Major Benjy, pointing with a shaking finger.

"Good God," said Major Benjy. "Pick up my ball, caddie." They scrambled down the steep dunes and walked across the sands to where lay this object which had attracted the Padre's attention. It was an immense kitchen table upside down with its legs in the air, wet with brine but still in perfect condition. Without doubt it was the one which they had seen two days before whirling out to sea. But now it was by itself, no ladies were sitting upon it. The Padre bared his head.

"Shall we abandon our game, Major?" he said. "We had better telephone from the clubhouse to the Mayor. And I must arrange to get some men to bring the table back. It's far too heavy for us to think of moving it."

∞

The news that the table had come ashore spread swiftly through Tilling, and Georgie, hearing that the Padre had directed that when it had passed the Custom House it should be brought to the Vicarage, went round there at once. It seemed almost unfeeling in this first shock of bereavement to think about tables, but it would save a great deal of bother afterwards to see to this now. The table surely belonged to Grebe.

"I quite understand your point of view," he said to the Padre, "and of course what is found on the seashore in a general way belongs to the finder, if it's a few oranges in a basket, because nobody knows who the real owner is. But we all know, at least we're afraid we do, where this came from."

The Padre was quite reasonable.

"You mean it ought to go back to Grebe," he said. "Yes, I agree. Ah, I see it has arrived."

They went out into the street, where a trolley, bearing the table, had just drawn up. Then a difficulty arose. It was late, and the bearers demurred to taking it all the way out to Grebe tonight and carrying it through the garden.

"Move it in here then for the night," said the Padre. "You can get it through the back-yard and into the outhouse."

Georgie felt himself bound to object to this: the table belonged to Grebe, and it looked as if Grebe, alas, belonged to him.

"I think it had better come to Mallards Cottage," said he firmly. "It's only just round the corner, and it can stand in my yard."

The Padre was quite willing that it should go back to Grebe, but why should Georgie claim this object with all the painful interest attached to it? After all, he had found it.

"And so I don't quite see why you should have it," he said a little stiffly.

Georgie took him aside.

"It's dreadful to talk about it so soon," he said, "but that is what I should like done with it. You see Lucia left me Grebe and all its contents. I still cling—can't help it—to the hope that neither it nor they may ever be mine, but in the interval which may elapse—"

"No! Really!" said the Padre with a sudden thrill of Tillingite interest which it was no use trying to suppress. "I congrat— Well, well. Of course the kitchen table is yours. Very proper."

The trolley started again and by dint of wheedlings and cunning coaxings the sad substantial relic was induced to enter the back-yard of Mallards Cottage. Here for the present it would have to remain, but pickled as it was with long immersion in sea water, the open air could not possibly hurt it, and if it rained, so much the better, for it would wash the salt out.

Georgie, very tired and haggard with these harrowing arrangements, had a little rest on his sofa, when he had seen the table safely bestowed. His cook gave him a succulent and most nutritious dinner by way of showing her sympathy, and Foljambe waited on him with peculiar attention, constantly holding a pocket-handkerchief to the end of her nose, by way of expressing her own grief. Afterwards he moved to his sitting-room and took up his needlework, that "sad narcotic exercise," and looked his loss in the face.

Indeed, it was difficult to imagine what life would be like without Lucia, but there was no need to imagine it, for he was experiencing it already. There was nothing to look forward to, and he realised how completely Lucia and her manoeuvres and her indomitable vitality and her deceptions and her greatnesses had supplied the salt to life. He had never been in the least in love with her, but somehow she had been as absorbing as any wayward and entrancing mistress. "It will be too dull for anything," thought he, "and there won't be a single day in which I shan't miss her most dreadfully. It's always been like that: when she was away from Riseholme, I never seemed to care to paint or to play, except because I should show her what I had done when she came back, and now she'll never come back."

He abandoned himself for quite a long time to despair with regard to what life would hold for him. Nobody else, not even Foljambe, seemed to matter at all. But then through the black, deep waters of his tribulation there began to appear little bubbles on the surface. It was like comparing a firefly with the huge night itself to weigh them against this all-encompassing darkness, but where for a moment each pricked the surface there was, it was idle to deny, just a spark that stood out momentarily against the blackness. The table, for instance: he would have a tablet fixed on to it, with a suitable inscription to record the tragic role it had played, a text, so to speak, as on a cenotaph. How would Lucia's last words do? "Just wait till we come back." But if this was a memorial table, it must record that Lucia was not coming back.

He fetched a writing-pad and began again. "This is the table—" but that wouldn't do. It suggested "This is the house that Jack built." Then, "It was upon this table on Boxing Day afternoon, 1930, that Mrs. Emmeline Lucas, of Grebe, and Miss Elizabeth Mapp, of Mallards—" that was too prolix. Then, "In memory of Emmeline Lucas and Elizabeth Mapp. They went to sea—" but that sounded like a nursery rhyme by Edward Lear, or it might suggest to future generations that they were sailors. Then he wondered if poetry would supply anything, and the lines, "And may there be no sadness of farewell, when I embark," occurred to him. But that wouldn't do: people would wonder why she had embarked on a kitchen table, and even now, when the event was so lamentably recent, nobody actually knew.

"I hadn't any idea," thought Georgie, "how difficult it is to write a few well-chosen and heart-felt words. I shall go and look at the tombstones in the churchyard tomorrow. Lucia would have thought of something perfect at once."

Tiny as were these bubbles and others (larger ones) which Georgie refused to look at directly, they made a momentary, an evanescent brightness. Some of them made quite loud pops as they burst, and some presented problems. This catastrophe had conveyed a solemn warning against living in a house so low-lying, and Major Benjy had already expressed that sentiment when he gave vent to that self-centred *cri du coeur*, "Thank God I live on a hill," but for Georgie that question would soon become a practical one, though he would not attempt to make up his mind yet. It would be absurd to have two houses in Tilling, to be the tenant of Mallards Cottage, and the owner of Grebe. Or should he live in Grebe during the summer, when there was no fear of floods, and Mallards Cottage in the winter?

He got into bed: the sympathetic Foljambe, before going home, had made a beautiful fire, and his hot-water bottle was of such a temperature that he could not put his feet on it at all . . . If he lived at Grebe she would only have to go back across the garden to her Cadman, if Cadman remained in his service. Then there was Lucia's big car. He supposed that would be included in the contents of Grebe. Then he must remember to put a black bow on Lucia's picture in the Art Exhibition. Then he got sleepy . . .

Chapter Eleven

THOUGH GEORGIE HAD THOUGHT THAT there would be nothing interesting left in life now that Lucia was gone, and though Tilling generally was conscious that the termination of the late rivalries would take all thrill out of existence as well as eclipsing its gaieties most dreadfully, it proved one morning when the sad days had begun to add themselves into weeks, that there was a great deal for him to do, as well as a great deal for Tilling to talk about. Lucia had employed a local lawyer over the making of her will, and today Mr. Causton (*re* the affairs of Mrs. Emmeline Lucas) came to see Georgie about it. He explained to him with a manner subtly compounded of sympathy and congratulation that the little sum of money to which Lucia had alluded was no less than £80,000. Georgie was, in fact, apart from certain legacies, her heir. He was much moved.

"Too kind of her," he said. "I had no idea—"

Mr. Causton went on with great delicacy.

"It will be some months," he said, "before in the absence of fresh evidence, the death of my client can be legally assumed—"

"Oh, the longer, the better," said Georgie rather vaguely, wiping his eyes, "but what do you mean about fresh evidence?"

"The recovery, by washing ashore or other identification, of the lamented corpses," said Mr. Causton. "In the interval the— the possibly late Mrs. Lucas has left no provision for the contingency we have to face. If and when her death is proved, the staff of servants will receive their wages up to date and a month's notice. Until then the estate, I take it, will be liable for the out-goings and the upkeep of Grebe. I would see to all that, but I felt that I must get your authority first."

"Of course, naturally," said Georgie.

"But here a difficulty arises," said Mr. Causton. "I have no authority for drawing on the late—or, we hope, the present Mrs. Lucas's balance at the bank. There is, you see, no fund out of which the current expenses of the upkeep of the house can be paid. There is more than a month's food and wages for her ser-vants already owing."

George's face changed a little. A very little.

"I had better pay them myself," he said. "Would not that be the proper course?"

"I think, under the circumstances, that it would," said Mr. Causton. "In fact, I don't see what else is to be done, unless all the servants were discharged at once, and the house shut up."

"No, that would never do," said Georgie. "I must go down there and arrange about it all. If Mrs. Lucas returns, how horrid for her to find all her servants who had been with her so long, gone. Everything must carry on as if she had only gone for a visit somewhere and forgotten to send a cheque for expenses."

Here then, at any rate, was something to do already, and Georgie, thinking that he would like a little walk on this brisk morning, and also feeling sure that he would like a little conver-sation with friends in the High Street, put on his thinner cape, for a hint of spring was in the air, and there were snowdrops a-bloom in the flower-border of his little garden. Lucia, he remembered, always detested snowdrops: they hung their heads and were fee-ble; they typified for her slack though amiable inefficiency. In order to traverse the whole length of the High Street and get as many conversations as possible he went down by Mallards and Major Benjy's house. The latter, from the window of his study, where he so often enjoyed a rest or a little refreshment before and after his game of golf, saw him pass, and beckoned him in.

"Good-morning, old boy," he said. "I've had a tremendous slice of luck: at least that is not quite the way to put it, but what I mean is— In fact, I've just had a visit from the solicitor of our lamented friend Elizabeth Mapp, God bless her, and he told me the most surprising news. I was monstrously touched by it: hadn't a notion of it, I assure you."

"You don't mean to say—" began Georgie.

"Yes I do. He informed me of the provisions of that dear woman's will. In memory of our long friendship, these were the very words—and I assure you I was not ashamed to turn away and wipe my eyes, when he told me—in memory of our long friendship she has left me that beautiful Mallards and the sum of ten thousand pounds, which I understand was the bulk of her fortune. What do you think of that?" he asked, allowing his exultation to get the better of him for the moment.

"No!" said Georgie, "I congratulate—at least in case—"

"I know," said Major Benjy. "If it turns out to be too true that our friends have gone for ever, you're friendly enough to be glad that what I've told you is too true, too. Eh?"

"Quite, and I've had a visit from Mr. Causton," said Georgie, unable to contain himself any longer, "and Lucia's left me Grebe and eighty thousand pounds."

"My word! What a monstrous fortune," cried the Major with a spasm of chagrin. "I congrat— Anyhow, the same to you. I shall get a motor instead of going to my golf on that measly tram. Then there's Mallards for me to arrange about. I'm thinking of letting it furnished, servants and all. It'll be snapped up at ten guineas a week. Why, she got fifteen last summer from the other poor corpse."

"I wouldn't," said Georgie. "Supposing she came back and found she couldn't get into her house for another month because you had let it?"

"God grant she may come back," said the Major, without falling dead on the spot. "But I see your point: it would be awkward. I'll think it over. Anyhow, of course, after a proper interval, when the tragedy is proved, I shall go and live there myself. Till then I shall certainly pay the servants' wages and the upkeep. Rather a drain, but it can't be helped. Board wages of twelve shillings a week is what I shall give them: they'll live like fighting cocks on that. By jove, when I think of that terrible sight of the kitchen table lying out there on the beach, it causes me such a sinking still. Have a drink: wonderful pre-war whisky."

Georgie had not yet visited Grebe, and he found a thrilling though melancholy interest in seeing the starting-point of the catastrophe. The Christmas tree, he ascertained, had stuck in the door of the kitchen, and the Padre had already been down to look at it, but had decided that the damage to it was irreparable. It was lying now in the garden from which soil and plants had been swept away by the flood, but Georgie could not bear to see it there, and directed that it should be put up, as a relic, in an empty outhouse. Perhaps a tablet on that as well as on the table. Then he had to interview Grosvenor, and make out a schedule of the servants' wages, the total of which rather astonished him. He saw the cook and told her that he had the kitchen table in his yard, but she begged him not to send it back, as it had always been most inconvenient. Mrs. Lucas, she told him, had had a feeling for it; she thought there was luck about it. Then she burst into tears and said it hadn't brought her mistress much luck after all. This was all dreadfully affecting, and Georgie told her that in this period of waiting during which they must not give up hope, all their wages would be paid as usual, and they must carry on as before, and keep the house in order. Then there were some unpaid bills of Lucia's, a rather appalling total, which must be discharged before long, and the kitchen must be renovated from the effects of the flood. It was after dark when he got back to Mallards Cottage again.

In the absence of what Mr. Causton called further evidence in the way of corpses, and of alibis in the way of living human bodies, the Padre settled in the course of the next week to hold a memorial service, for unless one was held soon, they would all have got used to the bereavement, and the service would lose point and poignancy. It was obviously suitable that Major Benjy and Georgie, being the contingent heirs of the defunct ladies, should sit by themselves in a front pew as chief mourners, and Major Benjy ordered a black suit to be made for him without delay for use on this solemn occasion. The church-bell was tolled as if for a funeral service, and the two walked in side by side after the rest of the congregation had assembled, and took their places in a pew by themselves immediately in front of the reading-desk.

The service was of the usual character, and the Padre gave a most touching address on the text "They were lovely and pleasant in their lives and in their death they were not divided." He reminded his hearers how the two whom they mourned were as sisters, taking the lead in social activities, and dispensing to all who knew them their bountiful hospitalities. Their lives had been full of lovable energy. They had been at the forefront in all artistic and literary pursuits: indeed he might almost have taken the whole of the verse of which he had read them only the half as his text, and have added that they were swifter than eagles, they were stronger than lions. One of them had been known to them all for many years, and the name of Elizabeth Mapp was written on their hearts. The other was a newer comer, but she had wonderfully endeared herself to them in her briefer sojourn here, and it was typical of her beautiful nature that on the very day on which the disaster occurred, she had been busy with a Christmas tree for the choristers in whom she took so profound an interest.

As regards the last sad scene, he need not say much about it, for never would any of them forget that touching, that ennobling, that teaching sight of the two, gallant in the face of death as they had ever been in that of life, being whirled out to sea. Mrs. Lucas in the ordeal which they would all have to face one day, giving that humorous greeting of hers, *"au reservoir,"* which they all knew so well, to her friends standing in safety on the shore, and then turning again to her womanly work of comforting and encouraging her weaker sister. "May we all," said the Padre, with a voice trembling with emotion, "go to meet death in that serene and untroubled spirit, doing our duty to the last. And now—"

This sermon, at the request of a few friends, he had printed in the Parish Magazine next week, and copies were sent to everybody.

∞

It was only natural that Tilling should feel relieved when the ceremony was over, for the weeks since the stranding of the kitchen table had been like the period between a death and a funeral. The blinds were up again now, and life gradually resumed a more normal complexion. January ebbed away into February, February into March, and as the days lengthened with the returning sun, so the mirths and squabbles of Tilling grew longer and brighter.

But a certain stimulus which had enlivened them all since Lucia's advent from Riseholme was lacking. It was not wholly that there was no Lucia, nor, wholly, that there was no Elizabeth, it was the intense reactions which they had produced together that everyone missed so fearfully. Day after day those who were left met and talked in the High Street, but never was there news of that thrilling kind which since the summer had keyed existence up to so exciting a level. But it was interesting to see Major Benjy in his new motor, which he drove himself, and watch his hairbreadth escapes from collisions at sharp corners and to hear the appalling explosions of military language if any other vehicle came within a yard of his green bonnet.

"He seems to think," said Diva to Mrs. Bartlett, as they met on shopping errands one morning, "that now he has got a motor nobody else may use the road at all."

"A trumpery little car," said Mrs. Bartlett, "I should have thought, with ten thousand pounds as good as in his pocket, he might have got himself something better."

They were standing at the corner looking up towards Mallards, and Diva suddenly caught sight of a board on Major Benjy's house, announcing that it was for sale.

"Why, whatever's that?" she cried. "That must have been put up only today. Good-morning, Mr. Georgie. What about Major Benjy's house?"

Georgie still wore a broad black band on his sleeve.

"Yes, he told me yesterday that he was going to move into Mallards next week," he said. "And he's going to have a sale of his furniture almost immediately."

"That won't be much to write home about," said Diva scornfully. "A few moth-eaten tiger-skins which he said he shot in India."

"I think he wants some money," said Georgie. "He's bought

a motor, you see, and he has to keep up Mallards as well as his own house."

"I call that very rash," said Mrs. Bartlett. "I call that counting your chickens before they're hatched. Oh dear me, what a thing to have said! Dreadful!"

Georgie tactfully covered this up by a change of subject.

"I've made up my mind," he said, "and I'm going to put up a cenotaph in the churchyard to dear Lucia and Elizabeth."

"What? Both?" asked Diva.

"Yes, I've thought it carefully over, and it's going to be both."

"Major Benjy ought to go halves with you then," said Diva.

"Well, I told him I was intending to do it," said Georgie, "and he didn't catch on. He only said 'Capital idea,' and took some whisky and soda. So I shan't say any more. I would really just as soon do it all myself."

"Well, I do think that's mean of him," said Diva. "He ought anyhow to bear some part of the expense, considering everything. Instead of which he buys a motor car which he can't drive. Go on about the cenotaph."

"I saw it down at the stonemason's yard," said Georgie, "and that put the idea into my head. Beautiful white marble on the lines, though of course much smaller, of the one in London. It had been ordered, I found, as a tombstone, but then the man who ordered it went bankrupt, and it was on the stonemason's hands."

"I've heard about it," said Mrs. Bartlett, in rather a superior voice. "Kenneth told me you'd told him, and we both think that it's a lovely idea."

"The stonemason ought to let you have it cheap then," said Diva.

"It wasn't very cheap," said Georgie, "but I've bought it, and they'll put it in its place today, just outside the south transept, and the Padre is going to dedicate it. Then there's the inscription. I shall have in loving memory of them, by me, and a bit of the Padre's text at the memorial service. Just 'In death they were not divided.'"

"Quite right. Don't put in about the eagles and the lions," said Diva.

"No, I thought I would leave that out. Though I like that part," said Georgie for the sake of Mrs. Bartlett.

"Talking of whisky," said Diva, flying back, as her manner was, to a remote allusion, "Major Benjy's finished all the pre-war whisky that Lucia gave him. At least I heard him ordering some more yesterday. Oh, and there's the notice of his sale. Old English furniture—yes, that may mean two things, and I know which of them it is. Valuable works of Art. Well I never! A print of the 'Monarch of the Glen' and a photograph of the 'Soul's Awakening.' Rubbish! Fine tiger-skins! The skins may be all right, but they're bald."

"My dear, how severe you are," said Georgie. "Now I must go and see how they're getting on with the inscription. *Au reservoir.*"

Diva nodded at Evie Bartlett.

"Nice to hear that again," she said. "I've not heard it—well, since."

The cenotaph with its inscription in bold leaded letters to say that Georgie had erected it in memory of the two undivided ladies, roused much admiration, and a full-page reproduction of it appeared in the Parish Magazine for April, which appeared on the last day of March. The stonecutter had slightly miscalculated the space at his disposal for the inscription, and the words "Elizabeth Mapp" were considerably smaller than the words "Emmeline Lucas" in order to get them into the line. Though Tilling said nothing about that, it was felt that the error was productive of a very suitable effect, if a symbolic meaning was interpreted into it. Georgie was considered to have done it very handsomely and to be behaving in a way that contrasted most favourably with the conduct of Major Benjy, for whereas Georgie was keeping up Grebe at great expense, and restoring, all at his own charge, the havoc the flood had wrought in the garden, Major Benjy, after unsuccessfully trying to let Mallards at ten guineas a week, had moved into the house, and, with a precipitation that was as rash as it was indelicate, was already negotiating about the disposal of his own, and was to have a sale of his furniture on April the first. He had bought a motor, he had replenished the cellars of Mallards with strong wines and more pre-war whisky, he was spending money like water and on the evening of this last day of March he gave a bridge party in the garden-room.

Georgie and Diva and Mrs. Padre were the guests at this party: there had been dinner first, a rich elaborate dinner, and bridge afterwards up till midnight. It had been an uncomfortable evening, and before it was over they all wished they had not come, for Major Benjy had alluded to it as a house-warming, which showed that either his memory was going, or that his was a very callous nature, for no one whose perceptions were not of the commonest could possibly have used that word so soon. He had spoken of his benefactress with fulsome warmth, but it was painfully evident from what source this posthumous affection sprang. He thought of having the garden-room redecorated, the house wanted brightening up a bit, he even offered each of them one of Miss Mapp's watercolour sketches, of which was a profusion on the walls, as a memento of their friend, God bless her . . . There he was straddling in the doorway with the air of a vulgar *nouveau riche* owner of an ancestral property, as they went their ways homeward into the night, and they heard him bolt and lock the door and put up the chain which Lucia in her tenancy had had repaired in order to keep out the uninvited and informal visits of Miss Mapp. "It would serve him jolly well right," thought Georgie, "if she came back."

Chapter Twelve

IT WAS A CALM AND BEAUTIFUL NIGHT with a high tide that overflowed the channel of the river. There was spread a great sheet of moonlit water over the submerged meadows at the margin, and it came up to the foot of the rebuilt bank opposite Grebe. Between four and five of the morning of April the first, a trawler entered the mouth of the river, and just at the time when the stars were growing pale and the sky growing red with the coming dawn, it drew up at the little quay to the east of the town, and was moored to the shore. There stepped out of it two figures clad in overalls and tarpaulin jackets.

"I think we had better go straight to Mallards, dear," said Elizabeth, "as it's so close, and have a nice cup of tea to warm ourselves. Then you can telephone from there to Grebe, and tell them to send the motor up for you."

"I shall ring up Georgie too," said Lucia. "I can't bear to think that his suspense should last a minute more than is necessary."

Elizabeth pointed upwards.

"See, there's the sun catching the top of the church tower," she said. "Little did I think I should ever see dear Tilling again."

"I never had the slightest doubt about it," said Lucia. "Look, there are the fields we floated across on the kitchen table. I wonder what happened to it."

They climbed the steps at the south-east angle of the town, and up the slope to the path across the churchyard. This path led close by the south side of the church, and the white marble of the cenotaph gleamed in the early sunlight.

"What a handsome tomb," said Elizabeth. "It's quite new. But how does it come here? No one has been buried in the churchyard for a hundred years."

Lucia gave a gasp as the polished lead letters caught her eye.

"But it's us!" she said.

They stood side by side in their tarpaulins, and together in a sort of chant read the inscription aloud.

THIS STONE WAS ERECTED BY
GEORGE PILLSON
IN LOVING MEMORY OF
EMMELINE LUCAS and ELIZABETH MAPP
LOST AT SEA ON BOXING DAY, 1930
"IN DEATH THEY WERE NOT DIVIDED"

"I've never heard of such a thing," cried Lucia. "I call it most premature of Georgie, assuming that I was dead like that. The inscription must be removed instantly. All the same it was kind of him and what a lot of money it must have cost him! Gracious me, I suppose he thought— Let us hurry, Elizabeth."

Elizabeth was still staring at the stone.

"I am puzzled to know why my name is put in such exceedingly small letters," she said acidly. "You can hardly read it. As you say, dear, it was most premature of him. I should call it impertinent, and I'm very glad dear Major Benjy had nothing to do with it. There's an indelicacy about it."

They went quickly on past Mallards Cottage where the blinds

were still down, and there was the window of the garden-room from which each had made so many thrilling observations, and the red-brick front, glowing in the sunlight, of Mallards itself. As they crossed the cobbled way to the front door, Elizabeth looked down towards the High Street and saw on Major Benjy's house next door the house-agents' board announcing that the freehold of this desirable residence was for disposal. There were bills pasted on the walls announcing the sale of furniture to take place there that very day.

Her face turned white, and she laid a quaking hand on Lucia's arm.

"Look, Major Benjy's house is for sale," she faltered. "Oh, Lucia, what has happened? Have we come back from the dead, as it were, to find that it's our dear old friend instead? And to think—" She could not complete the sentence.

"My dear, you mustn't jump at any such terrible conclusions," said Lucia. "He may have changed his house—"

Elizabeth shook her head; she was determined to believe the worst, and indeed it seemed most unlikely that Major Benjy who had lived in the same house for a full quarter of a century could have gone to any new abode but one. Meantime, eager to put an end to this suspense, Elizabeth kept pressing the bell and Lucia plying the knocker of Mallards.

"They all sleep on the attic floor," said Elizabeth, "but I think they must hear us soon if we go on. Ah, there's a step on the stairs. Someone is coming down."

They heard the numerous bolts on the door shot back, they heard the rattle of the released chain. The door was opened and there within stood Major Benjy. He had put on his dinner jacket over his Jaeger pyjamas, and had carpet slippers on his feet. He was sleepy and bristly and very cross.

"Now what's all this about, my men," he said, seeing two tar-paulined figures on the threshold. "What do you mean by waking me up with that infernal—"

Elizabeth's suspense was quite over.

"You wretch," she cried in a fury. "What do *you* mean? Why are you in my house? Ah, I guess! He! He! He! You learned about my will, did you? You thought you wouldn't wait to step into a dead woman's shoes, but positively tear them off my living feet. My will shall be revoked this day: I promise you that . . . Now out you go, you horrid supplanter! Off to your own house with you, for you shan't spend another minute in mine."

During this impassioned address Major Benjy's face changed to an expression of the blankest dismay, as if he had seen something much worse (as indeed he had) than a ghost. He pulled pieces of himself together.

"But, my dear Miss Elizabeth," he said. "You'll allow me surely to get my clothes on, and above all to say one word of my deep thankfulness that you and Mrs. Lucas—it is Mrs. Lucas, isn't it?—"

"Get out!" said Elizabeth, stamping her foot. "Thankfulness indeed! There's a lot of thankfulness in your face! Go away! Shoo!"

Major Benjy had faced wounded tigers (so he said) in India, but then he had a rifle in his hand. He could not face his benefactress, and, with first one slipper and then the other dropping off his feet, he hurried down the few yards of pavement to his own house. The two ladies entered: Elizabeth banged the door and put up the chain.

"So that's that," she observed (and undoubtedly it was). "Ah, here's Withers. Withers, we've come back, and though you ought never to have let the Major set foot in my house, I don't blame you, for I feel sure he bullied you into it."

"Oh, miss!" said Withers. "Is it you? Fancy! Well, that is a surprise!"

"Now get Mrs. Lucas and me a cup of tea," said Elizabeth, "and then she's going back to Grebe. That wretch hasn't been sleeping in my room, I trust?"

"No, in the best spare bedroom," said Withers.

"Then get my room ready, and I shall go to bed for a few hours. We've been up all night. Then, Withers, take all Major Benjy's clothes and his horrid pipes, and all that belongs to him, and put them on the steps outside. Ring him up, and tell him where he will find them. But not one foot shall he set in *my* house again."

Lucia went to the telephone and rang up Cadman's cottage for her motor. She heard his exclamation of "My Gawd," she heard (what she supposed was) Foljambe's cry of astonishment, and then she rang up Georgie. He and his household were all a-bed and asleep when the telephone began its summons, but presently the persistent tinkle penetrated into his consciousness, and made him dream that he was again watching Lucia whirling down the flood on the kitchen table and ringing an enormous dinner-bell as she swept by the steps. Then he became completely awake and knew it was only the telephone.

"The tarsome thing!" he muttered. "Who on earth can it be ringing one up at this time? Go on ringing then till you're tired. I shall go to sleep again."

In spite of these resolutions, he did nothing of the kind. So ceaseless was the summons that in a minute or two he got out of bed, and putting on his striped dressing-gown (blue and yellow) went down to his sitting-room.

"Yes. Who is it? What do you want?" he said crossly.

There came a little merry laugh, and then a voice, which he had thought was silent for ever, spoke in unmistakable accents.

"Georgie! *Georgino mio!*" it said.

His heart stood still. "What? What?" he cried.

"Yes, it's Lucia," said the voice. "Me's tum home, Georgie."

Eighty thousand pounds (less death duties) and Grebe seemed to sweep by him like an avalanche, and fall into the gulf of the things that might have been. But it was not the cold blast of that ruin that filled his eyes with tears.

"Oh my dear!" he cried. "Is it really you? Lucia, where are you? Where are you talking from?"

"Mallards. Elizabeth and I—"

"What, both of you?" called Georgie. "Then—where's Major Benjy?"

"Just gone home," said Lucia discreetly. "And as soon as I've had a cup of tea I'm going to Grebe."

"But I must come round and see you at once," said Georgie. "I'll just put some things on."

"Yes, do," said Lucia. "*Presto, presto,* Georgie."

Careless of his reputation for being the best-dressed man in Tilling, he put on his dress trousers and a pullover, and his thick brown cape, and did not bother about his *toupée.* The front door of Mallards was open, and Elizabeth's servants were laying out on the top step a curious collection of golf clubs and tooth-brushes and clothes. From mere habit—everyone in Tilling had the habit—he looked up at the window of the garden-room as he passed below it, and was astonished to see two mariners in sou'wester caps and tarpaulin jackets kissing their hands to him. He had only just time to wonder who these could possibly be when he guessed. He flew into Lucia's arms, then wondered if he ought to kiss Elizabeth too. But there was a slight reserve about her which caused him to refrain. He was not brilliant enough at so early an hour to guess that she had seen the smaller lettering in which her loving memory was recorded.

There was but time for a few ejaculations and a promise from Georgie to dine at Grebe that night, before Lucia's motor arrived, and the imperturbable Cadman touched his cap and said to Lucia, "Very pleased to see you back, ma'am," as she picked her way between the growing deposits of socks and other more intimate articles of male attire which were now being ranged on the front steps. Georgie hurried back to Mallards Cottage to dress in a manner more worthy of his reputation, and Elizabeth up to her bedroom for a few hours' sleep. Below her oilskins she still wore the ragged remains of the clothes in which she had left Tilling on Boxing Day, and now she drew out of the pocket of her frayed and sea-stained jacket, a half-sheet of discoloured paper. She unfolded it and having once more read the mystic words "Take two hen lobsters," she stowed it safely away for future use.

Meantime Major Benjy next door had been the prey of the most sickening reflections; whichever way he turned, fate gave him some stinging blow that set him staggering and reeling in another direction. Leaning out of an upper window of his own house, he observed his clothes and boots and articles of toilet being laid out like a bird's breakfast on the steps of Mallards, and essaying to grind his teeth with rage he discovered that his upper dental plate must still be reposing in a glass of water in the best spare bedroom which he had lately quitted in such haste. To recover his personal property was the first necessity, and when from his point of observation he saw that the collection had grown to a substantial size, he crept up the pavement, seized a bundle of miscellaneous articles, as many as he could carry, then stole back again, dropping a nailbrush here and a sock-suspender there, and dumped them in his house. Three times he must go on these degrading errands, before he had cleared all the bird's breakfast away; indeed he was an early bird feeding on the worms of affliction.

Tilling was beginning to awake now: the milkman came clattering down the street and, looking in amazement at his dishevelled figure, asked whether he wanted his morning supply left at his own house or at Mallards: Major Benjy turned on him so appalling a face that he left no milk at either and turned swiftly into the less alarming air of Porpoise Street. Again he had to make the passage of his Via Dolorosa to glean the objects which had dropped from his overburdened arms, and as he returned he heard a bumping noise behind him, and saw his new portmanteau hauled out by Withers rolling down the steps into the street. He emerged again when Withers had shut the door, put more gleanings into it and pulled it into his house. There he made a swift and sorry toilet, for there was business to be done which would not brook delay. Already the preparations for the sale of his furniture were almost finished; the carpet and hearthrug in his sitting-room were tied up together and labelled Lot 1; the fire-irons and a fishing-rod and a rhinoceros-hide whip were Lot 2; a kitchen tray with packs of cards, a tobacco jar, a piece of chipped *cloisonné* ware and a roll of toilet paper formed an unappetising Lot 3. The sale must be stopped at once and he went down to the auctioneer's in the High Street and informed him that owing to circumstances over which he had no control he was compelled to cancel it. It was pointed out to him that considerable expense had already been incurred for the printing and display of the bills that announced it, for the advertisements in the local press, for the time and trouble already spent in arranging and marking the lots, but the Major bawled out: "Damn it all, the things are mine and I won't sell one of them. Send me in your bill." Then he had to go to the house-agents' and tell them to withdraw his house from the market and take down his board, and coming out of the office he ran into Irene, already on her way to Grebe, who cried out: "They've come back, old Benjy-wenjy. Joy! Joy!"

The most immediate need of having a roof over his head and a chair to sit on was now provided for, and as he had already dismissed his own servants, taking those of Mallards, he must go to another agency to find some sort of cook or charwoman till he could get his establishment together again. They promised to send an elderly lady, highly respectable though rather deaf and weak in the legs, tomorrow if possible. Back he came to his house with such cold comfort to cheer him, and observed on the steps of Mallards half a dozen bottles of wine. "My God, my cellar," muttered the Major, "there are dozens and dozens of my wine and my whisky in the house!" Again he crept up to the abhorred door and, returning with the bottles, put a kettle on to boil, and began cutting the strings that held the lots together. Just then the church-bells burst out into a joyful peal, and it was not difficult to conjecture the reason for their unseemly mirth. All this before breakfast . . .

A cup of hot strong tea without any milk restored not only his physical stability but also his mental capacity for suffering, and he sat down to think. There was the financial side of the disaster first of all, a thing ghastly to contemplate. He had bought (but not yet paid for) a motor, some dozens of wine, a suit of new clothes, as well as the mourning habiliments in which he had attended the memorial service, quantities of stationery with the Mallards stamp on it, a box of cigars and other luxuries too numerous to mention. It was little comfort to remember that he had refused to contribute to the cenotaph; a small saving like that did not seem to signify. Then what view, he wondered, would his benefactress, when she knew all, take of his occupation of Mallards? She might find out (indeed being who she was, she would not fail to do so) that he had tried to let it at ten guineas a week and she might therefore send him in a bill on that scale for the fortnight he had spent there, together with that for her servants' wages, and for garden-produce and use of her piano. Luckily he had only eaten some beetroot out of the garden, and he had had the piano tuned. But of all these staggering expenses, the only items which were possibly recoverable were the wages he had paid to the staff of Mallards between Boxing Day and the date of his tenancy: these Elizabeth might consent to set against the debits. Not less hideous than this financial *débâcle* that stared him in the face, was the loss of prestige in Tilling. Tilling, he knew, had disapproved of his precipitancy in entering into Mallards, and Tilling, full, like Irene, of joy, joy for the return of the lost, would simply hoot with laughter at him. He could visualise with awful clearness the chatting groups in the High Street which would vainly endeavour to suppress their smiles as he approached. The day of swank was past and done, he would have to be quiet and humble and grateful to anybody who treated him with the respect to which he had been accustomed.

He unrolled a tiger-skin to lay down again in his hall: a cloud of dust and deciduous hair rose from it, pungent like snuff, and the remaining glass eye fell out of the socket. He bawled "*Quai-hai*" before he remembered that till tomorrow at least he would be alone in the house, and that even then his attendant would be deaf. He opened his front door and looked out into the street again, and there on the doorstep of Mallards was another dozen or so of wine and a walking-stick. Again he stole out to recover his property with the hideous sense that perhaps Elizabeth was watching him from the garden-room. His dental plate—thank God—was there too on the second step, all by itself, gleaming in the sun, and seeming to grin at him in a very mocking manner. After that throughout the morning he looked out at intervals as he rested from the awful labour of laying carpets and putting beds together, and there were usually some more bottles waiting for him, with stray golf clubs, bridge-markers and packs of cards. About one o'clock just as he was collecting what must surely be the last of these bird-breakfasts, the door of Mallards opened and Elizabeth stepped carefully over his umbrella and a box of cigars. She did not appear to see him. It seemed highly probable that she was going to revoke her will.

Georgie, as well as Major Benjy, had to do a little thinking, when he returned from his visit at dawn to Mallards. It concerned two points, the cenotaph and the kitchen table. The cenotaph had not been mentioned in those few joyful ejaculations he had exchanged with Lucia, and he hoped that the ladies had not seen it. So after breakfast he went down to the stone-mason's and begged him to send a trolley and a hefty lot of men up to the churchyard at once, and remove the monument to the back-yard of Mallards Cottage, which at present was chiefly occupied by the kitchen table under a tarpaulin. But Mr. Marble (such was his appropriate name) shook his head over this: the cenotaph had been dedicated, and he felt sure that a faculty must be procured before it could be removed. That would never do: Georgie could not wait for a faculty, whatever that was, and he ordered that the inscription, anyhow, should be effaced without delay: surely no faculty was needed to destroy all traces of a lie. Mr. Marble must send some men up to chip, and chip and chip for all they were worth till those beautiful lead letters were detached and the surface of the stone cleared of all that erroneous information.

"And then I'll tell you what," said Georgie, with a sudden splendid thought, "why not paint on to it (I can't afford any more cutting) the inscription that was to have been put on it when that man went bankrupt and I bought the monument instead? He'll get his monument for nothing, and I shall get rid of mine, which is just what I want . . . That's beautiful. Now you must send a trolley to my house and take a very big kitchen table, *the* one in fact, back to Grebe. It must go in through the door of the kitchen garden and be put quietly into the kitchen. And I particularly want it done today."

All went well with these thoughtful plans. Georgie saw with his own eyes the last word of his inscription disappear in chips of marble; and he carried away all the lead letters in case they might come in useful for something, though he could not have said what: perhaps he would have "Mallards Cottage" let into the threshold of his house for that long inscription would surely contain the necessary letters. Rather a pretty and original idea. Then he ascertained that the kitchen table had been restored to its place while Lucia slept, and he drove down at dinner-time feeling that he had done his best. He wore his white waistcoat with onyx buttons for the happy occasion.

Lucia was looking exceedingly well and much sunburnt. By way of resting she had written a larger number of postcards to all her friends, both here and elsewhere, than Georgie had ever seen together in one place.

"Georgino," she cried. "There's so much to say that I hardly know where to begin. I think my adventures first, quite shortly, for I shall dictate a full account of them to my secretary, and have a party next week for all Tilling, and read them out to you. Two parties, I expect, for I don't think I shall be able to read it all in one evening. Now we go back to Boxing Day.

"I went into the kitchen that afternoon," she said as they sat down to dinner, "and there was Elizabeth. I asked her—naturally, don't you think?—why she was there, and she said, 'I came to thank you for that delicious *pâté*, and to ask if—' That was as far as she got—I must return to that later—when the bank burst with a frightful roar, and the flood poured in. I was quite calm. We got on to, I should really say into the table— By the way, was the table ever washed up?"

"Yes," said Georgie, "it's in your kitchen now. I sent it back."

"Thank you, my dear. We got into the kitchen table, really a perfect boat, I can't think why they don't make more like it, flew by the steps—oh, did the Padre catch a dreadful cold? Such a splash it was, and that was the only drop of water that we shipped at all."

"No, but he lost his umbrella, the one you'd given him," said Georgie, "and the Padre of the Roman Catholic church found it, a week afterwards, and returned it to him. Wasn't that a coincidence? Go on. Oh no, wait a minute. What did you mean by calling out 'Just wait till we get back'?"

"Why of course I wanted to tell you that I had found Elizabeth in my kitchen," said Lucia.

"Hurrah! I guessed you meant something of the kind," said Georgie.

"Well, out we went—I've never been so fast in a kitchen table before—out to sea in a blinding sea-fog. My dear; poor Elizabeth! No nerve of any kind! I told her that if we were rescued, there was nothing to cry about, and if we weren't all our troubles would soon be over."

Grosvenor had put some fish before Lucia. She gave an awful shudder.

"Oh, take it away," she said. "Never let me see fish again, particularly cod, as long as I live. Tell the cook. You'll see why presently, Georgie. Elizabeth got hysterical and said she wasn't fit to die, so I scolded her—the best plan always with hysterical people—and told her that the longer she lived, the less fit she would be, and that did her a little good. Then it got dark, and there were fog-horns hooting all round us, and we called and yelled, but they had much more powerful voices than we, and nobody heard us. One of them grew louder and louder, until I could hardly bear it, and then we bumped quite gently into it, the fog-horn's boat I mean."

"Gracious, you might have upset," said Georgie.

"No, it was like a liner coming up to the quay," said Lucia. "No shock of any kind. Then when the fog-horn stopped, they heard us shouting, and took us aboard. It was an Italian trawler on its way to the cod-fishery (that's why I never want to see cod again) on the Gallagher Banks."

"That was lucky too," said Georgie, "you could make them understand a little. Better than if they had been Spanish."

"About the same, because I'm convinced, as I told Elizabeth, that they talked a very queer Neapolitan dialect. It was rather unlucky, in fact. But as the Captain understood English perfectly, it didn't matter. They were most polite, but they couldn't put us ashore, for we were miles out in the Channel by this time, and also quite lost. They hadn't an idea where the coast of England or any other coast was."

"Wireless?" suggested Georgie.

"It had been completely smashed up by the dreadful gale the day before. We drifted about in the fog for two days, and when it cleared and they could take the sun again—a nautical expression, Georgie—we were somewhere off the coast of Devonshire. The Captain promised to hail any passing vessel bound for

England that he saw, but he didn't see any. So he continued his course to the Gallagher Banks, which is about as far from Ireland as it is from America, and there we were for two months. Cod, cod, cod, nothing but cod, and Elizabeth snoring all night in the cabin we shared together. Bitterly cold very often: how glad I was that I knew so many callisthenic exercises! I shall tell you all about that time at my lecture. Then we found that there was a Tilling trawler on the bank, and when it was ready to start home we transshipped—they call it—and got back, as you know, this morning. That's the skeleton."

"It's the most wonderful skeleton I ever heard," said Georgie. "Do write your lecture quick."

Lucia fixed Georgie with her gimlet-eye. It had lost none of its penetrative power by being so long at sea.

"Now it's your turn for a little," she said. "I expect I know rather more than you think. First about that memorial service."

"Oh, do you know about that?" he asked.

"Certainly. I found the copy of the Parish Magazine waiting for me, and read it in bed. I consider it to have been very premature. You attended it, I think."

"We all did," said Georgie. "And after all, the Padre said extremely nice things about you."

"I felt very much flattered. But all the same it was too early. And you and Major Benjy were chief mourners."

Georgie considered for a moment.

"I'm going to make a clean breast of it," he said. "You told me you had left me Grebe, and a small sum of money, and your lawyer told me what that meant. My dear, I was too touched, and naturally, it was proper that I should be chief mourner. It was the same with Major Benjy. He had seen Elizabeth's will, so there we were."

Suddenly an irresistible curiosity seized him.

"Major Benjy hasn't been seen all day," he said. "Do tell me what happened this morning at Mallards. You only said on the telephone that he had just gone home."

"Yes, bag and baggage," said Lucia. "At least he went first and his bag and baggage followed. Socks and things, you saw some of them on the top step. Elizabeth was mad with rage, a perfect fishwife. So suitable after coming back from the Gallagher Banks. But tell me more. What was the next thing after the memorial service?"

The hope of keeping the knowledge of the cenotaph from Lucia became very dim. If Lucia had seen the February number of the Parish Magazine she had probably also seen the April number in which appeared the full-page reproduction of that monument. Besides, there was the gimlet-eye.

"The next thing was that I put up a beautiful cenotaph to you and Elizabeth," said Georgie firmly. " 'In loving memory of by me.' But I've had the inscription erased today."

Lucia laid her hand on his.

"Dear Georgie, I'm glad you told me," she said. "As a matter of fact I knew, because Elizabeth and I studied it this morning. I was vexed at first, but now I think it's rather dear of you. It must have cost a lot of money."

"It did," said Georgie. "And what did Elizabeth think about it?"

"Merely furious because her name was in smaller letters than mine," said Lucia. "So like the poor thing."

"Was she terribly tarsome all these months?" asked Georgie.

"Tiresome's not quite the word," said Lucia judicially. "Deficient rather than tiresome, except incidentally. She had no idea of the tremendous opportunities she was getting. She never rose to her chances, nor forgot our little discomforts and that everlasting smell of fish. Whereas I learned such lots of things, Georgie: the Italian for starboard and port—those are the right and left sides of the ship—and how to tie an anchor-knot and a running noose, and a clove-hitch, and how to splice two ends of fishing-line together, and all sorts of things of the most curious and interesting kind. I shall show you some of them at my lecture. I used to go about the deck barefoot (Lucia had very pretty feet) and pull on anchors and capstans and things, and managed never to tumble out of my berth on to the floor when the ship was rolling frightfully, and not to be seasick. But poor Elizabeth was always bumping on to the floor, and sometimes being sick there. She had no spirit. Little moans and sighs and regrets that she ever came down the Tilling hill on Boxing Day."

Lucia leaned forward and regarded Georgie steadfastly.

"I couldn't fathom her simply because she was so superficial," she said. "But I feel sure that there was something on her mind all the time. She used often to seem to be screwing herself up to confess something to me, and then not to be able to get it out. No courage. And though I can make no guess as to what it actually was, I believe I know its general nature."

"How thrilling!" cried Georgie. "Tell me!"

Lucia's eye ceased to bore, and became of far-off focus, keen still but speculative, as if she was Einstein concentrating on some cosmic deduction.

"Georgie, why did she come into my kitchen like a burglar on Boxing Day?" she asked. "She told me she had come to thank me for that *pâté* I sent her. But that wasn't true: anyone could see that it wasn't. Nobody goes into kitchens to thank people for *pâtés*."

"Diva guessed that she had gone there to see the Christmas

tree," said Georgie. "You weren't on very good terms at the time. We all thought that brilliant of her."

"Then why shouldn't she have said so?" asked Lucia. "I believe it was something much meaner and more underhand than that. And I am convinced—I have those perceptions sometimes, as you know very well—that all through the months of our Odyssey she wanted to tell me why she was there, and was ashamed of doing so. Naturally I never asked her, because if she didn't choose to tell me, it would be beneath me to force a confidence. There we were together on the Gallagher Banks, she all to bits all the time, and I should have scorned myself for attempting to worm it out of her. But the more I think of it, Georgie, the more convinced I am, that what she had to tell me and couldn't, concerned that. After all, I had unmasked every single plot she made against me before, and I knew the worst of her up till that moment. She had something on her mind, and that something was why she was in my kitchen."

Lucia's faraway prophetic aspect cleared.

"I shall find out all right," she said. "Poor Elizabeth will betray herself some time. But, Georgie, how in those weeks I missed my music! Not a piano on board any of the trawlers assembled there! Just a few concertinas and otherwise nothing except cod. Let us go, in a minute, into my music-room and have some Mozartino again. But first I want to say one thing."

Georgie took a rapid survey of all he had done in his conviction that Lucia had long ago been drowned. But if she knew about the memorial service and the cenotaph there could be nothing more except the kitchen table, and that was now in its place again. She knew all that mattered. Lucia began to speak baby-talk.

"Georgie," she said. " 'Oo have had dweffel disappointy—"

That was too much. Georgie thumped the table quite hard.

"I haven't," he cried. "How dare you say that?"

"Ickle joke, Georgie," piped Lucia. "Haven't had joke for so long with that melancholy Liblib. 'Pologise. 'Oo not angry wif Lucia?"

"No, but don't do it again," said Georgie. "I won't have it."

"You shan't then," said Lucia, relapsing into the vernacular of adults. "Now all this house is spick and span, and Grosvenor tells me you've been paying all their wages, week by week."

"Naturally," said Georgie.

"It was very dear and thoughtful of you. You saw that my house was ready to welcome my return, and you must send me in all the bills and everything tomorrow and I'll pay them at once, and I thank you enormously for your care of it. And send me in the bill for the cenotaph too. I want to pay for it, I do indeed. It was a loving impulse of yours, Georgie, though, thank goodness, a hasty one. But I can't bear to think that you're out of pocket because I'm alive. Don't answer: I shan't listen. And now let's go straight to the piano and have one of our duets, the one we played last, that heavenly Mozartino."

They went into the next room. There was the duet ready on the piano, which much looked as if Lucia had been at it already, and she slid on to the top music-stool.

"We both come in on the third beat," said she. "Are you ready? Now! *Uno, due, TRE!*"

Chapter Thirteen

THE WRETCHED MAJOR BENJY, who had not been out all day except for interviews with agents and miserable traverses between his house and the doorsteps of Mallards, dined alone that night (if you could call it dinner) on a pork pie and a bottle of Burgundy. A day's hard work had restored the lots of his abandoned sale to their proper places, and a little glue had restored its eye to the bald tiger. He felt worse than bald himself, he felt flayed, and God above alone knew what fresh skinnings were in store for him. All Tilling must have had its telephone-bells (as well as the church-bells) ringing from morning till night with messages of congratulation and suitable acknowledgements between the returned ladies and their friends, and he had never felt so much like a pariah before. Diva had just passed his windows (clearly visible in the lamplight, for he had not put up the curtains of his snuggery yet) and he had heard her knock on the door of Mallards. She must have gone to dine with the fatal Elizabeth, and what were they talking about now? Too well he knew, for he knew Elizabeth.

If in spirit he could have been present in the dining-room, where only last night he had so sumptuously entertained Diva and Georgie and Mrs. Bartlett, and had bidden them punish the port, he would not have felt much more cheerful.

"In my best spare room, Diva, would you believe it?" said

Elizabeth, "with all the drawers full of socks and shirts and false teeth, wasn't it so, Withers? and the cellar full of wine. What he has consumed of my things, goodness only knows. There was that *pâté* which Lucia gave me only the day before we were whisked out to sea—"

"But that was three months ago," said Diva.

"—and he used my coal and my electric light as if they were his own, not to mention firing," said Elizabeth, going on exactly where she had left off, "and a whole row of beetroot."

Diva was bursting to hear the story of the voyage. She knew that Georgie was dining with Lucia, and he would be telling everybody about it tomorrow, but if only Elizabeth would leave the beetroot alone and speak of the other she herself would be another focus of information instead of being obliged to listen to Georgie.

"Dear Elizabeth," she said, "what does a bit of beetroot matter compared to what you've been through? When an old friend like you has had such marvellous experiences as I'm sure you must have, nothing else counts. Of course I'm sorry about your beetroot: most annoying, but I do want to hear about your adventures."

"You'll hear all about them soon," said Elizabeth, "for tomorrow I'm going to begin a full history of it all. Then, as soon as it's finished, I shall have a big tea-party, and instead of bridge afterwards I shall read it to you. That's absolutely confidential, Diva. Don't say a word about it, or Lucia may steal my idea or do it first."

"Not a word," said Diva. "But surely you can tell me some bits."

"Yes, there is a certain amount which I shan't mention publicly," Elizabeth said. "Things about Lucia which I should never dream of stating openly."

"Those are just the ones I should like to hear about most," said Diva. "Just a few little titbits."

Elizabeth reflected a moment.

"I don't want to be hard on her," she said, "for after all we were together, and what would have happened if I had not been there, I can't think. A little off her head perhaps with panic: that is the most charitable explanation. As we swept by the town on our way out to sea she shrieked out—'*Au reservoir:* just wait till we come back.' Diva, I am not easily shocked, but I must say I was appalled. Death stared us in the face and all she could do was to make jokes! There was I sitting quiet and calm, preparing myself to meet the solemn moment as a Christian should, with this screaming hyena for my companion. Then out we went to sea, in that blinding fog, tossing and pitching on the waves, till we went crash into the side of a ship which was invisible in the darkness."

"How awful!" said Diva. "I wonder you didn't upset."

"Certainly it was miraculous," said Elizabeth. "We were battered about, the blows against the table were awful, and if I hadn't kept my head and clung on to the ship's side, we must have upset. They had heard our calls by then, and I sprang on to the rope-ladder they put down, without a moment's pause, so as to lighten the table for Lucia, and then she came up too."

Elizabeth paused a moment.

"Diva, you will bear me witness that I always said, in spite of Amelia Faraglione, that Lucia didn't know a word of Italian, and it was proved I was right. It was an Italian boat, and our great Italian scholar was absolutely flummoxed, and the Captain had to talk to us in English. There!"

"Go on," said Diva breathlessly.

"The ship was a fishing trawler bound for the Gallagher Banks, and we were there for two months, and then we found another trawler on its way home to Tilling, and it was from that we landed this morning. But I shan't tell you of our life and adventures, for I'm reserving that for my reading to you."

"No, never mind then," said Diva. "Tell me intimate things about Lucia."

Elizabeth sighed.

"We mustn't judge anybody," she said, "and I won't: but oh, the nature that revealed itself! The Italians were a set of coarse, lascivious men of the lowest type, and Lucia positively revelled in their society. Every day she used to walk about the deck, often with bare feet, and skip and do her callisthenics, and learn a few words of Italian; she sat with this one or that, with her fingers actually entwined with his, while he pretended to teach her to tie a knot or a clove-hitch or something that probably had an improper meaning as well. Such flirtation (at her age too), such promiscuousness, I have never seen. But I don't judge her, and I beg you won't."

"But didn't you speak to her about it?" asked Diva.

"I used to try to screw myself up to it," said Elizabeth, "but her lightness positively repelled me. We shared a cabin about as big as a dog kennel, and oh, the sleepless nights when I used to be thrown from the shelf where I lay! Even then she wanted to instruct me, and show me how to wedge myself in. Always that dreadful superior attitude, that mania to teach everybody everything except Italian, which we have so often deplored. But that was nothing. It was her levity from the time when the flood poured into the kitchen at Grebe—"

"Do tell me about that," cried Diva. "That's almost the most interesting thing of all. Why had she taken you into the kitchen?"

Elizabeth laughed.

"Dear thing!" she said. "What a lovely appetite you have for details! You might as well expect me to remember what I had for breakfast that morning. She and I had both gone into the kitchen; there we were, and we were looking at the Christmas tree. Such a tawdry tinselly tree! Rather like her. Then the flood poured in, and I saw that our only chance was to embark on the kitchen table. By the way, was it ever washed up?"

"Oh yes, without a scratch on it," said Diva, thinking of the battering it was supposed to have undergone against the side of the trawler . . .

Elizabeth had evidently not reckoned on its having come ashore, and rose.

"I am surprised that it didn't go to bits," she said. "But let us go into the garden-room. We must really talk about that wretched sponger next door. Is it true he's bought a motor car out of the money he hoped my death would bring him? And all that wine: bottles and bottles, so Withers told me. Oceans of champagne. How is he to pay for it all now with his miserable little income on which he used to pinch and scrape along before?"

"That's what nobody knows," said Diva. "An awful crash for him. So rash and hasty, as we all felt."

They settled themselves comfortably by the fire, after Elizabeth had had one peep between the curtains.

"I'm not the least sorry for having been a little severe with him this morning," she said. "Any woman would have done the same."

Withers entered with a note. Elizabeth glanced at the handwriting, and turned pale beneath the tan acquired on the codbanks.

"From him," she said. "No answer, Withers."

"Shall I read it?" said Elizabeth, when Withers had left the room, "or throw it, as it deserves, straight into the fire."

"Oh, read it," said Diva, longing to know what was in it. "You must see what he has to say for himself."

Elizabeth adjusted her pince-nez and read it in silence.

"Poor wretch," she said. "But very proper as far as it goes. Shall I read it you?"

"Do, do, do," said Diva.

Elizabeth read:

"MY DEAR MISS ELIZABETH (if you will still permit me
to call you so)—"

"Very proper," said Diva.

"Don't interrupt, dear, or I shan't read it," said Elizabeth.

"—call you so. I want first of all to congratulate you with all my heart on your return after adventures and privations which I know you bore with Christian courage.

Secondly I want to tender you my most humble apologies for my atrocious conduct in your absence, which was unworthy of a soldier and Christian, and, in spite of all, a gentleman. Your forgiveness, should you be so gracious as to extend it to me, will much mitigate my present situation.

Most sincerely yours (if you will allow me to say so),
BENJAMIN FLINT."

"I call that very nice," said Diva. "He didn't find that easy to write!"

"And I don't find it very easy to forgive him," retorted Elizabeth.

"Elizabeth, you must make an effort," said Diva energetically. "Tilling society will all fly to smithereens if we don't take care. You and Lucia have come back from the dead, so that's a very good opportunity for showing a forgiving spirit and beginning again. He really can't say more than he has said."

"Nor could he possibly, if he's a soldier, a Christian and a gentleman, have said less," observed Elizabeth.

"No, but he's done the right thing."

Elizabeth rose and had one more peep out of the window.

"I forgive him," she said. "I shall ask him to tea tomorrow."

Elizabeth carried up to bed with her quantities of food for thought and lay munching it till a very late hour. She had got rid of a good deal of spite against Lucia, which left her head the clearer, and she would be very busy tomorrow writing her account of the great adventure. But it was the thought of Major Benjy that most occupied her. Time had been when he had certainly come very near making honourable proposals to her which she always was more than ready to accept. They used to play golf together in those days before that firebrand Lucia descended on Tilling; he used to drop in casually, and she used to put flowers in his buttonhole for him. Tilling had expected their union, and Major Benjy had without doubt been on the brink. Now, she reflected, was the precise moment to extend to him a forgiveness so plenary that it would start a new chapter in the golden book of pardon. Though only this morning she had ejected his golf clubs and his socks and his false teeth with every demonstration of contempt, this appeal of his revived in her hopes that had hitherto found no fruition. There should be fatted calves for him as for a prodigal son, he should find in this house that he had violated a cordiality and a welcome for the future and an oblivion of the past that could not fail to undermine his celibate propensities. Discredited owing to his precipitate occupation of Mallards, humiliated by his degrading expulsion from it, and impoverished by the imprudent purchase of wines, motor car and steel-shafted drivers, he would surely take advantage of the wonderful opportunity which she presented to him. He might be timid at first, unable to believe the magnitude of his good fortune, but with a little tact, a proffering of saucers of milk, so to speak, as to a stray and friendless cat, with comfortable invitations to sweet Pussie to be fed and stroked, with stealthy butterings of his paws, and with, frankly, a sudden slam of the door when sweet Pussie had begun to make himself at home, it seemed that unless Pussie was a lunatic, he could not fail to wish to domesticate himself. "I think I can manage it," thought Elizabeth, "and then poor Lulu will only be a widow, and I a married woman with a well-controlled husband. How will she like that?"

Such sweet thoughts as these gradually lulled her to sleep.

It was soon evident that the return of the lost, an event in itself of the first magnitude, was instantly to cause a revival of those rivalries which during the autumn had rendered life at Tilling so thrilling a business. Georgie, walking down to see Lucia three days after her return, found a bill-poster placarding the High Street with notices of a lecture to be delivered at the Institute in two days' time by Mrs. Lucas, admission free and no collection of any sort before, during or after. "A modern Odyssey" was the title of the discourse. He hurried on to Grebe, and found her busy correcting the typewritten manuscript which she had been dictating to her secretary all yesterday with scarcely a pause for meals.

"Why, I thought it was to be just an after-dinner reading," he said, straight off, without any explanation of what he was talking about.

Lucia put a paperknife in the page she was at, and turned back to the first.

"My little room would not accommodate all the people who, I understand, are most eager to hear about what I went through," she said. "You see, Georgie, I think it is a duty laid upon those who have been privileged to pass unscathed through tremendous adventures to let others share, as far as is possible, their experiences. In fact that is how I propose to open my lecture. I was reading the first sentence. What do you think of it?"

"Splendid," said Georgie. "So well expressed."

"Then I make some allusion to Nansen, and Stanley and Amundsen," said Lucia, "who have all written long books about their travels, and say that as I do not dream of comparing my adventure to theirs, a short verbal recital of some of the strange things that happened to me will suffice. I calculate that it will not take much more than two hours, or at most two and a half. I finished it about one o'clock this morning."

"Well, you have been quick about it," said Georgie. "Why, you've only been back three days."

Lucia pushed the pile of typewritten sheets aside.

"Georgie, it has been terrific work," she said, "but I had to rid myself of the incubus of these memories by writing them down. Aristotle, you know; the purging of the mind. Besides, I'm sure I'm right in hurrying up. It would be like Elizabeth to be intending to do something of the sort. I've hired the Institute anyhow—"

"Now that is interesting," said Georgie. "Practically every time that I've passed Mallards during these last two days Elizabeth has been writing in the window of the garden-room. Frightfully busy: hardly looking up at all. I don't know for certain that she is writing her Odyssey—such a good title—but she is writing something, and surely it must be that. And two of those times Major Benjy was sitting with her on the piano-stool and she was reading to him from a pile of blue foolscap. Of course I couldn't hear the words, but there were her lips going on like anything. So busy that she didn't see me, but I think he did."

"No!" said Lucia, forgetting her lecture for the moment. "Has she made it up with him then?"

"She must have. He dined there once, for I saw him going in, and he lunched there once, for I saw him coming out, and then there was tea, when she was reading to him, and I passed them just now in his car. All their four hands were on the wheel, and I think he was teaching her to drive, or perhaps learning himself."

"And fancy his forgiving all the names she called him, and putting his teeth on the doorstep," said Lucia. "I believe there's more than meets the eye."

"Oh, much more," said he. "You know she wanted to marry him and nearly got him, Diva says, just before we came here. She's having another go."

"Clever of her," said Lucia appreciatively. "I didn't think she had so much ability. She's got him on the hop, you see, when he's ever so grateful for her forgiving him. But cunning, Georgie, rather low and cunning. And it's quite evident she's writing our adventures as hard as she can. It's a good thing I've wasted no time."

"I should like to see her face when she comes back from her drive," said Georgie. "They were pasting the High Street with you, as I came. Friday afternoon, too: that's a good choice because it's early closing."

"Yes, of course, that's why I chose it," said Lucia. "I don't think she can possibly be ready a whole day before me, and if she hires the Institute the day after me, nobody will go, because I shall have told them everything already. Then she can't have hired the Institute on the same day as I, because you can't have two lectures, especially on the same subject, going on in the same room simultaneously. Impossible."

Grosvenor came in with the afternoon post.

"And one by hand, ma'am," she said.

Lucia, of course, looked first at the one by hand. Nothing that came from outside Tilling could be as urgent as a local missive.

"Georgie!" she cried. "Delicious complication! Elizabeth asks me—me—to attend her reading in the garden-room called 'Lost to Sight,' at three o'clock on Friday afternoon. Major Benjamin Flint has kindly consented to take the chair. At exactly that hour the Padre will be taking the chair at the Institute for me. I know what I shall do. I shall send a special invitation to Elizabeth to sit on the platform at my lecture, and I shall send another note to her two hours later as if I had only just received hers, to say that as I am lecturing myself that afternoon at the Institute, I much regret that, etc. Then she can't say I haven't asked her."

"And when they come back from their drive this afternoon, she and Major Benjy," cried Georgie, "they'll see the High Street placarded with your notices. I've never been so excited before except when you came home."

The tension next day grew very pleasant. Elizabeth, hearing that Lucia had taken the Institute, did her best to deprive her of an audience, and wrote personal notes not only to her friends of the immediate circle, but to chemists and grocers and auctioneers and butchers to invite them to the garden-room at Mallards at three o'clock on the day of battle in order to hear a *true* (underlined) account of her adventure. Lucia's reply to that was to make a personal canvass of all the shops, pay all her bills, and tell everyone that in the interval between the two sections of her lecture, tea would be provided gratis for the audience. She delayed this manoeuvre till Friday morning, so that there could scarcely be a counter-attack.

That same morning, the Padre, feeling that he must do his best to restore peace after the engagement that was now imminent, dashed off two notes to Lucia and Elizabeth, saying that a few friends (this was a lie because he had thought of it himself) had suggested to him how suitable it would be that he should hold a short service of thanksgiving for their escape from the perils of the sea and of cod-fisheries. He proposed therefore that this service should take place directly after the baptisms on Sunday afternoon. It would be quite short, a few prayers, the general thanksgiving, a hymn ("Fierce raged the tempest o'er the deep"), and a few words from himself. He hoped the two ladies would sit together in the front pew which had been occupied at the memorial service by the chief mourners. Both of them were charmed with the idea, for neither dared refuse for fear of putting herself in the wrong. So after about three forty-five on Sunday afternoon (and it was already two forty-five on Friday afternoon) there must be peace, for who could go on after that joint thanksgiving?

By three o'clock on Friday there was not a seat to be had at the Institute, and many people were standing. At the same hour every seat was to be had at the garden-room, for nobody was sitting down in any of them. At half-past three Lucia was getting rather mixed about the latitude and longitude of the Gallagher Bank, and the map had fallen down. At half-past three Elizabeth and Major Benjy were alone in the garden-room. It would be fatiguing for her, he said, to read again the lecture she had read him yesterday, and he wouldn't allow her to do it. Every word was already branded on his memory. So they seated themselves comfortably by the fire and Elizabeth began to talk of the loneliness of loneliness and of affinities. At half-past four Lucia's audience, having eaten their sumptuous tea, had ebbed away, leaving only Irene, Georgie, Mr. and Mrs. Wyse, and Mr. and

Mrs. Padre to listen to the second half of the lecture. At half-past four in the garden-room Elizabeth and Major Benjy were engaged to be married. There was no reason for (in fact every reason against) a long engagement, and the banns would be put up in church next Sunday morning.

"So they'll all know about it, *Benjino mio*," said Elizabeth, "when we have our little thanksgiving service on Sunday afternoon, and I shall ask all our friends, Lucia included, to a cosy lunch on Monday to celebrate our engagement. You must send me across some of your best bottles of wine, dear."

"As if you didn't know that all my cellar was at your disposal," said he.

Elizabeth jumped up and clapped her hands. "Oh, I've got such a lovely idea for that lunch," she said. "Don't ask me about it, for I shan't tell you. A splendid surprise for everybody, especially Lulu."

∞

Elizabeth was slightly chagrined next day, when she offered to read her lecture on practically any afternoon to the inmates of the workhouse, to find that Lucia had already asked all those who were not bedridden or deaf to tea at Grebe that very day, and hear an abridged form of what she had read at the Institute: an hour was considered enough, since perhaps some of them would find the excitement and the strain of a longer intellectual effort too much for them. But this chagrin was altogether wiped from her mind when on Sunday morning at the end of the second lesson the Padre published banns of marriage. An irrepressible buzz of conversation like a sudden irruption of bluebottle flies filled the church, and Lucia, who was sitting behind the choir and assisting the altos, said "I thought so" in an audible voice.

Elizabeth was assisting the trebles on the Cantoris side, and had she not been a perfect lady, and the scene a sacred edifice, she might have been tempted to put out her tongue or make a face in the direction of the Decani altos. Then in the afternoon came the service of thanksgiving, and the two heroines were observed to give each other a stage kiss. Diva, who sat in the pew immediately behind them, was certain that actual contact was not established. They resumed their seats, slightly apart.

As was only to be expected, notes of congratulation and acceptance to the lunch on Monday poured in upon the young couple. All the intimate circle of Tilling was there, the sideboard groaned with Major Benjy's most expensive wines, and everyone felt that the hatchet which had done so much interesting chopping in the past was buried, for never had two folk been so cordial to each other as were Lucia and Elizabeth.

They took their places at the table. Though it was only lunch there were menu cards, and written on them as the first item of the banquet was "Lobster *à la Riseholme.*"

Georgie saw it first, though his claim was passionately disputed by Diva, but everybody else, except Lucia, saw it in a second or two and the gay talk dropped dead. What could have happened? Had Lucia, one day on the Gallagher Banks, given their hostess the secret which she had so firmly withheld? Somehow it seemed scarcely credible. The eyes of the guests, pair by pair, grew absorbed in meditation, for all were beginning to recall a mystery that had baffled them. The presence of Elizabeth in Lucia's kitchen when the flood poured in had never been fathomed, but surely . . . A slight catalepsy seized the party, and all eyes were turned on Lucia who now for the first time looked at the menu. If she had given the recipe to Elizabeth, she would surely say something about it.

Lucia read the menu and slightly moistened her lips. She directed on Elizabeth a long penetrating gaze that mutely questioned her. Then the character of that look altered. There was no reproach in it, only comprehension and unfathomable contempt.

The ghastly silence continued as the lobster was handed round. It came to Lucia first. She tasted it and found that it was exactly right. She laid down her fork, and grubbed up the imperfectly buried hatchet.

"Are you sure you copied the recipe out quite correctly, *Elizabetha mia*?" she asked. "You must pop into my kitchen some afternoon when you are going for your walk—never mind if I am in or not—and look at it again. And if my cook is out too, you will find the recipe in a book on the kitchen-shelf. But you know that, don't you?"

"Thank you, dear," said Elizabeth. "Sweet of you."

Then everybody began to talk in a great hurry.

Printed in the United States
by Baker & Taylor Publisher Services